PRAISE FOR SAINT DEATH'S DAUGHTER

"A tumultuous, swaggering, cackling story, a gorgeous citrus orchard with bones for roots. Miscellaneous Stones' journey into adulthood and power, sorting knowledge from wisdom and vengeance from justice, has an ocean's breadth and depth, its storms and sparkles and salt. Soaring with love and absolutely fizzing with tenderness and joy—I have never read anything so utterly alive."

Amal El-Mohtar

"To open a book by C. S. E. Cooney is to be seized by a narrative whirlwind. All around you are wonders, dangers, shattered mirrors, shooting stars; and the voice of the whirlwind, Cooney's prose, is a vast, note-perfect song. There's no voice like it. There's none richer in fantasy today."

Robert V. S. Redick

"*Saint Death's Daughter* is a triumph of a book, gorgeous beyond measure, fizzing with Cooney's love for language, her inventiveness in prose; it is also unbearably tender in how it addresses the idea of death and legacy, the love we can gather into a life before we curl to sleep in Death's arms."

Cassandra Khaw

"Cooney sets her budding young necromancer adrift in a dazzlingly dark, weird, engaging and strangely warm world alive with memorable characters, hidden secrets and sinister intrigues. This is a masterful work from a writer at the top of her game."

Howard Andrew Jones

"C. S. E. Cooney's prose once again delivers on the promise of the wild magic and music. *Saint Death's Daughter* will leave you feeling she's actually summoned a new world, and you might just stumble upon it around the next corner. Glorious."

Angela Slatter

"It feels like overhearing a conversation between Terry Pratchett and Susanna Clarke. A total must if you dig footnotes or fantasy."

Patty Templeton

"What happens if you are a necromancer born into a family of assassins—but you're literally allergic to death itself? *Saint Death's Daughter* is a whimsically gothy romp full of weird magic and intricate worldbuilding. Locked Tomb fans, you'll want to read this yesterday."

Nicole Kornher-Stace

"A luminous, chiming, bone-belled, ludicrous, austere, flamboyant, rhyming, reckless, affectionate novel; a giddy libation to a sly and shifting pantheon, a glittering ossuary-mosaic of incautious hope and over-generous loves, of gambling and falling and flying."

Kathleen Jennings

"Cooney's prose effervesces: each magnificent name, each glorious detail, each jig-and-reel phrase thrills like champagne bubbles on the tongue. Sumptuous, bawdy, and layered as a mille-feuille, this book is delicious, delectable, and impossible not to devour."

Lisa L. Hannett

"Gorgeous, sexy, cruel and compassionate and funny. Such rich, delicious world-building and frankly lovable characters (even the baddies are compelling!). I relished every word."

Liz Duffy Adams

"*Saint Death's Daughter* is filled with lavish world building, lyrical prose, and characters to die for. C. S. E. Cooney is a faerie queen barely trying to pass in the mundane world. This book is as luminous and flamboyant as she is."

Tina Jens

"A tantalizing hint at a fabulous backstory is followed by a mind-spinningly original bit of worldbuilding, and then that is in turn chased by an emotional arc so moving that I cried like a baby while reading at an airport gate, and nevermind all the people staring."

Caitlyn Paxson

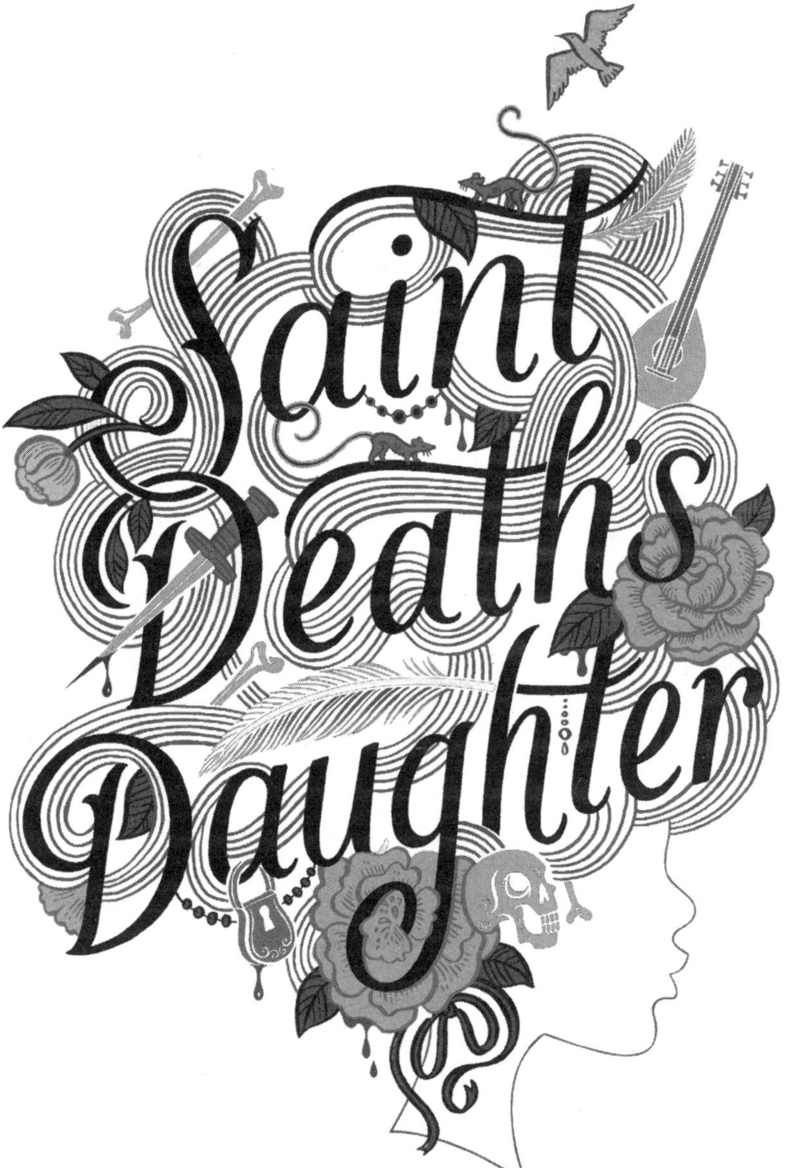
Saint Death's Daughter

First published 2022 by Solaris
an imprint of Rebellion Publishing Ltd,
Riverside House, Osney Mead,
Oxford, OX2 0ES, UK

www.solarisbooks.com

ISBN: 978-1-78618-470-2

10 9 8 7 6 5 4 3 2 1

A CIP catalogue record for this book is available from
the British Library.

Designed & typeset by Rebellion Publishing

Printed in the UK

SAINT DEATH'S DAUGHTER

C. S. E. COONEY

SOLARIS

For Jeanine Marie Vaughn

KEY TO DATES, GODS AND OTHER USEFUL TERMS

Days of the Week

Flameday, Brineday, Rainday, Rimeday, Luckday, Dustday, Hangday

Months of the Year

Winter: Vespers, Squalls, Barrens
Spring: Wells, Broods, Sporings
Summer: Flukes, Stews, Drubs
Fall: Chases, Embers, Umbers

The Twelve Gods of Quadiíb

Kantu, Flying God of Thunder
Ajdenia the Lizard Lady
Aganath, Queen of the Sea
Brotquen, Four-Faced Harvest Goddess
Kywit the Captured God
Amahirra Mirage-Shaper, Trickster God
Engoloth, God of War and Time (and Pepper)
Lan Satthi, the Notary God
Wykkyrri Thousand-Beasts
Sappacor, the Many-Gendered God of Fire
Yssimyss of Mysteries
Doédenna, God of Death

The Gods of Liriat

Sappacor (Old Sparks) and Doédenna (Saint Death)

Rulers of Liriat

The Blood Royal Brackenwilds

Their Left Hands

The Stoneses

PROLOGUE

Rainday 29th
Month of Embers, 413 Founding Era
121 days till Winter Solstice

Amanita Muscaria Stones
Care of Gyrlady Gelethai
Caravan School
The Traveling Palaces of Higher Quadiíb
Waystation VII

Nita,

They are both dead. Father, a month ago; Mother, last week.

While I was unable to change the fact of their deaths, I did my best to raise them up after. I followed Irradiant Stones's comprehensive treatise On the Benefits of Revitalizing Your Revenants While Their Flesh Is (More or Less) Fresh, which is—as texts on death magic go—fairly straightforward. Such a complex resurrection rite, however, requires a high holy fire feast, and alas, autumn equinox had already come and gone by the time they brought Father's body home. When Mother died, we were nowhere near a surge. My attempts failed.

Mostly failed. Father did open his ~~eyes~~ eye down in Stones Ossuary and blink a few times, but he had no more sense than a baby bird. Mother was more emphatic in her response; she spat black blood at me and cursed. (I could not understand the words. They were probably gibberish. The prevailing theory is that the dead lose their memory quickly, and without a mature necromancer's blood to spark it back, language is the first thing to go. My own blood, alas, will not attain full maturity for a few years yet.)

Neither of our parents' corpses stayed animate for more than a few minutes. Their remains turned to sludge soon after I performed the rite, and I did not have opportunity for further experimentation.

Now for more staggering news.

Just this morning, a woman named Sari Scratch arrived at Stones Manor—along with her three sons—and announced that she was calling in all our family's debts. I, not being aware that we had any, was disinclined to believe her, and opined that she and her progeny were all swindling imposters who would find no ready victim in me.

But, Nita, this Mistress Scratch merely smiled at me like I was a naughty yet adorably precocious child. She summoned from the depths of her coach an ordained notary priestess of Lan Satthi, whom she had chartered to verify our family's contract.

The contract was then explained to me in exhaustive detail by the notary priestess herself. When we came to its end, I saw what no forger could have hoped to accomplish: all of their names—signed in their blood. Such is the magic of Lan Satthi that I'd swear the ink was still wet, though the contract was dated four years ago. There was Father's signature, taking up half the page, Mother's so crabbed that I had to hold the sheet up next to my face, and Aunt Diggie's so jingled that it danced into the margins—one could practically smell the gin! The sigil of the god bound the whole contract so fast, four horses pulling in the four cardinal directions could not rip it asunder. Very professional magic.

That being settled, and me put in my place, Mistress Scratch introduced herself properly. She and her sons originally hail from Northernmost Skakmaht, but became full citizens of Liriat four years ago. I'd not met them before, because I never meet anyone, but I don't think even you could have crossed paths with them, Nita, for they moved to Liriat Proper a few months after you left for school. They've close business ties to the Blood Royal Brackenwilds, which is (I'm sure) how they met Father.

But allow me to sum up the nature of our debts while I still have it fresh in my mind. Between Aunt Diggie's gambling, Mother's special chemicals and weapons requests, Father's operas and races, and—pardon me—the cost of your schooling abroad, along with a host of other necessities and indulgences that attend the honor of our family being close intimates with the Brackenwilds, we are so deeply mired in debt that they'll be burning us for peat in another thousand years.

So long as Mother had her usual commissions coming in, and Father continued his work at Castle Ynyssyll, and Aunt Diggie was still moonlighting as leg-breaker for those gambling dens she frequented, we were able to keep up with the interest and our accustomed lifestyle. But now that all contracted parties have perished, one after another and in such short order, Mistress Scratch says that our assets belong to her firm. Even Goody Graves must stay with Stones Manor when it changes hands!

Mistress Scratch 'generously' (her word) offered a deferment on the debt pending your return to Liriat Proper, since you are, after all, the heir and of legal age to make decisions. She also told me privately that I, too, may stay with Stones Manor, if I so chose. She then invited me to marry whichever of her sons happened to take my fancy!

"Or all three of them," she said, "and have yourself a passel of spouses, just like the Blackbird Bride."

As fascinating as I find the political magics of Bran Fiakhna and her Parliament of Rooks, I have no desire to emulate her. However, it did not seem quite diplomatic to reject Scratten, Cracchen, <u>and</u> *Hatchet Scratch out of hand, so I told their mother that, given time—since I am only fifteen—it was not impossible I should come to regard any number of her offspring with affection.*

"It would be no bad thing," said she, "for us Scratches to unite our name with you Stoneses. No bad thing—for either family! We know all about you Stoneses. A byword in Skakmaht!"

I'll just bet 'we Stoneses' are a byword in the north, Nita—but it's not a word that anyone, even a Skaki, would say in polite company. Did Mistress Scratch think me ignorant of our history there? Perhaps. Perhaps she also imagined me easily buttered up by flattery, for immediately after her proposal of marriage, she began to make all manner of inquiries into our habits and traditions.

I told her quite firmly that the nature of my allergy was such that I could not disclose any details to her, and that she would do much better to consult with you upon your return. That is, if you plan on returning.

Nita, I understand that your expedition to Quadiíb is of paramount importance. Mother, Father, Aunt Diggie—even Blood Royal Erralierra Brackenwild!—could not have been more vehement on that point when you left four years ago. I would not have dared contact you had I not found myself in the direst of straits. I hope this situation constitutes what you would consider to be an emergency.

The fact of the matter is, if you do not come home, we shall be cast out of our house and lands.

Your obedient sister,
Miscellaneous Immiscible Stones
Stones Manor, Liriat

Part One
DEATH AND THE STONESES

CHAPTER ONE

The Heart of a Stones

Brineday 16th
Month of Wells, 414 Founding Era
3 days till Spring Equinox

IT WAS ALWAYS the same nightmare. Lanie must have had it a hundred times. A thousand.

Nita, stretched like a late afternoon shadow, tall and ever taller. Lanie, small for her age, made smaller by cowering.

But what alarmed Lanie most was her sister's air of tragic calm, so unlike the happy animal cruelty she usually exhibited. Grim and gigantic, Nita stooped down, snatching Hoppy Bunny from Lanie's grasp and swinging it to and fro by its stitched-on ears, her glowing yellow eyes following the pendulum. She hummed a little, tunelessly.

Then, both swinging and humming stopped.

With her huge hands, Nita began to twist. Lanie cried, *No! No!* but didn't actually make a sound. Nita twisted and twisted and *twisted* Hoppy Bunny's plush head until—POP!—the threads capitulated. Plump sock torso rent in two. A fountain of fine sawdust spilling out.

Next came Nita's voice, enormous, righteous, with none of her typical sharp glee. For once, she did not speak as predator to prey, and there was a tremble in her undertones that Lanie struggled to understand.

"Stoneses die young," her big sister explained patiently. "We have to grow up fast if we're to grow up at all."

Hoppy Bunny's sundered halves plonked to the ground. Lanie stared but did not dare cry. At best, Nita would laugh; at worst, Lanie would end up just like Hoppy Bunny.

Nita bent to pocket Hoppy Bunny's head (like Aunt Diggie, she always collected trophies), but instead of standing up again, she knelt before Lanie to stare at her straight on. Lanie shut her eyes before she could be caught in the yellow glare.

"I won't be here anymore to toughen you up, Miscellaneous," said Nita, and for the first time that Lanie could remember, her sister sounded afraid. "Put your toys away. Work hard. Write me often. Don't forget me."

Last, a terrible cold kiss on Lanie's brow.

Lanie was eleven when Nita left for school. And though she would regularly have nightmares about that day for years to come, what she always remembered when she woke up was this:

The *real* nightmare—Nita—was gone.

"WELL, MISCELLANEOUS! I'M home!"

Nita flung gloves, hat, and veil at Goody Graves the moment she sailed through the door. She swept Lanie into her arms. "Oh, I'm back! It's good to be back!"

Lanie peered out from her sister's formidable embrace to see Goody, stiff and antique as an old iron coat tree, covered in Nita's effects. At a massive eight-foot-something-or-other, Goody towered over Nita by a full head and shoulders, but seemed insubstantial as fog next to the living lightning strike that was Nita.

"Why are you just standing there, Graves?" Nita demanded, releasing Lanie abruptly. "Put my things away!"

Lanie stuffed her hands in the pockets of her canvas apron and stepped back, away from the coiled, crackling fury that lurked just under Nita's surface. From beneath her lashes, she watched Goody stolidly deciding whether to interpret Nita's command as 'drop everything on the floor and kick it under the bench,' or 'stuff them down Nita's throat until they disappeared.' Time to intervene.

Untucking a secret smile from the side of her mouth, Lanie flashed it at Goody before turning to distract her sister. "Welcome back, Amanita Muscaria. Stones Manor hasn't been the same without you."

It wasn't a lie—Lanie had no practical experience at lying—but it wasn't the compliment Nita took it for.

Nita grinned, and sank on to the vestibule bench to unbuckle her tall riding boots. "Been wretchedly lonely without me, Miscellaneous?"

"I certainly spend a great deal of time alone."

Goody's cold presence fell away from the vestibule as she stumped off to obey orders. Lanie knew she'd go to some trouble 'putting' Nita's things 'away' somewhere—and how! The cow byre? The privy closet? Lanie would find out later. At least the immediate danger of conflict had been averted.

Nita's gaze landed on her like a yoke. "Come sit," she said softly.

Lanie clenched her hands in her pockets and obeyed, trying not to wither. But Nita, like any extreme heat, was a desiccating force. She took after their mother, whose own mother had been half-Quadoni, a lion-colored people. Her wizard marks were also gold, but glitteringly metallic—a slash above her right eyebrow, another forming an almost complete ring about her throat. Her hair was the only soft thing about her, an opulence of golden spirals. (*Doll's hair*, Blood Royal Erralierra had once called it, tweaking a curl—nearly at the cost of her fingers.)

But where their mother had been cold, Nita flashed hot. She was easily irritated, sensitive to a fly's landing. To Nita, the world of Athe was peopled with flies. It was easy for her to look down on people, for—like their father—she was tall, lean, rangy, her carriage haughty. She had corded legs and hard arms and a pouncing walk. And her eyes, like their father's, were shark-black—until they weren't. Until they glowed yellow with her magic.

Lanie remembered how their father's one remaining eye had opened for her, down in the lacklight of Stones Ossuary, where she kept her workshop. His eye had not been black then—not anymore—but blue with ectenica from the resurrection rite. He had stared without sense, without breath, then died again.

Shying from the memory, she shifted on the bench, crossing her legs at the ankles and venturing, "That coat is very dashing, Amanita Muscaria."

It was the right thing to say; some tension in Nita's spine came unbraided. She brushed a hand down the peacock-colored velvet of her riding coat, with its cuffs embroidered in orange-red flames, and raised one plucked-to-filament-thinness eyebrow.

"Fine, isn't it? It's not Quadoni—velvet not being a popular textile in the desert. I bought it in Kalestis on my way back. One must dress. And how does your death magic progress, little sister?"

Lanie's palms sweated at the sudden turn. Nita hadn't even made it into the great hall, and already her interrogation had begun.

"Slowly," she replied.

Nita abandoned the straps, laces, and buckles binding her boots to her thighs and turned her complete attention on her sister. "Tell me."

"Let's see. Um. Well, last week in my workshop"—Lanie leaned back, casually, only narrowly avoiding bumping her head on a rusted brazier—"I mixed my blood with a mess of last winter's potatoes. The ectenica caught on like wildfire; the entire bin started bleeding blue light. Then the eyes of the potatoes began to grow, too fast to track, till they were as long as tentacles, reaching out for me. They were darlings—I wanted to keep them as pets—but ectenica never lasts for long. A few minutes later, the whole thing melted off into the most foul-smelling black sludge. I've been working on a way of *preserving* ectenica—starting small, you know: old vegetation, dead bees, that sort of thing—so I don't have to rely on my quarterly panthaumic surge to do all the heavy lifting. I'd love to perform more *permanent* acts of death magic without waiting three months between. And it gets tiresome, in the meantime, sticking myself with a syringe every time I want to do something small. But somehow, I don't know, I don't think potatoes are quite the right *medium* for stabilization..." She trailed off, embarrassed.

Blurting again. And to Nita, of all people! That was the trouble with being alone so much; Lanie was forgetting how to hold a normal conversation. Goody rarely spoke, and Grandpa Rad chattered so much there was no getting a word in edgewise.

"Progress indeed." Nita sounded almost proud.

"It's... coming along," Lanie agreed cautiously.

"Alas," her sister purred, bending over her boots, her smile a cream-licked curl, "that your undead potatoes could not save our parents."

Ah, this was more familiar. This glittering prick of failure. Lanie stammered, "I—I tried. I did try, Nita, but... It was off-surge—I didn't have a boost. No panthauma to help me, and my ectenica wasn't enough to keep them going. Worse than the potatoes. Much, much worse—the smell, you wouldn't... And then, *after*, there wasn't anything left..." She was talking too fast, forgetting to breathe.

Nita held up her hand, soothingly. "Hush, Miscellaneous. Hush, I know."

How could she know? Lanie wondered bitterly. Nita had only the smallest kind of magic. She used it well, of course, like any weapon in her arsenal—but it was just a tool to her, not an art. Not a *vocation*.

"So," Nita's voice caressed her, coaxing, "how did it happen? Our parents?"

Lanie crossed her arms over her chest, then immediately dropped them again. Nita tended to turn into a battering ram whenever she spotted a defensive wall.

"You want it chronologically?"

"As you wish." Nita shrugged. "Oh, but"—she waved her hand—"you can skip the part about Aunt Diggie. Mother wrote me all about *that*—how they found pieces of her scattered across the Diesmali Woods. Diggie's fault, of course. She liked putting her own skin in the pot. Said wagering was more thrilling that way—the stakes couldn't get any higher."

Lanie did not address that. She could not, not without making herself sick. The events Nita was asking her to recite would present difficulties enough; she was glad not to have to include the spectacular demise of Digitalis Stones in her upcoming report.

"Father first, then. Most of the details I got secondhand, mind," Lanie warned. "From Canon Lir."

Nita pressed her lips together, and Lanie froze. Her sister's jealous rages were quiet but devastating.

"Still exchanging letters with your chubby fire priest? And yet when I was in Quadiíb, letters from you were rarer than rain. Four years I was gone, but I can count on my two hands the times I received..." She stopped, visibly calmed herself, and gestured for Lanie to continue. "Never mind. The account!"

Lanie hastened on, not wanting to discuss Canon Lir with Nita, which would be a little like handing a baby sparrow to a catamount and telling it to take care.

"Late last year, Father was in Liriat Proper, attending Blood Royal Erralierra at the First Frost Harlequinade. It was the day after the high holy fire feast of Autumn Equinox. The whole city was still celebrating. The best-dressed clown in the Harlequinade was to be awarded a prize at the end of the procession—a cap with ass's ears and real gold bells. Father sat with Erralierra in the royal pavilion set up on Moll's Kopje. Each clown who passed before them made their genuflection for judgment. Near the end, a clown in orange and black motley, with a black and orange-painted face, leapt up from her knees to perform a dance routine with her baton. Said baton ended up buried in Father's eye. There was a blade," she explained, "concealed beneath a knot of ribbons. But the clown wasn't Lirian—she was *Rookish!* What they thought was face paint wasn't—it was her wizard markings. She belonged to the Blackbird Bride—one of her Parliament of Rooks. Canon Lir said that her face melted back into feathers when Erralierra executed her."

There, Lanie thought, that wasn't too bad, was it?

The toes of her left foot were numb, and she suspected a rash was starting under her right armpit, but Nita couldn't tell that just by *looking* at her. If Lanie could just hold still. And *not scratch*.

Nita was nodding, a remote expression on her face. "Surely the Blood Royal put the killer to the question before executing her?"

"In fact..." Lanie hesitated. Her throat itched, her sinuses prickled. It was a dangerous day for her to recall; this was going to get messy shortly.

Nita knew it. Her right eyebrow arched up, her wizard mark flashing at the movement, as she invited the whole tale and Lanie's allergy with it.

"In fact," Lanie continued, after a pragmatical clearing of the throat, "Erralierra asked Mother herself to perform the interrogation. *Bring all your skills to bear*, was the order. The clown—the Rookish wizard, I mean; the killer—arrived here at Stones Manor in a prison wagon that afternoon. Mother took her into her workshop."

So much Lanie had witnessed for herself but no more, for she had immediately left to visit her own workshop in the ossuary, staying away from the main manor house all evening and all night, even sleeping down amongst the bones. There she could not hear the screaming, nor feel the repercussion of the killer's pain in her own highly reactive body.

Nita's face was avid. "And what did Mother learn?"

Lanie licked dry lips, which prickled like impending cold sores. The nausea of memory was coming to a stormy boil in her stomach.

...Aba Stones, striding into the courtyard at dawn after her bloody work was done, a fug of exposed viscera and wet feathers following her like a trail of slime, blotting out her perfume of almonds and ice and kicking off one of Lanie's three-day migraines...

"*If* confession under torture can be trusted—"

"Of course it can!"

"—then," Lanie said, "the Blackbird Bride had *nothing* to do with Father's death. The clown who killed him was a young wizard, but recently inducted into the Parliament of Rooks. She wanted to impress her liege wife and queen, celebrate her new wings. Unnatural Stones being something of a celebrity—Brackenwild's Chief Executioner! The Left Hand of Liriat!—murdering him would bring her glory in the Parliament. You know the Rookish court; they're always vying for Bran Fiakhna's favor. The Blackbird Bride's got so many wizards dangling from her strings, she's like a spider with a bunch of marionettes."

"But was *Mother* content with the killer's confession?"

Lanie paused. *Aba* had been; *Lanie* was not. Grandpa Rad's declamations at the time had made her uneasy about the whole thing. He had ranted for days after the killer's execution, an endless lecture about the training all Rookish wizards receive before being inducted into Bran Fiakhna's Parliament. How *no wizard* who belonged to the Blackbird Bride would have acted *without* her knowledge or consent—or without her direct order. Rook, he said, had every reason for wanting to weaken Liriat's power base. Beginning with the Stoneses.

But Nita would no more want to hear Lanie repeating the ramblings of a ghost than Mother had. She didn't even believe in him.

So Lanie replied carefully, "Mother was certainly thorough about obtaining the confession."

"Good." Nita's voice hardened. "Now. How did Mother die?"

Lanie's throat crawled like poison ivy on a summer's day. Was it allergy, or guilt? She had nursed Aba while she could, but in the end, Lanie had been bedridden herself from such prolonged proximity to her mother's deathbed. When exposed too long to physical damage, her allergy began reproducing the symptoms of that damage until it laid her low. Contagious illnesses didn't count (Lanie was still susceptible to those, although she had so little contact with outsiders she rarely caught a cold), only damage caused by *intentional* violence—either self-inflicted or at the hand of an outside party. In Aba's case, it was the former.

"From what I could divine," Lanie swallowed to ease her tight throat, "shortly after we interred Father in Stones Ossuary, Mother ingested a quantity of a potion called 'Elixir of Adamant.'"

The label, as she explained to her sister, had been Leechese in origin, promising *Longevity, Clarity, and Invincibility*. The bottle was expensive, stoppered in crystal.

"But Goody and I analyzed the ingredients," she said. "Mere quackery."

Or worse, as she'd later theorized—deliberate sabotage. It had consisted of two parts briarbark syrup (for sweetness), one part alcohol (for kick), one part diamond dust (for murder).

Nita blinked as Lanie imparted all of this to her. From Nita, that was practically a flinch.

"Over a period of a few weeks," Lanie said in a rush, hoping to get this over with before her reaction became severe, "the diamond dust perforated and abraded Mother's organs. She was already blind and delirious from alcohol poisoning. What *I* do not know is if *she* knew what she was drinking. Or if she drank it believing the label, looking for some insurance against her own mortality. Father's death was... difficult for her."

The sisters regarded each other. Not quite three seconds passed. Nita's eyes were still black, but Lanie slid her gaze to the left and down, just in case. To her surprise, Nita brought her hands together in slow, loud applause.

"Oh, Miscellaneous! You *have* grown. Look at you—still on your feet after all that! Mother and Auntie used to sneer at your running noses, your headaches, how you vomited all the time." Laughing, she recalled, "Aunt Diggie used to call you *that mewling runt,* do you remember?"

Oh, Lanie remembered. She did not laugh, though she knew she should probably try. Thankfully, Nita didn't notice this time.

"Father told me once that what Mother always called your *weakness*—your allergy—was a sign of your power to come. Stoneses, he said, have been favored of Saint Death since the days of the Founding Queen. He said that your violent reaction to violence was the core of your necromancy—that one day your body would revolt so magnificently against death that you would raise the very dead themselves, call them forth from tombs and catacombs and bend them to your will!"

Nita laughed again, the sound rising like golden bubbles that skittered from the vestibule into the great hall. "I should have believed *him*, Miscellaneous, not Mother! We might have been better friends, you and I. You might have written me more letters when I went away, told me of your studies. I might have confessed to you how I... but"—she shook her head, controlling the strange tremor in her voice—"all *that* is over. I am home now. And you have welcomed me."

Lanie said nothing, uncomfortable with this new, confessional Nita. She wanted to go back to the library and curl up with a book next to Goody on the tiger rug. Even Grandpa Rad's dogmatic droning would be preferable to staying in this dusty black vestibule one minute longer.

Nita patted the basalt bench beside her. Rattled, Lanie sat.

"Had you been able to solicit my advice, Miscellaneous, I would have urged you not even to try and raise our dead. What do we want with them now? Would we have the inimitable Abandon Hope Stones, Royal Assassin of Liriat, and her husband Unnatural Stones, Chief Executioner, reduced to revenants? Living on nothing but your blood and their own memories, bound to your will like *that* great lump?" She indicated Goody Graves, who had silently re-entered the vestibule, and answered herself with a vehement "No!"

Lanie opened her mouth to impart a procedural correction on the various properties and provenances of panthauma versus ectenica (Nita obviously did not know as much about death magic as she thought she did), but her sister overrode her.

"No," she repeated, "it is best they are gone." Her nod was decisive. "I am even glad for it—for without your letter, I might have stayed in Quadiíb another year! A waste, believe me. Within *days* of arriving, I had already accomplished the primary mission our parents taxed me with: to discover the perfect stud horse for our stable. A man and mate worthy of Amanita Muscaria Stones, one who will renew the magic in our bloodline. It only remained how to extract him from his..."

Nita's gaze grew distant, almost drunken. Her throat moved. The glittering ring of her wizard mark seemed to strangle her. It was as if she were forcing down some mutinous mouthful.

"You perhaps recollect reading some mention of my mentor, Gyrlady Gelethai?" She opened her hand as if to usher the woman through the front door. "I wrote home regularly about her."

"I addressed all my letters to you in care of her, remember?"

"Ah, yes. That's right." Nita smiled, a bear-trap tension in her jaw.

Lanie had pored over all her sister's letters, hoping they might reveal some insight or observation about the world—especially Quadiíb!—that Lanie could dream on. She herself had never left the boundaries of Stones Manor, and never envied Nita so much as when she was sent away to the Traveling Palaces for her schooling. But Nita's descriptions consisted solely of the snubs and slights (real or perceived) that continuously assailed her from all sides; how it rankled her to stomach these insults from her teachers, classmates, and even random vendors at the marketplace; how she put herself to sleep at night by imagining infinite retaliations, like variations on a lullaby.

At one point, Aba had observed to Diggie—within Lanie's hearing—that this exercise of restraint was good for Nita, whose first response to an offense was usually to swing out like a trebuchet. What Nita *needed*, Aba stressed, was to learn the long, cold composure of vengeance. School abroad doubled as an intense course in deep cover in a foreign country. Nita would need these skills when she took over Aba's work as Royal Assassin to the Blood Royal Brackenwilds.

Before Nita's departure, Aba had arranged everything. She had written to the Traveling Palaces on her daughter's behalf, organized Nita's journey and citizenship papers (Quadiíb granted partial citizenship to any direct descendant of a full Quadoni citizen up to four generations after their death, including open admission into the Caravan School without having to put your name in the lottery), drilled her in languages and international policy, art, music, math lessons, history, cultural studies, and everything else Nita would need to know to pass for a scholar.

A scholar! Nita! How it rankled Lanie even now. The only joy Nita might ever take in a library would be burning it to the ground.

And yet, she grudgingly admitted to herself, Nita had endured her deep cover for four years. It was admirable.

"It was Gyrlady Gelethai," Nita said now, "whom Mother arranged to 'tutor' me in the ways of our Quadoni forebears. *Tutor* me? More like *thwart* me!" she burst out, a yellow beam flashing in her black eyes. "At every turn, she..." Her hands clenched in her velvet-covered lap. Her chin jerked up. She finished, softly, "But I triumphed in the end."

Lanie bent forward, elbows on knees. "I envy you."

It was a phrase calculated to soothe her sister, for whom the envy of others was ambrosia. But she meant it. To leave Stones Manor. To leave Liriat. To walk the Caravan School circuit, and study Quadic and ancient magic and who knew what else with the great Professora Ambassadors of Quadiíb! It had long been her own dream.

"You would have despised Quadiíb, Miscellaneous," Nita assured her confidently, her smile returning. "Gyrlady Gelethai disapproved of our entire house. I boasted of its storied past, the Northernmost War that we Stoneses helped to win, the death magic in our bloodline! Oh, yes. I told her all about *you*."

Curiosity sprang, thirsty and dry-clawed, to Lanie's throat. Studying her boots, she mumbled, "And... what did she say?" trying not to care about the answer.

Nita laughed, skinning off her boots one after the other. "Too much to remember. Gelethai talked too much. But she showed the *greatest* consternation!"

Lanie's shoulders slumped, and Nita laughed again, jostling her. "All right, all right, Miscellaneous, don't pout. How vain you've become! Let me see if I can recall."

Her voice took on a false Quadic cadence, and a tone at once strident and stuffy. "Your chances of surviving till your full maturation are *very* slim. Necromancers are rare and fragile, and the world is full of death. Especially for a Stones. She said growing up in a house swimming with death is tantamount to eating poison in your porridge every morning! Your allergy will make you frail, your vocation will bring you whisper-close to death, and even if you survive, it is always a fine line for any wizard to walk—that between magical vocation and magical obsession!"

Nita rolled her eyes and resumed her normal speaking voice. "She talked as if we hadn't put all precautions in place—giving you your own wing of the house, letting you take your meals alone, taking care not to expose you to the world too soon. She insisted you'd probably be dead by the time I graduated. But *you* lived."

"So far," Lanie agreed. Surviving till her fifteenth birthday had been a not unpleasant departure from what she herself had expected. Now that Nita was home, however, she wondered if she would make it to twenty.

"And now we can be friends," Nita announced.

Lanie jerked her head up so fast her spectacles slid down her nose. "Friends?"

Nita sprang up, buoyant on stockinged feet. "Friends—and partners! In three days, I shall present myself to Blood Royal Erralierra Brackenwild as candidate for Royal Assassin *and* Chief Executioner. She'll need both positions filled, you know, now that Father and Mother are gone. If I can earn double wages, we can pay off our debt to those abominable Skaki parvenus twice as fast. Erralierra knows my pedigree, and studying in Quadiíb taught me much. Though not"—that lioness's smile, those shark's eyes—"what it *tried* to teach me. Gyrlady Gelethai had *no idea* what to do with a Stones. She thought I should be interested in the *world*. As if any country but Liriat mattered!"

"I studied Quadic while you were away," Lanie said.

Nita turned to stare at her, and Lanie bit her tongue. Damn it duodecifold! She had not meant to blab it out like that. She'd *planned* to insert her burgeoning Quadic vocabulary naturally into the conversation, perhaps over dinner. Now she would just have to brazen it out.

"Could we speak it together sometime?"

Nita sent a short hiss whistling through her top front teeth. Not a real laugh, more of a scoff. "Really, Miscellaneous. I never took to the language myself. I could always make myself understood when I wanted. I just had to hold their gazes long enough." She winked. "*You* know."

Lanie did. Three seconds. Three heartbeats. That was all it took, and Nita could make you do anything. In any language. Not for long—but long enough.

"Apropos of that," Nita said brightly, "you must meet the father of my future children! The prize of my venture! I have to tell you, Miscellaneous—he was hard-won. But worth every wound."

"Oh?" Bemused, Lanie glanced over the rim of her spectacles to peer more deeply into the dim vestibule.

Nothing. No sign of Nita's hard-won human stud. Not even a sack to keep the pieces in. Catching the marbled blue glow of Goody Graves's eyes, she quirked her eyebrows in a question: *Do you know what she's talking about?*

On her most chipper days, Goody was slightly more expressive than an obelisk. But now, not so much as a single semi-petrified muscle twitched. Perhaps those uncanny eyes narrowed a bit? Goody was as clueless as she.

Lanie ducked back behind her lenses and refocused on her sister. Nita was rolling up the velvet sleeve of her riding coat. A silver-shot bracer shone upon her left forearm, laced tightly from wrist to elbow.

Though she recognized the bracer for what it was, Lanie could not actually *believe* what she saw. She had read about such objects, had traced several illustrated examples into her journal out of travel guides and histories of Quadiíb. But from all she had read, Lanie knew that such a bracer *should not* be ornamenting her sister's arm.

She pointed to it. "Amanita Muscaria—is that… Is that a *Bryddongard?*"

Smiling, Nita beckoned to her. "Come."

She walked the few paces out of the narrow, low-ceilinged vestibule and into the great hall. Lanie followed. The cramped entrance soared suddenly open into an echoing space. The floor and walls shone like a starlit lake, polished black rock with crystal chunks of feldspar glittering just under the surface. The rock flashed a deep blue wherever the morning sunlight slanted on it through the tall, narrow windows. Columns of the same darkly sparkling rock supported a coffered ceiling. Fifty feet above the paving stones, lacquered black with silver gilding, the ceiling was a piece of fixed midnight no matter the hour of day. In each of the sunken caissons, one of the twelve gods was etched, silver-on-black, along with Their attributes: Aganath with Her breastplate of shark teeth, Her harpoon, and Her glass coracle; Doédenna, Saint Death, with Her cowl of tiny bones, and a bird of smoke and air in Her cupped hands; Sappacor who bore the Triple Flame; Ajdenia, half-lizard, half-girl, scaled in emerald plating; Kantu the Thundergod with Her feather cape, beaked headdress, the lightning-sparking diamond on Her brow; all the others.

Nita raised her bracer high. It shone brighter than the faces of the gods. A light beamed out from it, piercing the gloom of the great hall, but in one direction only, like a polished mirror funneling sunlight straight into the eyes of an oncoming enemy.

It illuminated a bird.

Lanie stared at the handsome peregrine falcon who was caught on the beam's end, like a head on a pike. It was perched high above them, on one of the decorative spindles of iron railing that prevented persons on the second floor from plunging to their deaths on the flagstones below. (Not that it hadn't happened, but this way you really had to *try*.)

How the falcon had come to be there without Lanie noticing, she could not fathom. Had it flown through the vestibule and into the great hall while her head was bowed, while she was mumbling at her feet and avoiding Nita's gaze? Did *Goody* know it was up there?

She could not look away now, not for her life. So this was Quadoni magic! This was the Bryddongard spell!

As she watched, the falcon lifted off from the spindle. It wheeled through the vastness of the great hall with furious, forlorn swiftness. Nita's gaze tracked the gyration, a terrifying tenderness colonizing her face.

Witnessing that look, Lanie's blood turned to maggots.

Nita stretched her arm toward the bird. The falcon screamed.

Screaming was not the most uncommon of noises in Stones Manor. Lanie had grown up to all sorts of sounds of agony, many coming from the direction of Aba's workshop. She generally fled in the opposite direction of any screaming that was happening in her vicinity, because she did not want to spontaneously contract rope burns, or whip welts, or a hundred little cuts, or blood blisters, or stress fractures, or start swelling up in awkward places. She didn't love the sound of screaming; nevertheless, she was accustomed to it.

But today, when the falcon shrieked, all the hairs on Lanie's arms lifted.

Her sister called out in a ringing voice, "*Bryddon Bekkunnon Ne'hammanu!*"

It was Quadic—Old Quadic—the kind used only in ritual. Lanie knew a few words in Old Quadic, having received the language dry from books, enlivened occasionally by conversation with Goody Graves, who when she was alive had been Quadoni. Lanie was still mentally trying to translate the line when a particularly spectacular silver flash emanated from the bracer on Nita's wrist.

She winced, dazzled. Nita gasped in a kind of painful pleasure. The falcon, which had shot straight up toward the vaulted ceiling, dropped like an anvil.

It hit the floor.

And became a man.

CHAPTER TWO

The Art of Fascination

One. Two. Three...

Nita was there, kneeling at his side before the man even had a chance to uncurl. She grasped him by the chin and looked him deeply in the eyes. Lanie knew that look.

Three heartbeats passed.

"Easy," Nita whispered. "Be easy. Be mine."

And though the man was no longer a falcon, Nita had him hooded and jessed where he lay. He rolled over onto his side, groaning. He was not wearing any clothes.

Shocked at this new magic—it was like seeing a green sunset, or hearing a wolf talk to you—Lanie stammered, "But, Nita, I thought... I thought you *couldn't* become a gyrlady. You have to be Quadoni. Not like 'your grandmother was half-Quadoni' Quadoni, but born and raised. You..."

Nita's spiral curls bounced as she tossed her head. "Does he not have the finest shoulders you have ever seen? His shoulders are what first caught my eye. Or was it his calf muscles? Only see how shapely!"

The man's calf muscles were safe enough to look at it—if anything about this man was safe. Lanie doubted it. But she managed to imitate Nita's careless tone. "Yes. Indeed. Very shapely."

This temporarily placated her sister, but Nita's mood had started to darken. Lanie recognized the brittle quality in her sister's voice.

"No, you know, I do believe his forearms first caught my fancy!"

It would be wisest, Lanie knew, to dutifully admire his forearms. His teeth. The sullen scorch of his hair.

The babble that burst out of her instead was as involuntary as vomit. "But, Nita! Is he... He *is* a gyrgardi, isn't he? A Falcon Defender of Quadiíb? And that"—she pointed to the silver bracer—"that *is* his Bryddongard you're wearing, isn't it? The object that commands his change, that turns him into a bird and back? So... But that... Doesn't that *make* you his gyrlady? But for you to be a gyrlady... it's imposs..."

At her sister's swift glance, Lanie bit her tongue. Stop, she commanded herself. *Stop!*

All the precarious mischief in Nita's face was draining away, leaving it stark and icy. There she was. Amanita Muscaria Stones. Daughter of assassins and executioners. The nightmare.

"Run and fetch him something of Father's to wear, will you?" Nita not-quite-asked her sister. "We had to leave Quadiíb rather suddenly."

FASCINATION WAS NITA'S one talent in sorcery, for all she bore such flashy wizard marks. She had inherited it from their half-Quadoni grandmother, whom neither Nita nor Lanie had ever met.

The lady had either: 1) run away from Stones Manor after giving birth to Abandon Hope, or; 2) died in childbirth, or (mostly likely); 3) been murdered and secretly buried by her husband, Eleemosynary Stones, who'd hailed from a cadet branch of the family, and who was barely tolerated at Stones Manor as a freeloading sycophant right up until the day he just… disappeared[1].

Stonesish magic historically ran to necromancy, not fascination. But until Lanie had made her appearance on the scene, no necromancer had been born to the family for over a hundred years. Nevertheless, Nita did her best to bend her own talent toward violent ends. Most people used fascination for political advantage; it was the magical art of imparting influence, implanting suggestions, and commanding adoration—or, at the very least, obedience. Not so with Nita; she weaponized it, as she did with everything she touched, including herself.

The Blackbird Bride, Queen Bran Fiakhna of Rook, had ridden the riptide of her own formidable magic all the way to the throne. So skillfully did she wield her powers of fascination that wizards from every realm flocked to her, to fling themselves at her feet, and pledge their own magics in fealty. Her Parliament of Rooks consisted of four-and-twenty of the most powerful wizards from all branches of magic, bound to her body and soul as her espoused kin.

Compared to Bran Fiakhna's legendary fascination, Nita's talent was but the slenderest splinter. She could only fascinate one person at a time, never for very long, and she had but the one technique with which she tapped her magic.

But with that technique, and for a limited time, Nita could make you do pretty much anything she wanted.

She called it "The Glance of Three Heartbeats."

* * *

1 His disappearance went unmourned and uninvestigated. Rumor had it that his daughter and son-in-law had put their newlywedded heads together and done what Stoneses do best, before getting on with the business of conceiving Amanita Muscaria.

LANIE PASSED FROM the great hall, through the dining room, and into the circular morning room, exiting out the far side to take a short flight of stairs into the corridor that connected the main house to the northeast wing. She paused on the top step, squeezing her eyes shut for a second, like a diver about to plunge into a lake of swollen snowmelt. She wasn't exactly *afraid* of heights. But ever since Nita had fascinated her right out of a window, Lanie had been just the slightest bit *wary* of them.

She had been, what, all of six years old? Nita, twelve?

A three-second stare—that's all it took. Three heartbeats. *Ba-dum, ba-dum, ba-DOOM!* And Lanie just... jumped. Defenestrated herself. Catapulted right out of that little casement in the back servant's stair that led to the kitchen, and all the way down.

She could still recall with hideous clarity the gaseous golden giddiness that had effervesced through her every capillary. The longing that had filled her. How she had *wanted* to jump. How her desire to test the laws of gravity with her own body was fulfilled only at the bottom of her fall, when, reveling in two broken ankles and a sprained wrist, she looked up into the open window above her to see her sister peering down, black eyes dancing with strange yellow lights.

At which point, Nita had released the fascination.

Lanie remembered screaming. And she remembered Nita laughing, a sound as delicate and golden as her sorcery. Then she'd left the window. She'd left Lanie alone.

Goody Graves found her some hours later. Goody always found her eventually. But that was the day Lanie learned never to look into her sister's eyes if she could help it.

It was a lesson her sister's new... guest... could have used. Too late now, of course.

Nita must have thought a gyrgardi of Quadiíb the epitome of magic. Shapeshifter *and* warrior? The perfect addition to the Stones bloodline! She apparently had *no idea* that the transformative man-into-bird magic came from the *bond* between gyrlady and Falcon Defender—not the gyrgardi himself!

Gyrgardon weren't *innately* magical. Just the opposite! Even if one was born with magic, they poured it all into their silver bracer during the Rite of Bryddongard, which not they, but their gyrlady wore.

As for Nita's captive, his seed would produce nothing special. It would certainly do nothing to augment the magic in the Stones bloodline. Hadn't she known that? Surely she'd had opportunity enough to inspect that naked body fore to aft and find no wizard mark upon it!

But catch Lanie trying to tell her sister any of that. No, thank you.

She clattered up another flight of stairs, into the second floor of the northeast wing, where what had once been guest chambers later became Unnatural Stones's private rooms, and now were nothing.

She had not been inside them since her father's interment. The door was massive, planed from titanwood, ironbound. She laid a palm flat against it, sighed softly, but did not push.

Something rattled beside her. Lanie looked up.

Goody, looming like a cairn, unhooked a heavily decorated key from her chatelaine and handed it over in silence.

"Thank you," Lanie said gratefully. "I didn't see you there. This whole day's been very… distracting!"

Goody said nothing, which meant she was only a shade less talkative than normal. The corridor was too dim for Lanie to read the slow and subtle shifts of shadow that passed for expression on Goody's face. It would do no good to press her now—besides, there wasn't time. Suppressing another sigh, Lanie unlocked the door and pushed it open. Colors coursed out to greet her.

UNNATURAL 'NATTY' STONES had loved the opera, and the races, and masquerade balls, and anything that was outlandish and costly. Fine art covered his walls, some overlapping, with no attempt at coordination or curation. His chambers were stuffed with gaudily cheerful furniture made of the richest and finest materials. Natty had never been happier than when parading about in jeweled brocades and lustrous moiré (when he wasn't working, which of course required black—the deepest, velvetiest, gem-winkingest black!), smoking fine cigars from foreign lands, and killing people at the request of his liege lady: Blood Royal Erralierra Brackenwild.

He had loved the Blood Royal. More than his house, more than his children, more than his wife. His affair with Erralierra had been unabashed, indiscreet, and expensive. Lanie had seen just *how* expensive when Sari Scratch presented her with all the ledgers of their debt.

The lingering smell of her father, cologne and brandy and blood, overwhelmed her. She closed her eyes.

Natty and Lanie had not often crossed paths. That was to his credit. He had recognized his daughter for what she was when she was still a baby, and knowing that his presence in her life would only endanger it, he ordered that Lanie take her meals alone in her rooms in the southeast wing. He had brought in tutors for her who taught subjects other than the usual Stonesish arts (none of which Lanie could study without bleeding from eyes and ears or falling into convulsions), and allowed her free rein of the library (which he had moved, in its entirety, to her wing of the manor—a monumental task that required hiring ranks of strong servants and at least a dozen carpenters to build custom shelves). After that, he had pretty much ignored her—hoping that by doing so, he would ensure her survival.

But whenever Lanie *had* chanced to meet her father, the (necessarily) brief encounters had always been pleasant. He was friendly—even affectionate!

He seemed to regard her with awe and pride, and a great deal of blithe bewilderment.

She missed his singing in the house.

He had not sung much, toward the end of his marriage. He and Aba grew estranged, and Natty began spending more and more time at Castle Ynyssyll with his lover, the Blood Royal. By the time of his death, he hadn't visited Stones Manor in over a year, and without the head of the house to restrain her, Aunt Diggie's excesses had run unchecked. She'd turned the northwest wing of Stones Manor, where she was installed, into a gambling saloon, while Aba, glassy-eyed and chemically distant, ignored everything. Aba practically lived in her workshop, leaving it only to fulfill her commissions as Royal Assassin of Liriat, and these in such increasingly vile and public ways that those who wanted rather more prudence in their hired help began to look elsewhere.

Lanie forced herself deeper into her father's rooms, shattering memories with her body as she made a beeline for the wardrobe.

Stopped, as his ghost filled the full-length mirror.

No. Not a ghost. Only her own reflection.

If Nita, with her burnt-gold beauty, took after Abandon Hope Stones, then Lanie took after Unnatural. She was much shorter than he had been, but just as dark, her skin and hair black-brown—except for her left hand, which bore the largest of her wizard marks, and was entirely slate-gray, the color of a wet tombstone. She had another, smaller mark on her right thigh, also gray, but this one silvery, in a pattern like climbing ivy. Three of the toes on her right foot, and the great toe of her left foot, were also marked, as well as the dimples at the backs of both her knees. Her eyes were not black like Natty's, nor gray like Aba's, but a deep, clear brown. In her more hopeful moments, Lanie fancied she'd inherited her eye color from the notorious courtesan Delirious Stones.

Like Natty, Lanie was drawn to bright, busy colors—pinks and yellows, with touches of green and blue. (She never wore black.) When she released her hair from its everyday dozens of braids, it stood out around her head like a cloud—her father's favorite style. Mostly, she kept her braids bundled at the nape of her neck with a big ribbon, not because she didn't like wearing it undone, but because she wanted to save her unbounded hair for festival occasions.

Natty had been handsome though, which Lanie did not consider herself to be. She was scrawny, and—much to her dismay—had a tendency to break out into pimples about once a month. *Nita* had never had pimples. No Stones in the *history* of Stoneses had ever had pimples as far as Lanie could ascertain. Also, she perhaps had far too much forehead (on this, she was undecided; Delirious Stones had a lovely high forehead, so maybe Lanie's own was all right). And her spectacles were scratched, and her fingernails ink-marked, and her trousers perpetually stained with grass.

But never mind *that*, she told herself firmly. If I lollygag any longer, gawping at myself in the mirror, Nita will surely hunt me down.

Marching up to the wardrobe, Lanie snatched one of Natty's dressing gowns from the rack. An old forgotten favorite, a somethingth-anniversary gift from his wife, it had fallen into disuse long before his death. All his choicest belongings remained at Castle Ynyssyll, in the care of Blood Royal Erralierra Brackenwild—none of which she'd ever thought to return to Stones Manor or his family. The dressing gown's silver-on-green brocade was worn to tissue-paper thinness, the lustrous lion and monkey pattern dulled and sullen, the braided cuffs frayed.

Lanie held it to her nose briefly, breathed in, let it fall. Then, flinging the dressing gown over her shoulder, she glanced up at Goody.

"After all," she shrugged, "he doesn't have to *like* it, does he? So long as it covers him."

AMONG THE NUDE studies and anatomies in Stones Library, Celerity Stones's book of plates entitled *Barely There: The Exquisite Art of Excoriation, With (Predominantly) Live Models,* was the most infamous.

Celerity Stones had been Aunt Diggie's great aunt. (And Aunt Diggie—Digitalis Stones—was really Natty's mother's second cousin, but Natty always called her 'Aunt,' so Nita and Lanie had too.) A known genius in her day, Celerity had been much in demand for her pen and ink drawings, her sanguine sketches, her oils, watercolors, and illuminated calligraphy. Later, she won renown as an anatomical scientist. Very precise with spreader, saw, clamps, probes, and pliers was Celerity Stones. Not, however, very easy on her models[2].

Lanie could barely look at *Barely There;* she got blisters just from touching the book's binding. But she had peeked. And, of course, it was never easy to ignore her most famous work, *The Flayed Ideal*, which hung on the wall of Stones Gallery and had a way of glaring at you. Its exposed and accusatory eyeballs, rendered in oil on canvas with exquisite delicacy, followed you around the room—and very often out the door and down the hall.

When her father had left Stones Manor, Lanie's line of tutors dried up, and her studies became mostly autodidactic (if you didn't count Grandpa Rad's ranting and Goody's cooking lessons). This meant more death magic in Stones Ossuary (hurray!), not as much math (hurray!), Quadic whenever she could spare the time (mostly at night before sleeping), and sporadic forays into art history and biology (always enjoyable).

One thing that Lanie had learned while studying the latter was that

2 Indeed, the widow of the model for *The Flayed Ideal* became so distressed at the loss of her spouse to the cause of Art and Science that she had sneaked into Celerity's studio one night and left her own work of art: *Portrait of an Artist, Eviscerated*. Mixed media: flesh, scalpel, hurdy-gurdy, a few nails, a wooden frame. Thus, the end of Celerity Stones.

there was definitely a difference between *nudity* and *nakedness*. It was that very difference that was thwackingly borne in upon her now.

The naked man looked up when Lanie galloped down the short staircase from the dining room back into the great hall. The force and fire of his glare, more awful even than that of *The Flayed Ideal*, petrified her in place. She stopped one step shy of the main floor, Natty's old dressing gown slithering off her shoulder and onto the paving stones.

There was not such a green as his eyes in all the pages of all the books in Stones Library. His hostility stood out in every sinew, every line of his body. Lanie did not know how a man could keep all his skin on yet still look completely stripped. Had Nita called his shoulders fine? Lanie thought they were disastrous.

Nita. She had forgotten Nita.

The pitiless grip she still dreamed about closed on her wrist, and a dangerously dulcet tone inquired, "What are you thinking, Miscellaneous?"

Lanie breathed out, willing her wrist quiescent, her expression carefree, her voice light.

"I think your guest doesn't care for my choice of dressing gown. Does he fancy something finer?" She glanced doubtfully down at the heap of brocade at her feet. "It's a bit shabby, I guess."

Nita loosened her grip and laughed. "Oh, don't mind him. He's probably just used to being naked by now. I've kept him in his falcon form for most of our journey. He's half-feral."

Half? thought Lanie.

She fought not to roll her shoulders. If she rolled her shoulders, Nita would know she was tense and trying to relax. She had to relax without visible effort. "What's his name anyway?"

Nita regarded the man at their feet. "He has one of those stupidly unpronounceable Quadic names. But I suppose it could be shortened to something like Mak." She gave a short, sharp laugh. "Mak Cobb—that's Stonesish enough for going on with, don't you think?"

"Snappy." Lanie bent and scooped up the dressing gown, which she lobbed at the gyrgardi as if careless of where it fell. It fell within his reach.

He made no move to put it on. His gaze flickered to her hands instead: to her fingertips, which were, each one of them, tied up in bandages. Lanie squinted at the expression on his face—what was it? In his way, he was as difficult to read as Goody!

Fighting an urge to hide her hands behind her back, she flexed them instead. She had nothing to be ashamed of: the practice of death magic—off-surge—required a great deal of bloodletting. Her own, specifically. Only a necromancer's blood, when mixed with dead matter, could make ectenica, the undead material. Ectenica was the raw stuff of her medium, like clay was to a sculptor. But what was that look he was giving her? Recognition? Horror? Pity?

Gone now, whatever it was. But that glare was back, and Nita was laughing again.

"Snappy? So he is—if I don't stuff him full of rodents and rabbits. I can only feed him when he's in his falcon form. He doesn't... He won't *eat* when he's like this."

Lanie looked sidelong at her sister, whom she suspected was having some trouble holding this man to her will. Given half a second free from Nita's fascinating attention, this 'Mak' of hers would set his naked shoulders to the cornerstone of Stones Manor and collapse the walls atop their heads.

I should never have written her, Lanie thought. Better to be homeless than to have *him* here. Better to be married to Scratten, Cracchen, *and* Hatchet Scratch!

Nita crouched on the floor beside Mak. She fitted the silvery-green dressing gown over his shoulders, grabbing him by the chin when he twitched away from her touch, and murmuring until he grew calm again. When he was still, she cinched the dressing gown shut with the sash.

"I shouldn't keep him so long a falcon." Nita regretfully smoothed the brocade over his shoulders. "But there's nothing else to do. He won't *eat!* And he keeps trying to harm himself... Oh, he is intractable!"

Taking his face between her hands again, her nails biting deeply into his cheeks, she whispered, "Just you wait, Mak. Three days."

Mak's back was to Lanie, so she couldn't see what was in his eyes when he met Nita's gaze. But she did see his hands curling into fists, and Nita jumping to her feet as if snapped from a slingshot. Breathing sharply through her nose, she turned and stared directly into Lanie's eyes. One. Two...

Lanie looked down just in time.

"I am glad to be home," Nita said simply. "I can't tell you how much. Or what your letter meant to me, Miscellaneous—begging me to return. I would have returned for less, you know."

Lanie eyed the claw-like tension in Nita's hand as it stroked her silver bracer. She shifted her weight onto the step behind her, preparing to leap backwards in case Nita—or Mak—spontaneously exploded.

"You asked how I could possibly be a gyrlady," Nita went on. Lanie raised her eyebrows, surprised at the turn of subject. "You were right," she continued, "I'm not. Though I wear a Bryddongard and command a Falcon Defender, I am not and cannot be a gyrlady of Quadiíb. Mak"—she indicated the naked man—"*did* have a gyrlady once. My mentor at the Caravan School. Gelethai. She is dead now. So Mak is mine."

Lanie's nose began to bleed silently, copiously, dolorously. From the ferocity of her allergic reaction, she deduced three things.

One: Gyrlady Gelethai had died, violently and abruptly, at her sister's hand.

Two: Since it was antithetical to the sworn beliefs of the gyrgardon of

Quadiíb that they would stand by and permit their Gyrladies to come to harm without trying to stop that harm with their own bodies, then Mak had not only arrived at Stones Manor against his will, but he was only still *alive* against the sworn vows of his vocation, his religion, and the laws of his country.

Three: Nita would have ensorcelled Mak soon after receiving Lanie's letter late last fall. She had probably set her trap for the high holy fire feast at Midwinter, when the panthauma in the atmosphere surged, and the magic of the gods boosted the smaller magics of mortals. Probably she had meant her fascination to last an entire season. But Nita never had much magic to begin with—and now, with three days to go till Spring Equinox, her spell of fascination was beginning to fade.

Mak was fighting it. Fighting *her*. Bending his whole being to it. Nita must be renewing her fascination spell constantly, exhausting herself with each small, strenuous act of will—bleeding out *will* the way Lanie drew blood from her veins in order to make ectenica—as she awaited her next surge.

Lanie stepped away from her sister, stopping up her nosebleed with as little drama as possible. Being a necromancer meant needing as many handkerchiefs as hairs on your head, which, in Lanie's case, were innumerable.

"From the beginning," Nita murmured, lost in the gyrgardi's green glare, "Gelethai made it clear that I could never be like her. No matter how hard I studied, nor which of her high arts I mastered. She was never bold enough to say it to my face—but every day, in every way, she deliberately demonstrated her superiority. Flaunting her languages, her graces, her grasp of politics and trade. Her Bryddongard. I might have bested her in *sports*, had she deigned to compete in the field—but Gyrladies leave athletics to their gyrgardon. That's how I met Mak. He allowed me to hawk him—Gelethai had no interest in hunting, and he saw how restless I was. We spent hours together, bringing in meat for the Traveling Palaces. But he never looked at me the way he looked at *her*. The way they looked at each other, as if they knew all each other's secrets. As if they were inside each other's minds. They were never even *lovers*—can you believe it?"

Lanie swallowed, her throat too dry to answer. But Nita required no reply. She simply went on, "Gelethai laughed when I asked her how that was—laughed at *me!* She said it needn't be like that between Gyrladies and their Falcon Defenders; it was already *more* than that. She pitied me. She *dared* pity me! Because I could never be a gyrlady, never understand the bond she had with him. But *she* never understood that I didn't want her paltry title—not if she were *giving* it away. I didn't need it. I am Amanita Muscaria Stones."

Lanie's gaze roved desperately for something to alight upon that was not Nita or Mak. There: Goody Graves, standing beneath the Grand Staircase.

Goody's gaze cut to hers, the blue glow of her eyes the exact color of ectenica. It cooled her, like a breeze cutting through a conflagration.

"*I am a Stones,*" Nita spat. Lanie's head whipped back in her direction. Her sister's face blazed like a golden inferno. "And I made sure they all knew it by the time I left. Every patronizing, falcon-flashing, high-priced whore of Quadiíb."

With that, she snapped out the arm that wore the Bryddongard—"Mak! To me!"—and spoke three words in Old Quadic. A silver flash, and Mak melted from man to bird, leaving the old dressing gown in a forlorn puddle. He arrowed straight up from the floor to her left arm, where he mantled her silver bracer broodingly, as if it were prey. Face wreathed in a strained rictus that lacked joy or even satisfaction, Nita nodded to Lanie.

"We will see you tonight for dinner, Miscellaneous. Make sure Goody prepares meat. Venison stew—she can leave out the greens. No spices. Plenty of onion. I have been starving for proper Lirian food these last four years. Most Quadoni are vegetarians!"

Then she padded, stalking-quiet in her stockinged feet, over the glittering black flagstone. She did not, Lanie noted, head in the direction of her old bedchamber, but up the Grand Staircase towards Aba's rooms, workshop and all. No hesitation. No backward glance.

"Phew!" Lanie blew out her breath. Goody did not, but then, she never did. Picking up Natty's ancient dressing gown from the floor, Lanie strolled over to the staircase, where she leaned against Goody like a dog who wanted petting. "Well, Goody. We survived first contact."

Slowly, slowly, Goody's hand moved up to briefly press her braids. Lanie leaned in, hoping for more, but Goody let her hand fall again.

"What was that, do you think? That whole gyrgardi thing, I mean?"

"That?" Goody Graves's voice seemed to sound from the very bottoms of her feet. A flat, bone-cracking bass, with an echo at the bottom. "That, Mizka, was a travesty."

"What do you mean?"

For the flicker of a splinter of a second, Goody looked like she was about to say more. Instead, she shrugged her boulder-heavy shoulders and shambled off to the kitchen. Lanie hung back a second, glancing after her sister who had disappeared up the Grand Staircase.

If she liked you, Goody was the best cook in all of Liriat. And Goody *loved* Lanie. These blissful last few months, Goody had taught her hundreds of recipes—most of them Quadoni, all of them blessedly without meat. Without Natty and Aba and Aunt Diggie around, whose cumulative presence had caused in Lanie, since ever she could remember, low-grade nausea and a constant headache that made eating a repugnant duty, she had found herself—for the first time in her life—really hungry. She had been eating hugely, trying and tasting everything, and taking great pleasure in it.

But now Nita was back. And so was Lanie's bile.

Nevertheless, she thought she had better help Goody prepare tonight's dinner, or Nita was bound to get scorched bread and a rubbery stew of last year's apples. Which would make Nita furious.

Nita wanted dead deer; dead deer Nita would have. The last thing Lanie needed was her sister lashing out at the one person in the world who cared if Lanie lived or died.

Even if that person wasn't, precisely, alive.

CHAPTER THREE

The Sarcophagus of Souls

Rainday 17th
Month of Wells, 414 Founding Era
Two days till Spring Equinox

EARLY THE NEXT morning, Nita routed Lanie out of bed. Flushed, cheerful, with a hooded falcon on one arm and a dead squirrel swinging from her belt, she bid Lanie, "Come to breakfast, Miscellaneous!"

Lanie obeyed, mostly because she did not want Nita to touch her. So soon after killing that squirrel, Nita's hands would be full of death. The lightest of touches might set off Lanie's allergy. Even the lesser reactions—swelling, itching, sneezing, watering eyes, a dull headache—could lay her low for the day. And she had *plans*.

But it was, of course, impossible to actually eat breakfast. Lanie looked on, bilious, while Nita fed Mak—in his falcon form—bits of squirrel, all the time chatting amiably about her scheme for taking over Aba and Natty's former duties as Royal Assassin and Chief Executioner. Lanie kept her face open and encouraging, swallowing a sickening stream of free-running saliva, and taking deep, slow breaths through her nose.

"Oh!" Nita exclaimed, looking up at last from her wild-eyed raptor. "I forgot to tell you at dinner. I rode through Liriat Proper on my way home yesterday and requested an appointment with Erralierra. Her courier arrived this morning with my answer; she'll be coming here the day after tomorrow to discuss a few employment opportunities. She asks that you sit in on the meeting."

"But day after tomorrow is Spring Equinox!" Lanie protested, too loudly. The falcon's black head snapped toward her.

Lanie didn't ask *why* Erralierra wanted to see her; the Blood Royal always looked in on her whenever she came by Stones Manor. It had been generations since the Brackenwilds had their very own, homegrown necromancer at their disposal. The last one born was Irradiant Stones, who won the Northernmost War for Sosha Brackenwild a hundred years ago.

Nita's eyes were narrowing. "What does that have to do with anything?"

"It's my surge!"

"Yes. And?"

And I'll be *busy*, Lanie wanted to wail.

High holy fire feasts were so important. They were the four days of the year when the panthauma—the "All-Marvel," as the old texts called it, or "Gods-gift"—in the atmosphere boosted even the most minor magical acts to near-miracles. There was a limited opportunity to experiment with panthaumic surges, and the day after tomorrow—if she could marshal the concentration, which was always iffy on a surge-day—Lanie was planning on resurrecting a *whole family* of mouse skeletons she'd found preserved, in their entirety, beneath a couch cushion.

She tried a different tack. "Are you sure you want me there? You know I get a little... odd... on surge days. I don't want to embarrass you."

"You won't," her sister promised, "or you'll regret it."

Lanie nodded reluctant understanding, and Nita added briskly, "Our meeting with the Blood Royal will be at noon. It won't take but an hour or two, and then we'll both have all afternoon and evening free to practice our arts."

"All right," Lanie grumped. But she felt a stir of excitement as well. Erralierra never traveled to Stones Manor without a flight of advisors and secretaries and guards, including a contingent of fire priests, acolytes of the god Sappacor. Canon Lir was often among them. She had not seen Canon Lir for months and months, not since just after Midwinter, and it had been weeks since they'd last exchanged letters. Time was, not three days would go by without a letter between them, but they were both older now—and Canon Lir, at least, was busier.

"Also," Nita said, with less enthusiasm, "I'll be having a meeting just prior to that with Sari Scratch. About our debt."

Lanie groaned. Her sister continued inexorably. "You'll be joining me for that too." The *or else* was implicit.

"All right," Lanie said again, and sighed. "But if she brings Scratten, Cracchen and Hatchet along, it's *your* turn to fend off their matrimonial advances. Which," she reflected, "is sort of like fending off three very blond siege engines."

The glint in Nita's black eyes made Lanie's teeth tingle. "It has been too long since I have hunted big game. I've yet to bag a Northerner. Three of them, you said?"

"Triplets." Lanie's mouth felt like she had been sucking old bones, moss and all. But she managed to sound casual. She hoped.

"A matched set. Excellent!" Nita frowned at Lanie's plate. "Miscellaneous. Why aren't you eating?"

And that, thought Lanie, is my cue. Before Nita starts force-feeding me the rest of Mak's squirrel.

"I never eat breakfast," she lied. "Anyway, Amanita Muscaria, now that we'll be so busy first thing on surge day, I'll have to take most of today and tomorrow finishing up my prep. I'll see you later!"

"We'll take luncheon together!" Nita said quickly. "I want to tell you what I plan for *my* surge."

She stared with brooding fondness at the falcon, and Lanie noticed the shadows circling her sister's eyes, the same steely blue-gray as Mak's wings.

"I cannot wait for my panthaumic boost," Nita murmured. "Everything will be so much easier. See you at noon!"

NOON THE NEXT day perforce found Lanie in Stones Gallery, hiding out behind the Sarcophagus of Souls. Skipping lunch was no hardship; yesterday's experiment of trying to eat in her sister's presence left her feeling like she'd gulped down chopped-up worms (instead of a plate full of nothing, with a glass of juiced nothing, and a side of nothing-butter on nothing-bread). The last thing she wanted was to endure yet another lunch under Nita's gaze. Which would be difficult to avoid, since Nita seemed intent on keeping mealtimes sacred.

Why, Lanie didn't know. She'd never eaten with her sister before in all her life—or any of her family. They knew she couldn't.

"What are you doing?" asked the ghost in the padlock.

"Hiding from my sister," Lanie replied.

"What, again?"

"What do you mean *again?*" Lanie glared up from the floor to the Sarcophagus of Souls. The rusted padlock glowed down at her from its lid, now vaguely blue, now vaguely face-like: a long face with catfish whiskers and tiny spectacles as round and bright as bucklers. "I haven't had to do it for years!"

"*Years*. Ha!" The ghost yawned. Or rather, the padlock itself gave the impression of yawning: a faint blue gape of yawningness right around its keyhole. "Amanita Muscaria was in Quadiíb, what, four years only? That, girlie, is a hiccup in time. A burp. *Years*, she says. Let me tell you what *years* feels like."

In the shadow of the Sarcophagus, Lanie rolled her eyes. Then, rising to her knees, she popped her head up to peer around the gallery. All clear. Stones Gallery was as empty as when she'd entered it.

The gallery was a high-ceilinged room that ran the entire eastern length of the main house, terminating at the north end in the morning room and at the south end in the Solarium, which opened into the dining room and drawing rooms respectively. It was dim and dusty and stuffed with statuary and vitrines: plenty of things to hide behind—but none so large and splendid as the Sarcophagus of Souls. Mounted on a basalt plinth, it stood at the very center of the gallery: an altar to Stoneses past, and a monument to the greatest of them. Or so the ghost liked to claim.

He cackled now. "She always finds you in the end, you know."

Lanie shook her head. "I'm older now."

"So's she, girlie. So's she."

She crouched again, strategizing. She suspected that Nita would come at her from the Solarium, since that was at the back of the house, closer to Aba's—now Nita's—living quarters. Nita had spent most of yesterday and that morning in Aba's workroom, sorting through their mother's things. But she might rise up straight from her lunch in the dining room to search for Lanie—in which case, she'd be coming from the direction of the morning room, which opened onto the dining room.

Trust Nita to dine in state, even for a luncheon of cold meat and bread! Then again, the gallery's outer wall featured two more doors connecting to corridors leading into the northeast and southeast wings of the manor. While Lanie thought it was unlikely that Nita would approach from either of those, she knew—better than anyone—how unpredictable her sister could be, so she'd do well to keep an eye on all four points of entry. If only she had a circle of eyes set all around her head!

Instead, she had the Sarcophagus of Souls.

The main advantage of the Sarcophagus was its immense size. Another—and more to the point—was its deeper-than-natural shadow that extended like an aura all the way around it for several feet in all directions. The shadow was uncomfortably cold, blacker than ink but edged in eerie blue, and it murmured with uneasy voices. Lanie couldn't even see her own hand in front of her face when she sat in it.

Which meant that Nita wouldn't be able to see her either.

It *did* mean that she'd have to endure Grandpa Rad's incessant prattling at her—but at least he couldn't give her away. Nita had never been able to hear him. She had once accused Lanie of inventing the ghost to puff up her own importance.

"I always liked Amanita Muscaria," the ghost mused. "I wish *she'd* been born with your powers. Now *that* would be a vessel worthy of cultivating for my rebirth! Alas. I must wait till one or the other of you spawn someone rather more promising, for it would degrade me to possess a substandard soma such as yourself."

Grandpa Rad had waited his whole afterlife for another necromancer to be born into the Stones line, planning all the while to possess their body with his own soul, and once again walk the physical plane. Lanie, scrawny and snot-nosed, was deemed ineligible from the outset. He told her as much. Constantly.

She knew better than to argue with him. She knew that she should show a stony face like Goody Graves, and keep a stony tongue with it. After all, *she* had skin and *he* didn't; why should she let him get under hers? Her best vengeance was to treat him like a textbook, milk what mentoring she could from his boasts and scolds, and ignore the rest. Except...

Except, sometimes, she couldn't help herself. Like this time.

"If Nita had been born like me," she heard herself saying, "she'd be allergic to everything you say you like about her now."

"But," the ghost argued, "she would have had the *heart!* Your weakness isn't your *allergy!* Did I not have that same allergy in my youth? Did it not almost murder me a thousand times before I came into the fullness of my power? *All* necromancers are born with it. No, *your* weakness, girlie, is that you'd rather play in the dirt than study death magic with the greatest necromancer in history! You and your gardens. Growing your pumpkins and potatoes. Cooking lessons in the kitchen with that idiot revenant, who was worm-eaten when I was a lad. Don't think I don't know!"

"I study with you regularly!" Lanie protested.

"Not regularly enough!" the ghost thundered, the padlock clanging with resounding petulance against the Sarcophagus lid.

Silence. Slowly, Lanie leaned back against the basalt plinth that bore the weight of the Sarcophagus. Slowly, she breathed out.

The ghost said nothing. Grandpa Rad was sulking. He might not speak to her for days now. Oh, eventually he'd unpucker from his pout—he enjoyed talking far too much not to, and Lanie was the only one who could hear him... other than Goody Graves, who ignored him masterfully.

But relief lasted only a little while before guilt set in. She shouldn't have provoked him; Lanie *needed* the ghost to talk. Grandpa Rad was, indeed, the largest repository of necromantic knowledge at her disposal. He had left a stack of treatises and journals and personal correspondence to Stones Library upon his death, but his handwriting was execrable. Easier just to wheedle experimental spells out of him, flattering his prodigious ego whilst enduring his constant jabs at her person.

The flattery part was easy. All Lanie had to do was remind him of his past deeds.

THE GLORIOUS LIFE of Irradiant Stones—or 'Grandpa Rad,' a term Lanie used when she wanted to make his padlock clatter with rage—ended one night in a single act of death magic so sublime that it made the rest of his life seem retroactively dowdy by comparison. Irradiant used his own death to defeat the twenty-one powerful Sky Houses of Skakmaht, claiming a lasting victory for Liriat in the Northernmost War. Though this historic event occurred over a hundred years ago, Grandpa Rad (who had, for a ghost, an extraordinary memory) could recall it as clearly as the many little humiliations of Lanie's childhood—and took as great a pleasure in relating the one to her as the other.

During Irradiant's lifetime, the twenty-one wizard guilds of Skakmaht, called the Sky Houses, ruled the cities of the north from on high, governing their country from flying castles. They operated as individual structures most of the time, but once a year all the Sky Houses joined together in a single, colossal castle-entity called the Guilded Council, which would float in the clouds above Iskald, capital city of Skakmaht. Iskald was a city at the top of the world—physically, financially, and magically.

And it was Irradiant Stones who brought it down.

He was forty-six years old at the time, father of twelve fatal Stoneses, and feared by all who knew him. He was also the best friend and confidante of Blood Royal Sosha Brackenwild. So, naturally, when a spat between Sosha and the Sky Houses caused the Guilded Council to place an embargo on trade with Liriat, Irradiant Stones marched north with Sosha's army to seek retaliation.

The necromancer's presence ensured that any soldier who died on that brutally cold march—from lack of rations, improper equipment, exposure, disease—could be raised right up again and made to march as a member of the undead force. This would have been terrible for morale if Sosha had not pointed out to his living soldiers, quite practically, that while the undead could fight and loot tirelessly, *they* had no need for either treasure or renown. Now there would be twice as much of both to go around—and for half the effort!

The Lirian army ravaged Iskald. They hollowed out the glittering capital city like wood-boring beetles. They burnt buildings, raided supply houses, harried citizens, poisoned wells. Sosha Brackenwild took revenge for the embargo, his ax Drjōta ever thirsty. (Drjōta, endowed with ancient death magic. Drjōta, old as Liriat itself. Drjōta, whose blade brightened and sharpened the more it tasted flesh, whose edge, in Iskald, was never dull.)

When the wizard guilds heard of the attack on their capital city, the Sky Houses came soaring in from every quadrant of the Skaki heavens to join together in Guilded Council over Iskald. Their spells rained down on the encamped Lirian army. Icy nightmares crawled among the tents. Supply trains evanesced like mist. Weapons rotted, or turned against the hands that wielded them, or turned into something else entirely. Fevers and visions shook the living. Only the undead were unaffected, but even they, tireless under Irradiant's iron command, could not lay siege to the city-sized flying fortress high above them.

Sosha Brackenwild was losing the war.

But on the high holy fire feast of Midwinter, Irradiant Stones threw all his formidable power into a purely innovative act of magic. As a necromancer, he of course knew how to call the souls of the dead back into their bodies, animating them—temporarily—to obey his every command.

Now, he tried the reverse: calling forth *living* souls *out* of the bodies they inhabited.

With his powers enhanced by the panthaumic surge, when he called to them, the living souls of the Skaki sky wizards sprang to his summons like lightning to iron. They left their soul-scooped shells empty, their flesh frozen forever in time, never to die or decay. But even as Irradiant thrust the dazzlingly pure substances of thirty-one hundred wizards into the stone sarcophagus he had built for the purpose, the souls themselves burnt *him* to ash. Irradiant's body fell to nothing.

But he had predicted this development, and in the moment after his death, he retained enough command over his soul to seal the sarcophagus with it, and then inhabit the padlock that fastened the lid shut.

Upon Irradiant's abrupt demise, his undead force, bound to serve him by his blood, died as well. Only Sosha Brackenwild and a few survivors managed to return to Liriat, bearing the Sarcophagus of Souls with them. Shortly after that, the Blood Royal also died, alone, in his bed. Some said of pneumonia. Others said of proximity to a necromancer.

Skakmaht, without a centralized government, without its wizards, fell to disarray.

The great city of Iskald, in the shadow of an eternal eclipse, was never rebuilt, but left to lie in ruins.

Above the city, the Guilded Council hung like a meteorite that never fell. If it ever did, Iskald would surely be smashed beneath it. The Northernmost War was ended.

And Irradiant Stones had been bored ever since.

AT LAST THE story wound down, for Lanie-didn't-know-which-hundredth time. The padlock was once again a-twinkle with catfish whiskers—as if the ghost had never sunk into the sullens.

"So, girlie," said Grandpa Rad. "It's coming on surge-time. Tomorrow! Have you tried that exercise with the owl pellet yet?"

Ah! Lanie thought, stirring from the chilly stupor brought on by the Sarcophagus of Souls and its dusty old tale. At last! Something I'm *actually* interested in!

"I couldn't find an owl pellet," she said. "But I found nine whole mouse skeletons in the attics of Torr Digitalis."

"You'd do better to start with one," Grandpa Rad advised sourly.

"Nine is more fun."

"You'll regret it. You're not in your full power yet, girlie. You're, what now? Fifteen?"

"Sixteen soon," said summer-born Lanie.

But Grandpa Rad couldn't be bothered with meagre things like seasons or birthdays. He returned to his lecture. "Remember, *precision* is more important than *proportion*. Reassembling and reanimating a single mouse skeleton will require a great deal of delicacy and concentration. You might, eventually, with practice, be able to create a fair revenant out of nothing but ectenica—but anything you bind to undeath with your blood alone will never last for long off-surge. However, if you play your surge right, a *panthaumic* revenant should endure a full quarter—until the next high holy fire feast! And that's just early days. From there, you'll learn ways to extend the effects of panthauma—past even your own lifetime! Which surge is it tomorrow again?"

Grandpa Rad always knew when a surge was coming, but he could not differentiate between them, shackled to the padlock as he was.

"Spring Equinox." How Lanie longed for spring. Tomorrow, tomorrow, tomorrow, her blood sang.

"Right. Then. Use your vernal surge to raise up your little mousey whole. *One* mouse, mind! Trust me, girlie, you don't want nine undead mice scampering around chewing up the furniture for a whole season. Then, on your Midsummer surge, I'll teach you how to snuff it dead again. Keep a revenant around any longer and it'll start growing…"

A noise at the back of the gallery snagged Lanie's attention. She leaned forward on hands and knees to peep around the base of the basalt plinth. Movement.

"Rats," she cursed.

"No, no," Grandpa Rad objected, appalled, "rats are far too intelligent for *you* to be raising them up first thing. Just stick to…"

He trailed off as he too heard the voice, then uttered a loud, "Ha! Well, there you have it, girlie. *Told* you she'd find you."

CHAPTER FOUR

The Poison Cabinet of Delirious Stones

LANIE SLUNK LOW, belly-down, chin on floor, palms flat to either side of her face. The deep, cold shadow of the Sarcophagus of Souls covered her. She was like a fish head suspended in aspic. Black aspic. A really black aspic.

"This place is filthy!" Nita's disgust echoed throughout Stones Gallery. "It's disgraceful. How busy you must be all day *not* attending your duties, Graves. Miscellaneous has been much too lenient."

Abruptly, the tone of her voice changed from scourge to syrup. "Mak," she cooed, "I apologize on behalf of all my ancestors for the ramshackle state of Stones Manor. I'll not make you endure it a second longer. Graves!"

Lanie winced. She should spring up right now, put herself between Goody and Nita, distract her...

"Start on the floor," Nita ordered. "Sweep, mop, polish, wax. When you are finished, dust the vitrines, take a soapy rag to them, wash and dry them. After that, come find me for your next orders."

Goody Graves had a vast vocabulary of silences, and Lanie had spent most of her formative years learning how to interpret them. It was harder than learning Quadic from books; there was no lexicon in Stones Library for that particularly irritated absence of sound that meant: 'If you don't let the dough respire like I repeatedly instructed you to, Mizka, your bread will end up tasting like a brick of compost. But go on and do it your way if you must. I've no more to say on the matter.' By now, Lanie was fairly conversant in Goody's lacunae—and at the moment, the dusty parquet floor positively thundered with her speechless fury.

She thumped her forehead softly on the floorboards. She hated when Goody was angry. In certain moods—especially when Natty and Aba and Aunt Diggie were still alive—she'd not only refused to speak, she wouldn't even meet Lanie's eyes for weeks. It always felt like losing a limb.

Scooting forward on her belly, Lanie risked another peek. Nita was standing kissing-close to her Quadoni captive, whom she had released from his falcon form. Thank Saint Death—the man was draped in Natty's green-and-silver dressing gown once more, the sash doubled-wrapped around his concave belly, knotted fast. No more... nakedness.

Nita held his gaze, her black eyes sunk in gray hollows. Her lips had a chapped, bluish look to them, had peeled back slightly from her teeth like illustrations Lanie had seen of cholera victims.

Drained, she realized. Sucked dry. Spending too much magic off-surge. Nita should really know better. Couldn't she just... tie him up until tomorrow? But no; she needed to *control* him.

"Mak," Nita spoke slowly and clearly, never blinking, "you are to stay here in Stones Gallery. Study the portraits. Read the plaques. Learn my family history. It is yours now. Everything I have is yours."

Lanie gagged. The last thing on a long list of things she'd rather *not* be doing today was watching her sister flirt, especially with the cataclysmically furious man she'd ruined, kidnapped, and enslaved. But, praise be to Saint Death, Nita was already making her excuses.

"Tomorrow I'll be meeting with our creditors and my liege lady, and so I have many preparations to complete before day's end. I shall be back to fetch you for your dinner, Mak, never fear! There is so much game in the Diesmali; you'll have your pick of the finest, freshest meat."

Lanie made little flicking motions with her fingers, urging her sister's departure. But still Nita lingered, reluctant to leave Mak's side.

"I doubt Sari Scratch will agree to a complete remission, but a forbearance might be arranged. Her last letter implied heavily that much of our debt would be forgiven if I offered up my sister as collateral, but..."

The rest of what Nita said was lost to Lanie when Grandpa Rad started lecturing, "Those Scratches are Skaki agents for sure, girlie—didn't I say so when they first came calling? They want you for your magic. Not to *marry* you, whatever Mama Scratch says. Wed a Stones? After Iskald? Ha! A Skaki citizen—even displaced—would sooner breed with a plague carcass than a Stones. No, mark me, they'll be wanting to use *you* to crack open my dear old Sarcophagus of Souls and release their wizards back to the Sky Houses. They'll drain you dead to do it, girlie, and stomp your corpse to dust after. Oh, those Skakis have long dreamt of revenge for the north. They'll bed down any foreign government—Leech, Rook, Kalestis, Umrys-by-the-Sea—to gain a foothold in Liriat. My money's on Rook. Lots of activity up that way, ever since Queen Bran Fiakhna claimed her place as Blackbird Bride. But they can't outsmart us! Look at your sister's face. *She's* the Stones to keep Skakmaht in its place—which is stone-cold dead in the sky!"

Lanie tried to ignore the ghost's buzzing by focusing on Nita, who was explaining, frowningly, "Death magic is very rare, and in high demand. If Miscellaneous survives till her adulthood, I believe she will be someone of note. Father always said she would. And when she does, I'd rather she be a Stones than a Scratch withal."

"Your sister's got more faith in you than I, girlie," said Grandpa Rad.

This deserved no reply, so Lanie said nothing. But Sari Scratch certainly did make her uneasy, whatever her intentions, mostly because her behavior toward Lanie had been so very *motherly*. Lanie did not trust *motherly*.

But whatever Sari might be (and the woman was clever enough to be anything: agent of Skakmaht, tool of Rook, rising Lirian nobility, or all of the above!), she couldn't bring herself to believe that her sons, the Scratch boys, were anything but amiable lugs with half a brain to share between them. Well, *maybe* Cracchen had slightly more brains than his brothers. But his gain was Scratten and Hatchet's loss.

Come on, Nita! Lanie thought pleadingly. Will you never *leave?*

Moments passed as Nita stared at Mak, who returned her look, his own face blank. "I'd have *you* be a Stones too," she said, then—finally!—with a sigh, touched the back of her knuckles to his cheek, and left the gallery.

The only sound in the room was a broom brushing the floor. Goody could sweep with operatic aplomb, full of crescendo and opinion. But not today. Today the sweeps were short and sharp, like little gasps, or a jerk of the head.

Mak's shoulders crumpled first. His head bowed like a branch overladen with fatal fruit. Lanie watched as he bent to his breast, his arms coming up over his head as though to protect it from a wounding world, before his knees gave out and he crashed to the floor.

The *shh-shh-shh* of the broom bristles continued, only now they were tranquil as a lullaby. Goody Graves swept herself ever nearer to the gyrgardi, until she stopped, and squatted from her towering height to brush her heap of dust and debris into a pan. This brought her to Mak's level. She reached out a large gray hand to touch his shoulder. Mak looked up in despair.

His face! Lanie thought, wonderstruck. His face!

She shook her head, collecting herself.

His face, she observed, is much easier to look at when he's not confronting someone he wants to rip into gobbets.

The gyrgardi was of a height with Nita, a lean length of about six feet or so. Ceremonial scars adorned his face, small hook-like marks curving along forehead, cheekbones, and jawline. His complexion was a touch lighter than Nita's, a deep winter tawniness that would bronze in the summer sun. Ember-red hair flew out every which way from his head, bright as flame. The clear mineral green of his eyes was like the absinthe Aunt Diggie used to drink to celebrate a successful hit.

He gazed at Goody as if seeing her for the first time. Confusion crowded out despair, then cleared as he recognized her for what she was. Lanie expected revulsion and fear next: how most visitors to Stones Manor reacted to their undead housekeeper. Instead, reverence lit his cicatrized face.

"Elif Doéden!" he cried out in Quadic.

Hooking his hands at the thumbs, he pressed both palms flat against his chest. A bird with wings outspread. His head inclined in a sinuous dip. To Lanie's surprise, Goody returned the obeisance, taking it one step further by then unhooking her thumbs, uncrossing her palms, and proffering her open hands to him. The bass echo of her voice sounded from the bowels of her being.

"Gyrgardi iddin Quadiíb."

But Mak shook his head sharply. "No, lady," he spat in Lirian. "Not gyrgardi. I am this." His fists clenched, slamming against his breast. Once, twice, thrice. "I am *this* now. I am nothing."

Lanie muffled an 'Oof' as his self-violence bruised her own chest. Her contusions were only echo-wounds, an annoying symptom of her allergy, and she knew the marks would fade much faster than any real bruises she might get, from barking her shin or falling out of bed. Nevertheless, she resented him for hurting her, albeit unknowingly.

Mak brought the flat of his hand up before his face and held it there. Lanie identified the gesture as one of the sothaín attitudes. Her study of Quadoni movement meditation so far had consisted of copying all one hundred forty-four attitudes into her journal, and attempting the first set of twelve every morning. That was hard enough, and she was loath to move on to the next set without mastering them. She hadn't gotten to the attitude Mak was currently assuming, but that hand-to-face posture, she recalled, was one of grief. Twelfth set—the set belonging to Doédenna, god of Death. Big surprise.

Goody Graves moved her hand from his shoulder to his head, as if in blessing. Lanie frowned. Goody never touched anyone except her—and here she was, comforting a complete stranger! And, and... *speaking to him in Quadic!*

The words were soft, but Lanie, accustomed to Goody's silences, heard every syllable.

"Stoneses die young—and therefore thou must live. Outlive thy foe and dance upon her tomb."

Hearing those words was like swallowing a splinter of icicle. It scraped Lanie's throat and shriveled her belly. She shivered. She had never heard Goody speak so bitterly, or with such resolve.

But when Mak's hand did not waver from his face, Goody raised her own in solidarity. After a moment, she let it fall, and stood, and picked up her broom as if taking up a great burden once more. The shh-shh-shhing sounds started up again.

Mak finally emerged from behind his hand and slowly uncrumpled from the ground, taking a few aimless steps. He stopped, seemingly at random, before a large portrait of Ham-Handed Stones, and looked up.

But Lanie knew it wasn't random. He was only doing what Nita had ordered him to do. What she had *fascinated* him into doing. He was obeying. But she noted that he hadn't obeyed right away. He was still fighting her. He followed the letter of her command, but listlessly, with no real interest or attention.

She shifted her gaze to Ham-Handed Stones's portrait, trying to see it through his eyes. Not unworthy of attention. He'd been War Chief to Blood Royal Moll Brackenwild in the generation after Liriat's foundation. His portrait had pride of place in Stones Gallery, occupying a large rectangle of wall between Delirious Stones's poison cabinet and a more-than-life-size self-portrait of Celerity Stones. Ham-Handed glowered down at all he surveyed. He was beefy, beetle-browed, irate. His heavy jowls billowed with the most ferocious (and in Lanie's opinion, absurd) black sideburns that wanted (in Lanie's opinion) a stout pair of shears and a burly shepherd to keep them in line. Beneath his portrait, on two brass pegs, hung his sparth ax, dusty and disused, but ready. Killing-sharp.

After Mak had looked his fill on Ham Handed-Stones, he turned his attention to the other exhibits on display in the gallery, with the stoic air of a man paraded in front of his enemies before execution. He prowled the parquet floor with steps almost as silent as Goody's, first walking the length of the inner wall, then looping around and passing back up the outer one, studying the tremendous paintings in their ornate but tarnished frames, representing the celebrated spies, assassins, executioners, and royal revivifiers that bore the name Stones, as well as the vitrines beneath them containing various gewgaws and mementos from their (mostly) brief lives.

He passed, with only the briefest of pauses, several incredibly famous and important portraits: Opscheplooper Stones, who killed more friends by accident than enemies on commission; the triplets Iniquity, Propinquity, and Antiquity, who had founded the Lirian Academy for Young Cutthroats, and who'd all died together in their rooms when one of their students burnt it to the ground; Delirious Stones, author of the notorious memoir, *Adventures of a Courtesan Assassin,* posing in nothing but a bit of red ribbon and a powder puff; and—last and most magnificent of all—Quick Fantastic Stones, one of the First Founders of Liriat, Left Hand of the Founding Queen Ynyssyll Brackenwild herself. In the portrait, she stood with a hand on her young son's shoulder, on the wilderness site that would one day become Stones Manor.

Lanie, concealed in her sanctuary shadow, crawled around the perimeter of the Sarcophagus of Souls to observe Mak's progress. What had always seemed like a lot of ancestral junk bristled with new interest. She watched Mak study the contents of the grubby, spider-cracked vitrines, which she knew held in the main an array of weaponry: daggers, axes, dirks, long swords, needles, flails, star maces, war hammers, piano wire, boomerangs, bludgeons, crossbows, triple-bladed hedge trimmers, glaives and guisarmes. There were also the less traditional but no less effective boxes of nocuous chocolates, sticks of baneful incense, skin-eating massage oils, daintily embroidered smothering cushions, ivory-handled fans that opened into a splay of razorblades, assorted beakers, flasks, vials, hairpins, hatpins, and small tubes of toxic lipstick, usually in a signature shade of red.

By the time Mak had made a complete perambulation of Stones Gallery, stopping beneath Ham-Handed's portrait again to read the plaque detailing the spectacular manner of his death, Lanie's skull ached. What must he think of them all, these bygone Stoneses, murderous servants of the Blood Royal Brackenwilds since the establishment of Liriat? She had never before considered her life from a stranger's perspective. She was half-indignant (why didn't he *care?*), half-humbled (why *should* he care?), and wholly confused.

But no time to dwell on her feelings: Mak was on the move again. He had turned from Ham-Handed's portrait to Delirious Stones's poison cabinet, which he had completely ignored on his initial pass through the gallery.

Now he seemed to shake awake. The malaise of Nita's fascination shivered off his shoulders. His head rose. His eyes focused. He leapt forward.

Lanie scooted further back into the shadow, hugging her knees. If he was regaining his will, it was absolutely necessary that he not see her.

Now his nose was pressed to the glass-paned doors of the poison cabinet, his hands splayed to either side of his face like a child glimpsing his first snow through the nursery window. He made a sound somewhere between a sigh and a cry.

Goody Graves's sweeping slowed. Everything slowed. Except the gyrgardi.

He spun—lightly, so lightly, as if he were hollow-boned, as if it would be nothing to him to launch into sustained flight—and darted back to Goody Graves. He held out his hands to her, cupped in the shape of a begging bowl. She relinquished her broom to him, then turned her back, and grasped the handle of her mop instead. Following orders.

And what is *that* silence, Goody? Lanie thought, ears pricking. That's your silence for—what?—for, 'Do it if you must. But it is a shame and a pity and a *waste*.'

With that same light-footed, loping vigor, and a blaze of elation on his face, Mak turned the broom in his hands like a spear. Back he ran to the poison cabinet, gaining speed, never stopping until the blunt end of the broom staved in the glass doors.

Then, he was reaching through the shards.

Because his back was to her, Lanie could not see what it was, precisely, that he did next. She could only experience the echoes of it in her own body as her allergy took hold.

What was it? The nick of his skin with a finger-stinger[3]? A sip from a

3 Natty Stones had preferred a plain model for professional use, usually of brushed steel, with smooth joints and few embellishments. But there were other examples of finger-stingers in Stones Gallery, the most famous being Delirious Stones's 'spindle ring.' Gold-plated, studded with

slender vial? A long, purposeful sniff from a jar of caustic powder? He probably wanted to try a bit of everything in an orgy of thoroughness, just to make sure that it worked, ineradicably.

But Stoneses take special care of the tools of their trade, and the contents of the poison cabinet were no exception. Delirious, it was said, had never skimped on anything to do with love or death in her whole meteoric career.

No matter which vehicle to eternity Mak chose—whether inhaled, ingested, daubed, smeared, or jabbed—it would only take a second.

When he collapsed, Lanie felt the thump in her collarbones.

---

cabochon emeralds, it behaved like an ordinary ring until one depressed the central emerald, which triggered the telescoping needle concealed inside. The needle would slide out, three inches of polished platinum, the jut-end extending well over the nail of the wearer's forefinger, smeared with fermented frog poison.

CHAPTER FIVE

The Brinking

Being in such close physical proximity to Mak's death throes, Lanie's body produced its echo-wounds almost simultaneously. First, a sting sprang to her nose. Second, twin gouts of blood spurted from her nostrils. Bitter froth that burned like venom gathered at the back of her throat; she gulped hard as her air passages crushed closed. She had to get out of the gallery while she was still mobile—or Mak's passing might take her with him.

They're only echo-wounds, Lanie reminded herself, swallowing panic along with a mouthful of rotten fruit-, rotten egg-, horseradish-flavored saliva. They'll heal faster than real wounds. They'll only kill me if I remain too close to the source.

Stumbling to her feet, she lurched toward the nearest door. But in her haste, she had forgotten Mak, felled in his sprawl. She tripped over his feet. More echo-wounds flared up as she made contact with his body, and she collapsed to hands and knees beside him, feeling as though the top of her skull were sloughing off. Something not tears dripped from her eyes: something viscous and obscuring.

Mak's jaw locked as unknown poisons gripped his body, foam welling from nose and mouth. The corners of his eyes bled darkly. But the eyes themselves were clear and cold and open. And he saw her.

Mak saw her, and he turned his face to the wall—just as Aba had when she died.

Well, Lanie would not stand for it a second time. Not from *him*, who was not even kin, no matter what Nita said.

"No!"

The guttural, gravelly voice that burst from her throat surprised her. She had thought all those passages squeezed shut. But it wasn't an entirely foreign phenomenon; she had made similar noises a few times in her life now. They were what her screams had deepened into after Nita made her leap from that window; the noise she'd made the morning she found her kitten Katabasis dead in her little box (it was ricin that time—no animal lived long in Nita's house, nor any vulnerable thing Lanie loved too visibly);

and then, that time when Nita tore the cloth head off Hoppy Bunny's sock body, Lanie had gone to bed muttering in a voice like ground-up rocks: how she would learn so much death magic that her sister would never, *ever* be able to harm her or anything she held dear, ever again.

"Live!" Lanie commanded now, and it seemed as if her voice had doubled in its deepening, that she was speaking both with her throat and with something else, a second voice that defied physiology. Grandpa Rad never mentioned anything like it in his journals—but Lanie *knew* that her second voice was the sound of her death magic, just as surely as the smell of her death magic was citrus.

Mak was not all the way dead, not yet, so Lanie's death magic could not compel him to listen and obey. Even if he were dead, she knew that her voice alone could never do the trick of raising him back up. For that, she needed ectenica, and even ectenica—if he were well and truly dead—would not last long.

But one thing was certain: he was *dying*. Part of him was alive, but many tiny, invisible, vitally important parts of him were dead already. And as those parts of him were dead, Lanie could use them. She could mix her living blood with his partially dead matter, and make ectenica that would obey her. And maybe—just maybe—that would be enough to teach his living body how *not* to die.

Already Mak was beginning to buck and shudder. Lanie hastily spat a mouthful of blood into her gray left hand and smeared it onto the scarlet-flecked spume on his mouth. Flecks of their mingled fluids began to glow blue.

"Gyrgardi Iddin Quadiíb!" Lanie growled, still in that doubled voice. She set both her hands on either side of his face, her breath trembling on his copper-sparked eyelashes. "Live! Live, damn you!"

Moving her left hand from his cheek, she pressed it against his chest. The dark gray of her wizard mark seemed to rise from her skin, like a mist, like silvery dandelion fluff going to seed. His heartbeat scudded against her palm: erratic, weak, an exhausted fugitive pounding a barred door in a blizzard as a slink of wolves closed in behind him. Lanie's tears burned like scalding pitch. These, too, she directed into Mak's mouth, where they sizzled blue. Her own heart, mimicking his as it died, was an awkward butterfly fluttering feeble wings against a tightening net.

She lifted her fists and pounded his breast, as he had done. Three times. Her own chest ached in protest.

"Live!" she shouted, her voice huge now, filling Stones Gallery. "Live, damn it! Damn you duodecifold, Mak Cobb or whoever! *You will not take me with you!*"

From miles and miles away, she heard the ghost in the padlock shout, "Yes! That's the way, girlie! You show him!"

And then, a bright pink smell trumpeted up from the floor. The taste of death magic poured into her, as if she had dashed beneath a roaring waterfall of freshly squeezed grapefruit and opened her mouth. The tang cleared the rusty filth from her nose, the poison from her palate, expanded her throat, let her breathe again.

Her eyes flew open as if sparked apart by lightning. The room around her had turned yellow: the walls sloped away from the carpet at crazy angles, peeling back like petals and oozing a distorting amber sap that hardened and shone like jewels. This was the world as she saw it on a high holy fire feast day, when the panthauma of the gods boosted her own mortal magic. But she'd never experienced such a thing *off-surge* before, and never when merely making a simple ectenica.

Except, Lanie had never tried to make ectenica out of a (slightly) living person's matter before. Had she bungled something? Or did this phenomenon have to do with the proximity of tomorrow's surge?

She dragged her gaze back to Mak's envenomed body—and saw a lady kneeling across from her, right at his head.

The lady had a quiet brown face, cowled all in gray. The train of Her gray cloak was made up of thousands upon thousands of small, intersecting bones. It seethed out behind Her, swallowing the parquet floor with a faint clicking sound. She held in Her cupped hands a restless, wild, furious thing that beat and fanned its wings, that struggled and strained and *strove*.

Lanie had never met the lady before. But she had seen Her likeness in countless statues and murals and shrines. She *knew* Her. She knew that hoarfrost stillness.

"Back!" she growled, surprising herself. "*You stay back*. You're not invited."

Not the traditional way to talk to one's god, perhaps. Certainly not to Doédenna, Saint Death. But Lanie figured the lady was probably only phantasmagoria anyhow, brought on by whichever hallucinogenic toxin Mak had taken from Delirious Stones's poison cabinet and passed on to Lanie through her allergy.

And if She *weren't*, why then, Saint Death had already seen and heard everything under the starry spheres, and nothing Lanie said or did could possibly surprise or offend Her. At least, Lanie hoped not.

The hallucination/god considered her.

"I mean it," Lanie warned, speaking not only with her mouth but her *other* voice. "He's not for you. Not yet. And—in case you're considering it—neither am I."

When the lady said nothing, only tilting Her head as if to invite further comment, Lanie relaxed a little. The hallucination/god did not look unreasonable. But neither did She look like She was leaving.

Lanie tried coaxing instead. "Oh, come on. You'll get Your turn, Doédenna—eventually! What's a few more years between friends, hey?"

Doédenna smiled at her. It was a fond smile, broad and sudden and friendly in Her otherwise still face. And it was so very *particularly* directed at Lanie—with a wry squint at the corners of Her eyes, and the barest hint of a nose wrinkle—that Lanie grinned back.

We really *are* friends! she realized breathlessly. What's more—we always have been!

With a slight shrug, Saint Death opened Her palms and released the shadowy thing She held. The bird—if it was a bird; it certainly suggested a bird, one not unlike the peregrine falcon Mak became at Nita's whim, only this one was made of smoke—flew free, passing right through Lanie's breastbone and out the other side. It swooped three times around their heads, then dove straight down, through an invisible seam in Mak's clamped lips, and funneled down his throat, where it disappeared.

Saint Death smiled at Lanie again. She gave her a slight wave of the fingertips, followed by an even slighter nod that slammed Her cowl over Her face, concealing it in a caul of bone. Her infinite cloak collapsed around Her in a clickery-clackering heap. Then it, too, vanished—along with the smell of wild pink grapefruit and the deep yellow tint and the many-petaled walls.

Gone.

The world's rhythms resumed.

Mak's heartbeat drummed steadily beneath Lanie's left hand. The rigidity was fleeing his muscles. He sighed like a trusting child in his sleep.

"Well."

Shaken, but a little smug, Lanie wiped blood from his face, and from her own. "That's all right, then. We're okay, Mak."

She leaned over him, examining him for signs of consciousness. None so far.

"Next time you kill yourself," she whispered in his ear, "do it when I'm not looking."

Mak gasped, his eyes flying open.

Lanie reared back, reading in his face an indescribable horror at what she had done. She started to stammer an apology, hardly realizing why, but footsteps came thudding outside the gallery.

Lanie flung herself backwards and scuttled towards the plinth, where the deathly chill of the Sarcophagus of Souls awaited her.

On the floor where she left him, Mak was struggling to sit up, to meet his foe on his feet—but he was too weak; he had fainted dead away before Lanie had even reached the Sarcophagus's shadow and disappeared into it, curling herself pillbug-small.

Nita burst into the gallery, the Bryddongard blazing on her upraised arm, lighting up the dark room. After that first silver flash, the blaze narrowed to a silver beam, which began moving, scanning the long dimness of the gallery from one end to the other, at first indecisively, as if unsure there was anything left to find, and then with more confidence. Finally, it focused on the supine figure on the floor in front of the poison cabinet.

For a moment, all Nita could do was stare—at Mak, at the broom beside him, the shattered panes of the cabinet door—and then she ran to him, and flung herself to her knees.

"Goody! Goody—help him. Do something! Make him better! That's an order! A command! I conjure you, in the name of Even Quicker Stones!"

Goody Graves, compelled by the ancient spell that bound her to obey a Stones's command, set her mop in its bucket, lumbered over, squatted, scooped Mak up into her arms, and slung him over one massive shoulder. Nita sprang to her feet.

"Yes. T-take him to my bed. Fetch him whatever he needs. I will care for him."

At last—at last!—they were gone.

In the shadow of the Sarcophagus of Souls, Lanie rolled onto her back and expelled a shuddery breath. She was filthy, coated with blood and sputum and flop sweat. And she felt *raw*. Like someone had just skinned her with oyster shells[4].

She was also irritated at her sister. What, did Nita think Mak could swallow a regiment's worth of poison and survive it all by *himself*, suffering no worse a consequence than a certain poetic limpness? Yet Nita hadn't—not even once—glanced around to see if her necromancer sister might be skulking around in the shadows, saving the day.

Lanie harrumphed quietly to herself, the gravel gone from her voice. Grandpa Rad loosed a low whistle.

"Bless my soul or what's left of it. I must say, Miscellaneous Stones, for once in your life you've impressed me."

The shock of pleasure Lanie took from this acknowledgement was so sharp it felt like panic. "I have?"

"You brinked him, that's what you did."

She filed away this new vocabulary for reference. "I did?"

If the padlock had had eyes to roll, it would have rolled them. "*Brinking*, stupid! It's when you pull someone back from the brink of death. Very useful in my day. During the Northernmost War, we'd take any Skaki spy we'd seized and put 'em to the question. Sosha Brackenwild wanted information, certainly—but he also liked to toy with 'em. Didn't like it to *end*, if you see what I mean. So he'd bring those Skaki bastards right to the point of bleeding out. Then—just when they thought they could die and get away with it—Sosha would have me brink 'em. Bring 'em *all* the

4 Decortication by oyster shell was the manner in which Delirious Stones ultimately met her untimely death. She was mourned by dozens of nobles from the royal court at Castle Ynyssyll but not at all by their spouses, whom she had cuckolded, boastfully, repeatedly.

way back. Let 'em recover a bit. Do it all over again." The ghost chuckled dryly.

Lanie swallowed, tasting the after-echoes of the poison again.

"And so you've done today," he congratulated her. "Yon bird-man lives, no thanks to his efforts. Thought he could escape a Stones! Ha!"

If he'd been corporeal, Lanie was sure Grandpa Rad would have pumped his fist in victory.

"You did all that—and off-surge, too!—and I never even taught you how! Well, of course, you probably read all about it in one of my treatises. Not that I'll ever hear a word of thanks from you, ungrateful girlie that you are. But! Praise where it's due and all that. I'd do no less for a dog who finally did a trick right for the first time in his pathetic life. Well done, Miscellaneous Stones. Well done."

But, remembering the expression in Mak's eyes when he woke inside his living body, Lanie was not so sure.

CHAPTER SIX

A Scratch to Itch

Luckday 19th
Month of Wells, 414 Founding Era
High Holy Fire Feast of Spring Equinox: Dawn

Dawn of the high holy fire feast of Spring Equinox, and Lanie awoke feeling… odd.

She always felt a bit peculiar on surge days, sort of swoony and woozy, as if she and her shadow had swapped angles, so that she was the one walking sideways and with a fluid flatness, on a plane of yellow, jewel-like panels, under a yellow-petalled sky.

Panthauma boosted magic but shattered concentration. For most of her youth she'd spent her surges flat on her back, chanting nonsense rhymes up at her ceiling, only to wake the next morning wrung out, wet and ravaged as from fever.

But today was unusual.

Lanie felt less scattered—more abuzz, invigorated, ready to be up and doing. Today, she itched. A bone-deep itch, half-throb, half-tickle. As if her marrow itself had taken on the job of singing nursery rhymes so that her *mind* could be clear.

And that was good—because Lanie had much to do.

Hopping out of bed, she pranced up to the mirror and exclaimed, "To do! Ta-da! To be, to see, to fix, to mix, to meddle," and grinned at her reflection.

It was deep yellow, distorted. Today, her mirror was not glass backed with silver and mercury, but a huge citrine set in a golden frame, and her bedroom smelled like a grove of lemon trees, and she?

Why, she looked *ravishing*.

"You look ravishing!" she informed herself delightedly, tying up her braids in a yellow (at least, she thought it was yellow; wasn't everything yellow today?) ribbon. "Ravishing, and ready to meddle. To meddle, to meddle," she muttered, searching for a rhyme.

Her reflection offered helpfully, "Pedal? Settle? Kettle?"

She shook her finger at it. "No. Stop it, Miscellaneous Stones. Put the rhymes back in your bones. You have work to do."

"To do, ta-da, to work, to wake—to wake from the grave!—to amaze, to raise the dead!"

Did *she* say that, or did her reflection? Or was it all in her head? But Lanie was too busy to ponder too ponderously on the subject; she turned her back on the mirror and shrugged into her smock. Today was a day for work clothes, homespun by Goody's own dear hands. Dear, but unimaginative. If only she had some pink ribbons, or perhaps a sequined headdress, or...

"Why? So the Scratch boys will think you're preening for *them*?" (Her reflection again.)

"Not *them*," Lanie said. "But Canon Lir might come here."

"You're dreaming."

Whimsy wilted at the sharp tone of her voice—or was it her reflection's voice? Some smoke or fog cleared from behind her eyes, leaving only traces of lemongrass incense. Lanie shoved her feet into a worn pair of sandals, then kicked them off again with a cry of revulsion.

"Ugh!" What she really wanted was to be naked. Naked and dancing!

Or perhaps swimming. Yes. Yes, she should run outside right now to some secret glade of the Diesmali, where she knew—she just knew!—a pool of clear amber sap awaited her. She'd strip off everything. Dive in. Like swimming in honey. Float beneath a flowering yellow sky. And maybe Doédenna would join her this time, now that they were such good friends. Leave Her cloak of bone on the pebble shore. Slip right into the pool beside her, bare as a newborn babe. Wouldn't that be wonderful? Just Lanie and Saint Death, alone together, hand in hand, dreaming the whole day away...

"Stop it," Lanie commanded herself.

To her surprise—she obeyed. And so did her reflection. Both snapped to attention. All her racing fancies faded to background noise. She flashed a huge smile of triumph at herself, who in turn made shooing motions with her hands.

Lanie bowed. "All right, all right. See, I'm going now. Meet you in the ossuary!"

THE SOLARIUM, WITH its glass walls and southern sunlight, was all adazzle. Lanie was just stepping into it, still squinting from the dimness of the corridor that ran between her wing and the main house, when Nita pounced.

"Miscellaneous, at last! Where have you been?"

Lanie began to laugh. She wrapped her arms around her ribs, bent over her knees, and let it all loose—billows and billows of it, all her laughter adding to the luster of the room.

"Amanita Muscaria!" she declared when she could breathe again, straightening up and wiping her eyes. "You beauty! You look like royalty! You wear your vernal surge like cloth of gold!"

To Lanie's surge-struck eyes, Nita was like a golden statue with a blaze of light at her throat, at her brow, where her wizard marks normally only glittered. But they were a gold tipped in red. Definitely streaked with red all throughout. Really dark red. Getting darker. And somewhere beneath the beacon-bright wizard mark on her brow, Nita's mouth was a frown-shaped slash of perplexed scarlet.

"Miscellaneous?"

"Yes?" Lanie was starting to be concerned. No one, she opined, should be quite so *red* on a surge day.

"The Scratches are due here any minute."

"Oh, yes," Lanie recalled, smiling again. "Now, Amanita Muscaria, I promise you *most solemnly,* I will not marry any one of them today—nor even all three—no matter what Sari offers in return."

Canon Lir on the other hand, she thought, is another matter entirely. But what Nita doesn't know, she can't extract any solemn vows about, can she?

Nita's hands clamped around Lanie's shoulders. Hard.

"Ow," Lanie said mildly.

"Miscellaneous! Concentrate! What's wrong with you?"

What's wrong with *you?* Lanie thought. Don't you feel that? The All-Marvel, all around us?

But maybe Nita didn't feel the effects of the panthauma the way she did. Maybe she couldn't. Her sister had only a little magic, after all—ill-trained, hard-used. And she'd been draining herself off-surge to keep Mak under control. Maybe Nita was too tired and slow for the surge to lift her up today.

"I'm fine," Lanie said, more pityingly now, extricating herself from her sister's claws. Not because they hurt, precisely—nothing seemed to hurt her on surge days—but because Nita had *meant* it to hurt. On any other day, in addition to the finger-shaped bruises that would appear on her shoulders, Lanie would no doubt be doubled over sneezing and breaking out in hives. As far as her allergy went, *intent* to harm was only just slightly less harmful than being harmed directly.

"Are you with me?" Nita looked about ready to slap Lanie in the face. "Are you here?"

She tried to grab her again, but Lanie slipped out of reach as if greased with the richest, most delicious, most sunshiny-*yellowest* butter. She danced backwards and flung out her arms, examining herself thoroughly.

"All here! Axial and appendicular. All two hundred six bones of me present and accounted for. I was born with more than that, of course—we all are, you know—but at this point I'm pretty much ossified. More or less. I have a little ways to go. Not much."

Nita's red-streaked frown deepened, but before she could say anything, Goody Graves appeared at the door to the Solarium. Catching sight of her, Nita snapped around.

"Are they here?"

A slight jerk of Goody's granite-like chin indicated the room she had just entered from: the second best drawing room. The Scratches, it seemed, did not rate the great drawing room, or even the grand salon.

Nita caught Lanie by the shoulders and spun her till they were face to face.

Lanie looked down, noticing that the silver Bryddongard she wore *wasn't* silver today, but had all the depth, density, and swirling color-play of a fire opal. It made Nita's hand very hot and heavy on her, too. Much hotter and heavier than her other hand.

"That's so pretty!"

But Nita didn't hear her soft exclamation, being too busy squeezing again. "When we walk into that meeting," she growled, "you will not say anything. You will sit, and watch, and listen. Your eyes are uncanny at present—I've never seen them that color—so if you do nothing but stare, I'll consider you my asset. But if you open your mouth, or do *anything* to tip the negotiations in our creditors' favor, I will reckon you a liability and dispense with you accordingly. Do you hear and understand me, Miscellaneous Immiscible Stones?"

"Like a clarion," Lanie assured her. "Or a carrion crow. Clear as blood on snow."

Nita released her. "Not. One. Word."

Mischievously, Lanie buttoned her lips, added a few stitches, inserted a padlock, and slipped an invisible mask over her face, just to be sure. Then she adjusted her very real spectacles, and started marching off toward the second best drawing room.

Nita grabbed her by the back of the smock, shoved her aside, and went in first.

SARI SCRATCH SEEMED quite at home in the second best drawing room. She had selected a seat near the fireplace, a throne-like chair carved of elephant ivory, with black velvet cushions picked out in bone-white embroidery. It had a matching footstool, which she had made free with —as if she were already mistress of the house.

At least her soles are clean, Lanie thought—surmising that perhaps Scratten, Cracchen, and Hatchet had carried her in on a litter.

Mistress Scratch was tiny in stature but voluptuous in build, with the near-translucent whiteness of skin that most Skakis had. The delicate sag of her chin and the bags under her eyes were wrinkled like raw silk purses, her lips pale and unpainted, her eyes a glacier-bright turquoise-y white. Her boundless black curls probably owed more to chemistry than nature. Either that, or she knew a really spectacular wig-maker. Today she wore a wisteria-purple taffeta suit in the latest, smartest Rookish style (A sartorial choice that Lanie found interesting; was Grandpa Rad right about them being allies, or even agents, of Rook after all? Did Queen Bran Fiakhna bankroll the Scratches to operate in Liriat?) with black lace half-gloves and large purple sapphire drops in her ears. No particular panthaumic aura surrounded her, not a single extra blaze of yellow to indicate the presence of magic.

And why should there be? Lanie wondered. After all, there are no Skaki sky wizards anymore. Grandpa Rad saw to that.

Mistress Scratch was just what she seemed: a very rich woman who happened to be holding the two surviving Stoneses in the palm of her hand. And that was power enough to be getting on with.

"Hi there, Miss Lanie," one of the Scratch boys called out in greeting. "I like your smock."

"Don't suck up to her," said the second. "She's a *Stones*."

The third asked, in his Northern dialect that seemed slower and thicker than that of the others, and with what seemed like genuine curiosity, "Strong surge?"

Lanie turned toward the speakers. There they stood, all in a row, three identical tow-headed giants with their mother's ice-jewel eyes.

Cracchen, on the far left, was definitely the second speaker; he seemed smarter than his brothers, and could converse in words of more than one syllable. But he wasn't quite clever enough, or perhaps did not care enough, to conceal that ever-present edge of sarcasm.

Lanie thought that maybe the first speaker, the one who had greeted her by name, was Scratten, standing there in the middle. Scratten, she suspected, had a tiny crush on her—whatever Grandpa Rad said about all Skakis hating all Stoneses.

That left the question about her surge to Hatchet, on the right. She wondered why he'd asked. As far as Lanie had been able to ascertain from their previous meetings, Hatchet had nothing but a bird nest for a brain, and an unoccupied one at that.

But, heeding Nita's admonition to say nothing, she confined herself to a head bob for each of them. At least that way she didn't risk offending them when she got their names all wrong.

Sari, observing her keenly, pursued Hatchet's—possibly Hatchet's?—question. "You *are* having a strong surge. Ready to raise the dead, are you, Miss Lanie?"

Lanie, remembering the nine adorable mouse skeletons awaiting her attention, grinned. But Nita's quelling look compelled her to bite her tongue. She ducked her head modestly, strolled over to the window, and began removing handfuls of tiny bones from the pockets of her smock.

Laying them out along the windowsill, she separated them into stacks. Mandibles and skulls in one stack (mostly still attached to one another); scapulae in another; femurs in a third; tibias and fibulas together in the fourth; a heap of humeri; ulnas together with the radiuses, of course; all the pelvises like a pile of enormous-eyed needles; each of the sweet nubby little vertebra in an overflowing mound; and last, all the slender, exquisite rib bones bundled into a pyramid of pale eyelashes.

As she worked, she listened. But whatever Nita and Sari were saying could not possibly be as interesting as her project, and so she only paid them a sliver of her attention.

To the Scratches went the opening volley:

"Now that you are home, Mistress Stones," said Sari, "we can commence with the foreclosure proceedings. On the, shall we say, *powerful* advice of your Blood Royal Brackenwild, I have stayed my hand until this moment. But the contract states that after three lapsed payments, or upon the deaths of the signatories, your family's debt is due—*in full*—by the next high holy fire feast. *Both* of these events," she continued severely, "occurred before the surge last Midwinter. But, as Her Royal Highness pointed out to me, it is not good business practice to cast a child out of the only home she has known when her legal guardian is away at school. I have been lenient thus far, but you are home now and payment in full is due. Overdue, in fact."

"Tell me," Nita said, in a purring voice that was far more dangerous than a growl, "is it good business practice to offer your sons' hands—all six of them, I take it?—in marriage to said child, in exchange for debt relief?"

At the question, but even more at the *tone*, Lanie glanced up from her bones, which were just now under her ministrations beginning to gleam an opulent marrow-yellow.

Mistress Scratch was smiling at her sister, showing only the tips of her canines. "Miss Lanie is not such a child that she could not see the advantages of such a marriage. And it would be a true business arrangement, nothing unseemly—we'd see the contract drawn up proper as could be. True, she is a Stones and a necromancer: both assets in Liriat. But she is also impoverished, young, and in poor health. My lads are lusty and robust, eager, polite, and clean. The Blackbird Bride herself would be proud to take them for her espoused kin."

"Not at all, Mistress Scratch!" Nita loosed her golden bubble of a laugh, a sound like a lioness lashing her tail. "Bran Fiakhna only weds *wizards!* Her Parliament of Rooks would never support three talentless vacuums—however handsome; she is too practical. But your sons are," she added magnanimously, "very handsome indeed. I wonder why you did not offer them to *me?*"

Sari Scratch never lost her smile. "I did not want my boys returned to me in urns. Naturally."

"Naturally!" Nita laughed again.

Lanie wished she had brought plugs for her ears; her sister's laughter was very distracting. Nita laughing never meant anything good. On the contrary: it usually meant that Lanie would soon be tripping over somebody's severed limb, or slipping in a pool of arterial blood.

She twirled one of the mouse skulls on the tips of her fingers. When she held it up close to her nose and stared into its eye sockets dead-on, they seemed enormous, flickering with yellow fire, staring at her beseechingly. She plonked a kiss right atop that sagittal crest, and whispered, "Soon!"

"Miss Lanie." One of the Scratch boys sidled up to her. Which one? The brothers had shifted positions when she'd looked away, and now she'd lost track of her left-to-right ordering. "What are you doing?"

Impishly, Lanie jerked her chin at the wizard-gray thumb and forefinger of her left hand, which were pinched together as if holding an embroidery needle.

(She was, in fact, holding one, but the Scratch boy—whichever one he was—wouldn't be able to see it, because it was made of yellow fire, strung with yellow fire. A needle of pure panthauma, and thread of the same to go with it.)

Lanie took up one of the mouse vertebrae. It was, by the shape of it, a C1, according to Celerity Stones's anatomical reference charts. What's more, it was the *correct* C1, the *original* C1 that had once been attached to the mouse skull she next picked up. Lanie could feel its rightness all the way down to the tips of her braids. Then she took her needle and thread, the mouse skull, and the C1 vertebra, and she sutured them together.

To the Scratch boy's eyes, it would seem as if Lanie had floated the bones together mid-air, and secured them to each other like two magnets meeting.

Was it not beautiful? Did he not find her work absorbing, adorable, irresistible—like she did? Lanie glanced at his face to check.

His face, not unusual for the Scratch boys, was a blank. The triplets all fronted a facade like winter tundra, a barren sameness of expression that allowed nothing much to frolic on its surface. But his green-gray-white-blue eyes were opened slightly wider than usual, and there was something in them.

Not an *opinion*, exactly: it was more elusive than that. A hint of a glimmer. Sunlight flashing off shy ice. A mirror-glance of white fire. Almost as if, as if… he were surging along with her, but was deflecting, concealing somehow, his panthauma from her view. From everyone's view.

But when she blinked, it was gone.

Gone the glimmer, gone whatever interest or curiosity or compulsion had drawn him to her side. He withdrew a little, only a step or two. But it was as if he had stepped back into the ink-dark shadow of the Sarcophagus of Souls.

On any other day, Lanie might have tried seeking more information. Today, however, was a surge day. She knew she was seeing all sorts of things that weren't there, and this might be one of them. Might not. She simply wasn't all that interested—and besides, she had other, more engrossing objectives to pursue. She bent to her work.

The next time she looked up was in response to Mistress Scratch's rising voice.

"...not be re-negotiating anything, Mistress Stones. Your debt is due today in full. As you have not yet produced the funds, I take it that you do not have them. Therefore, I hereby give you and your sister seven days' notice to vacate the premises before I take possession of them. You and your sister are each permitted a single cartful of personal belongings, which may not include any furniture or items of magical significance. The rest belongs to me."

Items of magical significance.

Goody.

Sari Scratch was talking about Goody.

Lanie had already known, of course, that Goody was part of the package, part of the estate that her parents and aunt had frittered away with their excesses. That terrible knowledge was what had compelled her to write to her sister in Quadiíb. Had the Scratch's contract excluded the undead housekeeper, Lanie would've happily packed up a cart and trundled herself (and Goody) off to Liriat Proper, to beg Canon Lir for a place to stay and a job to do, something honest but out of the way, unlikely to spark her allergy, that would keep her fed and her and Goody in clothes and shelter. Never mind summoning Nita home—Lanie had always been better off without her.

But the contract was very clear. And there was no way Lanie was leaving Stones Manor without Goody. She couldn't.

The yellow-most edges of her vision were beginning to darken. Scarlet, blood-scarlet, black-scarlet. The half-completed mouse skeleton twitched in her palm as fury surged through her hands.

Her fingers sewed on, nimbly. Bones knitting together. Bones dancing together. Like lace. Like fire. Like lace and yellow fire and—

—there. Done.

Sweet, proud creature. How small and fierce. How ready to rise. If its little white bones had been friable before, now they were unsmashable, held fast in their glowing yellow net. And if its many parts had lain in quietude for years, now its tiny head lifted and sniffed the air with a nose that was not there. It *remembered* having a nose. It *remembered* smelling.

And that was good enough for the undead.

Lanie lifted it to her lips and murmured, "Go tell that Scratch woman Goody's *not* for sale!"

Straightway, the mouse skeleton leapt off her hand and ran at Sari Scratch, cheeping and squeaking. Or not squeaking, exactly: the noises it made were much deeper than they should have been—as if they were sounding out from the bottom of an oil jar.

To her credit, Sari did not scream, but stared down at her undead admonisher, first in incredulity and then—to Lanie's surprise—growing delight. She slid off her ivory throne, careless of the fancily flocked skirts of her suit, which had, upon closer inspection, a pattern of purple velvet birds applied to the purple taffeta: violet-backed starlings perhaps, or purple honeycreepers. Like the suit, the material itself was high Rookish fashion—aristocratic fashion—right out of Rookery Court. Bold, to sport such fashions in Liriat.

Lanie watched with narrowed eyes as Sari sank to hands and knees, stretching out a hand on the ground, palm-up, and crooning to the mouse skeleton in a surprisingly gentle voice, "Come here, pretty one. Come, uncannyling! Come to Mordda Sari!"

But the mouse, far from obeying, shied away from her, scampering back a few feet till it stood at a safe distance, whereupon it rose onto its hind legs and began scolding her again. Sari laughed, looking up at Lanie from the floor and shaking her head.

"I've never seen its like, Miss Lanie. And I've seen wonders."

Ever susceptible to compliments, and today even more so, Lanie beamed. She was about to thank her most graciously for the compliment, and to explain all about embroidering with yellow fire, and how delicate and perfect was this particular act of panthauma, when Nita's boot came down on the mouse.

Lanie gasped. She jerked away from the window and crossed half the room in a bound. She knew the mouse couldn't feel any pain. But still! The indignity!

Nita flung up a hand, halting her. Lanie strained, as if fighting an invisible barrier. But there was no barrier, only a small part of her that was still practical, that could still *fear*, holding her back.

Sari, who had not yet risen from her genuflection, craned her neck back to stare at Nita. "Now, Mistress Stones, was that really—"

She stopped. Nita was glaring down.

One.

Two.

Three.

Lanie shielded her eyes as her sister seemed to ignite, from her wizard-marks outward, until she stood at the center of her own conflagration.

From behind that pillar of golden flame, in a voice gonging like a golden bell, Nita demanded, "Was that really *what*, Mistress Scratch? *Necessary?* Oh, I think it was, don't you?"

No answer.

"It was necessary," Nita insisted, in that tolling golden voice.

"It was necessary," Sari repeated.

"It is *also* necessary," Nita said, smiling now, a smile that Lanie perceived as wreaths of golden flowers orbiting the pillar of flame, "to renegotiate the contract. Hand it up to me. Nice and slow."

Wordlessly, Sari handed her the rolled-up parchment she had carried into Stones Manor with her. It was bound in green ribbon—the color associated with Lan Satthi: god of Law, Memory, and Commerce. To Lanie's eyes, the parchment itself was a dazzling tube of spell-light. Algae-emerald-ivy-green. Shining.

"The contract," Sari said, in a fascination-thickened voice, "is signed in ink and blood, a drop each from your father, your mother, and your father's mother's second cousin. It was witnessed by an ordained notary of the god Lan Satthi, sealed in wax and viper venom. The house and all its assets are mine by *godright*. You cannot change that."

The contract flared with eager virescence, agreeing with all that Sari said, and binding Nita fast to it.

To Lanie's eyes, the contract was as bright as Nita was—if a decidedly different color. How dull and shrouded Mistress Scratch seemed in comparison!

Nita frowned. "Is it blood you want?"

She flipped a knife out of her belt sheath and carelessly sliced the tip of her pinkie, sprinkling her blood over the contract. The green light drank it greedily.

"Let Lan Satthi regard me as the newest signatory," she offered, "legal heir of those who signed before me. Stoneses pay their debts, Mistress Scratch—and so shall I. Not in full, not today. But I shall pay them off in the agreed-upon amounts, at the agreed-upon intervals. And there will be no more talk today of vacating the premises, in seven days, in seven weeks, or in seven months. Now. Sit down. And write it out."

Sari rose from the floor and sat in the black and ivory chair once more. Reaching over to a nearby console table, Nita produced inkwell and stylus, and handed them over. Mistress Scratch's fingers convulsed around the stylus, but there she paused, stirring in her seat like someone pinned underwater. She looked around, heavy-eyed, trying to blink.

Nita repeated, "Write it!" meeting her gaze more forcefully, and Mistress Scratch began writing.

Cracchen Scratch, when he saw what Nita was about, had initially charged at her, but then Nita had glanced at him. Not the Glance of Three Heartbeats—more like the glance of 'You come within spitting distance of a Stones, you'll find out what a Stones will spit at you, buddy, so back off.'

Cracchen did not back off, but he did stop charging. Whether this was due to Nita or to some subtle signal from his enspelled mother, Lanie could not tell. Scratten or Hatchet, whoever was standing behind the ivory throne, fidgeted. Both brothers glanced to the brother at the windowsill, where Lanie had been.

But Hatchet—or possibly Scratten—just smiled amiably back at them. He then shook his head in a gesture so slight that Lanie wondered if she had imagined it, and turned his back on the whole scene to play with her mouse bones like so many toy blocks laid out for his amusement. She wanted to snatch them from him. But she wanted to extract the whole—newly undead—mouse skeleton from under Nita's boot more. So she stayed where she was.

Nita, knife still in hand, kept all her attention on Sari. She was gathering her forces of fascination all about her, and when she was ready, she leaned in—*all the way in*. Lanie couldn't see her sister's eyes, but she wagered the shark-black sheen of them had gone as gold as a golden monarch—not the butterfly, the coin: the largest, shiniest denomination in Liriat.

"Lan Satthi has tasted my blood and recognized it as kin to the deceased signatories," she said. "You and I will sign the new terms. Both of us. Right here. Right now. You get your money, I keep my house. It's a mutually beneficial agreement."

"It's a mutually beneficial agreement," Sari agreed in a faint, far-off voice.

Nita smiled. Another wreath of blossoms circled the fire pillar of her magic.

Lanie drifted closer to the two women, hoping to somehow sneakily extricate her mouse skeleton from under her sister's heel while Nita was concerned with the business at hand.

But the panthauma had other ideas; it was alert to the marvelous, being part of the All-Marvel itself, and Lanie's attention followed where it led.

Just then, it led to Sari's handwriting, swirling away so industriously under the stylus. It was an elaborate, delicate calligraphy with more hoops, loops and curlicues than a piece of Umrysian lace woven by the holy urchins of Aganath, god of the Sea. Different from any script Lanie had studied: far closer to the codified cursive of the Quadoni alphabet than to the rough and squarish Lirian runes. But distinctly itself. Skaki script. A proud and patriotic hand.

Somewhere beneath all her giddiness, beyond her determination to rescue her newly resurrected murine friend, Lanie became suddenly, keenly interested in the *real* Sari Scratch. Who was the woman behind that handwriting? What did she want—besides everything the Stones family had ever owned? And why, come to think of it, did she want *that?*

"Please note in addendum," Nita dictated over the green-glowing contract, "that as long as we keep our payments current, you will not approach us in the street or trespass further upon our lands. All communications between our two parties will be in writing, delivered by courier, none of whom may bear the surname Scratch."

Sari said nothing, but scribbled away obediently.

Nita observed her work a while before adding, her voice hard, "Lastly: you and your sons will never, *ever* again approach my sister with your impudent propositions. Miscellaneous Stones, her person, her name, her *magic*, is not for sale. If your sons persist in wooing her"—her palm fell over Sari's hand, stilling it—"there will not be enough left of them to fill a barrel."

Sari did not look up, only nodded.

"My word on that, Mistress Scratch," Nita emphasized, releasing her. "Now. That's done. I want your boys as witnesses. Have them sign it—and seal it too. Mine won't be the only blood binding this contract."

At Sari's nod, Scratten, Cracchen, and Hatchet each filed over in a line to sign the new contract. Lanie watched them bend over the parchment, one by one, wanting to know once and for all whom was whom.

Cracchen signed his name first, a high pink flush upon his cheeks and forehead, his free hand curled upon the hilt of his dagger. Next came Scratten, with set lips and lowered eyes. It had been he, then, who'd been standing that whole time behind the ivory throne. Third was Hatchet, ambling amicably over from the window with no other expression on his face but agreeable stupidity.

Lanie blinked. So she was right then, and Hatchet *was* Hatchet—as she'd thought. But also *not* as she thought, for there was Hatchet's signature, in an even swirlier, prouder, more elaborate script than his mother's! And there *had* been that white glitter about him, hadn't there, like a patch of hidden ice that the sun had briefly found out?

Hidden magic.

He, like his brothers, added a drop of blood, coaxed from his fingertip at dagger point.

Well.

Well, well, well. Perhaps there was one baby bird in that tow-headed nest, after all.

"Miscellaneous," said her sister. "I want you for witness. Sign. Seal too."

Lanie wanted to demand Nita release her mouse first, but that small, practical part of her still held the reins somewhere at the back of her brain, so instead she simply plucked the glass stylus out of Hatchet's fingers, bent over the contract, skimmed the crabbed script and crossed paragraphs until she found the 'Witness the Following Seals and Signatures of the Party' section, and carelessly scrawled out her name. Capital M—(indecipherable squiggle), capital I—(inscrutable doodle), capital S, jab up, slash the t, o—flourish, n—flourish, e—flourish, swirl the s, swirl it twice, underline everything, underline it again, and swoop!

She used her own pocket syringe to extract a drop of blood for the seal, having a distaste of using Nita's dagger or anything the Scratches had touched. She was fastidious about her tools, and did not want an allergic reaction today of all days.

Her blood met the contract with a yellow sparkle, followed by green sparkles, like miniature fireworks. Like two gods meeting.

Before parting with it, Lanie gave the parchment a friendly pat, and murmured her respectful greetings to the god Lan Satthi. Her only familiarity with the god of Law, Memory, and Commerce came from flipping through old books, and studying the coffered ceiling of the great hall, where silver-on-black in Her sunken caisson, Lan Satthi grinned down at onlookers with hinged fangs, and keeled scales at Her throat, and egg sacs dangling from each wrist, one leg human, the other a giant rattlesnake's tail.

As the prayer left her lips, the contract stung the flesh of Lanie's palm. Greenly, but not meanly. A clean burn, like nettles. As if Lan Satthi had deigned, just for a moment, to return her greeting.

A second later, she forgot all about the strange sensation, for Nita lifted her foot.

Whooping delightedly, Lanie swooped down and scooped up her mouse, depositing it in her pocket. She retreated to the window before Nita could demand it back, and turned away, and willed everyone in the room to pay her no more mind.

"So!" Nita announced jovially, sitting back in a seat that matched Sari's and releasing her spell of fascination with an almost audible whoosh. "According to our new deal, I have until next surge—the high holy fire feast of Midsummer—to come up with our first payment. You'll be hearing from my bankers."

Sari was seated very still in her high-backed chair, slowly smoothing her fingers over the thick, curling sheaves of parchment. She hunched protectively over the pages, re-reading the old material and the new addenda of the contract closely, as if in disbelief.

But when she straightened up again, there was a look on her face that Lanie could only describe as triumphant.

"No," she said.

"No?" Nita repeated.

"No, Mistress Stones." And Sari arranged the stylus and inkwell neatly on the console table, set the contract between them, and then folded her hands and looked at Nita again—full in the eyes. Fearlessly.

Lanie gaped, amazed at the woman's audacity. Nita, too, seemed taken aback.

"I beg your pardon," she said, dangerously.

"Of course you have that freely, Mistress Stones," returned Mistress Scratch with preternatural calm, as if still under Nita's enchantment. "But that is the only thing you will get for free."

She was all tranquility, all placidity. But Lanie, watching closely, saw that Sari betrayed her excitement in a slight tapping of the contract, where the ink was still drying, against her knee.

"You see," she explained kindly to Nita, "it is true that you and I have just rewritten—with witnesses—the terms of this contract. And it is true that, as you dictated to me, the full debt left by your relatives has been transferred over to your name. All future payments, as you also dictated, will be your responsibility starting on the high holy fire feast of Midsummer, in three months' time. But in your haste"—and here she cast a pitying look at Nita—"you neglected to amend *in writing* the matter of the aforementioned three lapsed payments. Which were due, as I mentioned when this meeting started, last winter solstice. And, according to our contract—which you have now signed, irrevocably, in your own blood—those *back* payments, now transferred over to you, are due. Months overdue, in fact. And I am within my rights to demand immediate payment. Today."

And then Sari Scratch named a sum so vast that it seemed to suck all the air out of the room.

Nita, furious at having been out-maneuvered by a Skaki banker, and one just out of the throes of her own enchantment, grabbed the stylus again. She leaned over the contract as if to slash out the terms compelling her to pay the debt.

But a viridian radiance shot up out of the rolled-up parchment, driving Nita back into her chair like a battering ram. The legs of her chair even skidded a few inches, rucking up the carpet like sand after a storm.

Lanie clutched her stomach as the god-wave passed through her, almost knocking her off her feet. She glanced surreptitiously around, wondering if anyone else had felt it. But besides Nita, no one in the room seemed affected.

Except... Hatchet—ever so briefly—pinched the bridge of his nose.

"If you do not pay the sum owed us today," Sari added—and now she was the one smiling, as if Nita weren't about to shove the glass stylus up her nose and into her brains—"we will repossess the property in seven days. If you *do* pay the sum, of course, then your next payment will be due—as stated in the new terms—on Midsummer."

"The day isn't over," Nita said through gritted teeth. She staggered upright in her chair, the golden light now dimmed all around her. "You'll have your money—by *midnight tonight!*—damn you duodecifold! "

Sari slowly rose to her feet. "If you like. By midnight tonight, then, Mistress Stones."

"Now leave my house!"

Sari met Nita's eyes for a full three seconds, and beyond. Lanie could easily read her sister's expression, or rather, the colors that swirled around her. Cold calculation, red fury, and a longing—no, a *hunger*—to use all her skills to wipe Sari off the face of Liriat.

She could do it too, Lanie did not doubt; the Scratch boys were brawny and brave, and all three probably had a degree of thuggish cunning with hand weapons, but Nita was a *professional.*

And that was the problem. As a professional, Nita knew very well that Sari and her sons had risen high in Liriat. Doubtless more than a few people knew what business had taken them to Stones Manor that day, and would know to miss them if they did not return to keep their engagements that evening. She also knew that in the time she had been abroad in Quadiíb, the Stoneses had fallen from the inviolate position they once had enjoyed at Brackenwild Court. As much as she might regret it, Nita understood that the wholesale slaughter of the Scratch family would have deep—possibly fatally deep—repercussions. After all, if the thing could be done easily, would not Natty Stones have done it already? Would not have Aba?

And so, Lanie could actually *see* her sister deciding, in the skidding colors of the golden flames surrounding her, that quadruple murder, however tempting, was not worth the risk.

Sari held Nita's blazing gaze calmly: like her sons, as snow-faced and bare-swept as the Skaki tundra. Not breaking eye contact for a minute, she lifted the contract from the table and waved it gently back and forth in front of her face like a fan, blowing on the ink to dry it.

"Welcome home, Mistress Stones," she said, and let the contract fall from her fingertips, where it fluttered briefly and awkwardly, then splattered in a splay of pages on the floor. "It was... invigorating doing business with you."

Nita was speechless with outrage. Sari, ignoring her heaving breath, her yellow-eyed glower, bowed in the direction of the windowsill, where Lanie stood, pretending as hard as she could that neither she nor her mouse skeleton were visible.

"Miss Lanie, a pleasure. You enjoy your surge, now."

CHAPTER SEVEN

Substance and Accident

NITA COLLAPSED ONTO the ivory throne. She was sweating, limp, enraged. Even the wizard marks on her throat and brow looked dull, more like tarnished brass than gold.

But as soon as Goody had escorted the Scratches out of the room, she shook herself, plopped her mouse-crushing boots onto the footstool, and stretched her mouth in an exultant grin.

"There! We did it! Easy as breaking a baby's teeth."

Lanie glanced up quickly, but—wisely, she felt—refrained from questioning her sister's rapid revision of recent history. In the pocket of her smock, the mouse skeleton was still trembling in extremely low dudgeon.

Instead of answering, she went back to sorting bones on the windowsill. Hatchet had accomplished quite a lot in her absence: almost five more complete mice had been separated out into individual piles. He sometimes mixed up humerus with femur—but all in all, she was impressed.

"Did you see how I fascinated her?" Nita asked. "How she knelt at my feet? I would have managed it even without your trick with the mouse—but it was rather magnificent anyway, how we worked as a team."

Lanie's shoulders unhunched some. Her periphery started to glitter and twinkle like lemon zest. That edge of scarlet began to fade; her mouse began to calm. "It didn't like when you stepped on it."

"I could tell," Nita said wryly. "Your little revenant almost chewed through the sole of my shoe! It was like trying to stomp out a waterspout. Well done!"

With that praise, everything was sunshine and citron and citrine again. Lanie's surge rebounded from its subdued crouch and scampered in circles inside her. No new nursery rhymes yet, but she could feel a certain burbling chattiness flooding her banks. Cheerfully picking up the pieces of Hatchet's most complete mouse skeleton assembly, Lanie set to embroidering the bones.

"I'm not surprised," she remarked, "that your boot was having trouble. Of the three material states—life, death and undeath—undeath is physically the strongest."

Nita, who could not be less interested, thunked her head against the back of her chair. "That fucking Scratch woman! Won't she be surprised when I dump a load of Brackenwild gold on her doorstep tonight? She doesn't know who she's dealing with—talking to me like I was a child. But I've an appointment with Erralierra in an hour, and all will come out right. Miscellaneous!" She gestured to the floor at her feet. "Come over here by me."

"Light's better here," Lanie demurred.

"Graves," Nita called out, "light the fire."

At Goody's name, Lanie brightened and turned. When had she re-entered the room? Oh, how she *wanted* to show off her mouse to Goody! But not now. Not with Nita watching. Better if Nita didn't know how much she loved Goody. Nita hated whatever Lanie loved. Like Hoppy Bunny, like the kitten Katabasis...

Smiling, Lanie gathered up her materials with alacrity and went to sit on the hearthrug beside her sister—and, more to the point, closer to Goody. The mouse peeped out of Lanie's pocket to give Goody a good whiff, as if recognizing a thing as undead as itself.

Pleased to be obeyed, Nita laughed, the sound as effervescent as brisk wine. "I must say, Miscellaneous, a mouse is far more terrifying *without* its skin. I wouldn't want to wake up to that thing on my chest."

That *thing?*

Lanie thought, but did not say, that her new little friend was a *sweetheart*, and not in the *least* bit terrifying.

But instead of laying into her sister, which would do no good but much harm, she busied herself sewing almost invisible carpals to metacarpals to phalanges. She found she had to thin her fiery needle to the merest filament of flame, to slim down her thread to almost nothing, in order to work the tiny little bead-like bones, darling as anything.

"If only," Nita mused, "you could have made your creepy mouse skeleton the size of a horse! *That* would have given those Scratch bastards nightmares for months!"

"Oh, the undead only grow if they *stay* undead," Lanie explained earnestly. "Like Goody. That's why she's so tall. She's been undead so many centuries I'm surprised she doesn't hit the roof. But maybe she started out quite short?"

She looked over at Goody, seeking affirmation. But Goody said nothing. Did not even look at her. She was staring at the wall. Or maybe out the window? Yes, the window, the one overlooking Lanie's garden on the south side of the manor. Ah, the garden! Full of food! Beautiful food that Lanie could not eat in Nita's presence. Beyond the garden were the orchards, where wonderful, wonderful fruit grew.

Lanie realized she was hungry. Famished. Maybe she'd be able to eat lunch today, if she snuck it out of Nita's sight. Something creamy and sugary and zesty and spongy and—was she drooling?

She wiped her mouth.

Once she was finished with her project, she would escape Nita's clutches and hide herself away in the kitchen cupboard with one of Goody's cakes. A whole one. She would not share. Well, of course she'd share with her mice—if they wanted any. But the undead did not eat, not like that. At least, Goody didn't. She'd have to see if the mice were any different.

As she redoubled her efforts, fingers flying, Lanie realized that her mouth was already running, and had been for some time:

"I wonder if Goody's slow rate of growth has to do with the nature of her resurrection? Her servitude was meant to outlast the spell-caster's lifespan, so her undeath was—very unusually—tied not to a particular necromancer's blood *source*, but to the entire Stones *bloodline*. So long as our line continues, so does her undeath. That process may have stunted her expansion some..."

Nita flung up a hand. "You sound just like one of those Quadoni pedants at the Caravan School! They would never come out and *tell* me what fascination was, or how I could better use mine. Instead, Gelethai kept making me practice stupid sothaín, saying that movement meditation would help me 'find my stillness,' and that once I found it, we would start working on my technique." She snorted. "Four years of that! And then... to come home to *this!*"

Her snarl was back. Her panthaumic glow was going scarlet at the edges again. Time to redirect her attention.

"So," Lanie asked casually, "all that stuff you can do, you figured it out on your own?" (Of course she had. It was the same self-serving spell Nita had been casting since she was a child, just as impetuous and predictable.) "How admirable of you, Amanita Muscaria!"

Nita relaxed at the flattery. "I just go by instinct. If I *want* something enough, I can make someone else want it too. It all seems to go my way. For a time."

At the risk of being labeled a pedant again, Lanie ventured, "All twelve forms of magic have to do with substance and accident. 'Substance' being what a thing *is*—the term scholars use for the soul: will, memory, personality, experience. 'Accident' being what a thing *looks* like: physical bits like skin, bone, hair, fingernails, blood and other fluids. When I make ectenica, I mix my accident—my blood—with the accident of the dead. Their... leftover material. And then I impose my substance—my will—upon this mix to recall the substance of the dead back to its accident. Mixed together like that, life and death—will, soul, body, blood—we make ectenica. Undeath. But *your* magic, Amanita Muscaria, is *pure* will. It's like," she struggled, trying to frame her theory, "you project your living substance over another person's living substance—and bring it to heel."

Subjecting us, Lanie thought. Invading and overwhelming us—but not forever. All souls being equal, we can still eject your being from ours. If our wills are strong enough.

She had to believe that. She *had* to.

At her inattention, a fibula snapped off from its tibia. Lanie cussed softly. Nita glanced down at her with a crooked smile, more interested in the cuss than the lecture.

"Where did you learn that word?"

"Ghost," Lanie said shortly, fixing the breakage with a few stitches. There… and there.

"Not that old fib again!" Nita scoffed. "You and your ghosts. You're far too old for imaginary friends, Miscellaneous—almost sixteen! I was about that age when they sent me to Quadiíb."

She sat forward in her chair, elbows on knees, and brooded at Lanie, who refused to look up at her.

"Miscellaneous!" Nita suddenly sat back again, all magnanimity. "You mustn't worry that your magic isn't as powerful as mine. I'm older; my will is stronger. And recall: my magic came earlier than yours. I mean"—she laughed—"you were still raising potatoes from the dead till last year! Your weakness, your allergy, has kept you sheltered. But we can use that to our advantage. If no one knows you, or what you can do, then we can hold you over their heads as a threat. Meantime, you keep practicing." She gestured to the bones, who were becoming more and more mice. "You're getting very good."

Lanie bit her tongue, hard, before saying, very carefully, "Thank you."

She knew, if Nita did not, that the weaker a talent was, the earlier it manifested. Nita's power of fascination had not changed or grown since she was twelve. Four years in Quadiíb under the guidance of a great gyrlady, and she hadn't even begun to grasp the foundation upon which her ability was predicated, much less extend its potential.

But weak as Lanie had been at birth, stunted as she was from her allergy, and ailing from echo-wounds her whole life, she was yet getting stronger. Every year. Every day. And yesterday—not even a surge day, thank you very much—Lanie had, though Nita still had no idea of it, brinked her sister's captive gyrgardi Mak Cobb right back from the dead.

She slipped the second and third completed mice skeletons into her pocket, where they snuggled with the first against her hip. Three of nine.

Plucking needle and thread out of the air again, Lanie moved on. One foot. Two. Hook them up each with tibia and fibula. Then the femurs. The fragile pelvis. Maybe the pelvis was Lanie's favorite? No, how could she have a favorite bone? She could as soon choose a favorite cheese—and Lanie had never yet met a cheese she wouldn't happily die devouring! Did Goody have any ripe cheeses in the kitchen? Ah. Drooling again.

But she had been silent too long.

"What exactly are you doing?" Nita demanded, exasperated.

Lanie sighed at the interruption. A fourth mouse joined the others. It scampered about the pocket of her smock, chirruping and belling.

"Think of it," she explained, not looking up from her work, "as a kind of taxidermy. I'm re-stuffing a skeleton with its memory. The mouse is dead, but it *remembers* being alive. The reunion of substance—memory, will, the soul—with accident—the physical material—creates the third of the three states. Undeath. The dead who dream they are alive. Usually I have to use blood to make ectenica, but today, with panthauma everywhere..."

When she paused, breath spent, Nita leapt in, looking alarmingly thoughtful. "Panthauma is amazing stuff, isn't it?"

She didn't seem to want or need an answer, and as Lanie did not provide one, happily continued, "On my surge days, it's as if the will of the gods Themselves are amplifying my own. Their desires are mine. My needs, Theirs. Last Midwinter, the gods and I made Mak obedient to me. The Bryddongard I took from Gelethai did the rest to keep him in line. But *tonight*," Nita whispered, "I'll bring him under my total control. I'll wipe his memory clean. I will *will* it gone. Command him to forget Quadiíb, forget Gelethai, forget everything. Remember only me. Love only me. And then—oh, Miscellaneous!—then I will take him to my bed, and we can be true lovers. I will continue the Stones line as Mother and Father bid me do when they sent me away. All of Mak's many graces will go into the making of my child. I have waited so long."

Lanie, carefully—so very carefully—did not look up from her bones. "So that's your plan?"

"When my surge is at its highest," Nita said, "that's when I'll go to him." Swinging her boots off the footstool, she staggered to her feet, then put her hand out to steady herself on the chair.

"For now, though," she finished shakily, "I'll lie down. Remember, we have business with the Blood Royal in an hour. It is vital—*crucial!*—that Erralierra hires me today to fill both Mother and Father's positions, and also gives me an immediate advance on my wages. She owes us that much for stealing Father away. Damn that Scratch woman!" she snarled suddenly. "Damn that contract! Damn Lan Satthi and Her meddling—if it weren't for Her magic, I could've convinced Sari Scratch that she owed *us* money!"

"Remember how she knelt to you." Lanie almost choked on the words. "Remember how you had her at your feet."

"Right. That's right." Nita sighed. "Of course you're right, Miscellaneous."

Lanie watched as her sister gingerly removed her hand from the chair and took an experimental step towards the door. This time, she did not wobble. Much. But she listed as she walked, and weaved like one drunk, as she departed the second best drawing room, and left her sister, finally, alone.

* * *

All the citrus-tangy joy of Lanie's surge drained right out of her when she learned Nita's plans for Mak. She was in no danger of rhyming now. Even the thread of yellow fire in her hand was flickering in and out.

She concentrated hard on keeping that thin flame line alive.

"Come on," she coaxed it. "Come back!" She only realized she was crying when Goody knelt beside her like a silent avalanche and wiped the tears from her cheeks.

"Hello, Goody."

Lanie stared glumly at the tangle of thread and bone in her hand. Had she just attached a rib to an ulna? She'd have to start all over again!

Goody touched her chin with one cool and enormous gray finger. Lifting it gently but firmly, she held Lanie's gaze with her own glowing blue eyes. She said nothing. She said nothing so loud that Lanie shivered.

What *was* that silence? She cocked her head, ears pricked, listening hard into Goody's galvanized taciturnity.

Releasing Lanie's chin, Goody hooked her hands at the thumbs, and spread wing-shaped fingers over her chest. Finally, Lanie understood—though she did not want to.

"Yes, yes, all right!" she cried, frustrated. "I'll warn him, Goody, all right? You could've just said so; you're not *actually* made of rock, though I know you like to pretend. I don't suppose you know where he is? Or if he's even a man today? Maybe Nita's got him all hooded up and caged somewhere until her big moment. Wouldn't that be just like her?"

Goody nodded toward the window where she had been keeping watch all this while.

"Of course," Lanie muttered, huffily stuffing needle and thread and mouse bones back into her smock pockets. "Of course that's what you were looking at all this time. I should've guessed."

Mak was in the garden.

CHAPTER EIGHT

Sister of Mine Enemy

IF YOU PERFORMED sothaín correctly, your movements were liquid, limpid, graceful. You held each attitude for countless minutes, minding your breath, paying attention to everything, thinking purposefully about nothing.

Then, once you had achieved perfect stillness and were at one with the attitude you struck, you were supposed to flow from that attitude into the next, with 'the slowness of a pearl that sinks through oil.' (Or so Lanie's battered old manual on the ancient Quadoni practice instructed. As the text was written entirely in Quadic, she wasn't sure if she had translated the metaphor correctly, but there were plenty of pictures, so she kept trying to puzzle her way through.)

If you transitioned attitudes every five minutes, you could get through a set of twelve in an hour. There were twelve sets of twelve, which meant that it would take you half the day to move through all the attitudes, if you did them properly. Some of the great Quadoni practitioners spent their waking hours doing nothing but holding sothaín. They then presumably spent the next twelve hours sleeping it off.

Since discovering the slender manual in Stones Library three years back, stuffed on a shelf between two moldering tomes[5], Lanie had been practicing the first set of sothaín attitudes with Goody. Goody, of course, was a natural—or rather, a supernatural—at stillness, being both undead and formerly Quadoni. Other than her company, the only contribution to Lanie's sothaín studies Goody would give Lanie was this:

Where is breath?
In the stillness.
What is stillness?
Sothaín.

5 The first book was *Espionage, Volume I: The Pulchritudinous Art of Betrayal, Seduction, and Subterfuge*, a far fatter volume than the second book, its slim sequel, *Espionage II: Notes on a False Tooth*.

Goody, of course, didn't have any breath to speak of at the bottom of *her* stillness. And Lanie could never get her own breath quite right. Something always twitched or ached or fell asleep whenever she was holding an attitude. At least nowadays her limbs no longer shook like tree branches in a cyclone after only thirty seconds of posturing.

But despite its challenges, Lanie loved sothaín. She found she could set its silence against Grandpa Rad's dry lecturing, his never-ending criticism that drove the relentless pace of her studies but was never satisfied. The internal silence of sothaín, like the busily humming quiet of the garden, was also different from any of Goody's one thousand expressive silences, and brought Lanie rare contentment in a house where she could never satisfy anyone, least of all herself.

So why, she wondered, have *I* never thought to practice sothaín in my garden?

Mak, it seemed, had gone right to it. He was holding an attitude Lanie had not mastered yet, from the fifth set.

Each set of twelve attitudes was dedicated to one of the gods, and the fifth set went to Kywit, the captured god. It was a series of angular and twisted attitudes, suggestive of torture. You could not, just by studying the illustrations in the manual, intuit the narrative they were supposed to represent. But watching Mak move with agonizing slowness from one attitude to the next, Lanie finally understood how sothaín might be used, not merely as a practice to clear the mind or access hidden reserves of strength, but to express the profoundest depths of lament. The twelve attitudes of the fifth set went:

1. *Child is born; but mother dies to bear it.*
2. *Child's new mother hates, beats, and neglects it.*
3. *Child's new mother murders child most foully.*
4. *Child is cooked in soup, and fed to father.*
5. *Bones of child are buried in the tree roots.*
6. *Child and tree become a single being. (Captured God awakens, new and screaming.)*
7. *Captured God sends out its spirit winging. (Fire and shadow singing of its murder.)*
8. *Worshippers come kneeling to the tree roots. (Captured God grants gifts of bone and silver.)*
9. *They sacrifice their kin unto the tree, greedy for more gifts of bone and silver.*
10. *Captured God cries out, but goes unheeded.*
11. *Captured God grows strong from murdered children.*
12. *The sky goes dark with murdered, singing birds.*

Mak was just transforming from a dirty sack of sad, forgotten bones into a sturdy sapling whose branching arms were lifted beseechingly to the sky, when Lanie cleared her throat.

"Gyrgardi," she said in her faltering Quadic. "Greetings. Um."

Almost too slowly to see, Mak pulled himself out of sothaín. His expression, which was that of a young god born out of misery and into enduring agony, did not change. He looked at Lanie, his green eyes as clear as sap.

Lanie tried to marshal the correct vocabulary. She was still unsure of all her tenses, knew herself to be mediocre at the rhyme and meter that were as important to a Quadic sentence as its content. But she had to try. She'd promised Goody.

"My..." What was the word for *sister* again? Oh, well. "My father's daughter..." Lanie peered intently at Mak through her spectacles, eyebrows raised. Did he nod? Either that, or his jaw clenched involuntarily. "My father's daughter hath—"

Divided? Denuded?

"—*devised* a scheme. Tonight, on Feasting Fight... no, on *Fire Feast*..." Lanie cleared her throat, tried again. "Tonight, by surge and will, she'll make thee to forget. By fascination's force, thou shalt forget."

Lanie scrabbled through the flowers and thorns of his language for a word that meant 'everything.' She knew 'all.' But 'all' in Quadic meant the whole world and all the worlds beyond it. It didn't mean what she meant, which was 'all the things that make you *you*.' What she wanted was the Quadic word for 'substance.' For the soul.

Spreading her hands, she tried again. "Forget... *thyself*."

Mak's sharp face was like shards of glass. His green gaze pierced her. He asked slowly, "Lahnessthanessar?"

Old Quadic again. Ritual talk. The name of some spell, perhaps? Lanie thought she had encountered 'Lahnessthanessar' before—which book? which passage? where?—but seemed to remember it having something to do with music, not magic. Music. Was that right?

Lanie couldn't be sure. She wasn't sure of anything. Trying to communicate, in Quadic, to a hostile Quadoni, was shredding her confidence to cheesecloth. She was leaking vocabulary faster than she could talk—forget internal rhymes, least of all end ones! Shaking her head, squaring her shoulders, taking a deep breath, she tried again.

"She'll see that thou'lt obliterate *Quadiíb*. Forget thy home, thy name, thy friends..." She gulped and said a word out of rhythm: "Gelethai."

The murdered gyrlady's name gave her tongue the taste of profanity. Wretchedness etched itself anew onto Mak's forehead. He brought the flat of his palm a few inches before his face, the same sothaín attitude for grief he'd used with Goody Graves in Stones Gallery. The one from the twelfth set, dedicated to the god Doédenna, Saint Death.

At a loss for what else to do, Lanie followed Goody's example and mirrored his movement for as long as he held it. When Mak let his hand fall, so did she. They stood there, examining each other.

He looks more human now, Lanie thought. Less like a bird or a god or a wraith. Tired, sore... almost approachable.

In impetuous Lirian, she blurted, "Look, Mak Cobb or whoever, if you want to go back to the poison cabinet right now... I won't tell. I won't stop you this time, I promise. I just... I can't... can't *watch*. Okay? But if you'd prefer *that* to..." She trailed off.

Mak was shaking his head, his lips curling. Not in a smile. "Thy *sister*," he said in slow Quadic, putting a slight flex on the word she'd forgotten, "hath forbidden suicide. Her fascination's force I must abide. And as for what thou wilt and wilt not *watch*—child."

He held her gaze. Lanie remembered the bird. The gray shadowy winged thing that Saint Death had released back to Mak at her insistence. It had passed straight through Lanie's breastbone, into Mak's lips. His substance. His soul.

Watching her face closely, Mak nodded. "Thief of death," he said in a soft, steady voice, "corruptor of my will—thou stole *thy* choice when thou didst murder mine. My suffering is thine; thus, I rejoice."

And he turned his face from hers, withdrawing his contempt, his despair, his attention.

Lanie grimaced. Was it *her* fault that Nita had captured him? He—yes, and his dead gyrlady too, and his whole high-flown nation!—should've known better than to underestimate a Stones! Had Mak known Nita four years, let her fly him in the field, yet never *understood* her? And to blame Lanie for *saving* him! *Blame* her, when his death might have meant that *she* died too? Goody Graves had been right yesterday; Mak Cobb ought to want to outlive his foes and dance upon their graves! Where was his gumption?

Her internal surge reared up its sunflower head, nodding with ardent encouragement. It reached out citrusy, surge-y fingertips to tickle her everywhere, all the way up and down. It promised *faithfully* to give her all the right rhymes in *any* language she wanted—from Quadic quatrains to Skaki villanelles to Damahrashian rhyme-and-replace gutter slang—if only she'd just *please* get back to embroidering more mouse bones as soon as possible! So many tiny, perfect, awesomely irresistible little mouse bones to sew!

Lanie grinned at Mak, newly radiant and confident, taking him aback. She further startled him by pushing her spectacles firmly up her nose, hooking her thumbs together, and making him a traditional Quadoni bow—wings to breast and all. In a burbling-river rush of flawless Quadic, Lanie danced backward in her garden. As she went, she shot her parting crossbow bolt, using the couplet structure from Quadoni quest-poem cycles:

"Rejoice in thy capacity for thought. At midnight thou'lt forget—and be forgot."

CHAPTER NINE
The Brackenwilds

High Holy Fire Feast of Spring Equinox: Noon

LANIE WAS LATE to Nita's meeting with the Blood Royal. She had forgotten all about it; Goody had had to fetch her from her workshop in Stones Ossuary, which was way down past the bottom of the garden, beyond the orchards, practically at the mouth of the Diesmali—and a short flight of stairs underground.

It had taken Goody a while to get Lanie's attention, covered in undead mice as she was, playing with them on the ossuary floor beneath a chandelier of bones. Lanie had lit every single one of the one hundred forty-four candles on the chandelier for just this special occasion, and resented being asked to blow them all out and come away. Fortunately, she had several new undead mouse friends eagerly volunteering to do the job for her.

But Goody just said, "Your sister is not pleased, Mizka," in her voice that could split bedrock, and Lanie rolled her eyes and did as she was bid, deeply resentful.

It wasn't that she *hated* Blood Royal Erralierra Brackenwild. It was just… she didn't *like* her much.

"Let's face it, Goody," Lanie said, trudging back to Stones Manor at her side, "she looks like a chipmunk who stole all the best nuts from her friends. And she smells like the love child of a perfumery and a furriery. And she lies through her teeth."

"She is a politician, Mizka."

"I know—but does she have to *smile* as she lies?"

"She is," Goody repeated patiently, "a politician."

Perhaps Lanie could have forgiven the Blood Royal her, as she saw them, vices, had not Erralierra kept all of Father's nicest things after his death. As if *she* had a greater claim on them than his family! And the awful part was, Lanie sometimes felt that she *did*—for no one had loved Unnatural

Stones more than the Blood Royal of Liriat. Not even Lanie. Well—but Lanie had never been given a chance, had she? Because of Erralierra!

Or because of Lanie's allergy. Or the estrangement between Natty and Aba. Or… all of it, really. *Circumstances.*

And now, *circumstances*, that villain, was back to plague Lanie—on her surge day, too! After she had been so well behaved with the Scratch clan, *and* endured Nita's tantrum, *and* Mak's (perhaps understandable) rudeness to her, this was another distasteful chore that must be seen to before she could continue the work she liked best.

For comfort, she patted her pocket, the contents of which patted back with bony tails and foreheads and paws.

Since it was best to be unobtrusive when dealing with Blood Royals, who preferred all attention be on them—rather like Nita—Lanie decided to sneak into the great drawing room through the outside doors in the inner courtyard, rather than use the inside doors off the grand salon. Less of a chance of being noticed that way. But, lo! Her approach did not go unobserved.

To her delight—and immense chagrin—Canon Lir was in the inner courtyard, waiting for her.

They must have guessed her route, which should not have surprised her. Ever the strategist, Canon Lir. They had once challenged Lanie to a card-game-by-correspondence of Favors—a Rookish trick-taking game that was mostly bombast, bravado, and bluffing—saying that Lanie was the only person with whom they could conceivably imagine playing Favors long distance, and only because they knew her to be 'absolutely honorable.' At which point, Lanie could not have cared less if she won or lost, because Canon Lir thought her *honorable*, and wanted to play with her, and by all the smiles of Saint Death, she would give them the best game of their lives!

She lost, ultimately—but it took nine rounds, eighty-seven highly detailed letters, and two hundred sixty-one days all told.

Though they had been pen-pals since they were children (in the days Natty Stones still lived at Stones Manor, and Erralierra would come to visit him in the company of her fire priests, including the, at the time, extremely young Canon Lir), the Favors game had ramped up their correspondence to such a degree that by summer of last year, Lanie had come to expect to receive two or three letters a week, and to return the same. But since the end of autumn, their exchanges had cooled down. Other than a condolence card upon Aba's death, Lanie hadn't received so much as a few scribbled lines from Canon Lir in months.

At the thought, she skidded to a halt, suddenly shy. This movement sent five skittish mouse skeletons pouring from out of her pocket, scampering up her apron, and chittering for cover beneath her hair.

"Miss Stones!" called Canon Lir softly, rising from the bench they'd been lounging on.

Tongue-tangled, Lanie lifted her hand in a wave. In a moment of awful self-comprehension, she realized that not only had she forgotten to put on shoes or wash her face before leaving Stones Ossuary, but she was now wearing even fewer clothes than before! She was down to a long smock—which hung to her knees, but still!—and canvas apron, partially untied and sort of draped around her neck. All of her braids had come loose from their bright yellow bow and were clattering about her shoulders, a few now with mouse skeletons clinging to them like rope swings.

A Stones, caught without pants?

Surely this was the stuff of operetta, of buffoonery—not what one wanted when visiting with friends! Especially friends she very much liked, and admired, and... and she *ought* to go fetch her pants. If she could find them.

Only she was so hot. Surge-hot. Under her skin it was not spring at all, but summertime with a side of baked potato.

Lanie toyed with her apron strings as Canon Lir approached. Even staring fixedly at her feet, she could feel the high shine of their affection shedding its light all over her.

"Hello, Canon Lir," she whispered.

"Miss Stones. I must begin by begging your pardon. Do you despise me now? I know, I know, I have not answered your most recent letters—my remissness deserves your acute censure—but I assure you, I've started at least twenty dozen missives, and not finished a one of them, I've been that distracted. See here?"

From their yellow silk robes, they drew a thick packet of letters and offered it up to her like an oblation. Lanie's hands snaked out to snatch it up before she could stop herself—anymore than she could stop three inquisitive mouse skeletons from sliding off her braids and onto her shoulders, then running all the way down her arms to explore the packet. She put it—and the mice—back into her pocket without saying a word. Her mice would no more harm the letters than she would.

Canon Lir, who always seemed to understand everything at glance, now had mercy on her discomposure.

"You'll find in these unfinished epistles a little of everything that's been on my mind lately. Bristling with the latest gossip, of course—both castle and temple, I do not stint—summaries of all the books I've been reading; reflections on life and religion and magic; odes to my old farting dog—I love her, I wouldn't trade her for a puppy, I'm afraid she only has a few weeks left to live. But—and it is so embarrassing, Miss Stones—there's not a one letter here that doesn't break off just as I am about unleash some dazzling revelation, always mid-sentence! I've been so busy of late, I... But no more excuses! I brought you these fragments in the hopes that you'll forgive them. And me."

Lanie pushed her braids back over her shoulder, and adjusted her spectacles. Had a mouse skeleton found its way into her throat? It certainly felt like it.

"Thank you, Canon Lir. Nothing to forgive."

"Well," Canon Lir said, half-laughing, "if that's true, then why won't you look at me, Miss Stones?"

Lanie peeped at them from beneath her lashes. Canon Lir was, she was sure, the most beautiful person in Liriat, possibly the world. They were just about her height, plump where she was scrawny, coiffed where she was untidy, and impeccably clad in the petaled vestments of the fire priests of Sappacor.

Their moon-round face was painted like a shining disc of gold leaf, with a design of orange flames on cheeks and chin.

The only part of their skin left unpainted was their wizard mark, the Triple Flame of the many-gendered god of Fire in three shades of red, which they bore in the same place all fire priests bore theirs: upon their brow. Unlike wizards, who were born touched by their gods, fire priests received their marks upon the night of their initiation rite, when they transformed from lay disciple of Sappacor to fully dedicated fire priest. Even those born with no talent for bloodlighting magic would, at that moment, be able to wield their blood as flame—to greater or lesser degrees, of course, depending on skill, temperament, talent, and faith.

Canon Lir's lips were red, too. What went into that paint to make such a color, such a plump-ripe-apple, ruby-gloss red, Lanie did not know—but she could never see it without wanting to nibble it. Their eyes, heavily lined in black, were large and lustrous, the color of liquid copper. Great curly lashes, black-lacquered and gold-dusted, looked ready to fly off with every blink.

Those eyelashes blinked now. Those red lips smiled. Formed words. "Miss Stones?"

Lanie rubbed her nose, which glittered and tingled with the smell of strange magic. Not the lemon zest and lime spray of necromancy, no. No, bloodlighting smelled of wood smoke and lamp oil and white pepper incense, and the clean, hot scent of molten glass, and open flame. And so did Canon Lir.

Wait, but... had they just asked her a question? Yes—she rather thought they had. And here she was just smiling away at them. Possibly drooling. Belatedly, she inquired, "Sorry?"

"My mother and your sister await us." Canon Lir grimaced. "Not very patiently, either."

Lanie drooped, but Canon Lir gathered her elbow in their soft hand, and squeezed gently. The unpainted parts of their skin were a rich red-brown. Their shapely fingers terminated in long, gold-varnished nails, each thumb sporting a large ring of cabochon carnelian.

"I, too, would rather be back at the temple, performing bloodlight rites to my god," they disclosed in a conspiratorial murmur. "In most countries, the first duty of a sorcerer on a surge day is to their sorcery—that is, to the memory of their god—to the exclusion of all else. But we are Lirians, are we not, Miss Stones? And Lirians must bow to the Brackenwilds before they bow to their gods."

"*You're* a Brackenwild," Lanie reminded them. Not that she would mind bowing to Canon Lir in any number of interesting ways…

"Not since I was dedicated to Old Sparks as a child!" they laughed, using the pet name fire priests called their god. "We lose our surnames when we take orders. Well—ostensibly, anyway: what happens *practically* is a very different matter. But take heart, Miss Stones! We shall beard our various lionesses in the great drawing room together. Should we survive the encounter"—their red lips came very, very close to Lanie's ear—"you must meet me back here in the courtyard ere I depart. I have a gift for you."

"A gift?" Lanie was breathless, painfully pleased. "More than the letters?"

"Those!" Canon Lir scoffed. "Those are nothing. Scraps, unfinished, hardly worth your time or attention. No, this is much better. There's something I've been meaning to give you for ages. I found it in the temple vaults. My ommer—Eparch Aranha, I mean—said I may have it, though they recommended I hide it away and say nothing about it to Errolirrolin, lest he insist on liberating it from my possession and keeping it at Castle Ynyssyll as a Brackenwild heirloom." They smiled at her again, and her knees jellied. "And, I ask you, Miss Stones—what safer place could I find for it than entrusting it to *your* keeping?"

Lanie had never met Canon Lir's minutes-older brother, Errolirrolin Brackenwild, heir to the throne of Liriat. He was kept as closely confined to Castle Ynyssyll as she was to Stones Manor, and Erralierra guarded him jealously.

The Brackenwilds were notorious for always having twins, often several sets of them. Erralierra herself was the eldest of three identical pairs, none more than a year apart from each other. Her own twin, Canon Lir's ommer, was currently Eparch of the High Temple of Sappacor in Liriat Proper, the capital city; her other siblings were Blood Royal Plenipotentiaries in Leech, Damahrash, Umrys-by-the-Sea, and Quadiíb respectively. But other than Canon Lir, young Errolirrolin had no siblings.

And the reason for that was Jaor.

The winsome, wild son of Baroness Forthios, the late Prince Consort Jaor had been chosen for the Blood Royal when he was eighteen and she, twenty-six. But he had given his royal wife only one set of twins when Erralierra's spies discovered him to be part of a conspiracy to overthrow the Brackenwilds and divide the realm of Liriat amongst the nine baronies.

Lanie had heard the story from various sources. There was one tragic opera about it, and one comic opera (the latter focusing on the riotous romance between the Blood Royal and Unnatural Stones more than the messy politics), and the story went like this:

Erralierra had not yet left her childbed when she summoned her Chief Executioner Unnatural Stones to her side, and commanded him to pay the Prince Consort a visit at Forthios Manor. Her Chief Executioner was, as always, happy to be of service—and in this instance, perhaps more than ever.

That afternoon, a coach and six (matching blacks with silver manes) pounded up the gravel drive at the Forthios country estate. Unnatural 'Natty' Stones alighted from the coach, nobly but professionally attired in black brocade and black pearls, with darkly iridescent grackle feathers in his hat, and a black velvet ribbon binding back all his thick black braids. He presented himself to the major-domo and asked to speak with Prince Consort Jaor.

The major-domo, no fool or traitor, brought him directly to his young master, who promptly tried to climb out a window. But Natty, with a merry laugh, merely hauled the boy back into the room, and sat him down.

"There are two ways we can do this, my naughty little lad," said he, his husky tenor trained by loud singing and cigars. "We can do this right here and now, swiftly and gracefully, in the familiar splendor of your childhood bedroom—in this very plush, very comfortable chair, in fact." Natty held up a waxed cord with a loop on either end: very supple, very simple.

"Or," he continued, swinging the ligature like a pendulum, "if you prefer, we can do it in a few hours from now, in full view of a crowd gathered on Moll's Kopje, with your wife and newborn babies looking on from the windows of Castle Ynyssyll. I will drop you from the heights of Ynyssyll's Tooth onto the flagstones below—no great fuss, I assure you, but a lot of mess. Your choice!"

Unnatural Stones was a gentlemanly executioner. As Erralierra's official machine of death, he always gave the condemned a choice. (If, on the other hand, the Royal Assassin, Erralierra's *unofficial* machine of death, showed up at your house, she would not be announcing herself at the front door. Abandon Hope Stones would simply come to you in the dead of the night, and you would be sound asleep until you weren't, and after that, there would be nothing further to discuss.)

Prince Consort Jaor of Forthios was no coward, but he was very young. Hot-headed though he was, he was not so thoroughly convinced of his own convictions that they gave him courage enough for a death flight from Ynyssyll's Tooth. He chose the ligature, and neither Errolirrolin nor Canon Lir had ever known their father.

Shortly after her twins were weaned, Blood Royal Erralierra gave up the younger to the High Temple of Sappacor, dedicating them to blood and to flame, as was tradition to do with the second-born Brackenwild child.

Too busy governing Liriat and raising Errolirrolin to do the same, she took no part in parenting Canon Lir, who considered themself as much a temple baby as any orphan abandoned on the steps in a basket. However, being that the binding ties between the Brackenwilds and the fire priests were familial as well as political, Canon Lir did not grow up ignorant of or ignored by their progenitrix. As soon as they were old enough not to disgrace her in public, the Blood Royal selected Canon Lir to act as her personal page, later her amanuensis, to accompany her on visits such as this.

The first time Lanie had met Canon Lir, they were both about six years old, equally fascinated with each other from the moment Natty and Erralierra abandoned them together in Stones Library in order to purloin some quality private time in Natty's bedchambers—which were in a different wing of the house. Thus had their friendship begun.

"I really don't want to go inside," Lanie confessed now to Canon Lir, slipping her hand into the crook of their elbow. "My brain keeps talking to me in nursery rhymes, and I can't be sure I won't blurt them out by accident, inciting Nita to murder me in front of your mother. Also," she added meditatively, "I am not wearing any pants."

"Miss Stones, if you'd said nothing about it, I never would have noticed." Canon Lir winked.

Lanie giggled. The mouse skeletons snuggled the letters in her pocket. Arm in arm, the friends went together into Stones Manor.

"YOU'RE LATE, MISCELLANEOUS," Nita said flatly.

Her Highness Erralierra Brackenwild, Blood Royal of Liriat, Overlord of Ynyssyll's Tooth, Warden of the Diesmali Woods, Guardian of the Twin Rivers, waved her hand, overriding Nita's disapproval. She beamed at Lanie and Canon Lir where they stood, lightly linked at the elbow, on the threshold of the great drawing room. The barbecue rankness of her blood magic, so different from the delicate white pepper incense of her secondborn's, nearly smothered Lanie's happy surge.

"Lanie, honey! You're blooming! I've never seen you surge with such strength! How well you look—so much better than I remember!" She turned to smile at Nita. Perfectly round wizard marks, like two small cherry-red coins, accented the deep dimples on both of her cheeks. "How old is she now?"

Erralierra knew the answer, of course, for Lanie and Canon Lir were of an age, and the Blood Royal was a fiend for details. She stacked facts like coins, her memory a marauder's hoard. But it pleased her to needle Nita, whose patience had nearly run its ribbon to the raveled end.

"Fifteen," Nita replied.

"Fifteen! And still alive!" Erralierra marveled. "None of us thought she'd live to see double digits, did we? Oh, how my Natty worried for her. More ulcer than stomach some days, he was, pondering his poor daughter's survival. I cannot number the times I offered to have the sweet child stay with us at Castle Ynyssyll under the care of my finest physicians—and, of course, rather less exposed to her particular allergens—but, of course, Aba would not hear of it."

"Oh, Mother just doted on Miscellaneous," Nita lied.

"Such a dedicated parent," Erralierra lied right back, smoothly.

"Such a time we all had, twisting ourselves into hangman's knots trying to keep our favored child alive."

Lanie almost snorted. This, from Nita—who'd once tried to feed four-year-old Lanie a bowl of mushroom soup composed mainly of death caps!

"It takes a realm to raise a necromancer, they say," Erralierra agreed. "And how admirably we've all succeeded—so far."

The Blood Royal appeared to be enjoying herself hugely. She sat at her ease in a high-backed, half-domed canopy chair of tufted indigo velvet, her legs crossed at the knee, her fingers threaded in her lap.

With her silken trousers, embroidered slippers, and a great hat of gold netting that looked like a seeding dandelion, Erralierra was a study in extravagance. Her loose-swinging jacket was of claret-red satin, stiffly encrusted at collar and cuffs with thread of gold and rubies. Jewels flashed like fire against her long fingers. Though not as tall as Nita, the Blood Royal was somehow more immense—like a bonfire burning merrily in the middle of a room, attracting attention, admiration, and alarm. She had short-cropped, closely curled black hair, dark brown skin, a thick torso, mighty thighs, and sloping shoulders. Her eyes were brown with a hint of rust. She was smiling hard.

You could bounce a throwing star off that smile, Lanie thought glumly. And it would ricochet right back and shatter your teeth.

She glanced sideways at Canon Lir, who was glancing sideways at her. The corners of their painted mouth swept up like the curling prow of a ship, and Lanie felt instantly better. At least *Canon Lir* never looked like a chipmunk when *they* smiled!

"Now that you are home, Amanita Muscaria," Erralierra began, "and with a... consort... of your own"—she cast an incredulous glance at the peregrine falcon currently mantling the marble bust of Dowzabel Stones[6]—"surely you will want to set up household for yourself? Start

6 Dowzabel, dam of Irradiant 'Grandpa Rad' Stones, was best known for stitching a pair of genuine necropants out of her first husband's hide. In the peculiar way of necropants, its cured gonads produced for her, each time she reached deep into their sacks, so many gold monarch coins that in her lifetime Dowzabel became the richest woman in Liriat. As per usual for a Stones, that lifetime didn't last long: Dowzabel was found strangled by her necropants on the very night she announced the date of her forthcoming second marriage. After this, the treasured trousers yielded not so much as a single copper poppet (a denomination so low that even beggars gave

your nursery? Perhaps now is finally the time when our little Lanie can come home with me to Castle Ynyssyll. I have kept a suite of rooms ready for her—her father's rooms, in fact!"

"*Our* father's rooms," Nita said.

Erralierra ignored this. "Lanie, come here. Kneel by me. I want to have a look at you."

Lanie knelt, steeling herself not to flinch at Erralierra's unavoidable touch, no matter how her allergy responded.

But thank Saint Death for tender favors—no recent act of violence endowed those hands with allergens today. Erralierra had *flunkies* for that sort of thing.

"Ah, Lanie, honey. You look so like Natty," cooed the Blood Royal, her warm breath sweet and smoky, like cloves. "I miss him like I would miss my own left hand."

Lanie summoned a polite smile. She knew Erralierra liked her, though other than resembling her late father, she had never done anything to deserve it, and therefore found her affection suspect. If she'd had her druthers, Lanie would deflect all of the Blood Royal's fondness onto Nita, inspiring in her the desire to hire Nita to kill all sorts of people. All sorts of *very far away* people. That way, Nita would be constantly traveling for business, the Scratches would soon be paid what they were owed, and Lanie and Goody could remain together, alone at Stones Manor, like they were before Nita came home, perfectly happy to practice sothaín, bake bread, read books, tend the garden, and learn how to raise the dead. Not that Goody was very involved in the latter—but all the rest!

The peregrine falcon shifted on his perch, his eye catching hers. A thin ring of yellow around a black-amber void. Lanie quickly averted her gaze, lifting her face to the Blood Royal instead. Might as well try to do some good while she had her attention.

"I may look like Father," she said, "but you know it's Nita he mentored. Before she left, she took Father's full course of executioner's etiquette and protocol. And Mother did all her sharp arts training—marksmanship, evasion, interrogation, disguise. Plus, as you know, Nita is very fine at fascination: the same magic the Blackbird Bride uses! Mother was using her as a subcontractor by the time she was twelve..."

She trailed off, for the Blood Royal was shaking her head in a polished approximation of regret, even narrowing the inner corners of her eyes

---

it away) no matter what dark death-magic spells young Irradiant hurled at them. One night in a rage, he cut his palm over the necropants until his blood mixed with his father's dead matter, and the necropants burned with the intelligent blue aura of ectenica. Now that the necropants could communicate with him, Irradiant asked them *why* they no longer worked. The necropants replied: "*What e'er the magic that I enacted, 'twas all for love of Dowzabel.*" Then, sighing, the ectenical necropants sloughed off into slag and sludgy ash right there on Irradiant's workroom table.

in sympathy. "I am afraid I have already filled both positions of Chief Executioner *and* Royal Assassin of Liriat."

"*When?*" Nita demanded, much too loudly. "The positions were still open when I rode through Liriat Proper three days ago!"

"Why, just this morning, Amanita Muscaria," the Blood Royal replied coolly. "Before I came to see you." She tickled Lanie under the chin, rather in the manner of a woman with a favorite lap dog, and told her, "Go and stand by Canon Lir now, Lanie, there's a good girl."

Lanie scooted.

Nita was standing a respectful distance from Erralierra's blue velvet chair, having been invited no closer. Until that moment, she had been still, but now she stirred: a strange, sinuous movement that implied she had a crick in her neck that she couldn't quite pop, but would be more than happy to pop yours for you if you so much as looked at her the wrong way.

"And whom," she asked, "if I may be so bold as to inquire, Blood Royal, did you hire?"

"Two rising young luminaries in our immigrant community: Cracchen and Scratten Scratch."

CHAPTER TEN

Four and Twenty Blackbirds

"THE SCRATCHES ARE a prominent banking family in the capital city," Erralierra continued, aware but blithely unconcerned that Nita had just transformed into an active volcano right in front of her. "Skaki, originally. I think perhaps you have had some dealings with them already in the short time you've been back?"

Nita nodded.

Just like, Lanie thought, a volcano nods. Right before ejecting six miles of rock into the sky.

"Indeed, your family has for several years now enjoyed a healthy business relationship with Mistress Scratch. As have I! Of course," Erralierra laughed, slapping her knee, "I am not exactly clear as to which of her strapping sons I hired for which job! But I am convinced that both could do either equally. Or is it, 'either could do both'?"

Lanie's mischievous surge, rather like Nita's temper, suddenly boiled over, perhaps prompted by the tension in the room. She could not control the outpouring of rhymes, only the volume.

"Either could do neither," she muttered, "and neither could do naught! But ne'er could e'er do well—those ne'er-do-wells of Skakmaht!"

Canon Lir muffled a laugh, but placed a steadying hand over hers where it lay in the crook of their elbow.

"And what," Nita asked through clenched teeth, "are their qualifications—these immigrants, these *banker's* sons—to hold positions that the Stoneses have rightfully occupied since the founding of Liriat?"

Lanie's foot tapped, impatient with rhetoric. The answer was plain: how much of Erralierra's expensive gold embroidery and gem-encrusted cuffs was owed to Scratch coffers? Money was like magic for people who didn't have any. Sari Scratch, lacking the one, more than made up for it with the other. As for qualifications, Nita need look no further than a contract notarized by a priest of Lan Satthi—this one, Lanie was sure, with Erralierra's name and blood-print at the bottom of it.

"Their qualifications?" The Blood Royal issued another rolling laugh, punctuated with another percussive slap of the knee. "Well, let us count them. Cracchen Scratch captained a caravan guard unit for three years in Lower Quadiíb. Scratten Scratch was a soldier-for-hire to the Guardian Saint of Umrys-by-the-Sea. Most recently, both of them were personal bodyguards to our own Baroness Olithar out on our western borders.

"I'm afraid," she confided, "I poached them out from under Ollie after seeing them at their exercises. Both stripped to the breechclout! Strapping brutes! Such invigorating coloring, too—like an ice plunge after a hot steam! Such height and breadth! Not, I'm afraid, much in the way of *depth*—an asset, I fear, their profound mother did not pass on to her progeny. Bless her, Sari possesses enough for the whole family!"

Nita took a deep breath, still leaking magma. "You saw... Mistress Scratch... this morning?"

"She called on me right as I was leaving to come see you. I always make time to see her, you know: one of my closest advisors. Really, Amanita Muscaria!" Erralierra exclaimed. "My schedule is relentless—and never more so than on a surge day! The only reason I spared the time for you today was for the sake of your father. After our meeting here, I must join my son Errolirrolin at Sinistral Park for the vernal festival. We are slated to inspect the city lamps, see that they are all still burning high till the Bloodlighting Rite at Midsummer, then we must put in an appearance at several live concerts, three dinners, and five dances. So might we, if you please, address the business proposition you wished to discuss?"

Lanie watched Nita's gold-ringed throat work, as she realized how Sari Scratch had outplayed her. All her hopes of settling those three lapsed payments by midnight were crumbling like Dowzabel's necropants.

The next moment, Nita's expression went cold and smooth—except for a brief panthaumic flare just above her eyebrow.

Lanie jerked upright in surprise, snatching her hand from Canon Lir's elbow. It wasn't possible—couldn't be—but... her sister was about to fascinate the Blood Royal where she sat!

Erralierra saw it too; all joviality dropped from her face as she tracked Nita's magical flare with her own surge-struck eyes.

Moving calmly but efficiently, Canon Lir stepped away from Lanie and in front of Erralierra, interposing their body between hers and Nita's. Three other fire priests stepped away from the wall. The shorter skirts of their robes, their glinting mail shirts, and the coal-red glow of the wizard marks upon their foreheads indicated their rank as Bright Knights of the Triple Flame, the High Temple's military order.

The steel claws capping each of their fingertips folded into their flesh as their hands came together in prayer. Blood welled from those fresh wounds. From that blood, a blood-dark fire bloomed. Instead of liquid dripping down their arms, flames raced up to their fingertips, balanced on the blackening steel claws, rounded off into fireballs ready for throwing.

Nita quickly banked her leaping magic. Her magic was already stretched too thin from holding Mak in thrall. Besides, she was not the only trained killer in the room with a panthaumic surge at her behest.

She did the only thing she could; she fell to her knees and bowed her head.

"Forgive me, Blood Royal. My surge moved me to impulse, but I have mastered it. I confess," she laughed, unable to disguise her bitterness, "I am disappointed. I have lived in the Traveling Palaces and trained in their Caravan School for four years with the sole desire of returning to serve you, as my… my father did."

"My dear," said Erralierra very dryly (though Lanie could see, from her vantage point, that her hands had relaxed upon her knees), "no one can serve me as your father did."

Nita protested, "I didn't mean… I didn't think I could *replace* him! I only meant that I wished to dedicate my life to your service. The loss of our house and lands would be as nothing to me compared to the loss of your matronage. The Stoneses have always been bloodbound to the Brackenwilds. I"—she laid a hand over her heart—"have always been a proud patriot of Liriat. It's what kept me alive—functional—in Quadiíb, where I felt so lost."

Raising her left arm, but leaving her right upon her breast, Nita held it out in supplication.

"Liriat is my one true love. That—more than his etiquette or his technique—is what Father taught me. In everything he said or did, in all the songs he sang, he conveyed his love for realm. Like his character sings, in that opera written about you and him, your love for each other…"

To Lanie's surprise—to the surprise of everyone present—Nita opened her mouth and sang a snatch of melody, in a husky alto very close to what Natty's husky tenor once had been:

How piteous your look!
Your fingers cling to mine!
My words melt away—
What is left to say?
Who am I? Your servant!
Who are you? My queen!
My heart is in your hand!
My life is at your feet!
Now you know what I know—
What is left to say?
I hear what you speak
And seek to obey!

A risky move, Lanie thought, impressed. Very risky.

And yet—it was working. Erralierra's face was softening. She relaxed back in her seat, eyes half closed, and when Nita fell silent, bowing her head again, pursed her lips in thought for at least half a minute.

"I have in mind a project you might be perfect for," she told Nita slowly. "I only hesitated to bring it up because you are so newly returned home, and it requires a degree of travel."

"Oh?" Nita kept her head bowed, but every sorcerer in the room could see the hopeful glitter of her panthaumic aura.

"What has your sister"—Erralierra nodded at Lanie—"told you about Natty's death?"

Nita frowned, still not looking up, her golden glow taking on a calculating edge. "That a young wizard from Rook took it upon herself to impress the Blackbird Bride by killing a Stones. She was a new inductee in the Parliament of Rooks. Impulsive, heedless. Her daring meant her death—but she nevertheless dealt a double blow to you, for you lost both your executioner and a faithful... subject... that day."

"That is what your mother reported to me, yes, after she had performed the interrogation on the criminal. On Aba's word, I sentenced that wizard to death by boiled tar. A fitting end to our feathered friend."

Lanie's surge did *not* like that rhyme. Not in the least. The stench of tar dripped from her nostrils. Her sinuses swelled. She rubbed her nose. Her hand came away bloody. "Damn it duodecifold!"

Only Canon Lir heard her. Lanie sensed them looking over at her, doing a double-take at the sight of her no doubt impressive nosebleed. She squatted, aggrieved, tilting her nose back and fishing through her apron pockets. The mouse skeletons thought it was a game, and kept getting in her way.

From under the blue canopy of her chair, Erralierra continued her story, "The girl kept trying to transform, fly away, at the end. But she was too broken. In her final moments, she screamed out to her wife and queen. She called the name of Bran Fiakhna."

Canon Lir crouched down beside Lanie, quietly offering her the end of their belling sleeve. She smiled gratefully, but refused with a silent shake of her head, producing at last one of several handkerchiefs she always kept on her person. She was down from the usual half dozen to only three, as most of her pockets had gone missing with her trousers.

"Now, what I found extraordinary that day," Erralierra was saying, "was that, in the moment the young wizard shouted out to the Blackbird Bride, a great shadow fell over Moll's Kopje where the execution was taking place. It was as if a cloud—or perhaps a flight of birds—were passing directly in front of the sun. And when the sun shone again, the cauldron of tar was shattered. At the center of the breakage was a single blackbird—a blackstart, as it happened—who lay dead. Not a drop of tar clung to her! Now," she said, compelling Nita's gaze to meet her own, "what do you make of *that*?"

Nita's forehead wrinkled. "Who can fathom the ways of Rookish sorcery?"

"It was a blessing," Lanie piped up from behind her sodden handkerchief. "A mercy killing. It meant Bran Fiakhna was watching over the execution. *Obviously.*"

Nita glared at her for speaking out of turn. But Lanie was full of courage, for beside her Canon Lir was resting their hand lightly upon her back, right between her shoulder blades, listening intently to what she had to say. They gave her a little nod, inviting her to continue.

"It means Father's murder wasn't some heedless, impulsive act," she went on. "The Blackstart Wizard—that would have been her title, right? In the Parliament?—was *obeying orders*. She succeeded in her task. And the Blackbird Bride, her liege lady, was there for her at the finish, to end her suffering. To show *approval*."

As she spoke, Nita's furious scowl melted into a thoughtful frown. But it flashed to a scowl again when Erralierra applauded Lanie's deduction.

"Exactly, honey! I have allowed the—shall we say—*skewed* results of Aba's interrogation to remain as my *official* opinion regarding Natty's death: the killer acted alone—for personal, not political, gain. But ever since Blackstart's execution, darkly have I dwelled on the threat from Rook, and on the Blackbird Bride, who seeks to weaken me. Natty's death was but one instance of her interference. Twice have attempts been made on Errolirrolin's life. On my own as well. Even Canon Lir has not been spared her... attentions."

The hand on Lanie's back tensed, then relaxed again as Erralierra concluded, "And when Aba's death followed Natty's so closely, I knew my suspicions to be true. My assets, my fortifications, are most methodically being chipped out from under me. The time has come to *act*."

Lanie caught her breath. She knew her mother's death had been self-inflicted. The only mystery Lanie had perceived about it was whether Aba had poisoned herself on purpose or by accident.

But could Aba's 'accident' have been engineered? Had someone close to her, someone she trusted, knowing her predilection for recreational drug use, recommended Elixir of Adamant as the solution to her fears? What if they had offered it to her as a gift, citing its magical endowments: "Longevity, Clarity, and Invincibility"—three virtues that a woman whose husband had just been murdered, whose own life might be threatened, stood in desperate need of?

Lanie could see her mother swallowing that stuff whole, literally and figuratively. She just couldn't imagine who Aba would have trusted to that extent. She didn't have many friends. *Any* friends. Especially in the last years of her life.

"If there is any way I may help you to act, Blood Royal," Nita was saying eagerly, leaning forward on her knees, "please—please, let me serve you. Let me help you avenge Father's death!"

Clever Nita, Lanie thought, *not* to include Aba in her quest for vengeance.

Nita had been much closer to Aba than Natty, growing up. But none of that mattered now. Erralierra, who'd tolerated Abandon Hope Stones while she was courting her husband, had held her in open contempt ever since Natty had moved from Stones Manor into Castle Ynyssyll. The Blood Royal had only kept Aba in her employ because Abandon Hope Stones was, in fact, the best at her job. Worse than keeping her Royal Assassin close would have been to let her hire herself out to just any upstart from the baronies, or abroad, to Erralierra's enemies.

Nita was much like Aba, both in appearance and affect. She had inherited her powers of fascination from her mother's line. Perhaps it was this that influenced Erralierra's often peremptory treatment of her.

But Nita's aria seemed to have exorcised some of those phantoms from the past. Now, in the rolling tones of public oration, the Blood Royal began, "If you agree to my proposition, Amanita Muscaria Stones, history shall extol you as the most dreaded assassin of your illustrious line. More ruthless than War Chief Ham-Handed Stones, more cunning than Celerity Stones, more original than Irradiant Stones, and—as I am sure your Quadoni lover would agree"—a nod to the peregrine falcon on the mantle—"more beautiful than Delirious Stones, who slew men with her smile[7]."

Nita was ready—more than ready—to agree. It was all over her triumphantly blazing aura. But to Lanie's surprise, she bit her tongue and said demurely, "Name your terms, Blood Royal. And then, perhaps, you and I can discuss my fees."

Erralierra grinned, hard and feral, like a chipmunk about to go to war for the biggest nut of them all.

"I want you," she said simply, "to annihilate the Parliament of Rooks."

Lanie's nosebleed fountained up in blood.

Out in the courtyard, Canon Lir sat beside her on one of the long basalt benches, while inside the great drawing room, negotiations between Erralierra and Nita snapped back and forth like banners in the wind.

Lanie had finally escaped, but only after her nosebleed had soaked through all three of her handkerchiefs and most of Canon Lir's outer robe, lent for that purpose. Now they, like Lanie, were down a layer of clothing, though disappointingly (in Lanie's opinion) still completely covered. In addition to their long yellow skirts, Canon Lir wore a fitted mail shirt with a quilted gambeson beneath it. Neither garment had been previously visible under their outer robe.

Lanie indicated the mail shirt. "Are you taking orders with the Bright

7 In point of fact, Delirious Stones did *not* slay men with her smile. She killed with her kiss. The difference is significant, and mainly due to the toxins mixed in with her lipstick.

Knights?" Her voice sounded odd, each of her nostrils stuffed with bright silk.

Canon Lir smiled, the orange and red and gold disk of their face creasing shiningly. "No—Old Sparks forbid! I'm no warrior priest. But the Blood Royal has commanded that since... since a few attempts have been made on my life, I should not leave the temple unprotected."

Though their words were foreboding, their voice was like honey on the comb, sun-lashed and warm, sweet, full of life. The sound of it sent wave upon wave of pleasurable horripilation across Lanie's skin.

Since Canon Lir seemed hesitant to discuss the assassination attempts, and she couldn't very well ask for details—being, at this point, so sensitized that if someone swatted a fly in front of her, she'd probably black out—Lanie skirted around a direct reply.

"I hope the danger passes soon, what with the... the new plan." She paused a moment, then added grimly, "It's a large contract for one person. Even if that person is Nita. The Parliament of Rooks consists of how many wizards?"

"Four-and-twenty," Canon Lir said quietly. The black-and-gold fringe of their lashes swept down, concealing all expression in their copper-colored eyes.

"I know *why* the Blood Royal is making the attempt, but—but what good will it do?" Lanie burst out. "Wizards come from every realm to pay court to the Blackbird Bride. She'll replace the dead ones before they hit the ground. She'll never have fewer than twenty-four in her Parliament! What's the point?"

"Morale."

Lanie raised her eyebrows.

"The new wizards won't be her *first* choice, you see," Canon Lir explained. "No matter how many times Bran Fiakhna replaces them, they won't be her favorites: her 'espoused kin'—lovers and friends with whom she grew up, bred her children, shared the responsibilities of government, played games, ate meals, traveled. People she's made love to, made vows to. Any wizard new-come to her Parliament will be, merely, a replacement. Second best. A lesser power. A necessity. Liked, perhaps, but never loved. Or at least, never loved so deeply."

"Poor Bran Fiakhna," Lanie whispered.

"Poor Erralierra," Canon Lir countered neutrally, "who had only *one* love, and lost him. Because of Bran Fiakhna."

"But this isn't really about love, is it?" Lanie demanded. "It's about power. Rook versus Liriat. Bran Fiakhna made her move late last year; now it's for Erralierra to riposte. How long does this go on? Until we're annexed? Until we take the battle all the way to Rookery Court? Where does it end?"

Canon Lir spread their hands in a shrug. "The great political and military strategists of our time are asking these same questions. A hundred years ago, Liriat was a country to be reckoned with. We took down the sky wizards of Skakmaht in a single night, thanks to Irradiant Stones. After that, no power in any realm wanted to annoy us. We are a small nation, the youngest by several centuries, but we proved our ruthlessness in the skies above Iskald. Since then, however, many things have changed, not least—"

"No new necromancers were born in Liriat," Lanie said. Until her, that is.

"For one," Canon Lir conceded. "For another, Bran Fiakhna is by far the most powerful Blackbird Bride in recent history. Or ancient history, for that matter. She fascinated the throne of Rook before she turned twenty, and her hold on it has been uncontested in the decades since. Her Parliament is full. Her court is bursting with secondary and tertiary wizards awaiting her notice. She is restless. She is looking to expand her boundaries. We are her nearest border nation. The marches between us are flat, with well-maintained roads. We have very little in the way of a standing army. Our Diesmali is a treasure trove of titanwood timber and ore. Our farmlands are fertile. Two major rivers run through our capital city—which makes for rich trade. We would certainly be worth her effort."

Lanie muttered, "We're a backwater, basically." And if Liriat was a backwater, she lived in a sinkhole at the bottom of a bog.

The glittering tips of Canon Lir's fingernails flashed in another minuscule shrug. "Say rather, we are nice little asset awaiting a strong leader to come and pocket us. Meanwhile, Erralierra has been... *unlucky* in her reign. Strife amongst the baronies has made her insular. Public scandal has made her defiant—first, her husband's defection, then her affair with your father, and... and all that followed.

"Now she lives at the edges of her own extremes, has made a habit of truculence, scorn, the reckless squandering of cash. No, more than habit," they corrected themself. "She has made them *fashionable*. Discretion, diplomacy, economizing—these are to be scoffed at, considered weaknesses."

Lanie exhaled an impressed breath (as well as she could, through her blood-soaked wads). "You've thought this through."

Canon Lir laughed. "Well. I *am* temple-raised, and my ommer, the Eparch of Sappacor, *is* Erralierra's twin. I am constantly attending the Blood Royal at Castle Ynyssyll, and... and my own twin and I are very close. Not much occurs in Liriat Proper that escapes our notice."

"So what happens if Nita succeeds in"—Lanie's nose began tingling again, warning her—"in her mission?"

"Aside from provoking the furious indignation of the most powerful sorceress queen in generations?" Canon Lir asked dryly. "Well, *Erralierra* believes Amanita Muscaria's success will not only demoralize Rookery Court and debilitate its magical power base, it will also remind Bran Fiakhna that the Brackenwilds are not without allies. That there are Stoneses yet to be contended with. That when Stoneses and Brackenwilds act in harmony, Liriat is a country that cannot be conquered. Not by all the wizards—or wizard-birds—in the sky."

They paused, took a deep breath, and seemed to cast off their grave mantle of doubt and fear. Straightening up, they turned to Lanie, and turned the subject. "Miss Stones. Miss Stones, Miss Stones. Here we are, alone together as we seldom ever are, and what must we do but waste our precious minutes prating on about politics?"

"I don't mind," said Lanie, heartbeat quickening.

"But I promised you a present! And my time to bestow it upon you is almost out. We must not rush these things—for what is more sacred than a gift to one's friend?"

Lanie answered promptly, "A gift to one's friend on a *surge day*, Canon Lir!"

They laughed, and stood from the bench, gesturing for her to stay seated. Then, with a flourish, from the pockets of their yellow skirts they produced a small lacquered black box, presenting it to Lanie, who opened it.

Inside the box was a foot-shaped pendant, almost as large as the palm of her hand, of black walnut and hammered copper. The foot wore a sandal of blue enamel, with sapphires and rubies fitted cunningly over it. At the top of the wooden foot was inset a little crystal panel for peering inside. And inside the pendant, was...

"It's a toe bone!" Lanie exclaimed, delighted. "The hallux, right? The," she squinted, "left hallux?"

"Not just *any* left hallux," Canon Lir grandly informed her. "That, Miss Stones, is a reliquary containing the left big toe of Ynyssyll Brackenwild, Founding Queen of Liriat! Once, in Prince Sosha's day, it was stolen from the Brackenwild treasury, and sold in secret to a wealthy collector in Damahrash, who had coveted it all her life."

Taking the reliquary from her, they unclasped the chain it hung on and gestured for her to turn around. Behind Lanie, Canon Lir looped their arms over her head, and laid the reliquary against her throat, fixing the clasp in the back.

"After Sosha's death, the reliquary was recovered—a daring rescue, or 'heist,' if you will—and returned to Moll II, who bestowed it upon the then-Eparch of the High Temple of Sappacor. Ommer says the reliquary used to be kept under glass, locked up in their predecessor's private museum. But the whole place got a makeover when Eparch Aranha took over—they don't like having a lot of things about that constantly need dusting—and the reliquary was put away, left to attract cobwebs in a drawer somewhere. Which is where I found it. And thought of you."

Lanie wondered if her pupils were transforming into flowers and confetti, if her panthaumic aura were spitting fireworks, if her lips had reddened with all the kisses she wanted to press upon Canon Lir. She was barely able to form words of thanks, and the words that ended up burbling out of her mouth weren't the ones she was expecting:

"But... this isn't the only one, is it?"

Canon Lir threw back their head and laughed. "I *knew* you would sense it!" And they reached beneath their mail and gambeson and drew out a nearly identical reliquary: a foot-shaped pendant of black walnut and copper and enamel, with a little window of crystal.

Nearly identical, Lanie thought, but not *quite*.

Even without seeing it, she could sense the second bone, feel the shape of it in her own skeleton, and knew that it would prove to be—

"—the *right* big toe of Ynyssyll Brackenwild!" she and Canon Lir said at the same time.

"And now we match," Canon Lir pronounced, satisfied.

As the reliquary warmed against her skin, Lanie could feel the bone inside it thrumming. Then the thrumming turned into a keening. If she listened hard enough—if 'listening' were the right word, which it wasn't—she could hear both of the bones in their respective reliquaries ringing out to each other, as if they were not bones at all, but two tiny crystal bells in conversation. Those fragments of phalanx wanted nothing more than to reunite. With each other, yes, but even more, with the rest of the body.

And somewhere, very far away and faint, Lanie could almost hear the remaining remains of Ynyssyll Brackenwild calling out to them, calling them home.

Lanie reached to take Canon Lir's hand, a daring move that she would never, ever have attempted on any other day, at any other moment. But Canon Lir was smiling at her, and the bones were singing, and all her little mouse skeletons had crept out of her pocket to explore her new pendant.

And it seemed as if her mice were ringing too, a chiming handful of little crystal bells with long bony tails, and Lanie was glowing, she was a pillar of lemon blossoms and orange zest ...

But before her hand could quite make contact, Nita came dancing out into the courtyard. She hauled Lanie to her feet and swirled her around, laughing like a storm of lions.

"We have the money! The Blood Royal advanced me a sum on the understanding I'll leave next week for Rook. Sari Scratch can eat her heart and shit it out—we get to keep our home!"

A crop of blisters bubbled up on Lanie's arm where Nita gripped her, prickling and stinging. Nita's hands were full of joyous death, already itching to perform her duty to Liriat and the Blood Royal Brackenwilds.

She tried not to hiss in pain. "Wonderful, Amanita Muscaria! Congratulations. Just what you wanted."

"Yes," said Nita. "And after tonight—after I take care of Mak—I'll have everything I ever wanted. Everything!"

Lanie smiled weakly. "May I go back to Stones Ossuary now, please? I still have a few more things to do."

"Yes—yes, of course, Miscellaneous," Nita said, releasing her. "Run along and play with your bones." She beamed. "Oh, I am so happy! I don't know when I've been so happy! Four-and-twenty feathers to decorate my belt—plus Erralierra Brackenwild's matronage! The only thing that would make me happier would be slaughtering the Scratches in their beds. But I fear pissing off my Blood Royal." She smirked. "So they're safe. For now."

Lanie nodded along with this until Nita finished monologuing and dashed back into the house to see her guests off.

Finally, she was able to turn her attention back to Canon Lir. But they had heard Erralierra calling their name, and were already slipping away out of the courtyard, back inside toward the great drawing room. At the last moment, before disappearing into the house, they turned, and waved.

Lanie waved back, flapping the blood-spotted remains of Canon Lir's yellow robe like a flag. Canon Lir grinned, once more touched the reliquary around their neck, before tucking it back into their clothing, concealing it. Their secret. Nodding and grinning, Lanie did the same.

First thing tomorrow morning, she vowed, hurrying from the courtyard back to the ossuary, I'll read all of their letters through twice—no, thrice!—and begin my reply. But first, she would finish out her surge. She would wake the rest of her little friends from their (as it turned out) not-so-eternal slumber.

The more distance Lanie put between herself and Nita, the more her happiness flooded in, and with her happiness, a renewed swell of power, now enhanced by the gift Canon Lir had given her.

A toe bone! A toe bone of her very own!

Well, not her *very* own; it was Queen Ynyssyll's toe, after all—the sinister one, no less, for Canon Lir no doubt had remembered that Lanie was left-handed; that was *just like* them—and the rest of Queen Ynyssyll would probably thank her to return it someday, and maybe Lanie would—someday—when she was very old—but that was neither here nor there.

The point was... Really, the *point* was...

The urge to surge was about to converge.

CHAPTER ELEVEN

Ghostly Appetites

High Holy Fire Feast of Spring Equinox: the Hour before Midnight

NIGHT AT LAST, and Lanie was burning clear and true, her thoughts as crisp and crystalline as the star-capped night. A thin wind hovered just below freezing; frost sparkled on the mud and bloodwort and redbud trees.

As her surge crested toward midnight and came into the full glory of panthauma, so too did Lanie's fever. By now she had shed both apron and smock, wore only the lightest chemise for modesty's sake. Barefoot, she pattered across the garden, her footprints steaming on the grass. She entered the manor through the kitchen, navigating the unlit expanse of the great ante room, the great drawing room, the starry blue-black of the great hall, and the impedimenta-cluttered dining room, until she came to Stones Gallery.

She bumped into nothing, or if she did, felt nothing. A delicate parade of nine tiny mouse skeletons trailed after her.

Lanie was in love with each of them. She had already concocted several daydreams in which she and they and Goody all ran away from Stones Manor and started a circus. *Stones and Graves Present... The Reanimated Rodents of Resurrection Row!*

But, no.

No. She shook her head. The surge had stolen most of her brain for most of the day—as usual—and she was only now just getting it back.

"Moor yourself, Miscellaneous Stones," she said aloud. "You need your wits about you." And she shouldered open the carved double doors to Stones Gallery. "Grandpa Rad," she called out, "look at my—"

The rest of the sentence accordioned to a halt against her hard palate. The normal blue glow was gone from the padlock. Instead, a pillar of luminous vapor shot right out of its keyhole, billowing hugely, and resolving itself into the frail figure of a man with a closely shorn head, a set of carefully barbered catfish whiskers, and opaque spectacles like large pearls over the place his eyes should be.

The apparition bellowed, "Why so mealy-mouthed, girlie? Don't you recognize me?"

Lanie was careful not to fall back a step, like she wanted to, lest she trip over her mice.

"Why, Grandpa Rad," she said with what she felt was reasonable calm, "you're practically corporeal."

"You sound surprised, girlie. This *is* the vernal surge, after all," the ghost rejoined, slightly less testily than was his wont. He was pleased he'd startled her. "And I myself was—no, *am*—a necromancer of no mean stature. Since *you*, missy, are not nearly the runt you were last year, you are in the happy position of exuding enough panthaumic aura that I may siphon a significant portion of it off you! Hence, the meritorious result of me appearing before you as you see this evening. Come closer. I want to have a look at you."

Lanie took two more steps into the gallery. The ghost reached out to meet her, stretching the long blue light that bound him to the padlock thinner and thinner, letting it run its length almost all the way to the double doors. There he prowled around her in a tight spiral of light, examining her from all angles.

"Grandpa Rad?" Lanie asked, alarmed.

"You're not very tall, are you?"

She sighed.

"Can't be helped, I suppose," he muttered. "But we really should wait until your spots have cleared, before I..."

"Wait—what do you mean, 'wait?'" Lanie spun within that strange vortex of cold, cold light, trying to wriggle free. "Wait for what?"

"I would, of course, also prefer to wait till you've learned to dress better. Of course, if *I* had the dressing of us..."

Lanie dropped to her knees, hitting the floor and rolling out of the blue light as fast as she could.

Just in time, too. Skeletal mice scattered in all directions as the ghost's coils thickened and constricted all the way in. But Lanie's suddenly *not* being at the center threw the ghost off balance, and also alerted the Sarcophagus of Souls, which rumbled, as if just waking to the fact that the ghost was playing truant. The ice-and-ink shadow of its aura—which felt like the exact *opposite* of panthauma—shot out like a nest of snakes. It surrounded the thin blue light of the ghost and pulled it back toward the padlock, as if trying to suck it back inside.

Grandpa Rad was howling with laughter. Or just howling. "All right, all right! I was just testing you!"

Lanie did not know if he was talking to her or to the Sarcophagus. She was still trying to get her breath back.

"Did you just," she asked slowly, "try to inhabit my body as a vessel of your rebirth?"

From the center of the room, the ghost, now much diminished in size, turned the expressionless pearl disks of his spectral spectacles at her. His whiskers twitched. "Just stretching a bit. Just testing our—your—reflexes."

Lanie stared at him, breathing hard. Part of her was aflame with panthauma. Another part of her was deadly cold, still trapped inside the ghost's crushing blue coils. He'd just tried to *possess* her. Kill her where she stood. Meat-puppet her body around the realms of the world, blithe as you please. She'd read about a necromancer of their line—long before Irradiant's time—who'd done just that.[8] Lanie knew what *that* meant. No more Miscellaneous Stones.

A thought came unbidden to her then, one she'd never thought before. But Lanie was as sure of it as she was of Doédenna's face, smiling across at her from a cowl of bones. It was this: *I will learn from you, Irradiant Stones. And when I have learned enough, I will end you.*

"Anyway!" Grandpa Rad was saying. "Let's have a look at these critters of yours. I see you've ignored my advice about starting with just one and went for the whole mischief of 'em. How you think you can control nine of 'em, I'll never know. As the Quadoni sorceress-poet Salaci'ahn wrote, *Magic—like poetry—is what will suffice.*"

When Grandpa Rad resorted to quoting thousand-year-old verse, off-rhythm and badly translated from the Quadic, Lanie knew it was time to change the subject. Bending down, she scooped her armful of mice from the floor.

They ran up and down her arms, chattering and chittering, bringing an involuntary smile to her lips. But she dared not venture any closer to the Sarcophagus of Souls lest Grandpa Rad leap again.

"Aren't they adorable?" Lanie kept her voice light and steady, though her heart still felt like it was forging a piece of siderite. She wanted the ghost to know nothing of her plans for him, lest he plot to stop her before she was ready. "I'm thinking of naming them."

"Stupid idea," said the ghost. "Dangerous. They're not mice. They are only the dead *dreaming* they are mice."

"What does that make *you?*" Lanie flashed.

"Smarter than a rodent. Or a thirteen-year-old brat, for that matter."

"*Fifteen.*"

"Surge only lasts till midnight," he reminded her, as if Lanie didn't know that *in her bones*. "Better test 'em while you still have full panthaumic power. Put them to work! When you're done coursing them, bring 'em over to me, and I'll help you dismantle 'em." The ghost licked the leer of light that was his lips. "We'll let you keep one—just one!—for a full season of service. It'll last you till Midsummer, and then we'll put it down and start you on something more impressive."

---

8 The necromancer Halidom Stones famously mounted (i.e. 'took necromantic possession of') the shell of her cousin Halfendele Stones shortly before that lady expired of tuberculosis. Once inside her mount, however, Halidom realized that she hadn't left herself enough time to get back *out*, and thus the cousins share dates on a monument in Stones Ossuary.

Lanie's teeth clenched. Her brow furrowed. Her spectacles slipped down her nose, and she glared at the ghost over the tops of her lenses.

"Why can't I keep them *all?*"

The ghost cackled, his laughter high and humorless. "I commend your ambition, girlie—but your intellect leaves much to be desired. What, keep all nine? All infused with panthauma and your intent till the high holy fire feast at Midsummer? Don't you know what will happen? Haven't I drummed it into your skull by now?"

Lanie knew, but also knew he was going to explain anyway, and so said nothing.

"Every day that passes, each of your little revenants will grow denser and wilder—less likely to obey you, less easy to put down. And on that subject… Fond of them *now*, are you? Imagine making pets of them over the next three months, then having to terminate them on your next surge. Think you could do it? I don't. You're not at full power yet either, so they'll probably need to eat between surges. It's you they'll feed on. A nip here. A sip there. Maybe they'll get greedy. Maybe they'll start feeding from you as you sleep. Nine little mouse skulls lapping up your necromantic blood. Imagine the drain on you! And as they feed, they'll grow. The dead do go on growing. Take Goody Graves, for instance. In my day she was tall as a man—not the stone giant she is now. Tell me, girlie," the ghost asked maliciously, "do you *want* nine rodent skeletons the size of ponies galloping around the estate by the time you reach your majority?"

Yes! thought Lanie.

"No," she muttered, sullenly. She knew all this. The ghost knew she knew it. He was just tormenting her.

"Didn't think so." The ghost snorted. "Go on, girlie. Moonlight's wasting. Make 'em do something. And then we'll tear 'em down."

Lanie squatted, not quite setting her back to the Sarcophagus of Souls, but turning enough so that the ghost could not hear her or read her lips.

"Find him," she whispered.

The mice understood. Of course they did. They knew her thoughts, her heart. She and they were one. Each of them, one by one, gently bumped against her with skull or paw or tail, then scampered off, out the gallery doors. Lanie sank back on her heels, resting her elbows on her knees and her chin in her hands.

"Where did they go? What did they do? What are you up to?" the ghost demanded. His testiness was back, which satisfied Lanie no end. "What's going on, girlie?"

Lanie didn't answer.

It's probably too late, she thought mournfully. It's probably already over. No hope of stopping it.

But—just in case.

What possible harm could come from peeking?

CHAPTER TWELVE

The Undreaming

LANIE PRICKED HER ears. All eighteen of them. Not that her mice still had any actual ears, exactly. But they *remembered* having ears—and memory, for the undead, was enough.

"Mak! Here you are."

Nita's voice. Large as the sky. Well—wasn't everything, to a mouse?

Stones Gallery had disappeared. The ghost in his padlock, the Sarcophagus of Souls, the dusty parquet floor, the vitrines and their illustrious contents, the portraits, the poison cabinet: gone. Lanie found herself with an eighteen-eyed, panoramic—if low to the ground—view of Torr Digitalis.

The tower was named after Aunt Diggie, who had claimed it and the entire Northwest Wing when she had turned it into her very own gambling saloon. It was the only tower in Stones Manor, a drafty old pile in which Aunt Diggie had stuffed all her unwanted furniture.

But Nita and Mak were not inside the tower; they were atop it, on the battlements.

"It's so easy to get lost in this house, if you did not grow up in it," Nita said to her Quadoni captive. "But I can always find you, Mak. That's what I love most about the Bryddongard. It always knows where you are—and so do I."

Lanie's perception of her surroundings was fractured, many-faceted, topaz-tinted. The phenomenon would have delighted her more if she could have used it to examine pretty much anything other than her sister. But that was Lanie's fault. It was she, after all, who'd sent her mice to find Mak, all so that she might—what? Help him, somehow?

A stupid idea, Grandpa Rad would have said.

"Back in Quadiíb," Nita sounded more tentative than Lanie could remember ever hearing her, "you were the only one I met who was… who treated me like I… and all I ever wanted was to show you, Mak, to *prove* to you, that I—that my family, our storied past—was worthy of you."

Poor Mak, foolish Mak! To treat a Stones of Liriat with kindness. A not-quite-fatal-enough mistake.

"Oh." Nita laughed, a sound as bitter as Lanie's thoughts. "I know you're unhappy. Well—you proved it with your stunt in the gallery, didn't you? But you must know, Mak, that all my plans have been for you. To make you happy. Ever since Midwinter, when I took you as I did, not a night has passed but I've lain awake wondering what I might do to relieve you, to gladden you. I never wanted—I never wanted your misery, Mak. I think you would welcome death, even at my hand!"

All of Lanie's nine nearly invisible bodies shivered in apprehension, ready to run. She did not know what would happen to her if she witnessed Mak's death with the eyes of the undead.

Perhaps nothing. But she did not want to find out.

"Therefore," Nita breathed, stepping closer to the man on the battlements, "therefore, Mak Cobb, I have made my decision. I made it long ago, but tonight, it shall be realized."

Ah, so Nita was sticking to her original plan. Death would be better, Lanie thought. Death must be better—gentler—than this.

"Stop her," Lanie whispered. But she had no mouth. She had nine mouths, and they all whispered, "Stop her."

The new spring wind blew strong and cold across the heights of Torr Digitalis. Lanie's words, which were but the memory of a sound, were lost to it—and Nita did not hear her. But Nita never heard the dead, and did not believe in ghosts.

Mak, however, turned his head. His shadowed eyes sharpened. He peered past Nita's body and down, further down, until he was staring directly into the fiery gold eye sockets of a skeletal mouse.

He knows, Lanie thought, shrinking back.

But there was nowhere to hide. Mak's grim mouth grew grimmer, but there was also in his pale look something like entreaty. If looks could speak, she thought that his would say—softly, in Quadic:

Keep thou still, sister of mine enemy.

And though it was the hardest thing she had ever done—including trying to raise both her dead parents off-surge, down in the black-dark of Stones Ossuary—Lanie, at once sitting on the floor of Stones Gallery and also watching from the battlements of Torr Digitalis, kept still. And witnessed.

Nita was pressing Mak against one of the icy crenellations, her fists hard on the rocks to either side of him. She drove her forehead against his, making him breathe her breath.

"All you have to do is look at me, Mak. I can make all your sadness go away. I will fill you up with me, and you will be happy. I swear it."

The bird-shaped hole in Lanie's chest was starting to singe at the edges. But nothing of what Mak was feeling—or at least what Lanie felt he *must* be feeling—showed on his face. Nothing of his longing to accept Nita's offer. Nothing of his despair at the debacle Lanie had made of his attempt to end his own life. Nothing of the shrieking emptiness that had ravaged him in the wake his gyrlady's death. Nothing of his shame at failing her, of standing frozen solid by Nita's spell while she murdered his Gelethai.

But there was that hole in Lanie's chest, and it was Mak too. His fury. That cicatrizing lightning. That Nita, having laid waste to all else, would deprive him even of *himself*. Make of him some mindless marionette devoted to her doting—no.

NO AND NO AND NO AND…

A roaring filled her mind. Lanie did not know if the thoughts were hers, or his.

"You don't have a choice, really." Nita was no longer placating, no longer entreating. She was colder than the wind, colder than the stones of Stones Manor. "You *will* look at me. Look at me, Mak."

And then Mak made his choice.

His hands unclenched. For a moment, he kept them still at his sides, feeling the blood and strength flow into them. Then he lifted his hands, and deliberately, gently, touched Nita's face.

"Amanita Muscaria Stones," he said, in Lirian. "I am yours. I surrender."

His words acted like a barrel of broken ice poured over Nita's surge. The yellow beam in her eyes flickered to black. She reared away from him, gasping, "You… you what?"

"I am yours," Mak repeated. "I swear it. No more spells. I surrender."

He switched to Quadic, as if to emphasize his point. "By Bryddongard, I pledge my sacred troth: my loyalty is thine, my blood and bone. My body I commend to thy control, and thy command the mandate of my soul."

On Nita's arm, the Bryddongard flashed like an exploding star. The fire-opal-mercury-silver light of it dazzled all nine pairs of Lanie's undead eyes, and she reeled, and the mice reeled, and her mind filled with the sound of their chittering.

Mak had just bound himself to Nita, body and soul—before Nita had even had the chance to do it! He had agreed—had *promised*—to be her consort. Her body servant. Her something.

Something awful, Lanie thought. Something… not right, not right, not right.

Trapped in the hard circle of Nita's arms, Mak bowed his head over hers. He kissed her brow. Each eyelid. Her nose. Her chin. Her throat. With determined submission. With resignation and calm.

Nita lifted her face to his, eagerly.

Mak closed his eyes, and set his mouth upon hers.

LANIE'S EYELIDS SPRANG apart. Stones Gallery rushed back at her: the rusted weapons in their dusty vitrines, her haughty, painted ancestors with their scratched plaques and stale war trophies. All seemed leeched of color and dimension, afterimages only.

Reality was two mouths meeting. Reality was far and high-away, wind-scoured, witnessed by nothing now but stars.

As color slowly began to drain back into the room, so too did Lanie's awareness of her body and its place in physical space. She was in a corner of Stones Gallery, as far from the Sarcophagus of Souls as she could crawl, curled up into a ball.

"What happened?" the ghost demanded. He strained against the lashing shadows of the sarcophagus. "What did you see? Where were you? You were not here, in your body, so don't try to lie to me about that."

Lanie shielded her eyes from the blue phantom-fire that described the ghost, that blazed at his fury at being so bound. She did not answer him. She was too busy being revolted by the memory.

That noise Nita had made! That *noise* when he kissed her. When Mak had... capitulated.

She shuddered. It seemed to her that Mak was taking Goody's advice, after all—to outlive his foes and dance upon their graves. But oh, he was paying a high price for it.

So let him dance. He'd have earned it, if surrender meant what Lanie thought it did.

She startled upright. There was sound outside the door nearest to her, which opened into the morning room. Or—not a sound. More like a feeling, as of nine threads tightening. Like the warm anticipation of a beloved's homecoming (how Lanie had felt all week, counting the minutes till Canon Lir's visit). There was relief, too, in that anticipation. Relief from a breathtaking loneliness. Despair, too. For it was almost midnight. Almost over.

Not many seconds later, nine mouse skeletons presented themselves in a neat line at the threshold. They stopped, courteously awaiting invitation, paws shyly pausing, skulls just peeping in.

Rolling from her pill-bug ball to flatten herself out on the floor, Lanie stretched her hands to them.

"Come here, you darlings! Oh, I've missed you! I miss you already!"

She was, to her surprise, crying. She hiccuped, as an enormous pair of bare gray feet appeared in her line of vision, stepping silently behind the silent mice. Lanie craned her neck and smiled tearfully up at the housekeeper, trying to wipe her nose and eyes at the same time.

"Hallo, dear Goody. I haven't seen you since—when? Stones Ossuary? Just before the Blood Royal, I think. I've missed you too. I'm so sad right now. Tell me, Goody—why am I so sad?"

Her voice tectonically low, Goody replied, "You are tired. You are hungry. You are growing up."

"Did you see my friends?" Lanie brandished them for Goody's perusal, every finger but one clung about with curious explorers, all of them knit of fire-broidered bone. "Don't you love them?"

"Don't coddle them, girlie!" Grandpa Rad snapped from across the room. "No time for that. Keep the best one, get rid of the other eight, or you'll be overrun till Midsummer. Now come here and do exactly as I bid you."

Sniffing back another sob, Lanie encouraged the mice to run the rest of the way up her arms and swing from her hair. She dragged herself to her feet and trudged over to the freezing, blue-tinged shadow of the Sarcophagus of Souls, hoping to keep just out of reach of Grandpa Rad. At the very edge of the shadow, she sat again, cross-legged, coaxing the mice into the cradle of her lap.

"The undead," said the ghost at his most pontificating, "are the dead who dream they are alive. Like us, they dream the idea of themselves. Unlike us, it is not breath that sustains this dream, but memory."

Lanie kept her head bent, and refrained from reminding the ghost that he himself hadn't had any lungs to breathe with for over a hundred years.

The ghost continued, "Even now, even as they move and flirt and fuss at your fingertips, Miscellaneous Stones, those mice are not truly *alive*. They are merely *remembering* being alive. Remove their memory, cut them off from this dream of themselves, and they will die again."

"Yes, yes," she sighed. "But how?"

"Memory," Grandpa Rad tapped his own glowing blue head, "is seated in the skull."

"So?"

A mouse had scaled one of her braids again, and was nuzzling her scalp. Lanie disentangled it, and kissed its little skull, smiling despite her sadness.

"*So?*" The ghost's mockery was squealingly nasal for an entity entirely lacking sinuses. "So, girlie, it's simple. Just bite their heads off."

Lanie froze. "*What?*"

"Bite their heads off."

"Bite their… *what?*"

"Put it in your mouth, girlie, and chomp!"

"But…"

"It's nearly midnight," the ghost hissed, lunging at her. He was not quite able to slam his forehead, Nita-like, against hers, but he came close. "You think it's hard now? Wait till your estival surge at Midsummer. The mouse you choose to keep will have grown too big by then to fit between your jaws! You'll have to use a cleaver, perhaps a mallet. Right now, their hold on themselves is still quite light. I suppose you could *try* twisting the heads off," he added doubtfully, "but they look pretty sewn on. This is what happens when we let our amateur enthusiasms get away from us, hmm?"

Stricken, Lanie stared down at her mice. Then she looked up again—not at Grandpa Rad, but over her shoulder at Goody Graves.

Goody was right there, of course, kneeling right behind her, though Lanie had never heard or felt her move. Her glowing eyes were large as stars, their solemn tenderness staying Lanie's rising panic.

"Goody, Goody," Lanie implored her, "I don't have to, do I?"

"If you don't..." the ghost began in a dire voice.

But Goody Graves was already sinking into a crouch, putting the wall of her body between Lanie and the Sarcophagus. In her voice as soft and immense as a summer thunderstorm, she asked, "Are you prepared to take responsibility for nine of the undead? Nine of the undead, who will grow as you grow, and sup on your substance? Nine of the undead, who will live on in unending revenance after you die, if you do not finish them first? Where does it end for them, Mizka? When they have become so bewildered and feral, so enormous in undeath, that they are monsters only a magical army may destroy?"

Lanie's tears sizzled unchecked upon the knots of yellow fire that animated her mouse bones with the semblance of life.

Yes, I want this responsibility—she longed to say. And also, no, I'm not ready. And also, oh, I don't know.

But, really, her practical side told her practically, our answer isn't *I don't know.* It's simply: *Not yet.* I'm not ready *yet. Not yet* is bearable. Not this year. Not in this house. Not while the ghost tracks our every move. *Not for a good while yet.* But that doesn't mean, *Never.* And it doesn't mean *Goodbye, forever.*

Sorrowfully, Lanie raised the first mouse skeleton to her lips. Its eye sockets gazed up at her with adoration.

Her teeth parted. The mouse's jaw opened, in imitation. Her fingers trembled. The mouse's metatarsals trembled.

She laid her trusting darling upon her tongue.

"There is another way," Goody said brusquely.

Lanie blew out an explosive breath. Immediately, she spat the mouse skeleton back into her hand, where, caught off-guard by the cyclone, it did a backwards little somersault. Righting itself right away, it scampered in frantic circles around her palm, scolding her. Lanie tried to soothe it with caresses, but her attention was almost wholly on Goody.

Grandpa Rad glared whitely at the undead housekeeper. "How *dare* you presume to speak of these matters?"

Goody turned her head and said a single word, "Lahnessthanessar."

The effect it had upon Grandpa Rad's outrage was spectacular. It was as if a cloud rack had purposely crossed the sky to poise itself above a burning building, and then proceeded to dump not rain but seventy thousand tons of wet sand directly upon it. The ghost gaped at Goody. The great Irradiant Stones—at a loss for words!

Lanie watched, open-mouthed, as he retreated all the way back into his padlock, as if fleeing a pack of wolves.

Only after a few silent seconds did his lips jut out from the keyhole to say, sulkily, "You don't know the song of Undreaming. The Lahnessthanessar's the best-kept secret in the Traveling Palaces of Higher Quadiíb. Only the wisest Gyrladies are taught the melody. If *I* never learned it, revenant, *you* certainly never did."

"You never knew me in life," Goody said, with such withering sarcasm that Lanie was reminded of Mak.

Mak. Earlier that day. In the garden. Hadn't *he* said something about "Lahnessthanessar?" And she'd thought he'd meant music, but maybe he'd meant something else. Something Goody already knew.

She scooted closer, tugging at Goody's ragged hem, calling for her attention. "Tell me, Goody. Tell me about the Lahnessthanessar."

Goody looked down, and then, moving more quickly than she had in years, bent low and scooped Lanie up—with all of her undead creatures—into her undead arms, like she used to do when Lanie was a small child.

Lanie enjoyed the sensation of helpless nearness. She laid her face against Goody's breast, and smiled as her spectacles were knocked askew. Goody walked away from the Sarcophagus of Souls, taking Lanie with her. Affronted, Grandpa Rad sprang from hiding, trying to follow, but had only stretched the blue-lit length of himself a few feet from his padlock before the big black shadow of the sarcophagus yanked him back.

Setting Lanie back down in the corner, Goody sat before her, again screening her off from the ghost's view. She pitched her voice even lower than the bottommost tombs of the ossuary, so low that only Lanie could hear her, and asked the first question of a story Lanie knew well. (Goody had never been much for casual conversation, but—especially when Lanie was younger, so often bedridden from her unremitting allergy—she was a wonderful storyteller. There was a distinctive pattern to Goody's stories. They were always in Quadic. And they always were told in antiphony.)

Goody asked, "Who founded Liriat and called it home?"

Ah. "The Cornerstone Antiphony." There was only one response Lanie could make, only one way the story could go. She'd learned the words so many years ago now that she couldn't even remember when, and whispered them almost without thinking:

O, Yn'ssyll Brackenwild was Founding Queen
And Quick Fantastic Stones, her strong left hand.

Goody nodded her approval. Or rather, a tiny triangle in the lower right quadrant of her chin dented inward, and that was almost as good as a nod.

"*Whence came the Sorceress and Founding Queen*?" she asked.

Lanie answered promptly: "*From High Quadiib, whose roads the twelve gods walk.*"

Clipping the end of Lanie's sentence, Goody went on:

Why flee Quadiib and wander lonely wastes
Through deserts, marshes, steppes and woodlands lorn,

To pause at last their reckless, pell-mell pace
And summon Liriat by blood and storm
From out the bedrock of this savage loam?

Lanie paused, thinking, and replied with the Lirian version of the story, since saying it in Quadic would take twice as long.

"The two exiles left Quadiíb together, because the Quadoni—as a people—believe in balance. They worship all twelve gods, housing them in harmony inside the temple of their bodies. But Ynyssyll Brackenwild felt she had a predilection for Sappacor, god of Fire and Blood. She wanted to worship Them alone, to be flooded with Their particular powers. And her best friend—her oldest friend—Quick Fantastic Stones: she loved Saint Death. She wanted to dedicate herself to Doédenna, and with her dedicated love harness divine powers over the dead and the undead. But any worship that runs counter to the duodecifold religion was—is still?—forbidden in Quadiíb. So Quick Fantastic and Ynyssyll left together—and others with them—to make a place of their own, where they might worship as they pleased. And thus Liriat was founded by a bunch of ragtag radicals who disagreed with the Judicial Colloquium of Gyrladies. You were there too," Lanie reminded Goody.

A long pause. Then Goody asked, heavily, "Now tell me if thou canst: what was my name?"

That question used to stump her. But Lanie was ready for it now; Goody had asked it of her so many times.

"No one remembers it now, dear Goody. I'm sorry."

"I, too, have forgotten," Goody replied, in her deep-cracked Lirian. Pressing her cold, hard mouth to the top of Lanie's head, she whispered in Quadic, "But there is this I have not yet forgot: a song I learned back in those wild days, and sang to thee when thou wast sick and small. Think back and back, and sing it to me now."

Surprised, but willing, Lanie closed her eyes, reaching for the lullaby. Years since she'd last requested an evensong of Goody Graves, longer since Goody had offered one. But like the phrases of 'The Cornerstone,' a melody rose up the column of her throat, whereupon it burst upon her tongue, and unleashed itself into the air like startled starlings. She hummed the first phrase.

Goody—almost!—smiled. "That is it exactly, Mizka. Those are the first notes of the Lahnessthanessar, the great lullaby, the song of Undreaming, oldest of songs but one. It is all I remember from my time before—and it is yours."

Lanie nodded, and her nine mice all nodded along in perfect agreement, in perfect accord. Goody paused the length of a breath. But, of course, she did not breathe. Lanie felt as though she were leaning against a mountain that was gathering itself inwardly for some momentous decision.

"Now," Goody said in Quadic, "hast thou thy littlings held close in hand? Cling fast to them and feel their tender love."

As Lanie cradled those scampering handfuls to her breast, the mice curled their bony bodies against her, sweethearting love and devotion from out their very ribcages and tailbones, from every slender socket and delicate articulation, from each curve and knob and needle-like protuberance.

Goody bent her great head close to Lanie's, murmuring, "It wants a breath till equinox is o'er. Dost feel thy surge abound inside thee yet?"

For answer, Lanie consulted her left hand. Yes, her wizard mark was still expressing a sort of moonlight-barely-held-back-by-clouds opinion of itself. Yes. The bones beneath her skin still itched. A low, crawling, delicious itch.

And then, acknowledging her surge reactivated it: the yellow heat, the giddiness, the nursery rhyme babble at the back of her brain.

"Yes," she breathed, and heard her second, deeper voice stir within her. *Yes.*

Bless, confess, redress...

"Then sing to them the lullaby thou know'st," Goody advised her. "'Tis not a tune but memory you sing: the notes mean less than the remembering. Our song of memory is everything: the orison that dreams the dead to life. Thou holdest them in Sarcophagus song and in thy hands. Now bid them rest and leave their love to thee. To sleep is to forget—and in forgetting, the undead die again and quiet lie."

The instructions were clear. The song was simple. Lanie opened her mouth to sing.

She had a somewhat gravelly contralto that could catch a tune all right but rarely keep it. Not like her father's merry tenor, or Nita's rare golden alto, or even Aba's glassy soprano, which Lanie had heard but once, when her mother sang Natty's interment rite at the mouth of Stones Ossuary. Aba's voice had been as precise as her manicure, before the Elixir of Adamant had shredded the soft tissues of her throat.

But it wasn't her contralto that sang the Lahnessthanessar. Not really. The longer Lanie sang, the more she heard her *other* voice, the one that came from somewhere deeper than her lungs. The voice that talked to Saint Death Herself.

As *it* grew stronger, so too did Lanie's memories come foaming to the surface, tumbling along with images of her dead: Natty in his crypt, blinking his one remaining eye that glowed with its ectenical endowment; Aba on her marble tablet, bleeding black at the mouth, spitting unintelligible curses as she deliquesced; Aunt Diggie, whom Lanie had never tried to raise, because she'd only been found in pieces anyway.

But as she sang, she realized her song was not for them. Carefully, Lanie veered her lullaby away from her old, cold dead.

She shut her mind to their memories, and instead sang to her nine darling mice. She had known more love from them in a single day than from all her family put together for her whole life. And *that* would be how she remembered them (she sang), how her heart had leapt with gladness at first sight of them, how grateful she was for their help all that day and night, how honored she was to have spent this too-brief time with them, how she hoped to meet with them again in the everlasting hem of Doédenna's cloak.

"Hold up!" Grandpa Rad shouted from the sarcophagus. "Don't put them *all* down! Keep *one* active, girlie! What are you doing? Keep one back to *experiment* with!"

Turning her back wholly on the ghost, Lanie kept singing. How could she separate her sweet mice now, when she had brought them as a family back into this world? How would that one poor, lonely, lost thing bear it until Midsummer, with only Lanie for company, its sole purpose toil, its only hope a lullaby at last?

No. Not that. Not for them. Not for her beloveds.

Nine mice sighed without breath. Nine mice curled up to sleep in her hands—sleep, which, to the undead, was death. The yellow fire faded from their bones. Far away, in the grand salon, the clock struck twelve.

The last of her vernal fever leached out of Lanie. She shuddered, her own bones turned to icicles, her flesh to frozen meat. She cuddled closer to Goody Graves, whose chill was warm by comparison. Her hands convulsed, scattering hundreds and hundreds of tiny bones across the parquet floor. Over at the Sarcophagus of Souls, the ghost's blue light vanished deeply back into its padlock, but the ghost's voice remained blisteringly sonorous.

"Opportunity wasted, if you ask me. But the night's not been without its compensations—ha! The *Lahnessthanessar!* Damn me duodecifold! Had I but known you knew it, Graves, I'd've pried the tune from you with wrench and hammer back when I was living. The things I could have done with that song!"

"You," said Goody Graves, so quietly it might have been one of her silences speaking, "have done enough."

Part Two
STONES AND CROWS

Seven Years Later

CHAPTER THIRTEEN

The Harrier's Homecoming

Rimeday 6th
Month of Broods, 421 Founding Era
76 days till Summer Solstice

Out in the orchards beyond the back garden, Datu was singing her jump-rope song again.

Four-and-Twenty blackbirds
Shorn for their pelt
Four-and-Twenty feathers
On the Harrier's belt!

Lanie gritted her teeth, setting her folding stepladder on the ground. She stood beneath the stuffed boots of the garden's scarecrow and lifted her head to look at it: a motley fool, ragged-up in castoffs from fourteen generations of Stoneses. Its head was a sack—the old-fashioned kind, when headsmen used leather bags instead of baskets—still smelling of blood and sawdust. She and Goody had been piecing the scarecrow together over the past few days, readying it for her great experiment. The head was on its final fitting, Lanie painstakingly cutting two crosses into the leather for what would become its eyes, and then affixing, by means of a string, the fabled silver nose of Ostrobogulous Stones[9] to the center of the sack, and last, keeping in theme, drawing on a meandering red grin with Delirious Stones's dangerous lipstick. The eyes themselves would come last. Her masterwork.

First she killed the Kingbird
Magpie was next

9 A replacement for the one he lost to syphilis—a disease that did not, in most people's opinion, kill him quickly enough.

House Martin, Starling
Marked with an X!

Datu's infancy, reflected Lanie, had been bad enough. Screams pitched to break window glass. A totally unreasonable and utterly non-negotiable refusal to sleep for more than a few hours at a time. And then the diapers.

Saint Death, the diapers!

But it was only once her niece started walking and talking that Lanie understood the true meaning of despair.

Skimmer, then Bunting
Black Phoebe too
Lassoed a Lapwing
Ran her right through!

The child, naturally, had her father's facility with Quadic. Mak didn't speak anything else to her, although he never spoke anything but Lirian with Nita or Lanie. (When he talked to them at all. Which wasn't often.) Perhaps because of this, Datu was a fiend for rhymes. She rhymed all the time, in both languages. Rhymes like little needles zipping through Lanie's eyeballs. Rhymes like blisters bursting between her shoulders. Rhymes like shiny pink hives on the palms of her hands. *Allergenic* rhymes.

Wagtail and Warbler
Condor and Coot
Jackdaw and Blackstart
Ready, aim, shoot!

Stripping off her gardening gloves, Lanie rubbed her palms vigorously together. A few new itchy pink patches were only just beginning to blossom there.

"At least they aren't echo wounds," she muttered to herself.

To produce echo wounds in her aunt, Datu would have to hurt something in Lanie's vicinity. But unlike Nita, she didn't seem to have a predilection for animal abuse. Just violent rhymes.

Lanie's physical responses, therefore, were mere allergies. Mild ones, at that. Datu didn't even know her aunt was on the other side of the wall. Her little ditty held no real intent to harm, and that ameliorated the irritation somewhat... no matter that verse after graphic verse kept describing the many, *many* ways in which 'the Harrier of Rook' (as the Rookish newspapers referred to Nita, not knowing her real name) had gone about keeping herself gainfully employed these last seven years.

Seven years. The thought was like coming across a mold collective in the bread pantry when all you wanted was a muffin. Familiar, fated, never less than revolting. Seven years. Seven!

Has it really been so long, Lanie wondered, since Erralierra set Nita among the Parliament of Rooks like a catamount amongst the crows?

Had so many sunrises and moonsets and rhymes and *diapers* flowed through her life since her sister commenced her killing spree for the glory of the Brackenwilds?

Nita's body count was impressive—even for a Stones. Even more so when you considered that somehow, in the middle of all that murder, she'd found time to conceive a child and give birth to it. Which offspring she had promptly palmed off onto Lanie.

Myna, Anhinga
Raven and Rook
Grackle she'll tackle
But Swift she will cook!

Was it any wonder that Lanie was short on sleep—today and always? Childcare and household duties fully occupied her daylight hours, but she still had her own work to do. Every night for months now, she had been staying up till dawn, experimenting with ectenica in her workshop down in Stones Ossuary. And just that morning—that *very* morning!—her results had stabilized enough that she could test them out on her scarecrow. Her apron pockets bulged.

The Harrier's a-hunting!
Four left to go:
Cowbird and cormorant
Bobolink, crow!

Poor Datu! The child loved music, but Lanie herself could barely carry a tune in a tumulus, and her father did not often have the heart to sing. But that never stopped Datu. Whenever she was feeling noisy (like this morning, apparently), Datu would stalk around Stones Manor shout-singing in a sort of gruff but melodic roar. When she wasn't singing, she might be found dogging her aunt's footsteps, asking questions about everything and then arguing with the answers. Nor did she particularly appreciate being pointed to Stones Library where, Lanie assured her niece, the secrets of the universe awaited her undivided attention.

Datu *could* read, but whereas Lanie at her age (being, at the time, mostly bed-bound and short on entertainment) had already read thrice her weight in books, Datu did not seem able to settle to it for long. She'd sit and listen to Mak's stories for hours, though. Lanie's, too. Story time found Datu at her most tractable, a benison for which Lanie was grateful.

Had the singing stopped?

Poised on the lowest step of the ladder, Lanie paused, straining her ears. The child had gone stealthy.

Stealthy meant you wouldn't know Datu was behind you till she'd spitwadded the back of your neck with her blowgun—something she might do with extra vigor if you'd happened to have recently denigrated said weapon by referring to it as 'that pesky little peashooter,' and threatening to snap it in two.

The threat didn't bother Datu so much as the mislabeling: blowgun it was, and blowgun it *must* be called, no matter that Mak did not allow his daughter to use darts with it, much less ones dipped in curare, like the last set of darts he'd confiscated from her secret stash.

Stealthy meant be prepared for anything. Better to lure the child out into the open as soon as possible.

Quickly scaling the rest of the ladder, Lanie grasped the scarecrow's waist at the crux of its cross frame, where the ends of a billowing blue blouse that had belonged either to a remarkably impractical pirate or an adorably adipose poet had been cinched with a jaunty purple sash. More loudly and cheerily than either task or mood warranted, Lanie hailed it, "Good morning, Thrice-Digested Stones!"

"Is that his name?" asked a gravelly little voice from below.

Lanie did *not* jump. Certainly not. Any outward sign of surprise only encouraged the child. She pretended to fuss with the scarecrow's patched velvet trousers.

"*Her* name, in fact, and we must respect it—for she was our distinguished ancestor. Didn't I ever tell you the story of Thrice-Digested Stones, who was eaten by the *same* dragon three times and lived to tell the tale?"

"No."

"Really? Huh." Reaching into her pocket, Lanie brought out a handful of orblins.

"What are those?" Datu's voice was closer now.

"Magic."

Unlike her fib about Thrice-Digested Stones, this assertion was fact. But Lanie knew better than to try and lecture her niece about the technicalities of her work. Datu liked stories, not details, and occasionally emphasized this opinion with explosions.

Canon Lir, on the other hand, was always demanding details about the finer points of death magic from Lanie, and scolding her gently in letters when she was not more forthcoming. After her triumph that morning, she had written her friend a far more precise explanation about orblins than she dared declaim to Datu now.

Esteemed Canon,

For several months (well, years, but who's counting?) I've been bashing my brains against the difficulty of stabilizing ectenica so that it will last longer off-surge. I have discovered that by mixing my blood with bone dust and wet clay, I can shape a series of small spherical packages (or perhaps "vessels" is a better word), which, when baked, become delivery systems for tiny batches of dormant ectenica. Like stored medicine! Once activated by any of my body fluids—thankfully, saliva works just as well as blood—my "orblins," as I am calling them, have the ability to perform small magical tasks. Eventually a given task will drain an orblin of its death magic, and it will sludge off to the usual ashy slop, but this happens much more slowly than with raw ectenica. I am encouraged! I persist! I experiment with the scarecrow this afternoon.

More anon!

Misc. Stones

Datu pointed at the orblins in Lanie's hand. "Are those marbles?"

Lanie shrugged. "Not exactly."

"Are they rocks?"

"Clay."

"Are they why you have been going to the ossuary every night?"

Narrowing her eyes at her niece through her spectacles, Lanie demanded, "And how do you know where I go after you are *sound asleep in bed,* Sacred Datura Stones?"

Datu, with all the sangfroid of her six-going-on-sixty years, shrugged. But then she looked away. She knuckled one corner of her eye.

"Not sleeping well?" Lanie asked, more softly. She debated climbing down the stepladder, but decided Datu was far more likely to talk if some distance remained between them.

Datu was not a physically frail child; lifting her was like lifting a sack of cannonballs. She was stockily built, solid muscle, the result of two athlete parents and a childhood spent mostly outdoors. She might welcome touch during roughhousing, but barely endured it as tenderness—and only from her father.

"Nightmares?"

Nothing. Not even a shrug this time. Must be particularly bad, then. Lanie wondered if Mak knew.

"Hmm." She picked out two orblins from her handful, pocketed the rest, stood on her tiptoes, and affixed one each into the cut-out crosses that marked the scarecrow's eyes. "Want to see some of the fabulous death magic that your clever auntie has been inventing at the exorbitant price of delicious sleep?"

"Okay," Datu agreed, as if doing her aunt a favor. "But then you must come down from the ladder and tell me a story about Thrice-Digested Stones, Auntie Lanie. Her portrait does not hang in Stones Gallery."

Lanie shook her head sadly. "Think about it, Datu. If you went for a dive in a dragon's stomach acid and then came out the other end, you wouldn't want your portrait shown publicly either!"

"Yes, I would," announced the green-eyed contrarian. "I would want a horrible huge picture painted of me with lots of pus and dragon guts and I would hang it in the front vestibule where it will scare all the visitors."

Scaring visitors. That reminded Lanie. She turned back to the scarecrow. "All right. Let's see if this works."

Licking thumb and middle finger, she touched them to each of the orblins that she'd poked into the eye-slits of the leather sack.

Then she hummed a few bars of music in a voice so low that only the dead could hear it, setting all of her own bones abuzz, and whispered, "Wake up!"

The dull-gray clay spheres shimmered, glimmered, shone. Not gray anymore, but milky blue as larimar: curious, attentive, lit from within. The scarecrow's eyes stared down at her, almost alive, certainly undead. Lanie rested one hand on its stuffed breast, imagined she felt a heartbeat. Pure fancy.

"You're my eyes," she told the scarecrow, beaming up at its grinning face. "Some invader has been entering my garden at night and denuding it of vegetables. Analyze all nocturnal activity—prevent it if you can. I'll return tomorrow morning for your report."

The scarecrow nodded.

"You darling!" Lanie hugged it briefly, said, "Thank you!" and hopped down from the ladder, quite pleased with herself. Her hands no longer itched. She felt, in fact, phenomenal.

But Datu was fingering the black dagger at her belt, staring scornfully up at Thrice-Digested Stones, whose undead eyes burned benignly back at her. "I will stand watch for you, Auntie Lanie. I will be your scarecrow."

"You *are* very scary, Datu," Lanie assured her with complete sincerity. "But if it's simply a matter of beetles, that knife of yours won't do us much good."

"If it is beetles, I will squash them!" Datu stomped her foot suggestively.

Lanie snorted. "What if it's a deer?"

Her niece mimed a bow, pointed it at Lanie, and made the *ffpht-pock!* of an arrow released to its target. Lanie felt the shadow of Datu's intent pass right through her eye. A small, cruel thing.

"Deer stew," said Datu, satisfied.

Pressing a thumb to the ridge of her brow, Lanie asked sharply, "And if it's blackbirds?"

A small, cruel thing. She regretted it almost instantly.

Datu swallowed, her hand going to her dagger again. Her head lifted; she anxiously scanned the skies for any sign of blackbirds.

As Aba had been to her daughters, so Nita was to Datu—absent, mostly. In consequence, Datu remembered every sentence her mother had ever uttered to her, treasured every private moment grudgingly granted, hoarded any scrap of trash Nita let fall and called a gift.

The black dagger, for instance. Datu carried it everywhere, even sleeping with it under her pillow. It was a thing Nita had once tossed in her direction, careless of how it landed—though Datu had caught the wire-wrapped handle perfectly, with the grace, speed, and precision that came of her daily sothaín training—claiming that, with it:

"I slayed me the Warbler! Oh, you should have seen her, Sacred Datura! A raven-haired maiden, with eyes gray as icicles. She could raise the winds by whistling! A powerful wizard in the Parliament of Rooks. Favored concubine of the Blackbird Bride! But this bit of steel brought her down, Sacred Datura. And now it is yours."

But her mother's legacy amounted to much more than a dagger. Though by day, Datu would shout out her rhymes about blackbirds loudly and defiantly, by night, she would dream about the Parliament of Rooks coming for her: nightmares so terrible that they woke her up screaming.

"Are we done being out here now, Auntie Lanie?" she asked, her gaze still fixed on the sky.

What Lanie really wanted to do was stay and keep the scarecrow company a while longer. But she felt she owed something to Datu for speaking so heedlessly.

"I think so." Lanie checked her activated orblins one last time. They burned on, undimmed.

She nodded in satisfaction, climbed down her stepladder, and folded it up. Hopefully, the orblins would stay active the rest of that day and through the night before melting out of their cross-cut slits like black flies crushed in a mortar.

Turning to her niece, Lanie said, "Now, I promised you a story. Where were we?"

"Thrice-Digested Stones was eaten by a dragon three times and lived to tell the tale," Datu reminded her promptly.

"That's right." They began walking back toward the kitchen together: Lanie with her ladder tucked under her arm, Datu still nervy and clutching her dagger. "So, let's see, Thrice-Digested Stones was your Great-Grand-Uncle Recumbent Stones's third wife's youngest sister's brother-in-law's second cousin, and she was known for big game hunting, which, I have to tell you, got her into a lot of trouble..."

Goody Graves opened the kitchen door and stepped down into the garden. Her silence flowed out before her like a cold-water current, chilly and urgent. Datu, who had never taken to Goody, stepped closer to Lanie and clamped the hem of her canvas apron with pincer-like fingers.

"What is it, Goody?" Lanie kept her voice calm and pleasant, knowing that Datu was wound up like one of her own toy field gun cannons that shot real projectiles. She did not want to set her off.

But a faint, raised voice echoing down the corridor from the main house told her everything she needed to know—

—a split second after Datu took off running, shrieking, "Mumyu! Mumyu's back!"

CHAPTER FOURTEEN

Her Cup of Blood Is Spilt

"SAINT DEATH BLEEDS, Amanita Muscaria! What happened?"

Lanie checked herself at the doorway of what had been Aba's workshop and was now a more sedate anteroom to the state bedchamber where Nita and Mak slept[10]. She did not dare venture further into the room where her sister was stripping off her grimy clothes and drop-kicking them away, the better to review her wounds in the full-length mirror. Nita held another mirror in her hand, and was trying to examine the marks on her back.

Lanie's skin crawled. Hot welts began to score her body in sympathy to Nita's cuts: face and arms, between her shoulders, the tender flesh of her neck. If she stepped any closer to her sister, her echo wounds would open and start to bleed.

"Graves!" Nita barked, catching sight of the housekeeper looming behind Lanie. "Attend me!" Only then did she glance at Lanie, her eyes dull and bloodshot, sunk like black burrow spiders in their stolen snake holes. "An ambush," she spat.

From her perch on a settee nearby, Datu spoke up. "Look, Auntie Lanie! Mumyu's collected two more feathers. Cowbird and crow! Only two more to go!"

She announced it proudly; Mak had been working with her on arithmetic.

On her lap lay Nita's belt of feathers, mostly black, with variations. Datu bent over it, stroking it with reverent fingers, examining the newest and least bedraggled ones: the first, a darkly iridescent pinion with a faint sheen of rusty brown along one edge; the second, a long, strong, soot-black tail feather with a tip of pure white.

"But, Mumyu—I thought all crows were black?"

"Pied Crow," Nita said shortly, then hissed as Goody Graves cleaned a long scrape on her arm. "They're black and white." She pointed to the feather. "That was Prince Piceous—Royal Augur to the Blackbird Bride.

10 Most of Abandon Hope Stones's favorite instruments such as 'the Charring Bull' and 'the Iron Martyr' and 'Dunk, Dunk, Drown!' had been removed to Torr Digitalis with the rest of the old furniture, though the rope and pulley system for the strappado remained.

Her cousin. They grew up together. He trapped me!"

Her voice was like something that had been drawn and quartered, the pieces dragged for days in four directions over rough terrain. She cried out when Goody hit a sore spot. "*He trapped me!*"

"How?" Datu asked, eyes wide.

But Nita, jerking her arm out of Goody's grip to savagely wind the bandage around it herself, did not answer.

Datu bowed her head. Smoothing out the feather belt. she sang softly:

The Harrier's a-hunting
Right on track
Bobolink, Cormorant—
Watch your back!

Firmly lingering in the threshold, Lanie looked around. Where was Mak? He never approved of Datu playing with Nita's trophy belt, calling it "a foul, irreligious, unsanitary, *morbid* practice that gives the child nightmares which others must then manage."

To which Nita would reply, bitterly, "She's a Stones. We grow up quickly if we're to grow up at all."

But Mak was not currently present, and the window was open.

Probably, then, Nita's never prodigious patience for debate with the father of her child was all burnt up. She'd just Bryddongarded Mak willy-nilly into his bird form and sent him off into the sky.

In the last year or so, Lanie had begun wondering if maybe her sister wished that one of these days Mak would just stay gone—lose his way home, forget his human form, perhaps fall prey to some larger bird. But return he always did, bound by his vow to Nita—and by his love for his daughter. Whenever she knew her didyi was off hunting as a peregrine falcon, Datu would wait up in bed for him, insisting that when he came back, he would want to bid her goodnight. Which he always did, no matter how late Nita kept him jessed in that form. Datu's was a very particular bedtime ritual—and Doédenna help the whole household if it deviated from pattern.

Her wounds only half seen to, gauze bandages trailing after her, Nita started prowling the room like a caged lion. She paced several circuits before coming back to center and allowing Goody to resume ministering to her. She glanced at the feather belt in Datu's lap, then over to the doorway where she met Lanie's eyes.

"Prince Piceous," she repeated, in a desiccated voice. "I seduced him at a masquerade held at Rookery Court in honor of Bran Fiakhna's birthday. Fascinated him into taking me to his home."

Lanie felt her eyebrows shoot up, but Nita was no longer looking at her. "He is—was—the richest prince in Rook. His palace takes up half a city block! A known eccentric. All that space and what does he fill it with?

Animals! Some he uses—used—for his auguries, but mostly… mostly he just liked them. His bedroom was an aviary. Full of cages. Dozens and dozens. In each cage, a pied crow—his namesake. They spoke with human voices. But they weren't wizards, he told me. Just clever birds, like parrots. Their voices were strange. Deep." She shivered. "We—we started…"

Her gaze fell upon Datu, and suddenly her eyes became two barrels of burning pitch. "Go to your room! I don't want you here!"

Without a word, Datu put down the feather belt, slid off the settee to the floor, and quietly crossed the anteroom to the door. She passed her aunt without a word, and then, once she was out of her mother's sight, began to run.

Fists clenched, Lanie stepped over the threshold. "Amanita Muscaria!" Her welts began to seep. She did not care. "Every night for *eight months* she's asked when you'll be back. She worships you. And you just—"

"She won't anymore. Not now. Not when she knows." Nita raised her head from its broke-necked loll. She was weeping.

Lanie stopped advancing, nearly running into her own feet, which had turned into two lumps of ironwood. Her welts oozed freely.

"Back," Nita whispered. "Back up, Miscellaneous. A few more steps. There. Stay there. By the door. I need—I need you whole. There's work for us ahead. I need you able to work. Don't come too close."

As soon as Lanie resumed her original position, her echo-wounds began to close. Still furious, she folded her arms and glared at Nita expectantly.

Nita rubbed her face. "I seduced him. Piceous. He was utterly mine the entire time. I never lost him, not once that whole night. He was caught, Miscellaneous. *In the bag.* I had him naked beneath me and he never suspected a thing. Even when I gutted him, even when he was melting from man to crow to man again, faster than I could see, so fast he was a blur, his eyes held mine and they held no fear, only love, only devotion. He asked my name with his dying breath—said I was the most beautiful woman he had ever seen, said my touch was a caress. I had nothing to lose in telling him. We were alone. He was dying—whom could he tell? *I was holding his viscera in my hands.*"

Lanie's saliva tasted bright and coppery. Her own viscera were making unpleasant rumblings.

"So I told him. My name. He said it back to me, smiling. Then he said a word I didn't understand. Some Rookish charm. And that's when everything went wrong!"

Nita sat down suddenly, just folded up, right there in the middle of the floor, her half-bandaged wrist crooked up at an awkward angle. Goody, unperturbed, simply kept wrapping it in gauze.

"What went wrong?" Lanie asked, very carefully.

"Everything!" Nita shouted. "Everything, I tell you, everything! And nothing has been right since! First, all the pied crows in their cages started pecking at their doors. Which flew open. I didn't realize they weren't locked. That word he spoke? I think it was a signal. He'd trained them to come out at his command. Suddenly, the air was full of wings. Crows were flying all around, everywhere, black and white, crying out *my name,* and the prince's dying eyes were no longer on mine but following them."

"He was taking the auspices," Lanie murmured. Understanding dawned upon her, cold as the deadest day of winter. "Piceous was Bran Fiakhna's augur. Augurs prophesy by reading wing patterns. He needed his birds in flight in order to see the future."

"*My* future," Nita said grimly, yanking her arm back from Goody. She finished wrapping the gauze herself—much more sloppily than Goody would have done. "And the future of Liriat."

Her motions were jerky, inefficient. When she was done, she hurled the roll of bandages across the room.

"And then he *unfastened* from me!" she cried. "I lost him as thoroughly as I'd had him. That happens, sometimes, at death-tide. I couldn't get him back. Oh, but he took his time dying, that piebald prince! It was as if he *couldn't* die unless and *until* he had prophesied in full. I should have stopped him sooner—my knife was ready—I don't know why I… Except… Except, I needed, *needed* to hear what he was saying. He—he foretold the death of Erralierra Brackenwild. 'Her cup of blood is spilt,' he said, then went on about the fall of Stones Manor, and what would happen to… But that's when I silenced him for good, when he… I took my knife and… "

Lanie held up her hand. "I know."

She did, too. She knew precisely. Two slices: the first, practiced; the second, vicious. She felt them across her belly, across her throat. She backed up another step, until that thin, singing pain dulled down enough for her to ask, "What went wrong after that?"

Nita sprang to her feet. Forgetting her own prior warning, she pounced at Lanie. Took her by the shoulders. Shook her.

"You don't understand! The crows!" she rasped. "The pied crows know my name! They flew out the window—into the night, to Rookery Court—trained to make their report to Bran Fiakhna, no doubt. I couldn't kill them all."

Prying off her sister's fingers was impossible; enduring her touch was intolerable. So Lanie dropped, heavy and boneless, startling Nita into releasing her.

"I escaped." Nita turned her back, started gathering her dirt-matted hair into a ragged tail. "Barely. I laid false trails, Bran Fiakhna's birds harrying me at every turn. Everywhere, birds! They think I've gone into hiding in Quadiíb. They won't look for me here in Liriat. Not for a while yet. We have time to prepare."

She laughed, a terrible, dry, little sound. "Good thing too: the Parliament of Rooks is at full quorum again. As soon as ever I kill one of her consorts,

Bran Fiakhna replaces them. A new wedding practically before the funeral rites are over! She never seems *shaken!* Never at a lack. Rookery Court is rotten with wizards. But the new ones"—she shrugged—"are young, inexperienced. It's the old Parliament I fear. Those last two. Bobolink. Cormorant. I was saving them for the end, their powers being the most puissant. How do you flush out the Concealer? How do you chase down Time? I needed to study them further. And now I don't have the chance.

"Oh," she groaned, hiding her face in her hands, "I wish I'd never started this! Or that I'd finished sooner. Seven years! Only two wizards left of the original twenty-four, and no hope of getting to them now, or of being paid until I do. But if only I can regroup, Miscellaneous, I'm of a mind to finish this—no matter what the Blood Royal says." Growling, she finished, "He ordered me down. He wants to discontinue my mission!"

"Wait!" Lanie interrupted her. "Go back. The who? He? The Blood Royal?"

"Oh!" Nita stopped her frenzied pacing once again and slumped onto the settee, looking damp and dazed. "Didn't I tell you?"

Lanie's voice rose. "Tell me *what*, Amanita Muscaria?"

"I rode to Liriat Proper before coming here, to make my report to Erralierra. Canon Lir greeted me at the gates of Castle Ynyssyll; I'd sent a runner ahead to warn of my arrival. No one was being admitted to the castle—though they let *me* pass when I told them what I knew."

"Nita! *What happened?*"

Nita unburied her face from her hands and looked straight at her. "Blood Royal Erralierra Brackenwild was found dead this morning."

"YOU'RE *LEAVING?*" DATU'S gruff voice was much higher than usual.

"Not *leaving* leaving," Lanie reiterated. She was tense and tired. Once Nita's first floodgates of confession had burst, she had just kept on talking and talking. Then, there had been supper to get through—even more exhausting for its silence—with Mak staring stonily at the table and Nita jumping at every noise and no one eating much of anything. And though it was now Datu's bedtime, Lanie could foresee no rest for herself that night—or in the days to come.

"Just for the day," she promised her niece. "Your Mumyu and I will ride out to Liriat Proper at dawn tomorrow. We'll be back by tomorrow night. Maybe too late for stories, but I'll come and look in on you anyway."

"If I am asleep, you will wake me up and tell me goodnight," said Datu, dangerously.

"I will look in," Lanie countered, "and if you are awake, I will say goodnight."

"And," continued her niece, "*when* you wake me up to say goodnight, you will also tell me about what Liriat Proper is like, because we have never been."

As if Lanie needed reminding. Her stomach fluttered—but with dread, not excitement. After dreaming of going to Liriat Proper for years and years, it came to this: a royal request from Blood Royal Errolirrolin Brackenwild for the necromancer of Stones Manor to come to Castle Ynyssyll and investigate his mother's death. First and foremost, by asking the corpse herself the cause of it. It was possible, after all (if not likely, considering Nita's massive debacle in Rook), that Erralierra's death was due to *natural* causes. The Blood Royal wasn't terribly old, but she had lived extravagantly, eaten imprudently, drank voluminously, and daily endured the stresses of state. Would it be any wonder if her heart suddenly gave out?

Only… just now? Lanie thought. No.

"Maybe *I* can come with you instead of Mumyu," Datu suggested, in the manner of one issuing a command. Her face, innocent of any wizard mark but not of haughtiness, had assumed its empress look.

One corner of Lanie's mouth tugged up. "You may not come with me, Datu."

"Why not?"

Why not indeed? Lanie had asked the same thing earlier, near the end of their interminable dinner, breaking the silence to lobby for Datu—and Mak, and Goody as well—to ride with her and Nita into Liriat Proper tomorrow. All together. With the intention that the whole Stones family could plea sanctuary from the Brackenwilds. She felt uneasy leaving anyone behind. Stones Manor was so isolated, so infamous, its location marked on every map of Liriat as ostentatiously as any of the nine baronies. But all her efforts had yielded her was a flat "No" from Nita.

"Why not?" repeated her remorseless niece now. Datu was entirely capable of repeating those same two words for the rest of the night.

"Because," Lanie said, "the Blood Royal didn't invite you, and he'd think it was rude if I showed up to chat with his mother's cadaver with an audience in tow. Besides," she added reasonably, "you hate my death magic stuff. All necromancy and tedium, nothing to shoot at with your blowgun. You'd be bored."

Mollified at the use of the word 'blowgun,' Datu asked, "Auntie Lanie, are you going to bring the Blood Royal back to life?"

"Eh." Lanie made a seesawing motion with her left hand. "Briefly. Maybe. Sort of. But we're nowhere near a surge, you know. I'll see what I can do. Errolirrolin just wants me to ask her a few questions."

"What questions?"

Lanie considered this. She had never been consulted on a potential murder investigation before. This was the sort of thing Grandpa Rad was always training her to do (criminal inquiries being "the cash cow of the necromancy business," quoth he, "unless you're lucky enough to get involved in a major war, girlie…"), and for a first-time gig, the stakes could not be higher.

"Things like," she answered slowly, "did Erralierra see anybody come into her bedroom before she died? Does she remember eating or drinking or smelling anything that seemed a bit… off? Did she receive any threatening letters? Did she feel like she was being watched—more than usual, I mean? Did she or her fire priests notice any ominous portents in any of their prayers or dealings with the god Sappacor? Just… anything… unusual."

Lanie imagined Canon Lir standing beside her as she interrogated their late mother. How wise and warm, how reassuring they would be—astute and sensitive, even in the throes of their grief. Perhaps they might proffer up a few questions of their own, adding their keen insight, advising her when she stumbled, maybe even giving her the occasional, encouraging stroke on the back.

"Also," she added thoughtfully, "I will ask Erralierra if she has any last bequests to her children."

Datu, nightgown-muffled, blinked eyes like great green candle flames, her hair standing out like a red-gold thorn thicket around her brown face. "But," she pressed, "you will be back tomorrow night, Auntie Lanie?"

"Yes, Datu, I already told you. Anyway, be happy! You get your didyi to yourself all day."

But Datu only looked more troubled. "Where is Didyi?"

"On his way up to see you, I'm sure." Lanie was, in fact, not sure. Mak was late for Datu's bedtime ritual. Very unlike him. "He's probably having after-dinner drinks with your mumyu. You know she likes that."

Datu stared down at her coverlet. "Not anymore."

Sighing, Lanie propped her feet up on a stool and crossed her ankles. "Well, since he's being a dilatory didyi, we'll have to start story time without him. Unfortunately for Master Tardy Gyrgardi, he's going to be missing the initial degustation, mastication, and peristalsis procedure of Thrice-Digested Stones. But that's fine—we'll have two more rounds to catch him up later. Dragon digestion is a long, slow process, especially in winter, being as how reptiles are ectothermic—and don't get me started on their reproductive systems, Datu, because I am here to tell you that a dragon's cloaca is—"

"—not appropriate for a bedtime story," Mak interrupted her, striding into Datu's bedroom. He looked tousled and tired, but Datu's dark face eased immediately when she saw him, and Lanie realized just how worried her niece had been.

"Oh, you heard that, did you?" Lanie didn't budge from her armchair; Mak always sat on the bed. "How is it, Datu, that every time I mention a cloaca, your didyi just happens to walk through the door?"

Mak settled near his daughter's feet. "Remind your aunt, my plumula, that a story is more than a series of anatomical manuals."

He spoke Lirian for Lanie's benefit. Or as her punishment. Lanie was never quite sure. She would have liked nothing better than to converse with him in Quadic. With anyone, really.

"But Didyi," objected Datu, "I like it when Auntie Lanie talks about pus and things. Did you know that a dragon has a secondary set of saliva glands adapted to produce venom, and that when a dragon belches, its stomach acid reacts with the venom to produce a big flame, but that the dragon's mouth and throat are coated with flame-resistant mucus, so that the dragon doesn't burn itself, even though it can destroy a village just because it's feeling dis... dispestic."

"Dyspeptic," said Mak and Lanie at the same time. Mak's gaze slid to where Lanie lounged on the armchair. "Ridiculous. Dragons do not exist."

"Tell that to Thrice-Digested Stones," Lanie retorted.

"*He* does not exist either."

"*She*," Datu corrected him haughtily. "And she *does*, Didyi! I saw her. Auntie Lanie and Goody Graves made her out of some attic junk. She is our scarecrow, and her eyes are blue like Goody Graves's, and she is going to keep a lookout for blackbirds."

Mak said nothing.

He said nothing as loudly as Goody did.

Lanie shifted guiltily in her chair. Mak hated her death magic, hated even more that Datu had to see it, hated Lanie, hated everything.

Except Datu. Mak did not hate her. He adored her.

For Datu's sake, he redirected the conversation, visibly adjusting his mood and tone. His face lightened with one of his rare smiles, and he grasped his daughter's ankles under the blanket, asking gently, "Who made a maiden out of bloom and bud, and breathed this blossom-moppet into being?"

Ah. Those, Lanie knew, were the opening lines of 'The Flower-Hawk.' She smiled, her ears adjusting to the cadence of the Quadic antiphony. This was not one of Goody's tales; Lanie had never heard the story before Mak first began reciting it to Datu. Now she had it memorized. She could even guess the *reason* he chose it, and marveled at his quickness—sly Mak!—for 'The Flower-Hawk' was the closest thing the Quadoni had to a story about an undead scarecrow.

But instead of a creature slapped together of straw and old clothes and orblins, the protagonist—a maiden named Flaisalón—had been created from green growing things: from bloom and breath and magic. There were even birds in this story, but they were not blackbirds. Not to be *feared*. The birds he sang were always gyrgardon, the Falcon Defenders of Quadiíb. Mak was taking all of his daughter's daytime dreads and reshaping them into a beautiful nighttime myth, the same way he reshaped his body with sothaín into the very essence of his prayers.

Lanie's particular gift at bedtime was not her actual *storytelling*—Mak was right; she was hopeless at plot and character—but her ability to make the stories that she told, even the ones about fire-breathing dragons, endlessly clinical. Many a night she'd simply bored Datu to sleep, pontificating (doing her best Grandpa Rad impersonation) about the ins and outs of monster intestines. But Mak did her one better: he removed the monsters entirely, and sang his daughter to sleep with poetic parables instead.

Either way, Lanie figured, the end results were what mattered.

Settling back into her pillows, Datu stuck her right pinkie finger into the corner of her mouth, and around it, took up her part in the call-and-response, "'Twas Neesa breathed the girl-bouquet to life, wherefrom there sprang her doughty Gyrgardu."

Mak asked, "Wherefore did Neesa's Flower-Hawk take form, and wear her silver bracer all in joy?"

Datu replied. "Because she loved her maker like the sun, and wished her nevermore to be alone."

The story went on, telling of the loving friendship between Gyrlady Neesa and her Gyrgardu Flaisalón, the 'Flower-Hawk,' and their many adventures together among the Traveling Palaces of Higher Quadiíb. For years the two of them walked the roads of the Caravan School, seeking professorial positions at Waystation after Waystation—only to be rejected time and again because Flaisalón was "neither human nor a hawk in truth," merely flowers enchanted into a form that walked and talked and flew. At last, however, the wisest and wiliest elder of the Judicial Colloquium of Gyrladies summoned Neesa and Flaisalón to her tent.

She was dying, she told them. Only one herb could save her. Impotent in its preserved form, but all-powerful when fresh, this herb grew too far from their current camp to be fetched back before it wilted and its virtue was sapped.

Gyrlady Neesa was disinclined to be merciful. But her Gyrgardu Flaisalón did not hesitate. She plucked that precious herb fresh from among the petals of her own enchanted breast, and laid it upon the elder's tongue, even though the loss of it made her bleed thick green sap as from a mortal wound!

Then—miracle of miracles!—the ancient gyrlady arose from her death mat as sprightly as a child. She went to a secret place among her belongings, and from it removed a silver box, taking out an object locked inside it.

There, shining, the polished wishbone of a kestrel. This bone had been removed from the breast of her very own dear gyrgardi, who had died of old age the year before. The elder pressed the wishbone to Flaisalón's green and sticky wound. Right before their eyes, Flaisalón the Flower-Hawk transformed from girl-bouquet into girl-in-truth: a woman of flesh and blood.

Satisfied with the fullness of her life, the elder then lay down again upon her mat and died—but not before dashing off a stern note to her colleagues. On her written command, the Judicial Colloquium of Gyrladies elected

Gyrlady Neesa to take her place among them, with Flaisalón as a true member of the gyrgardon. And so they remained till the end of their days.

Gyrlady Neesa became legendary for her scholarship amongst the professora ambassadors of the Traveling Palaces. But it was to Gyrgardu Flaisalón that the needful and the holy of Quadiíb all flocked, for the woman who was once a girl made out of flowers was wisest of them all.

By the end of the story, Datu was asleep.

"SHE WON'T STAY down long," Lanie whispered as she and Mak tiptoed out of the nursery. "Not tonight."

Mak looked directly at her. A rarity.

"So," she continued, trying not to stammer, "while Nita is securing the house, I'm off to have a bit of reconnaissance myself, see which of her defense measures I can augment, what sort of safeguards I can put in place, that sort of thing. But just in case..."

"I will keep watch at Datu's door," Mak said in a low voice. "Unless I am called away."

Which might happen at any time, Lanie knew, depending on Nita's mood.

"Don't worry, Mak," she said, shoving a hand into her pocket and pulling out an orblin. "I'll leave one of these, just in case. It'll come find me if Datu wakes up and takes off on one of her midnight perambulations."

At the flash of unmitigated revulsion on Mak's face, Lanie felt her eager smile wither. But she kept her hand outstretched. "Guaranteed to lead us right to her."

He hesitated, dropping his gaze to the small clay object. His eyes closed. He nodded. Hardly daring to breathe lest he change his mind, Lanie licked the orblin to glowing blue life—or rather, undeath—and set it high on a shelf facing the nursery door. She stood beneath it, whispering the orblin to mindfulness, acquainting it with its new duties, and, finally, expressing her gratitude for its services—as she always tried to do with the undead, for Goody's sake. Well, except for Grandpa Rad.

Mak dragged a chair across the hall and set it just outside Datu's door. It was wooden and rickety and belonged in Torr Digitalis with the rest of the trashy old furniture. Lanie pointed to the loveseat occupying a cozy end of the corridor running between Datu's nursery and Lanie's bedroom. "You know, Mak, you'd probably be more comfortable in that."

Mak rubbed his tired face. "Exactly," he said, and sat down in the unforgiving chair, spine straight, hands on knees, like a strange sapling that had spontaneously grown up through the floor.

"Okay, gyrgardi. As you will. Just," Lanie added on her way out, "try not to smash that beak of yours when you face-plant."

CHAPTER FIFTEEN

Time-Hobble and Concealer

Luckday 7th
Month of Broods, 421 Founding Era
75 days till Summer Solstice

NOT LONG BEFORE dawn, Lanie waylaid her niece as she wandered into the anteroom outside Nita's bedchamber.

At first Datu did not realize she was caught. She stood, swaying slightly, blinking owlish eyes at her aunt, who was sitting, cross-legged and slouched, against the wall next to Nita's closed bedroom door, reading *How To Get Your Cadaver To Really Open Up: Advanced Interrogation Techniques for the Undead*, by Irradiant Radithor Stones.

A small pile of black sludge-ash-ooze was sizzling down near Lanie's left ankle. Her niece did not seem to see this, or to understand that it was what was left of the orblin Lanie had set to guard the nursery door.

"Good morning," whispered Lanie. "Are you even awake?"

The yawn resolved into a glare. "Of course I am awake," Datu retorted. "Why are you awake, Auntie Lanie? Why are you outside Mumyu's door?"

"Seemed like the place to be." Lanie kept her voice hushed. Nita's temper, uncertain at the best of times, would not be improved by being awoken a few short hours after finally collapsing in nervous exhaustion.

But Datu, skeptical, opened her mouth to demand further elucidation. Lanie cut her off. "Any Stones of any repute whatsoever ends up right here, just outside the state bedchamber, barefoot, in the darkest hours before dawn. Take yourself, for example."

Datu adjusted her toy crossbow in her arm, cradling it much like Lanie used to cradle Hoppy Bunny. "How"—yawn—"did you know I would come here, Auntie Lanie?"

"Because I am a true genius of my household," replied her aunt, softly closing her book and standing up. "I am a wizard of fell magics and towering repute, and my ways are mysterious. Now tell me, Sacred Datura Stones, what in Doédenna's name were you planning to do with *that*"—she pointed—"thing?"

Datu blinked down at her weapon. "I am going to protect Mumyu from blackbirds."

"Oh, if that's all." Lanie pointed to the settee in the middle of the room, where Datu had sat earlier that night watching Goody Graves tend Nita's wounds. "Do it there. Great view of the door."

Her niece climbed aboard the settee, crossbow in lap. Lanie sat beside her. "You know, Datu, after you went to bed, your mumyu and I went all over the manor. We barred doors, fastened windows, secured the cellars and the attic. Nita set booby-traps everywhere. If there's one thing Stones Manor is sufficiently stocked with, it's booby-traps. She gutted Torr Digitalis for all of Aunt Diggie's old gadgets. You never knew your Aunt Diggie—well, she was more of a cousin than an actual aunt, I guess, twice removed, maybe three or four; don't let's worry about genealogy just now—but she had all kinds of bear traps and bush meat snares, portable pits and explosive devices disguised as cupcakes and—urk—you know."

She stopped to gag; she was short on sleep, and the power of suggestion was giving her a bad case of burps. "That kind of stuff. *And* I posted my orblins as sentries all through the house."

To Lanie's surprise, the latter seemed to reassure Datu more than anything. Her shoulders relaxed about a quarter of an inch. "That is good," she said solemnly. "You have been working hard on those."

"They're like having extra eyes and ears everywhere," Lanie agreed. "I've got orblins looking out from every lintel, every windowsill. Like an army of little mouse spies—only without the mice. I even have a pair on the ramparts of Torr Digitalis, with a three-hundred-and-sixty-degree view for miles. No one can approach Stones Manor without me knowing. And even if they get past *my* spies, why, they'd just be setting off your mumyu's booby traps first thing."

Datu's heavy eyelids drooped, but she caught herself and shook herself out, determined not to fall asleep on her watch. "What is your book about, Auntie Lanie?"

"Research," Lanie said, as soporifically as possible. "Death magic stuff. For my job at Castle Ynyssyll in a few hours."

Her choice of reading material came recommended by the late author himself, when Lanie had consulted him after helping Nita lock down the house. But she didn't want to tell Datu about Grandpa Rad. Datu was unaware of the ghost, and that was better for all concerned, since any mention of him, or of Lanie's association with him, would be bound to throw both Mak and Nita into their respective temper tantrums, if for different reasons.

"Good reading, if I say it myself," Grandpa Rad had told her with his usual self-importance. Then added, in wheedling tones that had set off all of Lanie's alarm bells: "Say, girlie, any luck yet with our little ectenica-stability project? I know you've been tinkering with some notions down in Stones Ossuary—I've been sensing a great deal of activity coming from that area most nights, even all the way up here. If I weren't dead already, I'd be dying to know what you're up to down there..."

Lanie had lied without compunction. "No luck yet, Grandpa Rad."

If the ghost knew that she had indeed finally perfected a stabilized form of ectenica, he'd not only take all the credit himself, he'd pester her to stuff one of her precious orblins into the keyhole of his padlock straightaway, giving him 'that extra little boost' he liked off-surge. Lanie was not about to make *that* mistake again; the last time she'd tested out one of her prototypes on him, the ghost had grown so powerful he'd almost walked out of his padlock—and it wasn't even a high holy fire feast on that occasion.

Anyway, Lanie needed every last orblin she had.

Datu sniffed in sleepy disdain. "You are always reading about death magic."

Lanie shrugged. "Well, I like my work. You practice sothaín a lot; you know how it is."

"Only because Didyi makes me."

"I've seen you practicing when he's not around, Datu."

Datu rubbed her eyes but said nothing. Lanie went back to reading. Whatever his machinations, the ghost was right about one thing: *Advanced Interrogation Techniques* was good reading. She would be prepared for her appointment with the Blood Royal (or, more precisely, with his mother's cadaver) later that morning—if only she could manage to stay awake now. Sighing, she adjusted her spectacles and found her place on the page. But Datu was not in the mood to sit and watch her aunt read.

"Auntie Lanie, do you like anything else? Other than work," she added sternly.

Lanie shut the book, but kept her finger between the pages. "I like Goody. I like my garden..."

"You like Canon Lir," said Datu, who had long ago discovered what, exactly, could make her aunt squirm.

Lanie squirmed. "Sure. They're very... They're quite... likable."

She thought, but didn't say: I like Canon Lir too much. I live for the handful of minutes every few months I get to glimpse them. They've made the last seven years of my life not only bearable, but even occasionally enjoyable. How is it that they keep growing more interesting, more beautiful, more mysterious the longer I know them? They're the only person truly interested in me. Me, Miscellaneous Stones—not *Auntie*

Lanie, not *sister-of-mine-enemy*, not *future investment for the family fortune*. I'd rather hear Canon Lir say "Miss Stones" than any other two words in the world. I've saved all their letters in my underwear drawer, and if Datu ever finds *that* out—! Oh, yes. I like Canon Lir. I like Canon Lir the way the Holy Martyrs of Sappacor like self-immolation in the Triple Flame.

Datu demanded, "Do you like *me?*"

Startled, Lanie deflected the question with another question. "Why? Do *you* like *me?*"

"Sometimes," Datu replied.

Oh, the sting! But no less than she deserved for her own evasion. Well, Lanie would try for total honesty in return; it was the hour of the night for it. The silvered dark of the antechamber, the low lamp burning in the corner of the room, their whispered words, her weariness, and the precariousness of their situation, all conspired to turn Lanie loquacious.

"You know, Datu, I like *everyone* a lot more when I get at least six hours of sleep. I've not been sleeping much because of making my orblins, so maybe I've been irritable lately—and maybe I've made you feel like I *don't* like you. Which is just not true."

Datu did not blink, but something flickered in her eyes. Lanie added quickly, "Me being snarly is not your fault. It's mine—for working too much. Which I tend to do, don't I, because I like my work! Your didyi has an aphorism for that." She said in Quadic, "'The vicious circle of the heart's desire—'"

"'—consumes itself complete, as fire doth fire,'" Datu finished.

"Exactly. Even death magic—which I love—I sometimes also hate. Some nights, I look up at the bone chandelier in the ossuary, with all those empty eye sockets glaring down at me, dripping beeswax all over the floor, and I think, 'How did I get here? Why am I even doing this? Maybe I should run away and fry donuts for a living. That would be a good life.' But then some bit of bone shines out, singing to me, and I fall in love all over again. Maybe that's the difference. I don't always *like* death magic, but I always *love* it. I can't help it. Like Goody: I don't ever *not* love Goody. That's impossible. And" —to her surprise, she stammered a little—"and I don't ever *not* love you. Even when I'm irritable. I hope you know that. I don't say it often. Or ever, really. Your didyi's much better about that kind of thing, but..."

"Didyi," Datu said deliberately, "*always* loves me."

Lanie smiled wryly. "You're the only Stones he does."

It was this assertion, or perhaps her whole muddled attempt at expressing affection, that finally seemed to settle the child. Datu smiled to herself, as rare an expression for her as it was for her father, and began playing with her toy crossbow again: polishing the tiller on the sleeve of her nightgown, testing the tension of the string, cranking the cranequin, and checking her bag of bolts, which had been fitted by the original toymaker with small suction cups made out of gourds. Lanie devoutly prayed that Datu had not replaced them with something more pointy. Again.

But when she tried to go back to her book, Lanie could not focus on the words. The light was too low. Her eyes were tired.

She thought about Goody Graves. At Nita's command, she was patrolling the perimeter of the manor grounds, pushing a small demi-culverin before her like a wheelbarrow, ready to blast any invader she encountered. She thought about the scarecrow in the garden, reinvigorated with fresh orblins, asked to keep its eyes on the skies.

Lanie reached out with her thoughts to touch each orblin in its turn. She did not have to reach far.

Darkness, they reported back to her. Darkness and stillness and silence. Low clouds. A low mist.

It was so soothing that Lanie almost fell asleep right there. She stirred, turning to her niece, who was also awake, if barely.

"How'd you get past your didyi?" Lanie asked curiously. "I can't imagine he fell asleep at your nursery door. He really ought to have caught you sneaking out. I only stationed myself here as a secondary line of defense."

Datu glanced up. "Didyi is gone."

"Gone?"

Datu nodded. "Mumyu came. I heard them talking outside my room; it woke me up. He wanted to stay with me. She made him take falcon form. She said she needed his eyes outside."

Lanie knew better than to pull her niece in for a hug, no matter how bitterly dejected Datu sounded. The best way to comfort her niece was not to fondle her, but to distract her. Datu's rules were clear:

1) Never touch her without her permission.
2) Especially never touch her when she was hungry.
3) *Certainly* never touch her while she was armed.

Lanie faked a yawn that ended up being not so very fake. "Why don't you take first watch, Falcon's Daughter? I'll go back to reading. Poke me if anything weird happens."

Datu lit with the solemn radiance of duty. Bounding off the settee, she saluted with her toy crossbow—"I will, Auntie Lanie!"—and went to stand beside Nita's locked door. She moved easily into the first attitude of the seventh sothaín set, the one dedicated to Engoloth: One-Horned god of War and Time (and, strangely enough, Pepper). The first attitude was called 'Engoloth of the Ax Contemplates Cutting Down the Tree of Time,' the ur-parade rest.

Datu breathed out:

Where is breath?
In the stillness.
What is stillness?
Sothaín.

Lanie ducked her head to hide a smile. "That's my good scarecrow," she murmured. Then, fixing her focus on the page, she reached out with her mind to touch her orblins once more.

Darkness, they assured her. Silence. Mist. Nothing. Safe. Empty. Calm.

So why did she feel so uneasy?

THAT MOMENT *BETWEEN*, on the borderland of wake and dream, hovering like a teardrop on an eyelash. Aware of thought, lacking control. Oldest memories, excavated. Bright ideas blinking and winking, fireflies floating in a dark chaotic clarity. Urges at their vividest, most carnal. Lanie lived for these warm-bath reveries, in those precious few seconds before taking the plunge into total unconsciousness.

But that was *not* what was happening now.

For one thing, it came on too fast. One minute she was awake, reading a chapter called 'Playing with Pride,' which was about about flattering cadavers.[11] The next minute, she was... something else.

Not asleep. Not exactly. It was too sudden for that. Too... sticky. Something like... drowning. In honey.

Lanie fought for thought. But struggling seemed only to thrust her down further into the creeping treacle. She flailed but could not—quite—snatch back her connection to consciousness. Tried prying open her eyes. They would not come unglued. Some kind of trickling tackiness had crept in, gumming her eyelids, her mouth, her nostrils, her ears. A single heartbeat hung in her chest. The second heartbeat did not follow. Honey, not breath, moved through her lungs. Honey, not blood, pushed through her veins.

What is this? *What is this?* she screamed, or tried to.

No answer. Just a vast molasses downpour all around her, broken here and there by glowing blue eyes.

It was the blue of Goody's own dear eyes, lovingly re-created in every orblin Lanie had made. Blue spheres spinning on invisible axes, all rolling toward her. She felt them bumping her ankles, hopping into her lap, trying frantically to give her warning. They had all sped in, she knew—from every wall and lintel she had set them upon, from the heights of Torr Digitalis, from the very face of the scarecrow Thrice-Digested Stones. They had seen

---

11 *By flattering your undead corpse,* writes Irradiant Radithor Stones, *you reinforce its opinion of itself, bolstering its memory to the point where it may, in turn, reveal all of its secrets to you. If that doesn't work, try the opposite: insult and demean your cadaver, reduce it to the quivering memory of tears, until it tells you everything just to make you stop.*

something. Something glimpsed through the darkness, the silence.

Three shadows. Three birds on the wing.

The orblins chimed the alert, flaring like beacons. They transmitted image after image through the molasses.

But Lanie was stuck like a gadfly on a cobra lily. Impossible to act upon the information, even once she'd comprehended it. And comprehension came... so... slowly.

Eventually—minutes or hours later—the ectenica spent itself. The orblins dissolved to black sludge all around her, all over her, and upon her. And still Lanie could not move.

One thought, at least, was sharp and harsh, whipping through her molasses-gooed brains, returning again and again to true, like a boomerang. Datu's jump-rope rhyme.

The Harrier's a-hunting
Right on track
Bobolink, Cormorant—
Watch your back!

Watch your back indeed, Lanie thought bitterly. We watched from all directions, and still they found us.

Nita had promised—pacing, wild-eyed—that she had laid a false trail for the Parliament of Rooks. She'd sworn that she'd set the skies above Quadiíb a-swarm with wizard-birds chasing the shadow of the Harrier.

Liriat was supposed to be safe for the present. They were supposed to have more time, the Stoneses and the Brackenwilds, to plan a defense strategy against the Blackbird Bride's vengeance.

But here was Erralierra, dead. And here were three shadows, three birds, almost upon them.

Almost? thought Lanie. They're *already here!*

She strained and strained. Finally, the next thought came, and then the next. Like light filtering through a thick pane of old, warped glass, the images that her orblins had been beaming into her brain began at last to gleam through.

A bird: yellow nape, yellow breast, black below, black and white above. A bird who was also a human woman. Who was also, by her marks, a wizard. She had black and white hair, black skin with one big, beautiful, buff patch starting at the nape of her neck and spreading to her shoulders and upper back. Bright black eyes.

Lanie knew the woman because she knew the bird. The latter was a common enough sight in the meadows and hayfields that surrounded Stones Manor—but this bird was no normal bobolink, with its chirpy flirts and irrepressible burbles. This was Bobolink the Concealer, wizard of the Parliament of Rooks.

Bran Fiakhna's four-and-twenty espoused kin each had their own unique gift of sorcery. Every magic depended on the god the wizard worshipped, whence their powers derived, in addition to their own natural predilections and talents.

Upon their wedding day, the Blackbird Bride would pledge to her newly-sworn beloved a single feather of her own body, which was then sewn into the skin over the beloved's left breast, right over the heart. This feather gave the beloved control over their bird shape, and from that feather, they took their official title.

Sometimes a wizard died and another took their place. The new wizard's magic might be different in form or flavor from their predecessor's, but their title, and the bird shape that gave them wings, remained the same. This gave the Parliament of Rooks a sense of continuity and stability: no matter who fell, another bird would fly to take their place.

Bobolink the Concealer was one of the two remaining wizards of Bran Fiakhna's first Parliament—the one Nita had all but destroyed—and Lanie knew only a few basics about her kind of magic. Nita knew more. She'd spent the last seven years studying the Parliament: the pecking order at Rookery Court, their habits, strengths, and weaknesses, their ticks, secret desires, and hidden histories. She had with her own arts exploited them all. But Nita had been saving Bobolink and Cormorant for last—the final feathers for her trophy belt—because their magics were the most powerful.

Take the magic of concealment. One of the more slippery gifts of the trickster god, Amahirra: Mirage-Shaper.

What did it mean, then, when a wizard, as powerful at her art of concealing as Lanie was at her death magic, wanted to invade Stones Manor? How hard would it be, under cover of night, to bend the dark and the quiet and the mist around her, to move under it, projecting nothing but serenity even as she scaled the walls?

After all, Lanie reasoned slowly, if *I* wanted to enter a house, all I'd need were bones enough and the blood of my body. No lock in the realms could stop me.

Nor had all of Lanie's orblins or Nita's booby-traps stopped Bobolink the Concealer. Stones Manor was breached, and none within it the wiser. Except for Lanie. And *she* couldn't move.

But what was this other thing? This breathless blackstrap molasses spell? This reservoir of honey and syrup and jam she was drowning in? How long could Lanie thrash without breathing? How long would her single suspended heartbeat sustain her? How much time did she…?

Time.

The final images from the orblins reached her then—that same doubled view of bird and person.

First came the bird: a red-capped cormorant, large, gangly, pitch-black of body, with a red mask, a red beak, and red feet with red webbing. A black oil-slick of wings spread out behind it like a ragged cape in the wind. Then came the man, with his wizard marks ablaze. Black hair with red streaks, eyes like red embers. Black skin with slashes of red high on the cheeks, glowing like flowing lava.

This wizard was Cormorant, Time-Hobble to the Blackbird Bride.

A Time-Hobble's singular talent, Lanie knew, stemmed from the god Engoloth—and they needed no other magic.

The spell that any Time-Hobble must master in order to earn that title was known as 'Engoloth's Hourglass.'

It was an enchanted entrapment. A sap of slow motion that dawdled all the senses nearly to death, dragging you into its stillness as the rest of the world whipped on all around you, affording the spellcaster leisure to work uninterrupted—

—and just like that, the spell was ended.

Lanie's ears popped like blown-up bladders. Her lungs expanded; her heart crashed crazily in her chest. She tore open her eyes, clawed sensation back into her numb face, and gasped, "Datu!"

Her voice swam strangely in her ears. The sunlight stretched across the floor, lazy as a lynx.

When had that pre-dawn darkness advanced to full morning? Could it possibly be noon already? *After* noon? How long had she...

"Datu?"

Lanie stared around the room in a panic. But there she was, much as Lanie had last seen her, standing just beside Nita's door. Datu was still keeping watch all these hours later, pretending she was the god of War, holding sothaín perfectly.

Too perfectly.

"Datu!"

Lanie stumbled off the settee, immediately crashed to her knees, and crawled across the floor. Taking her niece by both arms, she shook her, trying to rouse her from the spell. Her hands seemed to stick to Datu's skin, but Lanie ignored the slurping sensation, and squeezed more urgently. Slowly, so slowly, Datu emerged from her stupor.

Lanie scanned her face desperately, and so knew the exact moment that the honey-thick glaze coating those green eyes cracked and crumbled away. She saw the pulse kicking up in her throat, and sighed in relief.

After that, Datu's recovery was almost instantaneous. She flowed out of sothaín so fast that her hand was on Nita's doorknob, her crossbow at the ready, and the door pushed open before Lanie could scramble after her.

"No—wait! Datu! Wait!"

But Datu was already inside, running.

CHAPTER SIXTEEN

"You, We Shall Keep"

Not a spiral of that boundless burnt-gold hair was out of place. Lion-colored skin ashen, wizard marks vanished—as if dusted off with a brush. Limbs arranged neatly, tidily, on the large bed, beneath a faded dressing gown. Frayed cuffs. Wide sash. Silver-maned lions and silver-furred monkeys transparent as ghosts against the green-sheened and cobweb-thin brocade. The robe was open.

Nita was split down the middle, gullet to gizzard.

One blackbird—or rather, a bird that was black, a black bird far too large to be a blackbird, a long-necked water bird with red mask and red crest, dark as a coastal midnight—feasted on her viscera.

Another, much smaller, bird—this one black and white, with yellow markings on her nape—sat on her chest, pecking at the meat of her tongue.

Nita's eyes had already been eaten.

The tattered feathers from her trophy belt surrounded her corpse like a dark nimbus. An accusation. A sentence already being carried out.

At her first sight of the birds, Datu had braked herself mid-stride. Lanie, on her heels, froze as well so as not to crash into her.

Datu's small face was calm and cold. She raised her toy crossbow, sighted down the bridge, and shot.

Lanie could not breathe. But it was neither the molasses-trap of the Time Hobble nor the paralyzing pain of echo-wounds that incapacitated her now. Her allergy never echoed the dead—only the stricken or dying. And her sister was not among these anymore.

No, it was fear that immobilized her. Fear for the child who, with her toy, was aiming at those bloody-beaked birds.

Datu's bolt caught the small one in the wing, knocking her aside. A perfect shot. But she had not, after all, removed the suction cups from her bolts; Bobolink the Concealer was merely startled. The blow, though harmless, broke the wizard's control, her concentration.

What she had been concealing came unconcealed.

Or rather, *whom*.

Lanie gasped when a tall, thin woman stepped out of the dense shadows near the bed, as if merely emerging from behind a screen, or having just turned a corner. One second not there; the next, possessing the room entirely.

"Hark," said the tall woman. "The Harrier's daughter has come."

Oh, the raw scrape of her voice! Lanie's skin pilled up like an old sweater at the sound.

"The blood of one lone daughter," the woman repeated, all soft rasp and razor edge, "to ransom two-and-twenty of our beloved dead. It is not enough to slake our thirst, little maiden. But it is a start."

Datu simply reloaded her crossbow and raised it again.

But Lanie shouted without sound, and lurched between woman and child, spreading her arms wide. She wished she had something sharp—knife, saw, ax—that she might cut herself open and bleed all over her dead sister, that the magic in her living blood might mingle with the cold sludge in Nita's veins, and make an ectenica to cover the corpse whole. Would that Nita might rise up a revenant and ravage this sorceress where she stood—and protect Datu! Protect her daughter from those who would murder her and drink her blood.

But Lanie had nothing to cut herself with. And Nita was too far away. Nor was it a surge day. Her bumbling, however, had distracted the tall woman's attention away from Datu.

Her Most Excellent Supremacy—the Rook of Rook, Keeper of the Seven Jetties, Splendor of the Glistring Sea, Her Sovereign Majesty, Queen Bran Fiakhna the Blackbird Bride—turned to Lanie, and smiled.

Oh, she was gorgeous—and gorgeously arrayed, her tunic of purple-black feathers the same nacreous black as her skin, her close-cropped hair, her finger- and toenails. All but the centermost triangle of her face, where she bore her wizard mark. It took the shape of an upside-down triangle: a straight line across her brow, two strong, slashing diagonal lines down each of her cheeks, a point at the cleft of her chin. Everything within that triangle was a pale, pearly gray. The Rook of Rook bore the markings of her bird shape, as did all the wizards in her Parliament. Her lips were gray, but the inside of her mouth was bright red. Her eyes, like silver coins rubbed smooth, had tiny pinprick pupils at their colorless centers.

One of Datu's suction-cup missiles bounced harmlessly off her feathered breast. She ignored it, still smiling at Lanie.

"You!"

The Blackbird Bride's face softened. Her harsh voice became the caress of eiderdown. "You are Miscellaneous Stones. We have heard tell of you, and"—gesturing at Lanie's left hand, and the rain-on-slate-colored wizard mark there—"of your great work among the tombs of your forebears."

Lanie's mouth was dry and cold. Her tongue stuck to her hard palate as if she had been licking old ice.

She thought desperately, Me? Who told Bran Fiakhna about me? And how could *they* have known about my work? I hardly see anyone!

"Long have we awaited you," the Blackbird Bride continued, stepping closer. "We have kept your seat at our table, thinking you would come to us in time. Surely you would fly to us, having outgrown this nest, and make your home at Rookery Court—as the most powerful wizards of every realm have done. Gladly would we take you in, and love you, and make you our own. We decided long ago, you see"—her smile widened; her teeth were lovely, sharp and white—"you, we shall keep."

Lanie's tongue was an ancient iceberg, but she forced the word past it: "Run."

The word was for Datu, but she did not look at her. Could not. At that moment, she would rather have put out her own eyes than take them off the Blackbird Bride. The woman's power of fascination was incredible—a sea-wave, salt-wet. Nita's own arts were nothing to it. Nothing. A tide pool next to an oncoming tide.

Yet, having lived so long with Nita, having learned early on in life to dodge a thousand lesser fascinations, Lanie found that she could just keep her feet after Bran Fiakhna sent that first, huge crash of fascination rolling over her. She swayed with it, half-seduced—but she did keep her feet.

"Run," Lanie choked out again. "Get Goody Graves."

"Can't," Datu replied, her voice flat and eerie. "They're blocking the door."

Ah. So Bobolink and Cormorant must have assumed their human shapes. Lanie could sense Datu just behind her—coiled, quiet, an adder at strike-point—and kept her arms stretched out, one palm bent back, one pushing forward, as if to thrust apart these two inexorable forces, Datu and Bran Fiakhna, by will alone.

"Was Nita"—Lanie stammered—"was she… asleep when… when you…?"

"No." A whisper, as if nothing louder could express her grief. The Blackbird Bride was shaking her head, tears standing out like stars in her eyes.

"No!" she shouted a second time—full-throated, a carrion cry. "Of course she was awake! *She* always took our beloveds awake, the better to watch them die, to look them in the eye as they adored her to the last. So was our Augur awake—our Piceous, our Pied Crow—when she slaughtered him. He sacrificed himself to learn her name, to prophesy her fall with his last breath. His crows brought the tidings to our bed, where we wept for seven nights and seven days for him—for his sacrifice. His sacrifice," she said savagely, "that we *forbade!* My Piceous! My cousin! My cradle-companion! My oldest friend. He gave his life to learn her name! Of course she was awake when we *gutted* her as she did him!"

In three strides she crossed the room and loomed over Lanie, looking down.

"And we will tell you this too: Amanita Muscaria Stones knew our power to the last. She loved *us* as she died. She thanked us for every slice."

Now came the echo-wounds—brought on by proximity as much as by suggestion. In one way, they were slightly less severe for the violence only being described to Lanie, instead of witnessed by her. But they were powerful nonetheless, for the violence had been enacted so very recently, and all the perpetrators were still in the room.

Lanie's stomach didn't fall open *exactly*—at least, she didn't think it did, but was too afraid to look—however, a jagged, stabbing pang did pierce her abdomen, followed by a searing line of pain that ended at her throat.

She doubled over, groaning. Stumbled backward.

But Lanie had not endured years of allergies and echo-wounds to be brought low by them now. Her stumble was controlled; it brought her closer to Datu. Draping herself over the girl's stiff shoulders as if for support, she pressed her mouth to Datu's ear.

"Climb," she whispered, then gave the child a hard shove toward the three open windows along the western wall.

Datu sprang through the casement like a cat, and swung herself into the ivy. Lanie blocked her niece's escape with her body. But she was small and the window was large, and she did not herself have wings.

Bobolink melted to her bird shape again and took to the air. Cormorant stayed by the door, blazing black and red, electing to keep his human shape. There was a smell of magic like burnt feathers, and Lanie knew some spell had been cast.

What spell? Hobble? Concealment? Something else? Would Datu stick like sap to the ivy, trapped in honey, caught like a butterfly in a spider's web—easy pickings for the red-and-black Cormorant? Or would Bobolink simply pursue her quarry all unseen—and spring out the moment Datu thought she'd reached safety, and strike the killing blow?

The Blackbird Bride stepped closer to Lanie, her slender hand with its long, tapering fingers outstretched.

Lanie could not back away. Did not want to. When that hand touched her cheek, she leaned into it.

The Blackbird Bride's gray mouth, full as a tulip, softened into a coaxing smile. "Doédenna's daughter. You understand us. We see you do. You know that we are all equal in the long train of Her cloak. You feel, as if they were your own wounds, how grievously we have been harmed."

Lanie nodded, not exactly against her will.

"You have witnessed, you have *seen*"—Bran Fiakhna gestured towards the bed, to the feathers surrounding Nita's corpse—"how your sister has wrenched our family asunder. No one may call them back—not even you, not though it were the high holy fire feast of Midwinter. We are owed a debt that can never be paid. We know that we shall never know true justice, or peace, or the contented joy that was ours in youth. All we ask, Miscellaneous Stones—and we ask it of *you*, of your tender, understanding eyes—is that you render unto us this child's death. The blood of the Harrier's daughter to set against the blood of my espoused kin."

At this, Lanie abruptly stopped nodding. But she couldn't shake her head, not when merely *not nodding*, in defiance of the Blackbird Bride's fascination, was bringing on vertigo and a migraine. But she'd let her skull peel apart at its sutures before agreeing to Datu's death. She'd let herself be damned duodecifold if she didn't die protecting that child.

What—that all those dirty diapers, those months of lost sleep, the daily battle of wills, the bedtime stories, those few heartbreaking, hard-won smiles over the last six years be for *naught?*

Never.

Not that Lanie could say as much, or anything. Bran Fiakhna was redoubling her efforts, and it was all Lanie could do to keep her feet.

"Her death is all we need to mend our broken heart. If you will but let us live in joy again," swore the Blackbird Bride, "then we will be most generous in our turn. Ours is an ardent heart; we will open it to you. Your children shall be ours; ours, yours. Friends you shall have, and a palace of your own. Our cousin's house stands empty; we bequeath it to you. We shall bind your magic to us; we shall live and act as one. We shall give you our own husbands and wives for your espoused kin. You shall choose concubines and cavaliers to fill the halls of your household. We will give you ourself, and the feather we have saved for you. You shall wear it upon your breast, and with it, command the skies. All the world shall see your ragged wings against the sun and know you for our own. Condor, we shall call you. King Consort of Rookery Court. You will want for nothing."

Lanie tried to buy Datu a precious few seconds more. That burnt-feather smell of magic was growing stronger.

Was it Bran Fiakhna herself, plying her powers of fascination? No, hers was the smell of the sea. And the Time-Hobble's smell was honey, was sap, was syrup—sweet with clover and wildflowers.

Bobolink, then.

Lanie could not see her—or anything but the Blackbird Bride. But did that mean Bobolink was already invisible? How long could such a spell last—off-surge, and after such a night's work as she had already done?

"If I agree," Lanie began, so slowly that she might as well still be caught in Engoloth's Hourglass, "would my capitulation also clear the Brackenwilds of their debt to you? For it is no coincidence, is it, that you are here, and Erralierra was found dead yesterday morning? 'Her cup of blood is spilt'—isn't that what your Augur prophesied? Erralierra's coffers gilded Nita's executions. Will Datu's death make all even for you? Or will Rook still take revenge upon all of Liriat?"

Bran Fiakhna closed the distance between them. She enveloped Lanie in the warm perfume and trembling softness of her feathered tunic, which Lanie could feel through her own rough smock and trousers.

"Beloved Condor," she with finality, "the fate of Liriat is not your concern."

The pity in her voice was sincere, even as she signaled to someone behind Lanie. A black and white and yellow bird—Bobolink—flapped past her shoulder, winking in and out of existence as she flew toward the window.

So, Bobolink the Concealer *was* tired. Exhausted, probably, from a long night's spellcasting. But Lanie did not think her exhaustion would be enough to stop her, to keep her from Datu.

She raised her hands, trying to catch the little bird, to bat her backwards, something. But she was too late.

The Blackbird Bride put a hand on Lanie's shoulder.

At once, Lanie crashed to her knees. She was suddenly out of breath, out of strength, wholly bowled over. It was as if a length of blue-black velvet the size of the sea had just dropped on her head. She sucked in a tiny gasp of air, all her lungs would allow. She would use it to scream, to warn Datu, to call for Goody, she would…

But before Bobolink could pass through the open window, could pursue her niece to the end, another bird flew in through it from the outside.

And it was a fatal swiftness, moving at the speed of death.

The falcon struck Bobolink with one closed talon. Bobolink toppled toward the ground, already dying, but Mak caught it before it touched the floor, and tore its little body in half.

Lanie screamed without breath, her entire body responding. But any wheeze or squeak of hers was drowned out by the Blackbird Bride's wail, a sound so awful the walls seemed to bend toward her.

Cormorant uttered a guttural grunt in answer to his liege lady, more like an enraged pig than man or bird. He gathered himself into his winged form. He was enormous—far larger than the falcon—but he was a water bird, meant to dive for fish, to absorb the sun's rays, to dry his stubby wings in a friendly wind. His flight was choppy, as hobbled as his enchantments. And he was already too late to aid Bobolink.

In hopeless rage, Cormorant the Time-Hobble launched his great bulk against the smallish peregrine. The air filled with high-pitched calls, and squealing grunts, and the beating of wings.

The Blackbird Bride followed the frantic battle with ferocious, silver-eyed attention. She crouched, her body bent forward, her hand still clutching Lanie's shoulder, as if to keep her down.

But Lanie, curled motionless on the floor, was not going anywhere. She herself could not watch the fight; she was done for. Echo wounds had taken control over her body; she could think of nothing else. The crushing weight of Bran Fiakhna's touch, the force of the falcon's first blow, Bobolink's vivisection, had felled her.

Lanie wrapped herself in agony around her own belly, where the largest of her echo wounds was spurting blood. Her skull crackled with each blow and peck above her; her vision snapped. Was she scored to the spine? Were her innards spilling out? Would she knit again when all this was ended?

Would—it—*never*—end?

Her body revolted. It began inching itself free from the Blackbird Bride's grip, dragging her with it across the floor.

The Blackbird Bride let her go. She was distracted; Cormorant had just sustained a deep wound in the shoulder.

Lanie squirmed, writhed, moved.

A little more...

A few more inches...

...just a foot or so closer until she came to the sundered carcass of Bobolink the Concealer.

One arm still clutching her belly, Lanie stretched out her other, reaching, reaching, grasping for the thing she needed.

And... there.

She slid the top half of the dead bird nearer to her, trying not to breathe too deeply for fear of vomiting up everything—small intestines included—and then, she opened her left palm on its slack beak.

Blood sprang bright to the cut, dripped over the wizard-gray skin of her left palm. She smeared her blood and the torn rags of her flesh over the black and white and yellow feathers. Then she scooped the dead thing close to her lips as it started to glow blue.

In a voice too low for the living to hear, Lanie sang the first brightdark notes of the Maranathasseth Anthem over the corpse.

If the Lahnessthanessar was the Undreaming, the oldest song but one, then—Goody had taught her—the Maranathasseth Anthem was the Undreaming's older sister—the Dreamcalling. The awakening. Goody had taught it to her only a few years back. Not only did it help her focus her powers, but whenever she sang the Dreamcalling spellsong, the results of her death magic made for stronger ectenica and sounder revenants. It was also the final secret ingredient in stabilizing Lanie's orblins; she'd sung it over the spheres as she kneaded her blood into the bone-dusted clay, sung it as she baked the clay till it was hard, and again when she licked the spheres to life.

Now Bobolink's top half twitched in her hands.

In response, the Blackbird Bride twitched too, her attention pulled away from the fight in the air to Lanie—on the floor, but no longer at her feet. Her beautiful gray face broke into a smile of such astonishing warmth that Lanie grew giddy. She only just stopped herself from offering Bran Fiakhna the severed corpse wrapped in her best hair ribbon.

Before she could recover from that smile, Bran Fiakhna was crouching beside her. This time, she kept her hands to herself, but her silver eyes were a caress.

"Beloved Condor! If we sewed Bobolink's two parts back together"—her voice eager, pleading—"and you, in your kindness, endowed her accident with the gift of your bespelled blood... would our beautiful one live again?"

"No," said Lanie, then changed her mind: "Well, yes. Sort of. But not for long."

Her fear was vanishing as her concentration split. One part of her voice, so deep it was inaudible—a sound not even the Blackbird Bride could hear—kept up the core-cracking line of the Maranathasseth Anthem. Her deep voice was singing the bird undead and undead. But she could not sing it alive again.

At the same time as her deep voice sang, her other, regular, talking voice added, "It's not life. Not really. Not like it was. The undead are not alive again. They are only the dead dreaming. Death magic grants only the third of the three states, and though it is the strongest, it is also the least stable."

Bran Fiakhna humbly bowed her head. "Yes. You must teach us. We see that you are holy. We see that you are learned, and peerless, and perfect beyond compare. We have never met your like. You, necromancer. Rarest of wizards. Rarest of birds."

Even now, covered with blood and sprawled before her sister's deathbed, Lanie was not immune to flattery. Who could grovel in the presence of such a woman and not want to be worthy of her?

"To do what you want," Lanie explained, like she would have done to Canon Lir, or to anybody who, unlike Datu and Nita, showed the slightest interest, "I would have to bind the substance back to its accident in such a way that each would sustain the other. Ectenica consumes the material it feeds on; it's like fire and kindling that way. For what you want me to do, I'd need panthauma—and a great deal of it, to reverse or repair this amount of damage, and make the entity functional again."

"You would need your surge," Bran Fiakhna murmured. "You would need a high holy fire feast."

"Yes," Lanie agreed. "But I don't think we can preserve Bobolink's accident till then. Not in the state she's in now. Any moment, she's going to sludge off to ash. That's always what happens with my ectenica. But not," she added, "before it does what I ask."

"And what is it," breathed the Blackbird Bride, her colorless eyes brilliant with calamitous curiosity, "that you ask?"

"*This!*"

Taking the bloody, blue-glowing ectenica in both her bloody, blue-glowing hands, she gave the thing a vicious twist.

"Go home!" Lanie commanded it. "Take them with you!" And she smashed the halved carcass to the floor.

The bird burst into runes. Slashes of scarlet, smears of viscera, a bit of beak, shattered plumes, all drifted to the floor. But not at random. The blue glow crawled from Lanie's hands out into the pattern on the tiles. Flaming veins of lapis lazuli spread throughout the room. The runes surrounded the other half of the small bird's corpse, and then the Blackbird Bride, and then, last, reached up into the air for Cormorant the Time-Hobble, where he yet grappled with Mak.

Lanie slammed her still-bleeding left hand upon the runes on the floor.

Bran Fiakhna, along with her last remaining consort of the original Parliament of Rooks, the few scraps left of Bobolink, and the glowing blue runes...

Vanished.

CHAPTER SEVENTEEN

Falcon Defender

In the stillness and emptiness of the room, the carnage on the bed was the stillest. The falcon screamed, flying in a tight loop around Nita's corpse.

Lanie pushed herself to her feet and approached the bed. Her body was quieting, her echo-wounds subsiding. Soon only the memory of being struck down, twice torn open and practically bleeding out, would remain. She was woozy; she'd have to remember to eat and drink to replenish her blood. Broth. Goody's cookies. Dark, leafy greens...

She avoided looking at Nita's face.

Gently, trying to touch it as little as possible, Lanie slid the silver bracer from her sister's stiffening arm. She checked to make sure the falcon had alighted somewhere—ah! There he was, perched on one of the bed's four titanwood posters, glaring at her—and balanced the Bryddongard in her right palm.

Her affinity for the dead, doubly sensitized at the moment, buzzed through her fingers. She could see—or maybe smell?—an unfamiliar ghost in the bracer. A partial one, anyway. A woman, smiling like a strawberry, expressive brown eyes rolling, brown hands drawing pictures in the air to emphasize the essence of whatever she was trying to convey. Gyrlady Gelethai—or the few scraps remaining of her substance, the soul-stuff she had entwined with Mak's own magic, when they had both bound themselves to the Bryddongard in sacred ritual.

Something of *Nita* was still in there as well: not so much a ghost as a dark vein of suppuration corrupting the ritual, invading the memory. The Bryddongard was a spell gone bad, like a limb marked by sepsis, needing severing.

Scraping a sour tongue over her teeth, Lanie pressed her cut left palm over the bracer and whispered, "*Bryddon Bekkunnon Ne'hammanu.*"

She felt the exact moment when a small part of herself—her death magic, her own substance, borne on her blood—slipped into the bracer as well. Getting crowded in there. Lanie could almost see Gelethai's reproachful look, Nita's dead black scowl. Then—both were gone. Flashed past. Passed right through her. Two ghosts, using her body as a doorway, stretching and bulging Lanie in ways she did not want to stretch or bulge, and she, disoriented by the silver dazzle, an ill fit for three. She wanted to hurl the Bryddongard away from herself, shake her skin free of its temporary occupation, but she could not—not while the spell was at work.

In the midst of this, the peregrine falcon launched himself from the carved poster and landed lightly on the floor on naked human feet.

Finally.

Lanie dropped the Bryddongard on the bed like it burned her. She turned her face to the wall as Mak began a desultory search for clothes.

Too soon, he was standing before her again. Trousers barely fastened, shirt hanging loose, Mak crowded in close, inserting himself between her and the wall, and staring into her face so intently that Lanie stumbled back.

Snatching up the Bryddongard, she held it out to him, as far from her own body as she could manage. "Take it! I don't want it! Don't you know that by now?"

Mak looked like he wanted to tear the bracer and her arm apart. His hands clenched against the action, but his intensity did not abate.

In Lirian, the words like hated weeds growing through his tongue, he said, "I must ask you to do something for me." His fists knotted tighter, knuckles gleaming white against his tawny skin. "Please."

Lanie almost cried, "Anything—just back off!" but bit her tongue and waited.

Mak took a deep breath. "The Judicial Colloquium forbids the gyrgardon from taking the Bryddongard for our own. I do not know if it would destroy me to try. But you are god-blessed, a scholar in your field, not unfamiliar with the structures of sothaín. Sothaín teaches us that the gods are friends to each other, family, twelve braided to make one—like the months who work together to make the year. If you ask"—he licked his lips—"ask Doédenna to intercede with Amahirra Mirage-Shaper and Wykkyrri Who Is Ten Thousand Beasts, whose magics bless the Bryddongard, ask that They make an exception in my case, I believe They will listen."

"You *believe?*" Lanie's voice broke, panicked. "I don't—I don't talk to Saint Death like that. I just, She doesn't... Mak, I only saw Her once!" she burst out. "I'm not even sure She's *real!*"

"What you do is real. Am I not standing here today," Mak demanded sternly, "and all because of your work? This"—he nodded at the Bryddongard—"is real. *I* am real. I am here. And I am asking you... I am *begging* this boon of you, aunt-of-my-daughter."

Aunt-of-my-daughter, Lanie thought dazedly, is an improvement over *sister-of-mine-enemy*.

...but his enemy is dead now, and the living child is the only bond between us.

A similar thought seemed to occur to Mak, for he shook his head so hard that Lanie fancied embers flew from his flaming hair.

"Please," he said again. "Try."

Lips pressed together, Lanie slid the silver bracer over his waiting right arm. She tightened knots and buckled clasps until it fit snugly. Her right hand shook and her left hand stung, as if the thing were made of hornets and nettles, not silver and leather, and then she asked, "Secure?"

Mak nodded tersely. He was sweating, a deep rift between his brows.

"You'd tell me if it's too tight?"

He shook his head and gasped, "Not tight!"

Lanie sighed. Whatever sensations he was experiencing, he wasn't about to tell her. Frowning, she took the bracer—and his arm—between her hands. Right hand on the bottom, left hand on top. The silver traceries warmed to her touch. No, not just *warm*. The silver was beginning to run, gleaming, along the leather. Threads of smoking liquid...

Mak made a noise like a falcon.

Lanie pressed her left hand, with its blood-smeared cut, hard over the fluid tracings. Instantly, she felt the Bryddongard buzz with recognition. She heard the sizzling of flesh but felt no pain—that was all for Mak. She sensed no ghosts this time, no internal spell-rot, no bulbous possession of her body. Just herself and this raw, deep, alien magic. And Mak, somewhere, suffering at the bottom of it.

"Saint Death," she said aloud, "it's me."

And up the Bryddongard blazed.

Her vision whited out: Mak, a mere silhouette before her. It was as if she and he stood at the center of a wide, white circle. Just beyond it, she knew—she knew!—*someone* was listening.

Lanie cleared her throat. "We've met before, Doédenna. Over this same man, in fact. Remember? I... I borrowed him back from You that day. Here he stands, a gyrgardi of Quadiíb, without a gyrlady. He has been"—she drew in a breath, remembering the Blackbird Bride's phrasing—"most grievously treated. My family has taken everything from him. I would give him this one thing back: power over his own Bryddongard, that it not be used against him again. Will You intercede on our behalf and ask the other gods to grant this?"

When the murmuring sprang up all around her, Lanie realized it was not just *one* entity standing outside the light, listening to her, but several. Had Amahirra and Wykkyrri, then, joined Doédenna for the intercession? Were there more? Perhaps as many as *twelve?* Lanie could not hear the details of the debate (if there was a debate), nor rightly know the moment when the murmuring voices reached some accord (if there was an accord). All her mortal mind could perceive was the white light shrinking suddenly down from an infinite circle to a nimbus containing only Mak's bracer-encased arm.

The Bryddongard was rapidly cooling under her palm. Then, like the white light, it too began to shrink. It tightened on Mak's forearm until he cried out, nearly jerking away from Lanie's grasp. Grimly she held on to him, digging fingers and heels in, watching the bracer as it sank into his flesh and fused with it. As it became nothing but a few faint silver traces etched upon his skin, like a tattoo tapped out in metal instead of ink. These lines caught the light as she released his arm.

Mak and Lanie each fell back a step, he against the wall, she towards the bed. The backs of her thighs brushed the mattress, but she managed to regain her balance right before collapsing on Nita's corpse.

Mak's left hand gripped his right arm. His eyes met hers, wide. "The power of the Bryddongard is still active!"

Lanie asked nervously, "That's... good, right?"

"I... I do not know. I would call it an abomination"—he shook his head—"but that the gods allowed—"

The door slammed open, and Datu charged in, black-bladed knife in hand. Goody Graves followed on her heels, wheeling the demi-culverin in before her. The long bronze barrel swiveled, seeking a target. The mouth of the bore gaped, cold as the void of space. Goody wore two bandoliers, each hung with round shot iron projectiles as big as melons. They did not even drag her shoulders down, though her step seemed heavier than usual.

"Where is she?" Datu glared about the room. She looked so like her father in his falcon form: except for the death-ash-chill-pale of her face, too like Nita's as she lay exsanguinated. "Where is the Blackbird Bride?"

For a brief, bleak moment, Lanie wondered if the child had perished out on the ivy after all, if it was her ghost who wielded that little black knife now.

But no, no—Datu was too much a thunderstorm, alive and crackling, moving through the room, wrenching aside curtains, scanning under sofas—even flinging open the wardrobe and climbing inside to search it. She ignored her father, her aunt. Murderous purpose rumbled off her body so seismically that Lanie felt as if she were standing on the cul-de-sac end of a bull stampede.

Finding nothing under the bed, Datu scrambled to her feet and advanced upon the mattress itself, intent on flinging back the covers and investigating what lay beneath. She saw her mother. Stopped.

The falcon fierceness left her. She slumped, grayed. Turning her head slightly, but not meeting her aunt's eyes, Datu asked, "Can you raise her?"

It was just that humble, hopeful tone the Blackbird Bride had used, right before Lanie had banished her back to Rook.

Carefully, so carefully, Lanie replied, "It's not a Fire Feast, Datu."

"We could put her on ice till Midsummer."

"She wouldn't keep."

"We could try."

"We could. But even if we did, and I used my surge to—to resurrect her... She wouldn't be the same. Not your mumyu. Only a revenant, with some of your mumyu's memories."

Datu was silent. Lanie tried breathing through her mouth to avoid the metallic, musty tang of blood and feathers that clung to the insides of her nostrils. Even so, there was a slight, sweet aftertaste on her tongue, a hint of salt: Bran Fiakhna. Jasmine, amber, and deep dark piles of midnight-blue velvet...

But she must *not* chase that lingering trail, lest she enthrall herself right out another window and all the way to Rookery Court. Which would mean, of course, abandoning Datu, Goody, Canon Lir, Stones Manor—everything—and for what? To be one of a pack of hounds bound to her mistress's scent? To be one ragged bird in a Parliament...

Condor, we shall call you. King Consort...

"I must exact vengeance." Datu was dreary, matter-of-fact. "I must storm Rookery Court and bring down the Blackbird Bride." She turned away from the bed and started for the door. "I must go now."

Arms outspread, Lanie leapt into her path. "Sacred Datura Stones! You will do no such thing!"

Datu's grip on her knife changed. "You cannot stop me, Auntie Lanie."

Lanie advanced another step. "Watch me."

But Datu flipped the knife, and held it against her own neck, screaming, "*You cannot stop me!*"

Lanie stopped breathing. Stopped everything.

Other than those hellish months of teething, and a few bouts of colic, as an infant Datu had been on the whole a calm, calculating child. What she was not, was a liar. She was not given to histrionics or hysterics. She wanted what she wanted and meant what she said. If she could not get what she wanted by demanding it as her due, she would simply, methodically, go about plotting how to acquire it for herself once your back was turned.

It was never tantrums you had to look out for with Datu. It was those sudden, prolonged silences. But that *scream*...

Datu meant to cut herself. Perhaps not deeply enough to do lasting harm. But deeply enough to open an echo-wound in her aunt's throat? Debilitate Lanie long enough to allow Datu to make good her escape? Certainly.

Though where Datu thought she would go, or how she thought she might get there, alone, Lanie did not know.

That didn't matter right now. Right now, the knife was at her niece's throat, and there was a threadbare line between *deep enough* and *too deep*.

Lanie let out her pent-up exhalation. Sought stillness in breath, sothaín. She stepped aside, allowing Datu to hurtle past her, toward the door, toward Rook, toward vengeance and death.

And right into her father's waiting embrace.

Mak disarmed his daughter with gentle agility, tossing the knife into one corner of the room and scooping her up.

Crushing her close, rocking her like a baby, he crooned in Quadic, "Be still, my plumula, and strive to breathe." He held her head to his shoulder as he used to do when she was tiny, no more than a girl-bouquet herself, a gathering of tender petals. "Or weep, if thou wilt weep, and cling to me."

Datu seemed to yield. Perhaps her lip even trembled.

Lanie did not dare to move. This was Sacred Datura Stones at her most dangerous. She braced herself instead, ready for any outrageous thing, and was therefore not surprised when her niece issued her next command:

"Graves, remove Didyi from my person. Do not let him touch me again."

CHAPTER EIGHTEEN

Retreat

A Stones commanded her: the ancient enchantment undergirding her undeath compelled Goody Graves to obey.

She set down the handspike of the demi-culverin and, as easily as he had taken Datu's knife, plucked Mak away from his daughter. He tried to knock her boulderish arm aside. It would not be knocked. He lunged sideways, grabbing for Datu. Goody took him by the collar of his shirt and threw him across the room.

Lanie flinched for impact, but Goody's aim was unerring. Mak landed softly, at the bottom of the mattress, hardly disturbing Nita's corpse. Rolling off the bed, he shook himself out, and started purposefully across the room. Lanie moved to block him. He seized her to put her aside.

She seized him right back, hissing, "Be still!"

Mak's whole body tensed. She had not voluntarily touched him since the day he had tried to kill himself in Stones Gallery.

Lanie lowered her voice even further. "Goody will tear you to pieces if Datu commands it."

"Then counter-command her!"

"I do not command her! I never will. *I will not do that.*"

The skepticism on his face pierced her more deeply than any of her echo-wounds. Her cheeks burned with shame and rage; her eyes stung unexpectedly. Turning her head, she wiped her nose on her shoulder, then bumped her spectacles back into place.

"Look, Mak. Datu's a Stones—"

"She's a little girl—"

"Right now, she's more Stones than girl. We have to treat her like one."

His jaw was clenched so tightly she feared it would shatter. "Then do thy utmost, scion of thy house," he whispered, and they released each other, both still vibrating with tension, to turn and face Datu.

Empty hands held out, palms up, Lanie assumed an attitude of supplication—the eighth attitude of the fifth sothaín set: 'Worshippers come kneeling to the tree roots.'

Datu glared coldly down at her. While Lanie and Mak had been busy whispering at each other, she had scaled Goody Graves like a mountainside. Now, she sat astride her shoulders, proud as a gyrlady hosting lessons from her golden howdah, while below her, a rumbling herd of elephants carried the Traveling Palaces on their circuits across Higher Quadiíb.

"Well, Auntie Lanie?" she asked. "Are you with me?"

Lanie cleared her throat. She knew she must proceed with extreme caution and cunning. The next few minutes would be a delicate business, calling for subtlety of speech, and a voice of ultimate authority—which would definitely be undermined by crackling, breaking, or squeaking. And Lanie's throat, smoked raw from this endless day, was unreliable at best.

"Have you ever heard, Sacred Datura," she began, "that old adage about revenge?" When Datu said nothing, Lanie recited: "'Vengeance is a bread best served stale.' Um—the better to choke your enemies with when you force it down their throats, I expect."

Datu's expression did not change, but her head did tilt slightly to the left. Lanie advanced. Just half a step. Palms up and open. She continued speaking, softly, Stones to Stones. Utterly reasonable. Utterly alien to someone like Mak, who could not understand that this was no occasion for soft Quadoni parenting.

"The Blackbird Bride is a fearsome enemy," she said, with utter sincerity. "She has a full Parliament at her command. And an army of lesser wizards begging for the scraps from her table. She is a foe full worthy of our… our *considered* strategy of retaliation. This will take time and study. I must… must seek out"—a vision of Grandpa Rad, swollen with surge and self-importance—"ectenical communication with the most vindictive of spirits, and compel them to mentor me in all the conceits of vengeance."

Vengeance was something Datu could understand, from a lifetime of Nita's stories. But Lanie wasn't really after revenge. All she wanted was power enough to stop the Blackbird Bride from hurting—from murdering—Datu. She cleared her throat again.

"*You*," she adjured her niece, "must practice the exercises and drills your mumyu taught you. You must learn every weapon, make *yourself* into a weapon. I, in turn, must learn to awaken an army of the undead."

If an army of the undead was what it took to stop Bran Fiakhna, so be it. No matter that she felt Mak's gaze boring into the back of her skull, no doubt promising himself that she would march with her niece at the head of an undead army over his cold, blue corpse.

"And when we are ready, Sacred Datura," she finished, "and only then!—we will march on Rook together!"

That, of course, was the lie, buried in all the truth.

Datu bought it. She had been hard-eyed up to this point, but the longer Lanie spoke, the more her look of stony disfavor ran molten from the fervor of the vision. Lanie dared her next step forward.

"So. Are *you* with *me*, Sacred Datura?"

"One year, Auntie Lanie." Datu's reply was clipped and fast. "Then we will march on Rook."

Ah. Lanie recognized this. The bargaining stage. This she could deal with. She advanced another step.

"It will take me two years at least to learn what I must. Besides—you'll barely be seven in a year."

"The seventh god is Engoloth," her niece retorted. "Seven is a good year to go to war."

Lanie countered, "Well, you'll still be seven when you're seven and a *half*. I promise you, we'll need those extra six months to prepare."

Datu made a few calculations in her head. She had been born just before Midwinter; her half-birthday fell in the summer months.

At last, she nodded. "That will be a good time to travel," she said. "We will not need to pack our coats."

Datu hated wearing coats.

Lanie exaggerated a sigh, and forced her shoulders to relax in a conciliatory shrug. That was hard to do with Mak behind her, steaming with rage at what he liked to call Lanie's 'utterly barbaric and incomprehensibly *Lirian* methods of childrearing.' But—thank Saint Death for small favors!—he said nothing.

"We'll both have to work very hard, and be very patient," she cautioned her niece. "It won't be easy."

"I will work hard, Auntie Lanie," Datu said flatly. "Will *you?*"

"I will. If *you* promise to cooperate with us now."

Two more steps forward. A half step beyond that. Lanie stood directly before Goody Graves, peering up into her niece's frowning face.

"You and I are allies in this, Sacred Datura. We need to work together. We need time. We need resources. We need a solid plan. And we *really* need"—Lanie emphasized these last words, the most important she had yet to speak—"to *go*."

"Go?" Datu sat back on Goody's shoulders. Bewildered exhaustion ghosted over her face. "Go where? Why?"

One more half step. There. Touching distance.

Lifting her empty hands, Lanie slowly, slowly, closed her fingers around Datu's small, bare, dirty, scratched-up ankle.

Careful, Miscellaneous Stones, she warned herself. Careful now.

"We have to leave Stones Manor before the blackbirds come back. We have to go somewhere they can't find us."

At this, Datu finally looked at her father, seeking answers in his face. "Where can we go, Didyi?"

Mak, who was still behind Lanie where she could not see him, did not answer.

Lanie waited, until she was sure he wouldn't, then said, "We'll have to go undercover for a while. Sound the retreat—"

Datu's chin lifted. "Retreat? Stoneses do *not* retreat."

Lanie squeezed her ankle again, ever so slightly. "Oh, I beg to differ, Datu. General Ham-Handed Stones himself, War Chief to Moll Brackenwild—Moll the First, that is—made a famous retreat at the Battle of the Poxbarge, when Umrysian mercenaries invaded Liriat Proper."

Datu unbent a bit, sensing a story. Lanie edged her body around so that Goody had to turn with her. This put Datu's back to the display on the bed and kept Mak in Lanie's sights. He was watching her, watching his daughter, lips pressed tightly together.

"Oh, yes," she went on, her gaze flashing back up to Datu's face, "it's in all the histories. The Umi mercs came upriver in war canoes, catching the outer settlements unprepared. To escape slaughter, Ham-Handed and his soldiers hid deep in the Diesmali Woods while the Umrysians dug in outside the city walls. Moll Brackenwild held Castle Ynyssyll for six months while Liriat Proper was under siege. But the mercs knew it was only a matter of time before they starved her out or she surrendered. In this, however, they were wrong. Ham-Handed's warriors—his Direwolves, he called them—nightly stole out of the Diesmali to harry the enemy. They disrupted supply lines, poisoned water supplies, set fire to tents, and such like. Eventually, with winter on the way, the Umrysians slunk home, much reduced. 'Gnawed at the edges,' is how the history books describe them."

Datu's eyes had gone round and solemn, like they always did when she was about to fall asleep. "Direwolves," she murmured. "Gnawed at the edges."

"They were like smoke"—Lanie husked her voice to a whisper—"but with more slink. Shadows moving through the shadows." With more gusto than she felt, she added, "Shadows with *teeth*."

"Retreat," Datu repeated, with considerably less hostility. She looked over her shoulder to Mak for guidance. His face gave nothing away. "Do we go into the woods, Didyi? Like we do when we are hunting?"

When it became obvious that Mak still wasn't going to answer, Lanie did. "No, Sacred Datura. We'll go..." And that was when she knew it herself. "We'll go *beneath* the woods," she said in a stronger voice. "And then beyond it—all the way into the capital city."

Where, she hoped, they would find help and succor.

"How do we do that?" Datu asked, and this time, her exhaustion and bewilderment made her face seem that of a wizened old woman, not a little girl.

"There's a path I know," Lanie explained, sweeping her gaze from Datu's face to include Mak and Goody. "A secret place. It starts in Stones Ossuary, at the bottom of a tomb. And it goes to Liriat Proper."

They all stared at her.

"What?" asked Lanie, suddenly uncomfortable. "It's just a secret passage. A kind of, of old tunnel. No one else knows about it—or if they do, they've been dead for centuries, so they won't tell unless I ask."

"*I* did not know about it, Mizka," Goody said, the basso sound of her voice after so much silence awful and ominous.

Lanie shrugged, not wanting to express how much or how often she had felt the need for a secret all her own, shared with no one else, not even Goody. "I read about it in an old book—years ago. I've only explored the tunnel a little, but it should work for us." she added, trying on a reassuring smile for her audience. It wobbled.

"Underground," Mak said flatly. Lanie braced herself against whatever was coming next. But he followed his terse statement with an abrupt, "Very well."

She started. "Very well?"

"Very well. We will take your tunnel and go to the city." He nodded at her, once and hard. He was still angry, she could tell. But he would stand united with her in this. She breathed a sigh of relief.

That was all Datu had been waiting for. She, too, nodded at Lanie.

"All right, Auntie Lanie. We will go there, into the ground. Goody Graves," she commanded, "you are to allow Didyi to touch me now."

Datu was looking at Mak as she spoke, was already reaching out for him, bending away from Goody's shoulders to be caught in his arms. Mak turned his back on her and opened the door.

"Come," he told them shortly. "There is much to do, and not much time."

CHAPTER NINETEEN

Door in the Bones

Dustday 8th
Month of Broods, 421 Founding Era
74 days till Summer Solstice

STONES OSSUARY, WHERE Lanie kept her workshop, comprised not just the bones of all the Stoneses who had been buried there since the Founding—a considerable number, but not a dizzying one—but the skeletal remains of upwards of forty thousand anonymous relics. These were the work of Gallowsdance Stones[12], who had, over the course of her lifetime, plundered a veritable amassment of bones from the catacombs beneath Liriat Proper, all for the sole purpose of interior decoration.

Bone mosaics decorated every wall. Stacks of long bones divided the vast underground chamber of the ossuary into a grid of smaller rooms that ordered groups of dead Stoneses by a cataloguing system known only to the late creator. Bouquets of artfully arranged bones flowered eternally from urns at the head of every crypt and cubby. Hanging mobiles of bone and stained glass twisted and turned from the barrel-vaulted ceiling (its arches inset with skulls), resulting in moving sculptures of fantastically finned, winged, spiked, and horned creatures that had never walked any world other than the realm of the imagination.

Both the artistic and criminal careers of Gallowsdance Stones were brought to an end circa 250 FE, when she was dragged in chains before Blood Royal Thirra Brackenwild to stand trial. The entire Magnum Concilium was convened, along with the Synod of Sappocor, for this was a religious as well as a civil matter, being that the crime was magical in nature. There was no question of Gallowsdance's guilt; no sooner had the charges been laid by the Grand Indicter (the desecration and vandalization of graves, and the removal of and tampering with human remains) than

12 Artist, eccentric, and the only necromancer of her line besides Quick Fantastic Stones to be tried for crimes against the dead.

Gallowsdance boastfully confessed to the whole, afterwards inviting her judges out on a day trip to Stones Manor, where she offered to present, as evidence, her masterwork: the ossuary[13].

The only information Gallowsdance never revealed during her trials was the manner in which she had moved forty thousand bones, give or take, in secret across the more than fifteen miles of public road that ran between Liriat Proper and Stones Manor. A conundrum to be sure: Gallowsdance was a notorious recluse, who, to the best of anyone's knowledge, never left her property at all. But on this subject, she kept silent until her execution.

Not, however, beyond it.

No sooner had her great-aunt's body been returned to the family crypts, but the budding young necromancer Marrowcrack Stones, never an admirer of her curmudgeonly predecessor, resurrected Gallowsdance and demanded to be told the secret.

This, the cephalophoric corpse gave up, easily and giddily, before subsiding into sludge. As the winning of the knowledge was vengeance enough for a lifetime of slights and rebuffs, Marrowcrack took it with her to her own grave. But she did leave a single reference to the incident, in code: an obscure passage at the back of one of her journals, shoved in a hollow space between Gallowsdance's recumbent cadaver monument (sans head, lovingly carved in black basalt), and her plinth. Lanie discovered the journal and had decrypted it by age eleven and a half.

"Apparently," she told Datu, Mak, Goody and the ghost of Grandpa Rad as they stopped at the bottom of the stairwell into the hillside ossuary, "she got her revenants to do all the work."

"They carried all the bones in here for her?" Datu asked.

"Oh, yes."

"Across the whole forest?"

"Well," Lanie said, "*beneath* it, anyway. But they had to dig a way for themselves first, you see. It's quite a nice tunnel, really," she assured them, for the seventh or seventeenth time; she'd lost count, "and no one else in the whole world knows about it. Granted, I've never explored it very far, but from what I could tell, the layout is spacious and tidy, no branching corridors or anything, and everything's all nice and"—she glanced at Mak, who'd made a small sound at the back of his throat—"shored up. It's even paved."

"Saint Death groans, girlie," Grandpa Rad complained from his padlock on high. "How you do natter on."

Lanie did not answer. She considered speaking to the dead in front of the

---

13 One municipal policy resulting from the Gallowsdance Trials was that the deceased of Liriat Proper were no longer buried in the catacombs, but cremated in the radiant ovens of the High Temple of Sappacor. Thus began a whole new fashion in funerary rites—extant to this day. While Liriat Proper would always revere its rare necromancers, its governing bodies thought it wisest to limit their potential resources.

living, who could not participate, rude. And Nita, at any rate, had deemed that rudeness worthy of punishment.

But she would not think of Nita. Not right now.

Datu gazed around at the ossuary from under her dark blue hood, wary but not without interest. She'd never been allowed to play down here, and since Lanie was rarely in her workshop except for when Datu was safely tucked in bed, she hadn't had occasion to come looking for her aunt as an excuse to poke around. She kept close as Lanie led them further in, constantly checking over her shoulder for her father, who did not make eye contact with her. To Lanie's relief, Datu didn't seem frightened or panicky. Unlike Mak.

He was pale as candle wax. As soon as they had descended the stairs, his eyes had gone glassy and strange, like the empty jeweled eyes of an effigy. But he did not argue, nor ask to turn back. Lanie just hoped that whatever fear had seized him would not overcome his reason halfway through their journey, when they were too far from any egress to allow him escape.

That, too, did not bear thinking on. No need to borrow another burden for her backpack. Lanie felt like she was carrying, in addition to all her worldly possessions, several anvils, her sister's corpse, and worse—the weight of Goody's disapproval.

Datu walked behind her aunt, hunched beneath a knapsack stuffed with every precious thing she'd been allowed to take with her. Her steps dragged; she wanted to walk beside her father, who was walking behind her, but he wheeled a barrow before him, full of food, bedding, and cooking utensils, and kept its length between them at all times. Lanie, in addition to her own pack, humped a large satchel of books, her syringe kit, and her sack of orblins. Goody took up the rear, bearing—at Lanie's behest—the greatest burden of them all: the Sarcophagus of Souls. It bent her almost in half.

Breath hitching with guilt, Lanie led them deeper into the ossuary, glad to be at the front of the procession and not at the back with Goody.

Goody was not happy with her—had never been *more* unhappy with her—but Lanie couldn't help that. The sarcophagus *had* to travel with them. She could no more leave it behind than she could leave Goody: not because of any affection she harbored for Grandpa Rad, but because he was the only one with the knowledge she now desperately needed: how to keep Datu safe from the Blackbird Bride. And, what was more—how to resist Bran Fiakhna's sensationally seductive powers of fascination.

But to remember those powers was to be seduced by them. Lanie shut the door on the smell of jasmine, of wet velvet, of the sea, the sea, and turning the key, shook herself free of those thoughts.

"Datu—look up," she said. "You don't want to miss it."

Datu obeyed, and even she—stoic as Engoloth on the eve of battle—gasped.

The bone chandelier of Stones Ossuary was the centerpiece of Gallowsdance's masterwork. With its eight branching arms festooned in femurs, its central column armored in dozens of wedge-shaped sacra—each evenly speckled with foramina like eight tiny windows—with its flat scapular plates at the end of each arm forming flower-like bases for the skully candle cups, and the chains all hung with pelvic girdles, and the delicate vertebra beading the bowl and finial, the chandelier was as elaborate as an ogress in a wedding dress. But instead of the usual smother of lace, pearls, veil, train, and the pure white blossoms adorning any blushing bride, this ogress instead dripped candle wax.

Lanie had often thought, in fact, that one might carve an entire second chandelier out of the wax the first had produced, and which hung like stalactites from the structure, distorting and metastasizing it.

"I used to think that thing was sentient," she confided to her niece. "That it grew bony eyeballs whenever my back was turned, and stuck waxy tongues out at me. Plus, it's a real pain to light."

"You might have brought a lamp in with you," Mak observed under his breath.

She glanced back at him, almost glad the chandelier had irritated him out of his silence. "I didn't think of it."

"No," he sighed. "Of course you did not."

Lanie stepped back, directing the others to go on before her, and adjuring them to sidestep the chandelier's monstrous offspring: a veritable mound of waxen stalagmites reaching pallid fingers up to its parent. The mound had grown in splendor and immensity with each passing century, until it rivaled the chandelier for magnificence. Many necromancers before Lanie had carved their cerographs onto its surface, or hidden small treasures to be encoffined forever by the drippings from above. She herself had buried the headless sock body of her favorite stuffed toy, Hoppy Bunny, somewhere near the top. Nita had kept Hoppy Bunny's head for a trophy, but had likely grown bored with it. Who knew where it was now? Probably disintegrating in a Quadoni ditch somewhere along the Caravan School road.

Goody lumbered by last, bearing the Sarcophagus of Souls like a basalt mausoleum upon her back.

Lanie paused before following Goody. She wanted to bid the waxen monster on the floor farewell. It saddened her to think that it would grow no taller. Who would light candles for the dead (or work into the small hours of the night by eerie chandelier light, until their eyeballs were twitching and they were more yawn than person) once she was gone? No one. There was no one left.

But enough of that. No time for grief. No time for wrath. Or panic. Or consideration. Only for action.

She turned her back on the chandelier, which had lit her midnight work for more than a decade, and locked it away in memory like she'd done everything else. The Blackbird Bride. The state bedchamber, where Nita lay beneath a length of clean linen. Everything she had seen and done over the last few days; she would deal with them later.

At the far end of the ossuary, the others awaited her in front of a great bone mosaic that stood out in relief from the plain stone wall. It depicted Doédenna, god of Death, in her cowl and cloak of bone that enveloped and enhaloed her. The cloak spilled out from the mosaic wall onto the surrounding walls in a pattern that had no seeming beginning or end. In her pale gray hands—made up of hundreds of actual carpi, metacarpi, and phalanges—Saint Death cradled, instead of her usual attribute of a bird, a small brass plaque, upon which a short verse was engraved:

I came to these wilds when I was ten
To build up a city from wood and fen
Now I am stronger than twenty men
Till Midsummer's Eve, when I die again!
—The Lay of the Undead Child[14]

Stepping forward, Lanie depressed Saint Death's sternum, and the wall with its mosaic swung inward, into darkness.

"Okay, everyone," she said cheerfully. "Ready?"

14 Written by Anonymous, circa O FE. Probably not by an undead child. Probably.

CHAPTER TWENTY

Oaths Underground

"What's going on?" the ghost asked from his padlock. His voice echoed in the darkness, thin and querulous. "Where are we? Where's my plinth?"

He sounded rattled, as if being transported from Stones Manor and then dragged miles and miles underground had somehow enervated him. But Lanie kept silent. She had dropped back from the lead, letting Mak march ahead with their lantern. There was only one direction he could go, after all, and Mak seemed to appreciate having open space in front of him. Datu trudged just behind her father, regarding his back with fixed contemplation. Mak still was not speaking to her.

Lanie lagged her footsteps, slowing to be closer to Goody, even if it meant perforce being closer to Grandpa Rad. She was hoping he would soon sink back into somnolence, or wherever he went when not pestering her.

She squinted over her shoulder, trying to make out Goody's shape. But Goody was invisible in the tunneling dark, doubly invisible beneath the creeping black shadow that perpetually surrounded the Sarcophagus of Souls. All she could see was that shadow's edge: the same sharp blue shine that lit Goody's eyes.

But then, a smaller blue flash caught her attention; Goody had lifted her head to stare at her—a terrible contortion for her bent-back state.

Flushing, Lanie quickened her pace again. Despite her fatigue and the weight of her pack, her guilt propelled her forward so rapidly that she was almost within range of Mak's circle of light when she heard him say to Datu, in Lirian:

"Sacred Datura. We will stop here and rest a while. Put down your pack and please come here before me."

Lanie stopped as if Nita herself had come back from the dead to command her. She could not be sure Mak was aware how near she was, but she knew that he would not want her for this. Dropping back against a wall, far enough away that the lantern light did not touch her, she slid her own pack off her back, and watched as Datu dithered and dug her feet in. Now that the child had the attention she'd been longing for, she—rightly—feared it.

"Sacred Datura. *Now.*"

"Why, Didyi?" Datu's usually husky voice had gone shrill.

Lanie stirred from her slouch, wanting to interfere. The child's fuse was burnt to candlewick-fineness; anything might detonate her. But... Mak had stayed his hand at Stones Manor, had let her try her way with Datu. She owed him this.

"You and I," he told his daughter, "need to discuss what happened yesterday."

"The blackbirds got Mumyu."

"After that," Mak replied, quiet but inexorable. "Come closer. Stand before me."

Stiff-limbed, Datu obeyed. She positively clanked with weapons. Some were her toys, others not. Lanie recognized several selections from the vitrines in Stones Gallery.

When he deemed her near enough, Mak sank to his knees, so that they were looking each other in the face. Datu dropped her gaze to the floor. The silence went on and on.

Finally, Datu broke it. "So, Didyi?"

"So." Softer now, but no less steely, Mak replied in Quadic: "Recall how thou took'st charge of that poor thrall—a woman more deserving of respect than all the Stoneses in their hall of death—and set her strength to smite me back from thee?"

Datu's head sank further as her shoulders rose in a shrug. She did not answer.

Mak went on, "It troubles me, my plumula, to think that thou wouldst harm whom only loves thee best. That thou, enraged, did order me struck down."

He broke rhythm, which the Quadoni only did when driving home a point. "Didst not do so?"

A pause.

"Aye, Didyi," Datu whispered.

Lanie, straining, could barely make out either of them. She glided closer to the lantern's glow, hardly breathing, shamelessly eavesdropping—a skill she'd developed while helping raise Datu.

After a long beat, Mak began again. "I know thy grief is avid, bitter, raw—but wouldst thou lose *two* parents in thine ire? How can I sleep for fear I'll never wake, or turn my back to thee who might lay siege? How can I trust thee now, my flesh and blood—when thou hast broken sacred trust with me?"

He ducked his head, as if listening for a response. He received none.

More sternly, he went on, "Then, dost thou see thy father as thy foe? Speak now, and I will take thee at thy word. If foe, I'll fly as falcon far and wide, keep watch on high and hide me from thine eye. No more thy didyi shall I be, but ghost: unseen but ever watchful at my post."

He broke rhythm again. "Is't thy desire?"

Datu glanced up, stark with terror.

Never, Lanie thought, not even when facing Bran Fiakhna with nothing but a toy crossbow, had she worn such a look.

Mak saw it too—instantly—and Lanie managed to just hold herself back, though her breath ached in her lungs.

He leaned forward, and asked again, perhaps more gently but just as formally, "Is't thy desire, my daughter?"

Datu's head sank again, her red-gold thicket of curls springing up like a veil of thorns. She seemed to have fallen asleep on her feet.

"Is't thy desire, my plumula?" Mak asked a third time, slightly louder now.

Datu didn't even start. Didn't make a noise. Didn't speak a word.

Mak sighed, nodded, straightened. "So be it, then. Thou shalt not see me more."

He stood up, clutching the arm that had absorbed the Bryddongard. The silver traceries caught the low light of the lantern.

The tension stretched. Lanie's nails dug into the palms of her hands. Her eyeballs pulsed; her ears rang; she realized she was not breathing. Then—

"No, Didyi!" Datu squeaked. She flung out her arms to hold him still. Mak stepped back, avoiding her touch.

"No, Didyi, what?" he asked mildly, in Lirian.

His daughter said, "You must not go. You *shall* not go. I forbid you to go!"

"Forbid? Another threat, Datu?"

One look at his face and she answered quickly, "No, no! Not a threat, Didyi!"

"I want your word."

Datu swallowed.

Mak's voice, harsh in its learned Lirian cadence, commanded, "You will *not* attack me or order me attacked. I will not fight you, blood of my blood, my heart's darling. If you want me to stay with you, Sacred Datura, to live with you as family, you will give me your word that we will resolve our differences through speech alone. I will not tolerate violence against my person—or *threat* of violence against my person. Not from you. Never again. Swear it."

Datu's eyes were like two pieces of a broken bottle. "I swear it," she whispered. "I swear it by Mumyu."

Mak's scarred face was grave. He nodded at her. "Very well. Then I also want your word on something else."

"Anything," Datu promised. "Anything, Didyi!"

"No, Sacred Datura. Do not swear a solemn oath empty of meaning.

Listen." He knelt again, and fixed her streaming gaze with his, and said, "All your life, you have seen your aunt with the Elif Doéden. Never have you seen your aunt command or compel her to do her will. If your aunt needs a thing done that only supernatural strength and peerless wisdom might accomplish, she asks the boon courteously, and gives thanks when the task is done. I do not want you, Sacred Datura, to ask the Elif Doéden for any favor lightly. Nor should you interfere with her at all without great need. But if you must, I want your word to do as your aunt does. You must *never* make the Elif Doéden your thrall again."

Datu's eyes were enormous. "But, Didyi... Mumyu—"

"Mumyu is not here," said Mak flatly. "Mumyu made her own choices, and her choices found her out. *We* are here. You and I and your aunt and the Elif Doéden. We are all here together in this place. We are in great danger. We must trust and respect each other. We must treat each other as allies. I want your word."

Datu coughed as if her throat were full of scree. "I give my word."

Mak made a bird of his hands and bowed to his daughter. "Then we have reached an accord, you and I. Now. When we have got to where we are going to, and the Elif Doéden has laid her burden down, what will you say to her?"

"I will say..." A shudder ran through Datu like an earthquake. She said, slowly, as if inventing a new language from the shards left in its wake, "I will say: 'Lady'"—Mak always called Goody Graves 'Lady,' not 'Goody,' or 'Graves,' or even 'Elif Doéden' to her face—"'Lady, an it pleaseth thee, forgive me.'"

Lanie's eyebrows flew up. She could not remember the last time Datu had apologized to anyone.

"Good," said her father. "Now. Walk with me, my plumula, and I will teach you the twelve apologies: starting with 'suriki,' which we use for our small but blundering transgressions, and ending with 'sa,' the most abject."

Datu asked, in a very small voice, "You will not leave me, Didyi?"

Mak answered readily, "I will not leave," and opened his arms.

Datu barreled into them, sobbing so loudly that the whole tunnel seemed to reverberate.

When her father began to croon one of his tender Quadoni lullabies to her, Lanie thought it best to leave them to their reconciliation. She crept back to Goody, who was taking her own rest against a wall. The tunnel was just a few inches shorter than she, so Goody was not able to stand upright. But with the burden of the Sarcophagus of Souls on her back, she could not do so anyway. Now the sarcophagus was resting on its side ten feet away, also propped against the wall, and Goody sat with her face turned away from it as if she could not bear the sight. Instead, she stared far ahead, to the speck of light that was Mak's lantern. Her shoulders braced the wall; she stretched her legs out fully before her. Though not tall, the tunnel was wide enough for a large cart (piled with bones pilfered from the catacombs of Liriat Proper) to be drawn easily through it by two skinny horses[15]. There were still wheel ruts in the dirt floor, though they had been made more than a century and a half before.

Lanie sat across from Goody. Her stomach was a noose with thirteen knots. She swallowed hard.

"Goody…" she began. "Tell me. If Datu asked you to do something—not *commanded* you, mind, just asked—would you be compelled to do it?"

Goody turned her head to stare at her. After a long moment, there was the barest twitch at the bottom left section of her chin, hardly visible in the darkness. But Lanie read it as clearly as if Goody had started jumping up and down, waving her hands, and shaking her head, shouting, "No!" No, Goody would *not* be compelled. And the way she was feeling about the child right now, Goody would in fact be strongly compelled to refuse outright anything Datu might ask her to do.

"But, so, Goody, when *I* asked you," Lanie continued, with a nervous glance at the Sarcophagus of Souls, "to do something that you plainly found revolting, to carry something you'd rather—if I'm reading this right—hack off your hands than touch, you picked it up and did it. Just as if I'd commanded you. You didn't even try to get out of it. Why?"

The steady blue burn of Goody's eyes regarded her. Goody's silence seemed to ask, "Why do you *think*, Mizka?" but she said nothing.

Lanie found herself in full sympathy with her niece, who'd had to endure similar silent treatment from her father all the past day. But she pressed, "Is it because of my death magic?"

That slight chin-movement, but in the opposite direction. A nod.

"So," she continued, "all this time, for all my life, I might as well have been ordering you around, for all the difference it made."

"It made," Goody said out loud, "a difference."

"Then could you have said no to me? If you'd wanted to?"

"No."

Lanie said desperately, bending forward over her knees, "Goody, I need Grandpa Rad. I don't *like* him—sometimes I hate him—but I need him now. I have nothing left. No books. No money. No resources. All I have is what is in my blood and what he can teach me. Surely you understand? Surely you know I'd never ask you to carry… to carry *that*… for any less a reason than life or death?"

Goody said nothing, her unblinking blue eyes betraying not even her feeling of betrayal.

"I'll make it up to you!" Lanie blurted.

---

15 The skinniest. Gallowsdance Stones had resurrected two nags for just that purpose.

Goody closed her eyes at this, and turned her face away again, this time in the direction of the sarcophagus. As if the weight of all those wizard souls, and the wintry shadow that haunted it—even the revolting phantom in the padlock sealing it off against all invaders—were preferable to Lanie's thin excuses and empty promises.

"No, no, Goody, I mean it," Lanie insisted. "I'm not just saying... Look, I *mean* it. Listen"—she set her elbows on her knees—"it's only for now. That's all it can be. Because of that duodecifold-damned contract. Remember? At Midsummer in a few months, all items listed in Sari Scratch's contract as belonging to Stones Manor are forfeit to her—with the exception of exactly one cartload of personal effects. That means that both you and the sarcophagus, by the magic of Lan Satthi, will be transported back to the house, and no power I can draw upon will be able to stop it. But if I, if I..."

Here she faltered, for saying what she meant to out loud seemed so irrevocable and awful, it caught in her throat like a bone and choked her.

But suddenly Goody Graves pushed off the wall, her great bulk moving noiselessly but gracefully, like a cloud falling through a mountain peak, and then she was kneeling in front of Lanie, taking both her hands in hers.

"Say it, Mizka," she said, in a voice so low and intent that Lanie thought her bones might break from the sound.

"If I release you," Lanie whispered, "if I sang the Lahnessthanessar for you before Midsummer's end, then the Scratches could not have you. The Sarcophagus of Souls will pass out of my hands, but no one could touch *you*, Goody. You'd return to the hem of Doédenna's cloak. You'd be free."

Many nights had Lanie lain awake thinking of making Goody this offer. She had been strong enough—necromantically speaking, anyway—to perform the task for several years now. She knew the melody of the Undreaming, as well as its counterpart, the Dreamcalling: the Maranathasseth Anthem. She knew them both so well that she could probably sing them in her sleep, in her deep voice that had nothing to do with her body and everything to do with Doédenna, god of death. But somehow, no matter what Lanie resolved to do before she slept, she would wake equally determined never to speak of it to Goody, to keep her near for as long as she lived, to treat her well, and when Lanie herself was near death, to release her then—but not a moment sooner.

But with every passing surge, Lanie had felt the guilt and wrongness of her own selfish determination eating away at her, felt the weight of Goody's watchful eyes as they followed her with an expression that Lanie knew was not—could not be—hope.

Goody's cold hands enfolded Lanie's—not pressing them, but entombing them, as if promising to keep them safe and quiet for all eternity. Her left hand responded more strongly than her right, tingling, almost burning with the cold.

"You would release me. You would do this, Mizka?"

"Oh, Goody!" Lanie felt sobs enough to rival Datu's rise up in her chest. All around her, the tunnel seemed so much darker, as if it were her entire future: an endless trek underground, alone. "I will! I will!"

And she meant it. She did. Though she did not know how she would endure it.

"Then gladly will I bear this house of death," said Goody in her beautifully antiquated Quadic, which she rarely spoke—even when Lanie asked. Rising and moving toward the loathed sarcophagus, she continued, "And in what time we two have left to us, we'll hold as precious every moment more, say what we must, and lay what ghosts we may—and gather strength to face Midsummer's Day."

With that, she hefted the Sarcophagus of Souls onto her back. Lanie was sure she heard a crack. Something deep and foundational. Her heart thudded as Goody stumbled, but she never made a sound, nor uttered a moan of pain or complaint. Rummaging in the sack she wore across her chest, Lanie came up with a handful of orblins, and licking each one to life, whispered the request, "Add your strength to hers." She pressed the whole handful into Goody's palm.

"Here, Goody," she said. "Pop these in. Chew. Swallow. They'll help."

This, unfortunately, roused the ghost.

"What's that sound?" demanded Grandpa Rad. "Who's chomping on crockery? Racket's loud enough to wake the dead." A pause. "Saint Death grew balls, girlie—where's the ectenica? I can smell it! Not fresh, but... strong. Very strong! What's going on?"

He was still too weak to emerge from his padlock even as an attenuated blue glow. The view from his keyhole, such as it was, might afford him a glimpse of the shored-up dirt ceiling and the topmost dark of the corridor, nothing more, and it drove him to howling that no one would explain any of it. But Lanie had no energy left over to flatter or cajole the ghost of Irradiant Stones. She knew she would have to find a way, at journey's end, to extract the knowledge she needed from him—though she dreaded whatever bargain his malice would inevitably drive her to make. But not right now. Not today.

Goody, meanwhile, ate as Lanie bade her do. With each crunch of her rock-like teeth, she pulverized the orblins, grinding the spheres into their component parts: clay, bone dust, Lanie's dried blood. Blue light leaked from between her lips as the dormant ectenica was released and awakened. Then her gray skin began to shine out in the darkness, the hard surface shot through with lightning branches of blue as fresh ectenica moved through the ossified channels that used to be her circulatory system. Even Goody's hair ran with electric currents, thickening and growing and curling, the tips sparking with energy before sputtering out. Her massive body, bent under the weight of the Sarcophagus of Souls, seemed to swell and broaden, and Goody, silent in her agony, now made a sound of relief as whatever had broken inside her was doubly—trebly—reinforced by Lanie's death magic.

"Better?" Lanie asked.

Goody, to Lanie's astonishment, smiled up at her with her entire face—*beamed* at her—and seemed to hitch the Sarcophagus of Souls to a more comfortable position on her back, as if carrying no more than a basket of eggs. "It is well, Mizka. It is very well."

But Lanie did not think Goody was talking about the effects of the orblins. She tried to smile back.

"I'm glad. Let's catch up to Mak and Datu, shall we? That is, if you're ready."

"I am ready, Mizka."

Lanie flinched. She knew exactly what Goody meant.

Part Three
BLOODLIGHT

Two Days Later

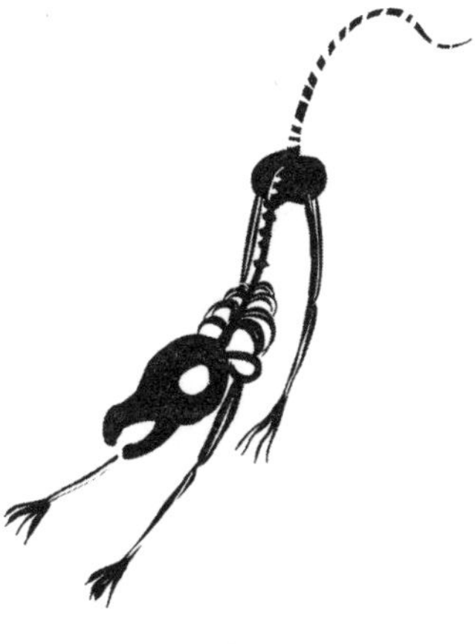

CHAPTER TWENTY-ONE

The High Temple of Sappacor

Flameday 10th
Month of Broods, 421 Founding Era
72 days till Summer Solstice

IN ALL HER twenty-two years, Lanie had mainly kept company with forty thousand skeletons (mostly furniture), a ghost (megalomaniacal), and a revenant housekeeper (seldom garrulous). She had interacted minimally with family members, seldom received visitors, and only upon the arrival of her infant niece six years ago did she begin associating daily with a living being whose presence (unlike Nita's) wasn't constantly insulting her body with echo-wounds, and who (unlike Mak) didn't wish her bricked up in a tomb with the rest of her ancestors. She had done fairly well—or thought she had—with human interaction, such as she'd always known it.

And so, Lanie had not expected her first day abroad—alone—in a bustling, dizzying, living city to all but vanquish her.

Several times she almost turned back from her undertaking. Lanie was not afraid of getting lost; that was perhaps the only thing about the capital city that did not terrify her. But her neck was sore from flinching at the bold regard of strangers. Her throat ached from choking down the odors of human ordure and the abattoir stench of Butcher's Circle and Fishmonger's Alley. Her body felt like it was slipping a bit more sideways every time she jumped at the cheerful cries of "Hoozzaplo[16]!"

But Lanie would not give Mak the satisfaction of a debasing surrender. He'd doubted—volubly, at length—her ability to find her way to the temple from their new home. (He'd not called it "home," of course. He'd used several very rude words, offending Lanie greatly, as the lodgings she'd procured for them were sound, snug, and inconspicuous, besides boasting a wide range of secret routes that they might take whenever they

16 "Hoods up below." A courtesy call to passersby when one is about to empty one's chamberpot out of one's window and into the open gutters.

wished to venture out unheard and unseen.) He'd protested Lanie's going out alone, was not altogether sure that her expedition was necessary or safe, and when she'd finally stormed out anyway, had flung predictions of such dire outcomes at her retreating back that she was *determined* to prove him wrong.

But the whole journey took several hours longer than she'd optimistically projected. Not because the path wasn't *clear* to her. It was. Always. If home—no matter what *Mak* called it—was a beacon at her back, then her destination was a twinkling, far-off star beckoning her onward. If home was a lusty-voiced chamber choir singing praises to Doédenna, then her destination was a faint but alluring solo, like one of Aganath's merrows, green-skinned and salt-eyed, singing sailors to their drowning deaths. If home was a giant web, then Lanie's destination lay at the other end of a single silken thread, and all she had to do was travel from web to thread to terminus: a bright-eyed spider, never faltering, connected to both.

Only, the thing was, as plain as her path might be to *Lanie*, it was *not* plain to this metastasized, tortuous, multi-level city she'd plunged herself into that she might require sidewalks—or boardwalks—or even throughways!—to get where she needed to go. Her route was therefore circuitous. Oh, it was one thing to *read* about the founding of Liriat Proper, to hear Goody's antiphonies and Grandpa Rad's meandering monologues. But it was another thing, Lanie discovered, to navigate the reality.

Four hundred years ago, a caravan of Quadoni exiles led by Ynyssyll Brackenwild and Quick Fantastic Stones emerged from a titanwood wilderness to this fertile stretch of land embraced by two rivers. The exiles then used their chaotic, newfound sorcery to call up a city from out of the very bedrock—smiting the naked granite with Sappacor's flames, forging it with Kantu's winds, and wearing it smooth with Aganath's waters—until the city took the shape of their desire: twelve concentric walls as thick as they were high, divided by twelve great boulevards shaped like a twelve-spoked wheel, and all of that raw rock honeycombed into living quarters, warehouses, shops, stables, and the like.

That was the basic plan. The skeletal structure. Then came the massive undertaking of laying the flesh of a functional city atop it. It was the work of years. Decades. Even as the original builders dropped dead from exhaustion and exposure and sickness, Quick Fantastic Stones raised them up again by the grace of Doédenna, and drove her revenants, obedient and inexhaustible, on and on, until—at last!—Ynyssyll Brackenwild had her seat of power: Liriat Proper. City of Bloodlight. City of Sorcery. Built on the backs of the living and the undead.

Liriat Proper today was all that, plus an additional four centuries of unplanned sprawl. Due to construction scaffolding, provisional bridges, pull rope elevators, and other towering structures that teetered above the original stone walls, the lowest streets never saw a dram of daylight.

Instead, they were lit by enormous red lamps set at intervals in the thick walls of the substructure. Easy, therefore, for strangers to lose their way, to disappear into the warren and, by some mischance or other, never emerge again.

But though a stranger, Lanie had something far better than a map to her name. She needed no compass, no native guide—for she still had the reliquary that Canon Lir had given her when she was fifteen.

It sang to her now.

It sang the bones of Queen Ynyssyll Brackenwild, which Lanie had left behind at the start of her journey. Those marvelous old bones, arrayed in the decay of glittering grave clothes, and tucked inside a splendid tomb chest, rested in the bottommost chamber of an obscure, antique chapel to Saint Death, hidden in a patch of wild parkland at the foot of Moll's Kopje.

Doédenna's secret chapel (which Lanie thought of as her new home, whatever *Mak* wanted to call it) was the nucleus of the network of catacombs running beneath the city. The catacombs went on for miles and miles, their corridors shaped like a twelve-pointed star, mirroring the original twelve boulevards above them.

Like Castle Ynyssyll, which stood atop Moll's Kopje at the epicenter of the twelve concentric circles it ruled over, Saint Death's forgotten chapel stood as sentinel over the invisible, gentle city of the dead. It was set directly above the Founding Queen's tomb, which was accessible by a small stair that plunged deeply into the underground from the inner sanctum of the chapel. But there was another, secret tunnel that led to that tomb as well: that of Gallowsdance Stones.

That second tunnel had led the refugees from their starting point at Stones Ossuary right to Queen Ynyssyll's old, splendid bones—a complete set, but for the two missing halluces of right foot and left.

The left hallux in Lanie's pendant reliquary sang the bones of the Founding Queen, but it also sang out, in longing and in love, to its missing twin. All Lanie had to do was follow that song, out of the underground, through the catacombs, and up into the city, to find that which she sought.

Her sweaty palm slipped against smooth black walnut and hammered copper. Her fingers cramped from clutching it close. But Lanie never loosened her grip, and the reliquary led her through arcades and esplanades, up stairways, down ramps, across boulevards throttled with stuttering traffic, and occasionally into a cul-de-sac, where the song's mischievous chiming seemed to indicate a desire that Lanie take the Z axis as the shortest route to her destination. Purposefully ignoring this advice, Lanie would just backtrack to some other path that did not require flight, and—eventually—the reliquary adjusted to her decision, and nudged her along the next-best of the remaining choices. Repeat, readjust, repeat, until—eventually—it guided her to the High Temple of Sappacor.

The temple took up three quarters of Fifth Circle. A red-lacquered colonnade ran the length of it, girded in trained ivy of a brilliant rust-orange stem and yellow leaf. The temple's façade was fashioned out of a garnet-veined red granite, and the roof soared higher than the highest street level, flaunting opulence in every golden dome and turret. Hundreds of long amber windowpanes, segmented like the abdomens of dragonflies, glazed the stone. But most impressive perhaps were the temple's incinerators—three colossal smokestacks scaled in gilded tiles that spewed tawny plumes into the cloudscape. This was the Triple Flame, where the fire priests burned everything from trash to scrap to bodies. Factories and mills flanked the temple complex on every side, powered by great engines running off waste heat from the incinerators.

Staring across the busy Fifth Circle boulevard to the temple's main entrance, Lanie had never felt so small, stained, or insignificant. Her ears were ringing. She was journey-jostled, bruised, twitchy. At any moment she feared bursting into panicked tears—turning tail—diving for the nearest bolthole, and burrowing her way back into the catacombs.

But in her hand, the reliquary sang out its excitement.

So Lanie shook herself out, and crossed the street, and slipped through the front doors of the temple—enormous, gold-lacquered doors, paneled in jewel-bright enamels that depicted Sappacor, god of Fire, in all Their forms—trying to look as if she belonged.

Immediately, the smoke of white pepper incense stung her nose. This, as much as the chiming and belling of Queen Ynyssyll's big left toe bone, spurred her on. She swiftly skirted the narthex, practically yanked along by the reliquary's increasingly agitated ardor until she came to the Holy Labyrinth of the Columbarium.

Open to the Public, explained a gold-brushed sign posted at the entrance. *Dawn till Sundown. Oblations and Bare Feet welcome. Food, Drink, Nudity Forbidden. Robes Provided for the Indigent at Temple Offices.*

Despite her nervous stomach, Lanie smiled as she passed the sign, wondering what happened to those inevitable tricksters or teenagers who shucked all their clothes at the entrance to the Columbarium and made a dash into its labyrinthine recesses. Would a dozen fire priests give chase? Would a golden gong ring out the alarum, summoning a platoon of Bright Knights, shining in their mail, fireballs flaming at their fingertips, to ferret out the trespassers? How high a crime was flashing the dead anyway? Perhaps the Eparch of Sappacor themself would sit in judgement of the naked person, exacting fines or volunteer time or however punishment worked hereabouts. Lanie would have to find out.

In its way, the Holy Labyrinth of the Columbarium was as confounding as the city streets: corridor after corridor of relentless red marble, all twisting and turning toward some hidden center that no pilgrim could ever quite reach. Niches carved in the floor-to-ceiling walls harbored urns uncounted, little golden birds in their sheltering dovecote.

As a necromancer, this offended Lanie to no end.

Homogenized memory, she realized indignantly, a little nauseated at the smudgy jumble emanating from the urns. None of the ash is purely from one person. The accident is all mixed up—I couldn't whip up a single batch of useful ectenica if I used a mountain of it!

Which, Lanie realized a second later, was probably the point.

That thought—and her sudden woe at all that *wastefulness*—startled her so profoundly that Lanie didn't realize the reliquary had led her right up to a blank wall, and was insisting she walk through it.

She stopped abruptly, venting a tiny, frustrated scream, and thunked her head against the cool red marble, kicking it a few times with her filthy boot—

—and then she saw it.

She loosed a low, slow breath.

"Got you," she said, and fingered the faint thread of an outline in the wall.

The wall was, in fact, a door. Further, what she had taken for another of those golden, birdlike urns was a doorknob. The reliquary had not led her astray.

Lanie twisted the bird-headed handle until the door swung inward, quickly slipped inside, and drew the door almost all the way shut behind her. Then she set off down the well-lit passageway. Needle-straight: no bends or branches. Like the tunnel leading from Stones Ossuary to Queen Ynyssyll Brackenwild's crypt, this passage had but one purpose—to cut through the tangle of the Holy Labyrinth of the Columbarium and conduct a traveler directly to the secret, glass-domed garden at the center.

At the end of the passageway, a glass door. Lanie pushed it open, and a steamy wall of humidity and flower smells rolled over her in greeting. The reliquary's song became so loud and insistent that it drowned out her anxieties, her irritation at Mak, her feelings of filthiness and dejection and failure. The last several hours of tense adventuring fell away. She stood still, and breathed, and smelled, and listened, and grew calm.

When she was calm enough, Lanie stepped into the garden, where she knew—in her bones—that she would find Canon Lir.

THEY WERE SPRAWLED, facedown and spread-eagled, before a statue of the Founding Queen.

Ynyssyll Brackenwild, Erralierra's illustrious ancestress, was looking much livelier than the physical remains Lanie had left back home in the tomb chest. Here were no old bones, but a woman in her prime, depicted in bronze: a warrior and a mother, wielding her great ax Drjōta in her right arm, and a squalling baby Moll in the crook of her left. The closed visor of her helm eternally concealed her features but never her identity, for the helm was crowned in the Lirian state regalia: a circlet of beaten silver lilies and iron spearheads.

Canon Lir's prone figure did not perturb the unflappable statue in the slightest. The statue presided over the ivy-occluded solitude of the garden: from the quiet fountains mosaicked in blue and green tiles, to the cultivated moss, to the lavender and rosemary and mint spilling from their fragrant containers, to the bier of Blood Royal Erralierra Brackenwild—a wooden frame set upon a wooden sawhorse, a plain white satin pallet stretched over the frame, and a body resting under glass.

Lanie stared. She had never seen Erralierra so… naked.

No, not naked. It wasn't that the late Blood Royal was *unclothed*. But her funerary garments, which would accompany her into the cremation chamber, were so utterly plain—raw cotton unadorned by jewel-work or crewelwork or even lace edging—that they seemed to render the once-extravagant ruler barer than would her skin alone. Her head, shaved of curls, was innocent of hat or headdress or crown. Her fingers and wrists were denuded of gems, her feet bare.

Lanie looked away, her gaze returning to the form stretched out upon the moss. Were they sleeping? Weeping? Their hands were locked over the back of their head as if warding off a terrible blow.

Too late, Lanie thought with a pang of pity like a hobnail spiking her breastbone.

She didn't think she'd made a sound, but Canon Lir raised their head. Slowly, they looked up, around, squinting in the late afternoon sunlight that poured through the glass dome above the garden. The Triple Flame on their forehead was dull, the wizard mark like a fire banked. The paint on their face was streaky and smudged, as if they'd slept—or not slept—all night in the garden, never leaving it to wash, or eat, or change robes, or reapply cosmetics. Their bloodshot eyes met hers, flashed wide.

"Miss Stones!" It was more crackle than voice.

"Canon Lir."

Lanie was proud of how steady she sounded, until she started to grin. It was a horrible, helpless grin; she had no power over it. All of its own accord, her mouth was stretching wide, wider, ear to ear, splitting her face in the biggest, giddiest, unseemliest grin she could remember wearing outside a surge day.

And then—worse!—she laughed. Though the noise came out half-sob, half-gasp.

At which point—and she was never able to explain how, since she did not actually see Canon Lir rise from the ground and fly across the garden to the glass door where she was standing—Lanie was lifted off her feet and spun around and around. And then every bit of her face was being kissed all over: her ears, her braids, her neck, her spectacles. Her reliquary banged against the identical one Canon Lir was wearing. An ecstasy of reunion—wood, metal, enamel, crystal pressing hard together, biting into the flesh of their wearers. New bruises like small footprints.

"You!" Canon Lir stepped back only to gather her unto their breast again. Their coppery eyes shone like sunlight striking off the domes of the temple. "You beautiful creature! Oh, you blessed, blessed, beautiful creature! Miss Stones! You are alive!"

CHAPTER TWENTY-TWO

Glass Houses

LATER, A RUSH of explanations: "When you never came for your appointment, my brother sent his Bright Knights out to Stones Manor, and they found your sister's body, but no trace of you, or your—"

And interjections: "—it happened so fast, we fled the same day, we didn't even have time to bury her, and besides, we thought if we made it easy for people to find her, then word would get back that—"

And exclamations of relief—of joy!—of delight!—in each other's merely being. In merely being *there*.

After all this, they stood, somber and silent, side by side at the bier. Hands clasped, staring down at Erralierra's body.

Canon Lir said quietly, "She passes through the Triple Flame tonight. I couldn't bear to abandon her, before..."

Releasing her hand to rub their face, Canon Lir seemed to wake to their disordered state: their tousled robes, chipped fingernail paint, the maquillage smearing their fingers like a massacre. They turned to walk stiffly to the fountain, where they began rinsing off and tidying their appearance.

Lanie trailed after more slowly, strangely reluctant to leave Erralierra's corpse. The solace she felt in the presence of actual dead matter, in its original and unadulterated accident, after having navigated so many corridors of amalgamated ash, was, to put it mildly, profound.

But she also wanted Canon Lir to know that she considered *them* far more important than dead people.

"Erralierra doesn't look right, somehow," she observed, passing Canon Lir a clean handkerchief as they groped for something to dry themself with. "Without all her... royal tackle."

"All that belongs to Errolirrolin now." Canon Lir did not sound envious, only weary.

They finished wiping their hands, and Lanie smiled as they absently tucked her handkerchief away. She hoped they would keep it always.

"And of course," they continued, "most everything *he* owns belongs to the Scratches. I advised him to sell off what he could, recoup some of his losses. But his debtors would not hear of it. And the Scratches have far more influence at Brackenwild Court than a humble fire priest"—they bowed bitterly—"be they ever so closely related to the crown. Sari Scratch would have Errolirrolin keep up the appearance of inexhaustible wealth, if for no other reason than to remind all those who behold him of those to whom *he* is beholden—and that it has been Scratch coffers that have for years covered Erralierra's excesses, when the state could bear no more."

Lanie found herself idly circling the fountain, dragging one dusty hand in the water, enjoying the cool, clean shock of it.

She would have to discuss water—and hygiene in general—with Mak. Later, when she returned to their tomb. A small creek ran through the cryptyard of the old chapel which stood above Queen Ynyssyll's resting place; it would likely be sufficient for their needs. But they would have to make sure to boil it.

Or! Or—and this was a thought that had occurred to Lanie during her infinite perambulations throughout Liriat Proper—what if she *happened* to drop an activated orblin into the water with a command to filter out and purify all the unwholesome corpse-y bits that happened to be floating within?

Mak would not like it of course, but it was a good idea, a brilliant one, and he didn't want to be dying of dysentery or other gastrointestinal complaints that arose from bad water. He would just have to live with it. And enjoy his healthy guts.

She paused at the far side of the fountain, closer now to Erralierra than to Canon Lir.

It troubled Lanie that she couldn't bring herself to move again. She was simply… too comfortable. The only way she could be any happier would be if she stepped closer to the bier.

But that, at least, she did not do.

"So what happens to Blood Royal Errolirrolin if he finds himself in arrears?" Lanie pitched her voice low on purpose, hoping Canon Lir would step closer to her, which they promptly did—another unutterable relief. "Will it be like with Stones Manor—will certain royal properties change hands? Ynyssyll's Tooth, for example? That would be strange. What would we call it, Sari's Tusk?"

Her soft laugh invited reply. But Canon Lir was silent.

"Or…" She squinted a little, trying to read their face. "Or does Sari get the whole realm? The nine baronies swear fealty to the Court of Scratch? A new Skaki Queen rules over all of Liriat? There *is* a certain poetic justice in that, I supp…"

She trailed off, aghast, when Canon Lir offered only more silence.

"What? All of *Liriat?* How much money did your moth…? Can the Scratches even *do* that?"

Canon Lir shuddered but said firmly, "No. It won't come to that. But it is true that the payment installments have less to do with accounting for every copper poppet than with a series of favors, concessions, and appointments that, in their vast accumulation, equal the approximate value of her debt. One of those installments, as you know, amounted to positions in Brackenwild Court for Sari's sons."

Lanie nodded in vague recollection. Many of the events that had occurred that fateful vernal surge seven years ago were hazy to her. Some of what she could remember, she'd actively tried to forget. Of her last encounter with the Scratches, what she recalled most clearly was Nita's boot cracking down on her valiant little mouse friend, and not lifting, and *not lifting*.

And she could recollect with startling clarity Hatchet Scratch's face, not as she knew it was, but instead dazzlingly clear and cold and white. She shook her head—it was as if she were remembering him with a wizard mark, only his wizard mark was not visible to the eye, but translucent like glass, water, or ice. Purest panthaumic ice.

But though the details of that long ago, pre-Datu day were fuzzy, the consequences were clear: Scratten and Cracchen had held their appointments as Royal Assassin and Chief Executioner ever since.

Between the two of them, they had put down a minor rebellion in the baronies and worked with the Lirian City Watch to apprehend a criminal organization of human traffickers in the Twelfth Circle slums. In both cases, they had made public examples of the ringleaders and private work of the rest. Erralierra famously did not want to waste prison space on either noble traitors or what she called 'slaughterhouse scum,' a term that defined any Lirian citizen who claimed an address of Eighth Circle or beyond. According to Nita's desultory but contemptuous reports, the Scratch brothers were much flattered and fawned over at Brackenwild Court, and somewhat feared by the general populace, but not truly dreaded. Not *adored*. Not like the Stoneses had been.

"Another of Erralierra's concessions to Sari," Canon Lir went on, "was a house in First Circle. Sari requested—and Erralierra granted—the Ambassadorial Palace of Skakmaht."

Lanie looked up. "Really?"

That, she knew, she would have to report to Grandpa Rad, for he would consider it significant, and perhaps be able to explain some of the legal and political ramifications of the move.

Canon Lir nodded. "But other than its prime real estate appeal, the house itself has no financial value. Negative value, in fact—for it was falling to ruin after lying empty a century. Hatchet Scratch has been staying there and renovating it—at his own expense—while his mother and brothers keep chambers at Castle Ynyssyll, sticking close to the web." They smoothed out the wrinkled silk of their garments. "No one knows what the Scratches mean by it. And yet, for this single concession of dubious merit, Sari forgave a considerable chunk of Erralierra's debt. The Blood Royal counted the cost cheap, but... I am not so sure."

Again, Hatchet's flashing face, like a mirror reflecting sunlight, played across Lanie's memory. His delicate way with bones. His placid demeanor, as he played stupid more brilliantly than his brutish brothers practiced it in earnest. His soft voice with its strong Skaki dialect, and the beautiful calligraphy of his hand...

Canon Lir wandered back to Erralierra's bier, which gave Lanie the permission she needed to stand opposite them, resting her hands on the wooden frame, her fingers lightly tapping the glass that separated her from the corpse.

Gazing somberly across at her, Canon Lir raised their eyebrows in a shrug. "So now we have Hatchet occupying the Ambassadorial Palace of Skakmaht—with all the associated intimations. And we have Sari, whose last installment from Erralierra won her a seat on the Administrative Council. Her next ambition, my brother tells me, is for a title. We have nine baronies already; Sari Scratch proposes ten. No need for a land grant, she assured him—or not much of one. After all, Stones Manor comes to her at Midsummer, and will serve nicely for her baronial estate."

The glance they cast at Lanie was fleeting but eloquent before those gold-tipped lashes swept down.

Lanie gaped at them. "*Baroness* Scratch?"

"But *only*," Canon Lir continued, "if the Blood Royal would be willing to 'throw in' that little stretch of Diesmali woodland between Stones Manor and the capital—land that has historically belonged to the Brackenwilds, held in common with the citizens of Liriat Proper. It is, oh, a mere matter of twelve thousand acres or so. Errolirrolin balks. But as for the title—and your house..." they trailed off.

Lanie felt her face go fierce, her voice savage: "Let them have it. Let them take everything. It's not like we can ever go back. Not while the Blackbird Bride is hunting us. Anyway, Datu will be better off changing her name, starting out fresh with her father... elsewhere. A different city. A different life."

She did not want to think about that. But she knew that Mak would not long tolerate camping out underground, drinking and washing with 'corpse water,' enjoying for his neighbors the contents of royal crypts and catacombs, and watching his daughter growing in darkness both without and within.

And yet, even knowing that with Datu's departure would go the last of her family, Lanie could not picture herself as anything but a Stones of Liriat. Necromancer to the Blood Royal Brackenwilds. It was what she had been born and bred to, what she had prepared for all her life: to come into her full power and serve her country, outshining even Irradiant Stones in the history books. She, Miscellaneous Immiscible Stones, would single-handedly save Liriat from something even grander and more dangerous than sky wizards in their flying castles. Side by side with Canon Lir, she would strive for the glory of Liriat, as close as Doédenna to Sappacor. Closer. Fire and bone.

She glanced up to find Canon Lir's steady gaze on her, as if they could read all her thoughts. As if they understood everything. *Everything*.

She flushed.

But her friend released her from any obligation to explain herself, and turned the subject with the delicacy of a diplomat.

"Shall we?" they asked gently, indicating Erralierra's bier. "You came all this way."

"To see you."

"And to do this. What Errolirrolin called you to do."

They were not wrong. Lanie licked dry lips, played with a hangnail on her left thumb. She wanted nothing more than to lift the glass and lay her hands upon Erralierra's accident. Still, she hesitated.

Beneath their paint, Canon Lir's ravaged face smoothed out into tranquil, expectant lines. "What is it, Miss Stones?"

"Could you... *not*... tell your brother I'm here?"

Gilded brows contracted, forehead wrinkle deepened.

Lanie swallowed. "Errolirrolin thinks I'm dead, doesn't he?"

"We all did." And just for a moment, the whole painted mess of Canon Lir's face trembled like a fountain troubled.

"I want to keep it that way."

"Why?"

She shivered at that spare, bare sound. She could not hear anything in their undertones; she did not know what Canon Lir was thinking. "I need time. I need a *plan*. I need to burrow away for awhile. Away from public—from *royal*—attention. Somewhere," she whispered, "safe."

"The Blood Royal will keep you safe." Canon Lir leaned over the glass toward her. "He deeply desires the harboring of you—just as Erralierra did but was so long denied. You will know every luxury, every protection. You and I, we would see each other every day. You would have servants to attend you, Bright Knights to guard you, and the great walls of Castle Ynyssyll—"

"—were breached," Lanie interrupted. "Not even the Blood Royal was safe, and I'd hardly be better guarded than she."

Canon Lir snapped back to true, spine straight. "There is yet no evidence of malfeasance..."

"I've the word of the Blackbird Bride herself."

"Fanfaronade," Canon Lir retorted. "At least six parties have already stepped forward to claim her death their victory—half of them anonymous, a few raving. It is an easy thing to boast, Miss Stones, when the deed is already done and the circumstances mysterious. But we do not even know that her death was unnatural—just untimely."

Lanie's hands tightened on the wooden bier. *She* knew, if Canon Lir didn't, that the Blackbird Bride was no swaggering braggart. *They* had not seen Bran Fiakhna's face, heard her shredded voice, the woe and rage in her silver-coin eyes…

"Well, as you said, that's why I'm here," she answered as calmly as she could. "I'll ask Erralierra what happened the night of her death, and then we'll know for sure. But, Canon Lir, if what we fear is true—that Bran Fiakhna executed Erralierra and Nita as vengeance for her murdered Parliament—then there's no safety on Moll's Kopje for me. Not in Tooth or Castle. Not under Errolirrolin's protection—no matter his desire. No matter how thick his castle walls."

Canon Lir pinched the bridge of their nose. "I do not know…"

"It's for your brother's own safety," Lanie pressed. "Once she hears I'm living at Castle Ynyssyll, the Blackbird Bride will lay four-and-twenty kinds of siege to it. You weren't there that day. You don't know how much she, she…"

"She wants you," Canon Lir whispered. Now Lanie heard the undertones, but did not understand them: guilt, sickness, fury, despair… envy? "Bran Fiakhna wants you for her own," they continued. "And her powers are such that once you are in her sights, *you* will want *her* just as desperately. And then she will be able to do what she will with you, for your will will be hers."

Heat rose again to Lanie's face. A bliss of brine and jasmine washed over her. She almost swayed, but her nails bit into her palms. "I resisted her! I broke her broken bird, and I sent her away!"

"*That* time."

This was so unfair, so unlike the Canon Lir she knew, that Lanie gasped, "Exactly! That time! Because she'd only brought two wizards with her, and by then one of them was dead. But, Canon Lir, I can't fight off the whole Parliament of Rooks. And if *I* can't protect Errolirrolin from Bran Fiakhna, he certainly can't protect *me*."

They stared at one another, each of them breathing heavily. Never once, in all their sixteen years of friendship, had they argued like this. Not once. Carefully, Lanie unclenched her hands. Both of them sighed softly, almost the same breath.

"And anyway," she said. "This is not just about my safety, is it? If it were, maybe I *would* give myself to her—offer myself as part of a peace treaty, or something. Just to end this whole… this whole…"

Canon Lir murmured, "…duodecifold-damned mess."

"Yes! But the thing is, I can't do that. Because aside from whatever she wants with *me*, Bran Fiakhna definitely wants to murder Datu. And the feeling, let me add, is mutual. As far as I can tell, I'm the only one who can protect her. Because," she swallowed, "you know, Bran Fiakhna doesn't have a necromancer at her disposal. No Condor flies in her Parliament. Which means…"

"You are unique," breathed Canon Lir. "Peerless."

Peerless. Bran Fiakhna's word for her.

Lanie shook her head. "It means," she said grimly, "that I'm an arsenal of unimaginable potential."

That was one of Grandpa Rad's favorite phrases for the necromancers of the Stones line, for himself in particular, and it made Lanie feel strange to use it now.

She shook her head, frustrated. "Even if I don't yet know how to detonate myself."

Canon Lir tried one last time, but their voice was quiet and lacked conviction. "If you go to my brother, I promise you, Errolirrolin will arrange safe housing and new identities, for you, your niece, and her father..."

"How safe?" Lanie demanded. "How safe can Errolirrolin make us, when, according to *you*, Sari Scratch has him in her pocket? And what if"—as Grandpa Rad had surmised—"the Scratches are actually agents of Bran Fiakhna, or at least her allies, working to achieve their own ends through hers? How long will it be till Sari asks Errolirrolin to 'borrow' me for some special necromantic favor—just one more way to work off his debt? And what if that favor is somehow detrimental to Liriat in a way none of us can foresee—what will I do then? Oh, Canon Lir, what if it's a surge day, and I'm not all the way in control of myself, and I, I..."

She jerked as Canon Lir touched her elbow. She hadn't noticed them stepping around the bier, reaching for her.

"Miss Stones," they murmured, drawing her close. White pepper incense. Sweat. Gold leaf. Greasepaint. "Miss Stones, we are both upset. We are not thinking clearly. And so, for now"—they drew in a deep breath—"for now, I will not disabuse those who think you dead of their mistaken notions. Castle Ynyssyll will mourn the passing of the great Amanita Muscaria, last of the Stoneses; and in the meantime, the truly greatest of the Stoneses and I will strategize about our next move."

Lanie tried not to melt into tears. "We will?"

"We will," Canon Lir repeated firmly, slipping their hand from her elbow, but not before giving it a warm squeeze. "Now. Let us perform our sad rite, and hear what, if any, insights Erralierra has to offer. Then you and I will sit down and eat something." A small smile came to their face—rueful, but bright enough to set Lanie aglow. "With food and rest, we will better be able to formulate our future plans with finesse and specificity."

That was more like the Canon Lir she knew. Her tears spilt over, a wave of relief and gratitude. But Lanie dashed them away, sniffing mightily.

"I would like that. Yes. Please. Let's do that."

Canon Lir bowed, and returned to their place opposite her. "But first—"

Lanie nodded, and set both hands upon the glass. "Ready? One, two, three, lift."

CHAPTER TWENTY-THREE

Erralierra's Last Advice

AND THEN, AT last—at last!—up went that stifling glass lid—light as a bubble, etched with frosted flowers—up and off the body, granting Lanie access and communion, and then she and Canon Lir were setting the lid down upon the moss—gently, gently—and Lanie was stepping in close.

She placed her left hand upon Erralierra's shoulder. Something deep—sweepingly, swimmingly deep—at the bottom of her belly relaxed. Her left hand tingled. She heard the deep chiming of bones. The first whiff of citrus teased her nostrils.

"Three days ago"—just three days? Lanie marveled—"when I was first preparing for this interrogation, I thought we would begin by discovering what happened to the Blood Royal on the night of her death. We will have her tell her story plainly, without interruption, then ask whatever clarifying questions we deem necessary.

"And then," she gestured to Canon Lir with her free hand, "if and when you are satisfied, I will step away—and you may have a word with her alone."

For a moment, Canon Lir's bloodshot eyes grew very large and round. Though Lanie had known them since their mutual childhood, Canon Lir had never seemed anything but completely self-possessed to her, their well-educated, sophisticated gravitas defying their years at every age. But now, looking terribly young, terribly lost, they whispered, "What shall I say to her?"

"Um."

Lanie wondered what she would have wanted from Natty or Aba, had she been strong enough at age fifteen to stabilize their ectenica. Had she bound their substance fast to their accident, and raised them up, and sat them down for an actual, honest-to-death-god conversation for once in their lives. Afterlives.

Too late for her now. But not for Canon Lir.

"You could ask her blessing?" she suggested. "Perhaps"—risking a grin—"beg that she might pass on the whereabouts of any secret caches of treasure she happened to leave lying about?"

Canon Lir's mouth twitched.

"Or perhaps," Lanie added more somberly, "she has some final advice for you and your brother, who must now carry on in her wake."

The twitch blossomed into a rueful dimple. "Her not inconsiderable wake."

She and they regarded each other, each nodding like two wise flowers in a rain. Then Canon Lir stepped back from the bier, and said, "Thank you, Miss Stones. I am ready."

So Lanie left Canon Lir to their own internal preparations, and gazed down instead at Erralierra's accident, sinking her whole consciousness into it. Memories of her time with the Blood Royal rose to the fore. Lanie could not regret never again encountering Erralierra's toothy, untrustworthy smile, or avoiding those avid, calculating eyes, or hearing that trained orator's voice lying to her. Lying to everyone, about everything, all the time. But the longer Lanie looked at her, the more kindly she felt.

And this, she knew, was dangerous. For Lanie did not *want* to love Erralierra, even now. And yet, she could not help it.

Canon Lir cleared their throat. Lanie brought her attention back up out of the corpse. "Yes?"

"If possible, Miss Stones, I... I would wish to arrange this conversation in such a way that Erralierra's body, or any conspicuous part of it, does not disintegrate in a suspicious manner. If my ommer—the Eparch Aranha—discovers that their royal sibling has deliquesced into a pile of post-ectenica sludge," they grimaced, "I fear that rumors of necromancy will inevitably follow. And since I have promised to keep your secret safe..."

"No, no. I see. Good point." Narrow-eyed, clinical, Lanie ducked her head to study the corpse more closely. She sucked her lower lip into her mouth. Bit down, released. Which gave her an idea.

"Her tongue," she decided. "Memory seated in the tongue will abet ectenical communication anyway. Plus, it's hidden."

She absently patted her trouser pockets for her syringe kit, then picked up her jacket and turned out every nook and cranny of it, only to realize that what she sought she'd unhappily left back at Queen Ynyssyll's tomb. She sighed.

"Oh, well. It's not necessary. It's cleaner and more efficient, but any sharp edge will do."

Silently, Canon Lir offered up their misericord[17]. The blade was slender as an icepick, with a decorative twist at the base like a small cyclone, a

17 The fire priests of Sappacor always carried this weapon with them as part of their vestments, though over the centuries its purpose had become more traditional than functional. It used to be that every fire priest was also a Bright Knight: a warrior who fought to drive the worship of the Triple Flame into every unbeliever's heart. Often forcibly. These days, fire priests were better known for their hedonism and peace-loving ways, and Bright Knights—at least in Liriat—were an elite force of priestly bodyguards for the highest-ranking clergy and their noble allies.

grip carved of ivory, and a creamy, cloud-colored pearl in the pommel. Lanie lost no time in nicking the tip of her middle finger and bending over Erralierra.

A slight, distressed sound across from her brought her glance up again. Canon Lir's face looked sick beneath the remnants of their paint.

"No, no, you mustn't worry," Lanie assured them quickly. "You keep your misericord quite keen; I hardly felt a thing. This? Is nothing. You've seen me bleed before, most copiously! Echo-wounds always produce more juice than these incidental prickles. Though—ha!—they do *heal* faster. Remember when you loaned me your robe for my nosebleed? I still keep a scrap of that silk by me, in a small box of my favorite things."

She watched with satisfaction as a look of delight and warmth returned to Canon Lir's face.

"Miss Stones," they said. "I am moved."

Lanie smiled at the tone of that 'Miss Stones.' She suspected Canon Lir of a gallant attempt at flirtation—even though with the greatest will in the world, neither of them was any good at flirting.

Still, it spiked the smell of citrus in the air, as well as her confidence, and Lanie thought she'd attempt a flirt herself.

"Well, it's only a very *little* scrap, Canon Lir. That's all that was left—after my very big nosebleed!"

"The biggest," they murmured.

But now the middle finger of her left hand was singing, *ready, ready, ready,* and Lanie became all business.

"Now if you will, Canon Lir—with all due reverence—open your mother's mouth for me? Thank you. All right, now you might want to look away while I... Yes, that's it. And now... Now, I'll just sing her a refrain of the Maranathasseth Anthem, shall I? Goody Graves taught it to me. An old Quadoni spellsong. The first ever uttered. A cry to Doédenna against death itself. Of course, I don't know if that's all true, but the song's origin is certainly of unfathomable antiquity.

"I learned its companion song first—though, like you, it was born second: the Lahnessthanessar, the *Undreaming*. Also called the Great Lullaby—for it can sing the undead to sleep again. But the Maranathasseth Anthem, which I will now attempt, is called the *Dreamcalling*, for it summons the dead back to their dream of life. Or so Goody says.

"All I know is, the melody focuses my death magic, and adds stability and durability to my ectenica—not to mention, oh, you know, *oomph*. It's how I finally perfected my orblins."

Lanie realized she was babbling, decided not to anymore, and bent to examine the blood spatter on Erralierra's tongue for ectenical change. Perhaps the slightest shimmering?

"It's... it's such a slippery little tune," she muttered, more to herself than to Canon Lir, who bent closer to hear her. "Like trying to isolate your earliest memory when you're not sure it even happened—but there's no one to corroborate it for you, so you can never be sure. Or like describing a dream; it's never quite the same in your mouth as it was in your mind. Even Goody only recalls the tunes in tatters.

"I will say that singing the melodies—or rather, *remembering* them—is effortless on a surge day. But, oh dear, in ordinary time, let me tell you... But no matter. Humming a few notes for you—I mean, for Erralierra—is my greatest honor."

She calmed her nervous babble, channeled it into silence, and the moment she did so, the ectenica caught. Cold-star snow-ember moon-frost kindled in the mouth of the dead Blood Royal of Liriat. The sight of it cooled Lanie's fevered thoughts, focused her mind. She breathed out.

Where is breath?
In the stillness.
What is stillness?
Sothaín.

In the stillness at the end of her breath, just prior to her next inhalation, Lanie tuned in to the twittering of her living bones, where the music lived. Ah, the tail of a trill! She hummed it back. The first four notes. Then the next four. Then the next. Twelve notes in all—barely a phrase—but surely as she was a Stones, that phrase was *ANTHEM!* was *WELCOME!* was *WAKE!*

Lanie doggedly kept the hum alive on her lips, like a bumblebee caught buzzingly between her teeth. Her deep voice sang counter to it, a sound only the dead could hear. Both her voices hummed, her whole body humming along, substance and accident together, until the blood throbbed in her newly cut finger.

Throbbed, too, where it flecked Erralierra's mouth, painted her cold tongue.

That tongue was now crawling with low blue light, the same spectral glow that illuminated Goody's eyes and clung to the padlock of the Sarcophagus of Souls. It quickened, an animating luster that took hold of its accidental fuel until it had lashed the tongue entirely.

And then, it *became* the tongue.

The ectenica writhed, wormlike, irate, in Erralierra's mouth, fast-flopping in every direction at once, scrabbling and squirming against the corpse's stiff cheeks like feet kicking at a confining blanket.

Lanie sucked in air like a swimmer at the plunge, then stuffed her left hand all the way into Erralierra's mouth. It stretched for her like obedient putty.

She caught the wriggling tongue in her fist, stilled its struggles, and began to pull. Stretched it. Worked it like luminous blue caramel. Shaped it.

Soon the thing she held no longer resembled 'tongue'; it hadn't been a tongue since the moment Lanie's blood met with the dead matter. No more flesh but ectenica: at once material and ethereal, dead matter and living blood combining into the third state, undeath. Ectenica swam up Lanie's fingers, twisted around her knuckles, her wrists. Cold electric cobwebs, popping and crackling in their eagerness to communicate.

Lanie smiled, just as eager—ecstatic—to oblige. "Erralierra Brackenwild. We wish to talk to you. We have questions, Erralierra Brackenwild."

Carefully, millimeter by millimeter, she released the ectenica back between Erralierra's lips. Ells and ells of it, a long ribbon of blue light unspooling from her left hand to coil tamely and snugly between the floor of Erralierra's mouth and her hard palate, like a snake in a shaft of sunlight.

When the ectenica was all in place, Lanie asked it, "Are you ready to talk, Erralierra Brackenwild?"

"I am ready to talk," the ectenica replied.

Lanie glanced up at Canon Lir, whose hands had tightened on the wooden frame of the bier. Their face was stoic, but their body was visibly shaking—from the beaded burls of black hair on their head to the gilded sandals on their feet.

But they gave a curt nod, so she began, "Tell us about the night you died."

The ectenica's report was pretty much what Lanie had been expecting: Erralierra had been reading in bed. A feeling—something like sleep, a lot more like drowning—overcame her. She could not move. Breathing was difficult. A sweet molasses stickiness between her and her next heartbeat. Two birds flew in through the window. A third bird, large and black with red markings, perched on the sill outside. The two birds inside the room vanished. In their place, two women stood over Erralierra's bed. Both of them bore the wizard marks of Rook. The tall one Erralierra knew, for they had met before. She would have spoken her name aloud—"Bran Fiakhna"—but at no time was released from that sensation of slow-squeezing sleep. Bran Fiakhna bent over her bed, whispered, "Two-and-twenty," and blew an iridescent dust from off the palm of her hand into Erralierra's face. What followed were hours of agony—or perhaps minutes, the ectenica corrected itself—and then, nothing. And now, this.

Lanie stood back. "Are you satisfied?" she asked, no longer addressing the corpse.

Canon Lir nodded without speaking.

"Do you have any more questions?"

They shook their head.

She hesitated, then asked, "Would you... would you like a private word with her?"

Hesitation. A quick jerky nod.

Lanie stepped away from the bier. "I'll let you say your goodbyes, then."

The glassed-in garden was not large, but Canon Lir's voice dropped to a whisper as they knelt beside their mother's bier, put their head next to the corpse's, and greeted it by name. The ectenica returned the greeting:

"Lir."

Lanie politely plugged her ears with her index fingers. But even that, though it stopped her from accidentally hearing Canon Lir's questions, did not mute Erralierra's responses.

Despite her best intentions, Lanie could hear every word uttered by the undead; it was a sound she received in her bones, not her ears.

Thankfully, Erralierra's responses to her secondborn were short and soothing. Yes, she loved them. Yes, she was proud of them. Yes, they had her blessing; she was confident they were clever and wily, wise and deep, would do their hard work remorselessly and well. Times boded to be dark and difficult for Liriat, the ectenica predicted, but it knew that Lir would keep the good of the realm foremost in their mind—as Erralierra had not.

After a quarter hour of this, Canon Lir bowed their head, said something that Lanie tried not to make out—"Thank you," perhaps, or "Goodbye"—and laid a kiss upon Erralierra's naked knuckles.

Lanie started making her way back from the fountain at that point, but Canon Lir was not quite done. They looked up suddenly, their troubled gaze meeting Lanie's. She replied with a tentative smile, and jerked her chin at Erralierra. This called their attention back to the ectenica that had been Erralierra's tongue, which was beginning to crumble at the edges. Lanie could almost taste the char.

She flashed a five-fingered warning. Canon Lir smiled crookedly, lifted a single finger in response, and turned to their mother's corpse. This time, they angled their shoulders so that Lanie could neither see their face nor read their lips, even if she'd wanted to. Bending low over Erralierra's body, they whispered something just above its mouth, before turning their ear toward its lips to hear the ectenica's whispered response. Whatever the question and its answer, they wanted to keep it as private, as secret, as possible.

But the ectenica's response rang throughout Lanie's whole body like the horns that heralded a high holy fire feast.

"Marry her."

CHAPTER TWENTY-FOUR

Queen Ynyssyll's Tomb

Rainday 27th
Month of Broods, 421 Founding Era
55 days till Summer Solstice

"No," the ghost persisted. "No more lessons."

Lanie did not bother looking up from her work. "I don't have enough orblins to trade, and it's too much of a drain to keep making them except for absolute emergencies. We'll have to work something else out."

Braced for argument, she went back to reviewing her stockpile of inactive orblins. She counted them out as meticulously as Mak counted out their coins, which they had even less of. They had some money from Nita's lockbox, and some from hocking whatever small household items they'd been able to carry with them on their flight, but Lanie did not dare go to the bank to inquire after any savings. It would announce their presence to all of Liriat Proper and beyond. Besides, all they had rightfully belonged to the Scratches. Interest accrued faster than Nita was willing to pay it down. She'd only ever liked to pay the barest minimum, preferring to spend her money on herself, her weapons, her travels, and her family.

On that point as well, Lanie had advised Mak to sell what he could as quickly as he could. Come Midsummer, she'd warned him, all that had belonged to Stones Manor, as listed in Sari Scratch's contract, would by the grace of the god Lan Satthi return to its rightful owners.

At first Mak had looked shocked. Then he had scowled at the necessity of such dishonest dealings. In the end, he had gone to Market Circle to do what he must. He'd wanted Datu to go with him, but the child had refused, stating that she did not like "leaving Auntie Lanie alone with all the dead people."

But of all the dead people in tomb and catacombs, Lanie only really worried about one.

"Fine, then." The ghost sniffed—as best he could with no nostrils, no lungs, and only an enormous rusted padlock for the expression of his umbrage. "You can't pay up? I'm not teaching nor telling you anything. Ever. Again."

"I don't know, Grandpa Rad. I don't think you can help it!" Lanie did her best to convey cheerful unconcern. "It's your nature, you know; you must pontificate. And I'm the only one who can hear you, besides Goody."

"Not that you ever *listen* to me—which, I tell you, girlie, you will live to regret, and die regretting, and spend the rest of your afterlife marinating in the bitterness of unfulfilled ambitions and shattered aspirations, and all because you were too stubborn to heed your betters!"

"You never know. I might change my ways and devote my undivided attention to your wisdom and perspicacity. Any day now."

"Not," cried the ghost triumphantly, "if I refuse to lecture you!"

"Yes, well, we'll see how long that lasts." Lanie adjusted her spectacles with an expression that she hoped conveyed indulgent complacence.

It drove the ghost straight into the sullens. With a, "Humph!" he subsided back into his padlock.

Lanie ignored him and continued her task of counting orblins. Or rather, she pretended to, but secretly brooded at the Sarcophagus of Souls.

This, at her direction, Goody had mounted atop the Founding Queen's tomb chest, and if Lanie regretted anything seventeen days into their new circumstances, it was that. She did not like to see the ghost of Irradiant Stones raised above Queen Ynyssyll Brackenwild in any way, but there were not many places in the underground royal tomb where the sarcophagus would comfortably fit, and Lanie didn't think it right to make Goody hump it all the way up into the chapel—if the tight, winding staircase would even support their combined weight and size, which she doubted.

Like the sarcophagus, Queen Ynyssyll's tomb chest was carved of basalt. Also like the sarcophagus, it was grand and imposing, large enough to house several generations of Brackenwilds rather than the sole progenitrix of the line. However, unlike the sarcophagus, which was rough-hewn and rather plain, the tomb chest was beveled, polished, and covered on every side by a scabrous gesso depicting the life and death of Ynyssyll Brackenwild. Deeply inscribed and minutely detailed as it was, the once-bright paint was long-since faded, the silver-gilt illuminations tarnished, and the gold-gilt details begrimed.

But Queen Ynyssyll's face emerged from the front of the tomb chest like the figurehead of a ship: instantly recognizable from a thousand lesser statues, with a serenity of countenance that belonged rightly neither to a living person nor to a dead one but to the rank of effigy itself.

Lanie found herself smiling at the Founding Queen's carved face, as at an old friend. The orblins rolled, cool and round, under her fingers.

Some of these she had designated as couriers, some as sentinels, some for further experimentation, some for emergencies, and the rest as water purifiers—an experiment that, if Lanie said it herself, had surpassed her idlest, wildest speculations.

As it happened, orblins worked even better than boiling. Because Lanie commanded them to, they cleansed the water of everything that was not quintessentially water: hard metals and other particulate matter (or so they conveyed to her through those strange flashes of insight that were like listening to a distant song, or seeing through somebody else's eyes). Datu claimed that water from Lanie's magically depolluted barrel tasted "flat" and "weird," and "like nothing, not even water," and called it "Auntie Lanie's deadwater." Mak, though he silently accepted it for washing, still preferred to use simple boiled water for eating and drinking.

But even carefully economized, there were not many orblins all told. Fewer than a gross. It made Lanie deeply uneasy. She would have to make more, and Grandpa Rad would be able to smell the ectenica on her, no matter how deeply she ventured into the catacombs to co-opt a chamber for her workshop.

As if reading her thoughts, the padlock on the Sarcophagus of Souls glimmered a sulky, sour blue. Shadowy shapes moved within the glow until a pair of lips formed, and immediately laid in to Lanie:

"Listen up, girlie. We had an arrangement, you and I—unspoken, perhaps, but age-old as apprenticeship itself, and ironclad as a blood-oath. You, the tedious canvas. I, the peerless painter. You, the blockish granite. I, the master architect. Obedience was to flow from you to me, and in return, the gratification of knowledge and the benefit of my incalculable genius would come back to you twelve-fold. In the beginning, I gave of myself without surcease or complaint, for I was assured of my reward come the day you entered fully into your power. Why should I have doubted I would receive my due? All justice and reason persuaded me that gratitude would forever behold you to me, your beloved teacher, the price of whose knowledge must be valued above first water diamonds. But that," said the ghost peevishly, "was before you *thwarted* and *deceived* me. You've freeloaded long enough, girlie! Pay up or make do."

"Grandpa Rad—"

"And another thing," the ghost interrupted irascibly. "Henceforth, you shall not address me by that vile appellation. You may address me as *Master Irradiant*, if you must address me at all, but don't expect an answer unless and *until* you are kneeling before me with a handful of orblins as oblation, ready and willing to learn from the only teacher in Liriat who can impart anything of value to you!"

Lanie sat back on her heels, arms crossed over her knees.

I will address you, she thought with a grim determination that surprised even her, however I please.

But she did not go so far as to say it aloud. Nor did she choose that moment to pit her will against the ghost's, to subjugate him as he always said a necromancer must subjugate the dead and the undead. That was coming, whether or not Master Irradiant Stones knew it, at Midsummer.

Just as she would release Goody to Saint Death's cloak when the midnight hour of Lanie's next surge crested upon her, so too would she take advantage of the high panthaumic tide to wrestle with what was left of the ghost. To try, if she might, to detach him from the object he haunted before it came into the Scratch family's possession.

Lanie had deduced years ago that it was probably to obtain the Sarcophagus of Souls that Sari had entered into a contract with Natty, Aba, and Diggie in the first place. Watching (and perhaps encouraging) the Stoneses' inevitable labefaction from afar, and then swooping in to fill the void they left, was just a bonus. As Lanie herself would have been—had she consented to Sari's scheme to marry her sons.

But the Sarcophagus of Souls was her true object; it was a funeral monument of great import to Northernmost Skakmaht. Should the death magic locking the Sarcophagus be cracked, and the wizard souls released, and the Sky Houses let to fly again, there was a chance the nation might begin to recover after all these years.

Lanie wished Sari joy of her imminent proprietorship. She even considered it a kind of remuneration for the wrongs Liriat had done to Skakmaht a century ago. And *she* certainly didn't want to lug around the Sarcophagus of Souls any longer, now that she had neither home nor any possessions left, and might at any moment need to flee her current situation. It had practically killed Goody to carry it for her that first time—and Goody was already dead!

But while it was one thing, she considered, if the *Sarcophagus* returned to Sari's hands on midnight of the next high holy fire feast, it was quite another to surrender the ghost of Skakmaht's greatest enemy into Skaki hands.

Whether such an arrangement would turn out the worse for Sari or for Grandpa Rad, Lanie didn't know. But she didn't want to find out.

What she did know was that Irradiant Radithor Stones was no ordinary ghost. Lanie had not herself encountered many as of yet, but she had read up on them and knew the thaumatological precedents.

A ghost was different from a revenant in that it had no physical accident of its own. It was pure substance—memory, will—attached to an object of significance, which stood in, in some ways, as proxy for its original accident. The object might be anything: the bed in which they'd died, a favorite locket or ring, a rocking chair. Whatever the object, the ghost imprinted upon it, feeding off its memories of that object, and letting those memories sustain its own idea of what it once had been in life.

But a ghost was very limited in its scope, for it could not move beyond the range of its object. Even if the object was quite large—a mountainside, a forest, a melancholy lake—the ghost was still bound to it, and bound to whatever changes that object underwent. If the object significantly changed—fell into disuse, was destroyed, or simply became imprinted with so many new memories that the ancient grip of the ghost lost its mooring—than the ghost itself unraveled. Its substance dissipated. A haunted place or thing came unhaunted, and Doédenna reclaimed her own—as was the natural way of supernatural things.

But Grandpa Rad had defied all that. He had created the object of his haunting himself, and created it to be unchangeable. He had, moreover, filled it with the souls of Skaki sky wizards—wizards who, after all this time, were *still alive*, but whose fleshly cases lay frozen in the flying castles suspended above Iskald—and had been leeching off this feast of undying (but not undead) substances ever since.

In other words, Grandpa Rad was powering his own afterlife with the equivalent of a great necromantic battery—which made him far more powerful than any other ghost or revenant that Lanie had read about or encountered. But did it make the necromancer's ghost more powerful than she was herself, a living necromancer?

She did not know. But Lanie did not want to risk losing to him before amassing all the panthauma granted her on a high holy fire feast. She had never forgotten—or forgiven—Grandpa Rad for once trying to take possession of her body, no matter that he'd always insisted it was only a test, that he'd never have gone through with it.

She did not intend to let him try again. She feared augmenting his powers off-surge by yielding even a small amount of her magic to his use. Even so small an amount as might be found, say, in a single orblin. Which was his price, he had declared, for a lesson in death magic.

But.

Lanie still needed to learn all of what Grandpa Rad remembered of his days as a necromancer—and she needed to learn it before Midsummer. The ghost was curiously parsimonious for such a loquacious and prolific entity. In life, he had written reams of material, but most of it was in code, and hardly any of it legible. In undeath, he could talk for hours, days, but only let fall a single useful fact, and that by accident, which Lanie would have to sift her notes for. She suspected his pedagogy was purposefully exhausting, that Grandpa Rad prided himself at wearing her down and teaching her as little as possible.

He was absolutely sure that Lanie would yield to his demand for her orblins eventually. She'd always yielded to him before.

This time, Lanie vowed, will be different. This time he'll be working for *my* scraps—if I can just convince him that I find him completely unnecessary.

After making him wait an excessively long time for a response, Lanie said, friendly and reasonable, "Dear Grandpa Rad! I really shouldn't be draining myself off-surge making orblins for you to snack on. I need to reserve them for my own use—not come to my estival surge poked full of holes like an ectenical cheesecloth. Canon Lir says it's very likely that the Blackbird Bride will use her own surge this Midsummer to strike at the heart of Liriat. Unless, of course, she can be made to treat with Errolirrolin—"

"Don't try to hornswoggle *me*, girlie," the ghost sneered. "You'd lavish your last drop of blood on that revenant Goody Graves if *she* asked you, and let Liriat fall to an army of blackbirds!"

"Are you still going on about that?" Of course he was; he'd not ceased complaining about it for weeks, long after the startling effects of the orblin faded from Goody's countenance. "That was an emergency! Goody was cracking under the strain from carrying *you!*"

"Your whole life is an emergency, Miscellaneous Stones," the ghost argued. "Which was why she was carrying me in the first place. Don't try to equivocate. We both know you'd've left me to the mercy of those Skaki spooks if you'd had any hope of fending off the Blackbird Bride on your own."

"But you're my family!" Lanie protested, going as innocently wide-eyed as she dared behind her spectacles. "I'd never leave you behind."

"Oh, *wouldn't* you?"

This launched the ghost into a fresh circuit of his usual complaints. Why had Lanie kept her formula for stabilizing ectenica secret from him all this time? Why had she not taught him the Maranathasseth and Lahnessthanessar spellsongs the moment she'd learned them from Goody Graves? Had not he, Irradiant Radithor Stones, shared his *life's work* with her? Had he not been attempting, all these years of his undeath, to drum a modicum of understanding into her skull, which was thicker by far than even his middleborn son's[18]—and that, he assured her, was saying something? Well, if *she* would be immoveable, so too would *he* be. Let Lanie just try to raise an army of the undead to march against Bran Fiakhna without his help. Let her try to take on the Parliament of Rooks—as he himself had taken on, and triumphed against, the Guilded Council of Skakmaht. They'd see who'd win out, and what the body count would be in the end. At least, *he* would see, laughing himself

18 Extramundane Stones, much to Irradiant's dismay, had taken his name all too literally. The only Stones to voluntarily leave Liriat upon attaining his majority, Mundy had shortened his forename and changed his surname to suggest ironically the one by which his august father most often addressed him. He had then moved to Leech and married a goose girl. Mundy thereafter lived out a prosperous four score and three years growing prize vegetables. His wife, Mistress Mudclopper, having been briefed on Mundy's family history, elected not to have children. Both Mudcloppers died content. The Stoneses never spoke of them.

deathless for the rest of eternity while she, Lanie, rotted in a ditch somewhere.

"Yes, yes, of course, Grandpa Ra—I mean, *Master Irradiant*," Lanie soothed him. "We'll talk more about this later."

"No!" the ghost insisted. "I've said what I've said! Agree to my demands, or lose everything you love to an enemy you cannot hope to defeat without my help. Think on *that*, girlie—if you're capable of such complex cogitations. I'm done with you."

This time, when he lapsed into silence, it rang with a finality that Lanie knew would last at least the rest of the day. She turned away from the Sarcophagus in relief, pressing her reliquary pendant to her chest hard enough to hurt. Her heartbeat pounded through wood and metal and bone, lending a pleasant percussive rhythm to the sweet duet that passed between the reliquary and the contents of Queen Ynyssyll's tomb chest.

The longer Lanie listened to the Founding Queen's bones, the more alert she became to the presence of the second reliquary, the twin hallux, moving around the city above her, going along with Canon Lir in their busy bustle, humming to itself. That awareness traveled back to Lanie through the miles and miles of bones that lay between her and Canon Lir, between herself and the daylit world.

The catacombs, too, in all their many osseous pieces, sang to her. Or rather, hummed. Or, perhaps—perhaps something between humming and *purring*. The sound, or sensation, Lanie imagined, was a little like lying out on a summer seashore, under a light breeze and a gentle sun. Or it was like being rocked to sleep in a hammock made of cats, under another pile of cats. This 'lure of the catacombs,' as Lanie had come to think of it, could suck her into hours-long reverie, out of which Mak or Datu had to physically shake her.

However, she was alone for the moment. She might have a chance to listen uninterrupted for a while. Grandpa Rad was unlikely to renew his ultimata till tomorrow.

But—

"Auntie Lanie?"

—it was not to be.

Lanie sighed. "Yes, Datu?"

"Who were you talking to?"

"Dead people, Datu. Just more dead people."

"What are the dead people saying this time?"

"Nonsense, mostly." Lanie grunted, forcing herself to her feet.

She'd woken in the dark, left their camp inside the chapel's main chamber to go into the inner sanctum, and thence to her workshop downstairs—far, far downstairs—in Queen Ynyssyll's tomb. Not that Grandpa Rad had allowed her to work, telling her nothing but talking without stopping, leaving her no time to read or write or even think. Nor could she do much of either, with such books and materials as she had been able to bring out of Stones Manor with her. What time it was now, Lanie scarcely knew, but she turned and attempted to smile at her niece.

"Nonsense," she repeated. "But I shall get the better of them, Datu, never fear."

But her expression must have conveyed something she did not intend, for Datu took a small step back, and said formally, "You are to come up to the garden now." She paused. "And you are to bring your gloves."

"Am I? Why?"

"Because Didyi wants to see us."

"Then why didn't Didyi come down to ask us himself?" Lanie asked as she fetched her gloves. They were thin and ragged. She hated wearing them, but they disguised her wizard mark, which must be what Mak intended.

Datu wasn't done rolling her eyes. "*You* know, Auntie Lanie. Didyi does not like dead people."

But Lanie understood that it wasn't the dead people Mak objected to—or not *just* the dead people. It was the underground itself. The lack of natural light, the lack of circulating air, the sensation of being trapped in stone, of being buried alive.

His fears went against all Lanie's own strongest predilections. Everything Mak hated about the underground, she loved. It made her feel snug, cozy, homey, even blissful. Except for wanting to escape Grandpa Rad's company, the longer Lanie spent in the tomb and exploring the surrounding catacombs, the less she wanted to emerge.

But Mak so seldom requested her company, and Datu was looking intractable, and, really, Lanie's curiosity was piqued. So she went.

Datu looked relieved at her acquiescence, even going so far as to nod approvingly and to take her by the hand. (This, Lanie suspected, was less affection than Datu urging her reluctant aunt upstairs with more speed than she would have preferred.)

"Ah," Mak greeted her as Lanie stumbled, blinking, into the harsh spring sunlight. Was it afternoon already? And fairly late in the afternoon, judging by the lengthening shadows. "You came."

"Saint Death weeps!" Lanie exclaimed. "When did it get so hot?"

"It is not so hot, Auntie Lanie," Datu protested. "It is just that you are cold and clammy from being with all the dead people."

Lanie rubbed her shoulders. They were sore: stiff as cairns.

"Odd," she said, a little peevishly. "I felt quite comfortable all morning."

"You were not comfortable," Datu informed her. "You were lazy. You need to do sothaín every morning with Didyi and me."

Lanie raised her eyebrows at Mak, who—to her astonishment—did not disagree. "That will be well," he said briskly. "We shall start tomorrow with the sixth set, dedicated to Amahirra Shape-Changer."

"Oh." Lanie squirmed. "Well, you know, I don't know that one very well—"

"Datu and I will show you," he said. "Tomorrow morning, first light. Outside," he added firmly. "But not today. I see you have your gloves. Good. This evening, we have business abroad."

"We do?"

"Yes," said Datu, and then, to Lanie's shock, beamed. "We are going out, Auntie Lanie! Didyi wants to show us my new school!"

CHAPTER TWENTY-FIVE

A Family Outing

TO LANIE'S CRY of, "Excuse me—what?" Mak replied, "Come. I'll explain as we walk."

But first he paused, looked her up and down, from her dusty boots to her tattered trousers and the shirt she couldn't be bothered to tuck in, and when his gaze rested on her face again, he said approvingly, "Ah. You washed your face. Very good."

"Yes?" Lanie said. "This surprises you?" (She never would have admitted it to him, but it surprised *her*. While she had indeed washed her face that morning, she was pretty sure it was the first time that week she'd bothered.)

The corners of Mak's eyes crinkled. "No. No, of course not."

"*This* way," Datu declared, already several steps ahead of them and impatient that they catch up.

What Mak and Datu referred to as 'the garden' was really a small cryptyard of old Brackenwild royals buried in the unkempt acres of wilderness that surrounded the chapel housing Queen Ynyssyll's tomb. The cryptyard was bounded on one side by a great stone wall, on the other by a moat, and the grounds that lay between had been neglected for more than a century.

Despite this lonely setting, the Brackenwilds did not slumber in solitude. The 'garden' was fertilized also by favorite pets, faithful hounds, prize horses, and preferred retainers, all buried there in the days before it was mandatory that Lirian citizens be consigned to the Triple Flame[19]. At the bottom of the garden, where weeds and wildflowers straggled into water reeds, was the moat. Across the moat was Castle Ynyssyll—twisting and jutting and curlicuing up from the green mound of Moll's Kopje, alongside the needle-like spire of Ynyssyll's Tooth—and there dwelt the living descendants of the Blood-Royal Brackenwilds still.

But Datu was leading them away from the moat, towards the wall. At first Lanie thought Mak meant them all to scale the immense iron

19 See footnote 13.

entrance gate, for it seemed sturdy and had footholds enough. It was also overgrown with briers, looked dangerously rusted, and was topped with spear-shaped finials that looked less decorative than deliberately hostile. Before she could voice an objection, Mak stopped beneath an ancient and gnarled sorkhadari tree, with its red-scaled bark and its blood-red berries. The tree's flat needles, so green they were almost black, fanned out from the branches in such profusion that its bushy crown reminded Lanie of her own hair whenever she brushed it loose from her braids.

The sorkhadari was, at Lanie's best guess, a thousand years older than Liriat Proper itself—and, moreover, was probably the reason the founders had chosen this location for their cryptyard in the first place. In olden days, the sorkhadari had been considered a sacred tree. Many legends still saw that tree as a place where one might encounter (or strike a bargain with) some divine entity.

"See, Auntie Lanie?" Datu cried over her shoulder. "It has got a lot of low branches! Even you can climb it!"

"Go on, Datu," Mak instructed, ready to boost her if she asked. She did not, but swung up into the tree, scaling it quickly till she came even with the top of the wall. She crouched there, waiting for her father's signal. He gave it, and she climbed down the branches overhanging the other side of the wall. They had obviously rehearsed this part.

Mak turned to Lanie. "I will go last," he said. At her questioning glance, he added, "I'll not take wing today."

It made sense; he couldn't very well take wing without leaving all his clothes behind, and unless he had caches of spares hidden around the back alleys of Liriat Proper, he'd be hip-deep in hoozzaplo in no time when he took human form again.

Lanie was growing more excited about their expedition by the minute. Her uneasiness at leaving the catacombs was fading; the sun no longer felt so grating, nor the bright air so stifling. Even the crowds and muck she'd encountered on her first (and last) attempt to navigate the city no longer seemed so terrifying. Company made all the difference. Still, she eyeballed the tree.

"Okay, then."

Back home at Stones Manor, Lanie had climbed all kinds of things—staircases, ladders, bookshelves—but it had been a long, long time since she had climbed a tree. To her astonishment, Mak stepped up and made a stirrup of his linked hands.

Lanie flushed in confusion. "No, no, thank you, Gyrgardi. Datu's right—the lowest branches are quite low."

Before either of them could embarrass themselves further, she followed Datu into the sorkhadari. But she had not scooted all the way onto the stone wall when she felt Mak's touch, so light she wasn't even startled, on her ankle.

"Please," he said. "Do not call me 'gyrgardi' today. It is of utmost importance that the… that Datu's potential schoolteachers do not guess what I am. If you will do me that favor, aunt-of-my-daughter?"

Lanie stared at his earnest face for a long moment, wanting to ask a hundred questions, but knowing that, even in the unlikely event he would answer them, Datu was on the other side of the wall, waiting.

"Of course," she said. "Mak."

He tilted his head as if about to tell her something. Lanie felt a frisson of fear, or something like fear.

Is he, she thought, about to tell me his name? Not the name Nita gave him—the only name I've ever known him by. His *real* name.

But then Mak jerked his chin, gesturing for her to go on. Lanie obeyed, stifling her curiosity.

Outside the cryptyard wall was the tree-lined boulevard of First Circle, clean and broad. Where the walls of the cryptyard ended, the even higher walls of the neighboring estates began. Behind them, set back on narrow but manicured lawns, were the domiciles of Liriat Proper's richest and most privileged families: the nobles of Brackenwild Court, foreign embassies, the palaces of merchant princes and military generals. The battlements and turrets of these orgulous edifices peeped above the trees, ringing the moat that surrounded Castle Ynyssyll, which towered over them all.

Ahead of them, Datu started singing a song that named all the trees she saw. Lanie didn't recognize the tune.

Titanwood, you are the tallest
Silktree, you're the first to bloom
Cobblebark, your trunk's the hardest
Quaketooth, how you shake and swoon
Sorkhadari! Sorkhadari!
Oldest of them all
Sorkhadari! Sorkhadari!
Never may you fall!

After several verses of this, Lanie asked, "Did you teach her that?"

"No," Mak said softly. "I just tell her the names. She does the rest. Like always."

Not for the first time, Lanie wondered if this was usual for a child. Any child. She only had Datu and her own memories to go by. Mak would know differently. Mak would know if Datu were strange or extraordinary or trailing behind where others dashed ahead. What was it that had made him seek out a school for Datu *now?*

The gate they would be taking, Mak informed them, was at the intersection of "First and Quarter Past." The layout of Liriat Proper, he elucidated, with its twelve concentric circles bisected by twelve major streets "made something of a monstrous clock" when you looked at maps of the city. The map did not at all match reality, but then (he shrugged) what map did?

He narrated the route he'd chosen as they walked it, pointing out landmarks of interest or spots of wildly creative graffiti or certain puddles in the street that Datu should *absolutely not*, under *no circumstances,* jump into. He'd obviously walked their route over several times already, and even more obviously flown over it.

As they walked and he talked, Lanie heard in Mak's voice a kind of admiration, grudging though it was, for Liriat Proper's rough layout. She had not thought Mak could like anything remotely Lirian, and the idea that he could, along with his present kindly manner and his willingness to talk to her at all, gave her mind a great deal of gristle to chew on.

She kept mostly quiet, confining her conversation to questions relevant to the urban geography.

Datu galloped ahead of them to the street called Quarter Past, following Mak's directions to take a right and head down the spike for Seventh Circle.

"Stop and wait before the underpass!" and "Do *not* cross the boulevard to Second Circle without us!" and once the inevitable "Datu! *Hoozzaplo!*"

Datu dodged the dangers that splashed down from the window above with admirable agility, her red-gold hair like a torch lit by bloodlight in the murk of Liriat Proper's understory. She moved easily through the late afternoon crowd, which thickened as they left the wealthy domesticity of the inner city. She was smooth as a pickpocket, slippery as a fish. Lanie's shoulders tensed every time she lost sight of her.

But Mak's sharp eyes tracked his daughter. Whenever Datu flew too far, his voice called her back, surely as a leash.

Not for the first time, Lanie marveled how Mak never seemed to mind leading from behind. She'd always privately thought of this as "Quadoni parenting" but now she wondered if it was, after all, just *Mak?*

"So," Lanie ventured, breaking her long silence, "what's all this about school?"

"I aim to register Datu at Waystation Thirteen," Mak replied, neutrally.

Lanie, wary that Mak's portcullis would crash shut if she said the wrong thing, spoke carefully. "That's... a departure."

Datu's education wasn't something they'd ever discussed with each other, although Lanie had once eavesdropped on a particularly epic argument on the subject between Mak and Nita. Historically, Stoneses were all educated at home by private tutors (in Lanie's case, mostly dead ones, via written or ectenical media). Nita had been an exception—and she would have been the first to say that she had proved the rule.

No, Nita had declared, Datu would be educated at home. Lanie would see to it that Datu learned all that was needful for a Stones to know. If

Mak might endeavor to teach the child her letters and numbers—proper *Lirian* ones—then Nita would undertake Datu's instructions in the killing arts. What more could a young person need?

Mak, it turned out, had strong opinions about that. But he had never conveyed them to Lanie. Until now.

His hands rose, shaped a response in the air that he did not voice, and fell again.

"It was not possible to send Datu to Waystation Thirteen. Before."

"Nita was… certainly set against it."

"She did not love Quadiíb. Nor anything that so much as trailed a scent of Quadiíb."

It was so wild an understatement that Lanie could think of no immediate response. Again, she began cautiously.

"I read all about Waystation Thirteen back when it opened a few years ago. Knowing how I… I enjoy the Quadic language, Canon Lir sends me—used to send—all the Quadoni ex-pat newspapers. I remember the journalists couldn't seem to make up their collective mind about whether the school should be celebrated as a multi-cultural institution or a hotbed of heresy."

"Newspapers," Mak murmured, "thrive on controversy. "

"Datu... doesn't."

He smiled—he actually smiled a little!—at that. "She will thrive at Waystation Thirteen. A traditional Quadoni school would not have done for her, not at this stage. *Traditionally*," he explained, "there are twelve Waystations along the Caravan School road in Higher and Lower Quadiíb. They started as caravanserai that were built up over reliable oases, places where the Traveling Palaces stopped to teach, take on new students and supplies, and release older erophains into the world when they were ready. Ylkazarra—Waystation One—is oldest and largest. A great city! It boasts five universities, twenty-seven colleges, at least a hundred trade schools. Of course, Ylkazarra is exceptional—"

He had been growing increasingly animated but now stopped talking abruptly. Lanie watched his face. Usually stern and colorless, it had begun glowing pink. Mak stared straight ahead, saying nothing for several minutes.

Finally, Lanie assured him, "I don't mind, you know. I love hearing about Quadiíb."

"I… I know."

Both of them knew, too, that Mak had always withheld his sacred memory of Quadiíb from her. It was a part of his ongoing vengeance, which Lanie at all times both resented and felt she deserved.

What does it mean, she thought, that he speaks to me of Quadiíb *now?*

The idea of his having forgiven her the wrong she had done him so many years ago almost frightened her. She skirted around the thought.

"Mak," she said, "I have to ask—is it… is it a good idea that Datu attend a public school—among strangers—at this present time?" She heard her own nervousness, almost querulousness. She sounded cowardly.

But Mak turned to her and said, in the gentlest voice, "Mizka."

Lanie looked up at him, startled. Only Goody Graves ever used that name for her.

"Sacred Datura is but one child. One child—with no friends and a great enemy. What I would give her *right at this present time* are great alliances, brilliant eyes and minds to watch over her, protectors who might willingly take her in should both you and I be—"

"I see," Lanie interrupted quickly. She didn't want even a hint or a suggestion of his to spark her allergy. She read in his face what he was remembering: Nita, laid out upon her bed, eyeless, tongueless, surrounded by feathers. Or perhaps they were only her own memories, crashing upon her like a tide of blood and brine and jasmine.

Mak met her eyes, still smiling a little, possibly in gratitude. "Do not let this trouble you too much prematurely," he advised her. "This is only our first foray into Datu's future education. Waystation Thirteen hosts a weekly cultural event in the brewpub below their establishment. I thought we might just go and… mingle."

"Mingle?" Lanie asked, fascinated and appalled. "Can we—I mean, Mak, can we even *do* that?"

"That, Mizka, is what we are going to find out."

CHAPTER TWENTY-SIX
The Lover's Complaint

"THAT MAN JUST took a pee, Auntie Lanie!"

Knowing Datu would always opt for a clinical explanation over a dramatic double-take, Lanie replied calmly, "Well, yes. We are just outside a brewpub, you see, and alcohol is a diuretic. The more you drink, the more you have to urinate, which often results in dehydration. This can cause headaches, nausea, and the sensation, I've heard it said, of your tongue turning into a bit of chalk wrapped in burlap."

"You've 'heard it said'?" Mak was directing that tender shoot of a smile at her again. "You do not speak from experience?"

"Well, no, I, not really, but, it's just"—Lanie stuttered, flustered; was Mak *teasing her?*—"Aunt Diggie used to host orgies in the northwest wing."

"Ah." Mak turned his face from hers.

A second later she heard him emit a small, helpless sound, somewhere between a squeak and a snort.

Clinging to the facts, Lanie explained to Datu, "You and your didyi never knew our Aunt Diggie. Inveterate gambler. Poor taste in friends. I was, I don't know, twelve or so, one night when I ran into one of her boorish guests. Or he ran into me. Some lout who had stumbled out of Torr Digitalis in search of a pot to piss in."

"Why did he not just use one of our privy closets, Auntie Lanie?" Datu asked practically.

"When you're that drunk, Datu..." Lanie hesitated. "Sometimes you make messes. And Saint Death smiles, his mess was *all over* the house."

"He did not find a pot, I take it," Mak murmured.

"Oh, he found pots all right," Lanie replied grimly, "and several planters, and a few vases, and various corners."

She bit her tongue before saying how he'd found her bedroom door too, but Lanie had locked it on Goody's orders. Goody told her she wouldn't be able to guard her door that night; Digitalis Stones had required her services as a bouncer.

"Is this my school?" Datu stared dubiously at the brewpub, which, with its green and yellow painted sign swinging from the awning, proclaimed itself *The Lover's Complaint*.

"No. That is." Squatting next to his daughter, Mak directed her attention higher—not to the brewpub, which stood at street level (and very likely was sunk beneath it), nor to the quaint blue-and-gold bakery built above that, but to a massive structure that had been built out from the very top of Seventh Circle wall.

It was one of the largest, fanciest buildings on the Seventh Circle 'skyway,' an elevated boardwalk overlaying the top of the wall and extending out from it, girded by permanent scaffolding. The building loomed over the lower boulevard like a very grand lady in full court dress. A very splendid, very frothy, very *pink* court dress.

Datu blinked up at it.

"Auntie Lanie!" She tugged her aunt's frayed shirt tails.

"Mmn?" Lanie turned from rapt contemplation of a bronze address plaque listing:

1. *The Lover's Complaint, Public House*
2. *Eidie's Unparalleled Breads and Pastries*
3. *Waystation Thirteen*[20]

"Auntie Lanie," Datu insisted, "I do not want to go to a school that is so... *that* pink."

Lanie smiled. Datu, in addition to never eating any one type of food that touched another type of food on her plate, and fastidiously avoiding contact with sticky substances, never ate or wore anything pink. She didn't like when Lanie did either. Lanie did it anyway.

"Whyever not?" she asked her niece now. "It's delightful."

Datu screwed up her face in distaste, and Lanie, who enjoyed teasing Datu a little but disliked arguments, instantly followed up with, "Never fear, Datu. I think your didyi said we're just going into the brewpub for now, not the pink place. The front door is right next to the, um, peeing man."

Datu looked to her father for confirmation.

He nodded. "There is a party starting there in a short while, my plumula," he explained. "With food." He paused, then added, "And music."

Something flared in Datu's shadow-sunk eyes. "Oh." She studied the door to the brewpub. Like the sign, its planks were painted yellow and green, which she seemed to find more acceptable than pink. "All right, Didyi."

---

20 Formerly, a brothel called the Pearl of Pleasure. Waystation Thirteen's new Quadoni tenants never got around to repainting the exterior, redecorating the interior, or replacing most of the signage in the propinquity of the property—possibly in the hopes of luring unsuspecting Lirians to higher education.

"'The Lover's Complaint'," Mak muttered to Lanie as they passed under the sign. "Is that a euphemism for one of your unmentionable Lirian maladies?"

"If so, I've not read about it," Lanie answered, reasonably sure that Mak was talking about venereal diseases, and that, if 'lover's complaint' was slang for one, Delirious Stones would have at least mentioned it in her memoirs. Probably more than once. "It's likely just double-entendre," she said airily.

Mak made that funny back-of-throat noise again. "Very likely."

Lanie stood aside to let him enter first after Datu. She had never seen Mak in such a good mood: smiling, teasing, almost—dare she say it?—laughing, and calling her *Mizka*, of all things: the very private, very tender nickname Goody had bestowed upon her in her infancy. Even Lanie didn't know what the name meant, though she knew it was of Quadic origin.

But here was Mak, using it as boldly as if she'd given him permission. But then, Mak had always liked Goody. Liked, and did *not* fear her. It was one of the things Lanie appreciated most in him. And perhaps a Quadic name passed more amiably out of his lips than a hated Lirian one—and a Stones-given name at that. Well, if Mak was determined on amiability, Lanie wasn't going to argue about it. Certainly 'Mizka' walloped 'sister-of-mine-enemy' in the lists—or even 'aunt-of-my-daughter,' which was already an unlooked-for improvement.

Sometime in the last fortnight, while she'd been preoccupied with her work in Queen Ynyssyll's tomb, something in Mak had changed. He'd been exploring his day-lit world, a free man, making his own decisions and coming to his own conclusions.

In some ways, Lanie thought she was meeting Mak tonight for the first time, here in the place and manner of his own choosing. After all, he might have visited the Lover's Complaint alone, or with Datu for sole company, leaving Lanie to the lure of the catacombs and the company of ghosts. He might have departed for good, bearing his daughter away with him (no matter her protests), in secret, taking his chance on speed and anonymity. And she, hard at work in the catacombs, would never have known until it was too late. Instead, he brought her here. For Datu's sake.

The Falcon Defender, she thought, is on the look-out for allies. And I'm one of them.

With that oddly cheering thought, Lanie followed him into the public house, albeit more slowly, and hung a moment in the vestibule, peering into the dark interior. The Lover's Complaint was roomier than Lanie had expected: the large tap room was sunk below street level, creating a cavernous coziness.

The thick darkness smelled of many ages of stale beer, of burning tallow, and sawdust, and fresh rushes, and warm pretzels. There were two enormous hearths on either side of the room, each burning merrily.

Three rows of long tables set end to end with each other, each big enough to seat at least eight people, ran the length of the room. Upon these, taper candles burned, shoved into old metal wine jugs or cheap glass vases, each as encrusted with wax as the chandelier in Stones Ossuary.

It was quite early in the evening—it might still be considered late afternoon—so the public house was light on company. One old woman, sitting at a corner table, ate pretzels and drank cider while reading a book. Lanie briefly envied her. A thin, red-nosed man was napping at the bar, where Mak had gone to sit. Nothing too… overwhelming.

Lanie drew in a deep breath and took a few steps further into the tap room. After all, the Lover's Complaint was a public house. She had as much right as anybody to be here. And Mak had invited her. She would *not* fail him. She would not fail Datu. She would—

"Auntie Lanie"—Datu interrupted this noble and determined flow of thought—"that lady over behind the bar says that food is free tonight for the party but drinks are not. There is a plate of pretzels, and a bowl of cheese, and that lady says to dip the pretzels into a bowl of hot cheese, and not to mind if I make a mess, because that is why there are napkins. That lady talks funny," she added. "Come and see!"

With this, Datu took Lanie by the hand and dragged her across the room to the bar. It was the second time that day that Datu had touched Lanie voluntarily.

Unusual. Perhaps, Lanie reflected, the child is entering a new phase of physical contact. Or perhaps, like her didyi, she is finding her own freedom in the daylit world. Or is terrorized by the possibility of losing herself in it.

Lanie squeezed her niece's hand—just a little, just in case it was the latter. Datu glanced up, but didn't remonstrate with her, and didn't loosen her grip.

Datu's 'lady' turned out to be the publican of the Lover's Complaint. Her hair was dyed as green as the sign, her eyelids painted that same glittering orange. She bore no wizard mark that Lanie could see.

But she was missing one of the fingers on her right hand.

Lanie knew that in some countries it was thought one could remove a wizard's magic by excising the god-marks from their skin. Patently ridiculous, of course, but…

She found herself rubbing her left hand with her right. Clenching her fists, she shoved them both into her trouser pockets.

The colorful publican was laying out platters of the promised pretzels on the long bar, each boasting a bread-bowl full of hot cheese at the center. Smaller plates of nuts, smoked sausages, pickled vegetables, brined olives, and hard cheeses came out next. All of it seemed on offer to all comers. Lanie supposed Waystation Thirteen was paying for it all, as they were the ones hosting what Mak had called a 'cultural night' at the brewpub.

Emboldened by her aunt's presence, Datu eyed the tall bar stool, backed up a few paces, and sprang up onto it with one of her elastic leaps. The publican widened her eyes in surprise, gave a low whistle, but otherwise kept to her tasks. Datu settled, and gestured imperiously for Lanie to join her.

Lanie glanced around for Mak, saw him chatting—chatting!—with a group of musicians setting up stands and chairs on a small raised platform near one of the hearths, and tried to catch his eye. It wasn't difficult; his body was angled so that he see the whole room.

He nodded at her, the slightest jerk of his chin, and gave her another of his small, new smiles. Then he turned back to his conversation.

Discomfited, Lanie scooted back around to focus on Datu, who was asking the publican what there was to drink.

"All depends, my giddy. What's your poison? Gin?" The woman winked at Lanie over Datu's head.

Datu noticed this but elected to ignore it. "What is gin?"

"It's pernicious. Tastes like prickleberries and turpentine. Some folks call it medicine. Others, ruin. Sells all right here, but small beer's better."

"I," said Datu, "do not like medicine. Or small beers. And," she added carefully, "I do not *think* I like gin."

The woman winked again, this time right at Datu, who blinked back at her. "Betchoo like limonana, though. Am I right?"

Before Datu could ask, she listed the ingredients: "Lemon, mint, twist o' sugar. Real sweet." She glanced at Lanie. "Comes in a bottle, corked and sealed, boiled to keep the rot off. No kick. Real safe. Drink it myself."

Lanie stared at the publican, utterly enchanted. She had never seen such a woman! Eel-thin, pale as sea-foam, her bones rising beneath her skin like half-submerged shipwrecks. She wore a stout pair of boots of rusty black leather, scalloped and scaled and fringed, with large buckles running the length of them in the shapes of anchors and figureheads and mermaids. Her apron was carelessly tied, her slithery clothes exposed bits of shoulder, belly, hip, and knee, but never all at once.

"Is limonana imported?" Lanie asked, warily playing with the coins in her pocket. The price of imported goods was a leap from poppets to eparchs.

"Nah," the publican assured her, "bottled locally. We get kids in here pretty often, 'cause of the bakery above us, and the school above that." She jerked a thumb ceilingward. "Students and teachers come down all the time for meal breaks. You want coffee and yer coffeecake, go upstairs to Eidie. But we got all the stick-to-yer ribs stuff down here."

Datu stated firmly, "I will have a limolala."

The woman raised her thin eyebrows at Lanie, who nodded. "Righty-oh, red pepper. One 'limolala' on the double."

Turning away to fetch them up, she showed a swoop of exposed back so fantastically tattooed, it was as if she'd sprung fully-formed from the dyer's baths. Datu's mouth dropped open.

She breathed, "Auntie Lanie. The lady has *pictures*. On her *body!*"

"Those are called 'tattoos,'" Lanie explained. Of course Datu wanted more information. Lanie wracked her brains. "They are like your didyi's facial cicatrices, or my earring holes: a kind of body modification done by ink and needle—though sometimes the piercing implement is thorn, bone, or shell, depending on the region or culture—for ritual purposes or personal embellishment."

"Very fine tattoos, too." Mak's voice behind them, making Lanie jump. "They are Umrysian work, like our publican's dialect—unless I miss my guess. May I sit beside you, my plumula?"

Looking pleased, Datu nodded graciously. Lanie took the next stool over from the one on Datu's free side, mostly so that she would not have to ask permission and seem Mak's mimic, or *not* ask and feel herself discourteous. Datu frowned at the empty space between them, and began to object, but her attention was reclaimed by the publican clomping back up to the bar. A tray bearing half a dozen sweating bottles full of pale green liquid balanced on her hip. She held a cane in her other hand, and moved slowly, favoring her right leg.

Lanie slid half-off her stool, asking, "May I help?"

The woman looked her over swiftly. There were lines on her forehead, at the corners of her mouth and eyes. Wise eyes, gray-blue. A brief flash of resentment, quickly snuffed. When she replied, her smile was a bit strained but not unkind.

"I'd take it."

Lanie ducked under the bar, grasped the tray, and transferred it to a cleared space next to a basket of shelled nuts. The publican came up beside her, nodded in approval, then leaned in and offered a hand. Her manner altered, became warmer, no longer so roguishly aloof. Her voice was softer, too, when she said, "Name's Havoc," not like she was announcing it to the world, but telling Lanie and Lanie alone.

Lanie thrilled to the sound. "I'm Lanie," she said. "Or… or Mizka, if you prefer. Or Auntie Lanie. Whatever you like."

"So many names," Havoc murmured provocatively. "Gotta getchoo one that's mine alone. You new to the old LP?"

"LP—oh, you mean the city?" Lanie laughed nervously. "I—yes, I suppose I am. A few weeks. I grew up in the country roundabouts. Not far… But…" She glanced around. "Not near enough either, I'm finding."

"How'd you hear about us?" Havoc's nose crinkled quizzically. "You *do* know whatcher in fer tonight, right?"

"You mean, the Waystation Thirteen gathering?" Lanie asked, laughing.

Havoc nodded. But here Lanie's tongue froze.

How should I answer? she thought. I have no *idea* what I'm in for, not really—except trying to 'mingle' with people I've longed to meet my whole life, and who would gladly string me up on the basis of my last name alone, thanks to Nita.

But since she couldn't say that (or anything else), Mak answered for her, smooth and friendly, his Lirian hardly accented at all.

"We have come on my suggestion, Mistress Havoc. I heard tell of my countrywoman hosting a weekly celebration on your premises, and wanted my daughter to experience that side of her heritage. Her exposure to Quadiíb and its culture has been a meager feast for any child, I fear. But, I thought, should Waystation Thirteen prove to be…"

Now it was Mak's turn to stop, suddenly unsure of his phrasing; he was still of two minds himself regarding the so-called 'hotbed of heresy' looming invisibly overhead like an alien pink sunflower.

The awkwardness was bridged with no more than a momentary silence; no one was more practiced at conversation than a publican. Havoc turned to Datu with a friendly grin. "Hey, ya! You fixin' to be an erophain, limolala?"

Datu refused to answer without more information. "What is an erophain?"

Havoc gestured toward the door. "Them."

Lanie turned, and almost wept at the sight.

CHAPTER TWENTY-SEVEN

Waystation Radicals

WHAT ENTERED THE room like a cloud of dragonflies was a thing Lanie had dreamed of seeing since childhood: a hoard of happy Quadoni students, dressed up for a party. They filled the room like a cool breeze, brightening even the furthest, darkest corners as if each carried with them their own particular lantern. They did not so much wear clothes as *perform* them: streams of iridescent ribbons pinned with sparkling broaches, chains of silver bells, knots of silken flowers, embroidered sashes, belts of gilded links.

Immediately, the erophains all shed their city-mucked boots in a merry heap by the door and crossed the room barefoot on light feet. Almost all of them carried instruments of one sort or another, and seemed intent on joining the other musicians at the platform, though several stopped at different tables to greet friends, or claim seats of their own. Two in particular were waylaid by the door by half a dozen patrons the instant they stepped in, and were laughingly answering a pelter of questions.

"Didyi," cried Datu in a tone Lanie had never heard from her before—one of *unmitigated delight*—"Didyi, they are all speaking Quadic! All of them!"

Lanie tore her eyes from the erophains to see how Mak would respond, wondering if his delight would match Datu's.

The shock on his face struck her like a backhanded blow. His long frame had shrunk down on his stool, as if he were making the smallest target possible of himself. His chest was neither rising nor falling that she could see; Lanie feared he had stopped breathing. Fat droplets of sweat rolled down his forehead into his eyes, and he did not blink them away. He stared down at the polished bar, as if counting each grain in the wood. Her regard of him seemed to touch off some instinct. Mak looked up, met her eye, and only then managed a harsh gasp.

Quickly, Lanie asked, "How's your limonana, Datu?" and moved one stool closer, trying to give Mak some time to recover.

"It is very good," Datu approved. "I will have another when I finish this." She held up her nearly empty bottle.

Imagining the sugar crash—but not before the fly-at-you-fast questions, the not-waiting-for-answers impatience, the darting-away-in-cartwheels-and-somersaults-and-wall-scalings—to come, Lanie sighed. "Made short work of that, didn't you?"

Datu absently smacked her lips, but she wasn't really listening; she was straining hard toward the erophains, leaning far forward in her seat, staring, trying to hear every conversation at once.

With a rueful smile, Lanie dug in her pockets for some coins, took Datu's hand, and poured them out into her palm.

"Okay. Listen up. You can buy what you like, but with two caveats. One: don't forget to tip Mistress Havoc. Two: save a little for the musicians if they put out a jar. That's to thank them for their playing. It's the polite thing to do."

She was proud at the note of authority in her voice, as if she'd been a weekly regular at the Lover's Complaint for Quadoni cultural nights. She would have to remember to thank Canon Lir for this handhold on normality. It was through their letters, and the newspaper clippings, contemporary novels, and current memoirs they'd always made sure to send her, that she even knew as much. Meticulous and generous, Canon Lir would describe everything from an intimate social outing with their fellow fire priests to the deep machinations of Brackenwild Court, knowing that Lanie starved for every detail. She felt surrounded by a lifetime of Canon Lir's letters. It was as if she moved through the world protected by the walls of an invisible library—only instead of the idiosyncratically Stonesish texts on necromancy and espionage and interrogation and assassination, what Canon Lir had given her was a lexicon of the very world she found herself in right now.

Datu's green eyes burned into hers briefly, hungrily. She contemplated the coins in her hand, calculating whether, if she did not buy herself another limonana, she might keep back that amount for her penny bank. Datu was ferociously protective of her allowance, and knew she wouldn't be getting any more until after their circumstances stabilized.

In the end, however, her sweet tooth won out. She climbed over three sets of stools to get closer to Havoc. Not only did Havoc fetch another bottle right away, but she helped Datu heap a napkin full of all the different foodstuffs on offer. Lanie looked away, smiling.

A shimmer. A twinkle. Across the room at the raised platform, the sound of instruments tuning. A trill of something light and flute-like. The twang of guitar. The scrape of a fiddle. The *doom-doom-doom* of a deep drum.

Then, a different kind of music—laughter—approaching the bar, enhanced by the melodic cadence of conversational Quadic.

The two women who had been stopped at the door were now approaching Havoc, who greeted them with a crooked grin. "Hoy, maties. Yer lookin' brighter than two mer-peacocks pullin' Aganath's glass coracle!"

"Hail, Havoc," said the older, plumper, smaller woman with the shaved-short haircut and a swoopy dyed-orange bang that broke dramatically over one brow. "Bless your prism eyes, that see rainbows trapped in the plain plumage of your fellows."

She spoke in clear though heavily-accented Lirian, her tiny dark eyes slanting into friendly slits when she smiled—which she apparently did so much that her face seemed to smile even at rest. She bore no wizard mark that Lanie could see, but wore a very different symbol of power—the Bryddongard around her right arm.

"Only my friends are rainbows, Tan," Havoc answered with a short laugh. "Most folks're plain enough. Speakin' of, meet my new friend Limolala."

Datu looked up, perfectly ready to accept this appellation—not least because Havoc had refused to take her coins when she wanted to pay for her second bottle of limonana. She said, in her most formal, most ornate Quadic, "Good greetings, countrywomen of Quadiíb."

Lanie could practically hear the buds unfurling in her vowels as Datu flew her fingers as wings against her chest and bowed.

"A friend of Mistress Havoc is my friend," Datu continued, "her boon companions compeers of my heart."

They were ritual phrases which Datu had learned by rote, but still it impressed Lanie that she had pulled them out so magnificently at the exact right moment. Datu was proud of herself too, Lanie could see, for she wore a pleased smirk, and did a little wiggle on her stool that had nothing to do with two bottles of limonana and everything to do with self-satisfaction.

"What have we here? A scholar in our midst?" asked the orange-haired gyrlady in surprised Quadic.

A thousand strong emotions had shaped her face into an expressive webwork of lines; her surprise seemed deeper than a younger countenance could produce, her pleasure an intenser pleasure, and even her keen interest shone like thousand-folded Damahrashian steel. She offered her hand for Datu to shake in the Lirian style, which Datu did just as naturally and (Lanie thought) just as smugly as she had performed her Quadic courtesies.

"To whom dost thou belong, young erophain?" the gyrlady went on.

Datu turned in her stool to point at Lanie and Mak, but changed the subject almost immediately, turning to the gyrlady's companion and asking her in Lirian, "What is that thing in your case?"

The younger woman—the first word Lanie thought of to describe her was 'radiant,' the second 'luminous,' and the third 'incandescent'—smiled sunbeamily down at Datu and answered in Quadic:

"Lovely Emaldissma is her name: friend in woe, close comfort far from home, muse and tyrant, lodestar and guitar. But wouldst thou help me tune her, erophain?"

Nodding eagerly, Datu leapt from her stool, then remembered herself, and dashed back to Mak and Lanie.

"May I help the guitar lady, Didyi? Auntie Lanie?"

Lanie watched Mak struggle to answer. His throat worked. He could not seem to look anywhere but down at the bar—except once, when he cast a sideways glance of mute agony Lanie's way.

"Yes, you may, Datu," Lanie said quickly. "But always stay where you can see us, and on no account are you to leave this room, or go off with any stranger, or take what they have to offer. If you do lose sight of us, find Mistress Havoc and stay with her till we come for you. Do you understand?"

Datu rolled her eyes—"Yes, Auntie Lanie"—and dashed back to the young woman, who met Lanie's gaze with a look of warm understanding.

She, too, bore no visible wizard mark. But there were other marks on her face, tiny sickle-shaped cicatrices that followed hairline and cheekbones. Mak had similar marks. The woman was a Gyrgardu, then. Bonded, of course, Lanie realized, to the orange-haired gyrlady.

Her eyes were some kind of shimmering. The dense gray luster of black pearls, fringed by thick black lashes.

Then she was smiling down at Datu again, bending down to whisper a question, or perhaps answer one. Datu made some half-shy, half-bold reply, and the young woman took her by the hand and led her to the stage, where the rest of the musicians were gathered.

Mak's gaze followed his daughter, so Lanie turned her attention back to Havoc and the gyrlady with the orange hair.

Havoc was busy with a patron, but the gyrlady was looking at her.

A bright, sharp shock, as if Lanie had touched a brass doorknob after shuffling around in wool socks all day. Sparks snapped from her lower back to the base of her skull. The smell of citrus stung her nostrils.

As if sensing her strong reaction, the woman's look of probing intensity vanished. Her gaze moved on—unfortunately, to Mak.

Lanie watched his shoulders creep up, his head sink heavily. He turned away from Datu, away from the bar, until he was entirely facing the back wall of the Lover's Complaint, left hand clutching his right arm, as if to hide what was already concealed by jacket and shirtsleeves: the silvery traces of his own Bryddongard, sunk beneath his skin. But the woman's gaze bored into him as if she could see through the fabric, through muscle and through bone, to the substance of him.

Again, she seemed to read Mak's discomfort, caught herself, withdrew her attention. Her piercing eyes met Lanie's once more.

Lanie couldn't school her scowl fast enough—even when the woman ventured a small smile and twitched her hand in an experimental salutation. Feeling far too peeled by that lancet-like curiosity to respond politely, Lanie gave a short nod, and touched Mak's elbow. He sprang from his stool as if galvanized by lightning, reaching back to grab Lanie by the arm and dragging her all the way to the front door of the tap room.

There he stood with his back to the crowd, facing the Lirian night, sucking down the outside air like it was the first he'd drawn in minutes.

"I cannot, I cannot," he murmured, over and over again. "I thought I could, but I cannot."

"I'll go get Datu," Lanie offered. "We'll leave right now."

Mak turned to look over his shoulder, just for a moment, just long enough to see his daughter perched on the edge of the stage, a drum in her lap. Her 'guitar lady' was teaching her a simple beat to keep. Datu was aglow.

"No," he said, and the word was agony. "No, she is happy. I knew it. I knew that this would be important. She must stay. We must stay. But, Mizka"—he turned his face to the open air, and practically moaned—"I *cannot!*"

"All right. It's all right, Mak." Lanie drew in a deep breath of her own. "This is not insoluble," she muttered, more to herself than to him. "It's just, I don't to want to be walking around with Datu in an unfamiliar city late at night. Too many things can go wrong. Nor," she added, "do I want to risk getting caught by First Circle Watch as we happen to be climbing a tree into an abandoned cryptyard in the richest part of town."

Mak opened his mouth. He shut it fast before his heaving stomach could betray him.

Lanie took him by the elbow and led him further into the short vestibule, keeping herself on the taproom side of the door so that Datu was never quite out of sight. He sank to a crouch and put his head between his knees.

"Don't say anything just yet," Lanie directed him. "Just listen. You know I can get Datu home safely, Mak. With your permission, I'll take her by way of… I'll take her underground."

She touched the reliquary hidden under her shirt collar, and Mak's expression went from nauseated to revolted.

"No harm will come to her," Lanie swore, "and we'll be home twice as fast. It's… it's a far more direct route that way, you know."

Mak withdrew his head from his knees and leaned it against the wall, passing a hand over his forehead.

"And," he said, "it does not… not sicken her. As it does me."

"In fact," Lanie said encouragingly, heartened by the strength returning to his face, "half of what you're feeling right now is probably just your thing about being underground. The Lover's Complaint is a bit, you know, chthonic. Sunken as it is."

Mak managed a short laugh. "Perhaps. Some. But not… not *all*, Mizka."

"I know," Lanie said. "I recall something about how you think you're an abomination in the eyes of conservative Quadoni. But remember, Mak," she leaned down and whispered, "these Waystation Thirteen people are a bunch of heretics. So you'll fit right in."

"Perhaps." Mak wiped his sweating face on his sleeve, heaved himself to his feet. "We shall speak more of this later, Mizka. For now—"

"Yes, yes—go. Before you fly apart."

Still, he hesitated. "Thank you."

"You're welcome, father-of-my-niece."

"Datu—tell her—"

"I will. Don't worry."

"And you'll—

"—be back before midnight. She never lasts much past ten, even after three bottles of sugar."

"I will be waiting." For a second, Mak's hand clasped her shoulder, and then he was through the door so fast Lanie barely saw him leave.

In almost the same instant, Datu was tugging at her coat hem, her voice high and strained. "Where is he? Where did Didyi go, Auntie Lanie? What happened? Did he see a blackbird?"

Turning quickly, Lanie knelt to be on a level with her. "No, no, nothing like that. No blackbirds. Remember how your Didyi gets a little shaky and pale underground?"

Datu nodded, eyes fearful, face ashen—and Lanie realized that however preoccupied she had seemed with the musicians, she'd been keeping one eye on Mak and Lanie the entire time.

Lanie held out both hands, palms up, and Datu unhesitatingly placed hers atop them. Her hands were sticky and hot, and they trembled.

"Well, I've been noticing that maybe your Didyi has some trouble when he finds himself in enclosed spaces. He gets sick—like the way I am with my allergy, you know? Except his allergy is different. He just needs some fresh air, and he'll... he'll be fine. But he says you and I can stay here at the party as long as you like, and you can play all the instruments, and ask about your school, and talk Quadic with your countrypeople, and then I'll take you home fast as anything. We," she imparted enthusiastically, as if conferring a rare and pleasurable privilege upon her niece (which Lanie rather thought she was), "will be traveling via one of my *secret passageways*."

Datu dropped her voice. "With the dead people?"

Lanie nodded. "You don't mind a few bones, do you, Datu?"

Or a few million. But she did not say that out loud.

"You will be with me the whole time?" Datu asked.

"I will," said Lanie. "And for a treat, I can tell you the whole story of Eliki Brackenwild and the riots at the Midwinter Rites—when all the bloodlamps of the capital city went dark."

Her niece looked dubious.

"*Or*," Lanie suggested smoothly, mentally flipping through Mak's gentler repertoire, "we can recite one of your Quadic antiphonies—like the one about the erophain who makes the first harp in the world all out of ice, and strings it with the winter wind, and sets it with the twelve brightest stars of night."

"I like that one."

"All right. It's a deal."

Datu pressed her palms firmly into Lanie's.

"Yes. Now," she said, shaking herself like a wet puppy, "come with me, Auntie Lanie," and she snatched her aunt's wrist in a sugar-grimed, cheese-slimed grip. "You will sit right by the stage, and watch the music, and hear me play the drum."

"Yes, ma'am," said Lanie, and followed.

LATER, IN HER letter to Canon Lir, she wrote:

> *...true to form, Datu was fast asleep by quarter till ten, but it took a whole five minutes to unwrap her from Duantri's guitar case, which she was holding like her toy trebuchet. Duantri offered us a bed in Waystation Thirteen—which used to be a brothel, Canon Lir; did you know??? It was called the Pearl of Pleasure, and Duantri says they've left most of the furniture 'as is' because Tan (that's 'Gyrlady Tanaliín,' the one with the orange hair and skewering eyes) thinks it's funny. But I refused, no matter how tempting. Mak would've torn himself right out of his skin if we'd not come home till morning.*
>
> *I've never seen Datu take to anyone the way she's taken to the young Gyrgardu Duantri. That's just as well, because it turns out that Duantri teaches Datu's age group. (Actually, they're not called 'age groups' at Waystation Thirteen; they're called 'flights,' but you probably already know that.) She'll get to learn things like the whole Quadoni canon of historical antiphonies, medical botany through the visual arts, and music. Couldn't you just turn gangrenous with envy? I could. Except why should I begrudge Datu the one thing I wanted most when I was her age? I just hope she likes school better than Nita did.*
>
> *Towards the end of the evening, I'd been helping Havoc behind the bar, and she let me keep all my tips! Which were considerable!*
>
> *(At least, I <u>think</u> they were considerable: to what shall I compare it? Professional necromancers won't get out of bed for less than twenty-five hundred monarchs a resurrection. That's five times what Nita charged per hit, because—after all—killing is something most anybody can do, and generally speaking, it can only be done once. But panthaumic resurrection is rare—and it's a renewable source of income. A spell set to last from one surge to the next can keep the gold tumbling in season after season. (So long as the living desire to keep their dead undead.) But what price a smile, an offer of pretzel and beer refills? (Re: tips: no, they <u>must</u> have been good, because even <u>Mak</u> was impressed.)*

Havoc asked if I would be coming back next week—and if I were, would I be willing to help her out again? Apparently Rainday nights at the Lover's Complaint are always mayhem, what with the erophains and the music and Quadoni culture lectures and everything. She'd been hinting around all night to discover whether or not I minded that maybe some of her spirituous liquors were perhaps not exactly what you might call 'legally imported' (DON'T TELL YOUR BROTHER I TOLD YOU; I AM HOLDING YOU TO THAT, CANON LIR)*, and I said of course I didn't, and how did she manage to smuggle them all inside the Lover's Complaint without the revenues officers any the wiser?*

I <u>*suspected*</u>*, you see, that smugglers run their contraband through the catacombs! And I was right! There are many more ways in and out of the city than by Gallowsdance's Tunnel of Doom—though I'm pretty sure* <u>*that*</u> *one's not been used since her execution. Except by us.*

So, anyway, I got a little sly, and told Havoc that I was fairly familiar with the catacombs myself, and that, in fact, I knew a shortcut home for me and my niece that way, if she wouldn't mind showing me the nearest entrance.

Canon Lir! There's one right in her cellar! Hidden beneath a stack of crates full of what your ommer might consider 'some dang fine demon grog!' (If, that is, Eparch Aranha of the Holy Temple of Sappacor were as given to using Umrysian slang as they are to drinking fine cognac.) It was all there: cognac, brandy, whiskey, you name it. Barrels of beer and wine, of course—but that's all local, or right from the baronies. And just <u>*shelves*</u> *of Datu's new favorite, 'limolala.' (I'm going to forget the real word soon if she keeps calling it that, and Havoc's no help, just egging her on.)*

What else? I'm giddy! And it's not just from lack of sleep or beer, though I've had plenty of both—the lack <u>*and*</u> *the beer—but, oh, from, from, just, I don't know,* <u>*people*</u>*. Real, live* <u>*people*</u>*, Canon Lir! And music. Everywhere! For hours! Guitars and drums and dancing—you know? And Mak has been so strange and kind all day and says I am to practice sothaín every morning with him and Datu, and Datu is so happy, and—I don't understand it at all, Canon Lir! How can the* <u>*worst*</u> *have happened and yet it's all so…* <u>*good*</u>*?*

I mean, for now. I know it won't last. But <u>*for now*</u>!

I wasn't halfway through the catacombs when Goody met us. Mak didn't even ask her to come. I swear, she just decided on her own. She always knows where I am—just like I always know where <u>*you*</u> *are, whenever you are wearing our reliquary. (I wonder how far that cord between us will stretch? Would I be able to find you on the other end of the world? Would running water or falling snow or dust storms obscure its signal? Perhaps we shall put it to the test by and by.) Goody offered to take Datu and carry her home for me! I was dreadfully grateful, I can tell you, because Datu is all muscle, and weighs more than a sack of cannonballs, and there are a lot of stairs from the catacombs up to the chapel.*

As we walked together, I told Goody all about tonight, just like I'm telling you—and, Canon Lir, she was so pleased for me! She asked me all sorts of questions! She's never this talkative. I think it was a combination of being away from Grandpa Rad, and the fact that on Midsummer, she and I must—

But I try not to think about that too much. Lest I despair.

Never mind! I hope that you and I will soon meet again! And well before Midsummer!

Perhaps you'll come to a Rainday culture night at the Lover's Complaint, and drink contraband brandy! I'll serve it to you myself, and even sit on your lap—but you must tip me handsomely!—and on no account are you to call me 'Miss Stones.' I'm trying to be inconspicuous!

Yours, very cordially (and by the way, you should try our cordial!),
Misc. Stones

Lanie waved the letter back and forth to dry the ink, keeping a surreptitious eye on the Sarcophagus of Souls. Grandpa Rad was still not talking to her, but that suited her at present. However stubbornly he meant to sulk in his padlock, she knew that he was just about wild to nose in on her doings and dealings.

Very deliberately, she withdrew a single orblin from her 'courier' stack, and licked it.

As it began to soften and glow, she set the orblin down upon her letter like a paperweight, with a whispered instruction.

Ectenica seeped like slow blue ink across the page, taking over the writing, the margins, the very fabric of the paper itself.

Soon, nothing of the letter remained but a thin sheet of spectral dazzle—and this not for long. It imploded with a soundless *pop*, leaving Lanie in the dark of Queen Ynyssyll's tomb—except for the padlock, which was blazing with ghostly curiosity.

"My letter will be appearing just now in Canon Lir's chambers," Lanie said aloud. "We've been experimenting. In a few minutes, they'll be sending one of their—"

A tiny, flame-red droplet appeared in the middle of the room, dancing and flickering as if glancing around inquiringly.

Lanie laughed, and beckoned, calling, "Here!"

The bright-lit drop bounced happily in the air, and then over to her, casting the trembling light of rubies all around it.

She touched one tip of her finger to it. The globule—blood? Fire? Both?—first flashed, then pulsed, then spoke with Canon Lir's voice. But for the slightly echoey quality, they might be in the same room with her.

"*I am in receipt of your message, Miss Stones—I will peruse it anon and reply at length in a more traditional manner. Call for my letter at the Lover's Complaint, care of your new friend, Mistress Havoc. Dream sweetly, sweetest of friends. Sappacor's blessings upon you.*"

The tiny red droplet flew to Lanie's mouth, and kissed it with an audible smack. A tingling—a smoky warmth upon her lips—and then the tomb was dark again.

"You want to watch it with that one, girlie. Fire priests are notoriously fickle," the ghost rasped.

"And necromancers are notoriously unstable," Lanie agreed. "Never mind that now, Grandpa Rad; I've decided something. I'm going to give you one of my orblins tomorrow."

The padlock fairly went up in a pillar of excited blue flames, but the ghost's voice was cautious. "Are you, then? What brought that—?"

Lanie interrupted, "I'll feed you half an orblin in good faith first. But then I want you to tell me, specifically and without any divagation into any personal reminiscences, how to identify a sorcerer—fire priest, holy urchin, Rookish wizard, gyrlady: *any* sorcerer—not by their visible wizard marks, but by their living bones."

"Ha!" the ghost laughed dryly. "For *two* orblins, I'll do you one better, Miscellaneous Stones. I'll tell you how to recognize a sorcerer by his living bones, *and* name the magic he'll wield against you for snatching that knowledge from him like some gutterlicking sneakthief."

"*Half* an orblin for the full theory and practice of identifying magic-users *and* their magics from both living specimens *and* fossils," Lanie countered. "Or half of *that* instead if you try to bargain me down further."

"Deal," said the ghost, trying to sound peevish but hardly succeeding even in masking his triumph.

But it was really Lanie who left the tomb victorious. On her pallet upstairs in Doédenna's chapel, where she lay awake a long while, listening to the sounds of Mak and Datu breathing, and the roaring, lulling lure of the catacombs below, like a beautiful beast humming beneath her, she dwelled, satisfied, on her day's work.

CHAPTER TWENTY-EIGHT

Raiment

Brineday 21st
Month of Flukes, 421 Founding Era
High Holy Fire Feast of Summer Solstice: Dawn

"When you were born," Goody told her, "I had loved nothing and no one for so long. I had forgotten my name, my language, my history, in the dry eternity of my servitude. No task brought me pleasure. Nothing moved me. I was animate but nearly mindless, unmotivated by anything but the compulsion to obey."

She spoke slowly, deliberately, the way she did everything, her voice so deep it seemed to come from beneath the grass. She and Lanie lay side by side on their backs: Goody with her hands folded upon her breast, Lanie's fingers intertwined behind her head, and the sorkhadari tree darkly luminous above them, not yet limned in any but the promise of daylight. The damp earth bent around their bodies like a table burdened by too great a feast, and when Goody turned her head in the grass to look at Lanie, the earth moved.

"And then..." she said.

Lanie closed her eyes, waiting. This was a story she had never heard before. The last story Goody would ever tell her.

"And then, twenty-three years ago, there was born to the Stoneses a sickly babe. A wasted, wretched, shriveled creature who could not sleep in a house that by day stank of death and by night rang with the cries of the dying. She could not bear the touch of her mother's cold hands or her father's rare caresses. Because of this, they ordered me to care for her. They were Stoneses; I was under their command. Care for her, they said, knowing I must obey. Well. You know, Mizka, and I know, that there are many ways I might have obeyed. I might have cared for her by throwing her down a well. Or bricking her up in the cellar. Or exposing her in the woods. Set against all the tales of all the necromancers of history—

especially those of *that* house—such actions might be considered care indeed. Call it, even, mercy."

Lanie shivered. She had borne witness to enough of Goody's interpretations of Stonesish commands over the years (hundreds, thousands, of them) to understand that Goody might have justified so much—or more—to herself.

"Instead, I cared for the babe by cleaning up her messes. Rocking her at night. Making sure that some of what she ate stayed inside her belly. I did this... *almost*... mindlessly." Goody paused. "But sometimes... sometimes, in my bleakest moments, sitting near her crib, covered in her drool and spit-up, listening to her beseeching, mewling, wordless whimpers, I remembered the faintest strains of a lullaby I once knew."

At this, Lanie opened her eyes. The dark needles and bright berries of the sorkhadari tree were beginning to sparkle with new light, but she was not sure if this was the breaking of dawn or of panthauma. She dared not interrupt Goody to speculate.

But she berated herself for never having conceived of it before: how, even as a helpless infant, Lanie had yet been bound to Goody—as a necromancer must always be to the undead. Her body, tiny and pitiful as it had been, was yet blessed of Doédenna, and would have exerted some influence or effect upon a revenant. Whenever her living fluids had come into contact with Goody's undead material—and however ungovernable and unappealing those fluids might have been—the result would still have created a pure ectenica. Which would, in turn, have renewed Goody's own substance, washing her in new strength and memory.

"I had not remembered anything of myself for so long," Goody continued. "I was like a scorched and salted battlefield pushing up its first wildflower. Even that lowly weed of a lullaby seemed to me a miracle. And so, remembering, I sang. And when I sang, the babe, at last, slept in my arms. That, Mizka, is when I recognized her. My language was slowly returning to me, and with it all the things I once knew. I knew her for what she was. What she could and *would* be to me. The daughter of my undeath. My hope for an end. This hope, Mizka—it was not... not a peaceful sensation, nor did it lighten my burdens. Indeed, with it came the whetted knowledge of my everlasting wounds, my unending durance, my thralldom, and such restlessness and loneliness and longing as I cannot now speak of. But if one thing made my terrible hope bearable, these twenty-three years, it was the love I felt for you, and from you for me. The surety of my love being returned. The surety that your love was true, and that once you came into your power, you would take my seed of hope and make it bloom, and lay it as a bouquet upon my final resting place."

Lanie could not answer this. She rolled over onto her stomach and wept into the grass. Her tears were hot; they scorched where they dropped.

No one, in all her life, had ever told her they loved her. Not in words. Not like Goody. And after tonight, would she ever hear such words again?

But if she failed Goody tonight, she might never hear them anyway, for she would have betrayed Goody's trust forever.

"I'll miss you!" The uneven ground of the cryptyard seemed to rise into her mouth to muffle her words. "I'll miss you so much. I'll miss you like breathing. I'll miss you like bread. I'll miss you like, like..."

Lanie couldn't finish, and Goody laid a hand upon her back, as vast and cold as the first stone to ever press a criminal to death. It silenced her.

"You have seen Doédenna's face," Goody whispered. "It is *my* turn, Mizka."

Lanie lay a long moment in the dirt before she mumbled in agreement. Gathering her up from the ground, Goody held her in her arms a while.

"Come," said she, almost a croon. "We will spend our day in joyful preparation. I shall sit beneath this sorkhadari tree and pray, remembering what of my life is still within my grasp, and also those points of my recent undeath wherein I sometimes felt joy. And you, Mizka, wipe your tears away"—she did this for Lanie, who sniffled—"and join your friends at festival. As you and they celebrate the gods in wonder, and as the gods turn their attention twelve-fold back upon you in blessing, so the tides of panthauma will crash ever higher, grow ever more marvelous. You shall return to me tonight at the height of your happiness, in the fullness of life and magic and the marvelous memory of the gods, and then you and I shall bid each other farewell. Truly," Goody murmured against Lanie's wet cheek, "truly, Mizka, we are blessed to have my hour come at a moment of our choosing. That is a rare gift in life—or, as I have found, otherwise."

It was the longest speech Lanie could remember Goody ever making, and the hardest to hear. Each word felt acid-etched in her memory. Certainly she had known enough of death—all of it shocking and ugly and cruel—to understand that tonight would be among the most beautiful of her life, full worthy of Doédenna who wanted to receive all Her people in gentleness.

Only, just... Goody! It was her Goody!

No, a voice at the back of her brain reminded her. It is *Her* Goody.

Remembering her god's face, Lanie's treacherous body was suddenly beset by eagerness, approval, encouragement—as if Saint Death Herself had joined with Goody in urging Lanie to keep her Midsummer promise. As Goody wished it, that internal joy seemed to convey, so too did She.

Lanie reluctantly nodded against Goody's granite breast, and sat up, wiping her face more thoroughly. "All right, Goody. It shall be as you wish."

Her voice trembled, but Goody tucked a finger under Lanie's chin, and smiled down as Lanie had never seen her smile. "I have a present for you."

Lanie was so startled, she hiccuped. "What?"

"Stay there," Goody commanded. "Close your eyes." She stood smoothly, like a monolith suddenly mobile, and disappeared behind the sorkhadari tree.

All was silent for some time. Lanie inhaled deeply: no hint of citrus, no tingle or tickle. No rhyme ringing in the cradle of her skull…

Except—? Oh. Except for the constant, light echo of Datu's silly tree song, of course. But that was not unusual even on a non-surge day. Under Gyrgardu Duantri's tutelage at Waystation Thirteen, Datu had set her little rhyme to music, bolstering the tune with a handful of chords she'd learned, accompanying herself by twanging away on the small cavaquinho her didyi had managed to purchase for her second- (or more likely sixth- or seventh-) hand from the rag-and-bottle shop on Market Circle. The child had been singing it nonstop for the last month and a half.

Sorkhadari! Sorkhadari!
Oldest of them all
Sorkhadari! Sorkhadari!
Never may you fall!

Lanie brushed new tears from her eyes, cursing herself for crying at a child's song. The next moment, she felt a heavy, silent tread come up behind her, and Goody's voice bidding her, "Open your eyes."

Lanie obeyed, as a waterfall of peony-pink, dahlia-coral, snapdragon-orange, and marigold-yellow silk fell into her lap, aglow in the breaking dawn. She stared at the piles and piles of silk, shining heaps and mounds of it: embroidered in contrasting jewel-blues and bright greens, bouncing with flounces, foaming with lace, running with ribbons, and festooned all over with enormous silk flowers.

Open-mouthed, she stroked the bright heaps and folds, and then, still gaping, glanced up at Goody, trying to gather wits enough to thank her.

But there came pouring upon her, in a secondary cascade of radiance, an onrush of panthauma like a fizzing citrus thunderstorm.

It was so sudden, so complete an envelopment, that Lanie could focus on nothing but those hundred zany pinwheels of fractured light.

Panthauma bubbled and glittered, capered and gesticulated, giggled and zinged and zanged. Lanie was dizzy with it.

Before she knew what was happening, Goody helped her to stand, and then helped her into the gown. In minutes, Lanie had been buttoned, clasped, and laced in pure panthauma, in silk and summertime and love and the work of Goody's hands. If lava were kindly, if rainbows were warm, if stars smelled of orange blossoms—these, then, Lanie felt, would be the raiment she stood up in.

"Weeks ago," Goody explained to her—and somehow it all rhymed and chimed in Lanie's ears, even though the words themselves were very plain—"when the gyrgardi went to market to find the child an instrument, I bid him bring me materials with which to make your festival dress. The child," Goody added conscientiously, "picked out the ribbons herself. She wished me to make that very clear to you. Here, too, are gloves."

Little yellow lace gloves, hardly there, like gauze, like mist. But they were enough to disguise the wizard mark on her left hand.

"The gyrgardi also found you a pair of slippers for me to make over. They are the correct size, but he apologizes that they must perforce also be secondhand."

To Lanie's surge-struck eyes, the slippers—another shade of pink, laced with coral and orange ribbons, with great floppy yellow silk flowers that trembled over the toes—appeared like two tiny fireworks that never lost their spark.

"I don't mind!" she gasped.

"That," said Goody, "is what I told him you would say." She produced another ribbon—pink satin this time, just a bit frayed at the ends—to tie around Lanie's neck. "Now sit you down upon this headstone, Mizka, and I shall unbraid your hair."

She did so, with great patience and gentleness, until Lanie's hair burgeoned up and around her head like a black gloriole. She set upon her brow a wreath of fresh peonies, made up of every sunset color, and fluffed a few of the silk flowers to bursting brightness at her shoulder, then stood back to inspect her handiwork.

"How glad thou mak'st mine eyes, thou girl-bouquet," Goody murmured in Quadic, her voice as deep as wells. "Now join thy friends and celebrate this day, and when the sky doth shroud itself in night, return to me and sing my lullaby."

"I will, Goody. I won't fail you. I... I... thank you!" Lanie flew back into Goody's arms, and held her tightly.

She clung until Goody turned her around and gave her a half-pat, half-push, expelling her from the shadow of the sorkhadari and into the blazing green garden, where Mak and Datu were awaiting her.

"Auntie Lanie!" Datu exclaimed disapprovingly from behind her red beard. "That dress is *pink!*"

CHAPTER TWENTY-NINE

An Estival Festival

High Holy Fire Feast of Summer Solstice: Midmorning

DUANTRI MET THEM at the door of the Lover's Complaint with many exclamations and embraces, and ushered them all inside the tap room, explaining that Havoc was still 'wiggling into her festival finery' and would be joining them shortly.

"Behold thyself!" she cried upon taking her first real look at Lanie. "A banquet for the gods! A cloud, a cake, a pastry of pure bliss! How shall thy canon look on sweetness thus, and not pounce straightway for thy sugar kiss?"

At this, Lanie's whole head grew so hot, she thought it would burst. "Datu!" She glared at her niece, who for her festival costume was arrayed as Engoloth, god of War, Time, and Pepper. She wore the whole traditional attire: beard, chainmail (scrap metal scavenged by her didyi), chaps, axe and all. "What have you been telling your teachers about me?"

"It was not a secret, Auntie Lanie!" Datu returned. "Canon Lir comes to see you at the Lover's Complaint every Rainday for Quadoni culture night, and Gyrlady Tanaliín says that while they are one of the politest young persons she has met, it is obviously not to hear the music and lectures they attend, but because you always end up sitting on their lap and whispering in their ear. Also, Duantri *asked* me, Auntie Lanie, and Didyi says I must not lie."

Now Lanie glared at Mak, who was trying not to laugh. She could not look at him for too long, though; he was too resplendent.

In Liriat, there were two modes of ritual habiliment for the high holy fire feast of Midsummer: 'flooping' and 'froofing.' Persons electing 'floomp' followed the sartorial edict to 'turn themselves inside out,' to become their own extravagant opposite—whatever that meant to them. 'Froofers,' on the other hand, strived to reveal, in the intricacy of their outerwear, their fanciest, happiest, most decorated inner self. These two modes were not always, or even often, mutually exclusive.

Today, Mak was both floomping *and* froofing, and his choices suited him as had no other attire Lanie had ever seen him wear.

She wondered if he had preferred this style of clothing in Quadiíb, and if that was another thing Nita had taken from him. Or was it one he had secreted from her, and was now reclaiming? At Stones Manor, he'd always worn hunting leathers or dun-colored castoffs. He had never incarnadined his cheeks and mouth—as he had today—with rouge and lipstick, nor shimmered those gold-green designs in looping swirls around his eyes and cheeks. A wreath of mauve and magenta zinnias crowned the flyaway flames of his hair, matching the gown of purple silk that left him bare at the shoulders, with deep slits at the thighs that went all the way to the floor. He'd tied a thin purple ribbon around his neck, and from it hung a small pearl drop—counterfeit, of course: most likely shell and fish scales, or perhaps glass painted with snail slime and egg white—trembling in the hollow of his throat. And the perfume of him…

Lanie returned her bemused gaze to Duantri, who was clinging to her arm, looking distressed. It took her a full three seconds to remember why.

"No, no, Lanie—blame them not! Forgive *me!*" pleaded the Gyrgardu in her slightly-awry Lirian. "I thought it not some heart-kept secret. It seemed to me a… a friendship of long-standing, yours with Canon Lir's, and I hoped one day to hear the story."

She squeezed Lanie's hand, waiting till Lanie gave a bashful nod of absolution, and upon receiving it, beamed sunnily and then adroitly turned the subject, sitting them all down at an empty table to await Havoc.

Havoc had closed the Lover's Complaint that day due to festival activities—and because she, along with her upstairs neighbor Eidie of Eidie's Unparalleled Breads and Pastries, would be catering the Waystation Thirteen party that night. But Havoc, Duantri, Lanie, and Datu had all agreed among themselves some weeks ago to walk together to Sinistral Park, where the Bloodlighting was to take place at noon. Tan would meet them all up later, after taking care of some last-minute party business. It was towards party matters that Duantri directed the conversation now.

"Canon Lir accepted Tan's invitation once they understood *you* were committed too, Lanie," she said, almost in the same breath as she had been exclaiming admiringly over Datu's costume. "They accepted on Eparch Aranha's behalf as well—the Eparch, I take it, is some kind of relative of theirs?" She rolled her eyes. "Talk of another fire priest with a serious case of heated loins—only Aranha's are all for Tan. Tan, of course, enjoys their bed-company and melancholy wit. The charm is real! But more than this, Tan enjoys their gossip. She hankers to meddle in local politics, you know. When we departed Quadiíb, she left absent her seat in the Judicial Colloquium, and even running Waystation Thirteen and teaching the elder erophains cannot be using half her energy or talents. And so, Aranha is often visiting us upstairs," Duantri finished on a little sigh.

Not in jealousy, Lanie thought interestedly—but as though Duantri doesn't find the Eparch of the Holy Temple of Sappacor nearly so entertaining as her beloved gyrlady does.

Lanie, like Mak, still dodged Gyrlady Tanaliín and her sharp, shrewd eyes whenever she could. Though both of them, like Datu, had long since melted into gooey puddles before Duantri's cheerful warmth.

Eparch Aranha, who seemed to Lanie no less piercingly watchful than Tan, was nevertheless easier to steer clear of, for they only occasionally attended Rainday culture nights with their niephling Lir, and that was for the sole purpose—so they proclaimed—of enjoying the sublime music of the erophains.

But whenever the Eparch's assessing eye fell upon her interactions with Canon Lir, Lanie felt it as a crawling sensation up her spine.

When she swished forward to serve or clear a table where Canon Lir was sitting. When she teased them about their fastidious habits (Canon Lir never drank anything harder than perry cider, and could nurse a single tankard for hours).

When Canon Lir pulled her close, to tip her outrageously, or slip a small gift into her apron pocket—a book, a ring, a bone—or tell her news of court: their concerns regarding the baronies, of Sari Scratch's ever-rising influence, how their twin Blood Royal Errolirrolin was planning to send a delegation to Rook in hopes of an alliance with the Blackbird Bride.

When, in exchange, while seeming to nibble their neck or nuzzle their ear, Lanie would hurriedly whisper her plans to return Goody to dust, what necromancy Grandpa Rad was teaching her in exchange for munching orblins, of Datu's lessons at the Waystation, and of Mak's work at the river docks.

Their exchanges would grow very heated, nor were any the less so for being minutely observed by multiple parties. Quadoni culture nights often ended with Lanie mussed, nonplussed, and beguiled, and Mak trying to chew his smile down to about half its knowing arc, and Datu looking revolted but also intrigued.

"I do not know the Eparch myself," Mak said quietly to Duantri, "but hope that you will find enjoyment at your own party. Despite the company."

He was still shy of speaking to anyone from the Waystation, and never spoke Quadic with any of them, but Duantri had responded to him from the start as though they had been friends since the creche. She gave him a merry look now—and Lanie started at the expression on Mak's face as he gazed back at the Gyrgardu: so clear and shining it was like a window you could fly right through.

"Certes," said Duantri, in Quadic, though out of rhythm for emphasis. "Though thou alas abstain'st from joining us."

Mak blushed. "It is a loud and rowdy crowd for some of us, and a late night withal."

"Watch out, Mak," Lanie said, grinning as his blunt sentences rounded out in rhymes. "Your Lirian's growing flowers."

Datu, watching and listening, and beginning to bristle, now hotly exclaimed, "But, Didyi, I *want* to go to the party! Auntie Lanie is going. Havoc and Duantri and all the erophains and everyone else is going. Gyrlady Tanaliín says it will be a *veritable orgy!*"

She pronounced that last phrase with gusto, having still only a vague notion of what an orgy actually was—though Lanie had tried her best to explain it to her in the most clinical of terms.

"Alas, Datu," her father responded somberly, "your aunt must represent us all tonight—the family ambassador, let's call her—for I must be at work tomorrow early at the docks." He glanced at Lanie. "Right about the same hour your aunt will be bedding down to sleep. So you must stand guard by day, like mighty Engoloth, and watch over her slumber."

A troubled darkness flickered momentarily over Datu's bearded face. Darkness and the thought of blackbirds. She moved away from Duantri's casual caresses to stand nearer to Lanie, plucking at one of the flowers on her skirt. *Not* one of the pink ones.

"You will come home tonight, Auntie Lanie?" Datu asked, not for the first time that day. "Gyrlady Tanaliín says the party will go on till dawn."

"I'll be home well before midnight, Datu," Lanie reassured her, as she had done several times on their walk over to the Lover's Complaint. "Remember, I've got a… a Midsummer rite with Goody this evening. It'll be private, but I'll be just outside in the garden. Probably done before you're asleep." Her throat tightened.

"What if," Datu asked, a little stubborn, a little sly, "*Canon Lir* asks you to stay and spend the night at the Waystation? In one of the pink rooms? How will we know you are safe?"

"I doubt they will," Lanie returned in a slightly sterner voice. "They will have their duties at the temple, after all. Midsummer is a busy time for fire priests. Like me, they'll just be stopping by the party for a short while. To be polite."

"I fear all that is true, Datu," Duantri sighed, "and not for trickery or show. Your Auntie Lanie and Canon Lir both are what Tan calls 'elusive beings.' It only spikes her curiosity, you know," she scolded Lanie, "which is already so great a power it could light Liriat Proper brighter than its cursèd bloodlamps!"

Lanie squirmed. "I really don't mean to be slippery," she lied, "and it's not that I *dislike* your gyrlady, Duantri, but—"

"Oh, I know. Tan knows too. She does try to rein herself in—only, she is a fiend for puzzles, my Tan—and you and yours must all *insist* on being so mysterious and intriguing! But I will not press you, for I love you, and we must all respect our sacred privacies."

Again, Duantri swiftly turned the subject to spare Lanie further embarrassment. "Canon Lir sent us their hostess gift well ahead of time! A dozen bottles of morats, bilbemels, and other metheglins right from their temple stores—along with a dark red bottle that utterly dreads me. I am afraid it is some kind of scorch mead, fermented with those peppers named after Damahrashian scorpions. Naturally, Tan is in a—what would you say? a tizzy?—a tizzy to try it. She..."

But then Duantri's mobile face went from scorch-wary to nova-bright, and she leapt up from her bench, declaiming in Quadic, "Lord Havoc! Merman of the briny deep! Pirate King and ravisher of women! Thou floomp'st alike to Aganath Herself!"

Havoc, just entering from her private chambers above the tap room, laughed. "Tits and pickles, Duantri! Ya know I don't speak high heathen. Talk urchin, wouldja?" She twirled for them all. "So. D'ya like my 'stache?"

Duantri affected a heavy Umrysian dialect, just enough like Havoc's own to be hilarious. "Aye, matie! 'Struth I like it mighty well. Um, mighty good?"

"Mighty fine," Datu piped in from between the two of them, where she had inserted herself. She watched their interplay like a spectator at a tennis court. Duantri obligingly returned the next volley.

"'Tis—it's—a 'stache of epic prow and bow. Bow and stern?" Duantri threw up both her hands in one of her happy, exaggerated shrugs. "Some kind of metaphor nautical, anyway! And who are *you* calling heathen, thou errant sea-worshipper?"

Havoc slid a wink Datu's way. Datu had been waiting for it, urgent but patient, like a hound expecting a juicy meat gobbet. Immediately she returned the wink with one of her own. She had been practicing her winking. Incessantly.

Lanie caught Mak's eye. They both smiled, then glanced away quickly so as not to burst out laughing.

"Nice beard," Havoc said, tilting her head at Datu's hennaed horsehair facial fixture. "Must be floompin' for Engoloth, big ol' red nest like that. Right?"

"Yup," Datu said, in her best 'deep gruff' voice. "Happy surge, Lord Havoc!"

"Happy High Tides to ye, Lord Limolala," Havoc returned, then swiveled to wink at Lanie next. "Heya, cookie!" she greeted her appreciatively. "Yer like a cloud o' orange spun sugar made love to a lemon lollypop, then had a raspberry sherbet baby in a flower bower. All that slurpability's makin' my mouth water."

Lanie laughed and curtsied, her own mouth suddenly full of the taste of pink lemonade. Or perhaps happiness. "I thank you kindly, Lord Havoc. You yourself are simply dashing. Duantri, I must be some kind of heathen too, for I find myself worshipping Havoc's mustache!"

Havoc twirled the waxed green ends of the handsome horseshoe on her upper lip. "Ain't heresy to recognize the divine, cookie," she drawled. "Don't I floomp like a champ? Tho' not," she added, giving Mak the once-over, twice, "as scrumptious as *that* fine gal over there. Hale and high tides to ye, Lady Mak. Holy smoked salmon! You smell like some dessert I'd love to scarf."

"Twelve gods," Duantri agreed, walking over to give Mak a deep sniff of her own, "if you will share, Lord Havoc, I swear I'll take my portion!"

Thus, Mak found himself beset by two floomped festival maids. First came Havoc—in her bandolier, bandana, an enormous galleon-shaped hat complete with sails and masts, a short-sleeved shirt (equal parts fishing net and bright patches), short red trousers, tall red boots, and a snug vest, pinned with a brooch the size of a breastplate. The brooch was bronze: a split-finned merrow with a saucy look on her face. Then, on her heels, came Duantri—in her sleeveless jacket of huntsman's mottle, ecru and brown and deep greens, braided up the front with spindle buttons. Her loose linen trousers were tucked into brown boots, her breasts were bound, and her black curls were scraped back and hidden beneath a jaunty cap.

"My lords," Mak murmured, and if his eyes half-closed as Havoc and Duantri began to nuzzle around his neck, he at least kept his feet. More or less.

But Datu, for all she adored Havoc and Duantri with a passion she rarely exhibited for anything but projectiles, did not like this. Not at all.

"Didyi is *not* food!" she protested, diving in and trying to wedge them all apart. "He just smells like dessert because we found some perfume oil in the rag-and-bottle shop. It is a mix of vanilla and nutmeg and almond and clove. Didyi says he used to wear something like that a long time ago, and wanted to try it again in case he still liked it. But, Didyi," she said to her father directly, having only partly succeeded in separating him from the predatory herd, "I do not think you should wear that perfume again, because it makes people hungry. Also"—she eyed her father's purple gown with new doubt—"I think that maybe you are too pretty in your new dress—"

"Yes, Mak," Lanie agreed, biting back another laugh. "It makes people hungry."

Mak snorted softly, but Datu's surly mood did not bear teasing. She hunched down in her chainmail, glowering, until her father—not without reluctance—extricated himself completely from Havoc and Duantri and put a table's length between his person and theirs. Still scowling, Datu muttered behind her beard, "Maybe Auntie Lanie and Didyi and I will just go to the Bloodlighting by ourselves."

Havoc and Duantri, who had entwined arms when Mak stepped away from them, now released each other. They did not even have to exchange glances to agree on a strategy; both, in their separate ways and roles—Havoc, as proprietress of a busy tavern, Duantri, as a teacher of young children—were masters at redirection. Havoc announced, "I'm gonna go get our picnic basket. Lady Mak, mayhap you'll lend me yer brawn?"

With a neutral nod, Mak joined her behind the bar, while Duantri perched on the edge of the table and began trying to coax Datu into a better mood.

"Dost chance to have thy cavaquinho by?" she asked in Quadic. "On feast days, revelers will pay for song, in coin and candy, drink, dance, and applause—and thou and I together singing true could rake in all the poppets of the park."

"I did not bring it," Datu said in stubborn Lirian. "Maybe I do not want to go to the park. Maybe I do not want a picnic anymore."

"Ah, truth be told," Duantri answered in kind, wrinkling her nose, "I don't really want to go either. *Lirian* rituals—all blood and fire, blah, blah, blah." She waved her hand, sounding just like Mak disparaging Lanie's necromancy, if a trifle more casually. Switching back to Quadic again, she said, "I'd lief by far attend the Merlintide."

Datu glanced up curiously from beneath her pasted-on bushy red brows. "What is that?"

"Oh!" Duantri exclaimed. "That's the falconry competition. I myself wanted to fly in it, but Tan told me it would be unfair to the other birds. But"—she lowered her voice—"if *you* flew me in my gyrlady's stead, Lord Limolala, Tan need never know!"

Looking more eager and alive than Lanie had seen her all day, Datu exclaimed, "What kind of bird are you? Are you a peregrine too?"

The gasp rasped, caught, in Lanie's throat. She could only be grateful that Mak had followed Havoc into the back storeroom, and had not heard his daughter expose him. Datu was not yet aware of what she had done, and Lanie did not know if she should react, or keep very still and neutral.

But Duantri, after only a short pause, answered in Quadic, "Not a peregrine—though that's a handsome bird! The first time Tan and I performed our rite, I did not know what shape would shape my flight. But lo! Aloft, I furled me fierce and small—and from my throat, I heard a kestrel call."

Datu was glowing with rare pleasure. "I will go with you to the Merlintide, Duantri," she told her teacher. "I will fly you as a kestrel."

Lanie cleared her throat. "Ahh, Datu... You might want to ask Mak—"

"Ask Mak what?" Mak had returned to the room. He was looked slightly more mussed than when he left, the paint on his lips smeared and haphazardly repaired.

When Datu laid her new plans before him, he was only—utterly—still for a moment, before smiling over at Duantri. "Of course. Datu must fly the Gyrgardu before she grows slack-mettled in her exile. But beware, Lord Duantri," he told her, "for if you lose to some Lirian bird, Quadiíb will never recover from the disgrace."

Duantri laughed in his face, and handed Datu the pouch she was carrying. Datu's exploration of it yielded a pair of short jesses of white horse skin, a stout glove, a lightweight hood and leash, a feathered lure, and binoculars.

As they watched the child examine each item with care, Duantri murmured to Mak, "Quadiíb, even Tanaliín, need never know."

"It will be our secret, then," Mak said, still smiling. "I hope you like pigeon."

"Oh, do we fly pigeon here?" Duantri made a face. "It is rabbit, generally, in Quadiíb."

"It is pigeon *this* year," said Mak. His voice went a bit distant. "Last year, it was blackbirds..."

Nita, Lanie remembered, home briefly for the previous Midsummer's Merlintide, had insisted on hawking Mak in the competition. She'd boasted to Blood Royal Erralierra of the bag of blackbirds she would bring in—implying, of course, that she would continue to do similar violence upon Bran Fiakhna's Parliament abroad. But (and Lanie had gotten most of the story later, in pieces, from different sources) Mak had bated from her fist, refusing to fly, and when Nita came home with him that day, incandescent with rage, she roared that if he wanted to sulk and take fits, he could very well do so in his falcon form and out of her sight. She did not activate her Bryddongard again until the day she left for Rook; it had taken Mak weeks to recover from being trapped in his other shape and neglected for so long.

By now Datu had packed all of Duantri's effects neatly back into their pouch. It was roomy enough, Lanie noticed, for all of Duantri's clothes once she'd made her change to kestrel.

Dancing up to her father, Datu begged, "Can we go now, Didyi? Can we go to the Merlintide?"

New plans quickly made, the picnic basket was split into portions for the two separate parties, and then it was time for farewells.

Lanie drew Datu aside, and said softly, "Hey, Datu. Maybe no more talk about your Didyi's falcon form? I don't think he wants people to know about his Bryddongard—especially not Quadonis. Also, the less in general that people know about us—about who we used to be—the better. Right?" It was not the first time they'd had this conversation, but it was never any less than a strain and a blight on any bright feeling.

Datu, crestfallen, bowed her head. "Oh."

But before her niece could edge herself off that dull gray cliff of despair, Lanie said, "Eyes up!"

Datu darted a glance ceilingward just in time to see—and catch—the coin her aunt had tossed at her.

"I've been saving that for you," Lanie said. She watched her niece closely. She'd traded a veritable pile of tips—small copper poppets, large copper eparchs, and bronze bannerets—for its equal in value: a single silver steeple.

It shone moon-bright in the palm of Datu's hand. Her eyes lit, greening again like summer leaves. Her brown face suffused with pleasure.

It was a huge amount, more than she'd ever been given for allowance or gift, more than she'd ever had at one time. She closed her fingers tightly about the coin, crossed both hands over her chest in a Quadoni bow, then sprang up, and unexpectedly hugged Lanie around the middle.

"Oof," said the cloud of peonies and silk, grinning down.

"Thank you, Auntie Lanie!" her niece said fervently, then ran across the room to Duantri and Havoc to show off her largesse.

Mak's voice startled her. "She will probably hoard it, you know."

Lanie whipped around to stare, her clothes making silk-and-air noises, gentling the violent movement. "It's hers to hoard," she replied. "But I hope you encourage her to spend it on something completely frivolous."

"Ah, of course," he returned politely. "Another cavaquinho, perhaps?"

Lanie rolled her eyes. Early last month, for several nights in a row, she had waged a heated campaign against what she felt was Mak's foolish notion of buying Datu a musical instrument. The expense, the noise, the upkeep—it was a rash idea, a reckless purchase. Datu had never played an instrument in her life; it would probably end up as very expensive firewood.

"I was wrong about the cavaquinho," she confessed at his sardonic look. "Datu loves that thing more than her artillery—which is saying something. Anyway, maybe she'll find some kind of pipe or penny whistle thing—"

"—a small drum or tambourine," Mak put in, "to torment us from our sleep."

"A fiddle?"

"Nay, a trumpet!"

"Accordion!"

"Bladder pipes—twelve gods forfend!"

Lanie grinned, conceding the game. Most likely, Datu would probably want to spend it on a dagger, or a bow, or a poison box ring, something Stonesish with the sole purpose of occision. But those purchases, she was sure, Datu's father would forbid.

"Whatever she likes."

"Never fear, Mizka. I shall adjure her to select some marvelous gift for herself on this most marvelous of days—courtesy of her loving aunt." Mak's tongue lingered reverently on 'marvelous,' impressing it with its most panthaumic sense: any marvel being but one piece of the godly All-Marvel surging on this day.

The word itself sent a sharp sparkle to the back corners of Lanie's mouth, flooding her tongue with the taste of blood orange and lime.

She laughed happily. "Have fun at the Merlintide, Mak!"

"And you, Mizka, have fun tonight at your—"

"Orgy," Lanie finished for him.

To her surprise, he grinned back. "Next year, *you* shall sit with the child overnight—and I shall attend the adult parties!"

Havoc crowed from across the room. "Bells, yeah! I'll buy yer first drink!"

"And I thy second drink, my Lady Mak," Duantri put in.

Soon, all together, the friends were walking out of the Lover's Complaint. Lanie took a deep, hot breath of the malodorous city air, all hoozzaplo and humanity.

Oh, how her surge was rising! Was gamboling—cheerful, reckless! Was rippling, tripling, stippling her arms with joyous prickles of delight. Was twinkling and tinkling in bright winks of pomelo, tangelo, citron, sweet orange. Was cresting in the very clothes she wore, was glancing off like light from Datu's eager face as Mak and Duantri each took one of her arms and swung her between them, was sliding down the swoops and loops of Havoc's green mustache as she crooked her left arm for Lanie to hook onto, and brandished her octopus-headed cane high in her right hand.

"Let's hoof it, cookie, or we'll miss the big Bloodlightin'!"

"Lead on, Lord Havoc! Lead on!"

CHAPTER THIRTY

Blood for Light

High Holy Fire Feast of Summer Solstice: Almost Noon

EIDIE OF EIDIE'S Unparalleled Breads and Pastries was big, bearded, and bedecked in a gown as fluffy, sparkly, and elaborately decorated as one of his famous powdercakes. Though he generally preferred skirts to trousers regardless of calendar day, Lanie had never seen him in something so sumptuous, so impractical, so diaphanously lavish as his dress today, covered with a little wisp of an apron that wouldn't protect him against anything stronger than a summer breeze.

"What a happy froof, Eidie!" Lanie cried. "You look ravishing!"

"Hail High Holy to you, Miss Lanie!" Eidie cheeped in his soft voice. He bore no wizard marks, but Lanie didn't think he felt the lack of them; his cakes were magic enough for most mortals. "And hail to you, Lord Havoc," he continued, curtsying his reverence to Havoc's mustache. "And where are the rest of you? Master Cicatrice, with his hair afire? Little Limolala and her littler guitar? That nice Quadoni girl who turns into a kestrel at full moon?"

Feeling in equal parts compelled to pontificate at length upon the true nature of the gyrgardon, their Gyrladies, and the Rite of Bryddongard, and to bite her tongue in half before she did so, Lanie ducked her head and let Havoc reply.

"All them birds're off to see the Merlintide, Aganath eat 'em," she said cheerfully. "Got me 'n' Lanie to keep you company, Eeds." She waggled her eyebrows. "And such grandio company it is. Look atcha. Sweeter'n molasses 'n' sassafras ice cream! I'd chomp you in two bites! Yer nice husband give you that dress?"

Eidie fluttered his eyelashes. "That he did, the foxy man. My apron too! Isn't it a treat?"

"Sure is." Havoc grinned. "Just like you. Makes me itch to tug the ribbons in yer beard, my lovely."

Beaming, Eidie beckoned them both beneath his airy awning to survey his baked goods. Cakes and crepes abounded. Plates of artfully arranged sugar cookies, frosted cookies, powdered cookies, wafer dips, puff-bites, Court of Kalestis cinnamon rolls, Skaki stuffed creams, and Quadoni caramel chews glazed with Umrysian glister-salt, decorated the tables. Presiding over them all like an empress was a tower of trays stacked with Eidie's most famous delicacy: the Triple-Chocolate Goblin Ball Truffle, which sweetmeat had made Eidie's Unparalleled Breads and Pastries a byword in Seventh Circle.

Eidie's strategy was to set up his booth near the largest fountain in Sinistral Park, where the heat of the Midsummer sun would surely bring parents—and their excited, over-warm children—to splash in the water. Such refreshing activity, he figured, would surely invigorate the appetites of all involved. And Eidie wanted to feed them all.

Clustered close to his booth was a face-painting and hair-braiding table sponsored by the Two-Night Footlight Theatre[21]. Actors and designers sat ready to decorate any citizen too poor or busy for a more elaborate floomp or froof (and, of course, to drum up business for their next show). Next to the Footlight's booth was a tent even larger than Eidie's, where workers from the Abrothoss Cider Mill filled eager comers' tankards with soft cider or applejack.

Between the Abrothoss wares and Eidie's, Lanie reflected, everyone in the park will soon be knocked flat on their backs after a brief, frenzied period of running around screaming.

Under the shade of Eidie's awning, she turned around and around, trying to see and hear and smell everything at once. Booths blazed with the colors of the Triple Flame, celebrating Sappacor, favorite god of Liriat Proper. Crimson and yellow and orange streamers snapped in the bright breeze from canvas roofs and tent poles, and billowed from centuries-old trees.

Along every gravel path wending through the greensward of Sinistral Park, more booths and tables invited revelers to food and drink and games. Vendors peddled pottery, jewelry, baskets, rugs, bonbons, hot sauce, home brews, ripe cheeses, hand pies, fried breads, roasting meats, and baked fruit, all vying for attention from the passersby and provoking an apparently universal appetite for everything at once.

Or, at least it did for Lanie.

She wanted to eat everything and everyone right down to the bone and suck the marrow clean. The sun warmed her scalp until she felt every strand of her hair as an individual hot wire. Her clothing was not just cloth anymore: it was petals bursting from her body; she was a flower, like Goody said, a girl-bouquet, open to everything, unfurling in her surge.

21 'One night for fright, one night to get it right,' went the Footlight's motto, a theatre infamous for short rehearsal periods and even shorter runs.

Havoc stumped up to her side, surveying the scene with prime satisfaction. "Fresh air. Like its own godsdamn miracle, ain't it? Enough to make a mer-gal trade her gills for legs. Every time I get all the way out here, I kick myself fer not comin' more. It's so pretty and fer everyone's use. But it ain't easy, cookie. Not with a game leg and a business to run."

"I've only ever read about it," Lanie confessed. "I didn't know it was so... big."

Outside Midnight Gate on the north side of the city, just beyond Twelfth Circle wall, Liriat Proper opened up onto its largest reserve, Sinistral Park[22], eight hundred acres of manicured grass, gardens, ponds, and paths, bordered by a stand of titanwood trees: all that was left of the old Diesmali in that area. That old growth separated the outer limits of the park from the spreading miles of Lirian farm- and pastureland mostly owned by the nearby Thallissar and Lanithall baronies, which were inhabited and worked by their tenants. Where at last the fields ended, the road north went on, cutting through a climbing straggle of uncultivated scrubland: the marches between Liriat and Rook.

The thought of Rook was like a mantle of icicles falling over Lanie's raiment, fencing her off from the sunlight.

She closed her eyes. When she opened them again, she scrutinized the crowd not as a giddy young woman at her first Midsummer Bloodlighting, but as a necromancer and a Stones.

She saw the bones beneath the skin.

One of the recent lessons Lanie had demanded from Grandpa Rad in exchange for orblins was how to ascertain, at sight, a wizard versus a non-wizard. The difference, he taught her, could be deduced from a person's 'deep accident'—their skeletal structure, in other words—in an exercise Grandpa Rad called 'waking to the bones.'

It was just one of the many death magics he had introduced her to over the last several months, all with the purpose, he'd told her, of her one day gaining mastery over another person's accident. After all, there might be circumstances wherein, if Lanie found herself short of materials to work her death magic with, she'd want to summon a skeleton to her side pronto. If said skeleton happened to still be residing inside a *living* body, well, sometimes that couldn't be helped, could it?

---

22 This was Blood Royal Sosha Brackenwild's single great civic contribution to his city. After its completion it was to be called, unsurprisingly, 'Sosha Park.' However, the longer he reigned, the faster and firmer his moniker of 'The Regent Sinister' stuck, being as how he favored chopping off the left hands of first-time offenders and hanging their severed appendages in garlands around his neck. Upon his death, which closely followed Liriat's victory over Skakmaht in the Northernmost War, his sister Moll II took over his reign. She dutifully completed Sosha Park (an expanded design, in time, and under budget)—along with two major bridges, the city's first public library, and a university—but renamed it 'Sinistral Park' thereafter. Moll II, history has it, was cheeky, and not very fond of her brother.

To Lanie's protests that the echo-wounds resulting from calling on a skeleton to rip itself out of its still-living casing would surely murder her, the ghost had merely pshawed: "The older you are, the more powerful you are, and the quicker you make of the work, girlie, the more paltry your echo-wounds become. Should only hurt a moment. Though there's always a mess to clean up after."

Upon that first lesson, he'd explained how the theory might be extrapolated. "Mastering another body's *accident* is one step further toward mastering the *substance* that animates it." He reminded Lanie that it was his own mastery over substance that had won the Northernmost War for Liriat, when he, Irradiant Stones, had called forth the collective soul-stuff from the bodies of the Guilded Council of Skakmaht, leaving behind mere shells of wizard flesh—alive but frozen, their wills and memories trapped forever in the Sarcophagus of Souls.

But in Sinistral Park, Lanie resolutely ignored the deep accident of the human bodies around her, and looked up instead. One of the first homework exercises Grandpa Rad had assigned her was to count all the birds in the sky.

Her awareness flashed sky-wide. She scanned for bones. Hollow bones but powerful, strutted and trussed for strength, full of air sacs to sustain lengthy flight. How many birds in and around Liriat Proper?

Millions. Well, millions of individual bones. But one million, two hundred one thousand, nine hundred ninety full and complete bird skeletons, to be precise. All of them *alive*. (Living bones had the blush and flush of flesh, to Lanie's deep sight. The bones of the dead glimmered like pearls.) Tears sprang to her physical eyes, which saw nothing but the dazzle of summer sky above, and little beads of clouds like white fewmishings.

But inside her bones, inside that marrow-rich, red-and-yellow darkness, she felt a million lighter bones fluttering and flirting, preening and scolding, taking wing. Mostly pigeons, of course. Some dozen pairs of hawks or so, nesting high on the scaffoldings or the ledges of the tallest buildings in the city. Sparrows, jays, robins, wrens. A few owls at the furthest edge of her awareness, where they lived in that old stand of titanwoods. All kinds of blackbirds.

Lanie stopped. Stiffened. The crowd flowed around her, noisy rosy clatter of bones that it was.

All kinds of blackbirds, she thought, and some of them are very near, pecking at the ground.

Ordinary blackbirds, eating the crumbs of one of Eidie's pastries, that a kneeling figure was feeding to them.

Ordinary blackbirds—all but one.

One particular raven. One raven, hopping closer and closer to the figure feeding it. A figure who bent close to whisper something at its earless head, which was cocked curiously to listen.

She could not hear them. All she could see, other than the fiery golden aura that surrounded the raven—revealing it to be a wizard-bird ablaze with its panthaumic surge—was the strangeness of the human figure. It glittered with its own particular cold light: sometimes silver, sometimes white, but always covert, like shy ice. Lanie could almost recognize the color of his magic; she had seen it before...

Someone jostled her arm, hard.

Lanie blinked.

Her deep sight winked out. She lost her lock on the two wizards, the kneeling human and the bird from Rook. Too much flesh in her way. Too many people, every which way. It was too hot, too bright. She had drifted from Eidie's tent. People were spilling out from under the awning, the place now stuffed with eager customers. Her knees were trembling, buckling...

Two sets of hands were suddenly supporting her elbows, steadying her.

She gazed woozily to her right. Havoc.

To her left...

A stranger. A gentleman. Small, dapper, double-chinned. Wearing a straw hat, a breezy tunic and trousers of undyed cotton, a short vest of amber silk, and a dark brown silk duster patterned in wine-pink embroidered roses, which swept the grass like a train. No visible wizard marks. He was carrying a sack stuffed full to bursting with Eidie's treats, and looking at Lanie in high concern.

Lanie blinked again, trying to focus on the stranger's strangely familiar face. But her focus went in too deep—went almost all the way back into her deep sight. It was as if she saw the skin of his face magnified under a lens of highly polished citrine: every blemish, every deep-cut line, every hair, every pore.

And then... his skin vanished altogether—even those twinkly eyes, like two jetty arrowheads. Lanie saw the shape of his bones—the depth and density, the gleaming fire-opal sheen of them. His bones were the same colors a Bryddongard took on when glimpsed with surge-struck eyes.

She knew the stranger at once.

"Gyrlady Tanaliín!"

Havoc snickered. "Tits and pickles!" She nudged Lanie in the ribs. "Yer expression's preciouser'n two men wearin' nothin' but the ribbons they won in a pissin' contest!"

Tan laughed—politely, carefully—eyeing Lanie with what seemed to be a truly outlandish concern. She doffed her straw hat. A fringe of brightly dyed orange bangs fell across a permanently furrowed forehead. One sparse brow quirked up like an accent mark. "I believe I startled you, Miss Lanie. My apologies."

Lanie squirmed, stammering, "No, no, Lady Tan—sorry, Lord Tan?—I..." The nervousness she always experienced under the keen knife of Tan's regard gripped her again, reigniting her fear of the wizard-bird she'd glimpsed a moment ago. "I thought—I thought I saw someone I knew. In the crowd. That's all."

"Not a welcome sight, I take it?" Tan asked.

"No. No, not... not welcome."

Say no more, Miscellaneous Stones, she told herself. Don't surrender to that hideous concern. It's nothing but vulgar curiosity.

After a lengthy pause, Tan pronounced, "I always find it best to eat something after I have had a shock."

She reached into the sticky depths of her burlap sack, withdrew a clump of caramel chews, and then, extracting one from its mates, offered it to Lanie. Not wanting to answer directly, Lanie popped the candy between her teeth.

At once, as the taste of burnt sugar and butter and cream burst upon her tongue, her surge rushed upon her, banishing all fear. The caramel melted, her molars worked, and her good mood whooshed back in, soaking her mouth with an afterthought of lime—the sweetest, juiciest lime in the history of citrus!

Popping her own candy between her lips, Tan reflected, "Everything tastes better on a high holy fire feast, doesn't it?"

"Yes!" Lanie exclaimed. "Everything tastes like citrus! A circus of citrus spins cartwheels on my tongue!"

Tan looked at her, too quickly, too sharply, but her voice, when she responded, was mild. "Citrus, is it? Most interesting, Miss Lanie."

She handed her another sweet, this time a powdercake: the perfect combination of deep-fried dough and the sifted softness of confectioner's sugar. Her voice was as deep, as sweet, when she asked in Quadic, "Or shall I call thee Flaisalón, fair maid, for all the silken flowers upon thy gown?"

Lanie recognized the name out of Mak's bedtime stories for Datu. She answered lightly, in her correct but awkward Quadic, "*Who made a maiden out of bloom and bud, and breathed this blossom-moppet into being?*"

Tan laughed with her whole body. "It delights me to hear a Lirian speaking Quadic! Most of your countrypeople dismiss our language as too difficult from the outset. But a few, like Canon Lir, speak it so adroitly! And poetically too—for they import words and phrases from the Lirian that shake the dust off our old tongue and put the the zest back in. It tickles me! Your accent is charming! It has an old-fashioned lilt to it; it reminds me of my great-grandmother—a darling but formidable woman—a gyrlady of the Judicial Colloquium right up until her death. She was my inspiration! Who tutored you?"

Goody, of course, was Lanie's earliest influence, and her Quadic was to 'old-fashioned' what fossils were to fresh bones. But Lanie was spared answering any more questions when Havoc clapped them both on their backs.

"Praise be to Aganath and stop yer yappin'! Yon Bloodlightin's a go!" Havoc linked her left arm with Lanie's right, keeping firm hold of her cane with her other hand.

Tan linked to Lanie's left, and the three of them joined the bouncing, gesturing, clamorous crowd that marched toward Midnight Gate.

The gates, which had closed fifteen minutes prior to noon for the ceremony, now stood wide open. A hush descended.

Standing just beyond Midnight Gate, a few steps inside the city, the Blood Royal of Liriat towered on gilded stilts over the ranks of his attendant fire priests. The stilts gleamed in the eye-watering afternoon light.

Errolirrolin was in full floomp, wearing a wild white wig wreathed in Lirian state regalia: the circlet of beaten silver lilies and iron spearheads that Lanie had last seen on a statue standing in the glass heart of the Holy Labyrinth of the Columbarium. His black mask had been cast of a crone's wizened face: a copy of the Founding Queen's death mask—which Lanie also recognized from her recent intimacy with Queen Ynyssyll's tomb. His hooped skirt was looped in lace and foaming with crimson panniers. He wore a stomacher of crimson velvet, and a stiff collar of gold lace that cradled his face like a large teacup.

As he was on stilts, the Blood Royal did not simply walk through Midnight Gate into Sinistral Park. He took it at a single, daring leap. Then he strutted backwards into the city, leapt out of it again, spinning thrice on one stilt right at the entrance of the park. His gait was angular and irregular but oddly graceful, like a praying mantis. He moved in such a way that made the joints at his shoulders and the hinges of his elbows seem better suited to a marionette than a man. His arms scooped up and swooped out; he beckoned to his attentive subjects, his fingertips like talons, scarlet-lacquered.

Follow me! the gesture seemed to say.

And the crowd obeyed.

Darting forward on his stilts, skirts flying, the cobwebby filaments of his white wig waving like ragged pennants about his head, Errolirrolin gathered up his people, and guided the dense press of them to the foot of the first lamp of the city. This was mounted in the outer rock of the Twelfth Circle wall, right above Midnight Gate. The lamp was enormous: the size of a large sow, its frame constructed of twisted black iron, its panes made of smoky glass. But the telltale red flame that was usually burning merrily away inside of it had gone dark the night before, at the Vespers Rite of Tenebrae[23].

23 Since the Vespers Rite of Tenebrae fell on the eve of the longest day of the year, nobody complained too much about those few short hours of inconvenient darkness. Some generations back, Eliki Brackenwild had tried declaring that the traditionally noontime Midsummer Rite

Midsummer's Eve was the time of year when a Blood Royal Brackenwild ritually severed their year-old magical sympathy with the one hundred forty-four bloodlamps in the city in preparation of the next day's fresh infusion. They, and the whole population of their capital city, waited out a day of darkness for the coming of the Midsummer's light. This year, of course, that sympathy had been severed upon the murder of Erralierra. In the months since, the fire priests of Sappacor had all but exhausted themselves keeping the bloodlights burning with their own regular donations. They were relieved to be laying down this burden at last. No one could keep the bloodlamps burning like the Brackenwilds, but it would not have done for Errolirrolin to have expended his precious blood off-surge.

Lanie stood on tiptoe—like everyone else—and waited breathlessly for whatever would come next. Then—

"Blood for light!" one of Errolirrolin's fire priests bellowed.

"*Blood for light!*" the crowd roared in response.

Was it Canon Lir who'd shouted? Lanie strained to see, jumping up and down, trying to snatch a better glimpse of the main players at Midnight Gate. But the crowd was too thick—and besides, all the fire priests were dressed in the same petal-yellow robes, their faces painted like gold disks, with swirling patterns in orange and red upon their cheeks, and their wizard marks uniform upon their brows: the Triple Flame. Rows of gilt-tipped hair knots abounded, and painted fingernails flashed, encrusted with elaborate jewels.

Lanie squinted, clutching her reliquary, trying to access her deep sight. She strained to hear the bone-chiming song that the twin halluces sang each to each. What she saw and heard instead—she thought—Lanie felt *almost* sure—was the god Sappacor.

Like a roaring bonfire, They blazed up from the yellow-robed bodies that surrounded the Blood Royal. It was as if Their priests were Their fuel, Their holy kindling, and They in turn illuminated what They consumed. God-light turned the gold paint on the fire priests' faces so harsh and bright, it was like solar flares. Lanie had to close her eyes for several seconds before she could see anything except the god's afterimage imprinted on her retinas.

"Blood for light!" another fire priest shouted, and tossed a clawed staff in the air, right at the Blood Royal.

Errolirrolin caught it with felicitous grace and gave it a practiced twirl,

---

should fall instead on Midwinter. He was a poet, and thought the visual metaphor of his blood lighting the winter darkness would have a moving effect upon his citizens. This effect turned out to be rioting mobs storming First Circle wall, and then Moll's Kopje itself. Before winter was over, Blood Royal Eliki had abdicated in favor of his twin brother, Blood Royal Kehleeli—Erralierra's sire—who promptly moved Vespers Rite back to Midsummer's Eve.

like a clown at First Frost Harlequinade. Then, righting the mighty staff, the Blood Royal used the clawed end to unlatch the door of the iron lamp. The smoky pane swung open, revealing the iron catch basin inside.

It's his first Bloodlighting, Lanie realized. He has to prove himself to his people, right here and now, openly. He must be perceived as fearless. He must show us how his blood is god-lit and blessed—like his mother's before him. And he has to do it now, under this vast, vast sky. Exposed to every wizard-bird hungering for his eyes and tongue. But surely his god is with him today. Surely today of all days...

"*BLOOD FOR LIGHT!*" the crowd screamed at the sight of the empty catch basin where no red fire burned.

The Blood Royal effected a start, as if shocked by the enormity of the noise. He even dropped his staff—right into the waiting grip of a fire priest below. Hooking one red-taloned hand behind his ear, Errolirrolin leaned forward, bending almost double over his stilts, his ancestress's death mask lending him the aspect of a deaf old woman straining to hear her whining grandchildren.

"Blood for light!" yelled his fire priests, helpfully.

But Blood Royal Errolirrolin shook his head, and cupped both ears now, gesturing for a louder, clearer response.

Thousands obliged.

"*BLOOD FOR LIGHT!*" they all shrieked. "*BLOOD FOR LIGHT!*"

Errolirrolin sprang upright again, and began prancing about—preening, patrolling, raising both hands in the air and shimmying bodily in victory. He'd heard them! He'd heard them! His people had spoken; he would obey!

Swagger-springing back to Midnight Gate, he cocked his head at a broke-neck tilt, swerving both arms—bent like boomerangs—in the direction of the lamp, forefingers extended, looking at the crowd as if to ask: *This? You mean this lamp here? This very lamp I see before me?*

His subjects howled incoherently—Lanie along with them, and Havoc too, and Tan, and everyone!—all pressing forward as one mass animal, thrusting out their own arms and pointing at the lamp, like an anti-cavalry company armed with long spears.

Again, the Blood Royal straightened up, nodding as if satisfied. He made huge shooing gestures to his fire priests. They rippled away from him like an ever-luminous pool, giving Errolirrolin a wider circle to work within.

The fire priests were greeted by the crowd they'd backed up into with wild embraces, kisses, back slaps, linked arms, held hands. They responded enthusiastically, redoubling every caress, smiling from their god-kissed faces that shone like a hundred small suns.

Lanie realized that Havoc was calling her name over and over again, one voice against a tide.

"Here, cookie! Cookie, look! Look what Tan snagged fer us!"

The gyrlady had apparently found and claimed a park bench, and was standing upon it, elevated above the crowd. She stooped to pull Havoc up beside her, but Havoc shook her head, nodding at her cane, planted firmly on solid ground.

In her stead, Lanie found herself being pulled up next to a grinning Tan, who asked, "This is your first time, yes?"

Lanie nodded enthusiastically, her surge fountaining up like a geyser. She wobbled, balanced buoyantly upon its crest. Panthauma splashed her legs, torso, breasts, neck: a blush of butterscotch, of buttercream, of tiger-tawny-amber-gold. Citrus overwhelmed her nostrils. Lemon. Grapefruit. Orange. Her vision blurred. It sharpened again the next moment into deep sight—but this time it was strangely warped and yellowed, as if glimpsed through a chunk of raw topaz.

And fast within those gem-cold facets, trapped and rapturous, the crowd seemed comprised not of the living but of the dead they would become. Lanie swayed for their stark beauty.

"Hey, cookie." Havoc, standing below the bench, set a friendly hand on her thigh. "Yer saggin' a bit. Y'all good?"

"Sure, sure." Lanie pushed her spectacles up her nose. She smiled, blithely if vaguely, but avoided direct eye-contact with her friend's bony eye sockets. Havoc was *hers*, was *alive*. Lanie did not wish to see her dead. Not today. Not ever! Though the beauty of the bones all around her almost—almost!—swayed her. Almost, she peered down.

No, don't look, Lanie told herself. Best turn your attention to the Blood Royal.

Unlike the rest of the cadaverous crowd, Errolirrolin's body had not thinned down to its skeleton self. Instead, the Blood Royal had become a towering pillar of fire. His wrinkled death mask shone like a black star, blank and beaming, red-lipped, wreathed in eyes. Errolirrolin Brackenwild had become Sappacor Themself, the many-gendered god of Fire—or as much of the god as his body could bear without combusting into sacrificial flames.

"*BLOOD FOR LIGHT! BLOOD FOR LIGHT!*" The frenzied roar blew like a backdraft over Lanie's senses, exploding her back to the surface of herself. To her relief and dismay, the threadbare bones of everyone around her were once more clothed in flesh and finery. The many-gendered god of Fire was just the Blood Royal after all, dressed up in his great-great-something-great grandmother's clothes.

Lanie rubbed her eyes. They felt dry as jerky, like she'd been racked up in a smoke house and cured alive[24].

"*BLOOD FOR LIGHT!*" the Lirians howled, and Lanie howled along, Havoc baying arcane Umrysian chanteys at her side, green-mustached

24 As had happened to Ham-Handed Stones's third daughter, Peccary Stones, at age four, ostensibly by accident.

face flushed and shining. Fists slammed the air. Feet stomped. Children were lifted onto the shoulders and backs of their guardians, screaming at the noise, and laughing too, and sobbing in hysterical elation. Floompers and froofers of all sizes and ages hurled themselves bruisingly against one another, ecstatic at the impact.

The mob made a massive but minute movement forward, eager to crush as close to their Blood Royal as possible. Ten thousand mouths, forty thousand limbs, a single ravenous organism.

The Blood Royal raised his arms to quiet them. The lacquered scimitars of his fingernails glittered with rubies.

For the second time, a profound hush fell over the revelers.

From a decorated sheath at his corseted waist, Errolirrolin removed a long knife. He brandished it in a sweeping arc above his head, the wicked serrations of its edge catching the afternoon glare. Unfurling the red talons of his free hand, the Blood Royal showed his open palm to the crowd.

This time, they did not roar. Only: the hush deepened. Only: a universal creak as they all leaned in, leaned on and over each other, like lodestone needles yearning north, like heliotropes to the noon sun, as if Errolirrolin alone could give them what they craved.

Once more the Blood Royal arced the knife high above his head. Once more he brought it down—and slashed open the palm of his right hand.

Lanie missed the exact moment he plunged his wounded hand through the panel of the lamp and let his blood drip into the catch basin until the puddle caught fire and burned high and scarlet.

She did not see the flames that leapt up to cauterize his wound, or how, when Errolirrolin withdrew his hand, it had become whole again by the grace of Sappacor.

She did not hear the crowd howling like hungry wolves, or witness them burst into tears of worshipful gratitude.

She noticed none of this because she was too busy looking down at her own right hand. Which, under her yellow lace glove, had split open like a ripe fruit.

The echo-wound in her palm erupted in a well of bright red blood that glittered with tiny yellow lights. Blood dripped all over her dress. Her new pink dress, that Goody had made for her. Her pink and yellow flowers. Her ribbons. Her slippers.

Lanie heard Havoc curse loud and long at the sight of it. She agreed with everything Havoc was saying—would have doubled down on it, if she could get her mouth to work properly—and she thought Tan must be saying something too, something quick and terse—an instruction, perhaps?—but could not quite catch the sense of it either.

She was too busy falling.

CHAPTER THIRTY-ONE

Bonnets and Veils

High Holy Fire Feast of Summer Solstice: Four Hours Till Midnight

"AT LAST! THE Twelve are blessed! She comes around!"

Duantri's voice. Breathless Quadic. Accompanied by a smoothing of Lanie's brow.

How tender she is, Lanie thought. How comprehensively she cuddles. No wonder Datu has thawed under her influence.

Cuddles, coddles, swaddles, cocoons, sang the rhymes at the back of Lanie's skull. (By which she understood that today was still today—a surge day—and not yet yesterday.) *Snuggles, bundles, canoodles, maroons...*

Marooned. On an island of affection. Far from Stones Manor and the things she'd once known. Thank Doédenna! What a burden that old pile had been. A heap of allergies and bad memories and things that could kill you if you looked at them sideways...

Lanie smiled to herself.

"Lookin' spryer fer damn sure," said Havoc's voice from her left. "A weensy smug, too—like a baby who's just passed a load o' gas."

Lanie's feet were wrapped in warm wet cloths. Gentle hands squeezed and massaged them. Careful fingernails scritched her scalp. Havoc had threaded her fingers through Lanie's left hand. She must still be wearing her glove on that side; she could feel the impression of lace against her skin. Good. So Havoc would perhaps not have noticed the stark, dark gray of her wizard mark swamping the skin of her hand up to her wrist. But her right hand was bare, and received, from time to time, the softest pat-pat of Duantri's palm.

Ah. That was the stuff. Thoroughly surrounded. The closest Lanie had ever come to this sensation of wellbeing was whenever she found herself within one of Goody's rare embraces. But *that* was more like being hugged by a sentient tombstone. These caresses, on the other hand, were such toasty trespasses, so warm, so invigorating, so alive!

And, Lanie realized, there are far too many caressing trespasses for just two sets of hands!

Not only Duantri and Havoc were there in the room with her, then. Who else? Who was at her feet, her head? She struggled to discern identities by touch alone, unwilling to open her eyes and end it all. It was too pleasant, for now, to remain pliant. The last time she'd felt such a lack of will, the Blackbird Bride was trying to seduce her at her sister's deathbed…

"At least the wound is closed." That was Canon Lir. Their breath on her face. Luminous mint. It was they who stroked her brow; they who scratched her head. Their lap of silk she lay in. Lanie snuggled deeper, with a grunt of contentment.

"And none too soon—all thanks to thy kind prayers," Duantri replied. "For t'was thy whispered words which closed her wound; thy fiery panthauma seared it shut."

"Not mine. Sappacor's mercy." Canon Lir's was a direct Lirian response to Duantri's flowering Quadic. Lanie wondered why they'd chosen to answer that way; Canon Lir did speak Quadic—and any number of languages besides—perfectly fluently. Perhaps they were nervous.

Havoc's fingers tightened on Lanie's left hand, a gesture of fierce protectiveness. "Old Spark's mercy's good enough fer me. Weren't any of Aganath's interferin'—that much I know. And whether it was you or yer god stopped that blood, I thankee both. I was so afeared I almost pooped out my brains."

Duantri pat-patted Lanie's right palm again, soft and anxious. "Our Tan is no mean healer in Quadiíb," she said, sounding near tears, "but nothing she could do would staunch the blood. Five times we changed the dressings on the wound, and still it spurted like some hellish font…"

"I am sure it looked worse than it was," Canon Lir assured her, still in Lirian. They spoke with their usual inexorable poise, but Lanie knew them well enough to hear the underlying tension in their voice. "See? She did not even need stitches. The cut is hardly noticeable now."

Lanie's thoughts muzzed and buzzed: An odd sort of wound, isn't it? Even for me. Echo-wounds don't usually bleed that long. Or refuse to close.

But then again, she reckoned more cheerfully, it *is* a high holy fire feast, and I am an acolyte of Saint Death. And one who has finally witnessed one of the Great Rites of Sappacor!

Perhaps by witnessing it with her deep sight she had inadvertently connected herself to the Bloodlighting Rite. What if Lanie's observation of Errolirrolin's first cut—precisely at midday of Midsummer's Day, with all that All-Marvel swirling around, inciting in Lanie fiery visions of colossal Sappacor and Their flame-faced priests—somehow started a cycle of sympathy between herself and the Blood Royal? One that did not end until each of the red lamps of Liriat had been lit? Had she received, then, not *one* echo-wound that mysteriously bled for hours, but one hundred forty-four *separate* wounds? Each in rapport with Errolirrolin's as he lit the city's lamps? Each appearing in the same place on her body, giving her hand no time to heal? If so, it must also have been that same panthaumic connection that had spared her from bleeding out. Errolirrolin was so god-ridden today that his wounds did him no harm. How could they therefore harm her, his echo?

Surely Lanie had not been in any *true* danger that day, for all the splatter and spectacle that had so frightened her friends.

Surely.

Though—she admitted to herself—I wouldn't've wagered on the chance in Aunt Diggie's gambling saloon.

"The cut is not so *noticeable* now," came Tan's voice from the foot of the bed. "But her right hand was much worse an hour ago—laid open from middle finger to wrist. That cut did in fact require stitches. However, every time I tried to sew it shut, my sutures sprang open again. I could see right down to the bones."

Lanie felt suddenly full of wasps. She suppressed an urge to kick Tan's massaging hands off her feet. Interfering know-it-all! Nosy inquisitor! Quadoni quack! Tan was too close to the truth, or had already arrived at it. Now, if it had been Lanie's *left* hand that were cut open, Tan would know her secret for sure. But it wasn't. It was her right, so her secret might still be safe...

Oh, dear. That foot rub felt *very* good. Perhaps she wouldn't kick Tan just yet.

"How quickly the wound closed once Canon Lir arrived," the gyrlady murmured. "But such things are not unheard of. Especially on a high holy fire feast."

She drew breath as if to say more. Canon Lir's legs tensed beneath Lanie's head. Lanie held her breath, waiting to be revealed.

But Tan's inhalation turned into nothing more dire than an exhalation. Her steady hands rested warmly on Lanie's ankles, forefingers pensively tapping the talus bones like tiny drums. Lanie vented a sigh of her own.

What were the chances that someone like Tan, a gyrlady, formerly of the Judicial Colloquium, professora emerita of Quadiíb, a woman worldly-wise and widely-educated, would understand the magical significance of a wound manifesting spontaneously in the wake of a witnessed injury?

All too high.

So, what would happen, then, if (when) Tan further deduced that Lanie was not only a necromancer, but (as this was Liriat Proper) a *Stones?* And not only a Stones, but the sister of gyrlady-murdering, gyrgardi-snatching, Parliament-hunting *Amanita Muscaria Stones*, the Harrier of Rook, notorious throughout the realms for her crimes?

Would Gyrlady Tanaliín, as Mak had done, loathe and fear Lanie on the basis of her antecedents? And would that loathing and fear corrupt even Duantri's radiant tenderness? Havoc's wry regard? Would Lanie have to forfeit all she had gained since losing everything—hope, house, and name?

It's time, isn't it? Lanie thought, and gummed her eyelids open.

The ceiling was pink. Deeply, adorably pink. A fleshy, wet-side-of-the-mouth pink, finished with a rosy opaline veneer. It was so unapologetically pink that it would've sent Datu gagging for the nearest chamber pot. But that very pinkety-pinkness also fueled Lanie's fading surge. It flashed up like a sun flare, the chime and rhyme of it bursting into gonging bells and trilling giggles, and Lanie broke into a grin so wide, she feared her face might split apart like her hand.

Canon Lir bent over her immediately. "Do you know where you are?"

"Waystation Thirteen," Lanie replied dreamily. She'd been here many times. Not this room. Downstairs, to drop off Datu for her lessons. The front parlor was the room she was most familiar with. It was pink and gold as well, full of vases bursting with ostrich feathers, and titillating knickknacks of suggestive shape and size, and bric-a-brac like the intricate mantel clock that revealed naked figures disporting themselves on a mattress at the top of every hour. Datu disapproved of the clock; she stated very clearly that she would not like to share her bed with so many people—or with anybody—and would kick anybody if they tried.

Canon Lir murmured, "The décor in this boudoir hasn't changed since it belonged to the Pearl of Pleasure."

Lanie appreciatively stretched her eyelids open wider. Squinted again, confused. While she could clearly see the decorative (again, quite naked, and very suggestive) corbels in the far corners of the room, with all their most protuberant bits gilded in gold paint, the living faces that were clustered around her were indistinct and featureless.

"What happened?" she wailed. "Why don't any of you have *faces?*"

"Hush, beloved." Canon Lir leaned over to stroke her cheek. "Your spectacles were crushed when you fell. We will see about replacing them for you. In the meantime, fear not. You are among friends."

Not budging an inch from Canon Lir's lap (just try and *make* me, she thought), Lanie blinked rapidly, re-analyzing the blobs around her.

There was the gold-faced blob, the curly-topped blob, the blob with the rainbow arms: Canon Lir, Duantri, and Havoc respectively, all where she had placed them by voice and touch. Clearest of all the blobs was Gyrlady Tanaliín, who sat furthest away, at the foot of the bed. She looked worn and worried, her short orange hair tousled.

At sight of the anxious furrow on that only slightly blurry brow, Lanie felt ashamed. Stretching out a toe, she tapped the gyrlady's thigh.

"Lady Tan, tell me truly—did I ruin your party?"

Tan practically melted with solicitude. Her black eyes softened and shone. She made a little sound in her throat, moving from the foot of the bed to stand at Duantri's side, and adding her own pat-pat-pats to Lanie's right hand. "Hardly. The party rages on below. This is one of our private rooms. We thought you'd be more comfortable here."

"What time is it?"

"Eight o' the clock," Duantri answered in Lirian, suspending her caresses to swoop closer to Lanie's ear. "Oh, Lanie! How my heart was struck with worry! At half past five, upon my return from the Merlintide, I found you here, in a swoon none could wake you from, tended to by Tan and Havoc and Master Hatchet, who had carried you back from the park..."

Lanie bolted up so quickly the blood rushed from her head. "Master Hatchet? Do you mean *Hatchet Scratch?*"

"Yeah, that's the one," Havoc supplied. "Been to the Lover's Complaint a few times. Massive. Blond. More muscles than a shellfish shack." She snorted. "One o' the triplets they all talk so much about. Seen one, they say, you seen all three. But I only seen one. I think."

A slight pressure from Canon Lir's hands sent her slumping back into their lap. Lanie reached to adjust spectacles that were no longer there, and groaned.

"Why *him?*" No doubt Hatchet had recognized her, even seven years a stranger, just as she had recognized him. No doubt he'd straightway left to tell his mother all about it, and Sari would summon up a wizard raven, and feed it all the news of Miscellaneous Stones's mysterious reappearance, and then *it* would fly to Rook and make its report to Bran Fiakhna. It could *not* be worse...

"Couldn't carry you home m'self, could I?" Havoc was answering Lanie's mostly rhetorical question. "Nor Tan neither. Like two middle-aged chickens, we were, thinkin' our chickie'd got bit by some giant invisible fox. But then that Scratch lad lumbered by—he was already sorta hoverin'-like, watchin' all that blood pourin' outta you with those weird Skaki eyes—so I sez to him, *Maybe you can use those big manly muscles o' yers for somethin' other than flexin' at mirrors. Do us a solid by carryin' her home fer us.* Plauds to him! Scooped you right up. Never minded the blood, neither—though he was froofed up fancy in white wolf pelts and egret feathers—in the middle o' summer, too!"

Lanie glanced worriedly up at Canon Lir's face-blob.

They responded by pulling their legs out from under Lanie's head, sliding off the bed, and then—happily—resettling themself cozily at her side. Stretching out full-length next to her, they snuck their arm under her shoulders, and crossed their ankles daintily, smoothing out their yellow silk robe so that it covered Lanie as well.

"Fret not, darling," they breathed, and gently kissed her cheek as she rested against them. "We will figure it out togeth—"

"Wait!" Lanie bolted up again. "What time did you say it was?"

Havoc laughed. "'Bout three minutes after the last time you asked."

"Just past eight," Canon Lir supplied.

"I need to go home." Lanie flexed her right hand. It was hardly stiff anymore, just sticky. Someone had rinsed off her whole arm, probably more than once, but there was still dried blood between her fingers.

Tan told her briskly, "That would be unwise."

Lanie snapped a scowl her way. "Lady Tan, I did not solicit your advice!"

The gyrlady put a hand to her orange hair, ruffled it once, and turned her face away. Duantri looked from her to Lanie. Bridging the fraught silence with her melodic Quadic, she ventured, "Wouldst thou enjoy a morsel or a drink?"

Just like that, the irritated wasps swarming Lanie's belly subsided. "No, I... Thank you, but... It's just, I really have to go..."

Duantri reached down and pulled up a sack-shaped blob from somewhere near her feet. From it, she drew another blob. By shape, it was either an unusually dark brown orblin or one of Eidie's Triple Chocolate Goblin Balls. When Lanie opened her mouth to protest, Duantri popped the blob right between her lips.

A fresh wave of panthauma hit Lanie, tongue-first. Her anxieties over Hatchet Scratch, the wizard raven, Goody, Grandpa Rad, the telling nature of the palm of her right hand, Tan's investigative inquiries, the threat of the Blackbird Bride—all washed away.

Her surge surged. Zing! Ping!

She reached out both arms for the sugar sack, which Duantri obligingly dumped out over Canon Lir's skirts. Lanie stuffed two, three, four sweet confections into her mouth without even looking to see which ones they were. It hardly mattered.

Food! Good friends! Silken laps! Had Lanie been worried? Why? It was the high holy fire feast of Midsummer! No trouble could touch her! Every problem had a panthaumic solution, every crisis a miracle to answer it! Snap of the fingers, sparkle of citrus—crisis averted!

Time? She had hours yet till midnight! *Hatchet Scratch?* Canon Lir said not to fret. *Goody?* Goody would keep! Goody always kept. That was her nature. Nothing was impossible for the All-Marvel. It moved through everything: the air, her hair, Eidie's sweets, all of Lanie's nooks and crannies, each and every corresponding area on Canon Lir's anatomy...

"Mmnph."

"That good?" asked Canon Lir.

"Mmnph." She leaned against their shoulder. Not as exciting as their lap, but perhaps she would be able to engineer her way back into that cradling warmth, given enough time, a little privacy, a little ingenuity.

Privacy. Ah, yes. A difficulty. But not an insurmountable one. A minor hurdle, really.

Canon Lir's hand glided down her spine and up again. She turned her nose to their neck, nuzzling them. A fire priest's neck, unlike their face, was always scrupulously bare of paint. Canon Lir's skin was soft and clean, moistened by the warmth and humidity of the room. As ever, the smell of white-pepper incense seemed to perfume their very pores. Lanie's mouth sprang with saliva. She turned her face wholly into the hollow of Canon Lir's throat, hiding it from the room. Their pulse beat wildly against her lips. Somehow they shifted again, squirming Lanie closer to them. She heard their light, quick breath. A melting heat from the wizard mark upon their brow, as though the Triple Flame were flame in truth. She could smell their own Midsummer surge on their skin, bright-hot, god-burnt-gold...

Lanie loved her friends. She did. Even Tan, maybe, a little, sometimes. But if they would all only just *go away*.

The room was very, very quiet.

Then Havoc cleared her throat.

"Say, Tan. Didja happen to make any, you know, *arrangements* about... millinery? Fer yer party?"

"Millinery?" Duantri repeated the Lirian word. "That is the business of bonnets and veils, is it not? Is there some kind of etiquette in Liriat Proper that stipulates a hostess must provide her guests with such items on Midsumm...?"

Tan interrupted with a short word in Quadic. It sounded to Lanie like she was trying not to laugh.

"Oh!" Duantri exclaimed. "Havoc, I mistook you! I thought you said *millinery*. You mean *prophylactics!*"

Lanie felt more than heard the chortle in Canon Lir's throat.

"Yeah, sorry," Havoc said none too contritely. "Local colloquialism. Guess a gal from Umrys-by-the-Sea could've been more clear. I meant, o' course, *bonnets and veils o' the loins*. But to get back to the point, Tan—ya happen to have any lyin' around? In case? Festival spirit and all?"

"In fact," Tan said, "we have several baskets of, as you call it, *millinery* downstairs. Our erophains are set up at different stations, giving them away for free. We are encouraging all of our guests to use them—even to take handfuls home for their friends. A party of this magnitude," she continued (in what Lanie thought of as Tan's professora-lecture mode, the gyrlady at her Gyrladiest), "is a shining opportunity for practical instruction in the prevention of disease and unwanted pregnancies. This Lirian penchant for irresponsible and unprotected intercourse is nothing short of appalling. I am hoping that by introducing Quadoni condoms to members of the First Circle elite, the rest of Liriat Proper will benefit from a widespread trickle-down effect."

Canon Lir shifted next to Lanie as they lifted their head from the mattress. "I have heard my ommer speak of your plans to educate the Lirian population in these matters. Eparch Aranha is very interested in the positive health ramifications that your Quadoni... millinery... might have for Liriat. Please know, Gyrlady Tanaliín, that the fire priests of Sappacor stand behind you."

While they spoke, their fingers were playing with the tips of Lanie's hair. Lanie's hair was practically purring.

"I know they do," said Tan with a smile in her voice. "I have been discussing the matter—lobbying, really—with Eparch Aranha these many months. They are considering co-funding a small prophylactics factory with me and a few of my investors. With the High Temple of Sappacor behind it, the venture should be a certain success. Aranha is a tease; they call it my 'practical curriculum for sexually transmitted education.' But, as you Lirians say, 'a salacious selling point is the first friend of social change!'"

Lanie lifted her head. "Wait. We say that?"

"Sex sells," Canon Lir translated.

"Oh, right."

She turned her head to catch Tan's eye. The gyrlady returned her gaze, eyes steady, face neutral, the beam of her curiosity and concern all but veiled.

Lanie ventured a small smile of apology. She had not behaved well, and could only hope that Tan would forgive her unutterable rudeness.

Not quite immediately, but not torturously long thereafter, Tan nodded back.

Lanie's surge, already bubbling, flowed over.

She ducked her head again, and pressed it once more into Canon Lir's neck, this time flicking out her tongue to lick a bead of sweat from the hollow of their throat. They jumped a little; their breath fluttered in her hair.

Lanie's hands knotted in their yellow silk robes. She wanted to peel them off. She wanted her oldest, dearest friend—who was *here*, in *bed*, with *her*—completely unclothed and at her fingertips. She could scarcely imagine what that might look like, feel like, even though right now there was only a thin layer of cloth between them. O, that the holy secrets of their body might at last be revealed!

Tan cleared her throat, this time with a note of command. Lanie lifted her head again, vision swimming. Before she knew what was happening, the gyrlady had lobbed a small package onto the bed.

"A sample of Quadoni millinery," she said. "High quality prophylactics, made of oiled silk paper. There are others less costly but still effective—of prepared linen or even a delicate leather derived from the intestines of sheep. But I have always preferred silk myself."

"More downstairs, you said?" Havoc asked, so interested that she was already walking out the door, not so subtly ushering Tan with her.

"Hundreds and hundreds," Duantri assured her, merrily following behind them.

"At last!" Lanie and Canon Lir blurted out when they were gone.

Laughing in surprise, they relaxed against each other. Only when she felt Canon Lir's body ease did Lanie comprehend how truly on edge they had been all that time.

"But reassure me once more," Canon Lir whispered, "are you *quite* well, Miss Stones?"

"Never better," Lanie swore. "I swear it by Doédenna's cupped hands. I don't know what Eidie put into those candies, but…" She set her lips to Canon Lir's ear and whispered, "My whole body is surging."

All the wasps in her breast had turned to honeybees: rumbling, tumbling, bumbling busily. She, their hive. She, a brood comb buzzing and regal, oozing golden honey, a home fit for a queen—or, at least, the twin sibling of a Blood Royal, reborn in fire.

"Mine is too." Canon Lir's voice was a blossom bursting with pollen, was a flower she wanted to crawl into. "But I do not think it is Eidie's candies that affect me thus, my beautiful friend, for I had none. Nor was it Midsummer the last time I saw you, or the time before that. And yet, I am heated through with that same longing, as ever I am when I am with you."

"So"—such great joy and relief, to be able to speak of these things freely, face to face, alone with them—"it's not just Midsummer?"

Lanie heard the tremor rippling through her confidence. So did Canon Lir, who placed one hand on her shoulder in reply, and one behind her neck, supporting her all the way down into the pile of pillows beneath them. All she could see of their face was a golden smear: it appeared smearier than usual, as if their once-perfect cosmetics had undergone a hard day's use. But their curly, ruby, slow-winding grin was, though blurry, categorically different from any other grin that had ever been directed at Lanie before.

And when Canon Lir slid their body down her body, all the way down to her ankles; when their reliquaries bumped in the middle with a vibrating chime; when Canon Lir stripped the damp cloths from Lanie's feet and stroked their fingers between her toes; when their warm breath sighed against the soles of her feet, a tremendous shudder wracked through her. Her head floated up from the pillows; she wanted to see their face.

A body's length away, Canon Lir came ever so slightly unblurred. Lanie could tell, at least, that they were smiling. And that the expression on their face was gentle, ardent, full of hope.

"It is not just Midsummer, Miss Stones," they told her. "Rather, it is that, wherever you are, *is* Midsummer."

And then they sucked her large toe right into their red mouth.

Falling every which way into a pink summer sky, Lanie thought: It doesn't take a prince, after all, to turn blood into light.

CHAPTER THIRTY-TWO

Bitter Doves of Ash

High Holy Fire Feast of Summer Solstice: The Hour Before Midnight

SILKY-SPINED AND SMILING, Lanie took the catacombs home. She skipped, she hummed, she hop-splattered through the puddly bits, she sang snatches of Datu's tree song, and the dark corridors echoed them back:

Sorkhadari! Sorkhadari!
Oldest of them all
Sorkhadari! Sorkhadari!
Never may you fall!

It was well before midnight. All right, perhaps not *well* before, but *sufficiently* before midnight. She was still in time for Goody, just as the panthauma had promised her. And oh, how marvelous was the All-Marvel, all the time, everywhere! In Lanie, especially. In what she had just shared with Canon Lir.

No. With *Lir*.

They'd told her—they'd insisted—that she call them Lir.

Well, then, you *must call me Lanie.*

Perhaps I will—in time—Miss Stones.

Her mind was clear, her heart serene. She was ready to sing the Great Lullaby, ready to give Goody over to the Undreaming. Today, Lanie knew she was loved. She had family; they had started the day together in festival celebration, in story and in song. She had friends, old and new. One of her oldest friends of all was newly become her lover; that was a joy as strong as its counter-strangeness, and a deep peace.

It was as if over the hours of her estival surge, all of Lanie's brittleness, her fear, her despair, had been heated through in some divine crucible. She'd been made molten, pliant, plastic—and now, made new: set singing into a shape of crystalline purity. In this shape, she knew she would be doing the most important work of her life. She would set her beloved Goody—her prisoner, her foster mother, her first friend, her thrall—free. And that was...

It was *good*.

Every step closer Lanie came to Goody, to that fulfillment, the better she felt. Faster, faster, ever more fleetly she moved—until she was running, practically flying. The green garlic glimmer of moss-fuzzed skulls lit her path, hundreds of them, neatly stacked, the bones of the catacombs flickering faintly to her surge-struck eyes. They seemed to croon at her, happy in her happiness. Vague but profound memories of their own first loves and lovers stirred as she passed them, half-enkindled by her presence.

Love was the Dreamcalling, love the Great Wakening, love the foundation of the Maranathasseth Anthem. It was the finest of all reasons to live—and after death, to live again.

Lanie blew kisses to her darlings as she ran. She loved them all, but tonight she owed them nothing. To Goody she owed everything, and Goody was waiting.

Here: the branching tunnel that led to a tunnel that led to a stair.

Here: the stair that wound from the catacombs up into the lower chambers of the old chapel.

Here: the corridor that led to the underground resting place of Ynyssyll Brackenwild, Founding Queen of Liriat.

Here: the door that opened into the tomb chamber...

Lanie entered, stripping the yellow lace glove from her left hand with her teeth. With her panthauma-enhanced vision, she could see her wizard mark exuding something like a starry fog, a moonlit mist—an extension of her touch, reaching out.

"Goody! Goody, I'm sorry I'm later than I—"

"Hello, girlie," said Grandpa Rad.

HE STOOD, FULLY manifest, in front of the Sarcophagus of Souls, hands on his hips, chewing his greeting around a mouthful of glowing blue goo.

"Having yourself a fine summer surge?" He grinned.

Lanie threw up her left hand in defense just as the ghost wrenched his mouth open wider than his whole head, and vomited rotten ectenica at her.

She had time to think:

—A human body yields one cubic inch of ash per one pound of weight. One pound of pure accident, reduced to a mere throat-full of char—

—before the ejecta made impact. It hit her with gale force, staggering her back. And then it kept coming.

From across the room, Grandpa Rad—no longer person-shaped, but a glowing rictus of disgorgement hovering balefully in the air—projectile-shoveled his sludgy mud of bitter black ash into Lanie's body by the barrel-full. The ectenical waste entered her through mouth and nose, through ears and eyes, through her very pores. She could not see, could not hear, could not breathe. She was *stopped up*.

Images of golden urns in their golden niches at the Holy Labyrinth of the Columbarium gleamed and glinted through the onrush of liquid ash. Each urn, in the shape of a dove, holding dozens to hundreds of cubit inches of ash. Each red marble wall, honeycombed like a dovecote into a hundred niches—and in every niche an urn. All of those many, many walls, twisting and twining in a labyrinth that guarded a secret glass garden heart. All those golden doves. So much ash. So many urns. Tens of thousands. Hundreds of thousands.

And Lanie, who could not breathe, *who could not breathe*, was choking on it all.

Panicked, flailing, nose and mouth and eyes running with black fluids, Lanie burst backwards out of the tomb chamber and into the empty corridor beyond it. She fell, retching. Gasping. Gasping. No air. No air.

Then—at last—a wheeze. Like a pinprick of air in her lungs. Enough. Enough to give her strength to retch still harder, to bring up more ash than was coming in. This, in turn, opened up another pinprick of space for her to breathe.

On hands and knees, coughing, sobbing, Lanie finally came to herself. She could hear Grandpa Rad cackling in the next room.

"Ha! Got you, girlie! Oh, I got you!"

Lanie's hands trembled. Her fingers, wrists. Her shoulders as she struggled to support herself even in this bestial pose. The tremors intensified. Now everything was shaking: knees, legs, stomach, elbows. She wiped her mouth, her nose.

Terrible.

Terrible black slime everywhere.

Where was Goody? In Queen Ynyssyll's tomb? Stuck in there with a ghost she loathed?

Cautiously, Lanie felt along the dark wall, grasping for handholds. She ripped several fingernails, but managed to gain her feet, only to collapse back against the stones and gasp for breath.

Bracing her lower back, she bent forward, gripped her knees, and spat. Oh, it stung. That foul, bitter stuff! She was used to old ectenica; this was what death magic became, off-surge, when the fuel ran out. This goop, this char: this substance and accident, severed each from the other, glued back together briefly by a necromancer's blood, then burnt out. The last taste of undeath.

But so much at once! It was like eating the world's despair.

Now that the ghost had fallen silent, Lanie's harsh breaths were the loudest thing in the corridor. Floors above, in the chapel to Doédenna, nothing stirred. Mak and Datu must be sleeping soundly after their all-day

Merlintide adventure. But even if they happened to wake, they wouldn't hear the ghost. They might hear *Lanie* if she screamed—but they might not, with all that flagstone between them. And Lanie did not have the energy, the will, to scream.

"Goody!" she croaked. "Goody!"

"Oh, she can't hear you, girlie." Grandpa Rad's voice sounded very close, as if he were standing just on the other side of the door.

Too close—Lanie thought. He's too close! Too far from the Sarcophagus of Souls. How did he stretch so far? *Why don't the shadows pull him back?*

She cleared her throat, spat again. "Goody!"

But it was Grandpa Rad who answered, in that artificially chatty whisper of his:

"I sent her away—a long way away—down Gallowsdance's tunnel. Gave her instructions to collapse it—on her own head, if need be. Served its purpose. No good leaving your flank unguarded, girlie. Should've taken care of it months ago. Might as well leave a note for those Skaki upstarts of yours, drawing them a map right to you. Yes, and the Blackbird Bride too! You'd like that, wouldn't you, girlie? For a woman like Bran Fiakhna to tickle your chin and call you her birdie."

"Goody!" The word loosed another throat-jarring fusillade of hacks and coughs. The effort sent Lanie sliding down the wall again, her sight darkening, a high whining whistle in her drowning ears.

But this time, her deep voice took up the echo, and lowly lowed the sound that only the undead could hear: "Goody!"

And somewhere, far below her, Lanie felt the catch of Goody's not-quite-breath as she heard.

"Too late," said Grandpa Rad, giggling. "Even at a run, she'll not make it back to you by midnight."

I can still sing, Lanie thought. Even if she's not here with me, I can still sing the Lahnessthanessar for her...

She sucked in a breath. For the first time, her lungs expanded as they ought to, and it was enough, *it had to be enough...*

Grandpa Rad walked out of the tomb chamber and into the hall, where he stood, hands on hips, grinning at her.

"Surprise!" he said, and leapt.

Lanie threw herself away from the wall and down the corridor at a darting weave. But her instinct had hurtled her in the wrong direction; the stairwell that led both down to the catacombs and up to the chapel was on the other end of the hall, as was the only other doorway: the one into Queen Ynyssyll's tomb. The ghost stood between her and any exit, dazzlingly luminous to her eyes but illuminating nothing else in the empty darkness. Lanie could not see it, but knew that she was heading toward a dead end.

Grandpa Rad followed more casually, popping another orblin into his mouth as he strolled forth. Lanie blanched when she saw it activate on contact with his manifestation's tongue. Nothing should be able to activate an orblin but her own living fluids. And where had he gotten that new orblin? She'd been doling them out to him so carefully, in halves or quarters. But here he had a sackful, which could only mean he'd breached her private stash.

It was as if the ghost could read her thoughts.

"Oh, this little thing?" the ghost asked, chawing horribly away at the orblin. "I had the revenant bring me all she could find. Placed your trust in the wrong fetch, didn't you? Graves is *nothing*—a *construct*—built to serve and obey. She ferreted out all your little caches and brought them right to me on my command. As for activating them; why, it was so simple, girlie, a dead child could do it. I kept that measly fragment of orblin you gave me this morning—your *Midsummer gift,* you called it, condescending little cunt—and held your saliva in stasis for later use. Think of it like kindling: whenever I want to activate a new orblin, I scrape off a drop or so of stored fluid onto it to make it catch. Only takes a little kindling for a mighty big bonfire, girlie."

The ghost's grin widened at the look on Lanie's face. He patted his swollen belly, which writhed and rippled like a pillowcase stuffed with beetles. "What with all your blood and death magic, I've fuel enough for a fine conflagration."

A snap of his fingers, and up flew a second orblin from the pouch attached to his belt.

Or—no, say rather, Lanie thought (that slim, not-as-panicked part of her brain that could still think)—say that it is Grandpa Rad's *memory* of his pouch, attached to the *memory* of his belt. Remember, Miscellaneous Stones, he is just a ghost. Substance without an accident, attached to an object. Made of memory and will—and Grandpa Rad has scads of both—but not illimitable. He has boundaries. Tethers.

She hoped.

Grandpa Rad had indeed manifested himself in such powerful detail and excruciating specificity that Lanie could see the fine stitching on his garments, the half moons of his cuticles, the wrinkles overlaying his bony hands. Never—not even on that long-ago night, when Lanie had fallen in love with nine mouse skeletons, and Mak had surrendered to Nita, and Grandpa Rad had tried to possess Lanie's body for his own—had she seen the substance of Irradiant Stones appear quite so *substantial.*

He wore an ensemble identical to the one sported by his portrait in Stones Gallery. This was probably because the ghost had been staring out his keyhole at that portrait for the better part of a hundred years, and his memory of those garments was freshly preserved. His legs were as long and thin as broomsticks, covered in both upper and lower stocks, before his thin ankles disappeared into clownishly enormous duckbill shoes. He wore a heavy silk shirt under a slashed doublet beaded in small pearls, each pearl as round and white as the lenses of his spectacles, which disguised eyes that were no longer there. Over his doublet, a skirted velvet jerkin and a fur-lined box coat made his otherwise attenuated figure strangely bulky—and of course, his enormous bloated belly strained against the confines of his manifestation, like a late-term pregnancy or malignant tumor. Even his catfish whiskers, rather than drooping in their usual fashion, seemed to have taken on an undeath of their own: with curl and sneer and opinion. Upon his close-shorn pate—Lanie could see the fine stubble, count the individual hairs—sat a tufted biretta with four stiffened peaks. The pom-pom of spectral light atop it bobbed in the air as the ghost turned to look at her.

Holding eye-contact with deliberate cheekiness, Grandpa Rad popped the orblin into his mouth—*crunch!*—and summoned up another from his pouch.

Crunch. Crunchety-crunch.

That sound. Clay shattering. Ectenica softening, activating, working. Lanie knew that an orblin had no features and therefore no expressions, was a sphere of fire-hardened clay and bone dust and her own blood. She knew that it had no lungs, no mouth, no lips. But she also knew that it was screaming.

Or maybe that was just her own mind. A sound like wind shrieking through broken glass. Lanie could not think through that noise. *She could not think.*

"So, girlie! How's your surge?" the ghost demanded gleefully. "Looking the worse for wear, I'm sorry to say. Don't you know to dress your best on festival occasions? But then, you always were such a tatterdemalion. Your father didn't have a drop of death magic in him, but he knew his fashion, I'll say that for him."

He took a step closer. The shrieking in Lanie's brain increased in volume. A wave of sickness washed over her. Grandpa Rad's range was wider than she'd ever seen it. Had he managed to detach his substance from its object? Was he even still connected to the Sarcophagus?

But—for all his slow stroll and air of imminent pounce—Grandpa Rad was pacing himself.

He's nearing the end of his tether (observed that practical sawed-off shard of Lanie), or he wants me to think so, in the hopes of luring me closer.

She squinted, focusing. The scream that was splitting her mind died back a little, and then utterly. She was thankful that she didn't need her spectacles to see the ghost. He was clearer and brighter than anything else in the corridor. She could almost believe that he was the only reality, that even *she* was a figment of his imagination.

He'd like that, she thought viciously, with a clarity that startled her. He'd like to be the only real thing in all existence!

Her rage augmented her deep sight, and Lanie finally saw them: filament-thin, viscerally sticky: the swarm of shadows she'd been searching for. They were hardly there, blue-black threads barely binding the ghost to the Sarcophagus.

A few times before, Lanie had seen them as mighty as tentacles, as threatening as thunderheads. Most often, they were just a lurking black leak, a dense aura that surrounded the Sarcophagus, something like the opposite of light. Now they were wispier and more friable than cobwebs.

Yet, they bound him.

Should she ever have leisure to count all those strands, Lanie wondered, would she come up with a number exactly equal to the sum of Skaki sky wizards lying frozen—not in undeath, exactly, but in *unlife*—in the Guilded Council above Iskald?

Irradiant Stones's death magic shackled their collective substance to him, and those fetters had held fast past his own death, far past the time even when he would have preferred them not to. It was as if the Sarcophagus of Souls itself fought now to keep him close. As if all the wizards trapped inside it were grimly determined not to let him loose, no matter how he plotted and schemed. If there was to be prison, it would be a mutual one.

"What are you gawping at, girlie?" Grandpa Rad chomped another orblin. "Shock is not a flattering look on you. But then," he sighed, "everyone but Sosha always underestimated me. To their doom."

Another orblin levitated from his pouch.

This time, Lanie flung out her left hand, rasping out, "Here!"

It flew to her, like a homing pigeon to its post. Her fingers closed around it. She felt a surge of confidence, of strength, as if it had given her a fresh infusion of her own blood. Stretching both of her hands out next, she shouted, "Come!"

The rest of the orblins—alas! so few!—erupted from the ghost's pouch. The movement shredded the pouch's tiny, ectenical stitches in a shower of blue sparks, dissolving the non-material entirely and leaving Grandpa Rad with a deflated rag of dimming light dangling from his belt.

He howled. Quicker than the space between winks, Grandpa Rad flickered forward, his clawed fingers mere centimeters from Lanie's throat. The movement must have cost him something; there was an overtaxed *creak* as thousands of thin shadowy strands stretched to the snapping point.

The ghost grunted, his attention turned momentarily inward.

Not a half second later, Lanie heard an even more ominous sound: the grinding of basalt against marble. It was the Sarcophagus of Souls, shifting on the Founding Queen's tomb chest. She heard it again, longer and more sustained. Grandpa Rad was *dragging* the thing towards him!

"How—?"

But the ghost, his grin returning, swiveled his attention back to her. He lunged again. His icy blue fingernails grazed her skin. Lanie's flesh went numb, and she knew that if he dug in any deeper, sharpened his substance and imposed it wholly upon her accident, her throat might unravel and burst apart. She jumped back again—but this time, her shoulders hit the wall. She had come to the corridor's end.

From Queen Ynyssyll's tomb chamber, the scraping and grinding noises of the Sarcophagus continued. The blue-black strands stretching between it and the ghost vibrated like strings on a phantom violin.

"Listen to them whinging!" Grandpa Rad chuckled, but plucked irritably at the shadows clinging to his substance. "That's Skakis for you, isn't it? You'd think they'd be glad to be rid of me after all this time. GRAVES!" he bellowed over the immense shoulder of his box coat. "Hurry it up!"

Involuntarily, Lanie glanced past him, peering down the corridor to see if Goody was standing there. Misdirection. The corridor was empty, Goody nowhere in sight.

The ghost sprang, and Lanie barely had time to dodge into a dusty corner of her cul-de-sac. He missed her by inches, passing partway into the wall and leaving a pale blue splattering behind that quickly flecked off to ash. Shakily, she tried to regain her balance, but before she could straighten from her stumble, the ghost's arms shot out, pinning her between them against the wall.

Grandpa Rad's precise manifestation of himself rippled. His chest expanded until it was swollen as bulbously tight as his gut.

And then, deliberately piercing the meticulous confines he'd set for himself, the ghost plucked the memory of his ribs free from the memory of his breastbone and began extruding them outward. He pushed the bones past the appearance of his skin, past layers of silk, through stiffened velvet and leather, until they closed around Lanie: a cage of ribs in truth, all glowing that sticky, shocky, static blue.

"Now," said the ghost, so close that Lanie could smell him, "either you give me what I want, or I'm going to vomit such a sludge of ectenica down your throat you'll perish of it. You'll die, Miscellaneous Stones, right here, tonight, all alone. And with you dies any hope that bitch Graves has of returning to Doédenna's cloak. I swear it by my own name."

To Lanie, who shrank from the lightning-blaze of those bony bars all around her, it was as if everything he was promising had already come to pass. Her throat squeezed shut at the thought of all his festering ectenica—so much of it that it would split her apart—pouring into her like sawdust into a stocking, burying her under its avalanche, never stopping, not even when she did. Her heart pounded, her head swam. Tears ran down her face.

The ghost leaned closer. "I want a vessel. I want free of this padlock, and that great lumpen thing I'm bound to. Why, I've practically sucked its substance dry. Don't know what those original accidents must look like, floating in the skies up north. Husks, I'd say. I've no use for them anymore. No, I want to *live*. I want to *walk*. And you, girlie, I'm afraid, are my only viable option. Now. Crack my lock. Break me free. Invite me into you. In return, I swear—as my first act as your co-host—I'll let you sing your revenant to sleep like you've both been pining for. Submit to me and I'll be generous. Anyway, I'm eager to learn the Lahnessthanessar firsthand. You've been so parsimonious about sharing. And that other one. The spell of spells. The Maranathasseth Anthem."

That was, of course, what he really wanted. And what Goody would have given her life—had she still had one—to keep from him.

Goody, Lanie thought desperately. The Lahnessthanessar. Is there still time?

There was, just. She knew it in her bones. She could sing it, right now. But Grandpa Rad would kill her as she sang; that much she knew. Lanie would surely strangle on the ash of his malice—but still she could sing the Great Lullaby, in her deep voice that needed no breath to bolster it.

She would die, but so would Goody. And wasn't that what Lanie had promised?

And yet, *after*...

The thin, logical voice at the back of her mind laid it all out for her: Grandpa Rad would keep going on, he and the sky wizards mutually enspelled until he found another vessel to possess. Perhaps that hapless future someone would not be as strong as Lanie, or would be more naive even than she.

And if Lanie died, then Datu would have no wizard blessed of Saint Death to stand between her and the Parliament of Rooks. Doomed to run and keep running all her life, she would always be looking over her shoulder, fearful of every blackbird, every passing cloud overhead. And then, there was Canon Lir...

No, Miscellaneous (Lanie's practical, reasonable, not-at-all terrifyingly calm voice told the petrified rest of her), what you have to do is deal with Grandpa Rad first. Then see to Goody, like you promised. There is still time. There has to be. And if not—

Lanie shoved the 'if not' into a box, and slammed the lid shut. There would be no 'if not.' She took her deep voice and its Undreaming, slid them deeper into her bones, and bid them both, bitterly, to bide.

At last, she found her speaking voice, though it was cold, crackingly cold, and not at all familiar to her ears.

"All the ectenica in you, Grandpa Rad," said that voice, very slowly, "belongs to me."

"Just like I said," boasted the ghost.

"Just like you said," she conceded. "*My* blood. *My* magic." And here, she grinned. Some distant, dreadful part of her was aware that her grin was identical to the ghost's, but the rest of her did not—could not—care.

"All the ectenica in you, therefore," Lanie concluded, "obeys *me*."

"What?" Grandpa Rad snapped, head rearing back, ribcage pulsing with such a light of indignation that Lanie's molars ached. "What are you—?"

Raising both hands to her chest, palms out, Lanie said, "Irradiant Stones—I *command* you to *back off!*" and pushed.

All twenty-four of the ghost's grossly manifested rib bones shattered. The ghost bellowed in surprise, blowing back several paces. His feet, in their elaborate duckbill shoes, with the squared-off toes and the fine leather slashed to display the even finer lining, flew out from beneath him. He did not land so much as float, flat on his back, disoriented, as if he had forgotten which direction was down, was *floor*. As if his memory had faltered, and with it, all sense of himself.

The ghost thrashed midair, limbs flailing. His doublet hung in tatters, showing the great gaping wounds in his sides where his ribs had been. But his bloated belly-gut-torso manifestation still burbled and strained, hard and taut as ever, dangerously full of old, fetid ectenica.

When he succeeded in slowing his out-of-control spin, Grandpa Rad caught Lanie's eye and remembered one direction at least: her.

With a sharp sucking pop, he thrust both fists into his main rotundity, sinking them up to the wrists. The swelling bobbed grotesquely, then, moving like a bolus in reverse, visibly engorged the ghost's chest, then throat, then head.

All the while, Grandpa Rad was unhinging his jaw again, *becoming* his jaw, readying himself to chunder a giant glopping mess of black sludge directly into the face of his great-granddaughter.

Lanie vaulted toward him, reaching her hands through the holes in his sides—which he had neglected, or perhaps utterly forgotten, to stop and patch up. There were holes in that part of his memory now—holes which Lanie had made—where once his ribs had been.

She wriggled her arms through those gaps, grasping for the big black bolus of old ectenica that churned so vilely within the ghost. She could sense, in the same way that she could sense her own heartbeat, that banked but still-burning fragment of orblin she had given him that morning, which he had hoarded, and was even now using against her.

She twitched her fingers towards it, beckoning. It flew back into her grasp, herding the whole ashen slurry of spent orblins along with it.

As Lanie jerked her hands from the holes she'd made, rotten ectenica jetted out of the ghost from both flanks, leaving him shriveled in mid-air like a punctured bladder. His head hung backward on his neck like a broken hinge. On either side of Lanie's feet, the black sludge piled up and puffed away like clouds of flies, of dust. It never touched her.

Whipping past the ghost, Lanie grasped a few of the black threads still doggedly binding him to the Sarcophagus. She gave them a tug. The ghost jerked, like a puppet on a leash, and let loose an awful groan.

Satisfied, she began gathering more and more of the threads together, all the while dragging the ghost down the corridor to Queen Ynyssyll's tomb chamber. The wispy, sticky strands thickened as Lanie shortened the distance between ghost and Sarcophagus. She braided the strands together into ever greater thicknesses: now cord, now rope, now cable. She crooned sub-vocalized encouragements at them, a variation of the Maranathasseth Anthem, channeling the last of her panthauma into their plaited strands: the taste of citrus, the chiming of bells, the chanting of children's rhymes.

As she worked the shadowy cables between her hands, she let them remember how *she* remembered them: as lashing tentacles of terrible justice, Grandpa Rad's indefatigable wardens, something to be feared by even he who had made them. The shadows slickened like exposed sinew beneath her fingers.

The black began to shine so darkly, it burned blue at the edges.

"No," the ghost wheezed. "No, don't suckle them! You don't know what you're doing!"

"Don't I?" Lanie asked, and it was as if they had swapped voices. Now it was she who chattered with terrible cheer, the ghost who hacked and moaned. "I'm thinking, Irradiant Stones"—she yanked the weakly protesting ghost across the threshold of the tomb chamber—"I'm thinking that we'll just bypass your padlock entirely. We're going to stuff you, just as you are, right into the Sarcophagus itself, and seal you inside with all those starving sky wizards you've been mocking all this while. You said you've surfeited on my ectenica—very well! How clever of you! We'll just rouse the shadows of your mortal foes with panthauma and bid them feast on your excess."

Grandpa Rad snarled and foamed, a ghost gone rabid. He had managed to pull his head on straight, but his jaw hung slackly, as if he had snapped the articulations to the skull. He hadn't, of course; he was not a physical being, but one of substance. It was his concentration that had snapped.

Still, he tried to fight Lanie as she dragged him toward the Sarcophagus, now sitting askew on Queen Ynyssyll's tomb chest. All the once-impeccable details of his clothes were running together, dripping off him like hot wax. By now the ghost had lost most of his shape—all but his face. His round spectacles glinted maniacally.

"I. Will. Have. My. Vessel!" The words were hiss and spittle, sparks and rage.

"You already have a vessel," Lanie reminded him. "And now, it's going to have you back."

In one last supreme act of will, the ghost made a nosedive for the keyhole of his padlock, forcing his collapsing substance through the rusted aperture. Abruptly releasing her cable of shadows, Lanie slammed her left hand over the lock, intent on drawing the ghost out of it and feeding him to the Sarcophagus, as promised. She sensed rather than saw the ghost flinging himself beyond her reach—back and down, and back and down, and back and down—into some unfathomable pit of his own digging.

She wanted to shout after him—something wild, vengeful, triumphant. She wanted him to know that she'd be back, that she was coming for him, that on the high holy fire feast of the Autumn Equinox she, Miscellaneous Immiscible Stones, would wrestle the remnants of Irradiant Radithor Stones, will he or nill he, into Saint Death's cloak for good. Her mouth stretched—a rictus—a grimace—a grin; she would scream her oath into his abyss so absolutely that he'd be hearing the echoes of it till her next surge.

The cold metal of the padlock disappeared from under the palm of her hand.

It was so abrupt, Lanie stepped back. She closed her eyes, opened them, looked again. She peered first at her hand, then at the place where the Sarcophagus of Souls had been, as if she had mistaken the evidence of her own sight.

She had not.

She could not believe how quietly, how unremarkably, it had happened.

There had been no sound. No thunderclap or great wind. Not even the smell of a strange god's magic—algae and snakeskin, nettle and venom—or the odd, green flash of spell-light. It was just... one minute, the Sarcophagus of Souls was there, crouched atop Queen Ynyssyll's tomb. The next—it wasn't.

Lanie's legs gave out.

She sprawled on the floor, colder than a corpse in a cellar, leaden as a coffin.

But why, she wondered, if I'm lead, am I shaking like the last leaves of a quaketooth tree in the month of Umbers?

She attempted to stand. To move at all. Could not. Could only stare at the ceiling of Queen Ynyssyll's tomb, trying not to think, trying not to *know* the one thing she knew for certain.

Panic and nausea, that skull-splitting shriek, all crashed down on her again. To escape it, to escape herself, Lanie cast her awareness away from her body.

Away and *beneath*.

But that sense of Goody sprinting up from Gallowsdance's tunnel at her call—that strengthening sense of Goody closing in, arriving in time, enfolding her, telling her that she was ready now, ready to sing—that *deep* sense of Goody that went far beyond either of their accidents, that was and had always been bound to Lanie's very substance—had evanesced like fog burnt off by strong sunlight.

It was midnight.

The festival was over.

Like the Sarcophagus of Souls, Goody Graves had been returned to Stones Manor.

Stones Manor, which was not *Stones* Manor at all anymore, being now the newly-bestowed baronial estate of Sari Scratch and her sons.

By the grace of the god Lan Satthi, the ancient bond between the Stones bloodline and the revenant Goody Graves was severed, utterly. Whatever was left of her, it belonged to the Scratches now.

Part Four
BONE-BOUND

Twelve Days Later

CHAPTER THIRTY-THREE

A Stones' Throw

Hangday 3rd
Month of Stews, 421 Founding Era
82 days till Autumn Equinox

"MIZKA, RECALL THAT… Mizka? *Miz*—Miscellaneous Stones!"

Lanie lifted heavy eyes from contemplation of her morning gruel. She found Mak regarding her across the rough boards they used as a table, his expression stern but not without concern.

At least, Lanie *thought* he was regarding her. But as her spare pair of spectacles was much older and cloudier than her old ones, irrevocably shattered at Midsummer, Mak's face was a bit of a blur. She squinted him into better focus.

His expression shifted, from concerned to expectant. He obviously wanted a vocal response today, so she replied wearily, "Yes, Mak?"

"I am reminding you that I will be away today. All day. And for most of the night. I need you," he explained patiently, "to look after Datu."

His words seemed to seep through miles of underground tunnels before they reached her place of comprehension. Lanie wondered how many times Mak had already reminded her. She hadn't slept in… she couldn't remember. Not much, in the last twelve days. (She was clear, at least, on the twelve days part. Lanie always knew where she was in relation to the last high holy fire feast and the next.)

Twelve days since Midsummer.

Twelve days since she had failed Goody.

"Datu," she repeated slowly, glancing over at the pallets on the floor: her own, unslept in; Mak's, trussed up in its neat roll for the day; Datu's, a sprawling nest of blankets and easy-to-reach weapons, with Datu forming a central lump beneath them. The lump did not stir at the sound of her name.

"Of course, Mak," Lanie said with more certainty. "I can look after her." The lump did not, after all, seem to require much looking after.

Mak flashed her a look, half-furious, half-tragic, that almost made her want to laugh, except for the line of worry bisecting his brow—as much for herself, Lanie thought, as for his daughter—which had deepened.

As abruptly as it bubbled up, the desire to laugh died out in her.

Datu had been rising later and later these days, ever since that morning after the high holy fire feast of Midsummer, when Lanie broke the news that Datu would not be returning to school. Now that Hatchet Scratch (and presumably, therefore, the whole Scratch clan, as well as their patroness, the Blackbird Bride) knew of Lanie's association with Waystation Thirteen, none of them would be able to visit that place again, nor drop by or work at the Lover's Complaint. Not even to bid their friends farewell. It was best, Lanie advised, to avoid Seventh Circle entirely.

The first thing Datu did, of course, was appeal to her didyi. But Lanie and Mak had already reached a unified decision on that front.

Or rather, *Lanie* had reached a decision, one which Mak had argued vehemently against in the dawn hours before Lanie broached the subject with Datu. He'd proposed that instead of abandoning their friends and disappearing from their lives, they take their tale to gyrlady Tanaliín. They ought, he said, to beg counsel of her and Duantri and Havoc, all of them, together, and strategize about their next move. *That* was the reason community existed, he'd told Lanie. Perhaps the *best* reason. So that, when disaster struck, they would not be alone.

Mak had spoken with a passionate earnestness that Lanie would have found convincing on any other morning—when she was not used up, bled out, wrung of magic, bereft of Goody, and at her wit's end.

Disaster *had* struck. They *were* alone.

And alone they should remain, for the safety of all concerned. Even the thought of appealing to Canon Lir for help horrified Lanie: in part, because it was due to their lovemaking that Lanie had come to Goody too late; in part because whatever protection was afforded to Canon Lir due to their status as a fire priest and a Brackenwild, it would not be enough if ever the Blackbird Bride got wind of Lanie's intimacy with them. Bran Fiakhna would not hesitate to use Lanie's lover as a lever to gain Datu. She would take Canon Lir apart, if it suited her ends.

So it did Mak no good to speak coaxingly of friendships and alliances, of strategies and the future. It was *not* an act of friendship to keep friends with a Stones. Lanie wouldn't wish her enemies on her enemies, much less upon her best friends.

When Mak seemed inclined to argue further, Lanie's temper—or something inside her, perhaps despair—snapped. Starting six generations back with Marrowcrack Stones[25], and moving down through Pannikel[26],

25 Devoured by undead squirrels.

26 Defenestrated, and when that didn't work, refenestrated to death.

Dowzabel[27], Irradiant[28], Rouke[29], and Unnatural[30], she reminded him, in excruciating detail, how each and every one of these august and storied Stoneses had died[31].

She then, perhaps unnecessarily, began to disinter Amanita Muscaria from the burial mound of their mutual memory. If she could *make* him remember the wreck Bran Fiakhna had made of her—that too-still body in its faded dressing gown, that eyeless face, that halo of black feathers—then he might subsequently begin to imagine (as she did, constantly) *Duantri* in Nita's place.

Or Tan, or Havoc, or Eidie, or Canon Lir. Or anyone whom they held dear.

But by the time she got to Nita, Lanie had worked her own allergies into a frothing frenzy. Rashes welted her neck and chest. Her numb right leg was buckling beneath her. Her nose was bleeding. Her whole body ached. Both eyes burned like fiery glass balls inside her skull. Before she could quite finish depicting her sister's death bed, Lanie began vomiting.

And then she fainted.

When she came to, Mak was silently cleaning her up. He said no more on the subject. Nor did he contradict Lanie when she dragged herself to Datu's bedside and told her the news. No more school. No more friends. No more long walks in the city. It was the chapel, the tomb, the catacombs. This was their world. This was their life.

In answer to Datu's protestations, all her father said was: "I am sorry, my plumula. But it will not be for long. I think it is time—yes, beyond time—that we left Liriat behind us. I have been saving up for the journey: just a little more and we shall have enough to go far from here. Perhaps it is best we cut ties now."

At which point, Datu smashed her cavaquinho.

The following scene was so fraught that Lanie did not have time to tell Mak that his idea of leaving Liriat Proper was ridiculous. Not just that—absurd! How could they leave *now*, with Goody enthralled to the Scratches, and Lanie honor-bound to rescue her?

But ever since that morning, Mak was gone more than he was at home. He sought day labor in the outer circles, places like Butcher's Circle and Fishmonger Alley, taking any work that paid a wage and asked no questions. Most nights, he contracted himself out to more nefarious jobs, crewing with a rough bunch of Twelfth Circle smugglers who made their monies on the margins of the law, transporting goods in and out of the

27 Strangled by necropants, see footnote 6.

28 Self-sacrificed to the Sarcophagus of Souls.

29 Had a live badger sewn into his belly.

30 Bladed baton through the eye, courtesy of a Rookish wizard.

31 And that was just the spear side of the family, always remembering there were Stoneses in the distaff line as well, albeit of a cadet branch.

city through the catacombs or on the dark banks of the Poxbarge and Whistlebelly rivers: goods that would never pay duties to the Revenues Office of Liriat Proper.

Lanie herself was busy minding Datu (mostly just watching the child drill herself in various target practices until she collapsed from exhaustion), not sleeping, pacing, and plotting how best to free Goody. So, what with one thing and another, she never found the time to tell Mak that of course they could not leave Liriat. Not *soon*. They would just have to lie low in the catacombs a while longer.

Lie, quite literally, low. At least in Datu's case.

Lanie didn't think the child meant to leave her pallet today. Well, perhaps she would join her niece in slumber. A few hours of sleep might clear the cobwebs from the catacombs of her brain. Suddenly, sleep was all she wanted, with the fierceness of thirst.

Mak's voice snapped her awake again. "Take Datu outdoors today. Go for a walk. You both need"—his hands lifted helplessly—"air. Light."

Lanie bristled. Or thought about bristling. It wanted too much energy. She concentrated on her gruel instead. It had gone cold and gluey. Even the lumps of dried fruit couldn't liven the taste.

"Well, you know," she replied, "that whole 'outdoors' part might present a problem."

Multiple problems. Chivvying Datu out of bed. Getting her dressed. Prodding her outside. Boosting her into the sorkhadari tree and over the wall. Such prolonged and sustained activities required motivation, energy, will—none of which virtues Lanie possessed in large quantities at present.

Even if she could conjure a little resolve for Datu's sake, what was resolve when set against the perils of travel? Resolve could not protect against exposure to unfriendly eyes, egress and ingress through the circular streets of the city, or magical murderbirds.

The next moment, Mak's scarred face was all but an inch from hers. He said, very softly, "You need to go outside."

Lanie stared. She had only ever heard him direct that particular tone of voice at Datu. A *fatherly* tone.

"You need to rest from… from this task you have set yourself. You need fresh air. Exercise. Even more so than Datu."

Startled by this solicitude, Lanie offered without thinking, "I could take her to the quarry lake at Sinistral Park."

For the first time in a long time, Mak smiled at her. She almost had to shade her eyes.

"Can you make it so far?" he asked.

"We can keep exposure to a minimum if we go underground," Lanie countered, as if bargaining.

The idea of strolling through the catacombs as opposed to the stinking city streets began, cautiously, to buoy her enthusiasm. She was sure she could get Datu to Midnight Gate via the bone roads, thus mitigating their risk of being spotted out of doors.

Mak hated the catacombs, had forbidden Datu to venture down into them without his presence (not trusting Lanie, perhaps, to keep her focus around so many of her beloved dead), but now he only shrugged unhappily.

"Yes, the catacombs are safest, naturally. So long as you spend your entire day down there… digging tunnels with femurs. Or whatever it is you do."

Lanie grimaced at his aggrieved tone. She much preferred his fatherly voice to his disparaging one: the one that hated her death magic as much as enclosed spaces.

Although… Mak's notion of digging tunnels with bones did put an idea into her head. Something had to be done about that tunnel—Gallowsdance's tunnel—that Grandpa Rad had made Goody collapse at Midsummer. It was not something Lanie could accomplish with her bare hands. But with enough bones...

She made a mental note to make an actual note to remind herself about this. Easy, these days, to forget.

"When I asked can you make it," Mak continued, gentling again, "what I meant was—can you make it that far on your own two legs?" When she frowned in confusion, he added, "It is a long walk."

"Oh." Lanie thought for a moment. "We'll take it in easy stages. Pack a picnic. We have all day, you said. And most of the night—not," she added quickly, "that I'll keep Datu out all night. Speaking of which, where will you be?"

"Trading with some flaskers up the Whistlebelly," Mak said. His gaze was steady, but she felt his shame. He hated smuggling, or any illicit work. "It is my last run. In a few days, we will all leave Liriat Proper."

Lanie dropped her eyes first. "We'll talk about that tomorrow."

Mak beamed, sunny with relief. "Good, Mizka," he said encouragingly. "That is good. Thank you. The quarry lake is a fine idea. You will enjoy yourselves."

Lanie returned a weak reflection of his smile, but felt oddly better because of it. "We will make every attempt."

Next, Mak went to squat beside Datu's pallet. In soft, coaxing Quadic, he sang to her: "Awake, my plumula! Arise and see: the summer grass and web-bespangled tree. Bestir thee all thy senses, limbs, and voice—and in this hopeful dawn, let us rejoice!"

Datu remained limp on her pallet, as broken as her cavaquinho—which her didyi, every night, worked to glue back together, piece by splintered piece. Lanie did not think it would ever be functional again, even if he did manage to rebuild the whole. But Mak needed to try. And Datu needed to see him trying.

"I love you, my plumula," he whispered. "I will be back tomorrow dawn."

"Tomorrow?" Datu's eyes bleared open at this, just in time for her father to kiss her forehead and both cheeks.

"Tomorrow," he promised, and left Doédenna's chapel for the graveyard garden.

When he was gone, Lanie marched up to her niece's pallet. Datu registered her presence, dismissed her as unworthy of interest, and shut her eyes again.

Lanie's eyes narrowed. She grunted, squatted, and then whisked away every blanket and stockpiled weapon on the pallet until there was nothing left but Datu.

"Up and at 'em, Slug-a-Bed Stones," she said. "We're going on a picnic."

THUNK-THUNK-THUNK.

Three of Datu's throwing knives thwacked in quick succession into the mossy side of a fallen tree trunk. The knives were small and light, with blades shaped like leaves that wanted to be diamonds, and metal hilts wrapped in simple black cord. The tree was a titanwood giant, which, having come at last to the end of its primordially long life, was gently decaying into a nurse log for the tender young saplings growing up all around it.

Dourly, Datu wrenched loose her knives of that fecund monument. Dourly, she shook them free of moss and spiders and splinters. Dourly, she marched off to a proper distance, and flipped her knives right-side ready, and began again.

Thunk! Thunk-thunk!

Fetch. Wrench. Shake. March. Flip.

Thunk-thunk! THUNK!

From her perch on a fat-bottomed, flat-topped boulder near the quarry lake's edge, Lanie watched her niece with both admiration and alarm.

Never did Datu remind her so much of Nita as when she practiced her sharp arts. That hypnotic focus. That quick, almost casual toss. That little kick of the back leg. The predatory flight of steel. Blue moss, micronizing. Wood chips, exploding.

How the knives always landed barber's shave close to each other. How Datu moved back further for each throw, or found rocks or logs to launch herself from to make her targets harder, or took her aim from a weaving run.

Datu was far more accurate with her knives than she'd ever been with her cavaquinho chords. But then, she'd been set to this sort of drill since before she could speak.

Thunk! Thunk! Thunk!

And again.

Sinistral Park was bounded on its northwest edge by a handsome stand of old-growth titanwoods, forming the dark and dense surrounds of an ancient granite quarry. Prized loose of its last usefulness years ago, it had abandoned itself to a quiet afterlife. Centuries of seeping groundwaters had decanted a lake into the gouged earth that was as deep and still as Doédenna's scrutiny. The surface of the water was preternaturally calm, webbed with delicate old-woman wrinkles interrupted by drifts of dragonfly, clumps of leaf, the balletic dance of water striders.

Were it not for Datu's incessant debasement of her nurse log via throwing knife, Lanie might have thought the whole scene serene. As it was, a small vein ticked uneasily at the corner of her right eye.

Datu's tongue was between her teeth. She was eyeing her target. Her shoulders relaxed as she concentrated.

Sultry as it was that afternoon, it was still rather cool for late Stews, notoriously the hottest month of the year. But this near the woods and water, the hard edge of heat was worn smooth, as if autumn had crept early to these shadowed places. The sun corralled the clouds like a bright dog her recalcitrant goats, and a flirty-skirted wind whisked up the smells of spruce and sedge, mint, marigold, and wild onion. Far distant in the welkin, a swirl of birds flew together, burst apart, and flew together again in never-repeating kaleidoscopic patterns.

Automatically, Lanie removed her battered spectacles and unfocused her eyes to behold those birds more deeply: to detect some flash of fulminating gold or other uncanny color-play of magic; to ascertain, in short, if any of those swarming dots were Rookish wizards, spying from the heights.

They were not.

Her breath puffing out in relief, she jammed her spectacles back on and looked around to locate Datu. Her niece was staring back at her across the rocky beach with fearful eyes, her whole face a question she did not ask.

Lanie forced a smile and a nonchalant shrug, and called, "Just swallows, Datu!"

Datu's expression shut like a bear trap. Betraying no sign of relief or anything else, she turned away and picked up her throwing knives again.

Sighing, Lanie continued her vigil, slipping down from the warm boulder to lean against it, arms folded.

The *thunk*ing started again.

This time, Lanie's allergies prickled. Datu was no longer seeing the titanwood as her target. In its place she was likely imagining a column of blackbirds—or perhaps the recumbent form of Bran Fiakhna herself. Waves of ill intent rose off her body with each toss of the knife, wrapping Lanie like a miasma. At every impact of Datu's blades hitting the tree-meat, Lanie felt a tap at her own breastbone.

THUNK-tap. *THUNK*-tap. *THUNK*-tap. Datu, knocking at Saint Death's door.

But the breeze soon brisked a new sound Lanie's way. Her ears pricked and she almost smiled. Datu was singing.

It was twelve days since Datu had done anything remotely musical, and Lanie couldn't help hoping that Mak's remedy of 'fresh air and exercise' was finally exerting its benisons upon his daughter.

But her heart sank again when she recognized the tune.

Not the sorkhadari song. Not any melody Datu had learned at Waystation Thirteen.

Four-and-Twenty blackbirds
Shorn for their pelt
Four-and-Twenty wizards
For the Harrier's belt!

Datu's voice was at its harshest, flattest: a voice that had rejected all erophain training, all of Duantri's merry melodic hints, her encouragements and adjurations to 'listen, in this symphony of sound: and hear the cadence of thy perfect voice.'

Datu's song meant business. Nothing more.

You hear a Stones sing like that, Lanie thought dolefully, it's probably the last thing you'll ever hear.

"*First she killed the Kingbird…*"

Thunk!

"*Magpie was next…*"

Thunk!

"*House Martin, Starling*
Marked with an—"

Something crackled in the underbrush beyond the fallen titanwood. Faster than an orblin under orders—so fast Lanie saw only the blur of her body—Datu sprinted forward, lifting her arm and hurling her last knife in the direction of the rustling.

It sliced through the green veil like silk. It landed wetly. A high, sharp cry answered.

"I got it!" Datu screamed. "I got it, Auntie Lanie! I saved you!"

CHAPTER THIRTY-FOUR

What Feeds the Gods

AN ECHO-WOUND SLASHED open on Lanie's side. She clapped a hand over it and began to run.

Near the boulder at the edge of the lake, she was still far enough away from whoever had cried out that her echo-wound was barely a scrape. But the ache in her chest deepened with every step, suggesting that the original wound was emphatically unsurvivable, and that whoever had sustained it would not be sustaining it for long.

Datu was plunging into the underbrush to count her kill. Shrill with victory, she bid her aunt to stay away—"Keep back, Auntie Lanie, because of your allergy!"—while she, Datu, investigated.

Lanie ignored her and staggered stolidly on.

The moment Datu disappeared from sight, her chatter died like a house blown down. Lanie, only steps behind, almost stumbled over her as she broke through the brush, for Datu had crashed to a halt.

It was a puppy.

Dog, Lanie thought, her thoughts sharp and thin as coffin nails. Maybe wolf. Maybe some hybrid of the two. On its own—too soon. Dam must be dead. Wandered off? Or an escapee from an unwanted litter, the rest drowned in some weighted sack tossed in the quarry lake.

It was only a little white fluff-ball of a thing. Gray mask. Black nose. Less than a month old—judging by the rounded head, the too-small ears, the pugged nose. But young as it was, the pup was nearer now to death than birth, and by Datu's hand.

Lanie's feet seemed to be sinking into the leaves, her entire body draining down to a wintry chill. The echoes rebounding off that tiny body filled her with an utter lack of air. To bleed out, after all, was very like suffocating to death. The body needed breath to survive, needed oxygen to circulate through the organs and feed the heart. Blood was the courier of air, of life, and this puppy's blood was pooling on the leaves.

"No," Datu moaned, falling to her knees in the bloody leaves. Blood everywhere.

Lanie blinked down at her. She had forgotten Datu. Bad, that. Had to remember. Had to *think*.

"No, no, no, no, no, no." Datu, dragging the small thing into her lap. Datu, cradling it with her whole body. "No, no, no. Please, no. No. Please."

Her distress was real, and shocking. So shocking, it penetrated Lanie's shock, pushed her out the other side of it. She lurched forward, though the mire sucked at her, trying to pull her back under.

Nita could never keep animals for long. They all ended up dead by hard use or abuse. Lanie had a kitten once. Katabasis Stones. Katabasis, who'd ended up poison-stiff in her padded box one morning. Ricin in her breakfast mash. Lanie found her like that, Nita smiling like a tiger over the still life. After that, Lanie made do with stuffed animals—and even then, Hoppy Bunny came to a headless end.

For these reasons, Datu never had a pet of her own. Lanie had just assumed that any animal in her care would end up like Katabasis: either because of Nita or because Datu might end up like Nita. Perhaps that had been a mistake.

Her niece was not smiling, tigerishly or otherwise. She did not regard the dying thing in her lap with ecstasy or triumph. She resembled her mother now only in her pallor, her brown skin drained of all color, vitality replaced by ashen lividity—as Nita had been when they found her dead among the blackbirds.

Datu lifted her head and stretched it back on her neck. An eerie keen sirened from her throat like an unmoored ghost. Higher and higher it wailed, as if seeking some window to break, some chandelier to shatter.

It's the sound Datu should have made *then*, Lanie thought, at Nita's death bed. But had not.

She collapsed in an ungainly sprawl at Datu's side. The canopy of trees pulsed and squeezed above her. Her lungs wheezed and rasped. Her heart was beating too fast, but also too lightly. Fluttering. But she couldn't back away to safety *now*. Datu was wailing, and Lanie had to comfort her. She threw her left arm unsteadily over Datu's shoulders.

Instead of rejecting her embrace, Datu leaned into it. "Help me! Help me, Auntie Lanie!"

Tears rolled from her eyes, snot from her nose, her body hot as fever. She was as blood-and-mud-matted as the thing in her lap, which she rocked like a baby, as she stared beseechingly up at her aunt.

But when Lanie took too long to answer, her wordless keening started again.

"No, no, no," Lanie whispered, tightening her arm around Datu's shoulders. "It's all right." Her breath whistled in her lungs. "It'll be over soon, and you'll be all right. I promise."

"No!" Datu screamed. "*No,* Auntie Lanie! *Help* me!" Her hand hovered over the third throwing knife, still embedded in the fur. She dared not to touch it. "Bring it back! Bring it back!"

"I can't, Datu. You know I can't. It's not a surge da—"

"Cut me open! Cut me open like you do you! Give it my blood!" She grabbed Nita's black dagger from its sheath at her belt and fumbled the blade over her wrist.

Lanie hastily snatched the weapon from her and tossed it aside. "Stop that!" she said fiercely. "You're not a necromancer. Hurting yourself *won't work*. It doesn't *work* like that, Datu—"

But Datu was gasping for air as loudly as Lanie, her whole body heaving. "I will share!" she pleaded with her. "I *want* to share, Auntie Lanie. Make it live. Please, Auntie Lanie. Please. Make it live."

Hunching protectively over the puppy, she whispered to it like a spell, "You are going to live. Auntie Lanie will help you live. I will take care of you my whole life. No one will ever hurt you ever again. I promise. I promise. Please. Please."

Lanie could not remember the last time Datu had said *please*.

She closed her eyes, forcing a breath through echo-lacerated lungs, and thought of three things at once.

First, brinking.

Bringing a body back from the point of death. Not resurrection, but the moment *before*. Irradiant Stones used brinking to pull tortured prisoners back from death so that Blood Royal Sosha Brackenwild could torture them all over again.

Lanie herself had brinked Mak after his encounter with Delirious Stones's poison cabinet. *That* hadn't been a surge day, had it? Nor had it been so much an act of magic as a... a petition. All right—say, a demand. Saint Death had been there, and Lanie had demanded that She *stay back!*

And Saint Death did stay back. And that was the first time Lanie had ever beheld Doédenna's face...

Second, the Rite of Bryddongard.

This was the ritual braiding of a fully accredited gyrlady of Quadiíb to her gyrgardon of choice, a bond set to last the mutual span of their lives. One of the greatest acts of Quadoni magic.

When Mak begged Lanie to bind his Bryddongard to his own flesh so that none could use it against him, Lanie had briefly entangled with that spell. His bracer had kept imprints not only of Gyrlady Gelethai's braided substance but of Nita's corrupting fascination as well.

In invoking Doédenna's intercession on Mak's behalf with Amahirra Mirage-Shaper and Wykkyrri Who Is Ten-Thousand Beasts—whose blessings enspelled the Bryddongard—Lanie had somehow ended up summoning all twelve Quadoni gods to the debate. She remembered an intense burst of white light, a collapse to singular blackness.

And then Mak's wings were his own.

That hadn't been a surge day either.

Third, Goody Graves.

Her Goody. A strict cord of undeath had bound Goody to the Stones family ever since the Founding of Liriat.

Lanie had been thinking of little else since Midsummer. That bond. What it meant.

It was not purely panthaumic; a panthaumic bond, like the Bloodlighting ritual, would've required quarterly renewals every high holy fire feast—or at least an annual renewal, in one great burst of magnificent expenditure.

Neither was the bond ectenical in nature; ectenica needed to be constantly reinvigorated by a living necromancer's fluids. Plus, an ectenical bond only lasted for as long as the dead accident did.

What Even Quicker Stones had wanted was for Goody to suffer, and to go on suffering, long after he'd turned to dust. Therefore her bond had to be *generational*, beginning with a necromancer but tied to the whole Stones bloodline. As long as there was a Stones to serve, there would be a Goody Graves to serve them.

He'd done it, too—but *how?* Lanie suspected he had stolen a page from the Rite of Bryddongard. He had soul-braided, not a gyrlady to a gyrgardon, but an undead creature to an entire family tree.

"Even if I'm wrong," Lanie heard herself saying aloud, "it's a sound thesis. I can improvise."

She was already, she noticed, speaking in her double voice. She had already begun working the spell.

Or *something*, she thought. Not a spell, exactly. More like a petition. A petition with a great deal of *specificity* and *impertinence*.

Doédenna didn't seem to mind Lanie's impertinence; it was her negligence Saint Death must despise.

And if it didn't work, at least Datu would see that her aunt had tried. Like Mak, with the shattered cavaquinho.

Scrabbling in the dirt for the black dagger with her right hand, she took Datu's wrist with her left. "I'm going to make a little cut on your finger. It will sting a bit. Are you sure you want this?"

Datu's face was like a cliff's edge before it crumbles. But she nodded, full resolute, and Lanie made the cut.

Datu's fingertip welled with blood. She did not gasp.

Casting the black dagger aside once more—far enough away that Datu could not causally reach for it—Lanie directed her niece, "Close your eyes. Think of sothaín."

She wracked her brains to remember the order of each set. So hard to think. "Second set. Dedicated to Ajdenia?"

Datu nodded.

"Ajdenia, the lizard god. Your didyi says she watches over all small things." The great god of prey, Lanie thought but did not say, and continued aloud, "Helper of the helpless? Devourer of Fiends?"

Datu nodded again.

"Close your eyes," Lanie repeated. "Run through all her sothaín attitudes one by one in your mind. Focus on them. That will help me."

Datu hesitated, looking doubtful, so Lanie half-shut her own eyes, assuring her, "A big help. Every act of sothaín is an act of prayer. That's what your didyi says. And we need all the gods we can get on this."

Mak's word worked where Lanie's did not. *Mak* had never disappeared for days into an underground workshop. *Mak* never broke vows to his best and oldest friend. No, Mak cooked dinner every night, and read his daughter to sleep even when she seemed not to listen. And when the Blackbird Bride sent Bobolink after Datu, it was Mak who in his falcon form had rent her in two.

Tears were still welling from beneath Datu's eyelids, but her breathing began to deepen. Her face became more serene.

She whispered, "Attitude One: The Lizard Suns Herself Upon a Stone. Attitude Two..."

With her niece distracted, Lanie squeezed out three drops of blood from the nick on Datu's finger into the palm of her own hand, still wet from clasping the bloody echo-wound in her side. That wound had not yet closed. It was a good sign, as far as it went: it meant that the tiny creature, though many-parts-dead, was not dead in *all* its parts. Some cellular life, some electric current, some *fluttering* still remained to it.

"Now," she charged her niece, her voice thin, the whistle in her breath very sharp, "focus on the sixth set of sothaín. For Amahirra Mirage-Shaper. Remember Them? Any of the attitudes representing chance or luck. We're going to need it."

"Attitude Six," Datu breathed. "The Trickster Wagers All For Love and Wins."

"Perfect."

Lanie set her hand upon the cord-wrapped hilt embedded in that dirty white fur. That wet, red fur.

A quick glance to make sure Datu's eyes were still closed, and she yanked out the knife. The echo-wound in her side spurted. Immediately, Lanie pressed her left hand—with her and Datu's mingled blood on it—upon the little beast's wound.

The first blue crawl of ectenica flared.

Never opening her mouth, Lanie adjured the ectenica in her deep voice to close the wound.

"Wykkyrri Who Is Ten Thousand Beasts," murmured Datu, her voice low and slow, rough around the edges from screaming, "help us. Attitude Eight: Wolf Am I, Wolf My Mother and Father."

She swayed in her trance. Lanie pulled her, unresisting, into her own lap. Her own breathing was slowing as well, but Lanie didn't know if that was the result of prayer or blood loss.

"Keep at it, Datu," she whispered. "This is your beloved. You are his mother and father."

Taking her niece's bleeding finger, Lanie pressed it hard into the bright blue ectenica, which had formed a funnel of cauterizing cobwebs that were quickly drawing the wound shut.

"Doédenna," Lanie whispered, and placed her wet, red palm over Datu's.

"Doédenna," Datu echoed, and sank still deeper into her sothaín trance. "Twelfth Attitude of the Twelfth Set: Who Is My Doorway Where the Dead Walk Through?"

But Lanie had not actually meant her niece to pray the twelfth reverence.

Merely, she had seen the gray wolf trotting up to them through the undergrowth, and spoke her greeting aloud.

Of course, She was not really a wolf. Not a *real* wolf. More like a plume of fog with lupine pretensions. Her ever-long tail was a dragging rattle of bones, extending as far as the eye could see. It disappeared into the brush, trawled the deeps of the quarry, and uncoiled in an infinite line across the far side of the rocky beach.

Great smoky ears were pricked with interest. Great smoky eyes—no pupils, no whites—watched Lanie, wild and wary. Reproachful.

Lanie swallowed. She had failed Saint Death at Midsummer. Failed Goody. Broken her promise. Yet here was her god anyway, come at her call. And here was Lanie, begging another favor—and not even on a high holy fire feast.

She wanted to apologize. But Doédenna wasn't wearing a human face today; it did not seem right to ply Her with human words. So she merely dropped her gaze in shame.

In Lanie's lap, Datu was slipping deeper and deeper into sothaín stillness. Her eyes were closed, her breathing steady.

A second wolf—or something like a wolf, but also like a fox, a dog, a jackal, a coyote—came trotting up behind the first. He was significantly larger and more substantial than His sister. His fur was a quilt of ten thousand different patches: pelts of all colors, stripes, spots, coarsenesses and consistencies. His ears were of two different lengths, His eyes of two different colors—and they were never the same color, no matter how often Lanie looked. Even His pupils changed their sizes and shapes. No set of paws matched. His tail was an enormous spray of tails, too many tails to count.

This, then, was Wykkyrri. Or one of Wykkyrri's many forms. Lanie felt His tread on the ground like an earthquake in her heart.

But He was not the last of the gods there that day. Upon Wykkyrri's motley head rode a small green lizard with lightning-white eyes. Her skin was armored in emeralds. Her claws were sickles of silver. Lanie recognized Ajdenia: the little god from a faraway desert, who had traveled all this distance in answer to Lanie's—and Datu's—pleas.

By this time, Lanie knew to peer around, searching out the fourth. She was uncertain what shape They would choose. Indeed, even when she spotted Them, They were half-shrouded by fogs and trees and Wykkyrri's tails, and seemed always too many paces away to perceive clearly.

The figure seemed human enough, a majestic pauper, dressed in ragbag splendor. They wore a pair of ass's ears, decorated with untold quantities of bells. The sweeping coat They wore trailed a spreading peacocky tail, but Their trousers were shredded and patched, and mismatched stockings peeped from mismatched old boots with toes cut out and heels flopping.

Who could this be but Amahirra Mirage-Shaper? Trickster, Shifter, Messenger to the Twelve. All Lanie could see of Their face was Their mouth: a great gibbous of glee. They grinned like They had a caper to cut and only Their grin to cut it with.

A feeling like a fizzing mixture of All-Marvel and hoozzaplo rose in Lanie's chest.

Four! she thought. Four of the Twelve! Four of Them at once!

But would They stay? Would They *listen?*

With her left hand pressed over Datu's, and both of them clutching the puppy's cooling body close, Lanie said, directly and defiantly into the four gods' faces:

"Growth of her growth. Life of her life. Shared blood, shared breath. Shared years, shared death. Let them be bound."

It was not the Rite of Bryddongard. It was not the ritual by which the Blackbird Bride bound the Parliament of Rooks to her service[32]. But Lanie's spell—her prayer—was a little like both of them. A little, too, like what Lanie imagined the binding of Goody Graves to the Stoneses' bloodline to be. Her spell stole parts from all of these bygone enchantments, but with an emphasis on brinking, and a double emphasis on binding the puppy to *Datu's* lifeline, that it might live as long as she lived and no longer. This dispelled with any need for panthaumic renewal or ectenical reinforcement from Lanie's own blood.

The gods stared at her in astonishment.

It was somewhat like standing in the glare of four self-aware suns. The only reason Lanie didn't burn to ash on the instant was because they all wanted to stare at her a little while longer.

---

32 The Covenant of Rooks was in fact a later derivative of the Rite of Bryddongard, several thousand years after the First Diaspora, but long before the Founding of Liriat. However—the prevailing belief amongst Rookish wizards being that the Blackbird Bride is the physical manifestation of all twelve gods at once, and Aganath in particular—it is not upon Amahirra or Wykkyrri whom the Blackbird Brides and their Parliaments call for the Covenant, but upon the Queen of the Sea, Aganath, who exerts Her fascination upon Her worshippers like the moon's pull on the tides.

And they? They brightened at her attention.

Overwhelmed, Lanie turned her face to Doédenna's, the only god she had ever called friend.

"Growth of her growth," she said again, in her deep voice, with all the conviction left in her. It was, it seemed, the *only* thing left of her after the gods' regard. "Life of her life. Shared blood, shared breath. Shared years, shared death. Let them be bound."

Doédenna did not answer. But in Lanie's periphery, Wykkyrri, that patchwork god, that wolf-dog-fox-jackal-coyote-flickering, bowed low—forelegs extended, rump in the air—and licked the pup's blunt white head with His rainbow-mottled tongue.

Head to toe He licked the tiny thing, and where He licked, the puppy's gray and white and black fur became strange and oversaturate. Spilled quicksilver. Moonlight-on-snow. The liquid black of boiling pitch. In Datu's lap, the small body—now gleaming, now shining, now uncanny in its colors—rose up into the air and rolled of its own accord, baring the wound in its side.

Datu was so deep in her prayers, she never opened her eyes. Her hand slid away from the wound, but did not break its contact with the furry body.

Seeing Her chance, Ajdenia, the lizard god, ran down the side of Wykkyrri's face, and jumped from His jaw to land lightly on the puppy's flank.

Her tongue slid out at once to lave the puppy's ectenical sutures. Being at least twice the length of her little green body—and possibly more at need—Ajdenia's incredible tongue encompassed both Datu's bleeding finger and Lanie's bloody hand as well as the death-wound, cleaning and blessing all three mortal creatures with its lavish lashings. She took their mingled blood into Herself, and with Her saliva changed it, returning the transubstantiated solution to the puppy's body.

Lanie trembled at that wet warmth, the power of that exchange. She felt Datu's deep shudder as well, though the child never opened her eyes.

When Ajdenia was finished, She turned and scurried back up Wykkyrri's muzzle to the top of His head, and the gash in the puppy's side had gone from ectenical-blue to the glittering green of emeralds. Her tongue had licked a new armor plating right into the fur, protecting that fatal vulnerability.

Then—fog-colored, mist-furred, smoke-footed, with Her endless tail of bone—Saint Death the Wolf advanced, approaching the puppy in Her turn.

Lanie watched her friend, tears rolling freely down her face, as Doédenna set to licking the puppy's sealed eyes.

Patiently, stoically, Saint Death the Wolf licked and licked and licked, until the delicate eyelids at last peeled open, revealing a marbled blue glow: the eyes of the undead.

Goody's eyes.

Saint Death the Wolf swiveled Her smoky head to stare at Lanie. That stillness, deeper than sothaín. That infinite reproach and disappointment.

Lanie swallowed another apology. She did not think Doédenna wanted her apology.

But to her surprise, the wolf padded a half-step closer, bent Her head again, and licked the echo-wound in Lanie's side.

The gory hole at once hushed closed, like a nursery door when the baby is finally asleep.

Then, as if startled by a distant shout, Doédenna shook Herself out and danced backwards into the woods. The rattle of Her tail followed last, then vanished.

Wykkyrri trotted after Her. He seemed, as He went, to take the form of a bear, a lion, a rattlesnake, a mink, an otter, a gazelle.

Whatever He became, Ajdenia remained perched upon His head, easy as a pilot at the prow of Her ship, sailing with Her face to the wind.

Lastly, and ever in the distance, the trickster Amahirra laughed. Their eye caught Lanie's through a fall of leaves, a splash of light, a thinning fog. They winked drolly, and made as if to swirl away in the twinkling tinkle of a million strange bells.

Instead, they feinted, danced forward, and gave the puppy a smacking kiss right on the nose.

"For luck!" boomed Amahirra.

The sound of Their voice knocked Lanie flat on her back. She had the presence of mind to keep hold of Datu, to cushion her from the fall, but only that.

"For laughs!" They laughed. "For the unexpected!"

Lanie rolled up as quickly, mindful of her niece and the puppy. But she was not quick enough to see Amahirra depart. She would never have been quick enough, no matter how fast she moved[33].

What she did see was the flash of color in her niece's lap as some movement there caught her eye: the too-gleaming fur, the emeralds that sealed the death scar, the little flanks as they began to rise and fall.

The puppy was breathing.

Lanie adjusted her awful spectacles, which had gone awry. She took them both in: niece and puppy.

Yes—the puppy's inhalations and exhalations were perfectly in time with Datu's. They breathed, like they slept, in perfect synchrony.

"Datu," she whispered in her niece's ear. "Open your eyes."

Two pairs of eyes opened.

33 Nobody, not even Even Quicker Stones, could have moved fast enough.

CHAPTER THIRTY-FIVE

The Empty Tomb

Hangday 4th
Month of Stews, 421 Founding Era
81 days till Autumn Equinox

"MAK, NO, IT'S not what you thi—"

"Sacred Datura, make your farewells to your aunt."

"Why, Didyi? Where is she going?"

"I'm not going anywhere, Datu—"

"Eek! Eek! Eek!" squeaked the puppy, paddling like a slow turtle until he emerged from Datu's grip and frantically flopped his stubby forepaws over her arms.

His head emerged next. He sneezed. The tip of his tongue stuck out.

Datu buried her face deep in his weird-lit fur until only her eyes showed. She sat cross-legged on her pallet, had shoved all her weapons into a pillowcase and hidden the pillowcase out of sight. She'd told her aunt that she didn't want the puppy to accidentally harm himself.

Lanie wondered if that was even possible.

She smiled down at both of them, realizing that she was sweating freely, that her smile felt ghastly, mask-like, then turned to Mak, and tried again. "See? He's harmless. More than harmless—absolutely adorable. Really, Mak, I prom—"

"Don't." Mak's face was as gray as Goody's.

"But it wasn't even a spell. I mean, not a spell like you're thinking. Nothing bad. Not," she reflected rapidly, "that you and I have actually ever agreed on the nature of magic, especially death magic, not that I know for sure if this *was* death magic—but never mind that for now. It was... it was a *miracle*, Mak! My own invention! I improvised—I petitioned! And, Mak, Mak, my prayers—our prayers—were answered. *Four gods!* Four gods were there, Mak! Like with your Bryddongard, remember, when all those gods answered Saint Death's intercess—"

"My Bryddongard"—Mak's voice rose—"is an abomination! *I* am an abomination! And now you have made *my daughter*—"

He stopped, swallowed. Severed himself from his unspoken sentence with a slash of his hands.

"Sacred Datura," he said with terrible, quiet calm. "Arise. Pack your things. We leave this moment."

Now even Datu's eyes disappeared into the puppy's fur. She did not answer him, or make a move to obey.

"Mak, Mak, Mak"—Lanie's ears filled with ringing thunderheads; her words tumbled out in a slurred rush—"you don't understand; he won't live forever—not like with Goody, don't worry about that. He's not bound in perpetuity, or, or bound to service. He's only... he's bound to Datu *specifically*. Like, like a companion. A friend. Her own gyrgardi. Except a wolf, not a falcon. Her Wolf Defender, if you will. Or, well, he will be. When he gets old enough to defend her. And he *will* grow—just like a living thing, but... only for the length of her life. He'll grow as she grows—no more than that—and when she dies, he dies. It's very... You see, it's really very elegant."

"Datu. Please. Pack your things."

Mak was bent to his task. Not looking at Lanie. Not looking at his daughter. His voice was like spider-cracked glass. First he nested the battered cooking pots, then bound their handles together with twine. He knotted the pots to his bedroll and heaved the roll into the wheelbarrow, followed by the food pack, the medicine pack, the flint and tinderbox, his and Datu's water flasks, their coin box, the tool bag, the lamp and lamp oil. His own clothes went in next, neatly rolled into his rucksack. Then came Datu's pillowcase of weapons, threadbare, spiky at the seams.

The chapel was stripped in less time than it took for the ringing in Lanie's ears to turn to roaring.

She seemed to lose time. She thought she blinked only once, but when she opened her eyes, she found the chapel all but emptied out, and there was Mak, kneeling beside Datu's pallet, gently nudging her off of it so that he could roll it up as well.

Bewildered, Datu stumbled to her feet, puppy held fast in her arms. The puppy was licking her neck in a way that obviously tickled her, and her expression went from crumbling cliff's edge to ecstatic delight, and then right back to cliff's edge again.

She glanced from father to aunt, her throat clicking. That first dangerous note of keening.

At the sound, all the numbness in Lanie's limbs spiked into sensation. Time became fluid once more. The roar in her ears diminished to a distant whistling.

Swiftly, she crossed the chapel and knelt before Datu, placing both of her hands on those huddled shoulders. The puppy's indiscriminate licking caught her in the knuckles. He sneezed, looked affronted, then went back to licking Datu.

"Hush. Hush, now, Datu. Listen to me. Just listen. Your didyi wants to take you out of this place. He's been thinking about and planning nothing else for all these months. You know that. Neither of you ever liked it here much, did you? All alone, with all those dead people in the garden, and under the stairs. But you know I love it, right? Just like... just like back home. At my workshop in, in the ossuary. Right?"

Datu, sucking her lips against a sob, nodded.

"Right, the ossuary, you know; and anyway"—Lanie gave her a reassuring pat—"you have your puppy to think of now. If he stays here, he might try to bury all those bones below-stairs. An infinite task! Terrible to tempt such a tiny thing like that. He'd have no time to play with you!"

"Eek!" said the puppy.

"Exactly," said Lanie.

Datu regarded her aunt. She frowned with her whole forehead, just like her father. She stroked the puppy's ears: the color of black ink swirled in liquid metal. He butted his skull against her palm as if determined to fuse the two together. "But, Auntie Lanie—"

"It's all right, Datu," Lanie whispered. "You need to get out of this place. You're ready. It's time. But I can't go yet. I can't—not because of you. Because of Goody. You know I can't leave Goody."

Carefully, Datu placed the puppy, belly-up like a baby, in one arm. His star-blue eyes winked adoringly up at her. He stuck his little paws in the air, and promptly fell asleep, panting rapidly.

"But we can wait? We can wait for you too. We can wait for Auntie Lanie, right, Didyi?"

She turned to her father, but Mak had already rolled the wheelbarrow outside, taking a pair of bolt cutters—a tool Lanie had never seen among his things—with him. He was walking across the garden toward the gate, and even in the darkness, Lanie could read his purpose. Mak would not be climbing the sorkhadari tree tonight, nor taking the bone roads below. He was cutting himself free of this place.

When he returned for the wheelbarrow and, presumably his daughter, Datu asked him, very sternly, "Why is Auntie Lanie not coming with us?"

Lanie shivered. It was a sweltering summer night, but she was cold. She folded her arms over her chest.

Mak stood just beyond the chapel doorway, in darkness. But the light from their camp stove fell across his eyes, which shone like shattered glass as he lifted his head, opened his hands, and cried, "Because she does not *think!*"

Datu's eyes went large as bruises. Lanie shivered again.

"Because," he continued, looking not at his daughter but at Lanie, "she has bound a *six-year-old child* to an undead thrall, without hesitation, without evaluation, without *permission* from that child's father; who, if asked"—a return of that caustic scornfulness that characterized their early acquaintance—"might have told her that this 'harmless' practice, this '*miracle*' of hers, which she claims to have invented today, is *not* unknown. It has been known in *civilized* countries for thousands of years, and has been *forbidden* for almost as long. Do you know why, you benighted Lirian?"

Lanie couldn't even shake her head, but that didn't matter; Mak's forefinger jabbed in the puppy's direction.

"Because while this preternatural creature may not rejoin the ranks of death until its new *life-source*—that is to say, my *daughter*—expires, the *reverse* is also true. The binding goes *both ways*."

That was when his voice broke, and the bright shards of his eyes splintered into tears, and he turned away.

Lanie tried to shake her head, but found she could not move. "No. No, Mak, the gods wouldn't have permi—"

Mak rounded on her again.

"Do you presume to know the minds of the gods?" His wet gaze scourged her. "How you do impress yourself, Miscellaneous Stones. Four gods, you say? Four who cater to your whims and answer to your call? That must seem like a banquet to a Lirian! You people, who eat fire for breakfast and death for dinner—your palate is *corrupt*. There are *twelve* gods for a reason. They keep each other in balance. *Four*, you say? Four is *chaos*."

Now, Lanie was no gyrlady, but it seemed to her, after all she saw done today, that it was Mak who was speaking heresy, not the other way around. The gods were gods, no matter in what number they gathered.

"Mak, just, if you'd been there—"

"Here is what I know, Miscellaneous Stones. What any child of Quadiíb knows, from all the cradle-tales we are told of old magic gone wrong. Should this creature"—he slashed a hand towards the puppy—"be captured by our enemies, should he be tortured, mutilated, drowned, smothered, butchered, then *my daughter* will share in its fate. No matter where she might be in the world. No matter how separate or hidden. No matter who guards her."

The binding goes both ways.

Lanie considered the potential ramifications, and felt her face go cold. "I didn't… I didn't know."

Mak grimaced. "*You know enough*. You know something of bindings. You know something of acting without permission." He made another slashing gesture, like he was trying to cut the night between them.

"You are not a fool, Miscellaneous Stones. Had you cared to do so, you might have extrapolated the consequences of today's work from a lifetime of observation, from mistakes you have *already made!* But you, like all necromancers before you, are selfish, monstrous, harmful, heedless, and utterly destructive in your pursuit of power."

"No, Didyi!"

Mak glanced in surprise at his daughter, whose voice was high and sharp, pitched like a puppy's yelp when a knife sinks in.

"That is not true," Datu told him passionately. "He was dead, he was *dead*, and I did it! It was an accident, I did not mean to, but I killed... I killed him, and then I made her raise him up again. I *made* Auntie Lanie do it, Didyi! She is not a monster; I am! *I am*, Didyi!"

Wordlessly, Mak scooped his daughter up into his arms. He held her close, pressed his forehead against hers.

"Meep!" said the puppy, and licked Mak's chin.

"Datu," he whispered, "you are no monster. You said it yourself; this death was unintentional. When accidents occur, we enter sothaín. We fit our forms to those of our gods. We hold ourselves in stillness and honor the unknowable. When we kill in the hunt, we invoke the Second Apology for those we take to eat, the Ninth Gratitude that we ourselves will be food in our time. The twelve gods remember our prayers and offerings, Theirs the World Memory from which the All-Marvel is made. You know some of this. There is more I will teach you. We enter our wretchedness and we grow wise; *we do not*"—he glared at Lanie—"look to necromancy to heal our dolor. Death magic always results in more death; it is a voracious discipline that loves only what it feeds on."

Lanie shook her head. She wanted to deny everything he was saying. He was not exactly *wrong*, but he was not exactly *right* either; it was all far, *far* more beautiful and tender and *complicated* than that. She wanted to debate with him, cite texts, quote Quadoni poetry, compare necromancy with other forms of magic, find some middle ground—but even if she could suddenly shape the right words, organize her arguments, call Saint Death Herself for witness, she was out of time.

From her father's arms, Datu stared desperately over at Lanie. She pushed away from his chest, began writhing so ferociously that Mak was forced to set her down lest she fall.

Backing away from both of them, she said, "I will not leave him here! I will never leave him! He is mine!"

"Yes, my plumula," Mak answered desolately. The corner of his mouth made a deeply unhappy tick. "He is yours, and you are his. There is no escaping that now, not till the end of your days. But none of us—not you, not I, not your creature—will stay in this place another night. Make your goodbyes to your aunt."

"No," said Datu, still backing away. "No, Didyi."

"Datu." He switched to Quadic. "No longer can we three be family."

Lanie heard herself make a noise. She heard the noise as if she were on the ceiling, looking down at herself. For some reason, she was sitting on the floor, her arms wrapping her knees, making a sound like coughing gravel. Datu stood near her, but was staring at her father, her head still shaking.

Just outside the door of the chapel, Mak spoke the first words of the 'Cornerstone' antiphony. Lanie knew it well; Goody had taught it to her her long ago:

"*Who founded Liriat and called it home?*"

When Datu refused to recite the response, Mak said it for her. But it was not the response Lanie had learned:

'Twas Ynyssyll, exiled Heretic
And by her side, the bone-bound mage she loved
Who only lived for death and what she wrought
With bodies raided from their graves and mounds,
Coerced to death yet not left underground.
And still, with every corpse she raised, she grew
In coldness, slipshod in her prayers, without
A care for life or breath or living friends
Her hunger heedless and without an end.

"That's not it." Lanie's head swung back and forth like a pendulum. Her skin felt acid-scalded all over, belly to brain. "That's not the verse I learned."

"You learned it wrong." Then, with a gesture, Mike wiped her out of his existence, and bent his whole attention to his daughter, who stood at the opposite end of the chapel, her back to the wall.

"The first necromancer of Liriat," he said softly, "was so bent on death, she *could not bend back*. There were not enough dead in the ground to satisfy her. She had to make more. She cut short the bright, brief lives around her, and raised them up, and sent them out to slaughter still more. And so raise *them* up, her newly murdered dead, and this continued until she was stopped. And the one who stopped her, who brought evidence of her crimes to the Founding Queen Ynyssyll Brackenwild, the one who called for Quick Fantastic Stones's execution? She was *herself* murdered for it, by Quick Fantastic Stones's son—who then, in the manner of his mother, compounded his crime by raising his victim up again and setting her to serve his family forever. *All* necromancers, Datu, walk the bone-bound way. It is the only way they leave open to themselves. It *always* destroys them." He stretched out one arm through the threshold, beckoning.

"My plumula. Listen and hear me. You are not safe when you are with your aunt. I am not safe. That creat… your pup is not safe. I tell you now, we would be safer walking unarmed into Rookery Court than should we stay here. Your aunt is dangerous. Even when she means to help. Even when she thinks her intentions are good. She is a Stones. But she is worse than the Stoneses who raised her—far worse than the worst killer among you: for she does not *leave* the dead to lie. She calls them back. She makes them *go on*."

Lanie touched her throat with her left hand. She covered her left hand with her right. She was making that sound again, the noise that was not a word. She willed the sound to shrivel like a forgotten mushroom, and herself with it.

Mak dropped his arm, stepped back further into the darkness of the cryptyard.

"My daughter," he said. "I would give my life for yours. If we stay, I fear I will. Now. Say goodbye to your aunt."

Lanie lost time.

Now Datu was on the floor with her, practically in her lap, the puppy between them. Lanie's lips were numb. She knew she must make an effort to say something. Anything. The first thing she thought of.

"This isn't goodbye forever, you know."

"No?" Datu's voice quavered. The puppy popped his jaw in a yawn that ended in an inquisitive yip.

"No." Lanie's lips flooded with sensation again. She felt them trembling. "Our blood, yours and mine, is what binds your beloved pup to life. Our blood, and the blessing of the gods. Remember how we prayed? I saw Their faces, Datu. They came because we begged Them, because They are merciful. And now, because my blood is part of your little one, wherever he goes, I'll feel him inside me. I'll know. I'll be able to follow the call of his blood—like a song. Like the chiming of bells… or a cavaquinho chord. He might even be able to find *me*, if you need me enough. Which means"—she paused to wipe Datu's face, and then her own—"we will *always* be able to find each other, no matter how far apart we are. Remember that. If you're ever lost or alone or in trouble, or… or you just need me. Send for me—send *him* to find me—and I'll come for you."

Datu nodded, barely.

"Do you believe me?"

Datu whispered, "Yes."

"Do you believe I'll come for you—no matter what?"

"Yes." Datu's voice was stronger this time.

Lanie set her cheek to Datu's cheek. Too quietly for Mak to hear, she asked, "Do you regret what we did today?"

"No!"

"Will you care for your pup to the best of your ability?"

"Yes!"

"Do you love him?"

In answer, the puppy tried to bury himself like a bone inside Datu's shirt—and Datu, raw to every new surprise, began to laugh.

The numbness washed away from Lanie's body. She was suffused with warmth, and an ache that was somehow better than feeling nothing at all, and her face smiled all by itself, without her having to force it.

"Then," she said, "it was worth it."

Some minutes later, the garden gate creaked shut.

CHAPTER THIRTY-SIX

A Token of Her Esteem

Luckday, 26th
Month of Drubs, 421 Founding Era
28 days till Autumn Equinox

"NO EYE TO see me. No ear to hear me. No nose to catch my scent. No tongue to taste it. No beast to note my passage as I pass them. No bird to take flight at my footstep. That the living feel my presence as the chill of the grave. That I walk as ghost, like the ghosts of my beloved dead."

The ectenica obeyed as it always obeyed.

When Lanie smashed her last orblin over her head, a cold trickle dripped down her scalp. The ectenical disguise would not impart invisibility on Lanie so much as inspire an avoidance of undesired attention concerning her. Most of the living, after all, did not like to dwell too long on the dead—outside periods of intense grief, or rituals set aside for such contemplation.

The trickle quickened to a downpour that flowed over her body in a wintry mix of ice and rain: a welcome chill on what was boding to be the hottest day of the year. Even the coolness of Queen Ynyssyll's tomb seemed unbearably stuffy to Lanie; she was thinking of moving her sleeping quarters down into the catacombs. But that seemed to want an inordinate effort on her part, and Lanie was otherwise occupied.

She was going to save Goody.

Save her. Murder her. Undream her from her undeath. Many ways to perceive the same end. She vacillated, depending on her mood.

As Lanie saw it, there was a *hard* way to go about rescuing Goody—and then, there was a *much harder* way.

Her first plan required a visit with Sari Scratch. Or whoever she was now. Baroness Something. Unfortunately for Lanie, nothing was ever easy, not even the less hard things, and Sari had been gone on a tour of the southern baronies for the last two months. Lanie knew that, because she had been dispatching her orblins as sentinels to spy at the gates of the Ambassadorial Palace of Skakmaht, and until that very morning, the orblins had reported back only empty rooms and servants' gossip.

But Lanie had not been idle whilst awaiting Sari's return. She had already begun laying a foundation for her second plan should her first (less hard, but not still not *easy*, damn it duodecifold) plan fail.

Her second plan involved clearing Goody's collapse of Gallowsdance's tunnel. Once she cleared it, she could walk those fifteen miles underground—untrammeled, unheard, and unseen—to what had formerly been Stones Manor, where Goody was held in durance vile. Earlier that summer, when Lanie set her orblins to sound the collapse, she'd discovered it went three miles deep. She had been clearing it, slowly, for the past two months, only...

Only... it was such an effort, and she seemed to be slowing down.

And now, with Sari returned to Liriat Proper, it was a good day to emerge, mole-like, from her burrow, and seek out a less resistant (though probably still resistant) path. Which was precisely why Lanie had decided to take her latest experiment in ectenical disguise out for a walk.

It was really quite a short stroll around First Circle boulevard from the cryptyard to the Ambassadorial Palace of Skakmaht.

Lanie walked out of Doédenna's ancient, overgrown chapel, scrambled up the sorkhadari tree, and leapt to the pavement on the other side of the wall.

The brown-and-buff linnet with his brave raspberry breast did not startle to flight when her racket disturbed his branches. But his feet curled convulsively around the branch he was perched on, and he swooned in sudden torpor, as if the summer world were suddenly seized in winter's chill.

The watchperson—a Bright Knight of the Triple Flame—making their rounds in that wealthy neighborhood, did not prick their fingertips to blood-red fire when Lanie brushed past. But they shivered. Tears stood out in their eyes, as if they suddenly recalled a terrible grief.

The feral cat, with raggedy ears and dragging belly, accidentally rubbed Lanie's ankle as she crept from pavement to gutter to explore some possible morsel there. Her torn ears flattened, her bowels loosened, her kitten-heavy body trembled, and she slunk quickly away, trying to escape forces she could neither see nor understand.

Mantled in gelid ectenica, Lanie ghosted by, and wondered what it would take to disappear from *herself* so easily.

But any steps she took in *that* direction, she knew, would not only *not* undo all the damage she'd already done, but would increase it tenfold. So she trudged on, leaving no footprints. A thin, phosphorescent film of azure encased her feet. It kept her lifted just off the ground—untethered, walking on air. If she weren't so anxious and tired, Lanie might have smiled in pleased surprise.

As it was, she couldn't bring herself to go so far as to smile. But as she floated—or skidded, rather—over the flagstones, she considered writing a treatise about her experience: 'On the Unexpected Side Effects of Ectenical Camouflage.'

Was it so unlikely, after all, that she might one day have progeny of her own? That these progeny might want to read of their progenitrix's redoubtable achievements?

But even trying to imagine it made Lanie want to lie down in the gutter and give up. No future existed beyond the next few hours. She had no goal but one.

First Circle being the innermost ring to band the bull's eye of Moll's Kopje, it was the smallest of the twelve concentric rings that made up Liriat Proper. Its fine estates were perforce excessively tall and thin. Most had sacrificed precious square footage of habitable space for the luxury of privacy. First Circle estates therefore boasted at least a strip of landscaping, usually lawn, often delineated by a hedge or wall or a slender copse of trees: anything to separate one from one's neighbors. The oldest residences were more like towers than houses, although unlike Ynyssyll's Tooth, these structures were built to be lived in, not simply used for observation or defense. Some of these tower houses were voluptuously round with onion domes, some sturdily square with crenellations, and some were octagonal with spires and crested rooftops.

Lanie's destination, the Ambassadorial Palace of Skakmaht, was a tapering stack of seven tiered octagons slabbed together of creamy travertine, its roof fanged in twisting bronze and copper shapes that looked to Lanie like winged serpents or mutant insects.

Before Sari had demanded the palace as partial payment for Erralierra Brackenwild's debt, the long-abandoned structure had been falling apart. It gleamed now as few buildings did in this city, what with all the smoke and soot flying about from the incinerators of the Triple Flame. Whether this uncanny cleanliness was a product of magic or industry, Lanie could not tell simply by looking. Perhaps she might, if she took the trouble to access her deep sight—but the thought of attempting it made her feel unutterably jaded.

Or perhaps that was the ectenica working on her, bitter and penetrating. Her disguise, as it lay atop her, felt as though it had frozen off the uppermost layer of her skin, leaving her raw to the elements.

She mentally added this side effect to her as-yet-to-be-written treatise.

Stopping at the iron gates outside the palace, Lanie gazed beyond them to the courtyard, where a stretch of warm red and black lava rocks was laid out in knotwork designs of more winged shapes, like those on the roof. The twists and turns made her dizzy when she stared at them too long, but still she lingered, her mind drifting as the ectenica seeped through her skin and into her bones. Thought, marrow, blood, heartbeat—all turned to ice. She could not be bothered to move. Could not indeed remember how.

But when a delivery cart pulled up, Lanie started at the sound. And when it was admitted into the estate by a worker in purple and black livery (Scratch colors, Lanie presumed), she doggedly followed behind it, her feet never quite touching the ground.

Staying well back, she scrutinized the worker over the tops of her spectacles. (Her stupid, cloudy, spare pair, which she hadn't yet replaced, which had already been hopeless and now were so scuffed and dirty as to be practically useless.) She could see better without them—at least, from a distance—but even so, after making a careful study of the wisteria purple material of his livery, she had difficulty making out the black shapes that flew over the material.

More dragons, Lanie thought. Like the roof. And the gate. And the black and red rocks. Dragons, or whatever.

The worker led the delivery cart to a fancy set of doors in the base of the palace, and from there, he and the delivery woman entered, each carrying a crate indoors. The bottommost chamber of the tower-like building was a storage room. Besides the casks and barrels and boxes, it boasted as its main feature a stone staircase winding around its outer edge. The second floor was servants' quarters, Lanie discovered as she followed along, and the third was the kitchen.

There, worker and delivery people stopped. There, Lanie left them and continued floating her way upstairs.

This should have been easier than walking. But as she spiraled up past the closed doors of what were probably bedrooms on the fourth and fifth floors, she thought that she had never felt so utterly exhausted. Icy sweat poured out of her but could not penetrate the barrier of ectenica. Instead, the sweat seemed to freeze against her skin in an underlayer of ice, until she was shivering as well as sweating.

The colder she became, the harder it was to think. Lanie had to force herself past the empty sixth-floor dining room, and on, and up, and on, and up, until, bleak, barren-hearted, and thoroughly winded, she finally attained the top of the tower.

In this bedroom-cum-study was Sari Scratch herself, working at a small desk that faced one of the eight floor-to-ceiling windows.

Each window conducted onto a small balcony with a delicate railing. Sari's window faced north, overlooking the First Circle treetops, the great wall of Second Circle, and the residences and businesses built atop the wall or high up against the other side. It was a bustling, busy view, but Sari was observing none of it. She sat, her back straight, her head bent, and applied herself to the parchment in front of her. Her memorable calligraphy flowed from the tip of a glass stylus, freshly dipped in a rich emerald ink.

Such a *Skaki* writing implement, Lanie reflected. Such a fragile, finicky thing, its tip likely to break at the first indelicate touch. Dangerous to sharpen, too—requiring sandpaper, a mask, and something to keep the tip wet so that glass dust didn't fly up into your everything.

Yet Sari's stylus itself looked, if not ancient, then at least antique, and she wielded it like it was an old friend, warmed to her hand. What would have shattered to a shard in Lanie's grip was an instrument of beauty in Sari's.

Lanie frowned. She remembered Sari as having a great deal more hair—masses and masses of it, all glossy ringlets, and such a uniform black that it seemed in retrospect an impossible color to achieve naturally. But the Sari sitting before her had almost no hair at all, only a few white wisps shorn close to her skull. A tattoo at the base of her skull looked very much like the winged shape on her workers' livery. Another dragon. It looked as if it had been there for a long, long time.

Presently, Sari set down her stylus in its crystal paperweight holder, and pressed the palms of her hands to her eyes.

When she let her hands fall, Lanie observed that Sari's pallor, always pronounced, seemed almost ghastly in its translucence, a marked contrast to the bruise-purple pits of sleeplessness or stress that surrounded her eyes. She heard the words came out of her mouth before she'd decided to speak them out loud.

"You look tired."

But Sari did not startle or stare, and Lanie realized her ectenica was still holding strong; Sari could neither see nor hear her. Even should she reach out and tousle those wispy white strands of hair, Sari would not register Lanie's presence as anything more than a foully cold wind. She might stand and shut the window. She might wonder why an arctic breeze had so abruptly disrupted the hottest day of summer, or note a melancholy turn to her thoughts. But she would not know the cause.

So Lanie said nothing more, only flexed her hands a few times, reminding herself how to move. Her body felt brittle, like an apple on the branch caught in a freezing rain: a glaze of ice on the outside, rotted to mush on the inside. If she moved too quickly, she feared she'd judder her essentials right out the bottom of her feet, leaving only a frosted impression of herself.

A glass Lanie. A ghost Lanie.

Nonsense, she told herself, and briskly shook all her limbs in defiance.

The movement hurt—which gave her a vicious sort of pleasure. She shook herself again, all her nerves sparking like a titanwood in a lightning storm. The second time was easier than the first. Lanie was still cold to the core, but at her surface, the glowing blue ectenica was beginning to crisp and blacken to a bitter char, which peeled up and fell from her skin in muddy clumps of ash.

Ack, but she was filthy! Bile rose in her throat, and with it, memories of Midsummer night—as if it was yesterday and not two months ago—when Grandpa Rad had buried her under his corrosive ectenica.

She held her breath, gulped, and caught Sari's shocked eye.

"I'm sorry," said Lanie when she could speak again. Strange, to suddenly be seen. She brushed at her clothes. "I didn't mean to startle you. I just didn't want to be inopportunely waylaid on my way to see you. We must speak."

Sari's ink-stained hand lifted to touch her bare head. Her gaze flickered involuntarily across the room, to something just beyond Lanie's shoulder. Following her line of sight, Lanie saw a privacy screen, partially obscuring a mirrored vanity, a cushioned stool, and a fully occupied wig stand.

She understood at once. "I... I'll just... step out onto your balcony for a few minutes, shall I?"

"Thank you," said Sari, her voice cool but controlled. "I am much obliged."

She took her time putting herself together, but if this was intended as deliberate malice, the effort was lost on Lanie. She was slowly thawing out on the balcony, remembering what it was to be alive and warm and wholly of the world again.

When Sari called to her to come back inside, she re-entered to see that the desk chair and vanity stool had been neatly arranged in the center of the tower room, not quite side by side, but not directly across from each other. Sari had exchanged her morning wrapper for a business suit: wide trousers, floppily tied cravat, loose vest: all of a rich purple cotton twill, with black trimming. To Lanie's surprise, she had left off her wig. But her face seemed less trampled, more energized (make-up, Lanie thought), and her eyes—that pale, glacial aqua color she'd passed on to her three sons—were alert.

"Please have a seat," she invited Lanie.

"Thank you." Lanie slumped tiredly down, wriggling her cold toes in her shoes. She lowered her gaze. She came as supplicant, after all.

"You look tired, Miss Stones."

Lanie barked out a laugh. "Yes, I... I'm not very presentable, am I? I've been digging. But I'm well enough." She set her hands on her knees, and tried to straighten her hunched back. Her body had bowed under all that ectenica. All that time on her hands and knees, deep underground. "It's... it's bizarre to see you again after so many years, Mistress—Baroness—Scratch."

Sari took this without apparent offense. "I regretted that our acquaintance was given no opportunity to flourish. However, your sister was quite explicit in the terms of our contract, and I was obliged to honor it." She raised an eyebrow. "But all of that ended at Midsummer, did it not?"

"Technically, it ended a few months earlier than that," Lanie replied. "When Bran Fiakhna and her Parliament gutted my sister in her bed."

"My condolences."

Lanie shrugged. "Stoneses die young."

"As a motto, I cannot say it recommends itself."

Lanie couldn't help laughing. "I never thought it aspirational, Baroness—just highly likely."

"It is, perhaps," Sari suggested gently, "not a prophecy you need go out of your way—as your sister did—to fulfill."

At that, Lanie's spine came all the way unbent. Her shoulders went back, her chin up. "I don't. Quite the opposite. I'd liefer run from danger as confront it. Nevertheless, I have been hunted."

Sari cleared her throat. "Say, rather, *wanted*."

"If I am wanted but my niece is hunted, then I am hunted too. Any danger to her body is a danger to my own, for I will stand between her and death as long as I am living."

Sari was silent.

Lanie flexed her stiff fingers again. Clenched. Flexed. Clenched. Relaxed.

"But all of that," she continued more carefully, "is beside the point, Baroness. My troubles have nothing to do with you. Or if they do"—her mouth twisted in a smile—"don't tell me. My only business with you has to do with the contract that my family signed with you. Now, I don't want to challenge any of that," she quickly added. "What's yours is yours, and long since due. But there's Goody, you see."

She leaned in, opening her mouth to explain, but Sari forestalled her.

"The revenant?"

"Yes. Yes, I—how is she?"

Sari's brows flew up in surprise. "How should I know? She is at Skrathmandan. I have myself only just returned to Liriat Proper from a tour of the southern baronies."

"Skrath… Skrathmandan?"

"We are calling our new estate after our family name in Skakmaht," Sari explained. "We were not Scratches till we came to Liriat. It is common, is it not, for an immigrant to change her name? Or"—pale lids drooped over pale eyes—"to have it changed for her?"

Lanie remembered Nita's casual bestowal of 'Mak Cobb' on the gyrgardi, declaring his Quadic name was unpronounceable. Nor had Lanie, in all the months since Nita's death, ever asked his true name, nor any questions about his past. She had been too afraid he'd turn cold again, and spurn their slow-warming friendship, or take Datu and leave her behind entirely…

With a hard blink, she refocused.

Another side-effect of ectenical disguise, she told herself: inattentiveness. Add it to stiffness of limbs and depression of spirits.

As effective as her disguise had been, and as amusing as levitation was, Lanie was rapidly coming to believe that covering her living body in undead material was perhaps detrimental to her health, both accidental and substantial. Or perhaps she was, like Sari had suggested, merely tired.

She had been digging for days. Weeks, perhaps. Time was strange in the catacombs.

Lanie attempted a pleasing, placating smile. "As to Goody—and her current place at, at Skrathmandan—I came here today hoping that you and I might… might come to some sort of… arrangement?"

Again, Sari let the silence flow from her. Lanie, who had grown to womanhood decoding the encyclopedia of all Goody's varied and complex silences, found this one to be of the patient but also not very easily convinced sort. Taking a deep breath, she made her case.

"Goody Graves has been bound to the Stoneses' bloodline since just after the death of Quick Fantastic Stones. Quick's son believed that Goody had betrayed his mother to her death—that it was by her evidence the Founding Queen found Quick Fantastic guilty and sentenced her to death by beheading—by the queen's own hand. So he—the son, that is, Even Quicker Stones—took revenge by executing Goody in turn. And then he laid a binding upon her corpse. Thus she became as you describe her: a revenant."

Sari asked curiously, "And was she? Guilty of treachery?"

"Yes. Probably. But whatever Goody did, Quick Fantastic Stones certainly deserved it. Necromancers are notoriously unstable—as I'm sure you've heard—and Quick was in the twilight of a very long life: a life in which she'd used herself and her death magic mercilessly. But Goody… whatever she did in her life—which she hardly even remembers at this point—she doesn't deserve to be left in this undying servitude. I have it my power… I *have had* it in my power," she corrected herself with painful deliberateness, "any time these last three years to release her back to death." Raising anguished eyes to Sari's watchful ones, Lanie whispered, "I didn't do it. I meant to, this last Midsummer, but I… I was waylaid. And I know, according to your contract, that she's your rightful property. But I've come to ask—to beg—that I might fulfill my promise and release her."

Sari maintained her silence, her icy face unreadable.

Lanie hesitated, then continued, picking at her dirty fingernails, "I have no money. My powers, such as they are, are not yet stable enough to sell for favors. But I'm learning. Every day, I'm learning. And... at one point," she stammered, "you intimated that… that my hand in marriage for your sons would not, would not be considered unwelcome…?"

Throat dry and face flushed, she faltered, caught on the thought of Canon Lir.

She had not spoken to them since Midsummer. They had sent her message after message: fiery beads of blood floating in the air above her head at night. But she had turned her face from them, and did not touch them, and eventually the blood-lit beads turned to a red smoke that sighed with Canon Lir's voice, but did not impart their waiting words to her.

Even if she were talking to them—even if they were continuing as friends and lovers—she could not see that her marriage to someone else would much matter to them. Fire priests themselves rarely married (no matter what advice a mother's corpse might spout under necromantic influence). Should Canon Lir ever be so inclined—and inclined in Lanie's direction—to matrimony, any previous connubial arrangements that Lanie had made on her own behalf would not impede their own union. They would understand. They *must*.

Multiple marriages, while not as common in Liriat as they were in Rook, were likewise not rare. In countries like Leech or Umrys-by-the-Sea, fidelity to a primary partner was rated chief amongst the virtues, whereas in Quadiíb—Duantri had told her—one might marry and divorce several times in one's life, or never marry at all but live in community with chosen family, and no one would wag a head at it.

Lanie wasn't sure what Skaki marriage practices generally entailed, but she did know that whatever else Sari was, she was a reasonable woman with an eye to her family future prosperity. Hope sparked in her when Sari at last began to speak, with considerable warmth and sympathy.

"I see that this business with the revenant is making you miserable, Miss Stones. Nor do I hold with indenture in my household. I'd by far rather have living workers about me, who are paid a living wage in exchange for their work. Most gladly would I offer you the opportunity to put the revenant down, particularly in light of what you are offering in exchange. I know very well what a rare gift is a necromancer's, and what it would mean to my family line to have death magic introduced into it. Were it solely up to me, I would claim you as my daughter before the day was out. However"—she paused, and Lanie braced herself, hope dying—"my earlier offer no longer stands."

Lanie sat back, breathless with disappointment.

Sari threaded her hands in her lap, prosaic and businesslike. "Miss Stones. You have, you know, a much greater offer of marriage on the table. Should you take it, all that I own would be yours for the asking, including your revenant. All of Liriat, perhaps. The Rook of Rook would stop at nothing to please you, her Condor."

As if Sari had cracked a dozen orblins over her head, releasing icy floodwaters of ectenica to drown her in, Lanie froze to her chair. She wanted to shake her head in denial, but she could not even move her head.

Sari went on, "Bran Fiakhna is a powerful foe, Miss Stones. But she is an even mightier ally." Her tones softened. "When I first came to Rookery Court with my three small sons—they were hardly more than toddlers at the time—Bran Fiakhna took us in. She did this, when no one else would have us, when we were starving and had nothing but the rags on our backs, when we had been hounded from every camp and slum and tenement that refused to tolerate another Skaki refugee. Every other realm thinks Skakmaht accursed, and believes that we who were born of it are cursed withal. We are given no chance to prove otherwise—even after a hundred years! But Bran Fiakhna gave us her matronage."

Lanie wondered if Sari performed this narrative often. It was polished to a shine, thoroughly conceptualized, and complete with the choreography. Cynically, she observed Sari shaking her head, affecting the bewildered wonderment of a music-starved child in her first luthier's shop.

"The great sorceress queen of Rook didn't even require an oath of fealty in exchange for the capital she lent me to start again. Merely, she requested that when the Sky Houses of Skakmaht rise again in glory, we who ascend with them remember that it was *she* who first lent us wings. I have never forgotten her words. And just look at me now, Miss Stones!"

Lanie's eyelids, which had grown heavy as her surname, shuttering so as not to give away the incredulity, distress, and fury she felt, now flew open in exaggerated obedience.

"It is twenty years," said Sari Scratch with an earnest intensity that was not, Lanie thought with dismay, at all a sham, "since I walked with nothing into Rookery Court. Only see how I am risen. In the decade and a half since coming to Liriat, I have attained the rank of baroness in the country that destroyed my own. The last heir of the Blood Royal Brackenwilds is indebted to me for life. The ancestral home of my people's greatest enemy has become mine own, and all his dark treasures therein, with the most powerful daughter of his line come begging for favors. *This* is what Bran Fiakhna has done for me. This, in turn, is what I shall do for Skakmaht—exalt it far beyond its former glory, and set it shining as a star in our firmament. Now *think!* Think, Lanie, what a wife Bran Fiakhna would be to *you*, should you take her as your Blackbird Bride."

Lanie adjusted her unadjustable spectacles, and thought on what she'd just heard. Some of what Sari had revealed was no doubt true—but not all of it, not by a cannon shot.

For what *reason*, after all, would Her Sovereign Majesty Bran Fiakhna, the Rook of Rook, Splendor of the Glistring Sea, et cetera, back a Skaki pauper to the tune of a barony, and not demand so much as an oath of fealty? She must have demanded something—or, if not demanded it, compelled Sari to offer it, in that way she had.

That crushing fascination. That sea-and-feather smell, and jasmine, and velvet. That husky voice that made an unbearable sacrifice seem but the paltriest of favors. How it was nothing to her, a mere nothing, to demand the murder of a child like Datu.

From *me*, the murder of a child, Lanie thought. From Sari—the *dedication* of one? A child who might, even as a toddler, have shown great promise as a wizard?

Lanie shuddered, thinking of a tiny Hatchet Scratch growing up in the shadow of the Parliament of Rooks. Sari's head rose, but it wasn't in response to Lanie's reaction. She was peering past her, looking across the room towards the door.

Below-stairs, somewhere at the bottom of the palace, a commotion. Voices. Footsteps. Growing louder. Coming closer.

"You have company." Lanie stood to take her leave. "I understand you won't help me. I'll not detain you any longer."

But she was too slow. Sari was already standing, moving toward her, taking possession of her dirty left hand and pressing something snakily cold into it. Lanie's hand convulsed with the impulse to cast whatever the thing was away, but Sari closed her fingers over the item, then wrapped her hand over Lanie's knuckles.

"Before you leave, take this treasure," she entreated Lanie. "Take it—as a token of her esteem. She entrusted it to me months ago, and asked that I might pass it on to you should the opportunity arise. She... she asked as well that I renew her protestations of continued passion and devotion." To her credit, Sari sounded vaguely embarrassed to repeat that last part.

Lanie stared down at the twinkling rope of gold, rubies, jet, garnets, and iron pyrite laying across her palm like a dead serpent. Every facet of every gem was sharp and clear to her eyes, despite her clawed and cloudy spectacles, and she realized she had gone into deep sight without even knowing it.

Some magic, some spell, she thought, is upon this necklace. But dormant.

She looked up. "Baroness Scratch, I didn't come here to pocket bribes from my Blood Royal's enemies. I came for one reason only—"

But Sari interrupted her. "The revenant Goody Graves will be yours, Miss Stones. Anything you ask will be yours—the moment you cede yourself and your niece to the Blackbird Bride. She is patient. She will wait for you to come to her. It is not you she is hunting, but the Harrier's daughter: a blood debt she feels is her due. But until you can agree to her terms, Miss Stones"—Sari loosed a short, regretful sigh—"I am afraid this conversation is over."

For a hard flash, Lanie wondered what it would be like to crack that whip of precious gems across Sari's haggish face. But the next moment, her own face echoed the welt of her violent intent. Her cheek stung, bringing her back to herself.

Instead of flinging the necklace away, she jerked her hand from Sari's and pocketed it. She would, of course, be examining the gems later and at length with her deep sight, searching for curses or tracking spells or other subtle enchantments that she might strip for her own better understanding of Parliamentary magic.

After that, she would strip the necklace down to its component parts and fence it for a queen's ransom—because whatever else the necklace might be, it was also terrifically, fantastically, dizzyingly expensive, and Lanie knew she would soon need to supply herself with things like food and soap and clothes that were not mostly holes again.

Eventually.

Before she could allow herself such luxuries as food and rest, however, she had some more digging to do. Petitioning Sari to release Goody to her had been, after all, only her first plan.

"Do convey my thanks to your mistress," she said in her driest voice.

Sari dipped her chin slightly and resumed her seat, just as the door opened and in walked Hatchet Scratch.

He immediately stepped to one side, ushering into the tower room the two people behind him: Eparch Aranha of the High Temple of Sappacor, and their niephling, Canon Lir.

CHAPTER THIRTY-SEVEN

A Diplomatic Mission

AT LANIE'S INDRAWN breath, Hatchet's gaze flickered to her. But he only gave her a short nod before kneeling beside his mother's chair and greeting her with an affectionate, "Mordda."

"Haaken."

Sari kissed his forehead, and once on each cheek. She followed this ritual with a request-inflected phrase in Skaki. It must have been a request to pour out drinks for their guests, because Hatchet immediately went to a small sideboard and began to do just that.

Lanie's gaze strayed to Canon Lir's face. It was turned from her, watching the interplay between Hatchet and Sari. But Canon Lir did stay lingering near the door, almost blocking it, even when their ommer the Eparch came further into the room and took the seat Lanie had vacated. If she left now, Lanie would have to pass Canon Lir on her way out. Perhaps, even, her sleeve would brush their sleeve. And then she didn't think she would be able to help herself. She would cast herself upon their breast and weep and weep and beg forgiveness for not answering their blood-borne messages, for not sending them word at the temple, for doing nothing to assure them of her well-being or their continued friendship.

No, she decided. Better not risk it.

Better stay where she was. Rooted to the floor. Hands in pockets. Fingers fisted over Bran Fiakhna's golden chain. If she kept very still, perhaps no one would much notice her, or at least they would pretend not to, and eventually Canon Lir would be called away from the door, and Lanie could make good her escape.

"Is it not rather early in the day for such strong spirituous liquors?" Eparch Aranha asked Hatchet when he brought them their cognac.

Hatchet just smiled, and the Eparch, no proof against that rare sight, sipped and protested no more. Canon Lir refused their drink politely. Lanie took her cup but did not drink it. Sari slammed hers back, and Hatchet, who had not poured for himself, returned to the sideboard and leaned against it, watching everyone.

Watching Lanie.

She caught his eye for a brief, skittering second. Was that a twinkle she detected? And if so, was it one of amusement or challenge?

Certainly Hatchet's former mask of cow-like placidity, which Lanie dimly recalled from previous encounters years ago, was utterly vanished now. His countenance was grave (but for that enigmatic twinkle), yet keenly attentive—and though she still had difficulty reading him, Lanie knew herself to be in the presence of a formidable intelligence. But the ambiguities of Hatchet Scratch were too much to cope with at present.

She ducked her head and turned her shoulder to him, only to find herself under scrutiny by the Eparch of the Holy Temple of Sappacor themself. Sighing inward, she met their gaze head-on.

"Yes, Eparch?"

"Now," Aranha mused slowly, "now, I have seen your face before, have I not? Under all that mud and soot?"

"Yes, Eparch." Back when she was helping out Havoc on Quadoni culture nights at the Lover's Complaint, Lanie had always worried that one day Aranha would look into her face and see her father mirrored there. But she needn't have stewed so—then or now. Eparch Aranha saw nothing in her but a dirty, ragged, hyperopic, hollow-eyed thing.

"Yes!" they exclaimed triumphantly. "You used to wait tables at that brewpub on Seventh! On Rainday nights, when the erophains played."

A dire thirst to return to those days made mudcrack of Lanie's throat. She swallowed. "Yes, Eparch."

"Yes," they reflected. "I recall that little red-haired daughter of yours used to run tame with the Quadoni musicians. I love to hear them play. Student of theirs, isn't she? Or"—they chuckled—"*erophain*, I should say, should I not, niephling?"

Canon Lir smiled. "That would be the correct Quadic term, ommer."

Sari was not smiling. She had glanced up sharply at the mention of Datu. "What brewpub is this?"

The Eparch laughed. "Oh, it has some gamy name, straight from the gutter. Must be a dozen like it in that neighborhood. The Paramour's Prognosis, or the Inamorato's Itch, or the like. Lord Haaken," they addressed Hatchet Scratch, "you remember it, surely?"

Sari's narrowed eyes widened in surprise as she swiveled to stare at Hatchet. But he simply bowed.

"I am afraid I cannot recollect it, Eparch," he said, his deep, slow voice that had more of Skakmaht in it than his mother's did.

Sari's shocked gaze locked on Lanie, who frowned. Why was Sari surprised—when Hatchet had discovered Lanie's connection to Seventh Circle almost two months ago? His coming to her rescue at Midsummer; his carrying her, bleeding, to the safety of Waystation Thirteen; his discovery of her close friendships with Havoc and Tan and Duantri and Canon Lir—those were all the reasons that she had pulled Datu from school. Lanie had known that if Hatchet knew about their refuge, their allies, then so too would Sari, and thus, the Parliament of Rooks, and thus Bran Fiakhna, whose greatest ambition was Datu's death.

But was it possible that the incident at Midsummer had gone no further than Hatchet?

If so, then…

Then Lanie had abandoned all their friends, ruined Mak's trust in her, and kept Datu holed up in that chapel—where she broke her cavaquinho, slept too many bleak hours, and destroyed countless tombstones with her throwing knives—for nothing.

That day at the quarry need never have come to pass. Datu would never have slain the pup. Lanie would never have had cause to raise him up. Mak would never have taken them both away.

And she, Lanie, wouldn't now be drowning in bone dust and grave dirt; and all because—Saint Death only knew why—Hatchet Scratch had kept his mouth shut.

She did not—could not—look at Hatchet. He did not look at her. Silence stretched taut.

Her patience snapped.

"The place is called the Lover's Complaint," Lanie told the Eparch, for Sari's benefit. "I don't work there anymore. My… the child no longer lives with me. She's long gone. With her father."

Sari's pale eyes flickered again at the bitterness in Lanie's voice. By the doorway, Canon Lir stirred slightly, a sound as soft as silk.

"Ah." Raising a painted eyebrow, Aranha murmured to their niephling, "Wasn't this young lady a favorite of yours?" in a wondering tone that intimated they could not conceive how such a thing had ever been possible.

Lanie felt Sari's attention move to Canon Lir with raptorial focus. But they, implacable behind their shield of gilt and paint, said merely, "Indeed. I knew her the moment I saw her. The barmaid who always brought me the perry cider I liked. Hello again."

"Hello," Lanie rasped out. "You tipped me a steeple once."

"No more than you deserved, I'm sure." With a nod of friendly dismissal, Canon Lir strolled over to a window with a southerly aspect, overlooking the rear aspect of Castle Ynyssyll, gray against the bright green of moat and kopje.

For a long moment, Lanie watched their back, ignoring the others in the room. Her shoulders crawled; she felt herself affixed in the sights of three separate crossbows. But when she looked up again, Hatchet was kneeling beside his mother's seat, unfolding a map between them, and Eparch Aranha was leaning forward in their own chair to peer over the map's edge.

The Triple Flame of their wizard mark was drawn down into a single burning point upon their brow. But their frown, Lanie thought, was not for her. The room had moved on to other business.

Sari asked her son, "Are all arrangements made to your satisfaction?"

"Yes, Mordda," Hatchet answered. "I stay at Castle Ynyssyll tonight, for our party sets forth for Rook at dawn."

Lanie started, blurting, "You're going to Rook?"

Hatchet turned to her, and bowed in that slight, polite way he had. This reverence obviously surprised Eparch Aranha; once more, their sharp but doleful coppery eyes flashed at her.

"Indeed, yes: I form one of Blood Royal Errolirrolin's courtship procession," Hatchet informed her.

"*Courtship?*" The word squeaked out of her with childlike incredulity.

Aranha snorted, "What, guttersnipe—do you live in a mine shaft, that you haven't heard? It's all the gossip in Liriat Proper!"

But Lanie ignored the Eparch, intensifying her focus on Hatchet until he answered her in full.

"The Blood Royal," he said in his measured tones, "sends his Minister Plenipotentiary and a full complement of royal guard to ride north and beg the Blackbird Bride for her hand. Should she so honor his proposal, Errolirrolin invites Rookery Court back to Castle Ynyssyll for the Midwinter revels, at which time the wedding will be held. Next spring, Rookery and Brackenwild courts together will embark on a year-long tour throughout the realms. This will quiet the unrest that has plagued Liriat, and reassure the subjects of Rook that all is amicable between their two great leaders again."

"But..."

Aranha harrumphed, offended at her interruption, but Hatchet, it seemed, had not finished answering Lanie's unfinished question. She was grateful; she thought for a second that she might actually like Hatchet Scratch, which of course put her on her guard again.

"Bran Fiakhna has so far responded favorably to Errolirrolin's overtures of peace. She collects wizards for Rook. The best of these are promoted to her Parliament, but Rookery Court and its environs abound in wizards of all variety. The new Blood Royal is known to enjoy Sappacor's favor; the bloodlamps haven't blazed so high since first I came to Liriat. Why should not Errolirrolin offer himself as a wizard worthy of her hand?"

"Why not indeed?" asked Eparch Aranha dryly. "Especially since, should he do otherwise, my nephew's alternative is to meet his mother's fate?"

Sari snorted. "The boy is no coward. But he's no fool either."

"Not at all," Hatchet agreed, though Lanie felt he was only still speaking for her benefit. "Errolirrolin has no interest in antagonizing the Blackbird Bride—as his mother clearly did. Erralierra's abortive attempts at enfeebling Rook through the slaughter of its greatest wizards only left Liriat vulnerable. Errolirrolin would mend that, if he can. In offering himself as lone phoenix amongst a menagerie of blackbirds, he hopes to beguile Bran Fiakhna's interest. Errolirrolin's coronation vows to Liriat—

sealed in blood and flame by Sappacor Themself—protect him from her fascination. He would be the one wizard at Rookery Court who could not be enspelled by the Blackbird Bride, nor compelled by oath to obey her, but who has chosen, willingly, to roost in her bosom."

"Just like Mak," Lanie muttered, rubbing her eyes. And just about as willing.

"What was that?" Sari asked sharply, but Lanie ignored her. Crusts of blackened ectenica were falling from her face.

She must look, she reflected, like a chimney sweep newly spewed from the flues of the Triple Flame. She tried calculating how long it had been since she had bathed.

The mental math renewed her bone-deep weariness, which had ebbed somewhat during her exchange with Sari, still more when the others had entered. Now Lanie imagined walking home, imagined hauling a bucket of water from the cryptyard stream and boiling it clean over a small fire in the chapel.

But first she'd have to light the fire. And even if she got that far, even if she managed to wash her body with harsh soap—did she even have any soap left?—she knew she'd never feel all the way clean.

She knew—she *knew!*—that neglect of *accident* was also neglect of *substance*. And that she needed to care for both if she wanted to keep going.

And she would keep going. She had to.

So, her first path to Goody dead-ended here, in Sari Scratch's eight-sided tower. Lanie had been preparing for that. She had already begun laying down her second path. She was digging out Gallowsdance's collapsed tunnel with her bare hands.

Well... with her hands, and her blood, and the bones of the dead.

And so what if she was using a great deal of death-magic off-surge. What of it? What *else* was death magic for?

At least today's visit wasn't a total loss. She'd had half a notion to try and gain an audience with Errolirrolin should her petition to Sari fail, see if she might offer her Stonesish services to him—some future grand act of necromancy wherein she, Miscellaneous Stones, would save all of Liriat and its peoples from its foes with her armies of the undead (or whatever)—in exchange for him interceding on her behalf with the Scratches.

Too late now.

Go to him *now*, and the Blood Royal would just sell her to the Rook of Rook along with himself, and be damned duodecifold the ancient lines of loyalty between his house and hers. What was left of their houses was up to them to save, separate and alone.

Her house was Goody. His, Liriat. And so.

More exhausted by the minute, Lanie backed toward the door. Canon Lir had not been guarding it for many long minutes, but she had been so distracted by Hatchet's news that she had forgotten to notice.

"Baroness Scratch," she said by way of farewell. "Eparch Aranha. Hatchet—or, I mean… is it, *Lord* Scratch now?"

"Lord Ambassador Haaken Skrathmandan," Eparch Aranha corrected her stiffly, as if it were something she and the whole world should know. "And I did not quite catch *your* name, girl?"

It was that 'girl' that did it—so close to Grandpa Rad's ubiquitous 'girlie' and in an almost identical tone of voice.

"Miscellaneous Stones," Lanie spat.

Aranha's golden mask cracked. Their mouth hung open.

She smiled maliciously.

Why should she not declare herself, after all? The Scratches knew who she was, and Canon Lir did too. Keeping Datu safe had been her primary reason for anonymity. Useless to keep pretending now. Useless, *and* counterproductive, when all she wanted was to blast that look of supercilious superiority off the Eparch's face.

Girl.

How *dared* they? Could she not summon the very skeleton from out Aranha's living flesh? Open her veins to their dying bones? Make undead their marrow—even as the rest of their accident fell to her feet and breathed no more? Did they not know her power?

Perhaps they did, a little.

Lanie did not realize she had stepped toward their chair until Aranha shrank back, which catapulted her spirits into even greater heights of courage. Flinging back her shoulders with flinty satisfaction, she pivoted, and marched herself right to the southern windows.

"Canon Lir. Will you walk me home?"

Canon Lir spun around, and smiled at her. "Certainly, Miss Stones."

Lanie's chest flooded with warmth. Her friend was gazing back at her with an undeniable, radiant affection that incinerated all their court-careful neutrality. *They* were not ashamed of her, said that glowing expression. *They* did not think her some dirty-faced, hoozzaplo-sucking guttersnipe of a *girl*. *They* were overjoyed to walk with her. And they were not afraid to show it.

When Canon Lir stepped forward and offered Lanie their arm, she accepted it gratefully. And when they covered her hand with theirs and squeezed, she felt her face almost break apart in its first real smile for… she couldn't remember how long.

Since Midsummer.

"Niephling," croaked Eparch Aranha. "But you told me… You said that, that the youngest Stones girl…"

Canon Lir said, very quietly, "*Enough.*"

Eparch Aranha shut their painted mouth so fast their teeth clicked.

Lanie stared at her friend in surprise. Never had she heard their mellifluous tones turn so cold or so sharp: the gold turned to steel, and the steel with an edge geometry that could split rock like lard. She hoped that they'd never turn such a tone on her—she didn't think she'd survive it.

But Saint Death smiles! How she enjoyed Canon Lir deploying that weapon for her benefit.

She leaned harder on their arm as they guided her to the door. For a moment, Lanie visualized all the stairs and courtyards and boulevards and walls and bridges between them and the place where they must bid each other farewell—almost as if she were Bran Fiakhna's Condor in truth, looking down upon the city from high on white-patched wings. And despite her fatigue, it seemed far too short a walk.

"Miss Stones!" Sari called out they made to exit. "Remember—it is within your power to resolve your present troubles. I shall await your word."

In answer, Lanie raised her left hand in its ratty fingerless mitten, but not in farewell. "Power, yes. Thank you for reminding me."

"I HAVE SOMETHING for you," Canon Lir began.

They had left First Circle, ducking down Quarter After to stroll arm in arm through the prosperous bustle of Second Circle. A few people paused to give Lanie startled looks, reminding her again how dirty she was, how tired she felt. But the presence of a fire priest of Canon Lir's splendor kept the rudesbies at bay.

"Something?" she asked, when Canon Lir said nothing more.

"A gift."

"A g-gift?" she stammered.

"Yes, I commissioned them for you, right after—" they began, just as Lanie said, "But... how did you know you would see me today?"

"I..." They hesitated. "I woke this morning with a sense of purpose not my own." They tapped their reliquary. "It was as if, for weeks, my reliquary had been sleeping, dull and dormant. But today it felt lighter, brighter, something a-thrum. I felt compelled, when Lord Haaken mentioned a visit to the Ambassadorial Palace today, to beg him allow me to accompany him there. I knew I would find you."

"You did?" Lanie asked in a small voice. She had not stopped leaning on their arm, and now Canon Lir covered her hand with theirs.

"Yes, I did. You seem surprised, my own dear necromancer. But I am, you know, a fire priest, and my god does, from time to time, deign to whisper in my ear. Or perhaps yours does. So... here, Miss Stones, come aside a moment. There's a bench beneath this tree. We don't start getting stingy on the benches till Fifth Circle at least, here in Liriat Proper. We shall sit, and I shall give you your present properly."

Lanie's heart hammered. For the first time in months she felt the faint, hopeful pinging of her reliquary. She thought Canon Lir must have felt it too, or something like it, for they reached inside their silken robes as if to press the pendant to their chest.

But she was mistaken; they were dipping into a concealed pocket and drawing out a small coffer, which they presented to her.

Lanie felt a spike of her delighted anticipation so poignant that she wanted only to prolong the moment. Canon Lir must have read that in her face, for they laughed suddenly, and teased her, "Go on!"

Obediently, Lanie took the coffer and lifted the hinged lid, then immediately gasped, "Oh!"

"Try them!"

She shook her head. "I wish I could look at them *and* wear them at the same time! How can these be for everyday use?" Nevertheless she slipped Canon Lir's gift onto her face, her vision sharpening and sparkling in time to see her friend affect a look of scandalized outrage. "What?" she asked.

"Have we not met, Miss Stones?"

"Too infrequently, Canon Lir."

"Do you not know me?"

"All my life." Lanie was growing more cheerful by the minute.

"Have you not found," they demanded, "in all these long years of our friendship, that I am a person fully prepared in any situation for any eventuality?"

"You are certainly efficient," Lanie admitted.

"And no less so today!" Canon Lir insisted. "Nor am I less cunning, thoughtful, or solicitous of your wellbeing than ever I was! And so I shall prove—momentarily."

Grinning like a mountebank hawking nostrums and emetics for the credulous passersby, they produced from another hidden pocket of their robes, a mirror no larger than an egg, backed in silver. Lanie was impressed.

"You do think of everything, don't you?"

"I try, Miss Stones. I try."

Peering into the mirror, she received the full impact of her own grin.

It was the prettiest pair of spectacles that ever a necromancer had received. The convex lenses were of purest crystal, ground thickest in the middle and set into gold-gilt frames decorated with cobalt blue enamel. Tiny red and purple enamel flowers and green vines twined all around the frames, and at the center of each flower a crystal chip was set, sparking rainbows in the sunlight.

But her first joy soon flickered. Lanie met her own eyes in the mirror, then hurriedly looked away. She was sick of herself, sick of a sight she found shabby and shameful.

She would gaze her fill instead at Canon Lir, and feast until surfeited.

But when she raised her head, and really *looked* at her friend, she saw that they too appeared as tired as she. As heartsore, as weary. The wizard mark on their forehead seemed tarnished, the Triple Flame gone brassy and a bit tired. Even their fingernails signaled some ongoing distress. They were not wearing their usual false ones: lacquered, filed to points, fantastically beaded. No, those were Canon Lir's natural nails, exposed. Clean but bitten to the quick.

"What's wrong?" Lanie's voice constricted to its smallest sound, only just able to squeeze past the tightness of her throat.

Canon Lir frowned down at the ground, and without looking, drew her arm once more through theirs, encouraging her to stand and walk once more with them.

"Well, Miss Stones," they began again, "I am shortly to be dispatched on a diplomatic mission." They cleared their throat. "I have been invested as Minister Plenipotentiary of Liriat, in order that I may offer the hand of my twin brother, Blood Royal Errolirrolin Brackenwild, in marriage to Her Sovereign Majesty Bran Fiakhna, the Blackbird Bride."

"Oh," Lanie whispered. "You're going too. With Hatchet Scratch. To Rook."

"Yes." They nodded, and sighed. "It is what Errolirrolin knows he must do. It is either propose marriage to Bran Fiakhna, or accept the total obliteration of Liriat. If Lord Haaken and I fail in our purpose, Rook will declare all-out war on our realm, and that's an end to us. Or so near an end it would take a hundred years for Liriat to recover—like Skakmaht when we finished with it. My brother hopes to buy Liriat the same as I would buy for you—time."

They stopped again, this time in the shadow of a covered bridge conducting from Second Circle to Third via 20th Till Boulevard. The nearest bloodlamp was too far away to light the tunnel entirely; its interior was dim, and even in this richer patch of the city, smelled of urine and churned mud. But at least she and Canon Lir were indisputably alone for the moment.

"I didn't know," Lanie told them, the darkness instantly dulling her voice and mood. Her exhaustion was twice as heavy in the dark. "I've been so... I've been otherwise occupied for so long, and I neglected you—I didn't even tell you about Datu—and now you are leaving, and I... I am so sorry, Canon Lir. I have wasted all our time..."

Canon Lir squeezed her arm. "You must know all is forgiven. You must know I trust you to have your reasons."

"You do?"

"Yes. We trust each other. Don't we, Lanie?"

Lanie looked for but could not see their face; the two of them had come about halfway through the dark tunnel. Light before them and behind them, but not where they stood. She felt rather than saw the dark rift in the damp wall to her left: one of the many boltholes from the surface streets of Liriat Proper down into the catacombs. The wet black passageway tugged at her gut, urging her bone-ward.

"I trust you, Lir," she said at last, trying to ignore the tug.

"Good. Now listen to me." Canon Lir's sweet summer voice had gone as gray and grim as she felt. "You must be well out of Liriat Proper by winter. Whether our mission fails or is triumphant, you have to be long gone from here. If we fail, Liriat Proper will be the most perilous place in the realms. If we succeed, we will be returning with Rookery Court for the revels. You must be so far vanished that there won't be even a trace—a scent—a sparkle—of you for Bran Fiakhna to sniff out. You must go where no wizard-bird can find you. Yes—and further than that. Stay alive, stay away, stay *yourself*. I love my brother; I honor his sacrifice. But I tell you now, Lanie, his sacrifice means nothing to me if it cannot buy you safety from the sphere of Bran Fiakhna's desire. I will *not* see the Condor's feather sewn into your breast. I will *not* see you her fourth-and-twenty espoused kin. Do you understand me?"

"Yes, Lir."

Lanie wiped her nose, which was dripping. So, she was surprised to find, were both her eyes. She had to remove her new spectacles to get at them.

"Will you," she hesitated, wiping the lenses on her grubby hem, "will you keep sending me messages? I won't ignore them anymore. I'll open every one, and, and when I have some... some blood and bone to spare, I'll write back, a proper letter, and send it via ectenica, like I used to do, back before, before Mid..."

But she couldn't finish the word, and Canon Lir was already shaking their head.

"On my road to Rook and back, invested with Errolirrolin's authority, I will never not be watched. Any blood magic I invoke—even what I practice in private—will be analyzed, reported, and investigated from source to terminus. I *will not*," they whispered, "be the proverbial trail of seed that leads the Blackbird Bride to your door."

Lanie blotted her raw face with her handkerchief again. "And our reliquaries? Must we give those up too?"

She could hear the rueful smile in their voice. "The bone inside my reliquary does not sing for me as yours does. It's not a magic that I possess. But then"—and they squeezed her arm again, drawing her close—"neither do any of the Parliament of Rooks."

A small hope flickered at her breast. Or perhaps it was her reliquary, singing.

"I do not therefore see the harm in continuing to wear my reliquary," Canon Lir continued. "I cannot, in fact, bear *not* to—for it reminds me of you every day, Lanie. But it won't be able to tell me where you are, or if you are well and happy, or even if you are alive, and I wish..."

"Wait." The command flew out of her mouth, but Canon Lir obeyed without objection.

Left-handed, Lanie clutched her reliquary like she wanted to clutch at them. She concentrated hard. She dove inward, to that place where her deep sight and deep voice came from: the luminous under-stuff of her own substance, which was seated in her body but not *affixed* there.

Very well. She would *unseat* the smallest fleck of it, and extend that bit of substance past her accident and into her reliquary. Into that fragment of bone taken from the Founding Queen of Liriat.

Her substance hummed, trapped in the pendant she wore like a bumblebee. It was willing to do her will, but unsure of what her will was.

And so, Lanie gathered her will with precision. Breathed. *Pushed*.

Her little sliver of substance understood. It leapt like a spark from a fire and caught hold of the nearest fragment like it: the bone in Canon Lir's reliquary.

This time, Lanie knew her friend could feel their reliquary respond—for she saw their robes kick out from their chest, as the bone inside their reliquary leapt.

"Oh!" said Canon Lir.

Then, more quietly, they added, "Do it again, Lanie. If you please. But… *less*."

With a small smile of acknowledgement, Lanie sank deeper into her own substance, sliced off an even smaller sliver of it, transfered that sliver to her reliquary again, and again thence to theirs, and *pushed*. This time, it was not so much the slamming of a brass knocker against a door, but the scratching of a fingernail in the dead of night.

"Yes," Canon Lir breathed. "Yes, I can feel that. But, I think, no one else will."

"It is something, at least," Lanie offered, her voice wavering at the end into a question, or perhaps a sob.

"It is a great gift, Miss Stones," Canon Lir told her, so warmly that their use of honorific and surname name seemed more like a caress than a formality. "For so long as you keep reaching out to me through our reliquaries, then wherever you go in the world, I will possess that which I would give my last breath to secure—the knowledge that you are alive."

"Alive," Lanie replied, "and thinking of you."

"And I of you. Always. But that you may be assured of, even without reliquaries."

She knew it was no lie, for the wizard mark on Canon Lir's forehead started to shine so brightly, it set the dim tunnel ablaze.

Lanie was reminded of the Midsummer Bloodlighting, when all the fire priests reflected the face of their god, their faces flaring up like torches, like mirrors a-glare with the white dazzle of reflected sunlight.

"So, this isn't goodbye. Not really," she said, even though it was, and she would have gladly swallowed her left arm to stop it. "We'll always have Queen Ynyssyll's toe bones, Canon Lir."

"And life can be long, Miss Stones," they replied. "And surprising. And resplendent with the possibility of reunion."

"Yes—but Stoneses die young."

It was the second time that day she'd said it, but now she felt the faintest stirring of rebellion at the idea, rather than a fatalistic acceptance.

"Perhaps, Miss Stones," Canon Lir suggested gently, "you might care to invent a new family motto? Something to go with whatever new name you choose for your new life. Something like—"

"—'outlive thy foe and dance upon her tomb'?"

"I would your future life and self will know no foes—but only dancing."

They drew her close to them, wrapping her in silken heat, sweet incense, tenderness, sadness, the smell of sweat.

"May Sappacor warm but never burn you."

"May Doédenna keep away from you and yours."

They leaned against each other, forehead against forehead. Lanie reached up to touch Canon Lir's face, feeling the gold paint flake off in her mittened hand.

And then they parted.

CHAPTER THIRTY-EIGHT

Collapse

Luckday, 9th
Month of Chases, 421 Founding Era
14 days till Autumn Equinox

DEEP UNDERGROUND, LANIE studied her work.

Her burrow through the collapse of Gallowsdance's tunnel was complete. At last.

It was not airy or open, as Gallowsdance's had been. It would not fit a cart pulled by two undead horses. It was slender, thread-like. It would fit only Lanie, and only if Lanie were crawling on her hands and knees.

But she had known how it would be the moment she had started this work. She knew that to create even this small of an aperture through the Midsummer collapse would require so much of her death magic off-surge that she had to be as sparing as possible with her resources. Bones she had in plenty. It was her own blood that was in too-short supply.

Every morning for months, she had carted bones by the armful to the site of the collapse. Every morning, she studded the wall of rubble with osseous fragments gathered from various parts of the catacombs. She never took more than a piece or two from any particular pile or crypt or cubbyhole. She wanted to respect her dead. They were all the family she had left, besides Goody.

Every morning, when her mound of rubble was thoroughly infiltrated with bone, resembling a child's proud mud cake decorated with tallow-yellow sticks for candles, Lanie would pause, and draw several tubes of blood from her arm. (A few weeks ago, she had to start switching between the basilic and cephalic veins of her right arm after her median cubital vein grew inflamed. This week, she finally changed over to her left arm. She was not, she found, nearly as deft with a syringe right-handed. But blood was blood, and it did the job, no matter how sloppily.)

She always drew just enough to fill a small bowl. And then, taking her aspergillum, she would swirl it around in her blood, brandish it above her head, and then swing it around in a series of arcs, splattering her blood about her until the bone-stuck dirt was freckled in red.

Until her red blood and the yellow bone and the black dirt began to glow blue with ectenica.

Then the whole mound became hers to command, for a time. Lanie ordered her ectenica to integrate with the dirt itself, to create for her a biddable slurry. Unlike an orblin's stabilized form, raw ectenica like this never lasted for long.

But it was powerful, and it was fast, and before it began to fall to sludgy ash, Lanie could basically command her tunnel to *burrow itself*.

The collapse was about three miles deep, or around 5,300 yards. She had been trying to worm through fifty to eighty yards a day. Sometimes she did more, sometimes less, and lately she had been growing so tired, almost too tired to go on, but she always pushed through.

She was impressed with her own engineering. The ectenica understood what she needed from it. Even after it sloughed off to ash, and the slurry hardened and dried, the new walls and floor and ceiling it left behind were smooth and hard and uniform, a strange sort of concrete that needed no shoring. Every morning, as Lanie crawled deeper into it to get to her next mound of loose dirt, she was grateful that the material was glassy and cool, like a polished jewel, like moonstone pavement, beneath her palms and knees.

Sometimes she was down there for days, digging. Day and night had no meaning anymore. Sometimes she woke and remembered she hadn't eaten, and then dragged herself back out of the tunnel and up into her workshop to sleep on her pallet. Food was more difficult to obtain than sleep; she had to actually go *outside* to find food. She filled her workshop with boxes of dried fruits and dried mushrooms, bulky sacks of nuts, hard cheese and hardtack, storing them in great quantities so that she wouldn't have to leave again.

And then, there were the days she lost.

But Lanie tried not to think about the gray spaces in her memory.

And anyway, a few fuzzy gray-outs in time were surely worth it—for now her tiny tunnel had finally opened up into Gallowsdance's larger one.

The last twelve miles to Goody were open to her, hers to traverse when she would. No wizard-bird to spy on her from on high. No travelers to stare at her as she trudged the packed gravel of Brackenwild Holloway through the Diesmali. No gates or walls or hedges or guard dogs or Scratch brothers to bar her from realizing her goal. She would go by Gallowsdance's tunnel to Goody, sneaking in like a thief in the night, and she would steal Goody's undeath from her, and then sneak back with none the wiser.

Now there was nothing but the long dark ahead of her, and Lanie did not mind the dark. The way was not strange to her. She had walked it before, with Mak and Datu and Goody and Grandpa Rad to keep her company.

It would be even faster going, alone.

The lightless path led in only one direction. No openings branched off to left or right. Nothing to lead her astray. Lanie reveled in walking upright, in the soundness of Gallowsdance's ancient structure. She walked as if in a dream, pausing sometimes to sit in the dark, and drink from her flask, or chew the leathery remains of her dried fruit and mushrooms, or sleep—or that thing that was not sleep, but was only gray, and strange, and lasted sometimes hours, sometimes days.

She did not know how long she traveled that dark road. But when she came to its end, Lanie found her hand lovingly pressed flat against the old wooden door leading back into Stones Ossuary. Saint Death's Doorway, she used to call it, when she was small. On the other side, the ossuary-side of that plain wooden door, hung the mosaic of Doédenna, with her cloak of bone that spread throughout the entire underground chamber.

Even having been absent from it these many months, Lanie was confident that even in total darkness, she could make her way across the ossuary to its entrance. She knew the ways of her old workshop like she knew the tangles in Datu's hair—and could navigate them far more easily.

On this side of the secret door, there was no hidden panel to depress. There was just a small latch to lift, allowing the door to swing silently toward her, into the tunnel.

But when Lanie lifted the latch, and the door swung open, there was nothing on the other side.

Nothing but dirt, pouring out in droves upon her.

Fine, soft dirt, loamy and sweet with petrichor, smelling faintly volcanic.

The smell, she realized, stumbling back from the lazy tumble of never-ending dirt, was a result of all the bone ash mixed into it.

She licked cracked lips, and contemplated the mound before her. Eyeless, it seemed to stare back at her, not in welcome but in challenge.

So she knelt before the door that opened into nowhere, and thrust her left arm up to her elbow into the dirt.

Reaching through her left hand with everything inside her, Lanie tried to extend the concentrated substance of her wizard mark well beyond the bounds of her accident. She sent it searching for something—anything—that she might recognize: the faint chime of a family skeleton; a chip from Saint Death's mosaic; a scapular pendant from the chandelier that had lit so many late nights in her workshop; even a fibula hollowed like a flute, attached to a sinew that strung it from the dark ceiling, where no wind ever whistled through it.

But there was nothing.

The Scratches had burnt Stones Ossuary to the ground.

Then they had razed the ruins. Raked them. Salted them. Prayed their Skaki prayers over the rubble. There was nothing left.

Worse…

Worse, when Lanie stretched her wizard mark as fully far as it would go—feverishly calculating how many bones she should return with on the morrow, how many bowlfuls of blood it would take to help her dig her way out of *this* mess and up onto the Skrathmandan property—she hit a ward.

It was… peculiar. Instantly recognizable. Like a particular flavor of ice she once had tasted, or a glass prison she once had visited, or a needle which once had pierced her flesh, and pumped her full of poison.

The ward was, no doubt, the work of Lord Ambassador Haaken Skrathmandan.

"Hatchet!" Lanie spat, as the whole left half of her body went numb. "Poxflake! Plaguejuice! Septicemic abscess!"

That was as far as she got before her mouth stopped working. The icy jaws of Hatchet's ward bit deeply. Had it been her actual flesh that made contact with it, her body would have stiffened on the spot and frozen clear through. And she would have died down there in the dark, preserved in icicle stillness, forever. And no one would ever have known what happened to her, or where to find her, or how she died.

Except, perhaps, Hatchet.

But Hatchet, Lanie thought, sly snow weasel that he was, would probably never tell.

Shambling-slow, she drew her substance back into herself. The left half of her body remained slumped like soft wax, swollen, semi-useless, filled with a fatty numbness sometimes painfully enlivened by the burning prickle of pins and needles. She lay in the dirt beneath Saint Death's Doorway, contemplating her newly bifurcated self, occasionally testing to see how much of her left side she could move. Eventually, enough feeling returned that she could labor her way up from the floor. Leaning heavily on the wall to her right, she dragged herself, limping, back through Gallowsdance's tunnel. Back the way she came.

More gray moments passed. Maybe days.

She ran out of food, water. She didn't think she slept—didn't remember ever going to sleep, anyway—but would sometimes open her eyes and realize she was sprawled on the floor of the tunnel. She did not remember how she got there.

And then, finally, she came to the end of Gallowsdance's tunnel, but not to the end of her journey.

She had forgotten, in the dark, about the collapse.

Now, confronting the tiny, smirking mouth of her own ectenical burrow, she stared at it, hardly believing that the worst was yet to come. Three more endless miles on her hands and feet, in the glassy cool coffin of her own making.

It was as if Mak's underground sickness had somehow passed into her. Lanie sat at the lip of her burrow, and set her head between her knees, and tried to breathe, though it felt as though her larynx had collapsed to the size of the eye of a needle.

"Tomorrow," she muttered in a voice like gravel. Perhaps it was her deep voice, which needed no throat to speak with. "We'll do it tomorrow."

And she curled up on the cold ground, and let the grayness take her.

CHAPTER THIRTY-NINE

Small Favors

Flameday 26th
Month of Chases
86 days till Winter Solstice

"LANIE. OH, LANIE."

Not so much words as a sigh. Footsteps, light vibrations. Maybe someone touched the pulse in her throat. Maybe they didn't.

"Do never fear"—it was a voice of breathless urgency, speaking a language Lanie knew but was not her own—"for I'll return forthwith, and with our friends to help bear thee away. In meantime, stay..." The stranger's—was she a stranger?—voice broke. "Oh, Lanie, try to *stay*."

A susurrus of wings. Wind of ascension. A cry from on high: the clipped call of *killy-killy-klee*.

TIME PASSED.

Or it didn't.

Lanie used to measure days by the leafy shadow of the sorkhadari as it moved across her body. Getting back up to the sorkhadari tree had been her only goal for so long. Once she made it that far, she'd just... stopped.

Dark. Light. Sometimes rain—which she felt as pressure, rather than temperature or wetness. Sometimes she opened her mouth and let the unwet wetness sluice through the dust of her throat.

She had been lying there for a long time.

Or she hadn't.

"TITS AND PICKLES!" A familiar curse, but Lanie could not place it. "How long's she been like this?"

"Too long, I fear." A third voice. Older. Sterner. "How she has wasted! Is she alone? Where are the child and her father?"

The first voice, the one with wings in it, replied: "I do not know, and dread the mystery. At all times secrets bided 'twixt those three."

A sweet breath stirred upon Lanie's cheek again. It almost made her want to breathe more deeply, which almost surprised her.

Stump. Stump. An uneven gate was approaching, the tinier footprint of a cane with it. A huff. A back-of-the-throat groan. The creak of a knee. Then a second, nearly-familiar hand touched her hair.

"Hey. Heya, cookie. Let's getcha up and outta this bonebox, eh? Happen I got a spare room with a door that shuts. Bed made up with yer name on it. What more could a gal want? Well, maybe a bath. And some of Eidie's fresh-baked bread."

"She will not be able to eat solid food just yet," warned the sterner, older voice. Meddlesome, bread-stealing, miserly voice. "Soup stock. Vegetable, I think. And dark, leafy greens."

That irked her. Lanie thrashed, internally. She tried to thrash *externally*, but her body didn't do as she bid it.

She wanted to demand *both* soup and bread, steaming and savory, warm and deep, stick-to-your-ribs, make-you-yawn stuff, that lasting fullness. Why not, when all she'd had for so long were fickle sunbeams and faded grass? And before that, hardtack and dried fruit, stale nuts with a fur of mold growing over them?

There.

Thrashing had accomplished something. Lanie managed to slit open her eyes. Three faces stared back down.

Ah, but this felt familiar too. Didn't it? The last time she had seen these faces, hadn't Lanie also just awoken from an injured sleep? And there they all were, then as now, each of them bright with their varied concerns?

Or perhaps *that* instance and *this* instance were the same. Perhaps it was still Midsummer, and there was still time—if she left right now—there was still time to go home and save...

But, no.

No, and no, and no. Lanie had tried and failed.

She'd tried everything, and every attempt had set her further back. Now the tunnel of herself had collapsed. The door was buried. She was sunk down so deep there was no digging herself out. No matter that she'd somehow managed to drag her battered old *accident* back up here, into the light; in *substance*, most of her remained behind, lying in the dark, gray and frozen beneath the catacombs.

And it was no more than she deserved. Lanie remembered *that* well enough.

Whoever these people were, whoever they thought they were to her or she to them, they shouldn't be here. Shouldn't be looking at her like that, whispering reassurances, trying to lift her from her grave beneath the sorkhadari tree. They should leave her to her rest, a shade amongst shades.

If she closed her eyes, they would all disappear. And then they would be safe again. Safe from her.

So she did.

HAVOC'S SPARE BEDROOM was austere: a cot, a much-battered and deeply rusted trunk[34], a few crates for bedside seating, a small table shoved up against a wall with a round, porthole window, and a shelf with a few curious books, which included: a stack of lovingly hand-bound poetry publications, an illustrated volume of mermaid lore, a complete nautical dictionary and etymology, and *The Book of Knots*.

Lanie didn't know what would kill her first: staying here, where her presence endangered everyone who succored her; or leaving—most likely on hands and knees, as she could not yet walk without aid. Leaving and setting off for she knew not where, to do she knew not what, with nothing to help her, and no one for company.

Mostly, she cried.

She lay in bed and sobbed until someone—usually Havoc or Duantri—came into the room with soup.

She had learned to recognize them again, though she did not speak to them, or even call them by name. She could not even look them in the eye.

But she ate what they brought her. And then, she slept. And when she woke, she cried again.

Until the day Gyrlady Tanaliín decided that she'd had enough.

TAN CAME IN armed with a vase of flowers.

Lanie lay in her cot, slitting her eyes against the effusive purple and yellow glare: asters, lilies, sage, goldenrod—all the smoke and ore of autumn. Just the goad she needed. Just the needle through her heart. The poisoned finger-stinger slipping under her skin. Autumn flowers to remind her how she had lost her entire autumn equinox—a whole high holy fire feast—down one of her numbing blinks between time. Disappeared. Gone.

---

34 The trunk had a checkered history: it originated as a storage chest for a captain on the seedier side of the seafaring industry; had safeguarded, in its time, illicitly acquired silver cups, emeralds the size of ostrich eggs, and ropes of pearls enough to depopulate whole oyster farms; and became, in its retirement at a Lirian brewpub, a repository for extra quilts. How it fell into Havoc Dreadnought's possession is a tale far too tortuous and beguiling for a mere footnote. For further reading, see *Havoc: How an Urchin of Umrys Lost a Finger, Kissed a Devil, and Let the Ocean In*.

She'd just… missed it. Failed to make use of her surge. Failed Goody. Failed everything. Again.

"Do you like them?" Tan set the vase on the desk by the window. "They made me think of you."

Tears rolled down Lanie's face, scalding her. Her skin was always cold these days.

"No?" Thoughtfully, Tan took a seat on the crate beside Lanie's bed, and crossed her legs, clad in embroidered trousers, at the ankles. "But you are not liking much, these days, are you? That would require too much energy."

Lanie would have liked to turn her head to the wall—but that would have required too much energy.

"Oh, I know you are pining for me to mind my own business," the gyrlady told her with a smile. "You hold me deeply suspect, believe me to be devious and prying—a ferret at your warren, hoping to scare up secrets like panicked rabbits. It is true that my inquisitive nature has been both helpmeet and hamartia throughout my life, but I am too old to repudiate it now, even for you. So I will tell you what I know."

Tan took a great, bracing breath.

Lanie held her own. An irritated flush was beginning to flood her extremities—the tips of her fingers, her toes—with a furious heat. Curiously, though, her desire to roll over and close her eyes was quickly melting into a desire to leap off the bed and shout and wave her hands until Tan *went away*.

"You, young lady, have been performing too much magic off-surge. Yes," she added, seeing Lanie's eyelids fly open, "I am well aware you are a sorcerer. We all know *that* by now, seeing as how we have each taken turns bathing you since bringing you home to Havoc's. You are fairly freckled with wizard marks—not even counting your left hand! Duantri and Havoc have a bet going as to your god. Duantri thinks you are a hetch of Four-Faced Brotquen—for your love of gardens and flowers and trees. Havoc has pegged you for a priestess of Yssimyss of Mysteries—which would, I concur, explain a certain 'aura of the unexplainable' about you. I hate to spoil their fun."

Tan leaned in closer, and Lanie wanted to shrink away, but could not.

"So I did not tell them," she whispered, "that you are a necromancer. And that your name is Miscellaneous Stones."

At the sound of her name on the gyrlady's lips, Lanie shuddered. She opened her mouth to repudiate it, but started coughing instead.

Tan patiently fetched a cup of water from the edge of the desk and held it to Lanie's lips until she drank and grew calmer.

"Why do you stare at me so, dear Lanie? As if I were about to start hurling insults and proselytizing Quadoni ways to you! It is true," Tan admitted, "that we do not precisely have sorcerers in Quadiíb… Not *officially*, anyway.

We pride ourselves too much on holding balance between the Twelve, paying our obeisances to each god in Their turn—but never devoting too much attention to any one of Them, lest Their attentions rebound upon us and we grow drunk with power. And yes, it is also true that the Quadoni tend to regard *all* Lirians—and not *only* Lirians, mind you, but Aganath's holy urchins in Umrys-by-the-Sea, and, of course, the entirety of Rookery Court—as dangerously destabilized by their respective reductive theisms. But that is not to say that we do not dabble in magic whenever it suits us. We are just as hypocritical as the next country."

Tan laughed at the startled expression on Lanie's face.

"Really, Lanie! Why do you think I *left* Quadiíb? The Judicial Colloquium of Gyrladies is the worst trespasser. What is the result of our smug self-regard and the high esteem in which general opinion holds us but an institution that has become conservative, piously pretentious, stodgy, unimaginative, and stuck in its ways? Intellectual complacence is the *opposite* of good pedagogy! So, yes, I will freely confess that we Gyrladies practice magic. The Rite of Bryddongard is but the best known of a thousand secret song-spells, and *that* rite is only known to the population at large because it is hard to conceal the fact that a six-foot Gyrgardu like Duantri turns into a six–and-a-half-ounce kestrel on the regular. But will we ever admit it? No!" she answered herself. "No, we are coy and sly! If caught out in a casting, we call it 'praying' or 'meditating' or 'miracle-making.' We swaddle our works in codified ritual and academic jargon so that idle onlookers are impressed and confounded!"

Lanie frowned in consternation.

But then how, she thought laboriously, if the Gyrladies of Quadiíb practice magic, do they stay in balance with the Twelve? Why would a god favor a worshipper who worshipped eleven other gods as equally with their thoughts and attention? Everything I know about the nature of magic makes it impossible.

Tan had her answer ready, though Lanie never asked her questions out loud.

"Oh, we do exactly as you Lirian sorcerers do, my plumula! But we do it by the *calendar*. Every month is dedicated to a different god, and thus, we only perform certain magics during certain months of the year. And we always make sure to bring ourselves *back* into balance with the Twelve on the high holy fire feasts. Those four days," she went on, "are the only time of year when we do *not*, in fact, ask our gods to favor us. Your Lirian practice of making your greatest magic on those days is completely bewildering to us Quadoni! Not to say blasphemous. But I do not like to use incendiary language. Now, I would like to ask you: do you know why we do as we do?"

This time, Lanie managed to croak out, "Is this Quadoni rhetoric? Do I wait for you to answer?"

The gyrlady snorted, commanding in Quadic, "Put up thy quills, thou porcupine! At ease! I truly cannot wait for thy reply."

Nonplussed, Lanie muttered, "You're asking me… if I know *why* all you Quadoni don't use magic on surge days?"

Tan beamed. "Exactly!"

"Because… because…" Lanie frowned, then burst out, "No! Of course I don't! It doesn't make sense *not* to! When people gather in great numbers, holding festivals across the land to celebrate the gods, the gods can't help but hear us all. They hear and remember Their creations. *Their* attention brightens on us, even as *our* attention summons Them nearer, and, and…" She trailed off, already exhausted. It was the most she had spoken in… she had lost track of the days.

Tan finished for her: "…and all creation grows more marvelous with the All-Marvel. And thus, the magic surges for all true believers, for magic is the memory of the gods."

"I was taught," Lanie tried again stiltedly, "I was taught"—she did not say by whom, hating the thought of him—"that on surge days, I was to make the most of my panthauma. That it is an incredibly potent resource, available to us for only a finite amount of time. *Not* to do use it would be… wasteful."

Her stomach panged at her wastefulness. Her autumn equinox, lost. Goody and any good that Lanie might do for her, lost. Tears sprang to her eyes, never far from the surface.

But Lanie found that she was somehow sitting up. She was swinging her legs over the side of the cot, leaning forward. Her knees and Tan's were practically touching. Tan even reached out and patted her leg briefly, saying, "That is certainly one way to think of it," her tone indicating that she didn't think much of that way of thinking.

"But here," she said a moment later, "let me give you a different notion," and then sat back on her crate, hands on thighs, to stare at the wall as if counting to ten in her language where even the numbers rhymed.

Lanie eyeballed her, feeling itchy and nervous, wondering if she should speak, ask questions, needle her. But before she could do so, the gyrlady finished setting her thoughts to order and cleared her throat.

"So. Let us, you and I, take a hypothetical Lirian sorcerer. For the sake of this thought experiment, let us say she is atypical amongst her countrypeople. Let us say that unlike *most* Lirian sorcerers, who traditionally dedicate themselves to Sappacor—Bloodlighters like the Brackenwilds, the fire priests and Bright Knights of the temple, even lowly street-performers who spin and eat fire for coin, or cabaret dancers who wear tiny points of flame and nothing else to tease their audience—alone of all of them, *this* Lirian sorcerer has dedicated her heart to the god of Death."

Tan's twinkly black eyes redoubled the sensation of beetles crawling all over Lanie's skin.

"Let us say further that this sorcerer's unusual devotion stems in part from a family legacy, in part from a habit of solitary study, and in part from a natural inclination towards, well, let us call it, *compassion*. Yes, compassion," she repeated, when Lanie shifted uncomfortably and made a small noise of protest, "for all things: living, dead, and in-between… the, um, *third* of the three states."

At the phrase, Lanie's heavy head lifted. It was the first time she had heard any living person other than herself speak it.

Tan's right eyelid shivered shut in a wink. "However our sorceress came by her devotion," she waved her hands, dismissing further conjecture, "it was very real, and it was all for Doédenna alone. She begged the impossible from, offered up the best of herself to, and poured out all her profoundest attentions and every last drop of her faith into this one lone god. And Doédenna, grateful for the single-minded devotion that so few have shown to Her, came to regard this sorcerer as Her dear friend.

"Now, Lanie." Tan cleared her throat again, earnestly and reflexively, and Lanie wondered if this was a habit of hers from her long years of lecturing. "*You* know and *I* know, that a sorcerer becomes the dwelling place that their god inhabits. A Blood Royal shares her palace. An herbhetch, her hovel. But whatever their state, lofty or low, they carry their god within them. Beautiful, no?"

Lanie was squeezing her hands so tightly together they were cramping. "What if all you have is an empty house?" she asked bitterly. "What if your god comes knocking, expecting a feast, expecting you to be arrayed in finery, ready to welcome Her with music and dancing, and all you have is a bare table and the rags on your back? What kind of a sorcerer does that make you? When you have nothing to give Her—because you have *already* given Her everything, and *it wasn't enough?*"

"I would say"—Tan's words were as careful as a thief's tread—"that perhaps this sorcerer is having a serious communication breakdown with her god."

Lanie snorted.

"Well, think about it," the gyrlady pressed, "here you have a sorcerer who has been asking her friend—her good friend, possibly her *best* friend—for favors her entire life! Maybe she started out small. Maybe her god was happy to grant those favors. Tiny tasks in return for *enormous* gratitude—which, as we know, is ambrosia to the gods. But as the sorcerer grew wiser and more learned, more ambitious, more desperate, so too did her favors. Perhaps they took on the form of demands. But what, in return, has *she* given to her god?"

"I've given up everything!" Lanie interjected. "Blood, safety, family—"

"A terrible return!" Tan retorted. "When all your god *really* wants is for Her young friend to ask Her, once in a while (perhaps as little as four days a year, for example), 'And what, my darling One, may I do for *You?*'"

"I don't have to ask!" Lanie shouted. "I know what She wants! I've always known it!" Heaving herself off the bed, she staggered toward the desk. "I can't do it. Every time I try, it's ruinous!"

"Have you tried," Tan inquired, careful again, "asking for help?"

"What? And ruin those who would help me? Lady Tan," she cried, "I don't know how you came to know what you know. But you don't know everything. You don't know what I can *do!*"

On the desk was a letter opener, which acted as paperweight to a stack of old broadsides. Havoc 'collected' these off walls and posts and doors where they'd been plastered, in order to re-purpose them for a variety of functions. "Blank backs're good fer everythin' from letter-writin' to wipin' my own blank back!" she liked to say.

The broadsides scattered when Lanie snatched up the letter opener and pressed her finger to its point. Her skin was less hardy than rag paper; it split easily, like old fruit.

Tan sucked in a breath. "Lanie, really, you do not have to prove any—"

"I have to," Lanie panted.

She slipped all too effortlessly into her deep sight, and right away heard the deep-down click of her second voice, the one that only the dead could hear. She hardly had to reach for this inward, downward access anymore; she'd spent so much of the last few weeks—months?—sliding, sinking, seeping, inch by fatal inch through Saint Death's doorway. It would be so easy, too easy, even now, to pass all the way through it.

"You have to see," she told Tan, "you have to understand."

And she squeezed a fat drop of her blood into the vase.

The way she was feeling, her blood should have come out a ghostly grayish pink. But it was red and rich, like Canon Lir's mouth, like their kiss, like the messages they used to send her by bloodlight.

Rich and red, like a gift, like a jewel for her god, her blood sank into the water, and the water immediately took on the hue of molten sapphires. The blue of Goody's eyes.

"Wake!" Lanie sang out. Just that single word. One note of the Maranathasseth Anthem.

The flowers heard.

First the green stems—wound-side first, where stem had been snipped from bush—ignited with ectenica. Then the glossy leaves caught blue and pulsed with eldritch light. Then the petals and pistols and stamens swelled with phantom fire. Lanie felt rather than saw Tan coming to stand beside her. She heard the in-draw of awed breath, the slow sigh of wonder. A quick prayer whispered in Quadic.

"Ectenica," Tan breathed, as if the word were one she'd only ever read and never spoken aloud. "What now? What happens? What may you ask of it?"

"Anything I desire," Lanie said mournfully. "For a short time."

Addressing the luminous flowers with weary tenderness, she said, "Do what you will—my beloveds."

Responding not to her spoken words, but to her second voice, the flowers writhed joyously in the glass vase. They were like dancing meteorites: bobbing and nodding and bumping and shirring. A few butted heads like kittens. Others nuzzled each other as if in recognition and entwined their stems like loving arms. A new scent pervaded the room. Not the sun-struck perfume of a living flower that flirts with bees and butterflies for the sake of perpetuation, but the unique fragrance of an undead blossom. Like a cluster of angelica trapped under ice, the greenwood musk of its umbels was more memory than aroma.

Tan shoved a hand into her fading orange hair. She had not dyed it recently; it showed a dark stripe of gray at the roots.

"Lanie, I tell you—save for my Duantri's face—I have never seen anything half so marvelous as this."

She touched one of the petals, and sucked in her breath at the icy silk of them, their sensuous and enthusiastic response.

"I can tell the ectenica to do anything," Lanie reiterated. "I could tell it to turn into a viper and sink its fangs into you and murder you. It would leave no evidence, no mark. Nobody would know."

Tan's fingers flexed as if she wanted to snatch her hand away. "You could do so," she agreed. "But you do not."

"Not this time," Lanie retorted. "But I will, one day. Watch me. That's what all necromancers do, Mak says. They go to the bad."

"That young man," Tan mused, "strikes me as a deeply traumatized individual."

Lanie's hands knotted. "Of course he is! He was my sister's captive for seven years!"

Tan gazed at her, sternly and long, "Duantri knew him for gyrgardon at a glance, even before we took a closer look at his cicatrization patterns. No gyrlady in evidence. A young daughter of certain age with Lirian matrilineage. The most fascinating… shall we call it 'panthaumic aura'?… lingering around his right arm. Those clues, coupled with years of rumors flying about this city regarding Amanita Muscaria Stones"—Tan's lip curled, not kindly—"her life and legend, and we were able to form a fairly accurate picture of his story. But a rough outline only. Poor boy. He never could look me in the eye, you know."

"I know."

"Then," sighed the gyrlady, "knowing the injuries done to him, perhaps it would be fair to say that your brother—that *Mak*," she corrected herself as Lanie shifted her weight, "for all his virtues, might not be an impartial judge when it comes to matters magical. Especially, perhaps, your own?"

She rubbed her fingertips together, frowning at the ash darkening her skin. Petal by petal, the glowing flowers beginning to crumble.

"Or *maybe*," Lanie retorted, "Mak is more right than you suppose! He's lived with me for seven years. He's seen me do things... things you cannot begin to extrapolate from your little thought experiment!"

The water in the vase, black now. The glass stained like the chimney of a lamp. The bitter stench of char. Bile rose in Lanie's throat. She backed away from the desk, gesturing to the mess she made.

"Do you see? I ruin everything I touch! Even though, even when... when it seems, seems so beautiful... so right... so *good,* at first?"

Her lips trembled. She drew her hand back into her body, and wrapped both arms around her ribs, shivering as the heat left her.

In response, Tan gave the sludge-filled, rot-spilling vase one final, thoughtful tap of the finger, then, turning, walked back to the cot, sat down, and patted the space beside her. Lanie elected to remain standing, as far from the vase of flowers, and the cot, as she could. This put her with her back to the door.

"Let me ask you something else." Tan paused, muttered 'hmm' to herself, and took another staring-at-the-wall-composing-her-thoughts moment.

Lanie wondered if Tan had to think out her sentences in Quadic first, then translate into Lirian before speaking, as Lanie would have to do were their positions reversed. She grew so engrossed with the thought of teaching necromancy to a roomful of Quadoni students that she almost jumped when Tan spoke again.

"Why do you think you are a necromancer?"

Before Lanie could answer, Tan shook her head, and said, "No. Let us go further," before clearing her throat with that same tic Lanie had noticed before. "Why do you think," she began again, "that the Stoneses of your line have *historically* given birth to necromancers, when, from what we know, it is the rarest and most delicate of magic? Why *them?*"

Lanie frowned. "Because Saint Death blessed us."

"Hmm," said Tan again. "Well," she coughed, "Saint Death certainly blessed *Quick Fantastic* Stones—not that that was her name *originally*, you know, back in Quadiíb, but that's a minor detail, of historical interest but not pertinent to us today. We know, as sure as anything, that Doédenna blessed Quick Fantastic *because* Quick Fantastic chose Doédenna above all other gods. So far, so much makes sense. But so... why, then, was her *son* also a necromancer?"

"Because, he... he learned his devotions at her knee?" Lanie said, hearing the doubt in her voice. "Quick Fantastic was... a charismatic character. Her son was very much attached to her. She was forceful, opinionated, an almost god-like figure herself. People admired her and feared her. But they loved Ynyssyll Brackenwild more, and made her their queen."

Tan smiled. "For my thesis, I studied Ynyssyll's diaries from her early days. Not anything from *after* her exile, of course. When you visit Quadiíb, you must stop by Ylkazarra First University and have a peep at our primary documents collection. Enrapturing! But, Lanie, we digress. Again."

Fixing Lanie with her disturbingly direct stare, she continued, "We now have a working theory about the first two necromancers of the Stones line. But now, Lanie, tell me: what of Quick Fantastic Stones's great-great-great-whatever-great grand-niece, twice-removed, adopted, only-grudgingly-bestowed-the-surname-Stones-by-marriage? Why did she *also* give birth to a necromancer?"

"Who?"

For a moment, Lanie thought Tan was referring to Lichwake Stones[35], but the antecedents were all wrong, and to the best of her knowledge, Lichwake never had any children. None that went by the name Stones, anyway.

"This grand-niece is a figure of conjecture only; I hyperbolize for effect! But do you see what I am driving at?" Lanie shook her head, but Tan was already answering herself. "Why are Stones *babies*—who have *no choice* in their gods—*born* as necromancers to your line? Why are *Stones* babies, like you, born with that—what do you call it?—that 'allergy' to violence, or what we might call 'an early, violent reaction against death,' *already inbred* in them?"

"Oh," Lanie stammered. "I... I understand what you're asking, Tan... but... the Stoneses have always loved Saint Death. And Saint Death has always loved us back. That's just how it's always been—ever since the Founding. Her love is passed on through our blood, which is why... why most of us are like... like Nita."

But her words were coming more and more slowly. "Like Nita," she continued, "we Stoneses are mostly assassins and... executioners. We are—were—the strong left hand of the Blood Royal Brackenwilds."

Tan nodded in approval. "Natural proclivity meets family custom! There is precedent. As the livestock butchers of Twelfth Circle inherit their trade from their parents, so too do the Stoneses inherit theirs. Your people are, in essence, professional butchers. But, Lanie. *Trade* is not the same as *vocation*, is it? *Sorcery* is a vocation. So tell me," she demanded, in another of her lightning-strike, bright-faced turns, "was your family particularly pious? Was, to take one example, Irradiant Radithor Stones—the greatest necromancer ever born since Quick Fantastic—a religious man?"

"Grandpa Rad?" Lanie scoffed at the thought. "He never prayed a day in his life. Or after."

The gyrlady looked startled, then stared at her for a long, meditative moment, as if wishing to pursue an all-new line of questioning, beginning with: Why was Lanie on familiar terms with a man who'd been dead for a century?

---

35 A foundling adopted by the triplets Iniquity, Propinquity, and Antiquity Stones. Also the arsonist behind the torching of the Lirian Academy for Young Cutthroats, in which blazing inferno Lichwake's (so-called) benefactresses perished.

But she didn't.

"Do you think," she asked instead, "that perhaps Irradiant Stones was secretly devout? That his parents taught him his prayers to Doédenna whilst dandling him on their fond knees?"

"How could they?" Lanie retorted. "He was orphaned as an infant—the youngest of a pack of siblings. They all grew up wild at Stones Manor, with a rotating roster of ommers, aunties, and uncles who leeched off the estate until the children grew old enough to drive them out. Or kill them off. As far as I know, it was mostly Goody who looked after them. Grandpa Rad was her nursling in particular."

Goody had rarely spoken to Lanie of those days, but taken collectively over the years, Lanie had gleaned a good bit of history from her terse remembrances. She'd also managed to decipher all of Grandpa Rad's compulsively-kept but nigh-impossible-to-read journals. Like Lanie herself, he'd never even left the grounds of Stones Manor till he was in his twenties—shortly after he and Sosha Brackenwild met for the first time by happenstance in the Diesmali.

The Blood Royal was out hunting. His favorite horse had broken a leg. Grandpa Rad offered to bayonet her when Sosha confessed he could not. Then he raised her up again so that the Blood Royal didn't have to walk all the way home. The friendship between the two men was instant and lifelong. Sosha, Grandpa Rad used to boast, even arranged his own marriage. He'd found Grandpa Rad the perfect wife: large fortune, low intelligence, fertile womb—and they'd all lived together at Castle Ynyssyll, two happy tyrants lording it over their prodigiously cowed families. Right up until the Northernmost War.

But Lanie didn't tell Tan any of this, because the gyrlady was practically snapping with excitement.

"Now we come to it!" Tan crowed.

"To what?" Lanie backtracked over her last words, wondering what she'd said to sharpen the gyrlady's focus to spindle's end.

"To Goody. Goody Graves, am I correct? That is what you call her? The legendary revenant of Stones Manor. You say her name in your sleep. Now, tell me, Lanie, about your Goody."

Time blinked.

The next thing she knew, Lanie found herself huddled on the floor, her head cradled in Tan's lap. She was sobbing again, numb in all her extremities.

"Lanie, Lanie," Tan crooned, her voice rough, as if she had been crooning for a while. "I know it hurts. I know. But this is it. This is the boil we must lance. You must speak of it, if you can. We are close to something now."

So Lanie told her everything, her cheek pressed against Tan's embroidered trousers. About Goody Graves. About Lanie's sickly infancy. How Unnatural Stones had declared Lanie's illness to be an early sign of her necromancy. How he had ordered Goody to tend to her, lest her allergy to her parents' profession and proximity finish her off. How Goody had done just that: attended her childhood sickbed, cared for her, sang to her, told her stories in Quadic. Comfortless herself, Goody had had no reason to offer solace to her enfeebled charge, but nonetheless she had given it. She applied wet cloths to Lanie's aches, caressed her matted hair, kept her in clean handkerchiefs, lit beeswax candles against nightmares, murmured assurances, sang lullabies, told stories, fed her, brought freshly cut flowers to her bedside—all while Lanie's fainting sicknesses, her swellings and outbreaks, her thunderous colds and flus, her sweats and wracks of fever, like storms, worsened, cracked, and finally passed.

Then she told Tan the rest.

Midsummer. Grandpa Rad. The Sarcophagus of Souls. Hatchet's ward. Datu and the wolf cub. Mak. Her descent. Her visit with Sari Scratch. Gallowsdance Stones's tunnel. Her walk to Skrathmandan. Hatchet's wards. The ice. The dirt. The dark.

By the time she finished, Lanie's burning eyes were drooping. She longed to crawl back into her cot and sleep. Instead, Tan propped her up and wiped her face.

Setting her hands upon her shoulders, she held Lanie's gaze. "Here is what I think," she said. "The *real* reason necromancers keep being born to the Stones line is *not* because the Stoneses are blessed of Saint Death. It is because the first necromancers of the Founding Era instigated a wrong long ago, and Saint Death wants to put to right.

"I believe that your Goody Graves—we must find her true name; I have some ideas about that—has been praying to Doédenna all these long years of her undeath. But she has been cut off from Doédenna; they cannot find each other. And because it was a Stones who severed them each from each, it must be a Stones to effect their reunion. Goody raised Irradiant from infancy. Perhaps because of this, feeling that he loved her best of all Stoneses thus far, Doédenna concentrated her greatest efforts on *him*. But Irradiant went astray. Raised without principles or role models, he fell in at a young age with a cruel and profligate friend who stripped him of whatever remained of his humanity.

"History," Tan reflected, "has nothing good to say about the Regent Sinister, Sosha Brackenwild. Even his sister, Moll the Second, laughed when he died[36]. After that, Doédenna was perhaps more careful in her choice of necromancers. When *you* were born, and put into Goody's care, Doédenna bent even more of Her concentration on you. She *brightened*

36 Moll II (who before her coronation was Canon Moll of the High Temple of Sappacor) was considered solemn, efficient, and kindly, but not much given to raucous mirth. The Brackenwild courtiers who reported hearing laughter echoing from the royal chambers at Castle Ynyssyll, where Moll II kept vigil at her brother's deathbed, could not actually swear it was *her* laughter; they had never heard such a sound before that night, nor did ever again after.

the potential She had planted in you with each passing year. And Goody did the rest, just by loving you."

This had the skin-peeling sensation of truth.

"But," she protested, "this is all conjecture!"

"Of course it is!" Tan said. "*I* am not in constant communication with Doédenna! *I* cannot presume to know the mind of the god of Death! Although," she mused, "come the twelfth month of Vespers, I intend to ask Her all about it. Sometimes She answers me in dreams, or comes to me in visions if I hold sothaín long enough. Exhausting, but worth the effort. *You*, however," she added, "may ask Her at any time. *Your* religion does not forbid chatting with the god of your choice no matter the calendar month! In fact, you're encouraged to do so!"

Lanie said slowly, "You want me to ask Saint Death about Goody? About the Stoneses being necromancers because of her?"

Tan's round face creased as it beamed. "It would be useful, would it not, to know where you came from? Why you are what you are? What hopes were placed in you from infancy—perhaps unfairly, but not, I might add, *unjustly?*"

Finding herself nodding along with Tan's enthusiastically bobbing head, Lanie almost flinched back when Tan leapt to her feet.

"Wonderful! You stay right here, in this room, and have a little talk with Doédenna. I, meanwhile, will pursue other avenues of research regarding your Goody's original identity. I want to know *who* she was, exactly, before she became slave to the Stoneses. I will also pursue my acquaintance with Sari Scratch—or, Baroness Skrathmandan, as she prefers these days. A formidable woman! Perhaps something might yet be arranged for you there. You see," she hinted slyly, "I have ties to Quadiíb that the Skrathmandan clan might covet for Skakmaht. Rook is a powerful ally, yes, but Quadiíb? Quadiíb could eat Rook for brunch! But let's not get ahead of ourselves. You, young lady, have some meditating to do."

"Yes," Lanie murmured, glancing away from the gyrlady to stare distractedly at the walls. They were already taking on the translucence and brilliance of citrine. This far from her next surge day, it was the very last thing Lanie had expected.

But she knew: her god was drawing near.

"Talk to Her," Tan urged Lanie, helping her to attain, albeit wobblingly, her feet. "Assure Her you're still working on the task She has laid out for you. That you haven't given up on either of them—not on Her, not on Goody. That you haven't given up *hope*."

"Haven't I?" Lanie asked.

"Have you?" Tan countered.

"No," Lanie sighed as the walls began to flash and glitter, and the air filled with the smell of lemons. "I suppose I haven't."

"Good!" Her small black eyes sparking suddenly, Tan looked up and around, and gave a deep, salubrious sniff.

"That! Is! *Marvelous!*" She shook herself like a wet robin. "I'll leave you to it, shall I? When you're ready, wash your face and come downstairs to the tap room for a late breakfast. Duantri will be down after her morning classes, and Havoc won't open to the public till noon. There will *lentils.* Spicy ones!" she added, shivering with decadence. "Delicious! And we *deserve* it!"

"Thank you, Tan." Lanie meant it with all her heart, but she also firmly shut the door behind the gyrlady the moment Tan stepped through, and resolutely fixed the latch.

For a moment, she let her left hand rest on the wood, watching the grayly glimmering color-play of her wizard mark begin to dance, as it reflected or responded to a light behind her that had not been there a moment before.

And when she turned around, she saw exactly what she expected to see, and also what she never could expect—not if she lived for ten thousand years:

Doédenna, god of Death, waiting for her.

Her hood and cowl shadowed that quiet brown face, those eyes like endless fog. Her cloak filled the tiny room, ivory-colored bones overlapping each other like scales, bones of every shape and size, bones from every beast imaginable, and exoskeletons, and ammonites, chitons and shells, sponges and luminescent algae, mites, bristle worms, black coral: all creatures who had ever lived and died were caught in her cloak.

"I missed our autumn equinox," Lanie said softly. "I regret that, more than I can say. But I promise You—I will make myself Your shrine at Midwinter. I shall be Your palace and Sky House and cathedral. And I promise You dancing. If You will still have me."

Saint Death smiled shyly.

In the glass vase on the desk, the black sludge of rotted ectenica gathered itself back together like a mandrake taking form. It stretched, it bubbled, it blossomed. It extruded flowers from itself, and those flowers turned the color of alluvial larimar, if larimar were made of moonlight instead of stone. A barely detectable scent perfumed the room, cold and faint and sweet: the memory of the woods in every season. This time, the petals did not blacken or slacken or fall to ash; they remained upright and trembling, chiming with their own music, alert to every tender word the god of Death murmured in answer to Her necromancer.

And when She opened Her arms, Lanie ran to Her, and hugged Her hard.

CHAPTER FORTY

Mizka and Jhímieti

Brineday, 18th
Month of Embers, 421 Founding Era
54 days till Winter Solstice

"I FOUND HER!" Tan crowed. "I found her! I found Jhímieti!"

Lanie bolted up from her bench and half-stretched, half-crawled across the trestle table to where Tan was poring over a stack of books she'd brought down to Havoc's from Waystation Thirteen. They had taken over one corner of the Lover's Complaint with their research materials. Behind the bar, Havoc's new part-time barkeep, a young man known amongst Seventh Circle artists for his ardent love poems, and for self-accompanying his recitations on goblet drum, flirted with Eidie and his husband unabashedly, which delighted both men to no end.

"Jhímieti?" Lanie repeated, her urgency cutting through the noise of the public room. "Her name is Jhímieti?"

Tan beamed at her. "A perfectly sweet name, is it not? I can translate the meaning for you if you like, but I shall have to make it a split couplet—no more than doggerel, really, and on the fly! But you will feel something of the parental sentiment behind it." She cleared her throat and began:

I sing thee, love thee, praise thy precious face
My child, my grace!

Lanie tried to imagine Goody as a baby. Couldn't. But she could—almost—imagine a young Quadoni mother, out on the dunes at dawn, with her new, tiny thing swaddled in her arms.

Shivering a little, she asked, "Where did you find her? How do you know it *is* her? That Goody is Jhímieti?"

Tan stuck a finger between the pages of her book to keep her place, flipped it shut, and showed the cover to Lanie.

The title was in Quadic. Loosely translated, Lanie thought it read something like, *A Cast of Hawks Let Fly: Stories of the Gyrgardon for Young Readers*.

"A child's book?"

"Falcon Tales!" Tan enthused. "Did you never read them? Never mind; one is never too old to begin! I practically forgot what I was looking for, so engrossed did I grow in these dear familiar tales—but I knew what I'd found the moment it crossed my eye. Ever since you told me your version of Goody's story, a notion has been chiming in my brain like..." Instead of finishing, she pointed significantly to Lanie's reliquary.

Lanie closed her hand over it. Without thinking, without trying, she sent a soft caress through the Founding Queen's left toe bone and into its matched pair—somewhere far, far away in Rook.

"You can read the story for yourself later," Tan continued, as Lanie opened the little book and squinted down at the text, trying to make out the Quadic. "Better yet—get Duantri to tell you some of her favorite Falcon Tales! She has them all memorized, and has adapted many into songs. For now, I will sum up the one I thought pertinent. It is one of our great tragedies! 'The Lost Gyrgardu,' it's called."

"So, was Goody... *Jhímieti*... a Gyrgardu?" Lanie leaned forward.

So much, so much of Goody would begin to make sense, if only that one little thing were true.

"Oh, yes! Not only was she Gyrgardu, but if memory of my thesis serves (and well it should, for my thesis was on this very subject), Jhímieti is our earliest recorded Gyrgardu to have sundered her Bryddongard bond with her gyrlady. These days, you know, Bryddongard divorces are rare, but when they happen, it is no longer considered the scandalous—or even blasphemous—act they used to be. But in *those* days! Ah, *that* was during the Second Diaspora, when Ynyssyll Fayyis—you would say 'Brackenwild,' a name she later chose—decided to break with the twelve gods and travel into the unknown with Sappacor for her sole guiding light. Her friends Kiqissim and Jhímieti—or, Quick Fantastic, and, if I am correct, your Goody—wanted to go with her. But Jhímieti's gyrlady, Mizka forbade—"

"Mizka?" Lanie interrupted sharply.

"Yes!" Tan crowed again. "When you told me it was your Goody's name for you, dear Lanie, that was my final clue! But what was I saying? Ah, yes. Mizka—the *first* Mizka, that is—didn't want to go into the wilderness with the three new-minted heathens. She declared rather that a Gyrgardu was supposed to stay with her gyrlady! But *Jhímieti* answered that she was no body-servant, paid to cater to Mizka's every demand; she had a right to fly where she would. And why, after all, should a gyrlady not follow where'er her *Gyrgardu* flies? To which Mizka replied that Jhímieti would *never* fly again—and with that, cast off her Bryddongard and crushed it underfoot! Probably," Tan mused, "it took a bit more spell-singing and a bit less stomping than the story has it, but we will leave that for now. The end of our Falcon Tale is a dire warning—in couplet form, of course."

Grabbing the slim volume back from Lanie, she flipped to the correct page. "Heroic couplet this time," she clarified, smiling over the pages at Lanie. "Bear with me while I translate."

And then the gyrlady stared into the middle distance in that way she had, until, without warning, she abruptly struck a dramatic pose, and with her fist raised before her face, declaimed:

O! wouldst we'd never met, thou Misbegot—
Whose name the falcons of Quadiíb forgot!
But Jhímieti, may they know thy shame;
The world o'er, let thine infamy inflame!

The gyrlady looked around and down for applause. She did not seem too disappointed to find only Lanie, who instead of clapping, was wiping tears from her eyes.

"Poor Goody! Poor Jhímieti!"

Tan clucked her tongue like a cavalier at her unruly horse. "Poor bitter old Mizka! In the disunion with her Gyrgardu, she would have lost not only her life-bonded partner, but her profession and her position of esteem. A Bryddongard divorce is not so *these* days—but in *those!* A grievous diminution of identity for Lady Mizka! I wonder if she ended up settling in a small village far from the Caravan School roads, nursing her resentment to the end. One hopes not. But! Aside from all that, I find this line of inquiry encouraging, do you not think?"

Lanie wanted to be encouraged. She wanted to imagine a reunion with Goody: meeting her one last time face to face, and calling her by her true name, and singing her the Lahnessthanessar at last.

But when she tried envision it, all she could see were Hatchet's icy wards, encircling the Skrathmandan estate, waiting to freeze her out. If his wards went as high into the sky as they went deep into the earth, she had no chance of ever seeing Goody face-to-face again. They would zap her where she stood, numb her, strike her like a giant icicle missile launch from a high-flying Sky House, and that would be the end of her. She did not think even the Great Lullaby could break through the barrier of Hatchet's Skaki magic—what though she found the courage to once again walk that long road from Liriat Proper to her old home, this time above-ground, exposed to the elements, scrutinized by the eyes of a dozen blackbirds—in order to sing it.

Tan fixed Lanie with her no-nonsense stare, and Lanie felt a prickle of irritation chafe her out of her cold, encroaching paralysis.

"We," announced the gyrlady, "have been at this for hours. You"—she pointed at Lanie—"are going to take a breather whilst I"—she pointed to herself—"ask that beautiful young man"—she waggled her eyebrows at the poetic young barkeep—"for an enormous hot pretzel!"

Left alone with *A Cast of Hawks Let Fly*, Lanie read the little fable silently to herself—slowly, because she could not read Quadic any other way—stroking Jhímieti's name every time she encountered it in the text.

When she finished, she looked up to see the eel-thin, slither-shape of Havoc standing just beside her.

But her smile faltered at the peculiar expression on her friend's face. "What is it?"

Havoc sank down onto the bench beside her. Propping her elbow on Lanie's pile of books, she sighed, "Cookie, you ain't gonna believe it till you seen it," and slid a folded letter over to her.

The seal was already broken, and Lanie saw that it had been penned in a careful but unmistakable calligraphy that was as distinctive as the woman who had written it.

Havoc Dreadnought, Proprietress
Liriat Proper, Liriat
Seventh Circle, Quarter Past, Level 1
The Lover's Complaint Public House

Mistress Dreadnought,

You do not know me, but perhaps you have heard the Skrathmandan name, or served one of my three sons in your establishment. Forgive the intrusion of a stranger writing to you, but the critical nature of my business compels me to so trespass upon your forbearance.

I believe that you have had in this past year some dealings with one Miscellaneous Stones, necromancer. You might know her by 'Lanie,' or by an entirely different name, but I believe when you see the sketch appended to this letter, you will recognize her immediately.

I assure you, my family wishes her no harm—quite the opposite. In writing to you thusly I am but seeking a means to contact Miss Stones and summon her with all speed to the Skrathmandan estates, where her skills are most urgently needed.

She will of course be amply compensated for any services she renders us. So too, if it is through your offices that this summons reaches her, shall you.

Thank you in advance for any assistance, and I must express again the extreme urgency of this matter.

Sari, Baroness Skrathmandan

* * *

When at last Lanie glanced up from reading the letter through for the fourth—fifth?—sixth?—time, she saw that not only Tan but Duantri—looking wind-blown and a bit wild, having just come in either from a flight or from teaching her rowdy crowd of seven year olds—were now clustered behind her, leaning in with Havoc and reading over her shoulder.

"Ah!" said Tan brightly. "I see our Havoc has had a letter too! Duantri just brought down another addressed to me at the Waystation."

"I must go," said Lanie. "To Skrathmandan. Today. Right now."

Something had happened with Goody. Something Sari could not control. Something very bad.

She glanced around the tap room blankly, as if expecting a means of travel to spontaneously appear before her and bear her away to what had formerly been Stones Manor, and then stood up abruptly, shedding concerned friends like flies.

But Duantri swooped in again, and grasped her arm, and said, in unexpectedly grim Lirian, "You mean, Lanie, that *we* must go."

Duantri in full Gyrgardu mode was a different creature from the warm, gentle music teacher of Waystation Thirteen. Nor was she at all like the radiant stage performer who enthralled her audience on Quadoni culture nights at the Lover's Complaint. Nor did she resemble the worry-ridden friend who for so many days and nights had sat vigil at Lanie's sickbed.

Here was Duantri, raptorial.

Except she was still very much in her human form. Relaxed but alert, her body completely still until it wasn't: when her head turned slowly, and her gray eyes, bright and alien, peered off into a distance Lanie could not fathom.

The Gyrgardu sat at the front of the sleigh with their driver, whose services Tan had hired from the Liriat Proper Public Mews. She was clad only in tunic and wrap, both the color of the snow that packed the Brackenwild Holloway, over which road their sleigh was briskly sluicing. The first snow of Liriat had fallen unusually early that year. It had not yet warmed enough again for the ice to melt.

Both that first snowstorm and the continuing cold fretted Lanie; were Mak and Datu caught out in it, travelers on a lonely road to some destination they had never even seen? Were they warm and safe and anonymous, somewhere in the southern baronies? Had they left the continent entirely? Or had they headed upcoast, closer to danger, closer to Rook, the very last place anyone would be bound to look for them, to find refuge in a tiny town of no particular name or fame, in Leech or Damahrash or Umrys-by-the-Sea?

From her heap of blankets, Tan nudged Lanie, nodding toward Duantri in the front seat. "Magnificent, is she not?"

Lanie grunted. She had always found Duantri more wonderful than words could say. So had Datu. So had Mak.

"Useless to try and get her attention in her present mood," the gyrlady sighed. "Duantri is an instrument tuned to our Bryddongard; she is hearing and seeing and sensing reverberations imperceptible to the rest of us."

Tan patted her arm, where her silver-embossed bracer was hidden beneath layers of wool. "I can feel our Bryddongard responding to her; it is very active, humming and warm. It enjoys Duantri's attention! Were I not accustomed to it, I'd find it all very distracting. But never you fear, Lanie; our Bryddongard will alert Duantri the very second I am in danger, enabling her to immediately take falcon form. For now, all is ready, waiting. Duantri keeps herself in a light sothaín trance. This, and the Bryddongard, enhance her awareness, her reflexes, her intuition, but"—Tan sighed again—"it makes her a very dull conversationalist."

Lanie was so wound up, she was practically thrumming. "Tell me, Tan"—she nodded toward the Gyrgardu, trying not to shiver even under all her layers—"if Duantri's like this *now*, doesn't that mean you're *already* in danger?"

Tan grinned. "No, dearest. It means *you* are in danger. Or she thinks you are, which comes to the same thing." When Lanie began to protest, the gyrlady continued, "Falcon Defenders join the gyrgardon not because they are bloodthirsty or ambitious or want to take part in some elite cadre of warriors. They go into the business—or, vocation, rather—because of their great hearts. Do you understand?"

Lanie began to shake her head, but thought of Mak, and changed the gesture to a slow nod.

"Oh, yes, I see you do," Tan said, squeezing Lanie's hand under their shared blanket. "It's like a gyrgardon is born wanting to save the world, save everyone. They love widely, deeply, devotedly. They are... how should I say it...? *service-oriented.* I think a gyrgardon chooses their gyrlady solely based upon... oh, I don't know... whomever they think might help them save the most people? Or whomever needs saving even more than the rest of the world? Some instinct, some hunter's sense of who might be lacking, or weak from want of love. Then, the gyrgardon swoops in! Their instinct is to fill that void. To befriend. To protect. To create family. All they ask for in return is that *we* help them do more of the same. That is why so many Gyrladies are teachers and professors, you know. Education is one sure way to save the world!"

Lanie turned the idea of a great-hearted, void-filling, service-oriented Mak over in her head.

She tried imagining Nita as he would have first seen her. Nita—who was all lack, all void. Proud. Alone. Unable to make friends, to speak the Quadic language. And young and beautiful to boot.

How he must have rushed in to fill her emptiness with kindness, Lanie thought. And now, here we all are. Or… were.

But before she could sink any deeper into these morose reflections, Tan's chatter snagged her wandering attention.

"…*says* she had several, to her mind, fine reasons for choosing me. She knew me to be a world traveler. She knew I had radical views about education across borders and cultures, et cetera, which she found appealing. But the real truth—she will never admit this—is also that I… well, I was not *well* when Duantri offered me her wings in service. Duantri is my second Gyrgardu, you know. Well," Tan scolded herself, "how could you know, when I have never told you?"

"Do you," Lanie asked, very softly, for Tan's voice had caught and wavered, "want to tell me now?"

With a sideways glance at her, the gyrlady answered with unwonted shyness, "It is not a thing I speak of often. When my first gyrgardi died, I no longer cared to be alive. That is not unusual for bonded pairs. It is the nature of the Bryddongard. But Duantri, a former student from my teaching days, sought me out after she graduated from the Gyrgardon Academy. She had heard something of my troubles, and came to camp outside my tent, day and night, declaring, 'I will have thee or no one, Tanalíín!" If she could not be my Gyrgardu, said Duantri, she would give up the gyrgardon forever! Despite my mood at the time—similar to the one we found *you* in lately, dear Lanie—I could not bear the idea of all that waste. So now"—she shrugged—"we are together. Scandalous, everyone said! She is far too young for me, far too *good* for me; she ought to have been paired with someone much closer to her in age and temperament, and yet…" Her gaze went almost as distant as Duantri's. "I would claw the eyes out of anyone who tried to take my Duantri away."

Lanie's eyes prickled and itched in faint echo of Tan's violent intent. She shut them. Imagined Gyrlady Gelethai trying to claw Nita's eyes out to protect Mak. Opened them again. Stared out over the side of the sleigh as the lengthening shadows rushed past until she could speak calmly.

"I don't like putting either of you in danger. Duantri should be looking after *you*, keeping *you* safe. Not rushing into potential peril with *me*."

"Yes, but," Tan said reasonably, "*I* am rushing into potential peril with you. And so, perforce, must she."

"But *you* are only here with me because *she* insisted on coming!"

"And if she had not, I would have."

"But you don't know what's awaiting us!" Lanie exploded. "What if Bran Fiakhna ordered Sari to abduct me, to throw me in a sack and drag me to Rook? What if she's decided I'm more trouble alive than I'm worth? Any of Sari's three boys could snap me in half and bury or burn me, no one the wiser. What if"—and here she faltered, remembering her last dawn in Stones Manor—"what if Bran Fiakhna sent her Parliament to take me down? We barely survived two of her wizard-birds, and that was with Mak in his falcon form—"

"We have Duantri, woman and kestrel," Tan soothed her. "Also," she added with a smile, "I am not helpless, you know!"

Lanie shook her head, still shivering, and fretted, "I wish you two had not come."

Now Tan sat up straighter, lost her cooing softness, said briskly, "If you, Miscellaneous Stones, think that either Duantri or I would let you journey alone to Skrathmandan—a place where you have suffered greatly, where no one has your interests at heart, where you are sworn to your god to sing the only true mother you have known from her long undeath—you have yesterday's fish for brains! To, um, coin Havoc's phrase. We are *not* those people. We never will be. Duantri and I chose you for our friend. We are here. You do not have a choice between having us with you or having no one. You have had enough of having no one. Do you understand?"

Before Lanie could answer, Duantri turned her head again, in extremely slow motion, this time craning to look over her shoulder at Lanie, curiously but impartially, like a kestrel spotting a grasshopper in the weeds. Lanie had a feeling that if she answered anything except, "Yes, Lady Tan," Duantri would pounce.

"Yes," she croaked, to both of them. "Yes. I understand."

She found she was clutching fast to Tan's hand. She could not remember reaching out to grip it.

Duantri nodded, again very slowly, and turned to face forward again.

"Good!" Tan settled into the tufted and buttoned leather of the squabs. "Now. Are we there yet?"

JUST AS EVENING fell, their sleigh approached the iron-and-icicle gates of Skrathmandan.

Fast, too fast—"Stop!" Lanie cried—and the driver clicked and *whoa*-ed, and the horses snorted and blew and obeyed, and the sleigh slid to a jingling stop.

Lanie stared.

She had never seen these gates before; they were a new installation since her departure and the Scratch's seizure of the estate. The worked iron depicted in repeating patterns what she had come to think of as 'Sari's dragons.' It was the same design she had glimpsed on the roof, lawns, and livery at the Ambassadorial Palace of Skakmaht on First Circle.

This close, and seen with proper spectacles, with the design rendered so large, Lanie realized that the creatures weren't dragons after all, just two ordinary animals—though fancifully stylized and entwined together in a knotwork of ardor or combat or both. The first animal was some kind of swan or crane or egret; the second a wild dog or, more probably a wolf.

But when she squinted at it, the two animals once more fused into one, and no matter what Lanie told herself, her mind insisted on dragons.

But more than this, Lanie knew on the instant that these gates were worked not of iron alone, and that these enhancements were, she was sure, of Lord Ambassador Haaken Skrathmandan's design.

She stared over the edge of the parked sleigh. She could feel Tan and Duantri and their driver watching her, awaiting her word to continue. But she was deep inside her deep sight, studying Haaken's spell.

She had met this same set of wards before, or a small part of it, down in the dirt and dark of Gallowsdance's tunnel. But here she could see plainly the effect it had upon living flesh, just as she had felt it in her own substance when she had attempted to worm her way through.

The gates were festooned in tiny frozen corpses, trapped in clear blue icicles.

Here were all the creatures, the beasts and birds and insects, who had blundered all unknowingly into Hatchet's—Haaken's—wards, and whose deaths, if she was correct in her reading of the spell, further fueled the strength of those wards.

So much, so far, she understood. But something—something terrible—must have broken through.

The gates stood open.

Or, one of them did. The other had been wrenched from its post and hurled several yards away.

Lanie scrambled down from the sleigh, absently instructing the driver not pass through the gates until she had a chance to examine them more closely. She was dimly aware of Duantri moving like a shadow at her side, and turned to address her, startled to find those oddly bright eyes staring right at her: if not quite blankly, then with an unblinking absence-of-Duantri-ness that she found disconcerting.

"The wards might still be in place—even if the gates aren't," she explained. "I don't want any of us to get zapped on the way through."

The destruction of the gates, alarming as it was, also comforted Lanie. It gave her to suppose that she had indeed been summoned here for the reasons Sari had proffered, and not any more nefarious purpose. And that meant, for the moment at least, that Tan and Duantri were somewhat safe in her company.

Safe from the Blackbird Bride, at least.

Not safe from... from whatever had uprooted several hundred pounds of worked iron and tossed it halfway across the lawn like a handful of weeds.

Her boots crunched in the snow. Charily, she approached the shattered gates, left hand extended, wizard mark extended past that.

The closer Lanie came to the gate left standing, the more her sense of Haaken's wards sharpened.

Closer, and she began to sense also the gate-shaped hole gaping at the center of his warding spell, like a spiderweb that was still attached at all its edges but missing its elaborate central stabilimentum. She felt the *lack* of the ward there like a tear at her center, through which there howled a hibernal wind.

Gulping hard, she shook herself and stood aside, turning to wave the sleigh through the broken gate. Duantri only followed when Lanie herself, with shoulders hunched and head bowed, also trudged after it, sticking close to her side like a white-wrapped ghost, silent and dogged.

By the time they all reached the portico, Scratten Scratch had flung open the heavy front doors and bounded outside to greet them.

He was bare-headed, but bundled in a coat of silvery fur. His face lit up when he saw Lanie, in a way that she found odd but also familiar. Vaguely she recalled suspecting a much younger Scratten of nursing an infatuation for a much younger Lanie—but she never expected him to have cosseted that tender flame for seven long years. It made his face, though identical to Hatchet's in *accident*, so *substantially* different that she knew she would never mistake him for his brother, even if she came upon them both at once.

He courteously handed Tan down from the sleigh, set her perfunctorily on her feet, and then launched himself at Lanie, crying her name in greeting.

"Thank the flying god of thunder you've come!"

Looming over her, wreathed in smiles, Scratten didn't seem to know what to do with his hands. Lanie watched him just barely restrain himself from taking both of hers in both of his and kissing them.

"I... we are... that is, Mordda—I mean, Mama—will be so pleased to see you! Come! Come in, where it's warm."

"Thank you," said Tan, with a sidelong wink at Lanie, and preceded her into the house.

Scratten was last to enter. Having directed their driver to take sleigh and horses to the stable, he followed his guests into the narrow vestibule, gesturing to its hooks and shelves and benches, and inviting them to dispense with their coats and boots. A new cupboard had been installed, one with dozens of cubbyholes that held house slippers of all sizes and colors: soft and warm, bright with embroidery. He offered a pair to each of them, but did not take any for himself, nor did he remove his boots or coat.

Lanie shoved her hands in her pockets, electing to keep all her clothes on as well, and followed Scratten from the vestibule into the sparkling black expanse of the great hall as Tan lagged behind to coo over the slippers. Duantri stayed back with her, so Lanie, for the moment, found herself alone with Scratten.

He turned, still smiling, and offered her the crook of his arm, like a lover inviting his beloved for a summer stroll. "Miss Lanie, allow me to take you up to Mama now. We are so grateful—so *very* grateful—that you've come!"

Keeping her hands firmly in her pockets, Lanie said politely, "I'll go where you take me, Scratten, but I can't take your arm. Sorry."

His smile fixed now, plastered over a pang of hurt, he begged her pardon, and blinked rapidly, looking elsewhere.

"Oh, it's not…" Embarrassed, Lanie glanced behind her into the dim vestibule, where Tan was still struggling out of her caped coat and boots, with Duantri's assistance. "It's nothing against you specifically. I have an… an idiosyncratic allergy. I thought you knew."

"I didn't," Scratten assured her. He locked his large, bright, sea-foam green eyes, full of hope and confusion, on hers. "Will you tell me?"

Lanie cleared her throat. "Your profession—"

"Executioner to the Blood Royal Brackenwilds," Scratten supplied proudly. "Like your own indomitable father, Unnatural Stones." And he laid a hand over his heart, as if remembering a fallen hero.

"Y-yes," Lanie stammered. "That. Well, it's… The necessities of such a… profession… leave certain, that is, invisible"—she searched for a more neutral word than 'stains' or 'contaminants'—"*marks*… on your hands."

"My hands?" Scratten stared at his hands as though for the first time.

Lanie nodded. "It was the same with my father. I'd get nosebleeds if he ever forgot and accidentally put an arm around me. He was an affectionate man, so, naturally, he shut me up in my own wing of the house for most of my childhood and did his best to ignore me. For my own good, you see."

Scratten's open countenance expressed such immediate pity and understanding that Lanie felt her cheeks heat. He made a brief scrubbing gesture, one hand over the other, before locking his wrists behind his back.

She felt her shoulders relax, and offered him a small smile. "Thank you."

They stood like that a few seconds, silent and staring, until, in a thoughtful voice, Scratten began, "You know, Miss Lanie… I take a great pride in preserving the dignity of my profession. I perform the Blood Royal's justices discreetly. I calculate my drop lengths meticulously. I try to extend, even to the most heinous of criminals, what mercy and gentleness I may. Should they care for snuff or brandy or a fine last meal, I do my best to accommodate them. The other kind of work—your mother's work—Cracchen was always better at it than I."

Lanie looked away, but everywhere she looked, she remembered her mother: a cold, golden presence in that great dark hall.

Lowering her eyes, she said carefully, "I have not encountered your brother Cracchen in a long time."

"Well, we look exactly the same," Scratten snorted. "But that's about the only thing we have in common. We—none of us, really—are anything alike."

"That, I believe," Lanie replied with a rueful grimace. She wondered if

Abandon Hope Stones's successor was still the nastiest of the triplets. At one point, she remembered believing Cracchen Scratch was the smartest, for his mean wit and sarcastic tongue. But that was before she'd discovered just how grossly Hatchet—beg pardon: *Lord Ambassador Haaken Skrathmandan*—had deceived her, with his deflections and his discretions, his wise, watchful eyes and his elusive Skaki wizardry.

And now, here was Scratten, surprising her still again—displaying a depth of sympathetic intelligence that she might expect from someone like *Duantri*, not from an upstart headsman from Northernmost Skakmaht!

But there. Nothing was as she thought it was; all her opinions were outdated; she was no longer a child, and must shed childhood's obsolete convictions.

The trouble was, she didn't know she had them until she ran smack into them, like a cobweb in a crawlspace.

"When I was younger—much younger," Scratten reminisced, "apprenticed to the executioner at Rookery Court, I used to have to look away at the moment of death. I'd have horrible nightmares otherwise. But my mentor… she said it was a shameful thing to do, that I must acquit myself with honor, and do my dead the respect of beholding them unflinchingly. So, I… I grew accustomed."

Lanie cocked her head at him. He was so tall, so well-scrubbed, so sinewy. With that grave, thoughtful expression, he looked a great deal like Haaken. She wondered what she might see, if she watched him at work with her deep sight.

Would Saint Death be standing at Scratten Skrathmandan's left shoulder? Did She keep vigil with him as he removed his shoes, picked up his sword of Damahrashian steel, and stepped quietly and quickly forward to deliver a swift beheading? Did She, perhaps, approve of this sweet-faced Scratch brother—for showing mercy in the act She otherwise abhorred: the cutting down of life before its time?

Lanie was curious.

Removing her right hand from her pocket, she offered it to Scratten. "Let's try."

Scratten beamed. "Really?"

"Really."

With an eagerness as gentle as it was urgent, Scratten received her hand in his. Immediately, a rash of gray-white spots popped up all over Lanie's skin, from the bumps of her knuckles to the band of her wrist, and all the way up to her elbow.

She sucked in a breath at the burning, itching, prickling tingle of it, and tugged at her hand. "Enough, please."

His eyes wide, Scratten released her. "That was so fast!"

She tried not to scratch herself, failed. "I guess you were at work this morning?"

"Yes—at Ynyssyll's Tooth, there was an—"

"Please. Don't. No details." Shoving her hand back into her pocket, Lanie stepped back from him. The itching subsided. Somewhat.

Scratten's chagrin was obvious by his bowed head and hunched shoulders, and Lanie felt a pang that had nothing to do with her allergies. She stepped closer.

"Listen," she said, bumping his arm with hers, making sure to keep several layers of cloth between them. "That was my fault. I wanted to see what happened. And *what* I saw," she added as he hunched further into himself, "is that you are a good and kind man. You are as much a disciple of Saint Death in your way as I am. And I laud you for it. I just can't... touch you. Well, not without gloves on, anyway."

At this, Scratten's bashful—almost worshipful—gaze finally rose to meet hers. "In Skakmaht," he murmured, "you know, we call Her—Saint Death, I mean—Erre'Elur. The Frost Queen."

"Erre'Elur," Lanie repeated. "Beautiful."

Scratten smiled, pleased at pleasing her. And then Tan swept in like the guest of honor at a masquerade ball, exclaiming over the black and silver coffered ceiling of the great hall, the depictions of the twelve gods, and the darkly glittering tiles that flashed blue whenever light from the sconces hit them a certain way.

"Magnificent!" she cried. Even blunted by soft-soled house slippers, orange with gold embroidery, her stride implied a bright herd of stampeding beasts.

Duantri, entering behind her, had shed her light wrap and her shoes. She stood in her tunic, barefoot and bareheaded, her glossy black ringlets clinging close to her scalp. She said nothing, and looked at everything, and even Scratten seemed wary of her.

"I love this room!" Scratten agreed. "It is my favorite!"

"Of course it is!" Tan said. "Won't you take my arm, Lord Scratten? These tiles are so slick, and my slippers are so soft!"

Beaming with solicitude, Scratten hurried toward Tan and offered her the arm that Lanie rejected.

"Mama's in the library," he said, conducting the gyrlady out of the great hall and into the grand salon. "She will be so pleased to see you all."

"A formidable woman!" Tan purred, flipping a rakishly dyed orange bang out of her eye. "Tell me all about her!"

They chattered on, drawing ahead as Lanie and Duantri fell in step behind them. Duantri slipped her arm around Lanie's waist, and murmured the first she had spoken since leaving Liriat Proper.

"But is't not strange to walk these halls again?"

Lanie glanced up. For all that the warmth in Duantri's voice was as encompassing as an embrace, her face was still stern and set, and her eyes were very bright and very wild, observing everything, ready for anything.

"Very," she answered.

"Ah," said Duantri, tightening her arm.

Her touch soothed the rash that Scratten's had incited. The last of the itch subsided to nothing. Gratefully, Lanie hugged her back, and tried not to look at the house that had been Stones Manor, either its changes or its samenesses, too closely.

"MISS STONES. GYRLADY Tanaliín. Gyrgardu Duantri." Sari scanned each of them in her turn. "Welcome to Skrathmandan."

Instead of sitting enthroned in one of the elaborately carved and cushioned chairs scattered around the library, she stood near the fire, one hand clutching the mantelpiece as if for support, the other fidgeting. Nervous energy rippled off her body like a hot-road mirage.

Cracchen, who was slouched against the doorjamb, cleared his throat as Lanie passed him by. When she glanced toward the sound, he drummed his fingers suggestively on the stock of his quad-barreled blunderbuss.

A ridiculous weapon. Lanie recognized it from her father's arsenal. Short range. Inaccurate. Kick like a freshly gelded bullock. Natty had only bought it because it amused him. Rolling her eyes at Cracchen's attempt at menace, she pushed her spectacles up her nose and decided to ignore him in favor of his much more interesting mother.

"Baroness Skrathmandan," she began, "how may I—?"

But Duantri, who never interrupted, interrupted. "What happened to your gate?" She spoke in Lirian, like iron spikes pounded in hard ground.

"My gate." And Sari sharped out a laugh that was not one. "Come, Miss Stones. Sit. Let me tell you about my gate."

She beckoned Lanie to a chair near the fire. Lanie sat, grateful when Tan claimed the seat next to her, and even more grateful when Duantri took up a post at the doorway that mirrored Cracchen's.

Cracchen glared at the Gyrgardu. Duantri ignored him beautifully. Scratten assumed his mother's position by the mantelpiece when Sari settled on a small sofa. He fixed his gaze on Lanie's face. She felt the weight of it like a second fire.

But she focused most of her attention on Sari, who was perched on the edge of her chair like she might fly off it at any moment.

For a moment, nobody spoke.

"You seem tense, Baroness," Tan observed, breaking the silence.

Sari barked out another not-laugh, and turned to Lanie. "Your revenant, Miss Stones," she said, "is out of control. She has *smashed* my gate. And much of my house. I want to hire you as a consulting necromancer before she brings the walls down. Tell me your fee, if you please. And then tell me, as succinctly as possible: how do we put her down?"

CHAPTER FORTY-ONE

Raising Tigers

LANIE SAT BACK, stunned. Tan shifted on her sofa cushion, obviously wanting to jump in with questions and challenges of her own. But somewhat to Lanie's surprise, she settled for a supportive squeeze of the knee, and that was what prompted Lanie to speak.

"When I came to you at the Ambassadorial Palace," she began, "you were unwilling to let *me* pay *you* to 'put Goody down.'" She grimaced at the phrasing, which made Goody sound like a dog, or a house in ruins wanting its final wrecking.

"The situation"—Sari's hands gripped her own knees—"has changed."

As if on cue, a muted crashing noise echoed down the corridor from the main house. The library was tucked snugly at the back of the southeast wing, just adjacent to where Lanie's old bedroom used to be. For any sound to have reached there at all from the main house, it would have to have been immense at its source.

"Is that—?" Lanie twisted in her seat. "Is that coming from the gallery?"

Sari briefly closed her eyes. "Yes. That is where we... trapped her." She drew breath to continue.

Another crash, muted, yet somehow still spectacularly loud, stopped her mid-breath.

From the door, Cracchen growled, "I tell you, she breaks that thing, Haaken is going to shit snowballs."

"That... thing?" Lanie asked Sari, leaning forward, "What thing?" She thought she knew, but she needed to hear it.

"Your revenant," Sari began again, glaring Cracchen down from across the room, "is drawn to the Almasquin." She seemed determined to proceed with the narrative at her own pace, in her own way. "You will know perhaps know it by a different name," she explained. "It is the black box of deathsleep that the demon Irradiant—"

"—the Sarcophagus of Souls, yes. Yes," Lanie mused, "it makes sense. It's the only other thing... like her... in the house."

"Your revenant wasn't like this when... when first she arrived at

Midsummer," Sari said. "She seemed stunned then, or in some sort of torpor. She sat in the kitchen, facing the wall, never moving. As weeks passed, we began finding her in slightly different positions, and then in different rooms. Often she was just standing in the garden, staring at nothing. Then, for several weeks, she never left the set of attic rooms I assume were the nurseries. One time, Haaken tracked her all the way to the family ossuary—

"Which you subsequently destroyed," Lanie murmured.

"But," Sari went on, "no matter what we did—command, cajole, or coerce—she never responded. She never so much as twitched."

"Bullets bounced off her." Cracchen snickered, thumping his shoulders restlessly against the wall.

Lanie's gaze narrowed on him, which just made him laugh again.

"All right," he said, holding up his hands, "sometimes big bits of her chipped off—but only when I used larger lead balls. Before you showed up, I was just about to break out the heavy artillery..."

"No one's interested in your artillery, Cracchen," Scratten said sharply.

"*Eventually*," Sari said, talking over both her sons, "the revenant always moved elsewhere on her own. She never did us any harm. Before he left for Rook, Haaken adjured us all to treat her like a ghost; and not"—her glare cut to Cracchen—"to *agitate* her."

"*I* say we blow a hole in the bitch," Cracchen put in. "Go in through the gallery wall. Take her down. Nothing in there we want anyhow—except the Almasquin—and she's been throwing it around for weeks. Not a dent on it."

"No one's tried firing a cannon ball into it yet," Scratten countered sarcastically. "Imagine Haaken's reaction if *you* ended up breaking the Almasquin before his return."

Cracchen's spine snapped straight. "Well, maybe Haaken's wrong about *that* too. Why should his opinion count for more than mine? Maybe blowing up that gods-damned thing would free the Guilded Council from their deathsleep. And even if it kills them all instead, well." He shrugged his burly shoulders. "After a hundred years? Maybe they'd thank us for it."

"That's not your decision to make—"

Cracchen interrupted, "Or maybe we blow a hole in this one!" He jabbed a finger Lanie's way. "A cannon ball with *her* name on it could end all our troubles. Maybe *she's* the one pulling that gray bitch's puppet strings—"

Scratten lunged at him. His long legs crossed the room in a few bounds. But Sari's voice, like ice cutting ice, stopped the potential brawl faster than thrusting a sword through a spoked wheel.

"Cracchen Uthpansel Skrathmandan! Scratten Murathan! Back! Back, I say."

Subsiding once more into his slouch, Cracchen smirked at Duantri, who was regarding him from her own post by the door with a pensive famishment, as if wondering whether he tasted as good as a mouse or a vole. Scratten, whose pale face had darkened to a red rivaling embers, spun around and returned to his place by the fire.

"So," Lanie said dryly, "this is all my fault. Of course."

Sari clutched the arms of her sofa with fists that wanted to fly out at something. "Miss Stones, if anyone is at fault, it is I—for not listening when you came to me at the Ambassadorial Palace. I thought to use your desire for the revenant to win you over for Bran Fiakhna. That scheme… recoiled. Not only is Bran Fiakhna *not* pleased"—for the first time her icy voice grew louder, outraged—"but she *intercepted* my message to my son at Rookery Court asking for his aid and advice in this matter, and sent a message of her own, *ordering* me to offer you the revenant as a bride gift. But—" Sari's pale mouth twisted. "I thought you might prefer to keep this matter transactional. Necromancy pays well—or so I'm told."

"Historically that's true," Lanie agreed. "I, personally, haven't found it to be so. It's cost me more than I've ever made off it."

She did not—she *would not!*—stick her hand into her coat pocket to fondle Bran Fiakhna's necklace, that 'token of her esteem.' But, oh, she wanted to. She always carried it with her; the cold golden snake of jet and onyx, garnet and pyrite clung to her fingers and warmed to her touch and reminded her, reminded her, of the power that was hunting Datu. She had tried several times to break the necklace into its components parts, or drop it down the privy or in the river. She could never quite manage it, but told herself it was just as well; she'd find a use for it someday.

Detangling her fingers from the chain, she removed her hand from her pocket and said, as briskly as Sari, "You say that Goody started acting up recently. How has her behavior changed since? When did it begin?"

"It began with Cracchen's bullets," Scratten said. He kept his back to her, and spoke softly, though she could tell he was still furious. "Until he started shooting at her, the revenant was mostly sluggish by day. She'd wander around a bit in the crepuscular hours, but it was at night she became most active. But when he started using her as target practice, it… roused her."

Sari winced slightly. Lanie could see, in the thousand new lines on her face, exactly how much sleep she had not been enjoying.

"But it wasn't until just before autumn equinox—a few days? A week, perhaps, before—that she began actively seeking out the Almasquin, and trying to destroy it."

Tan's eyes went to Lanie's. It was a few days before autumn equinox that Lanie had finally dug her way through the collapse in Gallowsdance's tunnel, and begun the long walk underground to Skrathmandan, and reached through the dirt and the dark and the ash of the old ossuary—and right into Haaken's wards.

Had Goody felt it, the moment Lanie's substance made contact with the wards?

Sari waved a tired hand. "We tried moving the Almasquin while she slept, or went torpid, or whatever it is she does by day. We had it carried down into the cellar—it took twelve hired men—and had new locks and bolts added to the cellar doors. But that same night, she woke and went right for the cellar, breaking down the doors."

"Barreled through them like a battering ram," Scratten said.

"Smashed a fortune in wine," Cracchen muttered.

Scratten took up the thread again. "So we tried hiding it in the woods, burying the Almasquin deeper than a grave. But the revenant dug it out that very night and tried to crack it open against a tree. We even rolled it out beyond the front gates, hoping that she might get hung up on Haaken's..." He stopped, looking guilty, and bit his tongue, as if he had been about to blurt out a secret.

"Haaken's wards," Lanie supplied. "His very zappy, very strong, very *Skaki* wards."

The glacier chips that were Sari's eyes glinted and warmed at this compliment to her absent son, but she did not confirm the wards' existence.

"But the gates only enraged her," Scratten went on. "She destroyed them like the cellar doors. Though," he added, slowing down, "I do think they *must* have hurt her, because after that, she went into her torpor for over a fortnight. That gave us ample time to move the Alma... the Sarcophagus of Souls... back into the gallery. We reinforced all doors and locks, boarded up the windows, and removed any items we thought might be of value. Then we left a single door open. Sure enough, as soon as she woke up again, she went straight for it. This time, we locked her in the gallery, and she hasn't tried to leave since. But every night, just as evening falls..."

The crash sounded again.

"And," Sari finished, "it's getting worse."

Lanie nodded again.

Goody may not be in possession of her full will and memories, she thought, but she knows she hates the Sarcophagus of Souls. And the ghost trapped inside its padlock.

She rubbed her hands together for warmth. Her left hand was freezing—but at least it wasn't numb. She realized that all the Scratches were looking at her expectantly—Scratten with an ardent trust she'd done nothing to merit; Sari warily and wearily; and Cracchen with something like hatred—and stopped rubbing.

"All right!" she said, and clapped her palms together to slam her thoughts into order. "Our best methods for dealing with a revenant—"

"Before you begin, Lanie," Tan interrupted her, almost apologetically, "why do you not discuss your fee with Baroness Skrathmandan? She did ask you to name it."

Lanie hesitated. She would have come to Skrathmandan for nothing. She would have come here even if it had been a trap set for her by the

Blackbird Bride. She was here for Goody. She had been ready to endure capture, imprisonment, indenture, or—twelve gods help her—marriage to all three Scratch boys, to help Goody.

But Grandpa Rad had once told her that a necromancer never got out of bed for less than twenty-five hundred monarchs. Of course, that was for a resurrection, not a laying to rest. But why not start high and bargain down?

"Five thousand monarchs," she said with as much authority as she could muster. "Or a future favor of equal value."

The corners of Sari's lips curled like calligraphy. "The latter terms are wide open to interpretation, Miss Stones."

Lanie shrugged. "An exchange of favors is not without precedent. We need only to look to your records with Erralierra Brackenwild to estimate certain favors' worth in gold. You did keep records, *Baroness* Skrathmandan?"

"Meticulously." said Sari, still looking amused, "Very well, a favor it is, then." She scrawled an extravagant IOU onto her notepad, and a few sentences of details, signed it, passed it around the room for witnesses, and handed it to Lanie, who gave it to Tan for safekeeping. "Continue, if you please."

Lanie cleared her throat. "So. The necromancer Irradiant Stones writes: there is only one way of dealing with a revenant. That is, remove its head. You don't, of course, have to be a necromancer to do this." She could already feel her cadence slip into something between Grandpa Rad in lecture mode and Gyrlady Tanaliín in lecture mode. But she couldn't seem to stop herself.

"Several things make this enterprise a tricky one," she went on. "First: the nature of the death magic worked upon undead creature—whether it is ectenical or panthaumic; second: the nature of the necromancer who first summoned it—how powerful they were or are, whether they themselves are still alive or are dead, and if the latter, how powerful were they in life, and how long have they been dead; third: the age, and therefore the size and strength, of the revenant. The older a revenant is, the larger it will be, and the harder its skin—for the undead keep growing after they die, and their outer layer thickens like a crust, becoming impervious to most elements. But there is another way, a gentler way to lay the undead to rest, and I—"

Duantri interrupted for the second time. "He left."

"Who left?" asked Tan, sitting up and glancing around.

Duantri jerked her head to the place Cracchen had been standing. "He left when you said to remove the head."

Scratten spun around and sprang away from the mantelpiece, cursing. He looked at his mother, who had also risen and was making for the door.

"He'll go for the ordinance," he warned Sari.

"Head him off at the arsenal, then, and try to hold him there. Sit on him if you have to—I'll be on your heels."

Lanie was familiar with the arsenal; it had been one of Nita's favorite places on the manor grounds, after Aba's old workshop. She remembered the demi-culverin Goody used to wheel around the grounds at night when Nita was feeling paranoid. But there were, she was sure, even smaller artillery that Cracchen could handle alone, or with a team of horses. Her stomach cramped as Scratten disappeared out the door.

Sari turned to face the room and said in a voice of unshatterable calm, "Please remain here, ladies. We will be back as soon as… as soon as Cracchen is calm again. It will not be safe for you to wander the manor without us."

"Loose cannons?" Tan guessed.

"Please excuse me." Sari exited and shut the door to the library.

Lanie heard the click as she locked it behind her. "She means Haaken's wards," she explained, rising from her seat and beginning to pace. "He's placed them all over—wherever he thought a defense was needed, or something precious wanted guarding."

She could sense the wards like wasp nests, hanging in all the nooks and crannies of the house, lurking at windows and under eaves, buzzing away busily in old cupboards and beneath stairwells. To race heedlessly through this house would inevitably be to run into one—as she had done once already underground, in Gallowsdance's tunnel. She didn't know if she could survive a second time.

"I do not like being locked in," Duantri commented, heading right for one of the library's windows and reaching for the latch.

"Stop!" Lanie cried.

Duantri obeyed, but turned in her slow, predatory way to stare, unblinking, at Lanie, as if daring her to make such a loud noise again.

"I have to check for wards," Lanie explained, and Duantri nodded.

There was one, as it turned out: a small one, tuned to the structure of the window glass. It was set to activate upon any forceful breakage from the outside.

"Go ahead and open it," Lanie said softly, in hardly more than a whisper. "But if you go out that way, Gyrgardu, I wouldn't re-enter the library by the same window—just in case."

"We will keep the window open for now," Duantri decided. She was still speaking only in Lirian, saying only what she must. "It is an eight-foot drop to the ground. A few feet of snow for cushion—if you need to exit in a hurry." Implying that she, Duantri, would of course not be walking at that point.

"Duantri… it's just us here. Why stick to Lirian, when we know you hate it?"

"She is scared," Tan called out from across the library. "Little to say and none of it beautiful. Thus"—she grunted—"*Lirian.*"

With an ostentatious grunt, she lowered herself to her hands and knees beside the fireplace. Lanie stood on tiptoe to try and see the gyrlady over the couch. "Tan, what are you doing?"

"The most exquisite rug! Dilapidated, but exquisite. I must examine it more closely. Now, I disapprove, of course, of big game hunting as a rule. But occasionally in Quadiíb, one encounters a tiger terrorizing the Caravan School roads—and then the gyrgardon will do what they must, as would the hunters of any tribe or village. But I do not suppose you have tigers this far west?"

"Catamounts, yes. Tigers, no." Lanie left the window to join her on the floor beneath the mantelpiece, where the ancient tiger rug was splayed in all its worn and well-trampled glory.

"You know," she said softly, "Datu used to pretend this was her pet kitty. She named it Stripes. She only knew about cats through Mak's stories and my books, so the sounds she made for it were idiosyncratic, to say the least."

Smiling a little, Lanie scratched the broad, buff bridge of its nose, just under the trident of dark stripes marking the top of its head. The glass eyes of the tiger rug glared at her, at nothing, in outraged fury: darkest amber with fixed black pupils, rimmed all around in black. They put her in mind of Datu's wolf cub, and the star-blue eyes of its undeath.

She thought of Saint Death's own eyes, which were sometimes brown like Lanie's own, and sometimes bone, and sometimes the color of a fog rising from the low places of the Diesmali. She wondered if the next time she beheld Doédenna, she would see a tiger's bright-burning eyes, and by this sign somehow understand Her more thoroughly.

Another crash from the distant gallery made both her and Tan jump.

Then, from outside the library's walls, came another sound. A boom. It shook books off the shelves, knickknacks off the side tables. The floor trembled.

A second second later, the boom was followed by a *crack*—like the moon splitting off from itself and plummeting planet-side into a mountain.

"He fired at the house," Duantri said from the window with absolutely no expression in her voice.

"He did not!" Creaking to her feet, Tan limped to the window and peered out. "He did! He fired right at the main house!" She clucked her tongue, sticking her head further out the window, and reported back over her shoulder, "One of the two young men—the hot-headed one—is standing out in the snow, far back on the east lawn. Reloading the smooth bore. In general I have tried to expunge the word 'idiot' from my vocabulary. But on this occasion, my Duantri, I cannot help but feel the strong need to reintroduce it. Just this once."

"You will remonstrate with yourself later, Tanaliín," Duantri murmured.

"Yes, but it would be so satisfying *now*."

Shouting in the distance had Tan sticking her head out the window again. A moment later, she announced (unnecessarily, for Lanie recognized the voices) that Sari and Scratten had finally caught up with Cracchen and were trying to reason with him. Soon, Cracchen's bellowing was overpowering theirs—though his exact words were unclear.

Lanie's fingers sank deeply into the tiger rug's fur.

"Goody!" she whispered. "Goody, hear me!"

No answer. Lanie tried not to panic. If Cracchen was reloading, it probably meant he hadn't taken Goody's head off with the first shot. Didn't it?

She tried again, this time using the name that had belonged to Goody before her death, before her undying servitude. It might be the only name she now remembered, all other bonds of memory being lost to her.

"Jhímieti!"

This time, she felt as well as heard it: her second voice, flowering beneath her first like a dark tide.

"Jhímieti, I am sent by your friend. I am sent by Saint Death for you. Do you hear me?"

A low, long groan answered her. Lanie felt it in her bones, like a fault line forming in bedrock.

Her fists closed involuntarily around the tiger rug's head. She came back to the surface of herself, surprised at the sensation of fur against her palm.

She had seen this well-trodden, toddler-gnawed, dusty-eyed, melancholy fury of a rug a hundred times—a thousand times!—before in her life. But now, for the first time, she was seeing it for what it was to *her*, a necromancer.

Dead accident. One of the two tools she needed.

Lanie glanced around quickly for her second tool—a knife, a letter opener, a mirror she could break, any sharp-edged instrument.

And, of course, they were everywhere. Once she started looking for them, she saw sharp things on every surface: on bookshelves, the writing desk in the corner, on side tables, as wall decorations. The library at Skrathmandan hadn't changed so much since its days as a Stones institution; Lanie could find what she needed twenty times over.

But she didn't stir from her knees. Didn't reach. Didn't ask.

She was remembering Saint Death's arms hard around her. Saint Death the Wolf, licking her wounds until they healed. Saint Death's eyes, so stark and wretched when She beheld what a ruin Lanie had made of her body's temple. Suddenly, the prospect of spraying her own blood all over one of Datu's formerly favorite toys—kindling it, transforming it, using it up till it fell to ash—became too sad to bear.

But Goody needed her. Goody had prayed to Doédenna for her—for centuries. Lanie was made for this. She was *made* for it. She must find a way.

Lanie stared at the tiger rug's head as if it were an oracle with the answers she craved. Her reliquary, which had worked loose from beneath the collar of her shirt, hung between her clenched fists, lightly knocking against the tiger rug's forehead. She wanted to hold onto it, wring it for what comfort she could, send the substance of a kiss through it—even though she would not be able to feel Canon Lir kissing her back.

Which gave her an idea.

Consciously relaxing her cramped fingers, Lanie forced her focus into her left hand. And then, she *poured.*

From some inexpressibly deep, potentially bottomless well within herself, she reached into her substance, drew it up from that place that was the all of her, and poured it out into her left hand. Her wizard mark, which on high holy fire feasts sometimes seemed to have about it a haze like mist on a swollen spring river, billowed up like steam from a hot tea kettle. She poured and poured her substance into her left hand, as the colorless steam swirled up and around her body like a current, like a cloak. She poured until she was surrounded by her own substance, until it hovered over the length of the striped rug like the tiger's own phantom. And then, when she felt she had poured out enough of herself, she began to *press it down.*

The haze that enveloped her acted like an additional limb—however vaporous and translucent—and because it belonged to her, it obeyed her edict: it sank right down into the striped pelt. From the flattened stub of the tiger rug's tail, to the clawless pads of its paws, to the mouth bared in perpetual belligerence, her substance fit itself to this new and extended physical form.

Lanie found herself stroking the pelt, humming the Maranathasseth Anthem to it, encouraging it to admix with her substance. But she hardly needed to do this; conjoining with the rug was as startlingly easy as tapping through her reliquary and into Canon Lir's, which she did every night before sleeping, and every morning upon waking, in order that they might know she was thinking of them.

In that sense, this was nothing new.

In another sense, the experience was wholly novel, merely because she was actually *thinking* about what she was doing, rather than leaning on instinct and desperation. She was inter-blending her substance—the living *substance* of a necromancer—with the dead material of the pelt.

She was making, in essence, a new kind of ectenica. One that she didn't have to bleed for. One that would leave the accident of the dead material unharmed by her interference once she released her substance from it. One that she might sustain for as long as she needed, off-surge, without weakening herself—so long as she maintained her will and her concentration.

This was close to the magic Grandpa Rad must have used when he called the living substances out of the Sky Wizards of Skakmaht, and bound them with his dying accident to create the engine of his own undeath, the Sarcophagus of Souls. Later (if there was a later), when she had time to think about all this more, Lanie would write all of this down. She would take Tan up on her offer to co-author a paper and submit it to the Judicial Colloquium of Gyrladies in Quadiíb for publication: *On Lirian Necromancy, Its Uses and Perils*.

But for now, she was fully occupied—being both herself *and* the tiger rug beneath her.

Being now her temporary ectenica, the tiger rug responded immediately to her will. And so, Lanie found herself rising into the air as she knelt on top of it. The rug had floated off the ground at her unspoken urging.

She heard herself crying out in a commanding voice, "Step aside, Duantri! I'm for the gallery!" before making at breathtaking speed for the open window.

The smell of citrus was everywhere, as if lemon trees were growing from out of the very library walls, as if their abrupt boughs were already laden with waxy yellow fruit, and their thick green leaves reflected the flickering flames of the fireplace.

And then, the smell of lemons mingled with the smell of snow.

Lanie tugged the tiger rug's ears to the right. They swerved together out of the library and into the newly fallen night, making their way around the corner of the southeast wing of the house towards the front of the manor.

Lifting her voice in a bloodcurdling scream, Lanie called the attention of all the Scratches on the eastern lawn to her levitation. She pointed in the direction of the gallery, then back at herself, and then she raised her fist in the air.

There, Lanie thought. If Cracchen fires again, it must be with the intent to murder *me*. And no matter how much he wants to, I don't think Scratten—or even Sari—will let him. This buys me some time.

In the distance, she heard Scratten exclaim her name in horrified recognition. Nodding to herself, Lanie took a much sharper right turn towards the main house—where a large, smoking hole gaped in the east-facing wall of the gallery.

Far behind Lanie, and unseen by her, a silver flash emanated from the library, like the light bouncing off a complex of war mirrors large enough to burn down a fleet of enemy ships. A shrill *killy-killy-klee* pierced the night as Duantri's garments fell, empty, to the carpet. Shortly after, Tan dropped down from the library window, floundered briefly in the snow, and then made her way, coatless, hatless, shod in a pair of embroidered house slippers, through the white mounds towards the main house. Circling the air above her head like a meteorite that never falls, the kestrel.

CHAPTER FORTY-TWO

Severance

Goody's agony pulled at Lanie like a lodestone tugging iron. From the moment she smelled lemons, Lanie knew that the doorway to Saint Death was standing open at her back, ready to welcome Goody inside it.

The world had become hard-angled citrine: very bright and very clear. The tiger rug flew on beneath her, taut and attentive, obeying Lanie's will like her own left hand. It was warm as her skin to the touch, in no danger of crumbling to blackened sludge as soon as her blood ran dry. An improvement over the old ectenica.

She zipped through the broken gallery wall and came to a hovering stop above the ruins. Leaning over the tiger rug's head, Lanie looked down and around for any sign of Goody. What she saw instead was rubble.

Rubble, everywhere. But surprisingly not all of it, or even most of it, was from Cracchen's cannon blast. Goody had destroyed the place. Not a portrait on the wall remained unslashed. Not a vitrine standing that had not been powdered to glittering dust. Delirious Stones's poison cabinet was upended; bottles and vials spilled out of it like strange innards. Weapons of every shape and size lay scattered and shattered on the parquet floor. Statues were toppled, plaques ripped off walls, mementoes shredded, and the great plinth that had once borne the weight of the Sarcophagus of Souls was cracked down the center like an altar abandoned by its god. The Sarcophagus itself was capsized on the north end of the gallery like a longboat after a hurricane, but otherwise seemed undamaged. Goody lay beneath it. Or part of her did. Lanie could not see her head.

She was so still.

Lanie did not remember directing the tiger rug to move, but suddenly she was there, floating over the place where Goody lay, and the rug was drifting down, down, ever so gently, but Lanie leapt from it as soon as she could safely do so, and half-stumbled, half-slid to her knees at Goody's side.

Goody's body, gigantic from its long undeath, yet seemed far smaller than Lanie remembered it. Her skin was the same slumping, spoiled gray color of a slag heap. Perhaps the apparent diminishment was an illusion, however; full half of Goody's body—everything from the waist up, including her arms—was crushed beneath the Sarcophagus of Souls. Lanie saw how the previously impenetrable surface of Goody's skin was pitted and chipped in places, and fractured in others, whole chunks of it flaking off like shale. Some of this was undoubtedly Cracchen's doing, but Lanie suspected that the majority of the damage had come because Goody was no longer bound to a necromancer's line. Over the years, Lanie's presence—not to mention her occasional gifts of orblins and the like—had probably enlivened and reinforced Goody's undeath. Not that Goody would have thanked her for that.

"Jhímieti," she called out in both of her voices. She placed one hand on Goody's leg, sent a faint thrum of her substance into it. "Jhímieti, I've come to free you."

Goody, lost beneath the hateful weight of the Sarcophagus of Souls, never twitched. Lanie knew—she *knew*—that she had heard Goody's groan back in the library, just after the explosion. She had felt Goody's agony during her brief flight through the snow. But now there was nothing. Had Goody's skull and neck been crushed? If so, was that trauma enough to unseat her memory from her accident? Had it killed her after all, if slowly? But surely Lanie would have felt *that* too, the whisper of Goody's passing?

A pang of loss rose up and choked her like rotten ectenica. Hot tears splashed onto Goody's legs; Lanie wiped her face, hating this new weakness of tears that had plagued her since autumn.

But, then, she thought, surely a necromancer's tears, like her blood, might rouse a revenant? Give her new strength, vitality enough to cast off the Sarcophagus of Souls, and let me see her face one last time?

One last time before Lanie sang Goody into her long Undreaming…

But Goody did not move.

"Miss Lanie!"

Lanie looked up to see Scratten barreling through the hole his brother had blown through the wall. He was red-faced from the cold, and from his high-speed bolt through the knee-deep snow, from his scrabble over the rubble. His fair hair was plastered against his skull, his shoulders heaved. When his pale gaze met hers, Scratten's relief was so great that he had to steady himself against the broken plinth. Heaving a sigh, he made his way across the room to her.

"She's not moving," Lanie said as Scratten drew close.

"Cracchen said he had a clear shot at her through the window. So—he took it." Scratten sounded painfully embarrassed. "Mordda is furious; the cost of demolishing and rebuilding this part of the house in addition to your consultation fee—which we will still pay, never fear—"

"She deserved better," Lanie murmured, her hand pressed to Goody's motionless leg. "She deserved me to… to sing… sing to…"

"I'm so sorry." Scratten squatted beside her. He did not touch her, though his face clearly expressed a longing to do so. "It could be," he ventured, "that she's just entered torpor again. She seems to do that when she's been wounded—like with Haaken's wards when she broke our gate. But she did it also to a lesser extent when Cracchen fired his blunderbuss at her. He used both snake shot and larger balls a few different times. In all cases, she shut down for a few nights."

"In some ways, that might be worse," Lanie said in a defeated voice. "She would have welcomed death either way. But that... that torpid state you describe would just prolong her misery."

As she helplessly patted Goody's legs, she began to notice that the places where her tears had splashed had streaked Goody's dry gray limbs with molten ribbons of lapis lazuli. She barely registered this before Goody gave a wild buck, and flipped the Sarcophagus of Souls off her body.

The black box skidded across the floor, splitting the wood as it went. Goody scrambled upright, her frantic movements sending Lanie tumbling after the Sarcophagus. She would have slammed into it hard enough to crack a bone if the tiger rug had not inserted itself between Lanie's body and the bulk of black stone. The rug cushioned her fall, but the breath was knocked clean out of her.

Lanie's glasses were thumped askew. She pushed them straight. Her vision cleared in time to see Goody, now fully upright, shake herself out like a beast unchained.

No longer did she seem small and frail—quite the opposite; she was swollen in feral enormity. Her face had the look of a great gray bear in a gladiator's pit: violated, brutalized, harassed past all bearing, and her eyes, bruised pearls with hardly any light left in them, fixed once more upon the Sarcophagus of Souls. Specifically, upon the padlock.

She did not see Lanie lying just in front of it. Or if she did, she did not register her as an object of import. Her expression, which for so many years had been so implacable, unreadable, was frozen in hatred. Her teeth were bared like the head of the tiger rug; her quarry was clear. Bending her head like a baited bull, Goody charged.

Lanie was not sure what Scratten meant to do. He had to have known he was no match for Goody; though he was almost seven feet tall himself, Goody towered over him, and was stone where he was flesh, and possessed of a far stronger accident than his own.

Perhaps Scratten thought merely to intercept her, to grapple with her just long enough to distract her and buy Lanie time to scramble out of the way. Perhaps he thought, even if Goody tossed him aside, that he would be able to find a safe way to land, and roll to his feet again, and shake off the impact, like he might after a brawl with his brothers.

Lanie was never to know.

Scratten ran to stand directly in Goody's path, planting himself in front of Lanie. His body was her wall. Lanie hauled herself to her knees, and the tiger rug slid beneath her. It scooped her into the air, and whisked her to safety—high, higher—ten feet, twenty—until she almost bumped the gallery ceiling. Her own frightened substance, mixed with the fatal reflexes and strength of the dead tiger, fought her to keep her safe and out of Goody's way.

When she tried climbing over the side of the rug, thinking to force it down with her weight until it dropped far enough that she could jump from it, the rug just wrapped itself ever more tightly about her lower body, cocooning everything but her arms and head. Dread made her desperate; Lanie struggled with it, but it was like struggling with herself. The more she fought, the less she was able to move. All she could do was scream:

"Scratten! Get out of her way! She can't—"

Scratten looked up at her from the gallery floor. Goody slammed into him. She lifted him in her arms. She bent him in half, first one way, then the other, and swung him down hard, dashing him to the floor. She trampled his body to get to the Sarcophagus; her left foot flattened his chest, her right his skull.

Both of Lanie's voices ground together in a wail of loss. The sound escaped her throat like a saw cutting through rock; she hardly knew what she was doing or how to stop herself. Her wail echoed through the gallery like a wound.

Even Goody seemed to hear it. She dropped the padlock she was squeezing in her fist, and looked to the ceiling, her dull eyes showing their first gleam of consciousness. Her face lost its rictus of fury; she looked—just for a moment—confused, sorrowful, and much more like herself. She stood very still in that moment, opening and closing those great, bloodstained hands which hung heavy at her sides.

Then a second wail joined Lanie's, cutting hers off. Sari Skrathmandan was kneeling by her son, who lay broken on the broken floor. She plucked at the silver fur of his bloodstained coat, at the parts of him that were still recognizable: his right hand, whole and perfect, his powerful thigh. Tan, crusted with ice and plodding from the cold, waded out of the snow and into the gallery the next moment, drawing Lanie's shocky gaze. Crashing against various impedimenta, but heeding none of them, Tan made her way to Sari's side. When she fell to her knees beside her, Sari crumpled against the gyrlady, and Tan wrapped her arms around her, her pale face a written record of her own dead.

BENEATH THE GALLERY ceiling, Lanie hovered.

Like one of Haaken's wards, she thought. Like a wasp nest in winter, gray and empty.

Clinging with both arms to the tiger rug's head, she pressed her face against it for comfort. The rest of the pelt scrolled around her body like a winding sheet. Her eyes were closed, her mouth and nose full of hard, warm fur.

She was waiting.

She was waiting for Scratten's death to blow through her like a typhoon.

It did not. She did not know why it did not. She had been so close to his death that she might even now be breathing his last breath. It was the first death she had ever witnessed with her own eyes—she, who'd been peripheral to death her whole life.

And it was Goody, who had…

Lanie should be riddled with echo wounds: her spine snapped, her skull caved in, her organs ruptured. Instead, her body had dropped neatly and without any fuss into one of its numb depths. All she felt was the sore, sorry absence of herself. That, itself, was nothing. She was used to that.

And yet—

BELOW, SARI SCREAMED, "My son! My son!" collapsed over the wreckage of his body like a castaway. Tan, who had become a whole-body embrace, pressed her cheek against Sari's, and was whispering something fiercely to her—comfort, promise, reason, nonsense; Lanie could not hear—moving whenever Sari moved, weeping with her. The gyrlady did not interfere with Sari in any other way, not until Sari flailed, and with wild hands ripped the wig off her head, then dug clawed fingers into her sparse hair and tried to tear it from her scalp. Tan caught her hands, kissed them, began whispering something else, something new, a humming of sorts, a keening hum, part lullaby, part dirge.

Lanie recognized the melody instantly. Though she had never heard that *particular* line of notes, not *precisely*, she knew it at once:

The Lahnessthanessar.

—AND YET, SHE thought, the numbness releasing her throat but leaving behind an awful ache—I can still sing.

She struck a fist to her chest, and knocked her sorrow into the future.

IT WOULD PERFORCE be different from Tan's, Lanie's Lahnessthanessar. Tan could only sing with one voice (though were it the month of Vespers, Lanie suspected the gyrlady might sing a doubled tune), invoking the ancient ritual of grief both to acknowledge Sari's sorrow and also, in some ceremonial way, to attempt to contain it. But when Lanie sang the Undreaming, it would move the spellsong out of the realm of ritual and into enchantment. The Lahnessthanessar, at full voices, would, upon reaching its crescendo, lay all the ghosts in the gallery to rest: Goody's ghost, that was glued to her petrified accident like a shroud rolled in resin; the ghost of Irradiant Stones, squirreled away inside his iron padlock, feeding off the captive souls of the Sky Wizards; and last, Scratten Skrathmandan's ghost, his substance too shredded and bewildered from the violent manner of his death to pass instantly through Doédenna's doorway. Lanie could just sense him, lingering near his bereaved parent as she embraced his shattered shell.

Lanie knew what her song could do. But the notes stuck in her throat.

The Lahnessthanessar had always been much harder for her than the Maranathasseth Anthem. Only with reluctance did it come to her mind and tongue, like a melody recalled on the brink of uneasy sleep, its provenance unprovable, the chance of reproducing it correctly—aloud and in full wakefulness—slim. More than this, fear of grief, like the fear of falling, stopped her. So much more joy in resurrection than in its opposite: and yet—

—and yet, this was the work that Doédenna had called her to do.

Tan had already done the hardest part by *beginning* it. All Lanie must do was sing one line—one note!—and the Great Lullaby would do the rest, inexorable as an onrushing tide.

That was what Goody had taught her. Goody, whom Lanie trusted above all people in Athe. Jhímieti, who had learned the oldest spellsong but one from her own gyrlady's lips.

Lanie closed her eyes. She drew in a breath. It came as a sob—ah! The first note.

How it formed in her throat perfectly. How its shadow shaped itself from the depths of her substance: a twinned note, one light and quavering, one gruff and relentless. Behind her voices and beneath them, a long chain of melody was already lining up in readiness, a whole symphony if she wanted it, hers to summon. All the eternal and ineffable music of the god of Death would ring at her request, if she but asked it.

The tiger rug relaxed as she relaxed. Lanie's substance, both without her body and within it, synced back with itself. They began to move as one. Her hands rested lightly on the tiger's head. Lanie raised her face to the ceiling, her eyes shut in concentration. The striped pelt uncoiled from her lower body. Together, they began their slow drift down.

AND THEN CAME Cracchen Scratch, roaring.

"STONES! YOU LOOK at me! Look me in the eye."

Lanie blinked, opened her eyes. She and the tiger rug were on a level with Cracchen's face. Or rather, on a level with all four barrels of his blunderbuss.

The gun was at full cock. Cracchen's eyes were wide and unblinking, with a sort of laugh in them, as if he had passed with a viper's speed through grief, punched through into rage, and out the other side into a strange glee.

His expression was familiar—Lanie had seen it often enough on Nita's face—a smile as thin and white as a razor's slash before it begins to bleed.

His intent moved through her like buckshot; Lanie could feel her body wanting to form blisters in all the places Cracchen sought to send his projectiles. But these sensations passed as quickly as a forgotten desire to sneeze. Above her, in the high gloom of the rafters, she heard the piercing *killy-killy-klee* of a hunting kestrel.

"You don't want to do that," Lanie said grimly.

The tiger rug trembled beneath her, not with fear but with rage. With readiness.

"Oh," he said. "I do," and fired.

The tiger yowled.

No sound but a flash of blue light.

The lead shot disappeared—disintegrated—and then, the tiger bit the blunderbuss in two.

Cracchen's face became all gape. The tiger rug reared its undead head, ready to rip off Cracchen Scratch's face with its undead fangs, and Lanie was about to let it, not knowing if her allergy would punish her later or if she had somehow moved beyond it.

She did not what she would have done, for the next second, a naked woman came tumbling out of the air.

The weight of Duantri's body sent Cracchen crashing down. He fell against the bust of Even Quicker Stones, sculpted of shining anthracite in the first generation of the Founding. The bust had fallen on its side during Goody's rampage, but the stand it rested upon remained upright. But when Cracchen fell against it, stand and bust both tumbled with him to the floor. The bust did not survive.

Cracchen pushed himself up, tossed down the remains of his blunderbuss on the floor, and rounded on Duantri. He looked, if anything, even more wildly gleeful. Here, at least, was a thing of flesh and blood. Something he could *fight*.

The Gyrgardu herself had landed in a one-legged squat, all her weight on her right foot, her left leg stretched before her, heel pressed to the floor. She held her arms out in front of her body, her right arm bent slightly more than her left. It was a variation on a sothaín gesture from the fourth set: 'The Four-Faced Harvest Goddess Falls to Rise.'

Cracchen moved in on her like a siege engine, legs kicking and fists swinging. It seemed a single blow from any of his limbs would crack Duantri like Goody had cracked Scratten. But as soon as he was close enough, Duantri seemed to fly up his body in a series of quick punches, as if each blow that landed lent her new wings. She caught his kicks in the dancing trap of her bare legs, tangling him, slithering her body around his like a snake until every way he turned he was turning against himself.

When he tried to lift her up and sling her away from him, she somehow managed to get under him, moving into his momentum, and launching him—or helping him launch himself—across the room.

He landed, much as Lanie had, near the Sarcophagus, but stopped short of crashing into it. Duantri had known just how to throw him, how hard, how far, even avoiding most of the broken glass on the floor, or the larger jagged objects that might have seriously injured him. Cracchen's breath was knocked out of him for the moment, that was all.

Straightening from her fight crouching, the Gyrgardu wiped a thread of blood from her mouth. She casually picked up Ham-Handed Stones's sparth ax from the floor, and shifted her grip on it. Her gaze tracked Cracchen's every twitch and groan. Lanie had no doubt that Duantri would blur back into action the moment he gave her cause.

But the sound of iron scraping stone swerved Lanie's attention away from Duantri and back to the Sarcophagus of Souls. It was flipped on its back like a monstrous cockroach, and Goody was straining against it, her legs braced against its black stone belly as she gripped its iron padlock in both hands. Arms rigid, she leaned back with all her weight, pulling like she would pull her own body to pieces before she'd let go. A final crack, and Goody staggered backwards. She held aloft the padlock, now ripped from its embedment, not in victory, but as if she wished to thrust it as far from her body as possible without losing her grip on it.

Goody regarded the thing with loathing as it pulsed in her hand like a violent star. Then she stuffed the whole padlock into her mouth.

Her granite-like teeth crunched on the metal. The padlock's radiance began to bleed from between Goody's lips, spilling its blue-white leakage out of her eyes, and from her nose and from her ears. The ghost of Irradiant Stones, shucked of his prison shell, began to expand into his new shape.

"No," Lanie shouted. "No!"

The doubled song of her deep voice faltered in fear. Even the tiger rug wrinkled beneath her, losing some of its tautness.

But Duantri caught Lanie's elbow, and whispered, "Sing, Lanie." Here, at last, was the true Duantri: the warm and coaxing teacher who had taught Datu to play the cavaquinho. "Sing the Lahnessthanessar with us," she said.

The Gyrgardu lifted her strong, young voice, with all its joyous training, to harmonize with Tan's keening.

Lanie's deep voice came in strong with the next phrase, a series of bass-bottom notes that shook the ground at Goody's feet. It was a divergence from the Lahnessthanessar—or perhaps a bridge—percussive with command:

Release the things that are not you. Let others bear the freight of chaos. Come unburdened to Doédenna. Let go.

Goody crashed to the floor like a titanwood falling, fist-deep in the splintered parquet tiles. Her head hung hung low. She retched and gagged and spat until every piece of the chewed-up padlock came clumping out of her mouth. No longer a single object, the foul pile gleamed and steamed, but the ghost of Irradiant Stones yet clung to its remains and not to Goody.

The hot glow faded from Goody's burnt-out eyes as she curled up in torpor, where, it seemed, the Lahnessthanessar could not reach her. But now, at least, Lanie knew how to wake her—with her tears, her touch, the pulse of her substance. And when the moment was right, she *would* wake her once more, if only to lull her back to sleep. Sleep, which, for the undead, was death. But not now. There was something she had to take care of first.

Crumpled, sundered, and deformed, up blazed the padlock once again, like druzy agate set aflame. From the blue dazzle, the faded silhouette of Lanie's great-grandfather began to take form: round spectacles, drooping whiskers, cruel mouth, unmistakable air of mockery.

Lanie bent over the tiger rug's head, her teeth bared like a tiger's teeth, and sped them both across the smithereened floor. She flung out her left arm to scoop up the ruined padlock. She was going to sing its occupant all the way back through Doédenna's doorway.

But the ghost was old. The ghost was ambitious. The ghost was afraid. And anything—*anything*—was better than the end promised by the gentle Lahnessthanessar. What Irradiant Stones found, nearest to hand, was Cracchen Scratch.

But Lanie, alive, quicker than he, moved at speeds no ghost could hope to match. He never would have made it—if the Sarcophagus of Souls itself had not decided to act. No more than Irradiant did the Sarcophagus want him lulled to his Undreaming so easily. Not without a chance for justice. For vengeance. With nothing left to fasten it down, the lid of the Sarcophagus blew off the top of the black basalt box.

A mass of roiling shadows tentacled out like a many-fingered hand. It grabbed for the ghost just as Lanie snatched up his padlock. The force of the flying lid flung her across the gallery. In panicked protectiveness, the tiger rug once again cocooned her almost entirely, leaving only a bit of her face exposed, so that she could see and breathe.

Of course, she dropped the padlock. The ghost fled its iron, jumping like a flea from it into Cracchen's stunned flesh, where he burrowed in through the center of his chest. The rack of black shadows, whose only wish was to detonate Irradiant Stones, to *atomize* him, recoiled from Cracchen's supine form. It wavered, split into filaments of uncertainty, as if the Skaki Sky Wizards who made up that terrible tangle were loathe to harm a single hair on the head of one of their own descended sons.

Writhing to work herself free from the rug, Lanie watched as a spot, invisible to everyone else in the room, began to form at the center of Cracchen's chest.

It glittered like an evil jewel, a luminous ellipsoid unfurling outward over his whole body in waves of sickly light. Soon, the creeping glow suffused him entirely, the way ectenica overtakes dead accident when a necromancer's living blood is spilt upon it.

But a ghost was not ectenica. A ghost was pure substance—memory and will—attached, not to its original accident, but to an object for which it bore some special sympathy: the object in this case being a Skrathmandan of Skakmaht, scion of a fallen Sky House that Irradiant Stones had once helped destroy. Sympathy enough.

The ghost stepped into Cracchen Scratch with the brazenness of a thief claiming an occupied house for his own. He thundered in, a hundred years undead, arrogant, more assured with every passing second. His substance *dominated* the terrified occupant, driving Cracchen into the very depths of himself, where Irradiant locked him in the dark, like he had the Sky Wizards deep into the shadows of the Almasquin.

Sari's cry when the Sarcophagus of Souls erupted was the only sound that had penetrated the protective layer of hide shielding Lanie from damage any worse than bruises. Sari shouted again when Cracchen—now mostly Irradiant—rose, glimmering, into the air. His feet dangled. His pale hair drifted up around his head like a halo. One eye had melted out of its socket, filled instead with blue flame. The other eye was still his own: icy aqua-green, mortal, and terrified.

Without the deep sight of death magic to call upon, Sari could not possibly know what was happening to her son. She could not see or hear the ghost. She could not see the glow overtaking Cracchen's body—only the effect it had on it: the levitation, the empty eye socket, the expression of pure terror. Nor could Sari see the shadows of the severed Sky Wizards that encircled her son like a tribe of lions. All of these events were invisible to her.

But Sari knew that her son was in peril. She tried to crawl across the floor to him, but she could not bear to let go of Scratten, whose corpse weighed her down.

Finally Lanie managed to battle herself loose of the tiger rug's panicked embrace. Spurring it back into the air, she rose to face the ghost. Her deep voice took up the Lahnessthanessar again. Her ravaged singing voice echoed it. Lanie looked directly into the blue-flame eye, and sang the Great Lullaby for her great-grandfather.

Her song was like a fishhook; the lure it dangled was irresistible; it *would* call the ghost out of Cracchen's sheltering body, as surely as the slow decay of the universe, and he would at last enter Doédenna's cloak for good.

Irradiant's face, clad in Cracchen's handsome accident, convulsed with fear. His body twitched uncontrollably. The blue flame flickered wildly in Cracchen's fire-scoured eye socket. His other eye, the human eye, rolled up in his head. The ghost knew that he could not stay within range of the Lahnessthanessar and not succumb to it. So he whipped his newly possessed self out of reach of Lanie's voices, out of the ruined gallery, out through the blown-out wall that Cracchen's cannon ball had made.

Flying as one body, Irradiant Stones and Cracchen Scratch fled the god of Death, pursued by a swarm of vengeful shadows, to a place where Sari's wail of despair could not follow.

Into the snow. Into the hematite sky. Into the north.

CHAPTER FORTY-THREE

Quietus

SARI WAS WHITER than Lanie had ever seen her. White like milk glass, like a lake in winter. She listened as Lanie explained what had just occurred, and seemed to sink deeper into herself, as her clothes darkened with her son's blood.

When Lanie was done talking, they sat in silence for a while. Sleet blew through the hole in the gallery wall. After a whispered exchange with Tan, Duantri left, and returned a few minutes later with an oil lamp from the library, and their coats and boots from the front hall. She was wearing her tunic again. When the light hit her face, Sari emerged from her long silence on a hitching breath that seemed to startle her.

"Will he ever come back?" she asked.

Lanie leaned back against Goody's bulk, across from the other women who were huddled around Scratten's body. She decided that Sari was speaking of her living son, not her dead one, and answered carefully. "He might in time fight free of his possession."

"And if he does not? If he *cannot?*"

Lanie felt herself nodding. She kept nodding until she forced herself to stop.

"If he cannot, it is likely that the ghost will... ride him... until his body is worn out. That might take years, even decades, depending on how hard he is used. After that, the ghost will probably dispose of Cracchen and find another, if he can." She grimaced. "Now that he has the way of it."

"Unless he is stopped," Tan put in, her voice as soft as Lanie's.

"Unless he is stopped," Lanie agreed.

"Will *you* stop him?" Sari croaked.

The day Saint Death embraced her—the day She brought the flowers back from ash—She had whispered in Lanie's ear, "*I have such work for you.*"

"Yes," Lanie said. "I will. I must. Listen, Sari." She leaned forward.

Sari lifted her gaze, meeting hers with such a hateful glitter, and yet such *hope*, that it momentarily stole Lanie's breath away.

"Irradiant Stones has entered Cracchen Skrathmandan's house. He has driven Cracchen's substance to the secret cellars of his own accident and sealed off Cracchen's access to the rest of himself. *But no house is completely sealed.* And Irradiant Stones will come to know that," she promised, "in the fullness of time. Even now, Cracchen will have begun to dig himself free—clawing at his foundations with his fingernails. He will give Irradiant such a fight as he has never seen since Iskald. That is the man—the warrior—you raised. But if Cracchen cannot free himself alone, Saint Death and I will do the rest. I will seek him out, and I will do the work set for me. And when I am done, your son will return to you. If—"

"—if your cure does not murder him first," Sari finished bitterly.

"I"—beneath her right hand, the fingers of her left hand curled—"I will learn to be gentle."

"Whatever my son does, from this day forward, it will be on you. Whatever that… that *thing* makes him do. It is on *your* head. You could have stopped this. You could have put her down"—Sari's chin stabbed like a dagger in Goody's direction—"anytime these last three years. That's what you told me when you came to me. But you did not. This is on you."

"And you," Tan put in, her voice low but firm, "could have given Lanie access to the revenant months ago. You decided to lick Bran Fiakhna's boots instead. That, Baroness, is on *you*."

"And this." Sari stroked a bloodied lock of Scratten's flaxen hair. "Whom shall I blame?"

Her gaze rose again. Met Lanie's again. Hers was not a question open to any other answer.

"I tried to make him leave," Lanie said. "I—"

Sari was not listening. She was smoothing her son's garments, murmuring, "He always wanted to be a hero. Like the Sky Wizards of legend. Like the ice giants, with their weapons made of frost and glass."

She kissed her son's hand. "He dreamed all his life of adventure, of noble sacrifice. But he stayed at my side despite that. Despite everything. He never complained. He learned this new language, accepted the change to his name. When we petitioned the Brackenwilds to change it back from Scratch to Skrathmandan, he said it was more trouble than it was worth. He *liked* Liriat!" she burst out, as if this were both insult and miracle.

"He had a joyful heart," said Duantri.

Sari's shoulders hunched. Again, she looked to Lanie, as if hers were the only face that anchored her.

"And now we must be enemies!" she cried, her voice as bewildered as a child's.

"You are not my enemy," Lanie replied. "I don't want that. I don't want any harm—any more harm—to come to you. Or your house."

"Then get out of my house."

Lanie pushed to her knees. "I will. I just need—"

"Get out of my house!" Sari surged up, her mouth a rictus, her hands claws.

But Duantri took hold of both her arms, and Tan's arms encircled her waist. They held her back as she struggled and thrashed, their faces full of sorrow.

"Five minutes!" Lanie begged her. "Five minutes, so I can sing Goody down. And Scratten, too. Sari, he can't linger like this. It isn't right. He'll grow confused. He'll be dissevered from Saint De… from Erre'Elur, if we don't sing for him. Please. Don't make me leave them out in the cold."

"Scratten?" Sari's voice was very small. "He's here?"

"He's here," Lanie said, and held out her left hand. She drew Scratten's shredded substance nearer, coaxing it into a more compact state.

There was a large piece of glass on the floor: a pane from Delirious Stones's poison cabinet. She picked it up and angled it in front of Sari so that it caught upon Scratten's shade. Blur, fog, shadow; but unmistakably he.

"Five minutes," Lanie whispered. "Please."

Instead of answering, Sari held out her hands for the pane. Lanie carefully handed it over, and Sari sank back down, holding the glass in her lap, poring over it with hungry eyes. Duantri kept a hand on one shoulder though, and Tan rested her chin on the other.

Duantri glanced across Scratten's corpse to Lanie and said softly, "And at the end of everything, I rest."

It was the first attitude of the twelfth set of sothaín, and Lanie felt the stillness of that phrase enter her. In that stillness, she heard the lowing of the Lahnessthanessar, like a wind blowing through the sinewy arches of a sorkhadari tree. It was still there, inside her. The song. Just below the surface.

But first, to wake Goody from her torpor. A different tune entirely.

Lanie began to hum.

"JHÍMIETI," SHE CALLED softly in both her voices, releasing the Maranathasseth Anthem back to its place of dancing. "Jhímieti, come to me. It's time."

Sluggish and colossal, Goody rolled over onto her back. The sleet blowing in from the hole in the gallery wall clung to her face and froze there, forming a crackling carapace of ice over the surface of her skin. Her eyes were pits, like the pit where her nose had been, and the hollow depressions that had been her ears. Irradiant Stones's substance had burnt them all away. And yet, there seemed in her expression some sign of recognition—not of Lanie, but of the name she had spoken:

Jhímieti.

Briefly, Lanie let her hand rise before her face in the Quadoni gesture for grief. All she could see were the lines of her own hand, her breath as it fogged against her palm. "Oh, Goody," she whispered. "Oh, Jhímieti. *Sa.*"

The twelfth and most abject of the Quadoni apologies was the truest word Lanie had ever spoken. It could be no louder than a breath; it was that fragile.

"Sa," she said again. Her voice ruptured on the repeat. She matched the broken word with another sothaín gesture—from the fifth set, belonging to Kywit the captured god: 'The Sky Goes Dark With Murdered, Singing Birds.'

Flinging out her arms like branches, she surrendered herself to the world's unending woes. Head thrown back, throat exposed, as if throwing her whole substance after that flight of phantom birds, she cried, "Sa!" a third time.

This time, she turned the cry into her Lahnessthanessar. Her second voice twinned in its drone, and Tan's weird, high keening sounded in counterpoint to Lanie's. Duantri joined in again, her voice darting like a swift through their intertwining lines.

All three sounds hung in the air, and together created a fourth sound, an overtone that hovered so delicately, so tremendously, over them all.

And burst.

And rained down such music that all their voices fell silent.

But the music went on.

The shredded remnants of Scratten Skrathmandan's substance lifted gracefully off the pane of glass where Lanie had caught it. He rose like mist into that music. Sari watched it happen in the reflective surface: her son—that spark of joy that was his alone, that had been his since babyhood—as he was borne through the doorway no living person could see. Then she let the pane of glass slide off her lap, and bent over her knees, and raised her arms to cover her head.

On the floor, Goody's furrowed face drank in the music. She made a sound—not groan or moan or sigh, but an utterance of unutterable relief—as waves of the Lahnessthanessar broke over her brow. Lanie stroked that beloved, brittle face, the hair that crumbled at her touch. She clung to Goody's long, strong fingers, like she had as a child. She wanted to apologize again, to never stop apologizing, for failing her at Midsummer. She wanted to tell Goody that she loved her. She wanted to thank her, to beg her pardon, to wish upon her the infinite peace of Saint Death's cloak. She wanted to ask that Goody remember her kindly when surrendering her memory back to the All-Marvel, the World Memory that belonged to the gods.

But nothing of this needed to be said. She had sung it all already. That longing *was* the lullaby.

Near the end, Goody lifted one large hand and laid it against Lanie's cheek. Her palm was not the arctic, unyielding surface it had always been; it was warm. A mother's hand. A final benediction.

Lanie leaned into it, and kissed her palm, and whispered, "Seroni seht."

Seroni seht, Mak had taught her, was what one said if—and only if—the twelfth and most abject apology, sa, had been offered and accepted, and forgiveness, granted.

Seroni seht, said the murderer, when given reprieve at the very foot of the gallows, a chance at new life.

Goody's hand on her cheek fell to ash. Lanie's tears ran black into her lap.

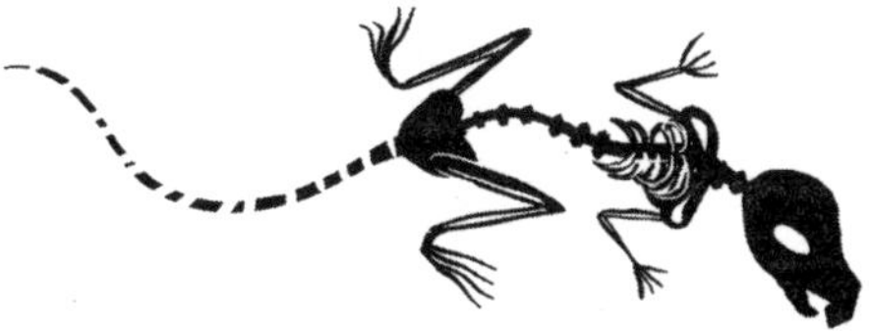

Part Five
THE BLACKBIRD BRIDEGROOM

One Month and Eight Days Later

CHAPTER FORTY-FOUR

A Stray Returns

Flameday 5th
Month of Vespers, 421 Founding Era
16 days till Winter Solstice

"But when we accompany Lanie to Quadiíb, what will become of Waystation Thirteen?" Tan fretted.

Her fretting was needless, fueled by wine. The decisions had already been made, their plans put into place. In a sennight, the Blackbird Bride would arrive with her nuptial procession and her new groom, Blood Royal Errolirrolin Brackenwild. But she would not find her 'Beloved Condor' within any of the Twelve Circles of Liriat Proper, for Lanie, along with Gyrlady Tanaliín and her Gyrgardu, would have already left the city the previous Dustday, on a riverboat making its way south on the Poxbarge River.

They were choosing to travel south rather than north, wanting to move away from the deepening winter rather than toward. When the riverboat reached the southernmost tip of Hannilor Barony, where the mouth of the Poxbarge emptied into the Glistring Sea, they would take the Isthmus of Ochre further south, then west into Lower Quadiíb. Lower Quadiíb, Tan had informed Lanie, was an entirely different world than Higher Quadiíb—culturally, linguistically, historically, and geographically—but, "well, you'll just see for yourself."

Ever since the decision had been made, Tan had been like an automaton that never wound down. She was already packed. She could barely stand to stay and finish the last bits of business left to her. Duantri, who was even more eager to leave, was also calmer and seemed to grow slower and more deliberate the more emphatic and worried her gyrlady became.

It had all come to a head that morning when Tan tried to pack Duantri's things for her. Duantri had calmly unpacked them all again, and then strewed everything all over the floor in pointed silence.

After that, they decided they needed an evening with friends, and a good deal to drink. A snowstorm had closed down most of the city's businesses that night, so Havoc and Lanie had hauled up the mulled wine to Waystation Thirteen, and they'd been drinking ever since.

Tan paced the pink and gold parlor, the wine having made her no less restless. It had had the opposite effect on Lanie, relaxing her to bonelessness. Havoc was curled on the couch beside her, amorous and affectionate. Duantri, with high roses in her cheeks and a dancing look in her eye, watched as Tan kept bringing up problems that she had already solved weeks ago.

"None of the erophains are quite ready, you know—though I place all my hopes in young Viquar. They have such administrative *potential.* It is just, I am not quite sure they yet have enough academic *experience*, and—"

"Oh, Tanaliín! My love! *Enough*, I pray!" Duantri cried in Quadic, slapping a pink satin cushion to the floor. The deeper she dove into her cups, the larger and more abrupt her movements became: the merry opposite of sothaín.

"Too long have we remained enmired here!" she continued. "The palace of our minds is *meant* to *move*—to walk the circuits and to soar on wings. We ventured west to build a nest for thought, and only see this aerie we have wrought!"

Her next gesture, requiring both hands and a dramatically pointed leg, encompassed the pink-and-gold receiving parlor and all the rooms of the Waystation beyond it.

"Our fledglings' feathers now must needs be dried, the skills we taught them likewise stretched and tried. And anyway"—she switched mid-breath back to Lirian—"if Viquar's inexperience worries you so, sign the property over to Havoc."

Havoc looked up, startled. "What now?"

"She will turn our school back into a brothel," Duantri went on cheerfully. "And be very rich and popular, and take for her lover the Eparch of the Holy Temple of Sappacor, and be made a baroness of this befouled city!"

Duantri had never made a secret of her homesickness, or of her dislike for Liriat Proper. She thought it needed, among other things: sewerage, an expanded university, and a better music scene. But her love for Tan was such that she would follow her gyrlady into a midden if Tan saw potential academics living at the bottom of one. (In Liriat Proper, the Gyrgardu rather thought she had.)

Havoc's sea-gray eyes narrowed in amusement. "Yeah, right. Might be I'd take ya up on that, goofbird. This place wasn't so bad, as brothels go. Put the 'pearl' back in Pearl of Pleasure." She tapped Lanie's nose. "You, though. Swear you'll come back and sample all my pearly wares once that Blackbird's forgot her crush on you."

"I will," Lanie promised. "I really, really will. If you scratch my head right now."

Havoc obliged, but addressed Tan: "Ya know, Lady Tan—whatever Viquar and the other erophains need, I got their backs. But tits and pickles, as fer runnin' the damned place, I got my hands full with the Lover's Complaint!"

"I do not expect you, Mistress Havoc, to run Waystation Thirteen," Tan informed her—but really Duantri—with a hint of haughty frostiness. "For one, you are *not* a gyrlady of Quadiíb. For two..." Distracted by Lanie's giggle, she said, "Well, she is *not*. And Viquar is not either, yet. Though they will be by the time we leave. A Gyrveard, I mean; they wouldn't use 'lady' unless they were floomping for festival, which they occasionally do. It has been many a long century since the Gyrladies of Quadiíb were solely Gyr*ladies,* but Quadiíb is slow to give up its more archaic linguistic traditions, as you might well imagi—"

Recognizing that Tan was about to launch into one of her lectures, Lanie interrupted, "Havoc, have we run out of wine?"

The answer was obvious. The glass carafe, which rested in the silver cradle of its warming stand, was empty, the tea light that had been burning beneath it all but snuffed.

Havoc gazed at the carafe with soulful and despairing eyes, and then heaved a deep sigh. "Ah, Cookie." She shook her head sadly. "I try takin' those stairs right now, I'd lose the only workin' leg I got. Not," she added slyly, "that I'm opposed to someone else goin' down and fetchin' her friends a refill. Big pot o' the stuff's just simmerin' away on my kitchen stove, waitin' for some bright young necromancer with a cute bow to claim it fer her own."

She tugged the pink ribbon in Lanie's braids until it came undone, then snapped it neatly away from her.

"Go on an' get us more wine, Cookie," she suggested. "Come back, an' I'll give ya yer bow back. And a kiss."

"How could I resist?"

Lanie heaved herself to her feet. She was not dizzy, just silky in her limbs. She tended to nurse her cup for hours, sipping from it only when she felt her mind drifting too far from the room and her companions. At those times, the taste of something warm and complex recalled her to herself, out of her encroaching sadness. Or worse, numbness. What better than Havoc's mulled wine to bring her back? It was a pleasure just to swirl it around and watch the colors. Better still to stick her nose in the cup and inhale: the chewy weight of the Abrothoss red—a barony famed as much for its wineries as its cider mills—star anise, cardamom, clove, cinnamon, Havoc's favorite smuggled cognac, briarbark syrup for sweetness, and the perfect finish: an orange slice that recalled Doédenna's own perfume.

"I'll be right back," Lanie said, taking the carafe. She heard the edges of her words softening. Not quite slurring. Not yet.

Duantri bounced up, smiling very kindly down at her. "But say the word and in thy stead I'll go—for thou art looking dreamy and beguiled. Methinks that if thou sink'st into the couch, thy louche and loving friend will scratch thy head, and send thee to a pleasant dream of bed."

"Volunteerin' me, are ya?" Havoc grinned. "All right, then. C'm'ere, Cookie. It bein' winter, there's fewer customers, and thus fewer dishes to wash. Hence, nice long nails on yers truly."

She wiggled her right hand, which, except for its missing pinkie finger,[37] sported very fine, very clean, very sharp nails indeed.

Lanie immediately thrust the decanter at Duantri and flopped down onto the couch again, declaring in Quadic, "Thou surely art a doughty sparrowhawk!"

This time, she heard herself slur. They all did.

"Yea, even into snow and cold I go," the Gyrgardu declared nobly, "for wine and spice and merry times must flow. I'll fetch us pastries powdery and sweet to slake my drunken hankering to eat. And eat, and eat," she added solemnly, like a bell ringing.

"And eat, and eat!" Lanie repeated in sing-song, waving one hand like a conductor's baton.

Havoc protested with mock horror, "Eatin' me outta booze and biz! Don't you all got food in your own kitchen or wherever?"

"Oh, we ran out of Eidie's pastries this morning," Tan explained. "Duantri tends to take the last of them and not tell anyone they are gone. But she knows where you keep your stash."

"All right, goofbird." Havoc narrowed laughing eyes at Duantri. "*Yer* on pastry run tomorrow. Refill my stash and yers, and I'll reimburse ya. Either way, get all yer favorites."

"Everything Eidie makes is my favorite," Duantri replied in Lirian. "I only have five days left to taste everything he makes before I shake this Lirian hoozzaplo from off my boots!"

"You are still here," Tan reminded her. "And we have no more wine."

Her Gyrgardu sighed wistfully, gazing out the door. "But the Lover's Complaint is so far away!"

"It ain't but a few stories downstairs!" Havoc protested. "Even I can make it!" She thumped her right leg.

"It's far enough," Duantri shivered, "when like a thorny branch, the wind doth pierce my heart and freeze my nips."

Havoc fell sideways on the couch, laughing. "Yer nips! That ain't Quadic."

"It is so Quadic!" Duantri insisted, in Lirian.

"I'll go, I'll go!" Lanie wallowed to her feet. It was harder this time. "We must... we must protect your nips!"

---

37 No two people ever received the same story regarding this missing digit. But every story always contained: a key, a saint, a seawall, a man in red, and a boat made all of glass. Havoc Dreadnought only ever told the true tale once, and never again. See Footnote 34.

Havoc flung herself across the couch and started tickling Lanie until she collapsed into the cushions again.

"Quick, Duantri—'fore she escapes and breaks her drunk neck on those stairs. Never mind yer nips! What're a coupla snow stiffies 'tween friends, eh?"

Duantri, assuming a scandalized expression, clasped her hands to her bosom, and dashed out the door.

But she was back sooner than any of them expected, carrying neither food nor wine.

At first Lanie mistook the muddy bundle for a small snow sculpture that had suffered the territorial spoliations of every free-ranging dog who trotted the spokes and alleys of Seventh Circle. But the expression on Duantri's face alerted her it was no such thing. She had only seen the Gyrgardu look like that once, at Skrathmandan.

And then, two filthy paws popped out of the bundle and flopped over the crook of Duantri's elbow.

A wet muzzle followed. Then, a pair eyes the color of a bluet damselfly as it catches the sun. His fur was a motley patchwork of black and white and gray, and even caked in mud and soaking wet, those lurid shades gleamed more brightly than the brightest colors in the parlor. A sort of saddle bag was belted over his waist, right over the place where his death wound had been crusted over with Ajdenia's emeralds. Lanie leapt to her feet. She immediately swayed, and Tan rushed to catch her.

"Datu?" she cried. "Was there any sign of—"

"He was alone," Duantri reported. "He was crying. Just outside the Waystation door. He came right into my arms."

Lanie sank, heavy, to the floor.

SHE SPENT THE next day fussing over the puppy and brooding over Mak's alarming letter, the sole content of that little saddlebag. The message had been rolled in enameled cloth that smelled strongly of linseed oil ("smells like home," Havoc said, not nostalgically), but the waterproofing wasn't perfect, and the writing was marred by large blots and splotches from the journey.

Mizka—

First, I must ask forgiveness for the way we parted. If we meet again, I will make the eighth (BLOTCH) *—ogy and hope for* (BLOTCH)

are sending you (BLOTCH) *—ar Stones* (BLOTCH) *—ccording to the directives you left with Datu, should she find herself in* (BLOTCH)

—ave been told there are three Parliamentary wizards in (BLOTCH) *—nocking at every door in the village.*

They are here for us. Datu is prepared. She has given the cub his instructions.

I know you will take care of him. You must, for he holds Datu's (BLOTCH) *in his gods-blessed body.*

I have come to love him as much as I love (BLOTCH) *and to better understand the words with which I chastised you, but with too much wrath and in too much haste:*

The binding goes both ways.

In Quadic, Mak added:

Please keep him safe, my heart's own cherished sister. And keep'st thou safe as well, and far from harm.

Makkovian Covan

Those last two words, *Makkovian Covan*, were a revelation. But Lanie forced herself to put that aside, on a shelf of herself that she promised she would one day return to. She then tried decoding the meaning *-ar Stones*, but couldn't quite manage it, due to the blotches.

The answer to that riddle, it turned out, lay not in the letter but in the puppy's collar. That slim leather braid was so slabbed with filth that at first Lanie had not distinguished it from the puppy's general coating of muck and debris.

But once he was scrubbed clean, Havoc (who'd fallen in love with him on sight) was the first to point out the bright, round tag hanging from his collar. The tag was pressed from what Lanie recognized as the silver steeple she'd given her niece on Midsummer. Both the iconography on the obverse side and the punch-mark on the reverse side had been rubbed smooth, the obverse then etched in minute, precise lettering with the words: *Underwear 'Undies' Stones*.

In the name, Lanie recognized Datu's sense of humor—even though, for as long as Lanie had known her, her niece didn't have one.

Only after the puppy was bathed and dried by Havoc's kitchen fireside, had endured a close interrogation from the necromancer who had brinked him from the abyss of death—"What happened? Where's Datu? Did you walk all the way from Umrys-by-the-Sea?" ("Swam, more like," said Havoc)—and been released when he did no more than lick Lanie and Havoc on every available surface, did Undies settle into the state that Lanie had come to understand as torpor. Just as she had observed in Goody at Skrathmandan, but doubly so: body slightly cooler than skin temperature; eyes open but fixed, the supernatural glow of them not snuffed but dimmed; heartbeat slowed to about twenty beats per minute; breath so light it did not fog the mirror Lanie held to his muzzle.

Undies must have expended a great deal of energy traveling to Liriat

Proper. Lanie was afraid that he had been drawing his energy directly from Datu. She hoped that by letting him sleep—or 'brumate,' as Tan termed it—Datu would be able to gain back any strength she might have lost.

And then, the day after the pup's first full day with them, on Rainday morning, the first wound appeared on his body.

WOKEN BEFORE DAWN by a sharp, pained yelp, Lanie scrambled through her covers to find Undies convulsing. Gathering him in her arms, she watched as a fine line of emeralds blossomed at his throat. Like a sickle. Like a smile. The jewels pulsed with a weird green glitter for a few seconds, then were subsumed back into his fur. They were like Aganath's icebergs that rise in defense of her island nation when enemy fleets threaten its shores, then fall again when the threat passes.

The puppy soon stopped convulsing. He sank into his silent brumation, and was so still his fur never trembled.

Later, sitting in front of a breakfast she could not eat, Lanie told Tan and Havoc: "I think he took a wound meant for Datu."

She caressed Undies' ears, gently. They were not cold like Goody's had been. She remembered how the puppy's body had matched itself to Datu's—breath, warmth, heartbeat—on the day that Lanie had bound them, life and undeath, to each other.

"And that means—"

"—some blackbird tried slittin' her throat," Havoc finished grimly from behind the bar. She'd be opening to the public in a quarter of an hour, and though she had scrubbed everything the night before, there were always surfaces, in her opinion, that needed polishing.

"And did *not* succeed," Tan added, seeing the gray look on Lanie's face.

"Not yet," Lanie whispered. "But how much life is shared between them? And how much undeath can sustain them? *This* is what Mak meant—this!—when he warned me that the binding goes both ways."

"There are stories. More in the nature of myths, really. About ancient sorcerers and the pacts they made with their death god."

Tan threaded her fingers together. Her face took on its faraway look.

"I was lately trying to recall the subject of Gelethai's thesis. I was one of the reviewers on her dissertation committee—oh, about a decade and a half ago. It was the last committee I ever sat on, before Duantri and I departed Quadiíb. Gelethai was studying Quadoni pre-history—those dark days before we came into balance with the Twelve. According to those myths, we Quadoni once had our fair share of necromancers..."

"According to you," Lanie interrupted, "you still do. But only in the month of Vespers."

Tan shrugged and looked secretive, which was mostly for show. Since the beginning of that month, she had been privately tutoring Lanie in the twelve sacred rites of Doédenna, each of which corresponded with one of the twelve attitudes in the twelfth set of sothaín. These were the rites the Gyrladies of Quadiíb practiced during Vespers—called in Quadic 'Edenna' and in Skaki 'Elurra.'

"In any case," Tan continued, "it is probably through Gelethai that young Makkovian Covan came to know those old tales. Though," she added with some asperity, "it sounds to *me* as if he understood them rather imperfectly. But the contents of his letter—such as we can decipher them—assure me that he has come to appreciate the complexities of death magic, rather than..."

She trailed off as Duantri blew into the Lover's Complaint. She did not enter by the front door but from the kitchen. Her black curls were windblown, her brown skin wet and flushed. She was not wearing any shoes.

Undies stirred in Lanie's lap, paws paddling. He shivered before opening his eyes and climbing up onto Lanie's shoulder to peer curiously over it.

"That's Duantri," Lanie explained quietly. "Remember her? And there's Tan. And your favorite—Havoc—right over there."

Havoc went from being 'right over there' to 'give me that puppy immediately' in a few steps. Taking Undies in her arms, she started crooning into his fur: "Heya, mutt. Heya, fuzz-face. You know, Master Underwear, sir, I ain't a cute dog person. I'm an ugly dog person. But I swear by my skivvies, yer enough to melt my wizened heart. Yeah. Yeah, go on lookin' at me like that, I'll give you anythin' you want. Includin' my skivvies. All right, you. Enough flirtin'. Go on back to Aunt Lanie now. Me, I gotta give Aunt Duantri a toddy."

Reluctantly, she handed him back to Lanie and pointed Duantri to a stool at the bar. "You," she ordered, "sit. Drink up. It's hot. Aganath's dorsal fin, Duantri—yer hardly wearin' a stitch!"

Duantri accepted the mug from Havoc's hand and drank thirstily, the bare skin on her arms rippling with pleasure as the warmth hit her. Tan came to stand behind her and rubbed her shoulders.

"Did you see them, beloved? How close are they?"

Duantri had been flying out every morning to watch the Blackbird Bride's nuptial procession make its way down the Leechward North, the road that led all the way from Iskald, ruined capital of Northernmost Skakmaht, to the Isthmus of Ochre in southernmost Liriat. It passed, inevitably, through Liriat Proper. The procession was a mile-long line of carts, carriages, coaches, and sleighs, and included several hundred nobles of Rookery Court, their servants and animals, and at least eight hundred horses. The northern baronies had been playing host to the procession on the final legs of its journey—bankrupting themselves, rumor had it, to entertain the Blood Royal and his Blackbird Bride—and in just five days' time, it would arrive at Liriat Proper.

Also in that procession, Lanie knew, were Haaken Skrathmandan and

Canon Lir. She dreaded the arrival of the first, longed for the second. But she herself would be gone from the city days before they next set foot in it.

"The procession continues apace," Duantri reported. "I flew out for two hours, maybe more. They are only fifty miles away now. They never travel more than twelve miles a day. Less, if the roads or weather are bad. Most of the Parliament of Rooks flies above the line, sometimes sending out single spies, sometimes branching out in formation. If I dared to come within a mile of them, they would surely mob me. Most of Bran Fiakhna's wizard-birds are large enough to eat me in my falcon form," she added philosophically, "so I kept well back and hovered. If they saw me, they did not think me worth chasing."

"Any sight of…?" Lanie bit her tongue. Surely if Duantri had seen either Datu or Mak, she would have said it first thing. And even if she had seen them, what could Lanie do about it? Her duty was to leave Liriat Proper with Undies safely in her charge. It was their best chance of preserving Datu's life.

Behind Duantri, Tan twitched. She drummed her fingers on the seat of a barstool and jittered one foot.

"I know we plan to leave the day after tomorrow," she said. "But perhaps we should see if we cannot book passage on another riverboat, one that departs tomorrow. Or tonight, even…"

"Tanaliín," Duantri said gently, "there are no earlier boats. You know this. We were lucky to find anything so late in the year. We were lucky," she added, "that the Poxbarge did not freeze over."

"It never freezes," Lanie said, surprised. "But then, I don't remember it ever being this cold."

As if the word were the thing itself, Undies started shivering in her lap. In another second, he was stiffening, panting rapidly. Lanie looked from Havoc, just going to unlatch her front door, to Tan, whose shrewd eyes were fixed on Undies' form. Lanie said quietly, "It's happening again. I don't want to distress Havoc, or upset her customers. I'd better go."

"Report back later!" Tan called after her as Lanie whisked the puppy from the tap room.

By the time she had sprinted down the hall and slammed the door to her bedroom, the puppy's fur had begun to smoke.

It was heavy smoke, black and oily. It belched sparks. It crackled, bloomed—but only for a few angry seconds. Then, abruptly, Undies was enveloped in emeralds. He became, as he lay in Lanie's arms, a jewel-encrusted statue of a wolf cub. Even his eyes were covered in emeralds, although Lanie could see, behind the faceted gems, the lights of them.

She collapsed on her bed, rocking back and forth, the cold, hard puppy pressed close to her breast. The tiger rug, which had followed her home from Skrathmandan, slithered up from the foot of the bed and draped itself over both her and the puppy, the entire striped length of it one long purr.

As she rocked, Lanie hummed tunelessly, helplessly. Neither the Maranathasseth Anthem nor the Lahnessthanessar could help Undies now. Or Datu either. Saint Death had done Her part for them already. This *was* the miracle. It was beyond the miracle she had meant to ask for, even.

And yet it was still not enough.

Phosphorescing faintly, the flowers in their glass vase chimed at her from the desk by the porthole window.

They had never faded since the day Saint Death brought them back. In their near-noiseless sound, Lanie could still hear her god whispering: "*I have such work for you.*"

"Keep her safe. I'll keep you safe." Lanie kissed the puppy's cold, green-glimmering brow with trembling lips. "Keep her safe. I'll keep you safe," she chanted, over and over again. "She won't have you both. She'll never have you both."

But running to the ends of Athe with Datu's undead wolf cub in tow wasn't a solution, and Lanie knew it. It was only a delaying tactic. Right now, the nature of Undies' resurrection was buying a captive Datu a little more time. It would be time wasted if Lanie used it to run, as Mak had wanted her to.

After what may have been hours, Undies' panoply of emeralds finally vanished back into his too-bright fur. The puppy squeak-whined, and looked up at Lanie with piteous white-blue eyes. He weakly licked her wrist before snuggling down into the tiger rug and slipping into his deepest torpor yet.

Lanie didn't think it was just her panic that she was seeing in his torpor a new, more exhausted stillness, an ebbing-away of that precious energy he was trying to preserve. His skin was cooler to the touch now, the light in his wide-open eyes dimmer. His heartbeat was at fifteen beats per minute.

That night, with Undies tucked away with Havoc in her kitchen, curled up snugly on the tiger rug and royally entertained by her sea-chanteys, stories of merrowmaids, of nokken knights astride their seahorse mounts, and other dreamfolk of the deep, Lanie went up to Waystation Thirteen. She sat Tan and Duantri down on their pink parlor couch, and stood before them in unconscious imitation of the portrait of General Ham-Handed Stones addressing his Direwolves at the Battle of the Poxbarge, her arms at parade rest, her feet wide apart.

Tan opened her mouth, but before she could say anything, Lanie cut her off.

"He's dying. Which means she is. Our original plan won't work. Neither will Mak's. We need a new one."

"You have one already," Duantri said softly.

"Yes." Lanie hesitated. "But you're not going to like the first part."

"What is the first part?" Tan asked warily.

"You have to leave without me."

CHAPTER FORTY-FIVE

Condor

Brineday 13th
Month of Vespers, 421 Founding Era
8 days till Winter Solstice

LANIE WATCHED LORD Ambassador Haaken Skrathmandan, formerly Hatchet Scratch, through the tower window of the Ambassadorial Palace of Skakmaht. Though she was bundled in winter coat, scarf (Havoc had knitted it herself), gloves, a hat pulled low over her braids, several pairs of stockings, and three layers of clothes, the fact was, that at seven stories up, at night, in winter, with a high wind blowing and no trees tall enough to break it, Lanie was colder than she had ever been.

Or perhaps the profounder chill came from her proximity to Haaken's wards. Lanie feared them almost as much as she feared the Blackbird Bride. Her left arm ached as if all her bones—humerus, tibia, and fibula, all the tiny carpals, metacarpals, and phalanges—were growing spurs and spikes, pushing her veins and muscles out of their way and bursting through her skin.

Ever since the ambassador's return with the nuptial procession the day before, his palace had shone to Lanie's deep sight. Magic lit it like moonlight beaming down upon some floating tower of ice calved from a mountainous glacier. Haaken had warded the place like a man who feared destruction from without and within. Like a man who'd lost not only his homeland, but both of his brothers and the house he had left them in, the house he had tried to make safe for them, and now ice was all the comfort and protection that remained. The only armor that might keep a death wound at bay.

Haaken's expression, on the other side of his tower window, was remote. He was bent over something on his desk, writing a letter, or perhaps building something. His wards fractured all the details, frosted over subtleties.

Lanie floated in the freezing darkness on the back of her tiger rug, watching him, dithering, shivering, wondering if she had the courage to knock.

No, not wondering. She knew she would do what she had come here to do. She just had to brace herself for it.

And so, although she feared them, Lanie drew close enough to Haaken's wards to smell them. The faint scent reminded her of Doédenna's resurrection bouquet: a memory of flowers, trapped in ice. She was close enough to feel the wards activating. A slow-moving shimmer moved through them, then a sliver of quickening silver that read her component parts: living accident (herself), dead accident (the tiger rug), and her substance, which flowed fluidly between both accidents.

She sensed in the wards an uncertainty, as if they could not quite decide what to do with her. They recognized her as a repeat offender; they knew that they had rebuffed her advances once before. If she reached out to touch them, they would doubtless zap her all the way back to childhood.

But Lanie did not think they would attack unprovoked. No doubt they were reporting her presence to the man behind the window.

When the wards dropped and the window opened, she loosed a sharp sigh of relief.

Haaken Skrathmandan looked her right in the eye. "Would you like to come in, Miscellaneous Stones?"

"Thank you, Ambassador," said Lanie, and flew into the tower room without further ado.

HE WAS AS pale as his mother had been when Lanie last saw her, dressed head to toe in heavy white velvet, broidered in silver. Silver egrets interthreaded with silver foxes. Or perhaps they were all dragons. His startling eyes were bloodshot and red-rimmed. His face seemed a different shape than she remembered it: hollowed out, those hollows filled with shadows. Fine lines etched his forehead and the corners of his mouth and eyes. A new razor sharpness honed his bones, as if he had been stropped by grief.

Lanie hopped down off the tiger rug. It furled itself into a roll and leaned against her leg. The tiger's glass eyes stared at Haaken, before turning its head to stare at something else. Something on the desk.

A pane of glass.

Lanie recognized it as a piece of Delirious Stones's poison cabinet. A very particular piece. It was this that she had observed Haaken working so intently on. He had apparently been wrapping the edges of the glass in jute rope, making a frame for it, and fixing the frame in place with a small pot of knacker's glue.

Lanie lightly brushed the pane with her fingernail. "It's empty, you know. He won't come back through this way."

"I know."

"Were you... were you hoping that it might be a window?"

Haaken joined her at the desk and held his hand over the glass. Not touching it, just holding it there. Soon, the broken pane was frosted over with snowflakes. They swirled and clustered and finally settled into the shape of Scratten's face. That sweet smile. That look of wonder. His final farewell.

"An impression remains," Haaken murmured. He did not at all talk like his brothers. His deep voice held the same strange, slow vowels and clipped consonants that Lanie sometimes heard in Sari's, when the baroness wasn't remembering to be careful. "As when a child presses their nose to a window pane, and later, when it is night and the glass grows cold, a warm breath might reveal the old print upon it."

He paused, then looked over at her again. "It is not a window. It is just a memorial."

And he had been weeping over it, Lanie knew. She took a respectful step back from the glass.

"I came," she said, "to request a favor. But before I do, I wanted to ask if you had any questions for me. While I did my best to explain to Sari what happened at Skrathmandan, I'm not sure what she retained. And I wanted to be sure you... you knew."

"Mordda retained enough," Haaken replied evenly. "Her account of events was precise, if not unbiased."

Lanie let out a soft, "Ha."

Haaken cocked his head at the humorless sound. His pale hair fell across his brow. It had grown longer since he had left Liriat for Rook with Canon Lir that summer. Long enough to braid. Both Cracchen and Scratten had kept theirs fighting-short.

"However," he said, turning slightly but keeping his gaze sidelong upon her, "I would not object if you were to tell me a more complex version of events. I would interview your tiger rug if I could glean from it a fresh perspective. I would speak with the two Quadoni women who accompanied you, and all the spirits in the Almasquin. I would even interrogate your great-grandfather's ghost, were he in my power." His mouth quirked, not in a smile. "Though that is not all I would do to him, were he in my power."

Lanie nodded. "Understood." Clasping her hands behind her back, she relayed the events of that night as simply and clearly as she could.

When she was done, Haaken paced the octagonal room in three slow circuits, head bowed, staring pensively at the floor. When he came to a rest, he commented, "Mordda is under the impression that you will soon go north. To exorcise the ghost possessing my brother, if you can."

"I can, and I will," Lanie replied grimly. "But my route must perforce be circuitous. I'll get there. I just... I have some business here first. Older business. I hope you know that I… that I don't lightly delay my work in the north."

Haaken's gaze met hers with what seemed to her sincere curiosity. "Do you think I do not know what it is," he asked, "to delay one's life-work in favor of former obligations? Sometimes we have promises to keep. Sometimes we ourselves are that promise, sworn by others, to others." His mouth twisted again. "But not for much longer."

"If your release from your prior obligation is imminent, I congratulate you." Lanie pushed her spectacles up the bridge of her nose. "Do you have any other questions for me? Wizard to wizard?"

Haaken took the pane of glass in its jute-rope frame and walked it over to one of the walls. He ceremoniously hung it on a nail apparently placed there for that purpose, and stepped back to stare into the transparent surface. His snowflakes had faded.

"Just one question," he said, his back still turned to her. "On a different subject. What of after? When you have sent Irradiant Stones through Erre'Elur's doorway. When Cracchen is free. What then?"

"After?" Lanie asked blankly.

"Indulge me."

She shrugged, even knowing he could not see her. "I find it hard to imagine surviving Irradiant Stones."

But that was a lie—or at least, not as true as it once had been. And Lanie owed Haaken, if she owed anyone anything, honesty. She began again.

"I've always thought, since I was a child, that I was meant to serve the Blood Royal Brackenwilds my whole life long. Just as soon as I was old enough. Powerful enough. The Stoneses have always done so, ever since the Founding."

Touching her reliquary pendant, which hung inside her winter gear, Lanie felt the black walnut and beaten copper, warm from lying against her skin. She wanted to trickle her substance through it and into Canon Lir's own pendant, to make it buzz against their breast. But they would not—could not—answer her in like manner. And that silence was growing lonelier every day.

Lanie saw that Haaken was waiting for her to finish.

"Service to the Brackenwilds, it turns out, is not to be my lot. I am called to Doédenna's service, starting with the north—if not ending there," she finished in a mutter. "Anyway, Errolirrolin Brackenwild has found himself a new sorcerous alliance in his Blackbird Bride. I'm sure he will not miss a mere Stones mucking about his cryptyard for materials."

She met Haaken's patient regard. She wondered if he, like his mordda, considered himself her enemy. Nothing was more likely. But there was that in his gaze which reminded Lanie of her friends. Haaken's was not a warmth like Duantri's, nor was there in him much evidence of the tenderness Mak was capable of. Haaken was more like Tan, with her beacon-black eyes that shone their penetrating lights on everyone with equal curiosity. Or like Havoc, ready with her wry smile and dry wit and her life's load of hard-bought wisdom. Or like Canon Lir, who, when you stood in front of them, no matter how you babbled, listened as if you were the only person in all of Athe.

Perhaps an enemy *would* listen like that, Lanie thought, in order to turn your words against you later. But she didn't think Haaken would.

He seemed to accept her answer as satisfactory. He walked back across the room, gestured for her to sit opposite him, and folded his hands on his desk.

"What is the favor you came to inquire of me, Miscellaneous Stones?"

She adjusted her glasses again, and considered asking him to call her Lanie. She did not. She did not think that he would oblige her anymore than Canon Lir ever did. "Information. Where is my niece?"

A fractional pause, before Haaken answered in his slow, steady way: "Ynyssyll's Tooth."

Lanie had to swallow several times before she could be sure of her voice. The tower at Castle Ynyssyll was where the Brackenwilds kept prisoners until they were executed. She cleared her throat. "And where is her father?"

"He is being kept under guard at the castle." Haaken looked down at his long hands. "He… the Blackbird Bride says she means to treat him well. When all of this is over. He will be released and"—another infinitesimal pause—"compensated."

Lanie let out a very careful, "Oh?"

"The Blackbird Bride," Haaken continued, "has stated publicly that she does not blame the gyrgardi for the death of her former Bobolink. That murder was committed, after all, in defense of his young—and in Rook that would be his right. But she is not without… subtlety. Or vindictiveness. And so, to ensure the safety of her new Parliament, she has"—his pauses were becoming smoother, shorter, less noticeable, but Lanie was onto him now; Haaken Skrathmandan found Bran Fiakhna's justice as loathsome as she did—"clipped his wings."

"She did *what?*"

Haaken vented a short sigh. Gesturing for her to stay seated, he rose and slipped behind a small painted screen.

Half-hidden behind the screen, resting on his mother's mirrored vanity table, was a long clear casket bound on both ends with short leather straps. The short straps were attached to a longer strap, such as a courier might wear slung over her chest. When he returned to his desk, Haaken was carrying the casket in both hands. He laid it down—across his lap, not upon the desk—with reverence. This close to it, Lanie noticed two things:

The casket was made, not of glass, but ice.

Inside the ice, preserved, was Mak's arm.

It was unmistakable. So clear was the ice, so perfectly pristine, that Lanie could see them gleaming: the silvery traces of his Bryddongard.

She did not know what of her shock showed on her face. Something must have, for Haaken said in a low, passionate voice, "I could not allow this gods-touched object to undergo further profanation. I have never seen its like. I cautioned the Blackbird Bride against dissevering it from its trunk. But *she*"—Lanie did not imagine it this time; she saw Haaken's lip curl with revulsion—"believes herself to be all twelve gods in one. She does not recognize any god but herself."

Lanie wanted, more than anything, to snatch that frozen casket from Haaken. She wanted to return the arm to its rightful owner. And then she wanted to watch as Mak took his falcon form and brought down four-and-twenty blackbirds—starting with the Rook of Rook.

In the last five days, Bran Fiakhna had tried slitting her niece's throat, setting her on fire, drowning her, smothering her, and pulling her apart, if Lanie had been correctly interpreting the shifting emerald armaments upon Underwear Stones's poor little body.

And now she had maimed Makkovian Covan for life.

Mak. Whose highest crime in youth had been being kind to a Stones.

She imagined Rook and falcon locked in combat. Pecking at each other. Plummeting through the air. She imagined falcon ripping the wings from Rook's body, the beak from her mouth, the heart from her chest. She imagined Makkovian Covan laying Bran Fiakhna's rookish heart in the palm of Lanie's hand. She imagined eating it.

The violence of her thoughts battered her body, but Lanie's allergy was no longer what it once had been. It calmed as soon as she did. It was almost too easy to be calm—or rather, to be numb and cold and ready to do whatever needed to be done.

"May I?" Lanie held out her hands. Haaken hesitated. "I will send it on to safety," she promised. The tiger rug nodded against her knee, quivering with readiness, already anticipating its next duty. "If… if I can win him free, I swear I'll reunite Makkovian Covan with his arm as soon as may be."

Haaken's mouth quirked again. This time, she was almost sure it was a smile. "Then I had better tell you how the thing is done, necromancer," he told her, "since you will not know which gods to call on, or which words to speak, when the time comes to do so."

"I'd appreciate that, sky wizard," Lanie retorted, "I'll convey your regards on that day."

But here she stopped, and abruptly discarded her nervous, furious glibness. Her left hand opened and shut, opened, shut.

She leaned over the desk suddenly and fiercely, and said, "Haaken Skrathmandan, I cannot thank you sufficiently here and now. But I *will* free your brother from my great-grandfather's ghost. I *will* do whatever I can to help wake the Guilded Council from their deathsleep. And if you ever call on me for aid, I *will* answer you. I swear it!"

"I know you will, Miscellaneous Stones," Haaken replied. "Why else do you think I am helping you?"

And then his mouth relaxed into its first true smile, and they nodded at each other.

"When do you go to Castle Ynyssyll?" he asked.

"Directly."

"Then I will be quick but thorough in my explanations. And, I believe"—his face was as cold and remote as the moon—"collector of the marvelous though I may be, I will stay far from Moll's Kopje tonight."

"*That*, ambassador," Lanie said, "would be for the best."

OF THE SEVERAL items of interest Haaken had relayed to her, foremost was this: rumor at the newly unified Brackenwild Rookery Court had it that the necromancer Miscellaneous Stones was seen boarding a riverboat with two Quadoni women four days earlier. The Blackbird Bride had been outspokenly disappointed about this. She had hoped to have Lanie as an honored guest at her wedding, which had taken place earlier that day.

Lanie did not mind having missed it.

She walked to the castle drawbridge from the Ambassadorial Palace of Skakmaht, the tiger rug being otherwise occupied. Nothing in First Circle was far from anything else in First Circle. As she approached the gatehouse, she saw that the usual guard had been trebled. Not only were there soldiers in Brackenwild livery, but Bright Knights from the Holy Temple of Sappacor were in attendance as well, and at least one Rookish wizard in his human form. None of them, it seemed, had been expecting her—which was just as Lanie had hoped—but the wizard knew her at once.

His eyes widened. They were pale gray—almost white—but for a thin band of black around his irises. His peculiar eyes, along with his wizard marks (wide stripes of slate-gray slashing sideways down his black face, a patch of gray covering the nape of his neck, and two more that bleached his hands to the beds of his fingernails, which were long and curved and glossy black) gave Lanie a clue as to his bird form. The black-and-gray feathers of his close-fitting tunic confirmed it. Even his hair echoed the theme: the front half of it was a crest of oil-slick black, the back half shone like gray quartz.

When he grinned at her—a very toothy grin—it was so winsome and unexpected that Lanie's own mouth twitched in response. He made her an utterly flamboyant, bow.

"Condor!" he said with a start. "You make me the happiest of men! Oh, how our glorious bride will shower me with favors and kisses! Oh!

That it was *I* who am chosen—I, the favored one!—who shall escort you to her side!"

"Jackdaw," Lanie greeted him, hoping her guess was correct.

It was, for he grinned again. "Spoken like a true king, Condor!" And then he giggled, perhaps the tiniest bit maliciously, but not at Lanie's expense.

"Won't Pied Crow cry a piebald tear that her auguries prophesied you not at all? You know, at first," he went on chattily, "when our bride assigned me to this, my lonely watch duty, out here in the dark and cold, beyond the pale—that is to say, beyond the moat!—with all these featherless nincompoops"—he indicated the Lirian soldiers and Bright Knights (most remained stoic, some muttered or rolled their eyes, giving Lanie the general impression that Jackdaw had not ceased talking since his arrival)—"I despaired! I believed our bride was displeased with me. And why?"

He dropped his voice to answer himself: "For that bit of fun I had imitating Eparch Aranha at banquet! A wonderful person—*such* a voice!—indeed, I meant no disrespect! Would that it had not been mistaken for such! But now I see that this punishment that sent me sulking like a child was really meant to honor me above all our spouses! For you—*you!*—are my reward. Even our Firebird—that is what we are calling our beautiful new Prince Consort, you know, though he is *not* an official wizard of our Parliament, nor never can be, due to some absurd prior vow he made to his so-called god of Fire for the good of Liriat—even he, *haughty* as he is, will look on me with amity and sweetness after tonight! For it is said he favors *your* family as his own left hand! Oh, I am the luckiest of birds! Do, *do* take my arm, Condor! See, it is most felicitous, most convenient! See I hold it ready for you, I—"

But when Lanie stepped forward to take his offered arm, Jackdaw shied away nervously, shrieking out a loud: "Kaar! Kak kak kak!" and crashing into one of the Bright Knights, who made no move to steady him. In fact, their fingernails flashed with fire, and Jackdaw barely escaped having his feathers scorched off.

Realizing that it was her own wizard mark that so affrighted him, Lanie didn't think it prudent to reach out and help him. He was wheezing, "Oh, my heart! My tiny lungs! Oh! My *air sacs!*"

Lanie hid both her hands behind her back. "How can I help you?" she asked as calmly as she could.

Cautiously peeking up from his pitiful crouch, Jackdaw flapped his hands.

"No, no, no. It's my fault, all my fault." He smiled tremulously at her. "You see, I am a coward. Without my mob, that is. A coward! And you—you're... why, you're just so terrible and grand!"

He's young, Lanie realized with a pang. He grew up in a court terrorized by the Harrier. And his magic is... his magic is...

Something he'd just said about imitating the Eparch gave her the hint she needed. Jackdaw magic was mimesis. This nervous, gallant little courtier's magic was a small thing: useful to entertain children, or serve an intrigue, or perhaps lambaste an enemy—so long as Jackdaw had a mob at his back to protect him against the consequences of his mockery. But mimesis was no match for death magic, and he knew it. He was sweating.

"What can I do to make you comfortable, Jackdaw?" Lanie asked. "For I've come to parley with Bran Fiakhna, and I intend to cross this bridge. On *your* arm, I hope?"

After exaggeratedly mopping his brow, Jackdaw bowed again. "So generous, Condor! So compassionate! Now... now, I do not suppose"—he gulped; Lanie watched the apple of his larynx bob up and down—"that you might give me your word—your *sacred* word, I mean, as the daughter of the Deathbird—your *word* of *bone*, I mean—that you intend to do me no harm?"

His eagerness, his extravagance, his desire to please her, moved her. Lanie couldn't help smiling.

Jackdaw flinched.

A Stones's smile carried a lot of weight. Especially in Rook. Especially after six years of Nita. There was an an old adage in Liriat: *If you're near enough to see a Stones smile, it's already too late to be pricing coffins.*

Lanie's smile faded as she imagined this young wizard's predecessor, the former Jackdaw. She had always avoided learning the details of Nita's work, but it had been hard to miss the dirty feathers hanging limply from her sister's trophy belt. She remembered the black and gray one clearly. Jackdaw was one of Nita's first kills.

It was not uncommon, she knew, for a Blackbird Bride to replace one of her deceased espoused kin with a close relative of the recently departed. Had Jackdaw's predecessor been one of his parents? An older sibling? An ommer? A cousin? And just how young must this gawky young man have been anyway, when Bran Fiakhna decided to sew her feather to his breast? Ten? Eleven? Just a few years older than Datu.

"I'll swear it, if you like," Lanie reassured the desperately smiling wizard. "I really don't mean you any harm. But"—here, she drew in a deep breath—"I can do you one better."

Lanie had already decided to do this in any case, either here at the drawbridge or further along. It was a risk—Tan had been against it from the start—but Lanie thought that she must take it, in order to gain the trust and access that she needed. To get close enough.

Here, in the dark, at the foot of the drawbridge, with Brackenwild guards and the temple's Bright Knights looking on, seemed as good a place as any to get it over with.

"For you, Jackdaw"—Lanie tried to catch and mimic some of his own grandiosity, hoping to flatter him—"for the great kindness you've already shown me, a newcomer to your Rookish ways, I, Miscellaneous Stones, necromancer of Liriat, left hand of Errolirrolin Brackenwild, do willingly put myself into your power."

He waited, mouth agape.

Lanie felt her lips curl in a very Haaken-like expression. "For *you*, Jackdaw," she said, "I, whom you call Condor"—stretching her mouth into a wider smile, she forced herself to finish—"am going to clip my wings."

Heart beating hard against her reliquary pendant, Lanie drew the other necklace out of her pocket. Rubies and garnets smoldered sullenly. Gold glinted. Jet winked. Iron pyrite reflected red lamplight like the windows of a secret city. In her palm, a rich clicker-clattering, as the gems fell against each other.

At sight of the snaky gold chain, Jackdaw tensed. He quivered. He hugged himself in excitement.

"I know what that is!" he exclaimed. "I know what that is!"

"I thought you might," Lanie murmured. She, like he, could not take her eyes from the thing.

"Oh, I do! I do! Did I not watch her make it? Did not we all? How she lavished it with her love! How she poured her most powerful enchantments into it! Oh, Condor! How clever you are! How courageous! Yes, *that* will do!"

Jackdaw was so happy, he seized her by her left hand, and twirled himself under it.

"What is it?" asked one of the Lirian guards involuntarily.

Jackdaw released Lanie, but kept dancing in place, clapping his hands in soft little tap-tap-tap-taps.

"Why!" he cried. "It is the token of our bride's esteem!"

"Take me to her, please," Lanie said, and slipped the necklace over her head.

CHAPTER FORTY-SIX

The Covenant of Rooks

WHEN THE SPELL hit her, she did not even know it at first. She was just, instantaneously, fathoms-sunk.

Fascinated.

What she saw, as it fell from everywhere to cover her completely, was a densely piled mantle of darkness, brine-purple, wine-dark, like a great destroying tidal bore before it makes landfall. The smell of the Blackbird Bride's magic filled her nostrils, flooded her mouth: wet feathers, wet velvet, salt wind, saltwater, jasmine, amber. She heard her heartbeat and nothing else.

And then, after twelve beats, she did hear something else: the chiming of the bone inside her reliquary pendant. With every beat of her heart, it answered, like a clapper hitting the sound bow of a bell.

She was not out from under it yet. No, she was still caught in the tide. But this, now—the sound of that tiny bone bell—was her lifeline. Her god, holding out Her hand. And she clung to it, with no thought or desire else beyond simply hanging on.

She was hardly aware of crossing the drawbridge under guard. Her boots slipped from time to time, but Jackdaw kept a delicate grip on her hand, which rested in the crook of his elbow.

He chattered continuously, advising her to, "Beware the ice, Condor! They say they've poured sand over the boards to prevent accidents, but I find it treacherous," and confiding, "we all *much* prefer to fly everywhere. Soon, when our bride has sewn her feather in you, you'll be able to join us aloft, and never walk anywhere again! Unless you *want* to, of course," he finished, rather resentfully picking his way through the snow.

They proceeded through the portcullis of Castle Ynyssyll's outer wall, which had been raised in anticipation of their approach. But instead of making for the castle, Jackdaw veered left, and steered her towards the slender tower of Ynyssyll's Tooth. As soon as they had crossed the bridge, his hopping and flinching and skittering askance had started up again. He kept glancing skyward, as if checking the weather.

Lanie was not yet in enough command of herself to follow his gaze, or to fully interpret her surroundings. But she could focus on Jackdaw, and eventually understand what he was saying after concentrating hard and committing his words to memory.

When he noticed her glassy gaze upon him, Jackdaw said uneasily, "It's nothing, really. Merely, I am being directed towards the Tooth. Why, I don't know. At this hour, everyone should be milling about the Brackenwild ballroom—such as it is—eating that awful orangey syllabub, and cringing as the orchestra—such as it is—warms up. We were promised a fête, you see. I, of course, was banned from tonight's festivities for my previous infraction, but before that happened, I had my suit and mask made specially, and when we have a moment of privacy, dear Condor, I shall show it to you!"

Crabwise and crookedly and not at all quickly, Lanie was edging back to herself. It was not hard to keep her face vacant, her smile vapid, her bearing puppet-like; it was in fact taking most of her strength not to slip back under the tide. But she was standing against it now. And angling, in her dogged diagonal, for the shore.

"Brace yourself, dear Condor," Jackdaw murmured, squeezing her arm. "We are about to have company. And," he added somewhat waspishly, "even though I naturally *love* and *adore* each and every one of them like my own, well, espoused kin—which they *are*—I am afraid we do not always agree, or see eye-to-eye on certain issues, or even have any great fondness for each other beyond what our bride bids us fabricate for the sake of peace and propriety. But never fear. I shall stay with you, at your side. Unless we're mobbed." He grinned in sheepish apology. "Coward, remember?"

Lanie's vague countenance vaguely smiled in response. She hardly even had to force it.

And then, four Rookish wizards fell from the sky.

Lightly they landed on naked human feet, forming a circle around Lanie and her escort. The night wind ruffled the feathers on their short tunics but did not raise gooseflesh on their bare limbs. They stood unflinching on the frozen ground, their scrutiny a flensing.

Another layer of Lanie's fascination fell away. She assessed their wizard marks and silently named them, chanting their titles in time to the chiming of Queen Ynyssyll's left toe bone:

Cowbird, Grackle, Lark Bunting, Blackstart.

Cowbird was a woman of delicate appearance, her skin of softest black, except for her face and neck, which were a rich river-bottom brown, and her hair, a halo of chestnut curls. She was lovely, but was not called the Parasite for nothing. When she drew upon her power, she was also drawing on the strength of any substance nearest her, sucking it dry to augment her own. Cowbird could go for weeks, months, without food or rest, and leave in her wake the line of desiccated corpses, barren patches of land, and stagnant bodies of water that had sustained her austerity.

Smooth, spare Grackle was tall and epicene, and glimmered all the colors of a speckled black opal. They were called the Amplifier, and had a talent for manipulating moods. They could soothe a fractious baby, or swell a staid dinner party into orgiastic action. If they stood above a battlefield and concentrated their powers upon their own warriors, those warriors would grow ravenous with bloodlust, berserking into apex predators whose only desire was to kill and die gloriously. Should they instead focus their powers upon their foes, their foes' greatest fears would swiftly overcome their senses; they would cower in shame, be unable to see through their tears, and wetting and shitting themselves, run in any direction but that of the front line. A formidable opponent.

Lanie did not think she needed to worry too much about Blackstart's magic. Though physically she was a giant—bold and sculpted, her upper body a dark gray shading to black, her lower body from belly to ankles the orange of sullen embers—her magic was that of Feastmaking. She was a provider, a multiplier of grains, a doubler of wine barrels. Lanie had read that the most powerful Feastmakers could enact the reverse of their calling as well—evaporating water at its source, rotting fruit and meat that seemed fresh, and hardening breads until they were like rock, inedible and unnourishing. But such strength of power was rare. If Blackstart had been a Famineer, gossip would have spread about it since her ascent to the Parliament of Rooks.

But Lark Bunting Lanie had heard of, and what she knew of him, she feared. He was black as a river at night, with moon-white arms and hands. Called the Flusher, he could sense hidden things, root them out. One clap of his hands, and the very maggots would rise up from the sunken carcass of some roadkill. One stomp of his foot, and foxes would bolt from their dens. One buzzy, insectile "Hweeee!" and a newly minted seven-year-old girl—a girl just like Datu—would unlatch her locked door, and voluntarily give herself up to the Rookish wizards who wished to kill her.

How could Datu have ever stayed hidden, with such a wizard on the hunt for her?

At least Lanie did not see Cormorant—the Time-Hobble—among them. At their previous meeting, Cormorant, the last surviving member of Bran Fiakhna's old Parliament, had eaten her sister's eyes while Lanie had been caught in his molasses-trap of slowed time. She was glad, for the sake of her continued pretense, that she did not have to face him just yet.

Unlike Jackdaw's delight at her unexpected appearance, these four new wizards did not at all seem pleased to see the necromancer Miscellaneous Stones. Even though she openly wore the Blackbird Bride's necklace. Even though its powers were obviously working. Even though, docile and vulnerable as she was, they might have fallen upon her and torn her apart, as from their expressions they clearly wished to. But they were skittish yet. And all of them were so very young.

Blackstart was first to speak.

"We've come to escort you and your girlfriend to the roof party, Jack." Her voice was sweet and high, incongruous in such a large body. A child's voice. "We wouldn't want you to lose her on the way."

Jackdaw tittered, "My prodigious sense of direction is matched only by my prodigious—"

"—folly," Grackle murmured.

Jackdaw glared at them and began to mutter, but at Cowbird's impatient prompting, he flounced in an about-face and cluckingly ushered Lanie through the door at the bottom of Ynyssyll's Tooth. With many a backward glance at the others following behind them, he tucked Lanie close to his side and narrated their journey up the cramped spiral staircase.

"Now, watch your feet here, Condor; the stones are slippery. There are two hundred and ninety-four steps to the roof of Ynyssyll's Tooth. The way is narrow and winding, as I have cause to know; we have been making this pilgrimage several times a day, by the graceful insistence of our bride, who insists we walk the entire way. This, she says, is to honor our Firebird, who—as I mentioned to you before, being a Lirian and a Brackenwild and a worshipper of a ridiculous god who cannot fly—has no wings. You will enjoy the sensation of openness when we reach the roof. It is a fine wide space, with a crenelated wall like a ring of teeth. Our bride, thankfully, does not insist we walk *down* again once we have performed our obligations on the roof, and I have taken many a refreshing plunge off the parapets, to my everlasting delight."

When Lanie, sweating and breathless, emerged on Jackdaw's arm from the gloom of the staircase, she felt like she was stepping into the sky. A blast of wind drove her back between two merlons of the wall, and almost right through the embrasure.

But a pair of strong arms caught her. Plucked her out of plummet's reach. Hauled her upright, held her. Lanie's tenuous hold on herself wavered.

She stared up in passionate admiration.

How had she forgotten the Blackbird Bride's magnificent height? Or how slender, how strong her body was? Seven feet at least, and straight as the pilum she wore in a sheath at her back. Alas for the cuirass that hid from Lanie's covetous gaze the soft plumage covering Bran Fiakhna's breast; she wished to lay her head upon it and be gathered snugly in. But the black leather scales of the armor were unyielding, the plated pteruges at shoulders and waist no pillow for a lover's head. Bran Fiakhna's close-shorn head was fitted with a bronze galea, its crest-holder rioting over with purple-black plumes. Winged cheek-pieces accentuated her high cheekbones, their silver-gilt steel no brighter than her eyes, which were fervent and unblinking as they stared down at Lanie, who swayed in her arms.

"Condor!" The Blackbird Bride's unmistakable rasp seemed louder than the howling night wind.

To Lanie's ears, it set up a sonorous echo—though the working part of her brain knew that this was a fascinator's trick and not an acoustic phenomenon. The sound of it froze every courtier of Brackenwild and Rook who were present, as well as every Bright Knight and wizard of the Parliament, so that they stood unmoving, inanimate, as if stuck to one of Haaken Skrathmandan's wards.

Lanie found her voice. "Bran Fiakhna."

But this time, it wasn't just her speaking voice she found. Her deeper voice unlocked beneath it, the doubled tones both reassuring her and clearing her head. She heard the howling of the wind again, and was once more able to process that those she had thought frozen in her periphery were in fact flickering with restless twitches and significant glances and exchanged whispers. Mostly, though, her attention was on the Blackbird Bride, whose face had broken into a wide smile at the sound of her name on Lanie's lips.

With a loving squeeze of Lanie's shoulders, Bran Fiakhna exclaimed, "Welcome! At last, welcome! And—ah!—wearing our token!"

Her cupped hand moved to the back of Lanie's neck. She adjusted the golden chain, smoothing out a few imaginary kinks and polishing a dull gem against Lanie's coat collar. Her warm fingers sent tingling waves of pleasure all the way down Lanie's spine, and further.

"I carried it with me," Lanie's surface voice responded, thin and distant, as her deep voice dropped down, and down, and down, sounding the deepest bowels of Moll's Kopje. "I kept it in my pocket, always. And remembered you."

That, she certainly had. And if Bran Fiakhna chose to take her words as a compliment, it would only work in Lanie's favor.

She did. Another radiant smile flashed out, making all the Rookish wizards on the rooftop sigh with delight. A wave of intense euphoria washed through Lanie's body as well, starting in the gold around her neck and spreading everywhere: pleasure such as she had not known since Midsummer, when she and Canon Lir took each other for lovers. As the sensations slithered to their deliciously drawn-out conclusion, Lanie was left feeling wrung-out and wobbly-kneed, throbbing at all her pulse-points, yearning for another chance to please her bride.

But then she caught sight of Jackdaw over Bran Fiakhna's shoulder. He looked so eager, so forlorn.

She heard herself commenting: "I've had a princely welcome. Jackdaw is the most chivalrous of courtiers. I owe him my timely escort to your side."

Jackdaw's face lit as Bran Fiakhna redirected her attention to him. Some of the oppressive pleasure in Lanie's body abated, and she was able to watch as the Blackbird Bride stroked the flesh of Jackdaw's neck with her sharp black talons, and sifted her long fingers through his parti-colored hair, bringing her soft gray lips to his ear and whispering until his eyes rolled up in his head and he swooned in her embrace.

Lanie used the last of her unburdened few seconds to glance around the rooftop—seeking the one person she had come here for. Braziers were lit at intervals upon the merlons, dazzling her eyes. But in all the play of light and dark, amongst all the milling dozens crammed together on the roof, she did not see anyone who looked in the least like a captive child.

She did see Eparch Aranha in their court dress of cloth-of-gold. They were wearing an elaborate headdress and such face-paint as was usually only reserved for high holy fire feasts. She noted several more Rookish wizards, too—though still no sign of Cormorant—and many Rookish courtiers who were dressed like wizards, but were obviously not. Unlike their magical counterparts, they shivered in their short feathered tunics, and were not barefoot and bare-limbed but wore fashionable shoes and feathered capes. Their careful face-paint was both too fanciful and too artistically symmetrical to be mistaken for wizard marks.

"Beloved Condor!"

Her attention snapped back to the Blackbird Bride. Bran Fiakhna was again standing too close, her long arm tightening around Lanie's shoulders—and with it, her formidable will. Lanie's eyelids fluttered shut. Without meaning to, she leaned into Bran Fiakhna's embrace, whose leather epaulettes creaked like small things being trodden upon.

"Soon—tonight, Condor—it is our dearest hope that we shall at last induct you into our Parliament. You shall be our fourth-and-twenty. Our final wizard."

Bran Fiakhna smiled ruefully. "Indeed we were sorry it could not be sooner, coinciding with this morning's wedding festivities. Doubtless our disappointment expressed itself in the rawness of our temper. Poor Jackdaw bore the brunt of it, alack! But we shall mend with him anon. The work is already begun! He knew. Oh, of all our espoused kin, Jackdaw knew our loving heart! One glimpse of you and all was forgiven, all was well! Our joy at the sight of your face will become the joy of all Rook and Liriat—amplified twelve-fold when we commence the Covenant of Rooks! What a bird you shall make!"

Lanie's knees were buckling under the onslaught of Bran Fiakhna's voice, from the fingers that gripped Lanie's neck, from the hand that ran up and down her spine. However, she managed to keep the bassoon-like drone of her deep voice tolling out from the bottoms of her feet.

"Tell me of this rite!" she gasped.

"The Covenant of Rooks?" Bran Fiakhna asked. "It is not so very complicated. You shall come to know it intimately soon enough. We shall pluck a feather from our breast, and sew it to your own with thread spun of our hair, dyed in our blood. Then you shall be named Condor in truth.

Your old name shall be erased, and with it your memory of all that came before. You shall be born into my arms anew. That lone feather shall multiply till it becomes a tunic fitted to your form. It will keep you warm and give you wings. You need never take it off. You shall never need more than that to cover you. Unless, of course," she laughed, "you wish it!"

In another world, Lanie thought, I, like Jackdaw and dozens before him, would have lain myself at her feet. I would have kissed the silver rings on each of her long toes. I would have *surrendered.*

"I know you are fond of bright colors, beloved," Bran Fiakhna was whispering, stroking the rainbow yarn of Lanie's scarf and cap. "Rejoice, then, in your coming shape! Condor's head is a flayed and naked pink, a true and noble pink. Your new wizard marks will reflect this." She laughed. "Such joy to think of you arrayed in Parliament colors! Such striking black and white feathers! Such a royal neck ruff! Such a wingspan that will o'ershadow the sun! All this shall be yours, and you shall be ours, and I shall know true happiness again. But one thing more we must attend to."

The Blackbird Bride raised her voice for everyone on the roof to hear, amplified its resonance until it once more drowned out the wind. "But one thing more before we enact the Covenant of Rooks and take you for our own!"

Now it was coming. What Lanie had been waiting for. What she had been expecting from the start. Still, the icicle chill that spiked down her spine startled her. She mourned the loss of warmth, of delight, of her desire to surrender.

But even as she mourned and grew cold, Lanie's deep voice redoubled. She could feel the dark prayer of it working, working, down in the depths below. In the crypts of the castle and beyond. In the catacombs of Liriat Proper.

"But one small matter," the Blackbird Bride said, coaxingly drawing Lanie's arms out to their full length as if in a dance. "One last boon we beg of you, my Condor, before our union is complete. We did want this thing done before you came to us. We wanted nothing to distract you or distress you at our celebration. Alas for unforeseen difficulties! Only you can help us. Only you are powerful enough—rare and clever enough. But we will help *you*," she assured Lanie. "We will give you all the succor of our flesh. We shall stand as buffer between you and any grief you might fear to feel. But it must be done."

Moving gently as a dreamwalker, Lanie detached her hands from Bran Fiakhna's grasp. "Your Maj—"

But a familiar voice interrupted her, whisking the words right off her tongue. "Your Majesty. Please."

There was no mistaking that voice. No one else could replicate its butter-silk, trumpet-colored, summer afternoon quality. And even if Lanie's ears had deceived her, the reliquary pendant had leapt at the sound of it like a trout at twilight.

She struggled to keep her face neutral and canted toward the Blackbird Bride, not toward the small sun that had come, blazing, to stand at her side.

Canon Lir. It was truly they. From what Lanie could observe in her periphery, they were dressed all in red and gold. They smelled of themself: of white pepper incense and beeswax and ink. They stood shoulder to shoulder with Lanie, and were smiling, as she was smiling, right up into the face of the Blackbird Bride. Their smile warmed their voice as well as their face, but Lanie could tell that it was the smile they reserved for court politics and temple diplomacy. Not for friendship. Not like they smiled at Lanie.

They stood near enough to touch her, but it was not Lanie they reached for.

"I beg you, your Majesty," they said, and all the ruby rings on their fingers flashed red in the firelight. "Have mercy."

"Husband," the Blackbird Bride replied, in the coldest tones Lanie had yet heard from her, "it cannot be. I will have the execution of Sacred Datura Stones."

CHAPTER FORTY-SEVEN

The Emerald Child

"MERCY, MY FIREBIRD?" Bran Fiakhna said with a corvine tilt of her head. "Did we not marry you and take your nation under our wing? *Your* nation, which sent the Harrier into Rookery Court to slaughter my espoused kin? We might easily have annihilated Liriat—starting with you, Errolirrolin, when you and your Bright Knights came begging at our gates. We have shown mercy. The life of a child is nothing to the millions of Lirian lives we have already spared for your sake. All we want now is the justice that is our due. Our Condor knows! She knows how long we have waited. Why else would she have come to us now, wearing my token, if not for this?"

"Why else indeed?" murmured Lanie through numb lips.

She turned, and looked for the first time upon the face of Errolirrolin Brackenwild.

Their face was naked of paint.

But then, perhaps they only wore it, Lanie surmised, when they were going around *pretending* to be a fire priest of Sappacor.

But no, they had not been pretending; their wizard mark was still there, smoldering beneath the fringe of rubies that fell across their brow.

Like their ommer, Blood Royal Errolirrolin Brackenwild wore cloth-of-gold. Collar and cuffs frothed with gold lace. There were gold buttons on their coat, gold buckles upon their shoes, and a sash of golden satin pinned across their chest, fixed in place with a ruby brooch shaped like the Triple Flame. Small ruby droplets hung from their ears. Their hair, grown longer even than Haaken's, was braided into slim, tidy black ropes, each terminating in a strand of jeweled and enameled beads.

Lanie dropped into a full and formal bow as befitted a subject to her sovereign, and then immediately destroyed the dignified effect by hissing, "Husband?"

Errolirrolin returned her bow, though theirs was abbreviated. When they moved, it was like the sun moved. They gazed at Lanie, calm as the death mask they had worn on Midsummer when with their own blood they had lit the red lamps of Liriat.

At least they were not smiling. At least they still considered her friend enough not to *smile* at her now.

"Our husband. Our Firebird," Bran Fiakhna reiterated.

Her voice had lost its coolness now that she was speaking to Lanie. She was all warmth, all sympathy. Her silvery regard was not precisely smug, but it was amused. Hers was the face of an adult watching a toddler taking her first tumble: a toddler who, plopping on her backside from the shock of it, starts to wail. The adult might comfort the child, croon at her, distract her. But she can't help smiling all the same, for she knows, with the monstrous, semi-divine confidence of adulthood, that the toddler is not *really* hurt, and will not be wailing for long.

"He did warn us," the Blackbird Bride said, "that news of his decades-long dissimulation might cause you, beloved Condor, a moment of consternation. We remonstrated with him long on the subject of his deceitfulness, and would have spared you this pain. After the covenant rite, with the love of all our Parliament set as ramparts to protect you, you would not have remembered that you ever loved him. But"—she shrugged her armored shoulders—"like all Brackenwilds, he is arrogant. He *will* think he knows best. As you see." Her tone implied that she, Bran Fiakhna, would soon break her bridegroom of this irritating habit.

"I do see," Lanie replied slowly.

And she did. She saw that Canon Lir—Errolirrolin—had stepped in to beg mercy for Datu. Either they had seen through Lanie's own facade, guessed that she was merely pretending to be Bran Fiakhna's thrall, and believed (rightly) that she had been about to let down her guise and confront her. Or they believed that Lanie was wholly fascinated in truth, ready to do the Blackbird Bride's bidding—even unto murdering her own niece—and wished to spare her, if they could, from the regret that she would face if ever she emerged from her enchanted state. They were friend enough for that. Whatever else they were.

Lifting her chin, she gave Errolirrolin a little nod, and looked them right in the eye. Something in the Blood Royal's face lit with a warmth that she knew they would as lief have kept hidden. But they concealed it quickly.

Calm and solemn as if nothing had passed between them, Errolirrolin said, "In my choice of bride, I did as my royal mother advised. After Erralierra's death, when you, Miss Stones, resurrected her tongue's sage counsel, I asked her what I must do to make our peace with Rook. This marriage was her answer. For my present happiness and for the peace in our nation, Miss Stones, I have you to thank."

Lanie stared. She remembered very well that strange spring day in Broods, wending her way through Liriat Proper for the first time, trying to find the High Temple of Sappacor. When was that, a century ago? But it might have been yesterday when Canon Lir flew to her across that glass garden, embracing her and kissing her, ecstatically relieved that Lanie had not been murdered along with her sister.

And yes, she did remember Erralierra's ectenica-lashed mouth whispering 'Marry her' from her cremation tray. Lanie had assumed, all these months, that the Blood Royal had meant marry *her*. Lanie. Miscellaneous Stones.

As if a Brackenwild would ever so lower themself! Even Erralierra had never married Natty Stones, whom she'd loved more than breathing. Stoneses *served* the Brackenwilds. They did not *marry* them.

Fury flashed in her, brighter than Bryddongard lightning. Fury and humiliation. Lanie did not know where to direct it. Nowhere was safe or fair. So she rounded on Bran Fiakhna and announced scathingly, "Brackenwilds are notorious for bearing twins. I hope you are prepared for that eventuality."

The Blackbird Bride laughed, her expressive face full of that awful, indulgent understanding. Of *course* Lanie must mourn her abortive first love before moving on to her next great love. A love far richer, deeper, subtler, wiser, and more beautiful than any childhood fancy whose death throes stung her now. She, Bran Fiakhna, would be that love. She was that love already. She was only waiting for Lanie to finally realize it.

"Ah, Condor!" she said. "We have borne our lot already. From now until our death, our womb shall have its rest. But wait until you meet our children! They did not accompany us to Liriat whilst the union of our nations is still so changeable and new. But there are nine of them in all—bright-eyed, brilliant, and mischievous—all waiting to love you as their Condor and King!"

But Errolirrolin had caught the question in Lanie's angry words. They answered it, as if continuing a friendly conversation over dinner.

"Erralierra did bear twins to Jaor Forthios, but one did not survive our birth. At the time, the baronies were in revolt. If they had known about my sibling's death, her enemies would have put it about that Erralierra's line was rotting, and Liriat with her. So she raised me in my dual role, castle and temple, Blood Royal and fire priest, and no one but my ommer ever knew." Glancing from Lanie to the Blackbird Bride, they added mildly, "I told Bran Fiakhna all of this, of course, when I pressed my suit at Rookery Court. I told her everything."

"Everything?"

Errolirrolin's eyes met hers, no apology in them. Lanie felt her stomach yawn open and fall away.

"How much you must love her," she managed to say, "to trust her with this secret no one else could know."

When had that curly mouth, once so full and so red, with such a promise of laughter in each up-tilted corner, gone so flat with resignation? When did those eyes, the color of copper poppets in the summer sun, begin to harbor such shadows? Or had they always done so, and Lanie been too imperceptive to observe it?

She must have made a noise without realizing it, for Bran Fiakhna moved in closer and placed a lulling hand on the small of her back. Wave after wave of compassion and compulsion encompassed her. Lanie was at sea, adrift.

But this time, with Errolirrolin so close, and their reliquaries singing to each other, she found her buoy almost immediately and clung to it.

Her teeth chattered. Lanie began shivering in earnest. She only hoped that the Blackbird Bride would take it for the trembling of desire. Not rage. Not resolve. Far below her, she felt her deep voice cracking something open, like a new fissure at the bottom of the sea.

Leaning back in Bran Fiakhna's arms, Lanie let her eyes slide half-closed. She saw that Errolirrolin was observing her without appearing to do so. That trick they had of peeking through their lashes. They noticed her noticing.

Very well, let them see. She was done with this charade. Almost.

Craning her neck back and feigning a fawning devotion, Lanie said, "Bran Fiakhna," and then, more softly, "Rook."

The Blackbird Bride practically melted with gladness and desire. "Yes, my Condor?"

"You have been the pinnacle of patience with me," said Lanie. "You have waited for me, wooed me. From the moment we met, *you* never hid who you were or what you wanted from me. Always, you were honest with me. I am tired of running. I want to rest. You wish the execution of the Harrier's daughter, Sacred Datura Stones. Very well. I shall take care of her. Where is she?"

Bran Fiakhna's triumphant smile shone from the inverted gray triangle of her wizard mark. The purple-dark plumes of her galea whipped in the wind. Stepping back from Lanie lightly as a dancer, she drew her black pilum from the sheath on her back, and, flattening her arm to extend the spear like a baton, pointed.

The courtiers on the roof who happened to be standing between the pilum and what it pointed to parted down the middle. When they did so, Lanie saw what she could not have seen before—what all their court dresses, furred cloaks and feathered mantles, hoods and headdresses had concealed: a rope.

A rope, as thick as a Skrathmandan's arm, knotted around one of the tall granite merlons of the battlement.

Lanie was grateful her face was numb. Grateful her belly had already taken that two-hundred-twenty-one-foot plunge down the length of Ynyssyll's Tooth to the flagstones below. All she wanted to do was fling herself at that knotted rope and haul whatever was swinging from the end of it to safety.

But she restrained herself. Any rash movement, any change of face or pace, and the shaft of that jetty pilum would crash down in front of her chest like the bar of a toll gate. The Blackbird Bride stepped up beside her, and bared her teeth at the merlon.

"There. In the crow's cage. She has hung all night and all day, and now it is night again. But still she will not die!"

Swiftly, she bent her head, and kissed the nape of Lanie's neck. Lanie's knees gave out entirely—she did not have to counterfeit that—but the Blackbird Bride held her upright.

"You know the reason for the child's unnatural survival, beloved Condor," she whispered. "We can smell your magic on her like a sun-drenched orange grove. It was you who did this. And it is you who must undo this, Miscellaneous Stones."

BACK HOME, LANIE reminded herself—back in the beery, pretzel-scented warmth of the Lover's Complaint, Havoc has barred her doors. Tonight, she is closed to all custom. She is huddled by the kitchen stove, pup in lap. She has wrapped him in blankets, for he is rimed up to his eyeballs in a frost of emeralds, cold and silent, barely breathing. Sometimes, the gems twinkle with his trembling, and within their preserving prison he squeaks his distress.

But Havoc is keeping him warm. And Undies is feeding that warmth into Datu. They are both doing their best, and they will continue do so for as long as they can.

As will I.

LANIE COULD NOT see the Blackbird Bride anymore, only sense her: a pillar of dark plumage and shining leather scales. Lips like warm gray tulips pressing more kisses to her neck. Teeth like sharpened pearls nibbling at her ear.

Someone emitted a tiny, high, breathless squeak, and Lanie knew it was she. But that was a sound she could ignore. It was not a sound that mattered. The sound she was making that truly mattered was soundless to almost everyone on Ynyssyll's Tooth.

But Errolirrolin stirred at her squeak. Or Lanie thought they did. They made no move to defend her, or to detach her from their new bride. But they did look her way. And perhaps, behind their unreadable royal accident, the red-gold flames of their substance were troubled. Perhaps.

Bran Fiakhna smiled against Lanie's throat, pleased at the response her caresses had elicited.

"Let us finish this," she whispered. "And then let us be bound."

Stroking Lanie on the cheek in the same fondling manner with which she had favored Jackdaw earlier, she gave Lanie a little push toward the merlon.

Release from that contact gave Lanie an intense relief. Bran Fiakhna's awareness followed her, but now her fascination was more like being lashed by a hail storm, and less like being dragged under by a riptide. This, Lanie could bear.

She picked her way across the snow-dredged flagstones to the knotted rope. She leaned into the embrasure, standing on tiptoe and craning as far as she could to peer down the side of the tower. She could just glimpse the top of the crow's cage swinging from the end of the rope. But the stones were too thick. She was not tall enough; she could not see.

All she could do was hear.

Her niece's howl was as hearty a sound as any aunt could wish for. Oddly wolf-like.

"I am Sacred Datura Stones! The Harrier's daughter! You think winter can kill me? A Stones is colder than winter!"

With none to see her expression but the indifferent night sky, Lanie felt her numb face crack into a smile that threatened the integrity of her skull. She sternly willed herself not to sob, or laugh aloud, or climb down the rope that very second—

"I am a *Stones!*" screamed her niece, with as fine a set of lungs as ever the descendent of opera-loving Natty Stones could have. "Engoloth eat you! When I come for you, your life won't be worth spit. *I will kill you with my spit!*"

Taking in a deep, nostril-pinching breath of air to cool her voice and deaden her nerves, Lanie called down to her: "Stoneses die young, Sacred Datura—but you may well be setting a record[38]."

The howling stopped. There was a short pause. A much smaller voice called out, "Auntie Lanie?"

"The one and only."

That was all it took for Lanie's echo wounds to open up. A blast of pure pain rocked her back on her heels. It was as if Datu, knowing Lanie to be so near, had loosed some desperate hold she had on herself and pushed all her agony upwards, trying to communicate her peril.

Lanie took it all in, drawing as much pain as she could off Datu. Her blood, and Datu's blood, the pup's blood—they were all intermingled in the spell that had brinked Mister Underwear Stones from death at the edge of the Diesmali. In Undies, Lanie's and Datu's living accidents had been transmuted to a conductor of the divine by the lips, tongues, and teeth of four curious gods. Lanie called upon that connection now. She entered into it once more and fully—though she predicted the cost to her own flesh would be dear.

First, the cold: barbed and brutal. Her clothes froze to her skin, as if, directly after trying to drown her, someone had hung her out in the wind,

38 This was patently not true, as Sacred Datura Stones would instantly have apprehended. See Peccary Stones, footnote 24.

hoping to speed her to her death. Second, loss of feeling in all extremities. The slow freeze at her core. Lanie sagged in the embrasure, the strength sapped from her limbs. Third, deep chafe marks on her wrists and ankles from the chains Datu wore. Her belly suddenly peppered open in puncture wounds. (Someone had apparently been using Datu for target practice.) Another, larger wound scored the center of her breast bone, where a blade much like the lozenge-shaped tip of the black pilum had stabbed Datu through.

Everything, everything, *everything* hurt.

But though they should have been, none of Datu's hurts were mortal. And almost as quickly as Lanie's echo wounds formed, the strangest of scabs clapped them closed again, glittering and green. These jeweled scales did not *pain* Lanie exactly, but they were uncomfortable and awkward. They did not sit easily upon her skin. If she hadn't already known what they were, they would have thrown her into a panic.

Lanie's teeth were chattering so hard they threatened to chip. Snowflakes stung her frozen eyes. Tears fell like needles. Nevertheless, she took in what pain she could for as long as she could. And below her in the crow's cage, she hoped—no, she *knew*—that Datu's agonies were easing.

All the while, as Lanie's body suffered, her deep voice swelled and swelled.

And then, she felt her legs and feet being seized. She did not struggle to fend off the grips of those half dozen hands; without their support she might have pitched over the side of the tower, unconscious and covered in her niece's wounds.

Now she was being heaved out of danger like a sack of soggy linen. Now plopped onto solid if slippery stones. Now left in a heap.

A red-gold sun knelt at her side. A gentle hand touched her face; hot enough to melt the thin layer of ice that had formed over her skin. Her blood heated deliciously. Her extremities tingled, but not painfully. Lanie allowed herself only a minute of this comfort before feeding most of it back through her connection to Datu in the crow's cage. She left herself only enough life and heat to function, to think, to act.

And then, the sun was eclipsed.

Dissolute drowsiness and pure poppy-syrup pleasure washed over Lanie once again. But this pleasure was almost malicious in its forcefulness—as brutal in its way as hanging a soaking-wet child out in the winter wind.

"We do not think, Miscellaneous Stones, that you have done what you promised. Quite the opposite, in fact."

Lanie opened her eyes and looked up forever. The Blackbird Bride, backlit by torchlight, was silhouetted against the night sky. Slim and straight as the pilum she held, Bran Fiakhna regarded Lanie somberly, the wizard mark on her face faintly luminous but no longer smiling.

Nothing for it, Lanie thought.

She tested her speaking voice, "Bran Fiakhna." The name came out surprisingly strong, even *Tan*-like. "I'm going to tell you something that you may not know. Possibly because most people find it difficult to articulate a complete sentence in your presence."

The Blackbird Bride's thin eyebrows winged high.

Lanie continued, "Executing a seven-year-old child for her mother's crimes isn't justice. It's wrong. *Nothing* you say to the contrary will make it right. No matter if your whole Parliament agrees with you. No matter if a Blood Royal Brackenwild has bartered this child's life for the safety of their realm. It will never be right. And I will never allow it."

A shocked silence reverberated across the top of Ynyssyll's Tooth—from the Parliament wizards, to the Bright Knights, to the courtiers of Liriat and Rook, to the Eparch of the High Temple of Sappacor. Even Errolirrolin was silent, watching Lanie with the remoteness of a star.

But why, Lanie wondered, are their arms pinned behind their back by Blackstart and Lark Bunting?

But she didn't have time to speculate about whether or not Errolirrolin had been struggling against the Rookish wizards to gain her side. The Blackbird Bride was lifting her sinewy arm—the one not carrying the pilum—and unfurling one slim and graceful hand to her newest bridegroom, beckoning them back to her side. Immediately, Blackstart and Lark Bunting released Errolirrolin, who smoothed their garments, stepped over to their bride, and lifted their own arm, that Bran Fiakhna might rest her regal hand upon it.

Lanie focused minutely on that point connection. The gold of Errolirrolin's sleeve. The glimmering moonstone on Bran Fiakhna's thumb. The ruby bracelet banding Errolirrolin's wrist. Bran Fiakhna's index finger, longer by an inch than her others, with its matte-black nail that was spikier than the spine of a fever tree. Bran Fiakhna's somber, tragic face. Errolirrolin's unreadable one.

Lanie's gaze wanted to linger there, but she wrenched her head aside. She made herself stare at Bran Fiakhna, who stared back, as if to look was also to devour.

Who knew how much of Lanie's words the Blackbird Bride had heard? Or hearing, comprehended? Certainly, Bran Fiakhna did not seem angered by them, only tortured by her own overwhelming love and longing for Lanie, and her desire to be adored by the powerful wizard whose wizardry she craved.

When Bran Fiakhna spoke, her voice was so rough and humble and human that Lanie's heart twisted within her. For the first time, the Blackbird Bride dropped her formal plural. This conversation was to involve no one else—no Parliament, no Firebird, no country but the air between them. It was for Lanie only.

"I see that you love children. I, too, love children. I have many heirs by my Parliament. I would eat the hearts of any who did them harm. Let me make a present to you. I shall give to you the very father of your niece, that you might bear your own children by him. Your two mingled accidents shall produce offspring close in likeness to the one you have lost. Do I not know your grief, Miscellaneous Stones? When your sister slaughtered my first Parliament, I knew such grief that I thought I could not bear it and live. Now we shall share that grief, you and I. We shall comfort each other, and in each other's arms know far greater joy than those who have never suffered loss."

Sickened, Lanie tried to sit up. She fell back again as Bran Fiakhna pounced on her. She straddled Lanie, her thighs pinning Lanie's to the cold stones, her hands tearing off Lanie's hat, and threading through her braided hair. She stared. And stared. Three heartbeats. Six. Twelve. Lanie sprawled beneath her. That silver-coin coldness. That frozen fastness. That drowning silver sea.

"Do not resist me," came the raspy whisper, just against Lanie's lips. "You do not know what I can do. What I *will* do, if you do not obey me. Look at me! Look into my eyes, Miscellaneous Stones!"

Lanie had never stopped shivering, but now it was no longer from pain or dread or cold. No. It was that, with each profound shout of her deep voice, she shook and shuddered with the force of it. Her call sounded out, again and again, slamming straight down from the top of Ynyssyll's Tooth to its deepest roots, from the heart of Liriat Proper to its furthest circle. Lanie stared at the Blackbird Bride with Saint Death's own eyes, but the Blackbird Bride did not know Who was looking back.

Inside her skin, inside her skull, wearing Lanie's accident for Her own, a quiet-faced woman shook out the folds of Her gray cloak. The cloak's infinite but invisible train spilled down the sides of the tower in a cascade of interlocking bone and shell and chiton, in a hundred million fossilized leaves from trees that the planet Athe knew only in its youngest days, in chains of long-extinct insects trapped in amber, in festoons of fangs that once had studded the jaws of leviathans, in a lacework of the claws of dragons—or things out of which dragons were dreamed; in the beads of embryos that had died when they were yet too tiny to be detected by the naked eye.

All of this, Doédenna's cloak, fell soundless and unseen across the circles of Liriat Proper. In an ever-widening ripple, it fell, and though no one alive could hear it, it clicked and clacked and creaked like winter branches in a winter wind. It dragged the city streets and sank beneath the stones and trawled the catacombs below. Saint Death's hem caressed the corpses stacked along those lightless underground avenues. Where Her cloak touched bone, spark after spark, quick and blue, leapt from one to the other, shedding an accumulation of substance gathered into itself for over four hundred years. Saint Death was lending it all back, spark by spark, to each of the accidents that had once had housed it.

"Obey me," said the Blackbird Bride on top of the tower. Her raspy voice was harsh, her breathing wild. She sounded as if she were shouting against a storm. But for once, Bran Fiakhna's fascinations were not closing easily over their target. She was struggling to hold Lanie's attention.

She did not know that it wasn't *Lanie* anymore whom she was forcing her attentions upon. Not *entirely* Lanie.

"Drop the shield you hold over your niece. Let me drive my pilum through her skull. Let me end this. I shall make you my own. You shall sit beside me on my throne, King and Condor, ruler over all of Rook and Liriat. All will be as I have promised—all of it and more!"

Taking Lanie's face in her hands, she squeezed it with strong fingers. "If you do not," she whispered, "*if you do not!* Alas for you! Alas for all of Liriat."

Lanie reached up with one snow-piled sleeve, adjusted her spectacles, and smiled.

Where is breath?
In the stillness.
What is stillness?
Sothaín.

The fourth set of sothaín belonged to Brotquen, the four-faced harvest goddess. Lanie, flat on her back on the wet stone roof, spread out her arms in Brotquen's sixth attitude: *The Queen of Reaping Welcomes All to Feast.* Open arms, open palms, fingers spread, eyes open, mouth smiling, legs wide. Body declaring welcome to everything under the sky. Body as inexhaustible hospitality. Merriment and play as long as a summer day. Flourishing fields. Orchards laden with fruit. Wells of pristine water. Granaries full. Wine cellars overflowing. Gardens bursting their boundaries. The table laid. Home, bright and gleaming. Welcome for all.

Welcome! Lanie called out silently.

Welcome! Saint Death sang in Lanie's deepest voice.

Together they sang the Joyful Threnody, the Dreamcalling, the Maranathasseth Anthem, oldest of spellsongs since the world was begun: *Welcome! Welcome! Welcome!*

Stillness cracked.

Something moved.

Everything moved.

This time, when Ynyssyll's Tooth shook to its foundations, everyone felt it. The winter-brown mound of Moll's Kopje heaved under its shroud of snow. The stones of Castle Ynyssyll groaned and shifted, disturbed by the unrest, and the frozen moat that surrounded it shattered from bed to surface. Chunks of dirty ice overflowed the outer banks, where naked willows swayed and tombstones toppled in the cryptyard outside Saint

Death's chapel, which housed the holy body of the Founding Queen. The shockwave continued, out and out, from First Circle to Twelfth. Every cobblestone, every bridge, platform, wooden walkway, cranny, cave, apartment, alleyway, every rust-and-tumble, brick-and-timber, clay-and-marble level of the city of Liriat Proper heard the music of the Maranathasseth Anthem.

And far beneath the city, the undead had heard it too.

In catacombs a-swarm with blue sparks, fireflies loosed by the god of Death, the undead heard the Dreamcalling.

And dreaming, they remembered.

And remembering, awoke.

And awoke.

And awoke.

CHAPTER FORTY-EIGHT

Wake the Bones and Make Them Walk

A CROWD OF skeletons erupted from the door in the tower floor.

Where scraps of sinew no longer affixed disintegrating bones to their natural neighbors, bands of star-blue fire bound them together. That same fire lit the sockets of skulls, the gaps of grins. In the emptiness between ribs, it flickered and pulsed in time with Lanie's heartbeat, which was going rather hard.

As more and more of them poured up onto the roof of Ynyssyll's Tooth, Lanie's nose filled with the scent of summer colors: lemon-yellow, lime-green, grapefruit-pink. Her vision fractured, faceted. The sensation of Saint Death residing inside her skull faded, but Lanie was not left alone. Now she saw, not only through her own eyes, but the eyes of all the undead.

But mostly, Lanie saw *them*. Her hundred thousand new friends. And she fell in love with what she saw.

"Welcome," she whispered.

No sooner did she speak than the skeletons were swarming her, efficiently jostling any impedimenta—human or otherwise—out of their way and back against the crenellated outer walls. Lanie heard the wailing and sobbing of terrified courtiers, smelled the strange magics of wizard birds and Bright Knights brewing on the wind. She did not care. She caressed whatever osseous fragments she could reach. Skulls butted and rubbed against her like kittens. Bony embraces lifted and cradled her.

Her arms were not wide enough to hold all of her undead, but she tried. They were so darling, so happy, so *hers!*

"Will you lift me higher?" she asked them, mostly to see them smile.

They were all smiles. *Would* they lift her higher? Would they *indeed?* O rapturous request! How high *wouldn't* they lift her?

In the space between two snowflakes, the eager skeletons had built a small siege tower of themselves, had swung Lanie up to their pinnacle, and surrounded her with a cage of their countless arms, hands, shoulders, and heads. From her new height, Lanie took stock of Ynyssyll's Tooth. More of Liriat's undead, with ever more incoming, choked the only exit from the tower (besides the final, fatal one).

Gouts of flame burst up here and there from the Bright Knights, but Eparch Aranha was shouting orders to "Stand down!" and these flickered out quickly.

All the wizards of the Parliament had taken wing, shedding their human forms and flocking to circle the air above the Blackbird Bride, warding her with their bodies and magics just as the undead warded Lanie.

There were ten-and-seven wizards in total, Lanie counted—not the full Parliament, but sufficient to present a problem once organized. She tried to calm the surge-like exhilaration rushing through her skull and decide on an order of operations.

Rescue Datu. Obviously.

(She wished she could tell Datu that help was already on its way. Following the path of the river back north to Liriat Proper. Roaring on the wind. Rapidly approaching.)

Rescue Mak.

(Voicelessly, she dispatched a squadron of skeletons to search Castle Ynyssyll, with orders to find him and secure his release, and further, to bear him to the Lover's Complaint and there stay put, standing guard at its several entrances—including the one in the cellar, that led in and out of the catacombs.)

Rescue Canon Lir—Errolirrolin—no, Lir!—*from whatever unseemly sacrificial fascination ritual it is that binds them in this marriage to Rook. Shake them, kiss them, make them see* sense!

(Lanie thought: This is a tricky ticket in its current position. Move it down a few points.)

Next:

Give the Rookish wizards a taste of Lirian death magic,

Thereby:

Driving Rook out of Liriat,

Thereby:

Rescuing Lir from their marriage, etc, see above.

But beneath her, all around her, Lanie's bony bearers were beginning to stir uneasily. A powerful smell of seawater and wet feathers fell damply through the falling snow. Lanie spun about in her lookout, her self-built tower spinning with her. She would know the scent of Bran Fiakhna's magic anywhere.

Even at this distance, the Blackbird Bride seemed so very tall. Growing taller, too—for her flock of wizard-birds was lifting her aloft, raising her to Lanie's eye level at the opposite end of the tower. Mid-air, with a bird beneath each of her bare feet, Bran Fiakhna shifted her stance. Her left foot slid forward. Her left arm thrust out before her. Right elbow snapped high. Right fist gripped the pilum just above her shoulder. The pilum locked into a position perfectly horizontal to the tower floor, which was now a good twenty feet below her. Bran Fiakhna re-spidered the fingers of her right hand until they held the shaft of the pilum like an overlarge stylus, her spine straight, her hips aligned with her target.

Their gazes met. Bran Fiakhna's expression was remorseful but resolute.

And then she let loose.

The jet-black spear arced high over the heads of the living and undead. A peerless throw, the pilum burned through the falling snow like a dark comet. Ribbons of magic—war-spells, curses, charms, whatever could be impressed upon it by the best and most bellicose of her Parliament—wrapped the speeding weapon with crackling energy. What could stop such a marriage of magic and velocity?

Nothing.

It was coming on too fast. Like a falcon in his stoop. Like Nita with her knives. As lovely, as lethal.

But a tall skeleton, clad in rotting silk and rusted armor, had been watching all this while. He had anticipated the attack, had scaled the lattice of ribcages, tibiae, fibulae, femurs, and humeri until he reached Lanie's tier. The moment that Bran Fiakhna let fly her pilum, he dove into the sky to meet it—and caught it with his face. The long black spear slid through the hole where his nose had been and right out the back of his skull.

It stopped there. Stuck. Quivering.

Pilum firmly lodged, and without looking at Lanie, the tall skeleton jumped down from her bone fortifications and landed on the back of a Bright Knight. The Bright Knight, a fine strapping warrior, crumpled beneath the skeleton's light, dry weight as under a load of masonry, covering their head and shrieking like a child waking from one nightmare into another.

Hovering above Ynyssyll's Tooth, the Blackbird Bride shouted to her Parliament, to the courtiers of Rook and Liriat, and to all the Bright Knights: "Their heads! Remove their heads! They are only the dead dreaming!"

Lanie cursed in Quadic. It was the tersest, worst word she knew—a word that rhymed with nothing, and could never be made beautiful.

So, Bran Fiakhna knew something of death magic after all. Had, in fact, learned something of it from Lanie's own lips, at Nita's deathbed all those months ago. And more of it from her faithful servant, Baroness Sari Skrathmandan, who knew all about the ways one might kill a revenant.

She cursed again, this time herself.

There came the stuttering scrape of many drawn swords. Snowflakes flurried and eddied as several blackbirds plummeted away from their bride to stand on two feet again. From the breasts of their feathered tunics—from out of their very flesh—the Rookish wizards drew strange black weapons, each branded with the wizard markings they bore on their skin. They, along with the Bright Knights bearing their swords of fire, advanced into the undead horde. Red-orange-gold stood back-to-back with brilliantly-marked black to lay about them. Even a few courtiers, those who had been wearing small daggers or jeweled sabers as a mostly decorative conceit, snatched weapons from scabbards to plunge into the fray. Anything was better than wailing in despair as the undead danced all about them.

The first skull rolled.

The thunk of it on the flagstones, muted by snow, fanned Lanie's fury into a high, white blaze.

"Disarm them!" she shouted. "Immobilize them. Bind them. Sit on them—I don't care! Don't hurt them, if you can help it. But keep your heads *on!*"

Her words were all but lost in the clank of steel on bone. But the undead heard her without ears, obeyed without voice. Blackbirds rose up out of the fracas only to rain down again from the sky, falling with blades in hand to take advantage from the air. Lanie saw Jackdaw, with his gray nape and silver-and-black hair, fighting in the shadow of his queen. His light eyes flashed with fear. Lanie felt a pang for him, for he had seemed gentle. He fought side by side with another wizard whose skin glimmered darkly iridescent brown-black, her spotted breast gleaming beneath the ruffled feathers of her tunic. Lanie didn't know which wizard-bird she was and didn't have time to guess.

Next came, winking out of invisibility, a black-and-white bird with a yellow cap—Bran Fiakhna's new Bobolink, whose power was Concealment—dropping down on the head of a skeleton too busy wrestling a Bright Knight to notice it. Lanie cried out. The skull rolled anyway, the blue flames that had illuminated its eye sockets snuffed out.

A moment later, her heart was struck with renewed dread even before she remembered why. And then she saw it—buffeting the edge of her vision—a great, ragged storm of black and red.

Hopping and pointing, Lanie screamed, "Time-Hobble! Knock him out! Knock him out!"

But it was too late.

Cormorant's time-trap oozed upon her. The mucilaginous nectar of thickened time dripped down, covering her, smothering her. Viscous lassitude crept unhurriedly through her veins. Her vision grew sticky. The top of her tongue adhered to the roof of her mouth. Every heartbeat pulsed honey: very sweet, very slow...

It's over, Lanie thought.

The thought hung suspended at the forefront of her mind, a molasses smear of perpetual despair.

But then—far too fast for Lanie's goo-caught gaze to track—a slender set of bones leapt to attack the wizard Cormorant.

This was not a human skeleton that came so energetically to Lanie's rescue, with a vigor that reminded her how undead, who stood outside time, were also outside Time-Hobble's trap. It was canine: a medium-sized hunting dog, with a gracefully arched neck, a proud, blunt skull, square muzzle, broad breast, and powerful haunches. The line of its vertebrae extended in an upswept whip of a tail. In life, it must have been so favored of its Blood Royal owner that in death it was buried with honors in the tumulus of Moll's Kopje.

A clever creature—even now, in undeath! It knew to keep a soft mouth when catching a bird, so as not to damage it. It caught Cormorant fast and sure, but also as gently as a net around a butterfly.

The wizard-bird hung limp and stymied from the bone dog's jaws. He lost focus; his Time-Hobble wobbled, came unstuck.

"Good girl!" Lanie cried, her breath rushing back into her lungs with gale-force. "Keep him still!"

Eager tail bones wagged with delight.

Wherever Lanie turned, she was at the center of a whirlpool of bone. Most of the skeletons who had reassembled themselves from the catacombs were bare of anything but themselves, and some were only partly reconstructed. But many hundreds—those who had come from cryptyard or kopje—still wore the rotting remnants of their burial garments. Some even carried items that had been buried with them.

One item in particular caught her eye.

"I beg your pardon!" she called to the bearer.

The skeleton turned to her with an air of courteous—even arrogant—expectancy. It was the tall one from before; Lanie recognized him by the black pilum jutting from his nose hole. When it saw whom addressed it, its demeanor changed. It bowed, grinning cheerily at her. Lanie found it a heartening sight.

"Will you please," she asked that friendly face, "climb down that rope"— she indicated the rope knotted about the merlon—"and cut my niece free from her cage? Then bring her back to me?"

If anything, the tall skeleton's grin grew wider and more cheerful. He nodded vigorously, and the pilum in his skull bobbed with the motion. From the holster slung across his back, the skeleton removed the item that had caught Lanie's attention: an ax big enough to rival the Founding Queen's.

Lanie's eyes widened.

It wasn't *like* the ax of the Founding Queen. It *was* the ax of the Founding Queen. Drjōta, Marrow Thirst, made for Ynyssyll Brackenwild by Quick Fantastic Stones herself, and passed on to her heirs.

Lanie had seen the fabled weapon depicted in portraits and on several statues. But she knew that this had to be the original—for the next thing that the tall skeleton did was to pluck a desiccated hand from a garland of similar grisly objects hanging around his neck and to feed it to the rusted ax.

The moment that the blade cleaved the withered flesh, its edges brightened and sharpened. The next moment, the flesh was entirely absorbed into it.

And only *then* did Lanie notice the tarnished silver circlet that sat upon the tall skeleton's brow. She almost choked.

"Sosha Brackenwild?"

Grandpa Rad's Sosha? The Regent Sinister?

Sosha grinned his skully grin once more before disappearing over the edge of the turret to swarm down the rope. Lanie stared, confounded. Sending the late Blood Royal Sosha Brackenwild after her niece was perhaps not the brightest decision she'd ever made. But even with help soaring in from afar, she did not like leaving Datu hanging in a crow's cage where any wizard-bird might get at her.

Anxiously she awaited Sosha's return, but it seemed only seconds later that his speared-through face reappeared in the embrasure. Datu was slung over his shoulder, hands and feet still bound, eyes wide open but body so limp Lanie thought she must be unconscious.

Shucking her coat, Lanie hastily gathered her niece into her arms. Datu's skin, like her puppy's fur had been earlier, glimmered with the faintest frost of emeralds. A cast of palest blue—ectenical blue—filmed the green of her eyes. But her eyes flinched slightly as Lanie directed Sosha to break her chains.

He did this easily—bright Drjōta sliced the iron like a cleaver through gossamer—and then stood back, regarding this paltry work with contemptuous amusement. Turning her back to him, Lanie wrapped her niece even more tightly in her coat, and tried to rub some warmth back into her. Datu did not endure this for many minutes before forcing her frozen mouth to voice her uppermost concern.

"Bluh-Bluh-Blackbird," her teeth were chattering like a windup toy, "c-cut Didyi. C-cut off-ff h-hih-his…"

"Don't worry. I have it," Lanie soothed her, still rubbing vigorously, "It's safe. I'll fix it. I promise."

She glanced over her left shoulder at Sosha, who stood taller than the Blackbird Bride. He presented, she realized, a formidable guardian—even more so than the one she'd originally had in mind. What with his ax and his crown and his being so tremendously undead, no one would dare challenge him.

"Blood Royal," she began, with a timidity she recognized but did not admire, "might you be so kind as to bear my niece to a brewpub called the Lover's Complaint? There you'll find a woman named Havoc; Datu will be safe with…"

Datu began squirming, trying to shrug off Lanie's coat while simultaneously throwing her arms around Lanie's neck in a panicked stranglehold. "L-let me s-stay. You puh-promised. When Muh-Mumyu d-d-died. Our v-v-v-vengeance."

But Lanie didn't think Datu was as interested in vengeance as in not leaving her aunt's side again—especially not in the company of a walking skeleton with the Blackbird Bride's spear stuck through his face. She set her forehead against Datu's. The child's skin was far colder than her own, the frost-gritted surface like a dusting of sugar. Pressing her palms to her niece's cheeks, Lanie willed her warm again. But she herself was cold through and through, in substance and in accident, and had no power to warm anyone.

Only Havoc's kitchen would do the trick. Only a blanket, or five. Warm food. A fire. Her didyi's arms around her. Her wolf puppy cuddled close. Lanie had to get Datu away. Away from all this undeath. Away from her.

"But I want to stay with you!" Datu wailed as Lanie unwrapped her arms from around her neck and tucked the coat more securely around her. "You p-*promised!*"

"I promised you an undead army," Lanie said in a stern voice. "Be content."

Ruthlessly, Sosha lifted Datu away from her aunt and slung her over his shoulder again. Stretching her neck, Datu directed an ectenica-glazed glare at her aunt. "Don't forget Didyi!"

Lanie rolled her eyes. "I didn't. He's safe at Havoc's. Waiting for you." Or would be, she thought, by the time Datu arrived.

The wild relief in Datu's face was worth everything. Her blue lips pinkened as her face broke into a smile. "Really?"

"Really!"

"Auntie Lanie!" Her niece had to shout the words as the distance between them grew. "It is a very good undead army!"

Grinning, Lanie shouted back, "I love you too, Datu!"

Bearing his small burden, Sosha Brackenwild plunged across the roof toward the door in the tower floor. His stride was long; he crossed Ynyssyll's Tooth in a few bounds. His fellow skeletons responded as elegantly as dancers, stepping out of his way without seeming to notice him at all.

But what Sosha did not see, as Lanie did from her lofty cradle of bone, was the Blackbird Bride cutting a swath across the tower.

When her spear had failed to meet its mark in Lanie, she had drawn from the feathers of her breast, from out of her very flesh, a blade of her own. It glittered as if cut from a single dark diamond. Those she slew by its edge—now twice-dead—piled up behind her: acephalous skeletons parted forever from their skulls, the animating fire quenched from their bones. Bran Fiakhna waded through her grisly harvest, fighting relentlessly, magnificently, moving almost too fast to track. More than half her Parliament was imprisoned in cages of bone, or shackled in chains of bone, with large femurs jammed between their teeth to prevent vocalized spell-casting. Those who had been trapped in their bird-forms were wrapped in the remnants of shrouds and stuffed, stunned, into ribcages.

But of those wizard-birds still free, all had taken wing again to keep out of arm's reach or range of various missiles—which included parts of the undead themselves, detached for the purpose. Lanie could deduce the reason for this magical withholding easily enough: the Blackbird Bride was pulling ever more strength and endurance from her Parliament. By the time she met Sosha Brackenwild over the door in the tower floor, she was practically snapping with power.

For the first time, Sosha's arrogant strut faltered. He backed away a few steps from the tower door, and shook his head in cowering denial. Lanie tried to feed him encouragement, fortitude, fearlessness—but encountered a baffling sort of block from his direction. No matter what she did, Sosha's patellae knocked, his pelvis quaked, his entire frame quivered.

Not lowering her guard, Bran Fiakhna commanded, "Put her down," and loosed a flood of fascination—not in Lanie's direction, but Sosha's.

Lanie was confounded. *That* won't work, will it? she thought, just as Sosha unslung Datu from his shoulder and dangled her between his bony hands. He held the child just a hair's breadth beyond the reach of Bran Fiakhna's sword, and rattled her like a rag doll, as if to ask, "What child? This child?"

Datu, her back to the Blackbird Bride, was facing Lanie but no longer seeing her, or anything. Her expression had drained of all meaning. She was far from herself, perhaps already entering a place of emeralds.

Swinging back her sword, the Blackbird Bride lunged.

Lanie cried "No!"—but Sosha only danced away again, Datu depending from his sinewless grip like a bit of refuse. He threw back his head as though in mocking laughter. The black pilum jutted from his nose and the back of his skull like the horns of some eldritch creature. Only then did he glance at Lanie. The blue-white fire in one eye socket winked drolly out for a millisecond.

And then, he tossed Datu over the side of the tower.

All the breath left Lanie's body. She might have pissed herself. She would find out later.

Lir shouted out.

(Oh, that sound! Lanie knew she would never forget it; all her life, she would love them for that shout. It told her how Lir would have rather thrown themself over the tower than watch her niece fall from it.)

Snapping loose from the bones cradling her, Lanie sprang down to the roof. Slipping and sliding in the trampled slush, her body feeling a hundred times lighter than it had for months, she ran to the edge of the Ynyssyll's Tooth and peered over it.

She was laughing even before she saw what she already knew was there, and yet—for that one appalling second—had doubted.

Lir met her at the embrasure, grasping her arms as if to pull her back from leaping. But Lanie tore herself free and pointed.

Floating a few feet below the tower's crenelations was Datu, in a coat far too large for her, curled limply on the back of the tiger rug. The tiger's head turned to Lanie, its glass eyes aglow with her own substance.

It's like—Lanie thought wildly—staring in a mirror at myself, but seeing a completely different face.

Part of her was always with the tiger rug: first flying back to the riverboat with Mak's frozen arm, delivering it promptly to Tan and Duantri with a note she had penned at Haaken's desk, and then, speeding back to herself where she waited on Ynyssyll's Tooth with a plan already in place to rescue Datu and remove her to safety.

But Lanie had also trusted that part of herself to let work autonomously, more like the way her breath or heartbeat worked than the conscious movements of her limbs or facial muscles. That being so, even knowing the tiger rug was speeding her way, with so many distractions and her attention split in so many directions, Lanie had not quite realized when it had arrived.

But the undead could always sense others of their kind. And so Sosha Brackenwild had done. Of course, how he had retained so much memory of himself, so much of his own will, as to defy a direct order from her, Miscellaneous Stones, and act according to his own mischievous strategy, Lanie did not know—and when she had a moment to breathe, she and the Regent Sinister were going to have *words!* Or *she* would, anyway. And he would stand there, tongueless and voiceless and penitent, and *take* it. After she thanked him, of course.

At her side, Lir was saying something to her. Lanie would have recognized their voice anywhere, and the tones of relief and joy filling it. But right now she heard it only distantly, like a bell ringing at the other end of the city. She knew that Lir had unfastened their golden velvet cloak, that they were clasping it around her shoulders, and peering into her face, and asking her questions. She was conscious of the smell of white pepper incense, and of an immense sense of loss.

But she was concentrating elsewhere. With the lightest push of her will, she sent the tiger rug and its invaluable burden speeding away—away from Tooth, away from Kopje, over moat and First Circle wall, away over the city, to Seventh Circle, to Havoc and the Lover's Complaint and home.

Away, away, away, and...

Safe.

Now to make sure she stayed that way.

Sidestepping Lir's embrace, Lanie whipped around and growled in both her voices: "Sosha Brackenwild! Hear me!"

The tall skeleton turned the remnants of his face to her. Snow crystals sparkled on his tarnished silver crown.

Locking her gaze with his eyeless sockets, Lanie pushed the best part of her will, her power, her identity—the deepest substance of herself—into his bones:

"The Blackbird Bride. Take her down."

The late, great tyrant of the realm of Liriat, now mounted by a necromancer of the deathly Stones line, was only too happy to oblige.

CHAPTER FORTY-NINE

An Age-Old Alliance

SOSHA BRACKENWILD TURNED. Lanie sat inside his skull like Saint Death. She watched through the windows of his orbits. He looked the Blackbird Bride up and down, just once. In the pith of his scrutiny was enough scorn to wither a stand of titanwoods.

The air above the tower crimped.

Sosha Brackenwild recognized the sudden sucking sensation as power being drawn down from many sources into one. It was almost palpable. He had witnessed such things on his campaign in Northernmost Skakmaht. He had observed Irradiant Stones with his undead, or the Sky Wizards with their ghost-powered contrivances. He knew what Bran Fiakhna was doing.

She was summoning the collective magics of her remaining Parliament into her body, her blade, into the very leather of her cuirass, transforming it into a substance that glinted like jet. She thrust her left hand again into the feathers of her tunic and from it plucked a buckler, hardly larger than a vamplate, that looked to be made of the same stuff as her blade.

Blackbirds began raining from the sky.

A few of their bodies were lucky enough to fall upon Ynyssyll's Tooth, where the undead caught them with gentle hands, and cradled them away as they swooned, drained. Others missed the tower entirely. Small feathered bodies fell, and fell, and fell. In her own flesh, Lanie felt the echoes of their hollow bones breaking on Moll's Kopje. Grackle. Skimmer. Starling. Lapwing. Swift. But these echoes soon faded as her seat in Sosha took ascendance.

With one hand, he jerked the pilum out of his nose hole. With the other, he drew Drjōta once more from its mighty holster. Brandishing both, Sosha Brackenwild crashed upon Bran Fiakhna like a meteor.

The first blow of that infamous ax bounced off her scaled cuirass. The armor's enchantment held. But the look on her face! Sosha could have fed off such a look for weeks. So. The armor might hold, but he could beat the body within it to jelly. All *that* would take was time.

And he, Sosha Brackenwild, being dead, was outside time. The wind was almost visible as the clouds shredded holes in the moonlight. It howled like spirits unmoored from their haunt, engirdling the tower in a second parapet. The stars glittered like the compound eyes of celestial flies, looking down on a sky suddenly empty of wizards.

Bran Fiakhna fought Sosha Brackenwild, alone.

She gave battle like the god her people called her—Twelve-in-One—with her blade of black diamond sharp enough to slice the night, and her buckler spitting dark sparks whenever it met pilum or ax. She whirled and wheeled like a machine made only of edges. Not seldom did her blade dip past Sosha's guard, grating through the spaces between ribs, glancing off his inferior armor. Ribbons of rotted silk flew from his body. She cleaved the steel plates that had once protected his neck bones. She might have killed him a dozen times over—had Sosha been a living man.

Instead, every blow she rained upon the dead Blood Royal invigorated him. He grinned and feinted, grinned and lunged, grinned, riposted, riposted, riposted, matching the Blackbird Bride blow for blow, and slowly but—more importantly—*unflaggingly* drove her across Ynyssyll's Tooth, from one wall to the next and back again, to no more purpose than exhaustion. Even as the borrowed strength drained out of her, his swordplay picked up speed. He had only been playing before; now he pressed her. Her form disintegrating from impassive to frantic, Bran Fiakhna parried his flurry of swings and thrusts. Under her cuirass, the plumage of her tunic steamed with sweat. Sweat ran beneath the rim of her galea into her silver-pale eyes, which were showing their whites all around.

The Blackbird Bride was slowing down.

Then Sosha whirled, getting in behind her, and slamming the flat of his battle-ax against her back. Bran Fiakhna staggered.

Lanie, her substance seated in Sosha's frame (and also watching from the shoulders of her bone guard, with Lir standing yet at her knee), followed the fight with shining pride. No wonder her great-grandfather had followed this man to Northernmost Skakmaht. No wonder Irradiant had raised dead warriors and felled whole cities in Sosha Brackenwild's name. He was magnificent—joyous!—with his necklace of severed hands rattling against his corroded mail, and his movements full of grace, and his eye sockets sparking with star-fire. Lanie, enthroned in his carcass (and looking on approvingly from her own far less interesting body) could have danced Bran Fiakhna right off her feet, right off the edge of the tower, right off the face of Athe—forever!

"Yes," Lanie urged Sosha in her deep voice. Without him and within him, she fed him her approval and encouragement, her anger and authority and pride, and the long, lonely autumn of her misery. The memory of Nita, dead. The memory of Datu and Undies, frozen in emerald. The memory of Lir, their face blank and bare, sun-like in rubies and cloth-of-gold. "Yes!"

"Lanie."

That voice. The color of dawn.

"Lanie, you have to stop."

That voice. A sound she would have cut off her own left arm to wake up to each morning.

"Stop this."

In the end, it was easy to ignore, that voice. All she had to do was push even more of herself outside of herself and into Sosha Brackenwild. Far enough from her body, she could not feel the echoes of Bran Fiakhna's labored breath in her own lungs, or how those bare, silver-ringed toes blackened from the cold and bled onto the snow.

Lanie minded none of it.

No! In fact, she would have *more!* More bone, more blade, more blood! More of Sosha's whirling dance! His joy in Bran Fiakhna's terror and pain. This, *this* was the woman who had driven her spear through Datu's chest. Who had ordered her shot at and drowned and hung out to freeze. Who had hurt Datu's own darling Undies—innocent, barely a baby. This was the woman who had hunted them from their home, who would enslave Mak's will to Lanie's, and Lanie's to her own, and grow in power, and put down any who defied her.

Was it any wonder Blood Royal Erralierra had sought to weaken the Blackbird Bride's power base in whatever way she could? She was a great ruler of her house! And as for her left hand, Amanita Muscaria Stones, she had died a *hero* of Liriat! When Sosha Brackenwild sat once more upon his throne, he would have a statue of Nita erected: and every year, pilgrims would come and gird it with a fresh belt of black feathers, four-and-twenty in all, reminding Rook that it would never again put its clawed foot on the neck of Liriat. And never, never again would Liriat grovel to this—or any!—sorceress queen.

But hands were squeezing Lanie's shoulders—her own shoulders, her *real* shoulders. For all that they were cold and stiff, they were still flesh, still hers, still with their muscles and blood-ways and *nerves*. They still responded to pressure. To heat.

Oh, that heat. Those fingers like red-hot irons clamped upon her. Scarlet flames ran up her neck and down both her arms, resting lightly on the surface of her skin, warming but not hurting her. The bloodlight did not even burn away the cloth of her shirt, so precise was Lir's control.

"Lanie. Please."

That voice, that voice. All the poetry she'd ever craved. To dwell just sidelong of its dear familiar mystery, to bask in its ever-deepening nuances, she would have traded her chance to walk alongside the Traveling Palaces of Higher Quadiíb.

But it had betrayed her, that voice. Deceiver, it had conversed with her at length, letting fall a thousand charming details, compliments, caressing words, had whispered love-talk in her ear at Midsummer, wretched farewells at summer's end, had bound her heart to its sound, while all the while—*all the while*—side-slipping what mattered most, slithering out of, glancing off of, obfuscating, or its opposite: concealing truth in light, not shadow. And worse—

"She *mutilated* Mak," Lanie spat. "Did you stand by and watch? Lir, she *tortured* Datu! She did her damnedest to make me her thrall—and you did *nothing!*"

"*You were not supposed to be here!*"

Lir's hot hands gripped her shoulders. Lanie was sweating from their nearness, their urgency. They spoke very rapidly, very softly.

"I only wished to buy you—and Datu—and Liriat!—*time*. It was all I had, and it was little enough. Once given, I had no currency left worth anything. I wagered it all on the chance of you *leaving!*"

Lanie lifted her hands to squeeze their wrists, her wizard mark livid in the darkness. "You gave her everything—Liriat, yourself, everything! You *told* her *everything!*"

"To save you. To save Liriat."

She would not look at them. To look upon them was to love them. To love them was to forgive them. And she was not ready, she *was not ready* for that.

"You'll see," she whispered. "I'll give you back Liriat—and all of Rook with it."

"Lanie."

Soft brown hands cradled her cheeks. That thoughtful, subtle round face drew nose to nose with hers. Their skin was like oven-fired clay. But Lanie was freezing cold. Even her sweat was sleet.

"Lanie, I ask you—I beg you—have mercy."

Was this not what she wanted? Had not Lir begged the Blackbird Bride for mercy—for the sake of Datu? And now they were groveling to Lanie—for the sake of the Blackbird Bride! Circles within circles. That was Liriat Proper. And Lir, always Lir, at its center. And here were Lir's lips, barely a breath away, that breath shared between them: smoke and citrus, molten glass, orange blossom.

Something unfroze in her. Lanie at last began to know true warmth again, starting with a pinch in her chest, a bead of bloodlight in her center darkness. And then, all the heat came flooding back in. She felt everything at once, so many echo-wounds it was like her body was an endless cavern of pain: broken birds, panicked courtiers, and Bran Fiakhna herself—whose great heart was failing her, whose lungs were failing her, whose strong arms were failing her…

Lanie began to weep. Lir brushed her tears away with gentle hands. They kissed the tender corners of her eyes.

Across the tower, a cry like a wounded crow rent the snow-laced night. Sosha Brackenwild had driven Bran Fiakhna to her knees.

Lanie wanted to look. She wanted to stare down at Bran Fiakhna from Sosha Brackenwild's long-dead face.

But Lir held her fast, and spoke fast, in that voice she could not help but helplessly love.

"Miscellaneous Stones. You are wonderful. You are brilliant and beautiful and strong. You love perry cider and boring your niece to sleep with anatomy lessons. You are a necromancer. You are Saint Death's daughter. You are my best friend and my beloved. You are not Sosha Brackenwild. You are not Irradiant Stones. If we have learned anything from our bloody history, let our lesson be that we are better—*you* are better—than those who came before us. You are more rational, more compassionate, more able to co-exist with the kindness of the world than with its cruelties. What you decide today will blaze a path for succeeding generations. You are not Quick Fantastic Stones. You are not Gallowsdance Stones. You are not your mother or your father or your sister—or any Stones before you! You, Miscellaneous Stones, redefine your name—as I shall mine. Ours, Lanie, need not be a path laid, paved, and bathed in blood. Therefore, Lanie, I beg you. I *beg* you. Stop. Stop this now."

Everything hurt. Even her tongue. Even her teeth. But Lanie, reluctantly peering up into those loving, desperate, coppery-brown eyes, felt warm again for the first time since leaving Havoc's kitchen. What was this warmth but the hearth fires of home?

She forced her cracked lips apart and spoke a single word, both her voices braided together, louder than a clap of thunder:

"Stop."

Sosha stopped, forced to obey her command. Somewhat. He took a half-step back from Bran Fiakhna, lowering ax and spear, and pivoting to glare eyelessly at Lanie. Flourishing his contempt like a well-timed acid splash, Sosha made a mocking little bow.

And then, deliberately and defiantly, he turned his back on her.

Lanie's gaze hardened. Her jaw clenched. She watched Sosha loom over the Blackbird Bride, who had fallen and who did not rise. The late Blood Royal's attenuated shadow seemed to cleave her in twain. Her head was bent, her shoulders heaving. Snow and blood trembled on her feathers, the gray markings on her face were masked in red from all the cuts he had dealt her. She was bleeding from several puncture wounds, a shallow slice to the neck. Sosha had been dealing her the same blows she had dealt Datu. And now he held his pilum posed for the killing blow—a single thrust to the chest.

Lanie bounded forward, screaming, "Stop!"

The pilum clattered to the ground.

But Sosha was strong in his undeath. The things of his life surrounded him: his silver crown, his garland of hands, Drjōta, Ynyssyll's Tooth, Castle Ynyssyll, even the sprawl of Liriat Proper beneath him. His dream of himself was inviolable. And in Sosha Brackenwild's dream, Stoneses served Brackenwilds—not the other way around.

He raised Drjōta high. He would *not* stop. He had never taken orders in his life and he would not start now. He would do as he had always done, as he had taught Irradiant Stones to do: precisely as he pleased.

Lanie's left hand swept up. Her deep sight saw what no one else on the roof could see: a hundred thousand fiery blue strands spinning out from her wizard mark, each with a terminus in one of Doédenna's beautiful revenants: those blue sparks of undeath which She had loaned back to them from Her cloak of bone.

Though there were many undead, and she was but one living necromancer, Lanie isolated Sosha's thread with unerring accuracy. She worked it between her fingers. She stretched it out longer, thinned it down further. In seconds, she had twisted his thread into a sort of lasso, which she looped—once, twice, thrice—around Sosha's neck.

Enraged, he clawed at his throat. He hacked at the strand that bound her to him with Drjōta's bright blade. But this was a thing even Drjōta's peerless edge could not cut. Once again he turned his empty eye sockets to her and glared. Leaving Bran Fiakhna on the ground, he spun and charged at Lanie.

Tried to charge her.

Tried to move. Found he could not. The more he strained against her thin blue thread, the tighter she pulled. The thread grew taut, like a crossbow cranked for murder.

Lanie jerked her left hand up and back. Sosha staggered. Lanie lashed his leash around her wrist, and dragged him over to her—long bones and silver crown and shining ax and all. And when the Regent Sinister, heaped up and intermingled and at all sorts of odd angles with himself, landed clatteringly at her feet, she planted a foot on his hyoid bone, grinding down.

"Take Drjōta," she told Lir.

Blood Royal Errolirrolin Brackenwild knelt beside their illustrious ancestor, the conqueror of Northernmost Skakmaht and the Bane of Iskald. Without cosmetics, stripped of all self-inculcated neutrality, they looked weary and sad. Drjōta gleamed in their grip, as if thirsting for a taste of fresh Brackenwild blood. Lir acceded. With a deft and practiced touch, they ran a single fingertip down the edge of the ax. A thin line of blood welled from their skin, only as deep and only as wide as a paper cut. Red flames sprang from the wound, bloodlight so bright that Lanie was sure a single drop could power every lamp in the city. Directing the red flames from fingertip to blade, Lir let the ax catch fire. Bloodlight blazed all along that silver-steel-starlight edge, setting it alight.

Drjōta sang out. After a century of starvation—and then a diet of a single withered hand, a few shallow cuts of a Rookish sorceress—this sip of living Brackenwild blood gave the ax an air of almost louche abandonment.

Sinking like a setting sun, Lir knelt at their forebear's side. Then, heaving a sigh and the fiery ax at the same time, they let the blade of Drjōta, Marrow Thirst, fall, and sever the neck of Sosha Brackenwild.

The Regent Sinister fell to fragments. The fragments fell to dust.

Lir, who—whatever else they were—was a true fire priest of Sappacor, spoke a prayer to their god, asking that They consign Sosha's malice to the Triple Flame. At prayer's end, they sprang to their feet, and with a look of loathing—and a much shorter prayer, or curse—they cast Drjōta onto the flagstones.

The flaming ax shattered into shrapnel. Like Sosha, the bright gleam of enchanted metal winked out. Old wood, old rust, fell to dust. Lir turned from the debris, and took Lanie's hands in theirs.

"Thank you," they said tiredly. "Thank you, Lanie."

Exhausted, impulsive, Lanie threw herself into their arms and held on tight. Oh, this scent of white pepper and sweat. Oh, this glowing skin. Oh, her friend.

"I've missed you, I've missed you!"

"I know, I know. I, too," Lir murmured. "I have missed you every day. I thought of you every day. Every moment. And every time you knocked"—they touched their reliquary—"a door to dawn opened in my heart."

"I was so lonely!"

"I, too, Lanie. I, too."

She touched her hair. She'd lost her hat. Her braids were frizzy, damp. "I'm a mess," she said, and hid her face in their shoulder again.

"Everything is," Lir agreed. "I am."

"No, no. But I can fix it, Lir. We can fix it together. Only tell me what you want. I'll give you anything you want!" Lanie hesitated. "I know… I know that you… that you've had to keep many secrets. From me. I'll try to understand. I promise I'll try."

Even Lir's saddest smile was a curly crimson ribbon of wonder. Their dimple peeped. "Oh, Lanie. You always understand so beautifully." They stooped in, peering more closely at her face, their fingers tightening on her shoulders. "I need you to understand me more than ever right now. Can you do that?"

"Of course! Just tell me what you want! What shall I do?" Lanie implored them. "Shall I drive Bran Fiakhna to our borders? Set our army of the undead to guard Liriat against further conquest? Whatever you ask, I—"

"Whatever I ask?"

"I swear it on Saint Death."

Lir was silent a moment, then whispered, "Thank you, Lanie. Bless you, Lanie."

At last they kissed her, sweet and clinging, and held her as close as two bodies could come without moving into each other. The heat of that kiss crested through Lanie like panthauma on a high holy fire feast. Even when it was over, the warmth of it went on and on inside her like a prayer.

Lir released her from their embrace, but they did not immediately step back. Instead, they bowed and kissed Lanie's hands, first one, then the other. Pressing her knuckles to their forehead, they prayed:

"May the Triple Flame light your footsteps all the long days of your life." And with a last hard squeeze of her hands, they let her go.

Just like that, Canon Lir disappeared, and Blood Royal Errolirrolin Brackenwild stood before Lanie once more. Quick as a flame flickering. Quick as a thought.

"Lir—"

Errolirrolin turned their back on her and walked across the silent tower to their wife, whom they helped to her feet. Bran Fiakhna stood, but leaned heavily against them, head lolling. Errolirrolin looked across the waiting sea of attendant bones and shivering bodies.

Meeting Lanie's gaze, they raised their free hand. It was as stylized and ostentatious a gesture as the Blood Royal's ritual dance last Midsummer, when they had worn the death mask of the Founding Queen and stood on gilded stilts above the cheering throng. They stretched their arm high above their head, spreading their fingers wide, the red flame of their blood dancing over their fingers.

"Miscellaneous Immiscible Stones," pronounced Blood Royal Errolirrolin Brackenwild, "wherein the House of Brackenwild finds you guilty of the charge of treason, of disturbing public order, disrupting the unity between our nation Liriat and her sister-bride Rook, of raising arms and enchantments against our lawful Wife and Queen and therefore against Us, and of causing violent hands to be laid upon Her Sovereign Majesty's sacred person, I hereby banish you from this day and forevermore from the realm of Liriat."

CHAPTER FIFTY

Saint Death, Will You Dance?

Rainday 14th
Month of Vespers, 421 Founding Era
7 days till Winter Solstice

EVERY TIME, SHE wondered how she could let her undead go. Yet before the night was over, she knew she must.

The undead bore her on their bony shoulders down the many steps of Ynyssyll's Tooth. They carried her across the moat, closing ranks behind her so that no Lirian soldier or Bright Knight (for there weren't any Rookish wizards left alive with any strength in them) could harry or harass her.

There, on the flagstones of First Circle, she found the people of Liriat Proper waiting for her.

Or rather, for *them*. Their woken dead.

She had never attended a First Frost Harlequinade herself. The only time she might have done so was this autumn past, but she had been too ill. It was the only holiday in Liriat dedicated to Doédenna alone, for the four high holy fire feasts were focused solely on Sappacor—even Winter Solstice, which in Quadiíb was held to belong to the twelfth god. But though Old Sparks held dominion over the hearts of Lirians, Saint Death remained their secondary founding god, and all Lirians knew to honor her. There were a few, perhaps, who even preferred her, in darkness, in secret, in the long watches of a Vespers night.

And earlier that night, when the catacombs trembled and the dead beneath the city awoke, the miracle on Ynyssyll's Tooth had brought Lirians flocking to their capital's center in open parade. They flooded First Circle, dressed like they would for the Harlequinade but more haphazardly, for they had grabbed whatever came most easily to hand: motley and paint, furs and brightly felted wools, horned headdresses, wreaths of evergreen, wreaths of holly and bloodberry, elaborate death's head masks crafted in

Doédenna's honor and set with lit candles.

There they stood, outside the drawbridge gate, in those black hours after midnight, waiting to greet their undead. Eyes glistening, they drank in the sight of the hundreds of skeletons crawling down the sides of the tower, then leaping the moat, or picking their way across the broken ice as lightly as water striders. But they watched most carefully the undead who had borne her on their shoulders across the slippery drawbridge, and it was these that the living first approached.

She was not sure what the living wanted with her, or with the undead. At first she feared this was to be another battle she must fight. But the moment she saw their festival dress, how even the raggedest among them were wearing their finest winter regalia, she relaxed. The living carried torches lit from the city's one hundred forty-four bloodlamps. The light fell upon their awed faces like the beaming approval of the god of Fire, who stood aside this night as humble spectator, watching as Their sister moved through Their city, mounted in the body of Her priestess.

That first moment, on the pavement of First Circle boulevard, living and undead stood separate—not quite fearful, but shy—of each other. Each side hesitant to make the first move. Each side longing to do so.

She did not know how to help them. Her hands rested lightly upon two smooth skulls, like the armrests of a throne.

And then, one of the vesper clowns, dressed in felted wool motley and wearing a cap with more petals than a peony, called out up to her, "Saint Death! Will you dance?"

She knew then that they did not see her for what she was: traitor, and exile, and necromancer of infamous surname, but who possessed nothing else of any worldly worth.

No, they saw a quiet-faced woman whose cloak of bone had come alive to dance with them all.

So she made the sign of the bird at her chest and answered softly, "Fool—I will!"

And dance she did. They all did.

Later, she could not remember how long it lasted. She did remember how she, along with the undead and all the vesper clowns of Liriat Proper, moved together as a single sinuous being, winding through the Twelve Circles in a cacophonous cocoon of sound made by every instrument imaginable, played as loudly as possible, with enthusiastic disregard for anything that hinted at rhythm or key signature. Those who had no instruments—a number which included all of the undead—joined in the jamboree any way they could: with pounding feet, clapping hands, sticks plucked from the gutters and scraped over ridges of exposed bone, tarsals clapping the naked curves of skulls—rat-a-tat, clatter-clat, rum-tum-tum-tum—the hoots and cries of living lungs mingled with the winter wind whistling through gaping grins.

The parade ended as all Proper parades must in Sinistral Park, which glittered in the snowlight. The dancers broke free of the line and piled their torches together for a bonfire, then ran for the woodpiles stacked outside Twelfth Circle wall for use of the poor and indigent. The bonfire grew mountainous. The dance grew riotous. Living and undead whirled with each other, and she stood at their center, turning around and around to watch the swirling and swinging and leaping and jumping that was spiraling on all about her.

Everyone—no matter how young or old, regardless of wealth or status, health or infirmity—everyone who beheld the expression on her face knew in their hearts that Doédenna, god of Death, loved them to every galaxy beyond the grave.

When it came time to end the dance, in the almost-dark of almost-dawn, she said, in a voice so low that it was lost to the noise and the laughter: "And now I shall sing."

Sing she did. The living did not hear her; they danced on. But it was not for the living that she sang the Lahnessthanessar, oldest of all the spellsongs but one. She sang for the undead. She sang the Great Lullaby as Goody had taught it to her, both in the beginning of Lanie's life and at the end of Goody's. A song of hush, of crèche, of snow falling on snow. The unknitting of noise itself.

It took but moments—a few phrases of music, that was all—and all the undead whom she had raised that night folded down where they stood. Snow on snow on snow. Blue sparks rose up as stars. Rose up, and returned to Doédenna's cloak.

When they noticed the thinning of their numbers, the slowing of their dance, the living finally stood still. Shoulders rolled back. Eyes opened, clear and wide. They watched in reverent surprise as their fallen companions sank beneath the snow and vanished into the frozen sod. Gone. Gone as if they had never been. Leaving no mark, no trace. Soundless as the hymn that sang them down.

When the last bone passed out of sight, the living—who, without realizing it, had reached out to hold the hands of lovers, neighbors, friends, strangers; who finding themselves wholly unable to witness these awesome events alone—gave a start, and smiled tremulously. They turned to each other with embraces and inarticulate murmurs. A few trudged to the bonfire and began to shovel snow atop it, until the red flames hissed happily and were smothered to sleep. Two by two, three by three, in large clusters and small, the citizens of Liriat Proper drifted back through Midnight Gate, back behind the walls of their city.

Their city. Where Lanie could return only briefly, and only to collect those she had promised to protect. Their city, which she must then bid farewell forever. It was over.

Except.

A shadow moved across the sky. The moonlight leached the striped pelt of its rich dark rust, but glinted in the glass eyes like another set of stars. Rippling like water, the tiger rug alighted upon the uppermost surface of the snow. So softly did it land, it left no print or mark beneath it.

When she did nothing but stare at it, the tiger rug undulated closer, and butted her thigh with its forehead until she climbed aboard. She sank into its rumbling warmth, and allowed it to bear her away from her unbearable solitude.

EPILOGUE

Salal

Rimeday, 26th
Month of Squalls, 422 Founding Era
55 days till Spring Equinox

A SMALL, BROWN hand caught her by the ankle. "Where are you going?"

"For a walk," Lanie told her niece. "A vigorous walk. Outside. Uphill. Alone. On dry land. Striding forth into the jungles of… wherever we are."

Tan glanced up from her bunk, where she was poring over her sea charts. "As of last night," she informed them with her usual bright precision, "we sailed past Ochre and are now following the west coast of Lower Quadiíb south. At dawn, we docked at Port Mohoon to take on supplies. In another week, we will have reached the southernmost tip of the Quadic continent, which we will sail around and thence up the east coast of Quadiíb until we reach Ylkazarra."

"Right," Lanie said. "Thanks." She turned to Datu. "You got all that? May I have your leave to go now?"

"Take Stripes," Datu demanded.

Undies yipped, aggrieved. The tiger rug was his favorite napping spot. His chew toy. His stalwart companion. He was loath to part with it even to please his beloved: his most worshiped and adored goddess-companion-sibling-queen, Sacred Datura Stones.

"The point of this exercise," Lanie explained, "is *exercise*. Not flying around on a rug. Besides. If Undies doesn't have Stripes's tail to teethe on, I shudder to think where he'll turn his attentions."

"My drawers," Datu said glumly.

The wolf pup's multicolored ears sprang up like shark fins in chummy waters. Not for nothing was he yclept Mister Underwear Stones! Drawers, even! Undies' predilection for said garments were Datu's original inspiration for his cleping!

"Stripes stays," Lanie said. "But *you* could come, if you want."

Datu shook her head, like she always did. "I must stay with Didyi."

"Duantri's shift with Makkovian will soon be over," Tan offered. "He is doing very well. Perhaps the four of us might venture together into the Mohooni markets this afternoon. We could meet you there, Lanie, on your way back from your walk."

Datu brightened. Lanie gave Tan a grateful nod. On paper, Tan and Lanie and Duantri all shared one cabin, Mak and Datu the other. But Mak, in whose battlefield body a high fever had vied with seasickness for long weeks of misery, had been in no fit state to care for his daughter anytime since their journey began. Tan and Duantri had been taking turns ministering to him, but when Lanie had tried volunteering, they quickly learned that Datu grew too agitated if both aunt and father were removed from her sight.

But now, by all reports, Mak was on the mend. Their ship was docked for the day on the main island of the Mohooni archipelago. And Lanie felt that she could—finally—take a few hours for herself. She needed to think—and not be observed thinking (by Tan), or be interrupted mid-thought (by Datu), or be sympathized with before she even understood her own thoughts (by Duantri). Seeing her niece occupied with wrestling Stripes's tail from Undies' mouth, Lanie tried to slip out of the room.

Datu's hand caught her ankle again, Stones-quick.

"When will you be back? Ow!"

The pup, apparently, had decided to substitute Datu's hand for Stripes's tail. Datu extracted her digits from his mouth and gave him a vigorous scrubbing behind the ears, but her other hand never loosed its grip on her aunt's ankle.

Undies rolled and writhed and made noises that intimated that if Datu ever stopped, he would either expire or perhaps gnaw off her hand, he couldn't decide which, only just keep scratching, never stop, please and thank you!

Lanie glanced helplessly at Tan, who rescued her again. "Dear Lanie, Duantri tells me there is a fine hiking trail that leads out of the Mohooni markets and into the jungle. The trail ends at a popular outlook on the cliffs. You'll be able to see the whole port from up there. On clear days, they say you can see past the Glistring Sea and all the way to Ama'al-hatir Ocean! Anyway, it's not a long trail—half a mile at most—though it is mostly vertical." She shuddered theatrically. "Duantri loved it."

"Half a mile?" Lanie considered the distance. She could feel her niece's piercing stare, so she squatted to meet it square-on. "Let's calculate, Datu. Thirty minutes for the first leg, because I'm out of shape. An hour of quiet contemplation, far out of chewing range of small fuzzy animals"—she wrestled the hem of her trouser leg from Undies' solicitude—"and then, say, twenty minutes back, all downhill. Give me my total?"

Datu gave her a dubious look; she always noticed when her aunt tried to slip in an arithmetic lesson on the sly.

"One hundred and ten minutes," she answered.

But the dent of worry that appeared on her brow panged Lanie. Datu's face had taken on its sunken, shadowy look. Her breath was coming in too rapidly and shrilly for Lanie's liking. Datu woke like that sometimes, wheezing and shivering, her face frozen in fear.

Doubtless Mak or Duantri would have known the perfect Quadic antiphony to calm her anxieties. But she, Lanie, would just have to do her best. Sitting on her heels, she jerked her chin toward the small porthole window.

"You know, Datu," she began, "this morning, when I was writing my letter to Havoc, I mentioned some old barrow mounds I'd noticed on those cliffs overlooking the bay. I think they're the remnants of ancient island villages, from back in the olden days of Port Mohoon—

"How olden?" Datu demanded.

"*So* olden," Lanie replied, aware of Tan's interested gaze sharpening on her, "that no one now remembers the names of those who died there." She shrugged, "At least, that's what Saint Death intimated, when I asked Her about them. I'm hoping Havoc can tell me more, when her letters catch up to us at Ylkazarra. She collects all sorts of sea lore. All I know for sure is that there are hundreds of ancient dead islanders—maybe more like thousands—buried in those mounds."

"Extraordinary," Tan murmured.

It was a compliment, but also warning: if Lanie did not wrap this up quickly, Tan would besiege her with a million unanswerable questions. For now the gyrlady was trying to restrain herself. She really was. She probably could even manage it—for about thirty more seconds, give or take.

"I'm telling you this, Datu, because I want you to know"—Lanie leaned in closer—"that if anyone gives me trouble today—but *anyone*!—I'll have help close at hand. You'll have Stripes and Undies, Tan and Duantri and Didyi, here on the boat. Out there on the cliffs, I'll have Saint Death and the barrow mounds—which, as you know, is all I need."

Datu's forehead was coming undented. "You'll call them if you need help?"

"I'll holler down the cliffs."

"And Saint Death will make them rise?"

"The barrow mounds will empty at our cries."

Datu smiled at Lanie's use of rhyme, even though they weren't speaking Quadic. "Blue fireflies," she whispered, and Lanie watched her remembering that night on Ynyssyll's Tooth.

"That's right, my plumula," she said softly. "Blue fireflies enough to light up this whole island."

Datu released her ankle.

Lanie brushed a curl from her ear. "Thanks. Give me a whole *two* hours before you start worrying too much. After all," she remarked with airy unconcern, "I might dawdle a while in the market. Maybe I'll see something Undies will like. New drawers. A petticoat. Some stays."

Finally, Datu cracked a smile. Her eyes were mostly clear of that brinking-blue glaze. They were very nearly almost all the way green again. Almost.

"He only likes them if I wear them first. Auntie Lanie, what are stays?"

"Gyrlady Tanaliín will tell you," Lanie promised grandly, and took advantage of Undies standing on Datu's lap and licking her mouth, prompting a fit of giggling, to make good her escape.

LANIE SCANNED THE skies. Nothing. No wizard birds anyway—though the island sported a species of black and white cormorant that was very handsome, as well as several gulls the color of volcanic ash. Nothing to worry or distress her. Nothing following her in the hopes of luring her back home again.

Not that she wanted anything like that. Damn them all duodecifold.

She played with the small velvet bag in her pocket. Entangled inside it were her reliquary and Bran Fiakhna's chain of gems and gold. Lanie no longer wore either. She did not in general even keep the bag on her person, but tucked away at the bottom of her trunk. Today she was contemplating hurling both necklaces into the sea.

Rituals were important.

Except that now, having come all this way, she did not want to let them go. Not Lir, not the Blackbird Bride, nor any part of her long road—bone road, river road, sea road—that had brought her to this moment.

So she sat very still on the beautifully carved driftwood bench, which some civic-minded Mohooner had erected at the outlook site on the head of the cliff, and she watched the waves. The wind moved through the stubble on her scalp—all that remained of her braids, which she had cut off, one by one, the day they left the river boat at the mouth of the Glistring Sea and set sail for Lower Quadiíb.

The wind was warm, even balmy, but she had not yet shucked any of her three layers of clothing, or her scarf. Many hours of basking in direct sunlight might thaw her out for a while, but overnight a deep chill would creep back into her body, seizing her muscles, aching in her bones, waking her with the shock of it. In that way, she was perhaps more like her niece than she cared to admit to either Tan or Duantri. Not that they hadn't guessed. They kept plying her with hot tea and soup, though the weather outside felt more like summer than winter this far south.

Thinking of the south made Lanie think of the north—the far north—Northernmost Skakmaht.

She thought of Grandpa Rad riding Cracchen Skrathmandan's corpus through the sky. She thought of that writhing mass of substance-tangled Sky Wizards pursuing him like a sentient storm. She remembered all the promises she had made to Sari Scratch—to fix what she had helped to shatter. But sometimes it seemed to her that she was only running further away…

"Mizka."

Lanie jolted so violently that her deep accident almost swapped with her surface. "Holy necropants!" she cried, and checked to make sure that she was still wearing her skeleton on the inside. "What are you *doing* here, Mak?"

The words were more blunt than welcoming—she was too surprised to modulate her tone—but Mak only smiled with one corner of his mouth, and shrugged with one shoulder, and asked mildly: "May not a brother visit his sister?"

Lanie sat up straighter on the bench. All right, so it wasn't just sunbeams and a balmy breeze that could thaw her frozen limbs. Now that her heartbeat was calming down, she was able to examine him with a tad more discretion and discernment. She crossed her arms over her chest.

"Tan said you were improving," she began doubtfully, "but—hiking a mile up a cliff?"

He stirred. "It is but half a mile."

"Still—"

"I had to get off that boat!"

"Yes." Lanie looked down at her lap. Both her hands were clutching the small velvet purse, twisting it between them. She had no memory of removing it from her pocket. She tucked it away again. "Me too."

"I have been lying in a stew of myself for weeks. Those berths—"

"I know!" Lanie groaned. "And in such close quarters. Duantri, though a darling—"

"Snores like a salamander with a head cold," he finished, and smiled again shyly, this time with his whole mouth. And his teeth. The sun burned brighter, and Lanie's face unfroze enough to return the smile.

"I am glad you're feeling better, Mak—Makkovian," she corrected herself.

"Thank you, Mizka," he returned with a thoughtful dip of his chin. "As am I glad… glad to be alive." Moving slowly, he walked the last few steps to the driftwood bench and sat down heavily beside her. Lanie saw then the gray-green cast to his pallor, his flop sweat and trembling. The empty shirt sleeve of his missing right arm had come untucked from his belt. It flapped in the wind.

And then she noticed the leather strap slung across his chest, and the object hanging from it. Mak was carrying Haaken's casket—that was to say, his own right arm, preserved in Haaken's spell—which Lanie had been keeping in the false bottom of her trunk. But Tan or Duantri (probably Tan), who knew all about the hiding place, must have felt it was high time to interfere in Lanie's business again, and told Mak where to find it, or fetched it to him herself. After all, according to the gyrlady's reasoning, Mak's arm was more *Mak's* business than Lanie's; he had a right to know of its continued existence.

Whatever Tan's intentions may have been, the repossession of his missing arm had driven Mak out of his sickbed, through a jungle, and up a cliff to find Lanie.

She felt her eyebrows winging high enough to exceed her hairline. "Are you all right?"

Mak followed her gaze to the casket, started, then looked up again. "Oh, this? Oh. Yes. I think so."

"Do you have any questions for me?"

He hesitated. "I do. Or... Tan told me some of it. She said Skrathmandan left instructions with you as to its possible..."

"Reattachment?"

He seemed relieved not to have to say the word first. "Yes."

"Yes," Lanie replied slowly. "Haaken talked me through it. He was, I think, indignant on your behalf and did everything he could to preserve your arm from corruption. It's incredible spellwork; I hope to learn the way of it... someday." She studied him. "You know, that casket isn't going to melt anytime soon. We don't have to do this right now."

Mak's shoulders hunched. "We set sail again on the evening tide. When is the next time we will be alone, you and I? Whether it works or does not, I would prefer to discover it now, in the open air. To be cooped up in a berth either for its success or failure, would feel like, like... panic. And if we fail, what do we do with the limb? Burial at sea?" He shuddered. "I would prefer to burn it."

"That is what Haaken advised," Lanie replied. "Fire would destroy the arm and its residual enchantments—both accidentally and substantially—so that it cannot be used against you in sympathetic spellwork, nor turned to any experimental usage by wizards who know no better."

Mak's face blanched to an even sicklier shade at the thought.

Lanie frowned down at her lap, where her fingers were now tightly inter-knotted. "Makkovian, are you sure you want me to try this? We could wait till we reach Ylkazarra, consult with the Gyrladies there—"

"No," he said. "It must be you."

"Why?" she asked bluntly. "The last time we spoke of my magic, you said that all acts of necromancy were vile, corrupt, and evil. And all necromancers as well."

Mak's head snapped up to look at her. "But... did you not get my letter? The one we sent away with the pup?"

"Oh, I got it," Lanie returned. "Some of it. The waterproofing… wasn't. Very."

"Ah." Mak nodded to himself. They both turned to face the sea again, and a hot wind blew through their silence. Presently, as if continuing aloud a conversation he was having inside his head, he said, "Yes, I should have begun with my apology. This occasion merits"—he cleared his throat—"salal. That is to say, the eighth of the twelve apologies. It is the one that means, 'I spoke then in haste and ignorance, but I know better now, and regret my words and actions more than I can say—except to say, salal.'"

Lanie was silent, sensing that however Mak's apology translated, he did indeed have more to say, and she needed to hear all of it.

"I left you, Mizka, all alone in that house of death. I left you with bitter words and under a stain of fear. Duantri has told me something of your autumn of illness, and… and the miracles you performed on the thirteenth of Vespers, at Ynyssyll's Tooth. For what you did that day for Datu—and for me—I… Well. I will make my thousand thanks to you over the many years of our friendship, I hope. Before my own illness, I had months to consider my behavior to you. What I thought was the single greatest evil that could ever befall my daughter turned out to be the saving of her. And not… not just because of the… the torments it enabled her to survive."

Mak shook his head as if to move through that memory before it choked him. "Before that, long before that, there was… Datu's joy in the pup. Her blossoming. If I hadn't seen it for myself, I could not have *imagined* it, Mizka—the change in her was so great. So sudden. I did not know my daughter until I saw how wildly she could love. Perhaps there was a part of me that had always feared a part of her. Feared that she would turn out like…"

"Like a Stones."

"Not every Stones," he remonstrated. "Like her mother." He swept the sweat from his brow with the back of his wrist. When he wiped his eyes too, Lanie had to look away, hiding her face as he finished:

"I return to Quadiíb no longer quite Quadoni. My head is filled with radical thoughts. My heart is certain of little but this: you, Mizka, are a true priest of Doédenna. The bond that lies between you and your god is for the good of this world. You *unbroke* Datu. Not only that, but you went alone to that tower to stand against the Rook of Rook and all her wizard birds…"

Behind her hands, Lanie bit her lip. She had never been alone on that tower—not once—but now was not the time to stop him. Not after so many months of silence, and so much rancor between them.

"Time and again, as I recovered on my sickbed, I have been asking myself, 'Makkovian Covan'"—here Mak slipped so smoothly into Quadic, Lanie imagined she was dropping feet-first into his thoughts—"'hadst thou an undead army called to heel, and came thou face-to-face against thy foe—the one who killed thy sister, stole thy love, exposed thy niece to ice and sky and wind, imperiled thee and sought thee for her thrall—wouldst *thou* have done as *she* did do that night? *No!*'" His switch back to Lirian was so vehement that Lanie jumped.

"No?"

"No. Not I. I," said Mak, "would have laid waste to those who did me harm. And so, laid waste myself." He paused to catch his breath, which was coming in shallow and fast, like his daughter's did when she woke from one of her bad dreams. "But *you*, Mizka—you defeated your foe so thoroughly that death became superfluous. You might have claimed the whole realm for your own. All of Liriat—and beyond. Instead, you laid your undead army to rest. I do not know how you did that. I could not have done. No necromancer in all the histories I have ever read—or heard said or sung—was able to do as you have done."

Lanie lifted her face. If it was time for confession, she would have hers too. "I wanted to destroy her," she said. "Her Parliament was falling, her power draining. I was so angry! I could have... But Lir—they asked me... they *asked* me, and I gave my word to them. I swore by *Saint Death* to do what they wanted. And to... to try to understand them. I didn't think," she burst out, "that they would *banish* me!"

"No," said Mak with utmost compassion. "No, Mizka, how could you have known?"

She began to weep then—stupidly, messily, mumblingly. Mak put his left arm around her shoulders, and she sobbed until she was almost as febrile and sweaty as he. But the storm was brief; it passed quickly and left her feeling embarrassed.

She pulled away, wiped her glasses, blew her nose, and sighed. "Oh, well. I *have* been trying to understand. I'm doing my best. Sometimes it all makes sense. Sometimes I think it never will. But let's leave it where it is for now; I'm not ready to pick apart that carcass anymore today. I am not the Condor she called me."

Taking a steadying breath, Lanie loosed it slowly. Her pounding heart was slowing again. She was calm enough to work.

"I don't know the hour. I imagine, if it gets much later, Datu might get frantic? So. While we still have some time, Makkovian Covan"—Mak smiled at her use of his full name, and she couldn't help but return it—"do you want to try this thing?"

They regarded the casket in his lap. "'This thing'?" Mak repeated wryly. "Yes. If you think that it is really possible."

"I am confident," Lanie stated, her voice gaining strength, "that I can follow Haaken's instructions for reattachment. Even so, I might fail. If I don't fail, I'm still not sure what will happen. All I know is... if we do this... we'll be calling the Skaki sky gods into our midst. They may be the same as our own gods with slightly different names, or they may be entirely different entities with agendas of their own."

She waved her left hand, which was already beginning to feel full and heavy, like a leaf laden with honeydew. "What I'm saying is—no matter what happens, Makkovian—if we try this, and it works, it will only have done so because some gods out there have plans of Their own. For you, I mean. You have to be ready for that. You have to be ready to *serve*. Knowing that, do you still want me to try?"

Mak's pallor was much improved after his rest on the bench, but his eyes were glass-glittering-bright. He regarded her with an expression that reminded her of his falcon form. But his voice, when it croaked out his "Yes," was more toad than raptor.

"Yes?" Lanie repeated, wanting to be absolutely sure.

"Yes, Mizka. Yes, my sister. I am ready. I trust you."

"You do?"

"Yes!" Mak shouted it with such exasperated affection that Lanie finally believed him.

The hot happiness of his trust unplucked another icy dart from its cold hold on her heart. Excitement and anticipation surged in her. Her left hand was like a warm and foggy morning at the edge of a cliff.

"All right!" She leapt from the bench. "Let's see what Haaken had in mind. Take off your shirt and hand me your arm."

Wordlessly, Mak obeyed, unslinging the strap of Haaken's casket from his shoulder and passing it over before turning his back on her and pulling his shirt over his head.

Pacing the ledge, Lanie ran her left hand over the cold surface of the casket. It sang like a crystal bowl beneath her fingertips, an echo of Haaken's spell. Her left palm tingled. She tapped a single fingernail against the ice, hearing it ring out a clear response. Haaken's wards lifted for her, a door of ice opening to invite her inside, and when she entered the spell, the casket evaporated under her touch. She was left holding Mak's right arm in both her hands, feeling the flesh of it—frosty but sound.

Lanie's nostrils pinched at the scent of ice, though there was no more ice in evidence. Haaken's magic had a dry sparkle, like effervescent wine. She sneezed in surprise, so hard it rocked her back a few steps. Alarmed, Mak caught her and guided her away from the cliff's edge, back to the bench.

This was just as well, because for Lanie the world was tunneling down into a prismatic blue-green oubliette. The Glistring Sea and the warm salt wind and the jungle-clung cliff had all disappeared, leaving her alone at the bottom of a glacier, looking up at a slice of illimitable sky.

She still sensed Mak beside her, but in substance more than accident, and kept her hand on him even after she was safely seated. She would need to be in contact with him for this.

Lanie closed her eyes to the cold ice-water world.

The substance in her hands sang to the substance seated beside her—the way Queen Ynyssyll's toe bones sang to each other in their separate reliquaries, the way both reliquaries sang to the rest of the Founding Queen's remains in her lonely tomb. All Lanie had to do was to reintroduce them. All she had to do was provide a bit of bonding glue of her own making and stitch the disparate pieces back together—like she used to stitch tiny mouse bones back into full skeletons.

Sightlessly, she reached out with the missing piece and fitted it back into the main puzzle, right where it belonged.

Mak screamed.

Lanie opened her eyes to find him on the ground in front of the bench, writhing. His spine was arched. His heels dug in the ground. The bandage at the stump of his elbow joint was unraveling like a ribbon in a high wind. She saw that the wound beneath it was clean; Bran Fiakhna's black sword had cauterized where it cleaved.

But Mak's right arm, though it clung doggedly and gummily to the side of his stump, remained frosty and blue, and would not reattach all the way.

Lanie slid off the bench and into the dirt beside him. Her vision remained cold and glinting. Her nose was frozen. She touched Mak's right arm with her curious left hand. Beneath the sheen of frost, the silver patterns of his Bryddongard flashed dully in response.

"What do I do?" Lanie asked her god, whom she knew to be everywhere at once, even in the ice. Yet it was ice, it seemed, that locked Her out, kept Her now from Lanie's side. A wall of perfect, preserving ice. "What do I do now?"

"I trust you," Mak whispered. His eyes, which had been fast shut, now peeled open. He stared straight up into Lanie's face. Once before, he had stared at her thus, on the floor of Stones Gallery. But this time, he did not turn his face away, wishing to die. This time, he smiled, though his lips were pale with pain.

"Doédenna. Erre'Elur. Lady of Doorways. I place my trust in you." Mak gasped as another convulsion of pain seized him, but he crossed his left arm over his body, and closed his left hand over Lanie's where it lay upon his right elbow stump, and he said in Quadic: "O blood and bone of mine, thou must not fear. But show Saint Death that She is welcome here."

Haaken's spell had needed only this: an invitation from the host body. Another open door.

It was as if Mak himself had lifted the last ward: the cold arm beneath their hands jumped, and slid into place, and sealed itself to Mak's stump.

His relief was so instantaneous, so intense that his head *thunked* back into the dirt. The golden color came flooding back into his face. The lines on his forehead and bracketing his mouth eased.

Lanie thought he fainted—until Mak bolted up as if the ground had belched him. He moved so quickly that her eyes crossed. She pushed her glasses up her nose and stared at him.

Clapping his left hand over his right arm, Mak explored the thick band of scar tissue ringing the skin below his elbow. The scar was blue-green-white, the colors shifting with the light. It glistened like frost. If she were meeting him for the first time, Lanie might have mistaken it for a wizard mark.

As for his Bryddongard, the silver lines that patterned his forearm had darkened to a vesper blue, a blue almost as black as the longest night of the year. It, too, reminded Lanie strongly of wizard marks—though of what magics and which gods, she did not know. She had the feeling that Mak would find out in time.

"My Bryddongard feels different!" Tearing his gaze from his arm, Mak stared at Lanie. "What does it *mean?*"

"I don't know!" The hectic flush was dying out of her. Lanie shook her head. "I'm sorry. I just don't know."

But Mak bent down to take her by the shoulder and jostle her out of her sagging state. He was smiling—excited, even merry. He looked ten years younger than any age Lanie had ever known him at. "No, no! Do not wilt so, my sister! This is not a cause for grief. Rather, as Tan might say, it is an excuse for experimentation—in the name of science!"

"Or… theology?" Lanie murmured.

"It need not be one or the other, Mizka; that's just your Lirian propensity for polarity. Remember, you are in *Quadiíb* now."

But there was a tease in his voice, and he was holding out his right hand to her, wiggling his fingers until she reached up and grasped him by the wrist. He yanked her to her feet.

"Whoa—!"

"First experiment successful!" Mak declared cheerfully. "Nothing fell off! Good work, Mizka. Now watch," he directed her. "With Saint Death's own eyes, my sister, watch what I do next. And tell me what you see."

He did nothing more than close his eyes, but Lanie felt it the moment he called upon his Bryddongard. The gathering of his will was like a wind blowing in from some new direction. But the flat, bright burst of sheet lightning that Lanie was expecting did not follow. Nothing followed. Not a beak. Not a talon. No rush of wings. No proud peregrine. Mak yet stood before her, a man.

She stared at him, stricken.

After a few seconds, Mak opened his eyes. Forehead furrowed, but smiling withal, he murmured, "The strangest sensation. It was as if—"

His head snapped back. He flung his arms out behind him but his breastbone strained forward as if yanked aloft by a giant hook. And then, from out of the center of his chest, there rushed a swift gray shape, half-transparent, a thing of shadow, of smoke.

It shot straight into the sky.

Lanie caught Mak as he stumbled. As he had done for her, she dragged him back from the cliff's edge, and sat him down on solid ground, and made sure he stayed there.

He sagged against her, and she locked her arms about his middle, but both kept their faces upturned, following the gray shape that soared overhead, swooping in a wide gyre above the cliffs.

Mak whispered, "Mizka. I can see everything. *Everything*. From up above!"

Lanie was shaking from head to toe, and all of it was laughter. She was laughing with her whole body—loud, giddy, terrified, happy—but after a few minutes, she tugged at Mak's arms and tapped on his shoulder, calling his name several times.

"That's enough for now, Makkovian! It's a good beginning. A good first experiment. But it's enough for one day. Come back!"

At first, Mak did not seem to hear her. But then he lifted his head, his neck straining, and let loose a piercing string of high-pitched, inhuman cries. In response, the ghost falcon plummeted down like pelting hail, so fast that it left a trail of vapor behind it, and swooped into the very center of Mak's chest.

He sucked in a breath. All at once, the rigidity left his body. His right arm slammed over his heart, as if to feel the bird trapped there. He twisted around on the ground to look at Lanie.

"What was that?" they asked together.

"A ghost!" Lanie guessed at once. "Or, maybe—the ghost of a spell!" She started bouncing in place. She couldn't help it. "It's like... like the spells on your Bryddongard, both the original and our alterations, died when Bran Fiakhna cut off your arm, and... and maybe Haaken did something to freeze the dead spells before they dissipated? Do spells have spirits? Did I—did we just—resurrect them—or? Was that it? What *was* that?" She laughed until her face hurt. "I have no idea!"

"Mizka," said Mak, laughing with her, "I do not know either! But what I feel is... What I feel..."

But Lirian was, of course, insufficient unto his needs. He slipped into his native Quadic, like a prayer.

"Saint Death hath made her aerie out of me."

HALFWAY DOWN THE cliff, they met the others on the narrow trail that wound through the lush undergrowth of the Mohooni jungle. Undies, having four legs, came galumphing up the soonest. No sooner did they meet him on the trail but he was yipping and whining around their legs, springing and sproinging, demanding pets, and licking anything that could conceivably be licked.

"Thou four-cursed bane and most infernal whelp!" Mak yelped. "So help me, gods, I'll soon have words with thee!"

But Undies, who knew Mak very well, merely puppy-panted at him, and wagged everything, and tried to lick his knee.

"Underwear Stones!" Lanie said very sternly, glaring down through her spectacles. "Calm down at once!"

To everyone's surprise—except Lanie's; she had been using her deep voice—the pup obeyed, and fell in step behind her.

"A miracle!" Tan called out as she approached them. She bore a stout walking stick, and her face was flushed, but she did not seem otherwise out of breath or upset. "You will have to teach me that trick—for those times he wakes me in the middle of the night to play."

Duantri, not far behind her, was bearing Datu on piggyback. When her luminous gaze caught sight of Mak and Lanie, she said over her shoulder, "But see, Datu—they're sound and safe from harm. I beg thee ease thy grip around my neck."

"Safe—and more than sound," Tan added, her small eyes sharpening as she took in Mak's shirtless state, the new seam ringing his right elbow, the new marks threading his forearm like a strange map. "Redoubtably sound, I should say!"

When Duantri drew even with Tan, she gasped. "Was not I right?" she asked her gyrlady in triumphant Quadic. "Didst not thou hear me say? Some new enchantment hath been wrought this day! Some wind there was that mingled wine and snow! That cry we heard on high, a falcon's call!" She switched to Lirian and crowed to Tan, "I *told* you so!"

All this time, Datu had been looking extremely anxious, but when she saw both father and aunt for herself, and saw Undies gamboling about them, her whole body went slack with relief. She slithered off Duantri's back as if worry alone had glued her there, and began scolding them both before her feet hit the dirt.

"Didyi! Auntie Lanie! You are *very* late! Auntie Tan says the tide is coming in in three hours and forty-five minutes and we did not want you to miss it… And Didyi, I think that you should not be out of bed so soon, but—*Didyi!*" she gasped. "Did Auntie Lanie raise your arm back from the dead? Can you fly again like before? Did Auntie Lanie give you back your falcon form?"

Mak glanced at Lanie, bright-eyed, and ceded her the stage. Lanie cleared her throat.

"Not exactly. I mean, yes, sort of, in a manner of speaking. But also, no. Makkovian himself won't be able to fly anymore. Not like he used to—

"Oh, no!" Duantri exclaimed involuntarily. Tan clucked her tongue. Datu glared fiercely at Lanie and opened her mouth as if to start scolding her again.

Mak stopped them all with a shout of laughter. They looked at him in astonishment—even Undies—and when he had all of their attentions, he began:

"My sister wrought a miracle in me, and thankless would I be to call it lack. I want for nothing more than what I have—and from this day, abundance is my creed. So come, my plumula," he opened his arms to his daughter, "and fly to me."

Datu needed no further invitation; she launched herself at him immediately, and Mak swung her in a wide circle before crushing her close. He smiled at them all over his daughter's red-gold mop, but it was Lanie's eyes he met and held.

"We need no wings between us, thou and I."

The End

ACKNOWLEDGEMENTS

WELL, MI ENJAMBRE. If you're reading this in 2022, this book has been a long thirteen (or seventeen-ish, depending on how you look at it) years in the making. I like to say that *Saint Death's Daughter* started life as a 50,000 word NaNoWriMo novel titled, ironically, *Miscellaneous Stones: Assassin* in November 2009. But really, it started four years before that, as a short story in Phyllis Eisenstein's Advanced Science Fiction Class at Columbia College Chicago, back in May 2005 (there was a robot butler named Graves; I remember very little else). But actually, it started even earlier than that, when Marie O'Mahony, née Cristina Marie Boothe, took me out to shoot guns in the Arizona desert, telling me, "You're a writer. You'll probably be writing about guns someday. You need experience shooting a gun."

What I experienced was a lot of sweaty palms and flinching at loud noises (even in my supposedly noise-canceling earmuffs, which maybe weren't working that day?) and a sense of explosive dread. I remember thinking: "Wouldn't it be interesting to write a character who is allergic to violence and therefore has to problem-solve in a totally different way and also projectile vomits every time she touches a weapon?"

It was then, and still remains (to my mind, at least), an interesting challenge for a fantasy writer—where epic battles must be epic, and when in doubt, insert tavern brawl!

Anyway. That's how it all started. Were it not for the following people (and many more, no doubt, whom I accidentally neglected to mention) this book in your hands might have withered and died at any number of crossroads along the way. Sometimes it takes a village to convince a writer to keep writing. My village spans a country, sometimes oceans and nations. And so, to this world village, I want to offer my thanks.

First, I want to thank those who were there for me from the first. I was never told not to write. I was only ever encouraged. I was only ever told to "follow your bliss and follow your dream." That, I have come to learn in my deep adulthood, is a gift more precious than debt forgiveness.

I can't thank you enough for that, family. Thank you—for listening to my stories and poems and plays, for sending me letters, for singing me songs, for giving me books, for taking me to the theatre, for finding all the wonderful schools and other learning experiences, for sending me abroad, for hosting house concerts, for attending my readings and performances.

Thank you especially: my mama, Sita; my papa, Rory Cooney; Terry Donohoo, my stepmother; my brothers—Joel, Aidan, Jeremy, Declan, and Desi; their wonderful, powerful partners—Nicole Cooney, MaLinda Zimmerman-Cooney, Rhiannon Parker-Cooney, and Martha Patty Hernandez Saray; all my aunties and uncles and piles (and heaps) (and scores) of cousins; Theresa L. Gerbig, who has been there since my birth; my nieces—Lenora Claire, Christiana Rose, Amelia Lynn, and LaLeta Louise; my nephew, Dega Vonn; my darling Mima, Mrs. Louise Riedel; my darling Grandma Marti, Mrs. Marti Larson.

Thank you too, my extended Phoenix (and formerly of Phoenix) friendship circle: especially Lydia Eickstaedt; A. J. Christiansen; Ben Christiansen; Sarah 'Beanie' Snow; Mary Davies; Arthur Wylde-TroutKornher-Stace; Ethan and Liz Sparks and their family; Daryl, Linda, and David Boothe. Thank you for showing up. Thank you for keeping the connection.

I want to thank my company of women—my shield sisters, my peers—with whom I perform, with whom I ascend, from whom I learn, and who I am always working to impress. I celebrate, admire, and adore you. May we meet next year on the Street of Many Porches. Thank you, (Kiri) Marie O'Mahony and (Mir) Miriam Grill, for sharing history and loyalty with me the longest. Thank you, my goblin girls and infernal harpies—I want to squeeze the ichor out of you!—for your adult friendship that keeps deepening and growing more rich and interesting: Caitlyn Paxson; Jessica P. Wick; Amal El-Mohtar; Tiffany Trent; Ysabeau Wilce; Nicole Kornher-Stace; Patty Templeton; Betsie Withey.

To my great mentors in science fiction and fantasy, I owe much that can never be repaid. Gene Wolfe and Phyllis Eisenstein were both very present for the beginning of this book. They are now gone, and my Earth is more barren. And so, to Rebecca Spizzirri and Therese Wolfe-Goulding, I want to say thank you for keeping me on as your honorary sister/cousin/friend. However that works.

Gene, his wife Rosemary, and Phyllis were an enormous part of my creative life in Chicago, but there were many others. Chicago folks—you were part of my formative years and continue to be essential: John O'Neill; Howard Andrew Jones; Tina Jens; Katie Redding (thank you for everything, always); Eric Cherry; Pete Thomas; Rebecca Huston; Dave Michelak; Geoffrey Winston Hyatt; Patrick Duvall; Frank Stascik; Allison Spangenberg; Max Ulve; Jenny Seay; Deb Lewis; Julia Borcherts; Shomari Black; Kelsey Huff; Cavan Hallman; Marissa McKown; Curtis Jackson; Marvin Quijada; ; Mike Martinez; Joshua Alan Doetsch; Karin Thogerson; Darci Stratton;

Martel Sardina; Brian Torney; Jahn Mitchell; Julie Barnett; Michael Penkas; Brendan Detzner; Janelle McHugh; Samu Rahn; Cynthia (Seven Deadly) J. Glasson; Joe Bonadonna; Dave Munger; Wayne Allen Sallee, Jude W. Mire and Jill Cooper; Shawna (Banana) Flavell; Sally Tibbetts (Kitchen Witch! Girl Detective!); Reina Hardy; Rory Leahy; Kyle Kratky; Megan Swanson; Gillian Hastings (Lumina!); Lea Grover; Stephanie Shaw (Mrs. Q!); and those whom my memory has failed.

Sometimes a writing group is for critique, sometimes it is for enthusiastic support, and sometimes it is for untangling knotty problems. Thank you to *all* of my writing groups, for all your many services, in person and online—especially the RAMP writers of New York City: Delia Sherman; Ellen Kushner; Liz Duffy Adams; Joel Derfner; Carlos Hernandez.

Thank you from my heart's depths, dear online writing community, for keeping me company during the pandemic, and holding me accountable through the slog of 2020 and 2021. To the Gumbo Fiction Cafe, I owe particular thanks. (Especially: Mike Allen, Patty Templeton, Tina Jens, Ambrosia Rose, Amanda McGee, Carrie Channel, Maria Schrater, Tazmania Hayward, Michael Fountain, John Dowds, and J9 Vaughn.) I must thank as well the Silent Writers Shift (especially Liz Duffy Adams, Carla 'La Carlotta' Kissane, and Professor Sean Elliot). Without your quiet, studious faces working away on the other side of Zoom, the final tail of this tale would have been a lot more arduous.

Speaking of New York! Thank you, New Yorkers and the New York-adjacent, for make living in this magnificent, overwhelming, and slightly terrifying city better than just bearable. Thank you for inviting me to your pie parties, for wandering musuems and parks with me, for feeding me fancy cheese and other fine things, and for riding your bikes long distances to visit. Thank you for playing games and breaking bread and sharing stories with me. Thank you especially: Katherine Vaz; Christopher Cerf; Fran Wilde; Meg Frank; Cameron Roberson (AKA 'Rob Cameron'); D. T. Friedman; Marty Cahill; Mac McAnally; Amanda Baker; Chris Kreuter and Alexandra Gardell Kreuter; Joshua and Amanda DeBonis; Gil Hova and Carrie Margulies; Mimi Mondal (fine company for theatre adventures!); Ellen Datlow; Matthew Kressel; Liz Gorinsky; DongWon Song; Sam Schreiber.

There were many groups of people along the way who bolstered my flagging spirits where this book was concerned. Thank you, Magill Foote and Grant Jeffrey, for designing a beautiful book trailer for an earlier draft of *Saint Death's Daughter* (when it was called something else) that made me want to live up to its vividness and artistry. Thank you to the members of my father's choir at St. Anne's Church (past and present), who warmly befriended me, and who remind me how holy it is just to lift my voice in song. Thank you to the theatre companies I have loved: especially, the Silent Theatre of Chicago; Flock Theatre of New London; and Upstart

Creatures of New York. Theatre brings me such a blazing joy, which—along with rage—is the finest fuel of art. Thank you, Mystic Aquarium and Tantor Audio, for giving me work when I came as a stranger to a faraway land. An artist needs a day job to keep a roof over her head (with a great garret view) in the most beautiful town she'd ever known (Westerly, Rhode Island).

To the writers, poets, thinkers, artists, and readers—near and far—who may or may not know how deeply they influence and inspire me, or how their letters, postcards, updates, tweets, messages, and *showing-up-ness* move me: Cassandra Khaw (part fox, part dark of the moon); Francesca Forrest (chronicler for dryads); Virginia Mohlere (part shark, all love); Elizabeth R. McClellan (poet and activist); S. J. Tucker (bards of gods); Cristina Quintero and her whole dang wonderful family; Margaret Hiebert; Jennifer Crow; Gwynne Garfinkle; Erik Amundsen; Sharon Shinn; Julia Rios (Voice of the Rainbow); Moss Collum; Cerece Rennie Murphy; Robert V. S. Redick; Karen Meisner; Pär Winzell; Christa Carmen (Dark Heart); Elissa Sweet (Lady of Flowers); Eric Michaelian; Dorian Mendez; Kelsey Alexander; Faye Ringel (my dear musical collaborator!); Zac Topping; Paul Magnan; Anne Flammang (long live the Depot!); Randee Dawn; Kathleen Jennings; Sara Logan; Jaymee Goh (for all the squeeing, really!); Bryce Parsons-Twesten (for the surprise texts); Brittany Warman and Sara Cleto (the Good Doctors of Carterhaugh); Jeanne Kramer-Smyth; Ken Schneyer; Dominik Parisien (Mockingbird); Elaine Isaak; Tina Connolly; Brandon O'Brien; Sonya Taaffe; Rose Fox; R. B. Lemberg; Mari Ness; Gemma Files; Lisa M. Bradley; Angela Slatter; Lisa L. Hannett; Lee Mandelo; Doctor Theodora Goss; Doctor Mary C. Crowell; Cat Valente; Heath Miller; Sally Brackett Robertson; B. Sharise Moore; Kenesha Williams; Dave Robson; Robert Peterson; Sally Rosen Kindred; Anita Allen; Ann Leckie; Martha Wells; Kay Kenyon; Sherry Thomas; C. M. Waggoner; Katherine Addison; Alix E. Harrow; Aliette de Bodard; Seanan McGuire; Sheree Renée Thomas. I know I have left people out, but this was not intentional. There are so many of you, and you are all so splendid.

Thank you one million infinities to my superagent, Markus Hoffmann of Regal Hoffmann & Associates—who is, by the way, the ***coolest***. Thank you to the whole fantastic team at Solaris/Rebellion. Thanks especially to my first editor, Kate Coe, for the loving my book (and its footnotes) (and the skeleton mice) the way I always wanted it to be loved, and to my second editor, David Moore, for his exquisitely close and careful reading. Thank you, Barry Goldblatt, for your early comments that informed the middle drafts of this book. Thank you, Audrey Niffenegger, for pointing me towards Markus.

Lastly but not leastly: thank you, Carlos Hernandez. My Carlos. My darling. Mi esposo. My famulus. Thank you for your keen eye, your sense of narrative balance, your enthusiasm for magic systems, your demand for emotional integrity in the characters you like best, and the way you have of drawing my bitterness "like poison from a wound" and leaving such sweet and loving kindness in its place. I shall not have to say, in the end, "They should have sent a poet." They sent me a poet.

C. S. E. Cooney
August 2021